THE GLADIATORS A TALE OF R

BY

George John WHYTE-MELVILLE

LONDON
W. THACKER & CO., 2 CREED LANE, E.C.
CALCUTTA: THACKER, SPINK & CO.
1901

CONTENTS

EROS

CHAP.		PAGE
I.	THE IVORY GATE	1
II.	THE MARBLE PORCH	6
III.	HERMES	15
IV.	APHRODITÉ	20
V.	ROME	28
VI.	THE WORSHIP OF ISIS	36
VII.	TRUTH	46
VIII.	THE JEW	55
IX.	THE ROMAN	61
X.	A TRIBUNE OF THE LEGIONS	71
XI.	STOLEN WATERS	81
XII.	MYRRHINA	86
XIII.	NOLENS—VOLENS	95
XIV.	CÆSAR	100
XV.	RED FALERNIAN	108
XVI.	THE TRAINING-SCHOOL	117
XVII.	A VEILED HEART	125

XVIII. WINGED WORDS	135
XIX. THE ARENA	144
XX. THE TRIDENT AND THE NET	155

ANTEROS

CHAP.	PAGE
I. THE LISTENING SLAVE	163
II. ATTACK AND DEFENCE	172
III. "FURENS QUID FŒMINA"	179
IV. THE LOVING CUP	186
V. SURGIT AMARI	194
VI. DEAD LEAVES	200
VII. "HABET!"	209
VIII. TOO LATE	214
IX. THE LURE	221
X. FROM SCYLLA TO CHARYBDIS	229
XI. THE RULES OF THE FAMILY	238
XII. A MASTER OF FENCE	245
XIII. THE ESQUILINE	252
XIV. THE CHURCH	260
XV. REDIVIVUS	269
XVI. "MORITURI"	280

XVII. THE GERMAN GUARD	286
XVIII. THE BUSINESS OF CÆSAR	293
XIX. AT BAY	300
XX. THE FAIR HAVEN	307

MOIRA

CHAP.	PAGE
I. A HOUSE DIVIDED AGAINST ITSELF	311
II. THE LION OF JUDAH	321
III. THE WISDOM OF THE SERPENT	330
IV. THE MASTERS OF THE WORLD	338
V. GLAD TIDINGS	345
VI. WINE ON THE LEES	352
VII. THE ATTAINDER	360
VIII. THE SANHEDRIM	368
IX. THE PAVED HALL	376
X. A ZEALOT OF THE ZEALOTS	384
XI. THE DOOMED CITY	392
XII. DESOLATION	398
XIII. THE LEGION OF THE LOST	406
XIV. FAITH	416
XV. FANATICISM	423

XVI. DAWN	427
XVII. THE FIRST STONE	435
XVIII. THE COST OF CONQUEST	440
XIX. THE GATHERING OF THE EAGLES	446
XX. THE VICTORY	453

THE GLADIATORS

Eros

CHAPTER I

THE IVORY GATE

Dark and stern, in their weird beauty, lower the sad brows of the Queen of Hell. Dear to her are the pomp and power, the shadowy vastness, and the terrible splendour of the nether world. Dear to her the pride of her unbending consort; and doubly dear the wide imperial sway, that rules the immortal destinies of souls. But dearer far than these—dearer than flashing crown and fiery sceptre, and throne of blazing gold—are the memories that glimmer bright as sunbeams athwart those vistas of gloomy grandeur, and seem to fan her weary spirit like a fresh breeze from the realms of upper earth. She has not forgotten, she never can forget, the dewy flowers, the blooming fragrance of lavish Sicily, nor the sparkling sea, and the summer haze, and the golden harvests that wave and whisper in the garden and granary of the world. Then a sad smile steals over the haughty face; the stern beauty softens in the gleam, and, for a while, the daughter of Ceres is a laughing girl once more.

So the Ivory Gate swings back, and gentle doves come forth on snowy wings, flying upwards through the gloom, to bear balm and consolation to the weary and the wounded and the lost. Now this was the dream the birds of Peace brought with them, to soothe the broken spirit of a sleeping slave.

The old boar has turned to bay at last. Long and severe has been the chase; through many an echoing woodland, down many a sunny glade, by copse and dingle, rock and cave, through splashing stream, and deep, dank, quivering morass, the large rough hounds have tracked him, unerring and pitiless, till they have set him up here, against the trunk of the old oak-tree, and he has turned—a true British denizen of the waste—to sell his life dearly, and fight unconquered to the last. His small eye glows like a burning coal; the stiff bristles are up along his huge black body, flecked with white froth that he churns and throws about him, as he offers those curved and ripping tusks, now to one, now to another of his crowding, baying, leaping foes.

"Have at him! Good dogs!" shouts the hunter, running in with a short, broad-bladed boar-spear in his hand. Breathless is he, and wearied with the long miles of tangled forests he has traversed; but his heart is glad within him, and his blood tingles with a strange wild thrill of triumph known only to the votaries of the chase.

"Have at him good dogs"

Gelert is down, torn and mangled from flank to dewlap; Luath has the wild swine by the throat; and a foot of gleaming steel, driven home by a young, powerful arm, has entered behind the neck and pierces downwards to the very brisket. The shaft of the spear snaps short across, as the thick unwieldy body turns slowly over, and the boar shivers out his life on the smooth sward, soft and green as velvet, that exists nowhere but in Britain.

The dream changes. The boar has disappeared, and the woodland gives place to a fair and smiling plain. Vast herds of shaggy red cattle are browsing contentedly, with their wide-horned heads to the breeze; flocks of sheep dot the green undulating pastures, that stretch away towards the sea. A gull turns its white wing against the clear blue sky; there is a hum of insects in the air, mingled with the barking of dogs, the lowing of kine, the laughter of women, and other sounds of peace, abundance, and content. A child is playing round its mother's knee—a child with frank bold brow and golden curls, and large blue fearless eyes, sturdy of limb, quick of gesture, fond, imperious, and wilful. The mother, a tall woman, with a beautiful but mournful face, is gazing steadfastly at the sea, and seems unconscious of her boy's caresses, who is fondling and kissing the white hand he holds in both his own. Her large shapely figure is draped in snowy robes that trail upon the ground, and massive ornaments of gold encircle arms and ankles. At intervals she looks fondly down upon the child; but ever her face resumes its wistful expression, as she fixes her eyes again upon the sea. There is nothing of actual sorrow in that steadfast gaze—still less of impatience, or anger, or discontent. Memory is the prevailing sentiment portrayed—memory, tender, absorbing, irresistible, without a ray of hope, but without a shadow of self-reproach. There is a statue of Mnemosyne at one of the entrances to the Forum that carries on its marble brow the same crushing weight of thought; that wears on its delicate features, graven into the saddest of beauty by the Athenian's chisel, just such a weary and despondent look. Where can the British child have seen those tasteful spoils of Greece that deck her imperial mistress? And yet he thinks of that statue as he looks up in his mother's face. But the fair tall woman shivers and draws her robe closer about her, and taking the child in her arms, nestles his head against her bosom and covers him over with her draperies, for the wind blows moist and chill, the summer air is white with driving mist, huge shapeless forms loom through the haze, and the busy sounds of life and laughter have subsided into the stillness of a vast and dreary plain.

The child and its mother have disappeared, but a tall, strong youth, just entering upon manhood, with the same blue eyes and fearless brow, is present in their stead. He is armed for the first time with the weapons of a warrior. He has seen blows struck in anger now, and fronted the legions as they advanced, and waged his fearless unskilful valour against the courage, and the tactics, and the discipline of Rome. So he is invested with sword, and helm, and target, and takes his place, not without boyish pride, amongst the young warriors who encircle the hallowed spot where the Druids celebrate their solemn and mysterious rites.

The mist comes thicker still, driving over the plain in waves of vapour, that impart a ghostly air of motion to the stones that tower erect around the mystic circle. Grey, moss-grown, and unhewn, hand of man seems never to have desecrated those mighty blocks of granite, standing there, changeless and awful, like types of eternity. Dim and indistinct are they as the worship they guard. Hard and stern as the pitiless faith of sacrifice, vengeance, and oblation, inculcated at their base. A wild low chant comes wailing on the breeze, and through the gathering mist a long line of white-robed priests winds slowly into the circle. Stern and gloomy are they of aspect, lofty of stature, and large of limb, with long grey beards and tresses waving in the wind. Each wears a crown of oak-leaves round his head; each grasps a wand covered with ivy in his hand. The youth cannot resist an exclamation of surprise. There is desecration in his thought, there is profanity in his words. Louder and louder swells the chant. Closer and closer still contracts the circle. The white-robed priests are hemming him in to the very centre of the mystic ring, and see! the sacrificial knife is already bared and whetted, and flourished in the air by a long brawny arm. The young warrior strives to fly. Horror! his feet refuse to stir, his hands cleave powerless to his sides. He seems turning to stone. A vague fear paralyses him that he too will become one of those granite masses to stand there motionless during eternity. His heart stops beating within him, and the transformation seems about to be completed, when lo! a warlike peal of trumpets breaks the spell, and he shakes his spear aloft and leaps gladly from the earth, exulting in the sense of life and motion once more.

Again the dream changes. Frenzied priest and Druidical stone have vanished like the mist that encircled them. It is a beautiful balmy night in June. The woods are black and silver in the moonlight. Not a breath of air stirs the topmost twigs of the lofty elm cut clear and distinct against the sky. Not a ripple blurs the surface of the lake, spread out and gleaming like a sheet of polished steel. The bittern calls at intervals from the adjacent marsh, and the nightingale carols in the copse. All is peaceful and beautiful, and suggestive of enjoyment or repose. Yet here, lying close amongst the foxglove and the fern, long lines of white-robed warriors are waiting but the signal for assault. And yonder, where the earthwork rises dark and level against the sky, paces to and fro a high-crested sentinel, watching over the safety of the eagles, with the calm and ceaseless vigilance of that discipline which has made the legionaries masters of the world.

Once more the trumpets peal; the only sound to be heard in that array of tents, drawn up with such order and precision, behind the works, except the footfall of the Roman guard, firm and regular, as it relieves the previous watch. In a short space that duty will be performed; and then, if ever, must the attack be made with any probability of success. Youth is impatient of delay— the young warrior's pulse beats audibly, and he feels the edge of his blade and the point of his short-handled javelin, with an intensity of longing that is absolutely painful. At length the word is passed from rank to rank. Like the crest of a sea-wave breaking into foam, rises that wavering line of white, rolling its length out in the moonlight, as man after man springs erect at the touch of his comrade; and then a roar of voices, a rush of feet, and the wave dashes up and breaks against the steady solid resistance of the embankment. But discipline is not to be caught thus napping. Ere the echo of their trumpets has died out among the distant hills, the legionaries stand to their arms throughout the camp. Already the rampart gleams and bristles with shield and helmet, javelin, sword, and spear. Already the eagle is awake and defiant; unruffled, indeed, in plumage, but with beak and talons bare and whetted for defence. The tall centurions marshal their men in line even and regular, as though about to defile by the throne of Cæsar, rather than to repel the attack of a wild barbarian foe. The tribunes, with their golden crests, take up their appointed posts in the four corners of the camp; while the prætor himself gives his orders calm and unmoved from the centre.

Over the roar of the swarming Britons sounds the clear trumpet-note pealing out its directions, concise and intelligible as a living voice, and heard by the combatants far and wide, inspiring courage and confidence, and order in the confusion. Brandishing their long swords, the white-clad warriors of Britain rush tumultuously to the attack. Already, they have filled the ditch and scaled the earthwork; but once and again they recoil from the steady front and rigid discipline of the invader, while the short stabbing sword of the Roman soldier, covered as he is by his ample shield, does fearful execution at close quarters. But still fresh assailants pour in, and the camp is carried and overrun. The young warrior rushes exulting to and fro, and the enemy falls in heaps before him. Such moments are worth whole years of peaceful life. He has reached the prætorium. He is close beneath the eagles, and he leaps wildly at them to bring them off in triumph as trophies of his victory. But a grim centurion strikes him to the earth. Wounded, faint, and bleeding, he is carried away by his comrades, the shaft of the Roman standard in his hand. They bear him to a war-chariot, they lash the wild galloping steeds, the roll of the wheels thunders in his ears as they dash tumultuously across the plain, and then ... the gentle mission is fulfilled, the doves fly down again to Proserpine, and the young, joyous, triumphant warrior of Britain wakes up a Roman slave.

CHAPTER II

THE MARBLE PORCH

It was the sound of a chariot, truly enough, that roused the dreamer from his slumbers; but how different the scene on which his drowsy eyes unclosed, from that which fancy had conjured up in the shadowy realms of sleep!

A beautiful portico, supported on slender columns of smooth white marble, protected him from the rays of the morning sun, already pouring down with the intensity of Italian heat. Garlands of leaves and flowers, cool and fresh in their contrast with the snowy surface of these dainty pillars, were wreathed around their stems, and twined amongst the delicate carving of their Corinthian capitals. Large stone vases, urn-shaped and massive, stood in long array at stated intervals, bearing the orange-tree, the myrtle, and other dark-green flowering shrubs, which formed a fair perspective of retirement and repose. Shapely statues filled the niches in the wall, or stood out more prominently in the vacant spaces of the colonnade. Here cowered a marble Venus, in the shamefaced consciousness of unequalled beauty; there stood forth a bright Apollo, exulting in the perfection of godlike symmetry and grace. Rome could not finger the chisel like her instructress Greece, the mother of the Arts, but the hand that firmly grasps the sword need never want for anything skill produces, or genius creates, or gold can buy; so it is no marvel that the masterpieces and treasures of the nations she subdued found their way to the Imperial City, mistress of the world. Even where the sleeper lay reclined upon a couch of curiously-carved wood from the forests that clothe Mount Hymettus, an owl so beautifully chiseled that its very breast-plumage seemed to ruffle in the breeze, looked down upon him from a niche where it had been placed at a cost that might have bought a dozen such human chattels as himself; for it had been brought from Athens as the most successful effort of a sculptor, who had devoted it to the honour of Minerva in his zeal. Refinement, luxury, nay, profusion, reigned paramount even here outside the sumptuous dwelling of a Roman lady: and the very ground in her porch over which she was borne, for she seldom touched it with her feet, was fresh swept and sanded as often as it had been disturbed by the tread of her litter-bearers, or the wheels of her chariot.

Many a time was this ceremony performed in the twenty-four hours; for Valeria was a woman of noble rank, great possessions, and the highest fashion. Not a vanity of her sex, not a folly was there of her class, in which she scrupled to indulge; and then, as now, ladies were prone to rush into extremes, and frivolity, when it took the garb of a female, assumed preposterous dimensions, and a thirst for amusement, incompatible with reason or self-control.

There is always a certain hush, and, as it were, a pompous stillness, about the houses of the great, even long after inferior mortals are astir in pursuit of their pleasure or their business. To-day was Valeria's birthday, and as such was duly observed by the hanging of garlands on the pillars of her porch; but after the completion of this graceful ceremony, silence seemed to have sunk once more upon the household, and the slave whose dream we have recorded, coming into her gates with an offering from his lord, and finding no domestics in the way, had sat him down to wait in the grateful shade, and, overcome with heat, might have slept on till noon had he not been roused by the grinding chariot-wheels, which mingled so confusedly with his dream.

It was no plebeian vehicle that now rolled into the colonnade, driven at a furious pace, and stopping so abruptly as to create considerable confusion and insubordination amongst the noble animals that drew it. The car, mounted on two wheels, was constructed of a highly-polished wood, cut from the wild fig-tree, elaborately inlaid with ivory and gold; the very spokes and felloes of the wheels were carved in patterns of vine-leaves and flowers, whilst the extremities of the pole, the axle, and the yoke, were wrought into exquisite representations of the wolf's head, an animal, from historical reasons, ever dear to the fancy of the Roman. There was but one person besides the driver in the carriage, and so light a draught might indeed command any rate of speed, when whirled along by four such horses as now plunged and reared and bit each other's crests in the portico of Valeria's mansion. These were of a milky white, with dark muzzles, and a bluish tinge under the coat, denoting its soft texture, and the Eastern origin of the animals. Some[pg 8]what thick of neck and shoulders, with semicircular jowl, it was the broad and tapering head, the small quivering ear, the wide red nostril, that demonstrated the purity of their blood, and argued extraordinary powers of speed and endurance; while their short, round backs, prominent muscles, flat legs, and dainty feet, promised an amount of strength and activity only to be attained by the production of perfect symmetry. These beautiful animals were harnessed four abreast—the inner pair, somewhat in the fashion of our modern curricle, being yoked to the pole, of which the very fastening-pins were steel overlaid with gold, whilst the outer horses, drawing only from a trace attached respectively on the inner side of each to the axle of the chariot, were free to wheel their quarters outwards in every direction, and kick to their heart's content—a liberty of which, in the present instance, they seemed well disposed to avail themselves.

The slave started to his feet as the nearest horse winced and swerved aside from his unexpected figure, snorting the while in mingled wantonness and fear. The axle grazed his tunic while it passed, and the driver, irritated at his horses' unsteadiness, or perhaps in the mere insolence of a great man's favourite, struck at him heavily with his whip as he went by. The Briton's blood boiled at the indignity; but his sinewy arm was up like lightning to parry the blow, and as the lash curled round his wrist he drew the weapon quickly from the driver's hand, and would have returned the insult with interest, had he not been deterred from his purpose by the youthful, effeminate appearance of the aggressor.

"I cannot strike a girl!" exclaimed the slave contemptuously, throwing the whip at the same time into the floor of the chariot, where it lit at the feet of the other occupant, a sumptuously-dressed nobleman, who enjoyed the discomfiture of his charioteer, with the loud frank glee of a master jeering a dependant.

"Well said, my hero!" laughed the patrician, adding in good-humoured, though haughty tones, "Not that I would give much for the chance of man or woman in a grasp like yours. By Jupiter! you've got the arms and shoulders of Antæus! Who owns you, my good fellow? and what do you here?"

"Nay, I would strike him again to some purpose if I were on the ground with him," interrupted the charioteer, a handsome, petulant youth of some sixteen summers, whose long flowing curls and rich scarlet mantle denoted a pampered [pg 9]and favourite slave. "Gently, Scipio! So-ho, Jugurtha! The horses will fret for an hour now they have been scared by his ugly face."

"Better let him alone, Automedon!" observed his master, again shaking his sides at the obvious discomfiture portrayed on the flushed face of his favourite. "Through your life keep clear of a man when he shuts his mouth like that, as you would of an ox with a wisp of hay on his horn. You silly boy! why he would swallow such a slender frame as yours at a gulp: and nobody but a fool ever strikes at a man unless he knows he can reach him, ay, and punish him too, without hurting his own knuckles in return! But what do you here, good fellow?" he repeated, addressing himself once more to the slave, who stood erect, scanning his questioner with a fearless, though respectful eye.

"My master is your friend," was the outspoken answer. "You supped with him only the night before last. But a man need not be in the household of Licinius, not have spent his best years at Rome, to know the face of Julius Placidus, the tribune."

A smile of gratified vanity stole over the patrician's countenance while he listened; a smile that had the effect of imparting to its lineaments an expression at once mocking, crafty, and malicious. In repose, and such was its usual condition, the face was almost handsome, perfect in its regularity, and of a fixed, sedate composure which bordered on vacuity, but when disturbed, as it sometimes, though rarely, was, by a passing emotion, the smile that passed over it like a lurid gleam, became truly diabolical.

The slave was right. Amongst all the notorious personages who crowded and jostled each other in the streets of Rome at that stormy period, none was better known, none more courted, flattered, honoured, hated, and mistrusted, than the occupant of the gilded chariot. It was no time for men to wear their hearts in their hands—it was no time to make an additional enemy, or to lose a possible friend. Since the death of Tiberius, emperor had succeeded emperor with alarming rapidity. Nero had indeed died by his own hand, to avoid the just retribution of unexampled vices and crimes; but the poisoned mushroom had carried off his predecessor, and the old man who succeeded him fell by the weapons of the very guards he had enlisted to protect his grey head from violence. Since then another suicide had indued Vitellius with the purple; but the throne of the Cæsars was fast becoming synonymous with a scaffold, and the sword of [pg 10]Damocles quivered more menacingly, and on a slenderer hair than ever, over the diadem.

When great political convulsions agitate a State, already seething with general vice and luxury, the moral scum seems, by a law of nature, to float invariably to the surface—the characters most destitute of principle, the readiest to obey the instincts of self-aggrandisement and expediency, achieve a kind of spurious fame, a doubtful and temporary success. Under the rule of Nero, perhaps, there was but one path to Court favour, and that lay in the disgraceful attempt to vie with this emperor's brutalities and crimes. The palace of Cæsar was then indeed a sink of foul iniquity and utter degradation. The sycophant who could most readily reduce himself to the level of a beast in gross sensuality, while he boasted a demon's refinement of cruelty, and morbid depravity of heart, became the first favourite for the time with his imperial master. To be fat, slothful, weak, gluttonous, and effeminate, while the brow was crowned with roses, and the brain was drenched with wine, and the hands were steeped in blood—this it was to be a friend and counsellor of Cæsar. Men waited and wondered in stupefied awe when they marked the monster reeling from a debauch to some fresh feast of horrors, some ingenious exhibition of the complicated tortures that may be inflicted on a human being, some devilish experiment of all the body can bear, ere the soul takes wing from its ghastly, mutilated tenement, and this not on one, but a thousand victims. They waited and wondered what the gods were about, that divine vengeance should slumber through such provocations as these.

But retribution overtook him at last. The heart which a slaughtered mother's spectre could not soften, which remorse for a pregnant wife's fate, kicked to death by a brutal lord, failed to wring, quailed at the approach of a few exasperated soldiers; and the tyrant who had so often smiled to see blood flow like water in the amphitheatre, died by his own hand—died as he had lived, a coward and a murderer to the last.

Since then, the Court was a sphere in which any bold unscrupulous man might be pretty sure of attaining success. The present emperor was a good-humoured glutton, one whose faculties, originally vigorous, had been warped and deadened by excess, just as his body had become bloated, his eye dimmed, his strength palsied, and his courage destroyed by the same course. The scheming statesman, the pliant courtier, the successful soldier had but one passion [pg 11]now, one only object for the exercise of his energies, both of mind and body—to eat enormously, to drink to excess, to study every art by which fresh appetite could be stimulated when gorged to repletion—and then—to eat and drink again.

With such a patron, any man who united to a tendency for the pleasures of the table, a strong brain, a cool head, and an aptitude for business, might be sure of considerable influence. The Emperor thoroughly appreciated one who would take trouble off his hands, while at the same time he encouraged his master, by precept and example, in his swinish propensities. It was no slight service to Vitellius, to rise from a debauch and give those necessary orders in an unforeseen emergency which Cæsar's sodden brain was powerless to originate or to understand.

Ere Placidus had been a month about the Court, he had insinuated himself thoroughly into the good graces of the Emperor. This man's had been a strange and stirring history. Born of patrician rank, he had used his family influence to advance him in the military service, and already, whilst still in the flower of youth, had attained the grade of tribune in Vespasian's army, then occupying Judæa under that distinguished general. Although no man yielded so willingly, or gave himself up so entirely to the indolent enjoyments of Asiatic life, Placidus possessed many of the qualities which are esteemed essential to the character of a soldier. Personal bravery, or we should rather say, insensibility to danger, was one of his peculiar advantages. Perhaps this is a quality inseparable from such an organisation as his, in which, while the system seems to contain a wealth of energy and vitality, the nerves are extremely callous to irritation, and completely under control. The tribune never came out in more favourable colours than when everyone about him was in a state of alarm and confusion. On one occasion, at the siege of Jotapata, where the Jews were defending themselves with the desperate energy of their race, Placidus won golden opinions from Vespasian by the cool dexterity with which he saved from destruction a whole company of soldiers and their centurion, under the very eye of his general.

A maniple, or, in the military language of to-day, a wing of the cohort led by Placidus was advancing to the attack, and the first centurion, with the company under his command, was already beneath the wall, bristling as it was with defenders, who hurled down on their assailants darts, [pg 12]javelins, huge stones, every description of weapon or missile, including molten lead and boiling oil. Under cover of a movable pent-house, which protected them, the head of the column had advanced their battering-ram to the very wall, and were swinging the huge engine back, by the ropes and pulleys which governed it, for an increased impulse of destruction, when the Jews, who had been watching their opportunity, succeeded in balancing an enormous mass of granite immediately above the pent-house and the materials of offence, animate and inanimate, which it contained. A Jewish warrior clad in shining armour had taken a lever in his hand, and was in the act of applying that instrument to the impending tottering mass; in another instant it must have crashed down upon their heads, and buried the whole band beneath its weight. At his appointed station by the eagle, the tribune was watching the movements of his men with his usual air of sleepy, indolent approval. And even in this critical moment his eye never brightened, his colour never deepened a shade. The voice was calm, low, and perfectly modulated in which he bade the trumpeter at his right hand sound the recall; nor, though its business-like rapidity could scarce have been exceeded by the most practised archer, was the movement the least hurried with which he snatched the bow from a dead Parthian auxiliary at his feet and fitted an arrow to its string. In the twinkling of an eye, while the granite vibrated on the very parapet, that arrow was quivering between the joints of the warrior's harness who held the lever, and he had fallen with his head over the wall in the throes of death. Before another of the defenders could take his place the assaulting party had retired, bringing along with them, in their cool and rigid discipline, the battering-ram and wooden covering which protected it, while the tribune quietly observed, as he replaced the bow into the fallen Parthian's hand, "A company saved is a hundred men gained. A dead barbarian is exactly worth my tallest centurion, and the smartest troop I have in the maniple!"

Vespasian was not the man to forget such an instance of cool promptitude, and Julius Placidus was marked out for promotion from that day forth. But with its courage, the tribune possessed the cunning of the tiger, not without something also of that fierce animal's outward beauty, and much of its watchful, pitiless, and untiring nature. A brave soldier should have considered it a degradation, under any circumstances, to play a double part; but with Placidus [pg 13]every step was esteemed honourable so long as it was on the ascent. The successful winner had no scruple in deceiving all about him at Rome, by the eagerness with which he assumed the character of a mere man of pleasure, while he lost no opportunity the while of ingratiating himself with the many desperate spirits who were to be found in the Imperial City, ready and willing to assist in any enterprise which should tend to anarchy and confusion. While he rushed into every extravagance and pleasure of that luxurious Court—while he vied with Cæsar himself in his profusion, and surpassed him in his orgies—he suffered no symptoms to escape him of a higher ambition than that of excellence in trifling—of deeper projects than those which affected the winecup, the pageant, and the passing follies of the hour. Yet all the while, within that dainty reveller's brain, schemes were forming and thoughts burning that should have withered the very roses on his brow. It might have been the strain of Greek blood which filtered through his veins, that tempered his Roman courage and endurance with the pliancy essential to conspiracy and intrigue—a strain that was apparent in his sculptured regularity of features, and general symmetry of form. His character has already been compared to the tiger's, and his movements had all the pliant ease and stealthy freedom of that graceful animal. His stature was little above the average of his countrymen, but his frame was cast in that mould of exact proportion which promises the extreme of strength combined with agility and endurance. Had he been caught like Milo, he would have writhed himself out of the trap, with the sinuous persistency of a snake. There was something snake-like, too, in his small glittering eye, and the clear smoothness of his skin. With all its brightness no woman worthy of the name but would have winced with womanly instincts of aversion and repugnance from his glance. With all its beauty no child would have looked up frankly and confidingly in his face. Men turned, indeed, to scan him approvingly as he passed; but the brave owned no sympathy with that smooth set brow, that crafty and malicious smile, while the timid or the superstitious shuddered and shrank away, averting their own gaze from what they felt to be the influence of the evil eye. Yet, in his snowy tunic bleached to dazzling white, in his collar of linked gold, his jewelled belt, his embroidered sandals, and the ample folds of his deep violet mantle, nearly approaching purple, Julius Placidus was no unworthy representative of his time and [pg 14]his order, no mean specimen of the wealth, and foppery, and extravagance of Rome.

Such was the man who now stood up in his gilded chariot at Valeria's door, masking with his usual expression of careless indolence, the real impatience he felt for tidings of its mistress.

[pg 15]

CHAPTER III

HERMES

It was customary with the more refined aristocracy of Rome, during the first century of the Empire, to pay great respect to Mercury, the god of invention and intrigue. Not that the qualities generally attributed to that power were calculated to inspire admiration or esteem, but simply because he had acquired a fortuitous popularity at a period when the graceful Pantheism of the nation was regulated by general opinion, and when a deity went in and out of fashion like a dress. At Valeria's porch, in common with many other great houses, stood an exquisite statue of the god, representing him as a youth, of athletic and symmetrical proportions, poised on a winged foot in the act of running, with the broad-leaf hat on his head, and the snake-turned rod in his hand. The countenance of the statue was expressive of intellect and vivacity, while the form was wrought into the highest ideal of activity and strength. It was placed on a square pedestal of marble immediately opposite the door; and behind this pedestal, the slave retired in some confusion when a train of maidens appeared from within, to answer the summons of Julius Placidus in his chariot.

The tribune did not think it necessary to alight, but producing from the bosom of his tunic a jewelled casket, leaned one hand on the shoulder of Automedon, while with the other he proffered his gift to a damsel who seemed the chief among her fellows, and whose manners partook largely of the flippancy of the waiting-maid.

"Commend me to your mistress," said Placidus, at the same time throwing a gold chain round her neck on her own account, and bending carelessly down to take a receipt for the same, in the shape of a caress; "bid her every good omen from the most faithful of her servants, and ask her at what hour I may hope to be received on this her birthday, which the trifle you carry to her from me will prove I have not forgotten."

[pg 16]

The waiting-maid tried hard to raise a blush, but with all her efforts the rich Southern colour would not deepen on her cheek; so she thought better of it, and looked him full in the face with her bold black eyes, while she replied: "You have forgotten surely, my lord, that this is the feast of Isis, and no lady that *is* a lady, at least here in Rome, can have leisure to-day for anything but the sacred mysteries of the goddess."

Placidus laughed outright; and it was strange how his laugh scared those who watched it. Automedon fairly turned pale, and even the waiting-maid seemed disconcerted for a moment.

"I have heard of these mysteries," said he, "my pretty Myrrhina, and who has not? The Roman ladies keep them somewhat jealously to themselves; and by all accounts it is well for our sex that they do so. Nevertheless there are yet some hours of sunlight to pass before the chaste rites of Egypt can possibly begin. Will not Valeria see me in the interval?"

A very quick ear might have detected the least possible tremor in the tribune's voice as he spoke the last sentence; it was not lost upon Myrrhina, for she showed all the white teeth in her large well-formed mouth, while she enumerated with immense volubility those different pursuits which filled up the day of a fashionable Roman lady.

"Impossible!" burst out the damsel. "She has not a moment to spare from now till sunset. There's her dinner,[1] and her fencing-lesson, and her bath, and her dressing, and the sculptor coming for her hand, and the painter for her face, and the new Greek sandals to be fitted to her feet. Then she has sent for Philogemon, the augur, to cast her horoscope, and for Galanthis, who is cleverer than ever Locusta was, and has twice the practice, to prepare a philtre. Maybe it is for *you*, my lord," added the girl roguishly. "I hear the ladies are all using them just now."

The evil smile crossed the tribune's face once more; perhaps he too had been indebted to the potions of Galanthis, for purposes of love or hate, and he did not care to be reminded of them.

"Nay," said he meaningly, "there is no need for that. Valeria can do more with one glance of her bright eyes, than all the potions and poisons of Galanthis put together. Say, Myrrhina—you are in my interest—does she look more favourably of late?"

"How can I tell, my lord?" answered the girl, with an [pg 17]arch expression of amusement and defiance in her face. "My mistress is but a woman after all, and they say women are more easily mastered by the strong hand, than lured by the honey lip. She is not to be won by a smooth tongue and a beardless face, I know, for I heard her say so to Paris myself, in the very spot where we are now standing. Juno! but the player slunk away somewhat crestfallen, I can tell you, when she called him 'a mere girl in her brother's clothes' at the best. No; the man who wins my mistress will be a man all over, I'll answer for it! So far, she is like the rest of us for that matter."

And Myrrhina sighed, thinking, it may be, of some sunburnt youth the while, whose rough but not unwelcome wooing had assailed her in her early girlhood, ere she came to Rome; far away yonder amongst the blushing vines, in the bright Campanian hills.

"Say you so?" observed the tribune, obviously flattered by the implied compliment; for he was proud in his secret heart of his bodily strength. "Nay, there was a fellow standing here when I drove up, who would make an easy conquest of you, Myrrhina, if, like your Sabine grandams, you must be borne off to be wed, on your lover's shoulders. By the body of Hercules! he would tuck you up under his arm as easily as you carry that casket, which you seem so afraid to let out of your hand. Ay, there he is! lurking behind Hermes. Stand forth, my good fellow! What! you are not afraid of Automedon, are you, and the crack of that young reprobate's whip?"

While he spoke, the slave stepped forward from his lurking-place behind the statue, where the quick eye of Placidus had detected him, and presented to Myrrhina with a respectful gesture the offering of his lord to her mistress—a filigree basket of frosted silver, filled with a few choice fruits and flowers—

"From Caius Licinius, greeting," said he, "in honour of Valeria's natal day. The flowers are scarce yet dry from the spray that brawling Anio flings upon its banks; the fruits were glowing in yesterday's sun, on the brightest slopes of Tibur. My master offers the freshest and fairest of his fruits and flowers to his kinswoman, who is fresher and fairer than them all."

He delivered his message, which he had obviously learned by rote, in sufficiently pure and fluent Latin, scarcely tinged with the accent of a barbarian, and bowing low as he placed the basket in Myrrhina's hand, drew himself up to his [pg 18]noble height, and looked proudly, almost defiantly, at the tribune.

The girl started and turned pale—it seemed as if the statue of Hermes had descended from its pedestal to do her homage. He stood there, that glorious specimen of manhood, in his majestic strength and symmetry, in the glow of his youth, and health, and beauty, like an impersonation of the god. Myrrhina, in common with many of her sex, was easily fascinated by external advantages, and she laughed nervously, while she accepted with shaking hands the handsome slave's offering to his master's kinswoman.

"Will you not enter?" said she, the colour mantling once more, and this time without an effort, in her burning cheeks. "It is not the custom to depart from Valeria's house without breaking bread and drinking wine."

But the slave excused himself, abruptly, almost rudely, losing, be sure, by his refusal, none of the ground he had already gained in Myrrhina's good graces. It chafed him to remain even at the porch. The atmosphere of luxury that pervaded it, seemed to weigh upon his senses, and oppress his breath. Moreover, the insult he had sustained from Automedon, yet rankled in his heart. How he wished the boy-charioteer was nearer his match in size and strength! He would have hurled him from the chariot where he stood, turning his curls so insolently round his dainty fingers— hurled him to earth beyond his horses' heads, and taught him the strength of a Briton's arm and the squeeze of a Briton's gripe. "Ay! and his master after him!" thought the slave, for already he experienced towards Placidus that unaccountable instinct of aversion which seems to warn men of a future foe, and which, to give him his due, the tribune was not unused to awaken in a brave and honest breast.

Placidus, however, scanned him once more, as he strode away, with the critical gaze of a judge of human animals. It was this man's peculiarity to look on all he met as possible tools, that might come into use for various purposes at a future and indefinite time. If he observed more than usual courage in a soldier, superior acuteness in a freedman, nay, even uncommon beauty in a woman, he bethought himself that although he might have no immediate use for these qualities, occasions often arose on which he could turn them to his profit, and he noted, and made sure of, their amount accordingly. In the present instance, although somewhat surprised that he had never before remarked the slave's stalwart proportions in the household of Licinius, whose [pg 19]affection for the Briton had excused him from all menial offices, and consequent contact with visitors, he determined not to lose sight of one so formed by nature to excel in the gymnasium or the amphitheatre, while there crept into his heart a cruel cold-blooded feeling of satisfaction at the possibility of witnessing so muscular and shapely a figure in the contortions of a mortal struggle, or the throes of a painful death.

Besides, there was envy, too, at the bottom—envy in the proud patrician's breast, leaning so negligently on the cushions of his gilded chariot, with all his advantages of rank, reputation, wealth, and influence—envy of the noble bearing, the personal comeliness, and the free manly step of the slave.

"Had he struck thee, Automedon," said his master, unable to resist taunting the petted youth who held the reins; "had he but laid a finger on thee, thou hadst never spoken again, and I had been rid of the noisiest and most useless of my household. Gently with that outside horse; dost see how he chafes upon the rein? Gently, boy, I say! and drive me back into the Forum."

As he settled himself among the cushions and rolled swiftly away, Myrrhina came forth into the porch once more. She seemed, however, scarcely to notice the departing chariot, but looked dreamily about her, and then re-entered the house with a shake of the head, a smile, and something that was almost a sigh.

[pg 20]

CHAPTER IV

APHRODITÉ

A negro boy, the ugliest of his kind, and probably all the more prized for that reason, was shifting uneasily from knee to knee, in an attitude of constraint that showed how long and tiresome he felt his office, and how wearied he was of Valeria's own apartment. Such a child, for the urchin seemed of the tenderest age, might be initiated without impropriety into the mysteries of a lady's toilet; and, indeed, the office it was his duty to undertake, formed the most indispensable part of the whole performance. With a skill and steadiness beyond his years, though with a rueful face, he was propping up an enormous mirror, in which his mistress might contemplate the whole galaxy of her charms—a mirror formed of one broad plate of silver, burnished to the brightness and lucidity of glass, set in an oval frame of richly chased gold, wrought into fantastic patterns and studded with emeralds, rubies, and other precious stones. Not a speck was to be discerned on the polish of its dazzling surface; and, indeed, the time of one maiden was devoted to the task alone of preserving it from the lightest breath that might dim its brightness, and cloud the reflection of the stately form that now sat before it, undergoing, at the hands of her attendants, the pleasing tortures of an elaborate toilet.

The reflection was that of a large handsome woman in the very prime and noontide of her beauty—a woman whose every movement and gesture bespoke physical organisation of a vigorous nature and perfect health. While the strong white neck gave grace and dignity to her carriage—while the deep bosom and somewhat massive shoulders partook more of Juno's majestic frame than Hebe's pliant youth—while the full sweep and outline of her figure denoted maturity and completeness in every part—the long round limbs, the shapely hands and feet, might have belonged to Diana, so perfect was their symmetry; the warm flush that tinted them, the voluptuous ease of her attitude, the gentle languor of her [pg 21]whole bearing, would have done no discredit to the goddess, hanging over the mountain-tops in the golden summer nights to look down upon Endymion, and bathe her sleeping favourite in floods of light and love.

Too fastidious a critic might have objected to Valeria's form that it expressed more of physical strength than is compatible with perfect womanly beauty, that the muscles were developed overmuch, and the whole frame, despite its flowing outlines, partook somewhat of a man's organisation, and a man's redundant strength. The same fault might have been found in a less degree with her countenance. There was a little too much resolution in the small aquiline nose, something of manly audacity and energy in the large well-formed mouth, with its broad white teeth that the fullest and reddest of lips could not conceal—a shade of masculine sternness on the low wide brow, smooth and white, but somewhat prominent, and scarcely softened by the arch of the marked eyebrows, or the dark sweep of the lashes that fringed the long laughing eyes.

And yet it was a face that a man, and still more a boy, could hardly have looked on without misgivings that he might too soon learn to long for its glances, its smiles, its approval, and its love. There was such a glow of health on the soft transparent skin, such a freshness and vitality in the colour of those blooming cheeks, such a sparkle in the grey eyes, that flashed so meaningly when she smiled, that gleamed so clear and bright and cold when the features resumed their natural expression, grave, scornful, almost stern in their repose; and then such womanly softness in the masses of rich nut-brown hair that showered down neck and shoulders, to form a framework for this lovely, dangerous, and too alluring picture. Even the little negro, wearied as he was, peeped at intervals from the back of the mirror he upheld, fawning like a dog for some sign of approval from his haughty, careless mistress. At length she bade him keep still, with a half-scornful smile at his antics; and the sharp white teeth gleamed from ear to ear of the dusky little face, as it grinned with pleasure, while the boy settled himself once more in an attitude of patience and steady submission.

Nor was Valeria's apartment unworthy of the noble beauty who devoted it to the mysterious rites of dress and decoration. Everything that luxury could imagine for bodily ease, everything that science had as yet discovered for the preservation or the production of feminine attractions, was there to be found in its handsomest and costliest form. In [pg 22]one recess, shrouded by transparent curtains of the softest pink, was the bath that could be heated at will to any temperature, and the marble steps of which that shapely form was accustomed to descend twice and thrice a day. In another stood the ivory couch with its quilted crimson silks and ornamental pillars of solid gold, in which Valeria slept, and dreamed such dreams as hover round the rest of those whose life is luxury, and whose business is a ceaseless career of pleasure. On a table of cedar-wood, fashioned like a palm-leaf opening out from a pedestal that terminated in a single claw of grotesque shape, stood her silver night-lamp, exhaling odours of perfumed oil, and near it lay the waxen tablets, on which she made her memorandums, or composed her love-letters, and from which, as from an unfinished task, the sharp-pointed steel pencil had rolled away upon the shining floor. Through the whole court—for court it might be called, with its many entrances and recesses, its cool and shady nooks, its lofty ceiling and its tesselated pavement—choice vases, jewelled cups, burnished chalices, and exquisite little statues, were scattered in systematic irregularity and graceful profusion. Even the very water in the bath flowed through the mouth of a marble Cupid; and two more winged urchins wrought in bronze, supported a stand on which was set a formidable array of perfumes, essences, cosmetics, and such material for offensive and defensive warfare.

The walls, too, of this seductive arsenal, were delicately tinted of a light rose-colour, that should throw the most becoming shade over its inmates, relieved at intervals by oval wreaths wrought out in bas-relief, enclosing diverse mythological subjects, in which the figure of Venus, goddess of love and laughter, predominated. Round the cornices stretched a frieze representing, also in relief, the fabulous contests of the Amazons with every description of monster, amongst which the most conspicuous foe was the well-known gryphon, or griffin, an abnormal quadruped, with the head and neck of a bird of prey. It was curious to trace in the female warriors thus delineated, something of the imperious beauty, the vigorous symmetry, and the dauntless bearing that distinguished Valeria herself, though their energetic and spirited attitudes afforded, at the same time, a marked contrast to the pleasing languor that seemed to pervade every movement of that luxurious lady reclining before her mirror, and submitting indolently to the attentions of her maid-servants.

These were five in number, and constituted the principal slaves of her household; the most important among them [pg 23]seemed to be a tall matronly woman, considerably older than her comrades, who filled the responsible office of housekeeper in the establishment—a dignity which did not, however, exempt her from insult, and even blows, when she failed to satisfy the caprices of a somewhat exacting mistress; the others, comely laughing girls, with the sparkling eyes and white teeth of their countrywomen, seemed principally occupied with the various matters that constituted their lady's toilet—a daily penance, in which, notwithstanding the rigour of its discipline, and the severities that were sure to follow the most trifling act of negligence, they took an inexplicable and essentially feminine delight.

Of these it was obvious that Myrrhina was the first in place as in favour. She it was who brought her mistress the warm towels for her bath; who was ready with her slippers when she emerged; who handed every article of clothing as it was required; whose taste was invariably consulted, and whose decision was considered final, on such important points as the position of a jewel, the studied negligence of a curl, or the exact adjustment of a fold.

This girl possessed, with an Italian exterior, the pliant cunning and plausible fluency of the Greek. Born a slave on one of Valeria's estates in the country, she had been reared a mere peasant, on a simple country diet, and amidst healthful country occupations, till a freak of her mistress brought her to Rome. With a woman's versatility—with a woman's quickness in adapting herself to a strange phase of life and a total change of circumstances—the country girl had not been a year in her new situation, ere she became the acutest and cleverest waiting-maid in the capital, with what benefit to her own morals and character, it is needless to inquire. Who so quick as Myrrhina to prepare the unguents, the perfumes, or the cosmetics that repaired the injuries of climate, and effaced the marks of dissipation? Who so delicate a sempstress; who had such taste in colours; who could convey a note or a message with half such precision, simplicity, and tact? In short, who was ever so ready, in an emergency, with brush, crisping-iron, needle, hand, eye, or tongue? Intrigue was her native element. To lie on her mistress's behalf, seemed as natural as on her own. He who would advance in Valeria's goodwill, must begin by bribing her maid; and many a Roman gallant had ere this discovered that even that royal road to success was as tedious as it was costly, and might lead eventually to discomfiture and disgrace.

[pg 24]

As she took the pouncet-box from one of the girls, and proceeded to sprinkle gold-dust in Valeria's hair, Myrrhina's eye was caught by the gift of Placidus, lying neglected at her feet, the casket open, the jewels scattered on the floor. Such as it was, the waiting-maid owned a conscience. It warned her that she had not as yet worked out the value of the costly chain thrown round her neck by the tribune. Showering the gold-dust liberally about her lady's head, Myrrhina felt her way cautiously to the delicate theme.

"There's a new fashion coming in for headgear when the weather gets cooler," said she. "It's truth I tell you, madam, for I heard it direct from Selina, who was told by the Empress's first tirewoman, though even Cæsar himself cannot think Galeria looks well, with that yellow mop stuck all over her head. But it's to be the fashion, nevertheless, and right sorry I am to hear it; nor am I the only one for that matter."

"Why so?" asked Valeria languidly; "is it more troublesome than the present?"

Myrrhina had done with the gold-dust now, and, holding the comb in her mouth, was throwing a rich brown curl across her wrist, while she laid a plat carefully beneath it. Notwithstanding the impediment between her lips, however, she was able to reply with great volubility.

"The trouble counts for nothing, madam, when a lady has got such hair as yours. It's a pleasure to run your hands through it, let alone dressing and crisping it, and plaiting it up into a crown that's fit for a queen. But this new fashion will make us all alike, whether we're as bald as old Lyce, or wear our curls down to our ankles, like Neæra. Still, to hide such hair as *yours*;—as my lord said, only this morning"—

"What lord? this morning!" interrupted Valeria, a dawn of interest waking on her handsome features; "not Licinius, my noble kinsman? His approval is indeed worth having."

"Better worth than his gifts," answered Myrrhina pertly; pointing to the filigree basket which occupied a place of honour on the toilet-table. "Such a birthday present I never saw! A few late roses and a bunch or two of figs to the richest lady in Rome! To be sure, he sent a messenger with them, who might have come direct from Jove, and the properest man I ever set eyes on."

And Myrrhina moved to one side, that her lady might not observe the blush that rose, even to her shameless brow, as she recalled the impression made on her by the handsome slave. Valeria liked to hear of proper men; she woke up a [pg 25]little out of her languor, and flung the hair back from her face.

"Go on," said she, as Myrrhina hesitated, half eager and half loth to pursue the pleasing topic.

But the waiting-maid felt the chain round her neck, and acknowledged in her heart the equivalent it demanded.

"It was the tribune, madam," said she, "who spoke about your hair—Julius Placidus, who values every curl you wear, more than a whole mine of gold. Ah! there's not a lord in Rome has such a taste in dress. Only to see him this morning, with his violet mantle and his jewels sparkling in the sun, with the handsomest chariot and the four whitest horses in the town. Well! if I was a lady, and wooed by such a man as that"—

"*Man* call you him?" interrupted her mistress, with a scornful smile. "Nay, when these curled, perfumed, close-shaven things are called men, 'tis time for us women to bestir ourselves, lest strength and courage die out in Rome altogether. And you, too, Myrrhina, who know Licinius and Hippias, and saw with your own eyes two hundred gladiators in the circus only yesterday, you ought to be a better judge. Man, forsooth! Why, you will be calling smooth-faced Paris a man next!"

Here maid and mistress burst out laughing, for thereby hung a tale of which Valeria was not a little proud. This Paris, a young Egyptian, of beautiful but effeminate appearance, had lately come to Italy to figure with no small success on the Roman stage. His delicate features, his symmetrical shape, and the girlish graces of his pantomimic gestures, had made sad havoc in the hearts of the Roman ladies, at all times too susceptible to histrionic charms. He lost nothing, either, of public attention, by bearing the name of Nero's ill-fated favourite, and embarked at once, unhesitatingly, on the same brilliant and dangerous career. But although it was the fashion to be in love with Paris, Valeria alone never yielded to the mode, but treated him with all the placid indifference she felt for attractions that found no favour in her sight. Stung by such neglect, the petted actor paid devoted court to the woman who despised him, and succeeded, after much importunity, in prevailing on her to accord him an interview in her own house. Of this he had the bad taste to make no small boast in anticipation; and Myrrhina, who found out most things, lost no time in informing her mistress that her condescension was already as much misrepresented as it was misplaced. The two laid their plans accordingly; [pg 26]and when Paris, attired in the utmost splendour, arrived panting to the promised interview, he found himself seized by some half-dozen hideous old negresses, who smothered him with caresses, stripped him from head to foot, forced him into the bath, and persisted in treating him as if he were a delicate young lady, but with a quiet violence the while, that it was useless to resist. The same swarthy tirewomen then dressed him in female garments; and despite of threats, struggles, outcries, and entreaties, placed him in Valeria's litter, and so carried him home to his own door. The ready wit of the play-actor put upon his metamorphosis the construction least favourable to the character of its originator; but he vowed a summary vengeance, we may be sure, nevertheless.

"I think Paris knows what you think of him only too well," resumed Myrrhina; "not but that he has a fair face of his own, and a lovely shape for dancing, though, to be sure, Placidus is a finer figure of a man. Oh! if you could have seen him this morning, madam, when he lay back so graceful in his chariot, and chid that pert lad of his for striking with his whip at the tall slave, who to be sure vanished like a flash of lightning, you would have said there wasn't such another patrician in the whole city of Rome!"

"Enough of Placidus!" interrupted her mistress impatiently; "the subject wearies me. What of this tall slave, Myrrhina, who seems to have attracted your attention? Did he look like one of the barbarians my kinsman Licinius cries up so mightily? Is he handsome enough to step with my Liburnians, think you, under the day-litter?"

The waiting-maid's eyes sparkled as she thought how pleasant it would be to have him in the same household as herself; and any little restraint she might have experienced in running over the personal advantages that had captivated her fancy disappeared before this agreeable prospect.

"Handsome enough, madam!" she exclaimed, removing the comb from her mouth, dropping her lady's hair, and flourishing her hands with true Italian emphasis and rapidity,—"handsome enough! why he would make the Liburnians look like bald-headed vultures beside a golden eagle! Barbarian, like enough, he may be, Cimbrian, Frisian, Ansibarian, or what not, for I caught the foreign accent tripping on his tongue, and we have few men in Rome of stature equal to his. A neck like a tower of marble; arms and shoulders like the statue of Hercules yonder in the vestibule; a face, ay, twice as beautiful as Pericles on your medallion, with the [pg 27]golden curls clustering round a forehead as white as milk and eyes"—

Here Myrrhina stopped, a little at a loss for a simile, and a good deal out of breath besides.

"Go on," said Valeria, who had been listening in an attitude of languid attention, her eyes half closed, her lips parted, and the colour deepening on her cheek. "What were his eyes like, Myrrhina?"

"Well, they were like the blue sky of Campania in the vintage; they were like the stones round the boss of your state-mantle; they were like the sea at noonday from the long walls of Ostia. And yet they flashed into sparks of fire when he looked at poor little Automedon. I wonder the boy wasn't frightened! I am sure I should have been; only nothing frightens those impudent young charioteers."

"Was he my kinsman's slave; are you sure, Myrrhina?" said her mistress, in an accent of studied unconcern, and never moving a finger from her listless and comfortable attitude.

"No doubt of it, madam," replied the waiting-maid; and would probably have continued to enlarge on the congenial subject, had she not been interrupted by the entrance of one of the damsels who had been summoned from the apartment, and returned to announce that Hippias, the retired gladiator, was in waiting—"Would Valeria take her fencing-lesson?"

But Valeria declined at once, and sat on before her mirror, without even raising her eyes to the tempting picture it displayed. Whatever was the subject of her thoughts, it must have been very engrossing, she seemed so loth to be disturbed.

[pg 28]

CHAPTER V

ROME

Meanwhile the British slave, unconscious that he was already the object of Valeria's interest and Myrrhina's admiration, was threading his way through the crowded streets that adjoined the Forum, enjoying that vague sense of amusement with which a man surveys a scene of bustle and confusion that does not affect his immediate concerns. Thanks to the favour of his master, his time was nearly at his own disposal, and he had ample leisure to observe the busiest scene in the known world, and to compare it, perhaps, with the peace and simplicity of those early days, which seemed now like the memories of a dream, so completely had they passed away. The business of the Forum was over: the markets were disgorging their mingled stream of purveyors, purchasers, and idle lookers-on. The whole population of Rome was hurrying home to dinner, and a motley crowd it was. The citizens themselves, the Plebeians, properly so called, scarcely formed one half of the swarming assemblage. Slaves innumerable hurried to and fro, to speed the business or the pleasure of their lords; slaves of every colour and of every nation, from the Scandinavian giant, with blue eyes and waving yellow locks, to the sturdy Ethiopian, thick-lipped, and woolly-haired, the swarthy child of Africa, whose inheritance has been servitude from the earliest ages until now. Many a Roman born was there, too, amongst the servile crowd, aping the appearance and manner of a citizen, but who shrank from a master's frown at home, and who, despite the acquirement of wealth, and even the attainment of power, must die a bondsman as he had lived.

Not the least characteristic feature of the state of society [pg 29]under the Empire was the troop of freedmen that everywhere accompanied the person, and swelled the retinue of each powerful patrician. These manumitted slaves were usually bound by the ties of interest as much as gratitude to the former master, who had now become their patron. Dependent on him in many cases for their daily food, doled out to them in rations at his door, they were necessarily little emancipated from his authority by their lately acquired freedom. While the relation of patron and client was productive of crying evils in the Imperial City, while the former threw the shield of his powerful protection over the crimes of the latter, and the client in return became the willing pander to his patron's vices, it was the freedman who, more than all others, rendered himself a willing tool to his patrician employer, who yielded unhesitatingly time, affections, probity, and honour itself, to the caprices of his lord. They swarmed about the Forum now, running hither and thither with the obsequious haste of the parasite, bent on errands which in too many cases would scarce have borne the light of day.

Besides these, a vast number of foreigners, wearing the costumes of their different countries, hindered the course of traffic as they stood gaping, stupefied by the confusing scene on which they gazed. The Gaul, with his short, close-fitting garment; the Parthian, with his conical sheepskin cap; the Mede, with his loose silken trousers; the Jew, barefoot and robed in black; the stately Spaniard, the fawning Egyptian, and amongst them all, winding his way wherever the crowd was closest, with perfect ease and self-possession, the smooth and supple Greek. When some great man passed through the midst, borne aloft in his litter, or leaning on the shoulder of a favourite slave, and freedmen and clients made a passage for him with threat, and push, and blow, the latter would invariably miss the Greek to light on the pate of a humble mechanic, or the shoulders of a sturdy barbarian, while the descendant of Leonidas or Alcibiades would reply in whining sing-song tones to the verbal abuse, with some biting retort, which was sure to turn the laughter of the crowd on the aggressor.

If Rome had once overrun and conquered the dominions of her elder sister in civilisation, the invasion seemed now to be all the other way. With the turn of the tide had come such an overflow of Greek manners, Greek customs, Greek morals, and Greek artifice, that the Imperial City was already losing its natural characteristics; and the very language was so interlarded with the vocabulary of the conquered, that it [pg 30]was fast becoming less Latin than Greek. The Roman ladies, especially, delighted in those euphonious syllables, which clothed Athenian eloquence in such melodious rhythm; and their choicest terms of endearment in the language of love, were invariably whispered in Greek.

That supple nation, too, adapting itself to the degradation of slavery and the indulgence of ease, as it had risen in nobler times to the exigencies of liberty and the efforts demanded by war, had usurped the greater portion of art, science, and even power, in Rome. The most talented painters and sculptors were Greeks. The most enterprising contractors and engineers were Greeks. Rhetoric and elocution could only be learned in a Greek school, and mathematics, unless studied with Greek letters, must be esteemed confused and useless; the fashionable invalid who objected to consult a Greek physician deserved to die; and there was but one astrologer in Rome who could cast a patrician horoscope. Of course he was a Greek. In the lower walks of criminal industry; in the many iniquitous professions called into existence by the luxury of a great city, the Greeks drove a thriving and almost an exclusive trade. Whoever was in most repute, as an evil counsellor, a low buffoon, a money-lender, pimp, pander, or parasite, whatever might be his other qualifications, was sure to be a Greek. And many a scrutinising glance was cast by professors of this successful nation at the Briton's manly form as he strode through the crowd, making his way quietly but surely from sheer weight and strength. They followed him with covetous eyes, as they speculated on the various purposes to which so much good manhood might be applied. They appraised him, so to speak, and took an inventory of his thews and sinews, his limbs, his stature, and his good looks; but they refrained from accosting him with importunate questions or insolent proposals, for there was a bold confident air about him, that bespoke the stout heart and the ready hand. The stamp of freedom had not yet faded from his brow, and he looked like one who was accustomed to take his own part in a crowd.

Suddenly a stoppage in the traffic arrested the moving stream, which swelled in continually to a struggling, eager, vociferating mass. A dray, containing huge blocks of marble, and drawn by several files of oxen, had become entangled with the chariot of a passing patrician, and another great man's litter being checked by the obstruction, much confusion and bad language was the result. Amused with the turmoil, and in no hurry to get home, the British slave stood looking [pg 31]over the heads of the populace at the irritated and gesticulating antagonists, when a smart blow on the shoulder caused him to wheel suddenly round, prepared to return the injury with interest. At the same instant a powerful hand dragged him back by the tunic, and a grasp was laid on him, from which he could not shake himself free, while a rough good-humoured voice whispered in his ear—

"Softly, lad, softly! Keep hands off Cæsar's lictors an' thou be'st not mad in good earnest. These gentry give more than they take, I can promise thee!"

The speaker was a broad powerful man of middle size, with the chest of a Hercules; he held the Briton firmly pinioned in his arms while he spoke, and it was well that he did so, for the lictors were indeed forcing a passage for the Emperor himself, who was proceeding on foot, and as far as was practicable *incog.*, to inspect the fish-market.

Vitellius shuffled along with the lagging step of an infirm and bloated old man. His face was pale and flabby, his eye dim, though sparkling at intervals with some little remnant of the ready wit and pliant humour that had made him the favourite of three emperors ere he himself attained the purple. Supported by two freedmen, preceded and followed only by a file of lictors, and attended by three or four slaves, Cæsar was taking his short walk in hopes of acquiring some little appetite for dinner: what locality so favourable for the furtherance of this object as the fish-market, where the imperial glutton could feast his eyes, if nothing else, on the choicest dainties of the deep? He was so seldom seen abroad in Rome, that the Briton could not forbear following him with his glance, while his new friend, relaxing his hold with great caution, whispered once more in his ear—

"Ay, look well at him, man, and give Jove thanks thou art not an emperor. There's a shape for the purple! There's a head to carry a diadem! Well, well, for all he's so white and flabby now, like a Lucrine turbot, he could drive a chariot once, and hold his own at sword and buckler with the best of them. They say he can drink as well as ever still. Not that he was a match for Nero in his best days, even at that game. Ay, ay, they may talk as they will: we've never had an emperor like *him* before nor since. Wine, women, shows, sacrifices, wild-beast fights;—a legion of men all engaged in the circus at once! Such a friend as he was to *our* trade."

"And that trade?" inquired the Briton good-humouredly enough, now his hands were free: "I think I can guess it without asking too many questions."

[pg 32]

"No need to guess," replied the other. "I'm not ashamed of my trade, nor of my name neither. Maybe you have heard of Hirpinus, the gladiator? Tuscan born, free Roman citizen, and willing to match himself with any man of his weight, on foot or on horseback, blindfold or half-armed, in or out of a war-chariot, with two swords, sword and buckler, or sword or spear. Any weapon, and every weapon, always excepting the net and the noose. Those I can't bear talking about—to my mind they are not fair fighting. But what need I tell *you* all about it?" he added, running his eye over the slave's powerful frame. "I must surely have seen you before. You look as if you belonged to the Family yourself!"

The slave smiled, not insensible to the compliment.

"'Tis a manlier way of getting bread than most of the employments I see practised in Rome," was his reply, though he spoke more to himself than his companion. "A man might die a worse death than in the amphitheatre," he added meditatively.

"A worse death!" echoed Hirpinus. "He could scarce die a better! Think of the rows of heads one upon another piled up like apples to the very awnings. Think of the patricians and senators wagering their collars and bracelets, and their sesterces in millions, on the strength of your arm, and the point of your blade. Think of your own vigour and manhood, trained till you feel as strong as an elephant, and as lithe as a panther, with an honest wooden buckler on your arm, and two feet of pliant steel in your hand, as you defile by Cæsar and bid him 'Good-morrow, from those who have come here to die!' Think of the tough bout with your antagonist, foot to foot, hand to hand, eye to eye, feeling his blade with your own (why a swordsman, lad, can fence as well in the dark as the daylight!), foiling his passes, drawing his attack, learning his feints, watching your opportunity; when you catch it at last, in you dash like a wild-cat, and the guard of your sword rings sharp and true against his breastbone, as he goes over backwards on the sand!"

"And if *he* gets the opportunity first?" asked the slave, interested in spite of himself at the enthusiasm which carried him irresistibly along with it. "If your guard is an inch too high, your return a thought too slow? If you go backwards on the sand, with the hilt at your breastbone, and the two feet of steel in your bosom? How does it feel then?"

[pg 33]

"Faith, lad, you must cross the Styx to have that question fairly answered," replied the other. "I have had no such experience yet. When it comes I shall know how to meet it. But this talking makes a man thirsty, and the sun is hot enough to bake a negro here. Come with me, lad! I know a shady nook, where we can pierce a skin of wine, and afterwards play a game at quoits, or have a bout of wrestling, to while away the afternoon."

The slave was nothing loth. Besides the debt of gratitude he owed for preservation from a serious danger, there was something in his new friend's rough, good-humoured, and athletic manhood that won on the Briton's favour. Hirpinus, with even more than their fierce courage, had less than the usual brutality of his class, and possessed besides a sort of quaint and careless good-humour, by no means rare among the athletes of every time, which found its way at once to the natural sympathies of the slave. They started off accordingly, on the most amicable terms, in search of that refreshment which a few hours' exposure to an Italian sun rendered very desirable; but the crowd had not yet cleared off, and their progress was necessarily somewhat slow, notwithstanding that the throng of passengers gave way readily enough before two such stalwart and athletic forms.

Hirpinus thought it incumbent on him to take the Briton, as it were, under his protection, and to point out to him the different objects of interest, and the important personages, to be seen at that hour in the streets of the capital, totally irrespective of the fact that his pupil was as well instructed on these points as himself. But the gladiator dearly loved a listener, and, truth to tell, was extremely diffuse in his narratives when he had got one to his mind. These generally turned on his own physical prowess, and his deadly exploits in the amphitheatre, which he was by no means disposed to underrate. There are some really brave men who are also boasters, and Hirpinus was one of them.

He was in the midst of a long dissertation on the beauties of an encounter fought out between naked combatants, armed only with the sword, and was explaining at great length a certain fatal thrust outside his antagonist's guard, and over his elbow, which he affirmed to be his own invention, and irresistible by any party yet discovered, when the slave felt his gown plucked by a female hand, and turning sharply round was somewhat disconcerted to find himself face to face with Valeria's waiting-maid.

"You are wanted," said she unceremoniously, and with an [pg 34]imperious gesture. "You are to come to my lady this instant. Make haste, man; she cannot brook waiting."

Myrrhina pointed while she spoke to where a closed litter borne aloft by four tall Liburnian slaves, had stopped the traffic, and already become the nucleus of a crowd. A white hand peeped through its curtains, as the slave approached, surprised and somewhat abashed at this unexpected appeal. Hirpinus looked on with grave approval the while. Arriving close beneath the litter, of which the curtain was now open, the slave paused and made a graceful obeisance; then, drawing himself up proudly, stood erect before it, looking unconsciously his best, in the pride of his youth and beauty. Valeria's cheek was paler than usual, and her attitude more languid, but her grey eyes sparkled, and a smile played round her mouth as she addressed him.

"Myrrhina tells me that you are the man who brought a basket of flowers to my house this morning from Licinius. Why did you not wait to carry back my salutations to my kinsman?"

The colour mounted to the slave's brow as he thought of Automedon's insolence, but he only replied humbly, "Had I known it was your wish, lady, I had been standing in your porch till now."

She marked his rising colour, and attributed it to the effect of her own dazzling beauty.

"Myrrhina knew you at once in the crowd," said she graciously; "and indeed yours is a face and figure not easily mistaken in Rome. I should recognise you myself anywhere now."

She paused, expecting a suitable reply, but the slave, albeit not insensible to the compliment, only blushed again and was silent. Valeria, meanwhile, whose motives in summoning him to her litter had been in the first instance of simple curiosity to see the stalwart barbarian who had so excited Myrrhina's admiration, and whom that sharp-sighted damsel had recognised in an instant amongst the populace, now found herself pleased and interested by the quiet demeanour and noble bearing of this foreign slave. She had always been susceptible to manly beauty, and here she beheld it in its noblest type. She was rapacious of admiration in all quarters; and here she could not but flatter herself she gathered an undoubted tribute to the power of her charms. She owned all a woman's interest in anything that had a spice of mystery or romance, and a woman's unfailing instinct in discovering high birth and gentle breeding under every [pg 35]disguise; and here she found a delightful puzzle in the manner and appearance of her kinsman's messenger, whose position seemed so at variance with his looks. She had never in her life laid the slightest restraint on her thoughts, and but little on her actions—she had never left a purpose unfulfilled, nor a wish ungratified—but a strange and new feeling, at which even her courageous nature quailed, seemed springing up in her heart while she gazed with half-closed eyes at the Briton, and hesitated to confess, even to herself, that she had never seen such a man as this in her life before. It was in a softened tone that she again addressed him, moving on her couch to show an ivory shoulder and a rounded arm to the best advantage.

"You are a confidential servant of my kinsman's? You are attached to his person, and always to be found in his household?" she asked, more with a view of detaining him than for any fixed purpose.

"I would give my life for Licinius!" was the prompt and spirited reply.

"But you are gentle born," she resumed, with increasing interest; "how came you in your present dress, your present station? Licinius has never mentioned you to me. I do not even know your name. What is it?"

"Esca," answered the slave proudly, and looking the while anything but a slave.

"Esca!" she repeated, dwelling on the syllables, with a slow soft cadence; "Esca! 'Tis none of our Latin names; but that I might have known already. Who and what are you?"

There was something of defiance in the melancholy tone with which he answered—

"A prince in my own country, and a chief of ten thousand. A barbarian and a slave in Rome."

She gave him her hand to kiss, with a gesture of pity that was almost a caress, and then, as though ashamed of her own condescension, bade the Liburnians angrily to "go on."

Esca looked long and wistfully after the litter as it disappeared; but Hirpinus, clapping him on the back with his heavy hand, burst into a hearty laugh while he declared—

"'Tis a clear case, comrade. 'Came, saw, and conquered,' as the great soldier said. I have known it a hundred times, but always to men of muscle like thee and me. By Castor and Pollux! lad, thou art in luck. Ay, ay, 'tis always so. She takes thee for a gladiator, and they'll look at nothing but a gladiator now. Come on, brother; we'll drink a cup to every letter of her name!"

CHAPTER VI

THE WORSHIP OF ISIS

It was the cool and calming hour of sunset. Esca was strolling quietly homewards after the pursuits of the day. He had emptied a wineskin with Hirpinus; and, resisting that worthy's entreaties to mark so auspicious a meeting by a debauch, had accompanied him to the gymnasium, where the Briton's magnificent strength and prowess raised him higher than ever in the opinion of the experienced athlete. Untiring as were the trained muscles of the professional, he found himself unable to cope with the barbarian in such exercises as demanded chiefly untaught physical power and length of limb. In running, leaping, and wrestling, Esca was more than a match for the gladiator. In hurling the quoit, and fencing with wooden foils, the latter's constant practice gave him the advantage, and when he fastened round his wrists and hands the leathern thong or *cestus*, used for the same purpose as our modern boxing-glove, and proposed a round or two of that manly exercise to conclude with, he little doubted that his own science and experience would afford him an easy victory. The result, however, was far different from his expectations. His antagonist's powers were especially adapted to this particular kind of contest; his length of limb, his quickness of eye, hand, and foot, his youthful elasticity of muscle, and his unfailing wind, rendered him an invincible combatant, and it was with something like pique that Hirpinus was compelled to confess as much to himself.

At the end of the first round he was satisfied of his mistake in underrating so formidable an opponent. Ere the second was half through, he had exhausted all the resources of his own skill without gaining the slightest advantage over his antagonist; and with the conclusion of a third, he flung away the *cestus* in well-feigned disgust at the heat of the weather, and proposed one more skin of wine before parting, to drink success to the profession, and speedy employ[pg 37]ment for the gladiators at the approaching games in the amphitheatre.

"Join us, man!" said Hirpinus, dropping something of the patronising air he had before affected. "Thou wert born to be a swordsman. Hippias would teach thee in a week to hold thine own against the best fencers in Rome. I myself will look to thy food, thy training, and thy private practice. Thou wouldst gain thy liberty easily, after a few victories. Think it over, man! and when thou hast decided, come to the fencing-school yonder, and ask for old Hirpinus. The steel may have a speck of rust on it, but it's tough and true still; so fare thee well, lad. I count to hear from thee again before long!"

The gladiator accordingly rolled off with more than his usual assumption of manly independence, attributable to the measure of rough Sabine wine of which he had drunk his full share, whilst the Briton walked quietly away in the direction of his home, enjoying the cool breeze that fanned his brow, and following out a train of vague and complicated reflections, originating in the advice of his late companion.

The crimson glow of a summer evening had faded into the serene beauty of a summer night. Stars were flashing out, one by one, with mellow lustre, not glimmering faintly, as in our northern climate, but hanging like silver lamps, in the infinity of the sky. The busy turmoil of the streets had subsided to a low and drowsy hum; the few chance passengers who still paced them, went softly and at leisure, as though enjoying the soothing influence of the hour. Even here, in the great city, everything seemed to breathe of peace, and contentment, and repose. Esca walked slowly on, lost in meditation.

Suddenly, the clash of cymbals and the sound of voices struck upon his ear. A wild and fitful melody, rising and falling with strange thrilling cadence, was borne upon the breeze. Even while he stopped to listen, it swelled into a full harmonious chorus, and he recognised the chant of the worshippers of Isis, returning from the unholy celebration of her rites. Soon the glare of torches heralded its approach, and the tumultuous procession wound round the corner of the street with all the strange grotesque ceremonies of their order. Clashing their cymbals, dashing their torches together till the sparks flew up in showers, tossing their bare arms aloft with frantic gestures, the smooth-faced priests, having girt their linen garments tightly round their loins, were dancing to and fro before the image of the goddess with bacchanalian energy. [pg 38]Some were bareheaded, some crowned with garlands of the lotus-leaf, and some wore masks representing the heads of dogs and other animals; but all, though leaping wildly here and there, danced in the same step, all used the same mysterious gestures of which the meaning was only known to the initiated. The figure of the goddess herself was borne aloft on the shoulders of two sturdy priests, fat, oily, smooth, and sensual, with the odious look of their kind. It represented a stately woman crowned with the lotus, holding a four-barred lyre in her hand. Gold and silver tinsel was freely scattered over her flowing garments, and jewels of considerable value, the gifts of unusually fervent devotees, might be observed upon her bosom and around her neck and arms. Behind her were carried the different symbols by which her qualities were supposed to be typified; amongst these an image of the sacred cow, wrought in frosted silver with horns and hoofs of gold, showed the most conspicuous, borne aloft as it was by an acolyte in the wildest stage of inebriety, and wavering, with the uncertain movements of its bearer, over the heads of the throng. In the van moved the priests, bloated eunuchs clad in white; behind these came the sacred images carried by younger votaries, who, aspiring to the sacerdotal office, and already prepared for its functions, devoted themselves assiduously in the meantime to the orgies with which it was their custom to celebrate the worship of their deity. Maddened with wine, bare-limbed and with dishevelled locks, they danced frantically to and fro, darting at intervals from their ranks, and compelling the passengers whom they met to turn behind them, and help to swell the rear of the procession. This was formed of a motley crew. Rich and poor, old and young, the proud patrician and the squalid slave, were mingled together in turbulent confusion; it was difficult to distinguish those who formed a part of the original pageant from the idlers who had attached themselves to it, and, having caught the contagious excitement, vociferated as loudly, and leaped about as wildly, as the initiated themselves. Amongst these might be seen some of the fairest and proudest faces in Rome. Noble matrons reared in luxury, under the very busts of those illustrious ancestors who had been counsellors of kings, defenders of the commonwealth, senators of the empire, thought it no shame to be seen reeling about the public streets, unveiled and flushed with wine, in the company of the most notorious and profligate of their sex. A multitude of torches shed their glare on the upturned faces of the throng, and on one that looked, [pg 39]with its scornful lips and defiant brow, to have no business there.

Amongst the wildest of these revellers, Valeria's haughty head moved on, towering above the companions, with whom she seemed to have nothing in common, save a fierce determination to set modesty and propriety at defiance. Esca caught her glance as she swept by. She blushed crimson, he observed even in the torchlight, and seemed for an instant to shrink behind the portly form of a priest who marched at her side; but, immediately recovering herself, moved on with a gradually paling cheek, and a haughtier step than before.

He had little leisure, however, to observe the scornful beauty, whose charms, to tell the truth, had made no slight impression on his imagination; for a disturbance at its head, which had now passed him some distance, had stopped the progress of the whole procession, and no small confusion was the result. The torch-bearers were hurrying to the front. The silver cow had fallen and been replaced in an upright position more than once. The goddess herself had nearly shared the same fate. The sacred chant had ceased, and instead a hundred tongues were vociferating at once, some in anger, some in expostulation, some in maudlin ribaldry and mirth. "Let her go!" cried one. "Hold her fast!" shouted another. "Bring her along with you!" reasoned a drunken acolyte. "If she be worthy she will conform to the worship of the goddess. If she be unworthy she shall experience the divine wrath of Isis!" "Mind what you are about," interposed a more cautious votary. "She is a Roman maiden," said one. "She's a barbarian!" shrieked another. "A Mede!" "A Spaniard!" "A Persian!" "A Jewess! A Jewess!"

In the meantime the unfortunate cause of all this turmoil, a young girl closely veiled and dressed in black, was struggling in the arms of a large unwieldy eunuch, who had seized her as a hawk pounces on a pigeon, and despite her agonised entreaties, for the poor thing was in mortal fear, held her ruthlessly in his grasp. She had been surrounded by the lawless band, ere she was aware, as she glided quietly round the street corner, on her homeward way, had shrunk up against the wall in the desperate hope that she might remain unobserved or unmolested, and found herself, as was to be expected, an immediate object of insult to the dissolute and licentious crew. Though her dress was torn and her arms bruised from the unmanly violence to which she was subjected, with true feminine modesty she kept her veil closely [pg 40]drawn round her face, and resisted every effort for its removal, with a firm strength of which those slender wrists seemed hardly capable. As the eunuch grasped her with drunken violence, bending his huge body and bloated face over the shrinking figure of the girl, she could not suppress one piercing shriek for help, though, even while it left her lips, she felt how futile it must be, and how utterly hopeless was her situation. It was echoed by a hundred voices in tones of mockery and derision.

Little did Spado, for such was the eunuch's name, little did Spado think how near was the aid for which his victim called; how sudden would be the reprisals that should astonish himself with their prompt and complete redress, reminding him of what he had long forgotten, the strength of a man's blow, and the weight of a man's arm. At the first sound of the girl's voice, Esca had forced his way through the crowd to her assistance. In three strides he had come up with her assailant, and laid his heavy grasp on Spado's fat shoulder, while he bade him in low determined accents to release his prey. The eunuch smiled insolently, and replied with a brutal jest.

Valeria, interested in spite of herself, could not resist an impulse to press forward and see what was going on. Long afterwards she delighted to recall the scene she now beheld with far more of exultation and excitement than alarm. It had, indeed, especial attraction for an imagination like hers. Standing out in the red glare of the torches, like the bronze statue of some demigod starting into life, towered the tall figure of Esca, defiance in his attitude, anger on his brow, and resistless strength in the quivering outline of each sculptured limb. Within arm's length of him, the obese, ungraceful shape of Spado, with his broad fat face, expressive chiefly of gluttony and sensual enjoyment, but wearing now an ugly look of malice and apprehension. Starting back from his odious embrace to the utmost length of her outstretched arms, the veiled form of the frightened girl, her head turned from the eunuch, her hands pressed against his chest, every line of her figure denoting the extreme of horror, and aversion, and disgust. Round the three, a shifting mass of grinning faces, and tossing arms, and wild bacchanalian gestures; the whole rendered more grotesque and unnatural by the lurid, flickering light. With an unaccountable fascination Valeria watched for the result.

"Let her go!" repeated Esca, in the distinct accents with which a man speaks who is about to strike, tightening at the [pg 41]same time a gripe which went into the eunuch's soft flesh like iron.

Spado howled in mingled rage and fear, but released the girl nevertheless, who cowered instinctively close to her protector.

"Help!" shouted the eunuch, looking round for assistance from his comrades. "Help! I say. Will ye see the priest mishandled and the goddess reviled? Down with him! down with him, comrades, and keep him down!"

There is little doubt that had Esca's head once touched the ground it had never risen again, for the priests were crowding about him with wild yells and savage eyes, and the fierce revelry of a while ago was fast warming into a thirst for blood. Valeria thrust her way into the circle, though she never feared for the Briton—not for an instant.

It was getting dangerous, though, to remain any longer amongst this frantic crew. Esca wound one arm round the girl's waist and opposed the other shoulder to the throng. Spado, encouraged by his comrades, struck wildly at the Briton, and made a furious effort to recover his prey. Esca drew himself together like a panther about to spring, then his long sinewy arm flew out with the force and impulse of a catapult, and the eunuch, reeling backwards, fell heavily to the ground, with a gash upon his cheek like the wound inflicted by a sword.

"*Euge!*" exclaimed Valeria, in a thrill of admiration and delight. "Well struck, by Hercules! Ah! these barbarians have at least the free use of their limbs. Why, the priest went down like a white ox at the Mucian Gate. Is he much hurt, think ye? Will he rise again?"

The last sentence was addressed to the throng who now crowded round the prostrate Spado, and was but the result of that pity which is never quite dormant in a woman's breast. The fallen eunuch seemed indeed in no hurry to get upon his legs again. He rolled about in hideous discomfiture, and gave vent to his feelings in loud and pitiful moans and lamentations.

After such an example of the Briton's prowess, none of her other votaries seemed to think it incumbent on them to vindicate the majesty of the goddess by further interference with the maiden and her protector. Supporting and almost carrying her drooping form, Esca hurried her away with swift firm strides, pausing and looking back at intervals, as though loth to leave his work half finished, and by no means unwilling to renew the contest. The last Valeria saw of him [pg 42]was the turn of his noble head bending down with a courteous and protecting gesture, to console and reassure his frightened charge. All her womanly instincts revolted at that moment from the odious throng with whom she was involved. She could have found it in her heart to envy that obscure and unknown girl hurrying away yonder through the darkening streets on the arm of her powerful protector—could have wished herself a peasant or a slave, with some one being in the world to look up to, and to love.

Valeria's life had been that of a spoiled child from the day she left her cradle—that gilded cradle over which the nurses had repeated their customary Roman blessing with an emphasis that in her case seemed to be prophetic—

"May monarchs woo thee, darling! to their bed,

And roses blossom where thy footsteps tread!"

The metaphorical flowers of wealth, prosperity, and admiration, did indeed seem to spring up beneath her feet, and her stately beauty would have done no discredit to an imperial bride; but it must have been something more than outward pomp and show—something nobler than the purple and the diadem—that could have won its way to Valeria's heart.

She was habituated to the beautiful, the costly, the refined, till she had learned to consider such qualities as the mere essentials of life. It seemed to her a simple matter of course that houses should be noble, and chariots luxurious, and horses swift, and men brave. The *nil admirari* was the maxim of the class in which she lived; and whilst their standard was thus placed at the superlative, that which came up to it received no credit for excellence, that which fell short was treated with disapproval and contempt. Valeria's life had been one constant round of pleasure and amusement; yet she was not happy, not even contented. Day by day she felt the want of some fresh interest, some fresh excitement; and it was this craving probably, more than innate depravity, which drove her, in common with many of her companions, into such disgraceful scenes as were enacted at the worship of Juno, Isis, and the other gods and goddesses of mythology.

Lovers, it is needless to say, Valeria had won in plenty. Each new face possessed for her but the attraction of its novelty. The favourite of the hour had small cause to plume himself on his position. For the first week he interested her curiosity, for the second he pleased her fancy, after which, if he was wise, he took his leave gracefully, ere he was bidden [pg 43]to do so with a frankness that admitted of no misconception. Perhaps the only person in the world whom she respected was her kinsman Licinius; and this, none the less, that she possessed no kind of influence over his feelings or his opinions; that she well knew he viewed her proceedings often with disapprobation, and entertained for her character a kindly pity not far removed from contempt. Even Julius Placidus, who was the most persevering, as he was the craftiest, of her adorers, had made no impression on her heart. She appreciated his intellect, she was amused with his conversation, she approved of his deep schemes, his lavish extravagance, his unprincipled recklessness; but she never thought of him for an instant after he was out of her sight, and there was something in the cold-blooded ferocity of his character from which, even in his presence, she unconsciously recoiled. Perhaps she admired the person of Hippias, her fencing-master, a retired gladiator, who combined handsome regularity of features with a certain worn and warlike air, not without its charm, more than that of any man whom she had yet seen, and with all her pride and her cold exterior, Valeria was a woman to be captivated by the eye; but Hippias, from his professional reputation, was the darling of half the matrons in Rome, and it may be that she only followed the example of her friends, with whom, at this period of the Empire, it was considered a proof of the highest fashion, and the best taste, to be in love with a gladiator.

Strong in her passions, as in her physical organisation, the former were only bridled by an unbending pride, and an intensity of will more than masculine in its resolution. As under that smooth skin the muscles of the round white arm were firm and hard like marble, so beneath that fair and tranquil bosom there beat a heart that for good or evil could dare, endure, and defy the worst. Valeria was a woman whom none but a very bold or very ignorant suitor would have taken to his breast; yet it may be that the right man could have tamed, and made her gentle and patient as the dove. And now something seemed to tell her that the void in her heart was filled at last. Esca's manly beauty had made a strong impression on her senses; the anomaly of his position had captivated her imagination; there was something very attractive in the mystery that surrounded him; there was even a wild thrill of pleasure in the shame of loving a slave. Then, when he stood forth, the champion of that poor helpless girl, brave, handsome, and victorious, the charm was complete; and Valeria's eyes followed him as he dis[pg 44]appeared with a longing loving look, that had never glistened in them in her life before.

The Briton hurried away with his arm round the drooping figure of his companion, and for a time forbore to speak a word even of encouragement or consolation. At first the reaction of her feelings turned her sick and faint, then a burst of weeping came to her relief; ere long the tears were flowing silently; and the girl, who indeed showed no lack of courage, had recovered herself sufficiently to look up in her protector's face, and pour out her thanks with a quiet earnestness that showed they came direct from the heart.

"I can trust you," she said, in a voice of peculiar sweetness, though her Latin, like his own, was touched with a slightly foreign accent. "I can read a brave man's face—none better. We have not far to go now. You will take me safe home?"

"I will guard you to your very door," said he, in tones of the deepest respect. "But you need fear nothing now; the drunken priests and their mysterious deity are far enough off by this time. 'Tis a noble worship, truly, for such a city as this—the mistress of the world!"

"False gods! false gods!" replied the girl, very earnestly. "Oh! how can men be so blind, so degraded?" Here she stopped suddenly, and clung closer to her companion's arm, drawing her veil tighter round her face the while. Her quick ear had caught the sound of hurrying footsteps, and she dreaded pursuit.

"'Tis nothing," said Esca, encouraging her; "the most we have to dread now is some drunken freedman or client reeling home from his patron's supper-table. They are a weakly race, these Roman citizens," he added good-humouredly; "I think I can promise to stave them off if they come not more than a dozen at a time."

The cheerful tone reassured her no less than the strong arm to which she clung. It was delightful to feel so safe after the fright she had undergone. The footsteps were indeed those of a few dissolute idlers loitering home after a debauch. They had hastened forward on espying a female figure; but there was something in the air of her protector that forbade a near approach, and they shrank to the other side of the way rather than come in contact with so powerful an opponent. The girl felt proud of her escort, and safer every minute. By this time she had guided him into a dark and narrow street, at the end of which the Tiber might be seen gleaming under the starlit sky. She stopped at a mean-looking door, let into a dead-wall, and applying her [pg 45]hand to a secret spring, it opened noiselessly to her touch. Then she turned to face her companion, and said frankly, "I have not thanked you half enough. Will you not enter our poor dwelling, and share with us a morsel of food and a cup of wine, ere you depart upon your way?"

Esca was neither hungry nor thirsty, yet he bowed his head, and followed her into the house.

CHAPTER VII

TRUTH

The dwelling in which the Briton now found himself presented a strange contrast of simplicity and splendour, of wealth and frugality, of obscure poverty and costly refinement. The wall was bare and weather-stained; but a silver lamp, burning perfumed oil, was fixed against its surface on a bracket of common deal. Though the stone floor was damp and broken, it was partially covered by a soft thick carpet of brilliant colours, while shawls from the richest looms of Asia hung over the mutilated wooden seats and the crazy couch, which appeared to be the congenial furniture of the apartment. Esca could not but remark on the same inconsistency throughout all the minor details of the household. A measure of rich wine from the Lebanon was cooling in a pitcher of coarse earthenware, a draught of fair water sparkled in a cup of gold. A bundle of Eastern javelins, inlaid with ivory and of beautiful finish and workmanship, kept guard, as it were, over a plain two-edged sword devoid of ornament, and with a handle frayed and worn as though from constant use, that looked like a weapon born for work not show, some rough soldier's rude but trusty friend. The room of which Esca thus caught a hasty glance as he passed through, opened on an inner apartment, which seemed to have been originally equally bare and dilapidated, but of which the furniture was even more rich and incongruous. It was flooded by a soft warm light, shed from a lamp burning some rare Syrian oil, that was scarcely to be procured for money in Rome. It dazzled Esca's eyes as he followed the girl through the outer apartment into this retreat, and it was a few seconds ere he recovered his sight sufficiently to take note of the objects that surrounded him.

A venerable man with bald head and long silvery beard was sitting at the table when they entered, reading from a roll of parchment filled to the very margin with characters in the Syriac language, then generally spoken over the whole of Asia Minor, and sufficiently familiar at Rome. So immersed was he in his studies, that he did not seem to notice her arrival, till the girl rushed up to him, and, without unveiling, threw herself into his arms with many expressions of endearment and delight at her own return. The language in which she spoke was unknown to the Briton; but he gathered from her gestures, and the agitation which again overcame her for an instant, that she was relating her own troubles, and the part he had himself borne in the adventures of the night. Presently she turned, and drew him forward, while she said in Latin, with a little sob of agitation between every sentence—

"Behold my preserver—the youth who came in like a lion to save me from those wicked men! Thank him in my father's name, and yours, and all my kindred and all my tribe. Bid him welcome to the best our house affords. It is not every day a daughter of Judah meets with an arm and a heart like his, when she falls into the grasp of the heathen and the oppressor!"

The old man stretched his hand to Esca with cordiality and goodwill; as he did so, the Briton could not but observe how kindly was the smile that mantled over his serene and gentle face.

"My brother will be home ere long," said he, "and will himself thank you for preserving his daughter from insult and worse. Meantime Calchas bids you heartily welcome to Eleazar's house. Mariamne," he added, turning to the girl, "prepare us a morsel of food that we may eat. It is not the custom of our nation to send a stranger fasting from the door."

The girl departed on her hospitable mission, and Esca, making light of his prowess, and of the danger incurred, gave his own version of the night's occurrence, to which Calchas listened with grave interest and approval. When he had concluded, the old man pointed to the scroll he had been reading, which now lay rolled up on the table at his hand.

"The time will come," said he, "when the words that are written here shall be in the mouths of all men on the surface of the known earth. Then shall there be no more strife, nor oppression, nor suffering, nor sorrow. Then shall men love each other like brothers, and live only in kindliness and goodwill. The day may seem far distant, and the means may seem poor and inadequate now, yet so it is written here, and so will it be at last."

[pg 48]

"You think that Rome will extend her dominions farther and farther? That she will conquer all known nations, as she has conquered us? That she means to be in fact what she proudly styles herself, the Mistress of the World? In truth, the eagle's wings are wide and strong. His beak is very sharp, and where his talons have once fastened themselves, they never again let go their hold!"

Calchas smiled and shook his head.

"The dove will prevail against the eagle, as love is a stronger power than hate. But it is not of Rome I speak as the future influence that shall establish the great good on earth. The legions are indeed well trained, and brave even to the death; but I know of soldiers in a better service than Cæsar's, whose warfare is harder, whose watches are longer, whose adversaries are more numerous, but whose triumph is more certain, and more glorious at the last."

Esca looked as if he understood him not. The Briton's thoughts were wandering back to the tramp of columns and the clash of steel, and the gallant stand made against the invader by the white-robed warriors with their long swords, amongst whom he had been one of the boldest and the best.

"It is hard to strive against Rome," said he, with a glowing cheek and sparkling eye. "Yet I cannot but think, if we had never been provoked to an attack, if we had kept steadily on the defensive, if we had moved inland as he approached, harassing and cutting him off whenever we saw an opportunity, but never suffering him to make one for himself—trusting more to our woods and rivers, and less to our own right hands—we might have tamed the eagle and clipped his wings, and beat him back across the sea at last. But what have I to do with such matters now?" he added, while his whole countenance fell in bitter humiliation. "I, a poor barbarian captive, and a slave here in Rome!"

Calchas studied his face with a keen scrutinising glance, then he laid his hand on the young man's shoulder, and said inquiringly—

"There is not a grey hair in your clustering locks, nor a wrinkle on your brow, yet you have known sorrow?"

"Who has not?" replied the other cheerfully; "and yet I never thought to have come to this."

"You are a slave, and you would be free?" asked Calchas, slowly and impressively.

"I am a slave," repeated the Briton, "and I shall be free. But not till death."

[pg 49]

"And after death?" proceeded the old man, in the same gentle inquiring tone.

"After death," answered the other, "I shall be free as the elements I have been taught to worship, and into which they tell me I shall be resolved. What need I know or care more than that in death there will be neither pleasure nor pain?"

"And is not life with all its changes too sweet to lose on such terms as these?" asked the older man. "Are you content to believe that, like one walking through a quicksand, the footsteps you leave are filled up and obliterated behind you as you pass on? Can you bear to think that yesterday is indeed banished and gone for ever? That a to-morrow must come of black and endless night? Death should be really terrible if this is your conviction and your creed!"

"Death is never terrible to a brave man," answered Esca. "A Briton need not be taught how to die sword in hand."

"You think you are brave," said Calchas, looking wistfully on the other's rising colour and kindling eyes. "Ah! you have not seen my comrades die, or you would know that something better than courage is required for the service to which we belong. What think ye of weak women, tender shrinking maidens, worn with fatigue, emaciated with hunger, fainting with heat and thirst, brought out to be devoured by beasts, or to suffer long and agonising tortures, yet smiling the while in quiet calm contentment, as seeing the home to which they are hastening, the triumph but a few short hours off? What think ye of the captains under whom I served, who here at Rome, in the face of Cæsar and his power, vindicated the honour of their Lord and died without a murmur for His cause? I was with Peter, I tell you, Peter the Galilean, of whom men talk to this day, of whom men shall never cease to talk in after ages, when he opposed to Simon's magic arts his simple faith in the Master whom he served, and I saw the magician hurled like a stricken vulture to the ground. I was present when the fiercest and the wickedest of the Cæsars, returning from the expedition to Greece, wherein his buffooneries had earned the contempt even of that subtle nation of flatterers, sentenced him to death upon the cross for that he had dared to oppose Nero's vices, and to tell Nero the truth. I heard him petition that he might be crucified with his head downward, as not worthy to suffer in the same posture as his Lord—and I can see him now, the pale face, the noble head, the dark keen eye, the slender sinewy form, and, above all, the self-sustaining con[pg 50]fidence, the triumphant daring of the man as he walked fearlessly to death. I was with Paul, the noble Pharisee, the naturalised Roman citizen, when he, alone amongst a crowd of passengers and a century of soldiers, quailed not to look on the black waves raging round our broken ship, and bade us all be of good cheer, for that every soul, to the number of two hundred and seventy-five, should come safe to shore. I remember how trustfully we looked on that low spare form, that grave and gracious face with its kindly eyes, its bushy brows and thick beard sprinkled here and there with grey. It was the soul, we knew, that sustained and strengthened the weakly body of the man. The very barbarians where we landed acknowledged its influence, and would fain have worshipped him for a god. Nero might well fear that quiet, humble, trusting, yet energetic nature; and where the imperial monster feared, as where he admired, loved, hated, envied, or despised, the sentiment must be quenched in blood."

"And did he too fall a victim?" inquired Esca, whose interest, notwithstanding occasional glances at the door through which Mariamne had gone out, seemed thoroughly awakened by the old man's narrative.

"They might not crucify him," answered Calchas, "for he was of noble lineage and a Roman citizen born; but they took him from amongst us, and they let him languish in a prison, till they released him at last and brought him out to be beheaded. Ay, Rome was a fearful sight that day; the foot was scorched as it trod the ashes of the devastated city, the eye smarted in the lurid smoke that hung like a pall upon the heavy air and would not pass away. Palaces were crumbling in ruins, the shrivelled spoils of an empire were blackening around, the dead were lying in the choked-up highways half-festering, half-consumed—orphan children were wandering about starved and shivering, with sallow faces and large shining eyes, or, worse still, playing thoughtlessly, unconscious of their doom. They said the Christians had set fire to the city, and many an innocent victim suffered for this foul and groundless slander. The Christians, forsooth! oppressed, persecuted, reviled; whose only desire was to live in brotherhood with all men, whose very creed is peace and goodwill on earth. I counted twenty of them, men, women, and children, neighbours with whom I had held kindly fellowship, friends with whom I had broken bread, lying stiff and cold in the Flaminian Way on the morning Paul was led out to die. But there was peace on the dead faces, and the rigid hands were clasped in prayer; and [pg 51]though the lacerated emaciated body, the mere shell, was grovelling there in the dust, the spirit had gone home to God who made it, to the other world of which you have not so much as heard, yet which you too must some day visit, to remain for ever. Do you understand me? not for ages, but *for ever*—without end!"

"Where is it?" asked Esca, on whom the idea of a spiritual existence, innate from its very organisation in every intelligent being, did not now dawn for the first time. "Is it here, or there? below, or above? in the stars, or the elements? I know the world in which I live; I can see it, can hear it, can feel it; but that other world, where is it?"

"Where is it?" repeated Calchas. "Where are the dearest wishes of your heart, the noblest thoughts of your mind? Where are your loves, your hopes, your affections, above all, your memories? Where is the whole better part of your nature? your remorse for evil, your aspirations after good, your speculations on the future, your convictions of the reality of the past? Where these are, there is that other world. You cannot see it, you cannot hear it, yet you *know* that it must be. Is any man's happiness complete? is any man's misery when it reaches him so overwhelming as it seemed at a distance? And why is it not? Because something tells him that the present life is but a small segment in the complete circle of a soul's existence. And the circle, you have not lived in Rome without learning, is the symbol of infinity."

Esca pondered and was silent. There are convictions which men hold unconsciously, and to which they are so accustomed that their attention can only be directed to them from without, just as they wear their skins and scarcely know it, till the familiar covering has been lacerated by injury or disease. At last he looked up with a brightening countenance, and exclaimed, "In that world, surely, all men will be free!"

"All men will be equal," replied Calchas, "but no mortal or immortal ever can be free. Suppose a being totally divested of all necessity for effort, all responsibility to his fellows or himself, all participation in the great scheme of which government is the essential condition in its every part, and you suppose one whose own feelings would be an intolerable burden, whose own wishes would be an unendurable torture. Man is made to bear a yoke; but the Captain whom I serve has told me that His yoke is easy and His burden is light. How easy and how light, I experience every moment of my life."

[pg 52]

"And yet you said but now that death and degradation were the lot of those who bore arms by your side in the ranks," observed the Briton, still intently regarding his companion.

A ray of triumphant courage and exultation flashed up into the old man's face. For an instant Esca recognised the fierce daring of a nature essentially bold, reckless, and defiant; but it faded as it came, and was succeeded by an expression of meek, chastened humility, whilst he replied—

"Death welcome and long looked-for! Degradation that confers the highest honours in this world and the next!—at least to those who are held worthy of the great glory of martyrdom. Oh! that I might be esteemed one of that noble band! But my work will be laid to my hand, and it is enough for me to be the lowest of the low in the service of my Master."

"And that master? Tell me of that master," exclaimed Esca, whose interest was excited, as his feelings were roused, by converse with one who seemed so thoroughly impressed with the truth of what he spoke, who was at once so earnest, so gentle, and so brave. The old man bowed his head with unspeakable reverence, but in his face shone the deep and fervent joy of one who looks back with intense love and gratitude to the great epoch of his existence.

"I saw Him once," said he, "on the shore of the Sea of Galilee—I that speak to you now saw Him with my own eyes—there were little children at His feet. But we will talk of this again, for you are weary and exhausted. Meat and drink are even now prepared for you. It is good to refresh the body if the mind is to be vigorous and discerning. You have done for us to-night the act of a true friend. You will henceforth be always welcome in Eleazar's house."

While he spoke, the girl whom Esca had rescued so opportunely entered the apartment, bearing in some food on a coarse and common trencher, with a wineskin, of which she poured the contents into a jewelled cup, and presented it to her preserver with an embarrassed but very graceful gesture, and a soft shy smile.

Mariamne had unveiled; and, if Esca's expectations during their homeward walk had been raised by her gentle feminine manners, and the sweet tones of her voice, they were not now disappointed with what he saw. The dark eyes that looked up so timidly into his own, were full and lustrous as those of a deer. They had, moreover, the mournful pleading expression peculiar to that animal, and, [pg 53]through all their softness and intelligence, betrayed the watchful anxiety of one whose life is passed in constant vicissitudes and occasional danger. The girl's face was habitually pale, though the warm blood mantled in her cheek as she drooped beneath Esca's gaze of honest admiration, and her regular features were sharpened, a little more than was natural to them, by daily care and apprehension. This was especially apparent in the delicate aquiline of the nose, and a slight prominency of the cheek-bones. It was a face that in prosperity would have been rich and sparkling as a jewel, that in adversity preserved its charms from the rare and chastened beauty in which it was modelled. Her dress betrayed the same incongruity that was so remarkable in the furniture of her home. Like her veil it was black, and of a coarse and common material, but where it was looped up, the folds were fastened by one single gem of considerable value; and two or three links of a heavy gold chain were visible round her white and well-turned neck.

Moving through the room, busied with the arrangements of the meal which she must herself have prepared, Esca could not but observe the pliant grace of her form, enhanced by a certain modest dignity, very different from the vivacious gestures of the Roman maidens to whom he was accustomed, and especially pleasing to the eye of the Briton.

Calchas seemed to love the girl as a daughter; and his kind face grew kinder and gentler still, while he followed her about in her different movements, with eyes of the deepest and fondest affection.

Esca could not but observe that the board was laid for three persons, and that by one of the wooden platters stood a drinking-cup of great beauty and value. Mariamne's glance followed his as it rested on the spare place. "For my father," said she gently, in answer to the inquiry she read on his face. "He is later than usual to-night, and, I fear—I fear; my father is so bold, so prompt to draw steel when he is angered. To-night he has left his sword at home; and I know not whether to be most frightened or reassured at his being alone in this wicked town, unarmed."

"He is in God's hand, my child," said Calchas reverently. "But I should not fear for Eleazar," he added, with a proud and martial air, "were he surrounded by a score of such as we see prowling nightly in the streets of Rome, though they were armed to the teeth, and he with only a shepherd's staff to keep his head."

"Is he, then, so redoubtable a warrior?" asked Esca, on [pg 54]whom good manhood seldom failed to produce a favourable impression. While he spoke he looked from one to the other with increasing curiosity and interest.

"You shall judge for yourself," answered Calchas, "for it cannot now be long ere he return. Nevertheless, the man who could leap down from the walls of a beleaguered city, as my brother did, naked and unarmed; who could break the head off a Roman battering-ram by main force, and render that engine useless; who could reach the wall again with his prize, covered with wounds, having fought his way through a whole maniple of Roman soldiers, and could ask but for a draught of water, ere he donned his armour, and took his place once more upon the rampart, is not likely to fear aught that can befall him from a few idlers in a common street-broil. Nevertheless, as I said before, you shall judge for yourself."

"And here he is!" exclaimed Mariamne, while the outer door shut to, and a man's step was heard advancing through the adjoining apartment, with a firm and measured footfall.

She had been pale enough all night in the eyes of Esca, who was watching her intently; but he thought now she seemed to turn a shade paler than before.

[pg 55]

CHAPTER VIII

THE JEW

The man who entered the apartment with the air of one to whom every nook and corner was familiar, must have been fully three-score years of age, yet his dark eye still glittered with the fire of youth, his thick curling beard and hair were but slightly sprinkled with grey, and the muscles of his square powerful frame seemed but to have acquired solidity and consistency with age. His appearance was that of a warrior, toughened, and, as it were, forged into iron, by years of strife, hardship, and unremitting toil.

If something in the line of his aquiline features resembled Calchas, no two faces could have been more different in their character and expression than those of Eleazar and his brother. The latter was all gentleness, kindliness, and peace; on the former, fiery passions, deep schemes, continual peril, and contention, had set their indelible marks. The one was that of the spectator, who is seated securely on the cliff, and marks the seething waters below with interest, indeed, and sympathy, but with feelings neither of agitation nor alarm; the other was the strong swimmer, breasting the waves fiercely, and battling with their might, striving for his life inch by inch, and stroke by stroke, conscious of his peril, confident in his strength, and never despairing for an instant of the result. At times, indeed, the influence of opposite feelings, softening the one and kindling the other, would bring out the family likeness clear and apparent upon each; but in repose no two faces could be more dissimilar, no two types of character more utterly at variance, than those of the Christian and the Jew.

As Eleazar's warlike figure came into the light, Esca could not but remark with what a glance of mistrust his quick eye took in the presence of a stranger, how the strong fingers closed instinctively round the staff he was in the act of laying down, and the whole form seemed to gather itself in an instant as though ready for the promptest measures [pg 56]of resistance or attack. Such trifling gestures spoke volumes of the character and habits of the man.

Nevertheless Calchas rapidly explained to his brother the cause of this addition to their supper-party; and Mariamne, who seemed in considerable awe of her father, busied herself in placing food and wine before him, with even more alacrity than she had shown when serving their guest.

The Jew thanked his new friend for the kindness he had rendered his daughter, with a few brief cordial words, as one brave man expresses his gratitude to another, then fell to on the meat and drink provided, with a voracity that argued well for his physical powers, and denoted a strong constitution and a long fast. As he took breath after a deep draught of wine in which, though he pledged him not, he challenged his guest to join, Calchas asked his brother how he had sped in the affairs that kept him from home all day.

"Ill," answered the other, shooting from under his thick eyebrows a penetrating glance at the Briton. "Ill and slowly, yet not so ill but that something has been gained, another step taken in the direction at which I aim. Yet I have been to-day in high places, have seen those bloated gluttons and drunkards who are the ministers of Cæsar's will, have spoken with that spotted panther, Vespasian's scheming agent forsooth! who thinks he hath the cunning, as he can doubtless boast of the treachery and the gaudy colours, of the beast of prey. Let him take care! Weaker hands than mine have ere this strangled a fiercer animal for the worth of his shining skin. Let him beware! Eleazar-Ben-Manahem is a match, and more than a match, for Julius Placidus the tribune!"

Esca glanced quickly at the speaker, as his ear caught the familiar name. The look was not lost upon his host.

"You know him?" said he, with a fierce smile that showed the strong white teeth gleaming through his bushy beard. "Then you know as cool and well-taught a soldier as ever buckled on a sword. I wish I had a few like him to officer the Sicarii[a] at home. But you know, also, a man who would not scruple to slay his own father for the worth of the clasp that fastens his gown. I have seen him in the field, and I have seen him in the council. He is bold, skilful, and he can be treacherous in both! Where met you him last?" he added, with a searching glance at Esca, while at the same [pg 57]time he desired Mariamne to fill the stranger's cup and his own.

The latter proceeding engrossed the Briton's whole attention. It was with the utmost carelessness that he replied to the question, by relating his interview, that very morning, with the tribune at

Valeria's door. He scarcely marked how precisely the father noted down the name in his tablets, for the daughter's white arm was reaching over his shoulder, so close that it almost touched his cheek.

It was indeed well worth Eleazar's while to obtain information, from whatever source, of any influence that might affect those in authority with whom he was in daily contact at Rome. His position was one which called for courage, tact, skill, and even cunning, to a great extent. Charged by the Supreme Council at Jerusalem, then in the last stage of perplexity and sorely beset by Vespasian and his legions, with a private mission to Vitellius, who much mistrusted the successful general, he represented the hopes and fears, the temporal and political prosperity, nay, the very existence of the Chosen People. Nor to all appearance could a better instrument have been selected for the purpose. Eleazar, though a bigoted and fanatical Jew of the strictest sect, was a man of keen and powerful intellect, whose obstinacy was open to no conviction, whose perseverance was to be deterred by no obstacle. A distinguished and fearless soldier, he possessed the confidence of the large and fighting portion of the nation, who looked on Roman supremacy with abhorrence, and who clung dearly to the notion of earthly dominion, wrested from the heathen with the sword. His rigid observance of its fasts, its duties, and its ceremonials, had gained him the affections of the priesthood, and the more enthusiastic followers of that religion in which outward forms were so strictly enjoined and so faithfully observed; while a certain fierce, defiant, and unbending demeanour towards all classes of men, had won for him a character of frankness which did him good service in the schemes of intrigue and dissimulation with which he was continually engaged.

Yet perhaps the man was honest too, as far as his own convictions went. He esteemed all means lawful for the furtherance of a lawful object. He was one of those who deem it the most contemptible of weakness to shrink from doing evil that good may come. Like Jephthah he would have sacrificed his daughter unflinchingly in performance of a vow; nay, had Mariamne stood between him and the [pg 58]attainment of his ambition, or even the accomplishment of his revenge, he would have walked ruthlessly over the body of his child. Versed in the traditions of his family and the history of his nation, he was steeped to the lips in that pride of pedigree which was so essential a feature of the Jewish character: he was convinced that the eventual destiny of his people was to lord it over the whole earth. He possessed more than his share of that haughty self-sufficiency which bade the Pharisee hold aloof from those of lower pretensions and humbler demeanour than himself; while he had all the fierce courage and energy of the Lion of Judah, so terrible when roused, so difficult to be appeased when victorious. In his secret heart he anticipated the time when Jerusalem should again become a sovereign city, when the Roman eagles should be scared away from Syria, and a hierarchy established once more as the government of the people chosen by Heaven. That he should be a second Judas Maccabæus, a chief commander of the armies of the faithful in the new order of things, was an ambition naturally enough entertained by the bold and skilful soldier; but, to do Eleazar justice, individual aggrandisement had but little share in his schemes, and personal interest never crossed those visions for the future, on which his dark and dangerous enthusiasm so loved to dwell.

It was a delicate matter to intrigue with Vitellius in Rome against the very general who held supreme authority, at least ostensibly, from the Emperor. It was playing a hazardous game, to receive power and instructions from the Council at Jerusalem, and to use or suppress them according to the bearer's own political views and future intentions.

It was no easy task to hold his own against such men as Placidus, in the contest of *finesse*, subtlety, and double-dealing; yet the Jew entered upon his perilous career with a strenuous energy, a cool calculating audacity, that was engraved in the very character of the man.

Another draught of the rich Lebanon wine served to improve their acquaintance, and Eleazar, with considerable tact, drew from the Briton all the information he could obtain as to the habits and movements of his antagonist the tribune, while he seemed but to be carrying on the courteous conversation of a host with his guest. Esca's answers, notwithstanding that thoughts and eyes wandered frequently towards Mariamne, were frank and open like his disposition. He, too, entertained no very cordial liking for Placidus, and experienced towards the tribune that unconscious antipathy which the honest man so often feels for the knave.

[pg 59]

Calchas, meanwhile, had returned to the perusal of his scroll, on which his brother cast occasional glances of unfeigned contempt, notwithstanding that the reader was the person whom he most loved and respected on earth. Mariamne, moving about the apartment, looked covertly on the fair face and stately form of her preserver, approving much of what she saw; once their eyes met, and the Jewess blushed to her temples for very shame. So the time passed quickly; the night stole on, the Lebanon was nearly finished, and Esca rose to bid his entertainers farewell.

"You have done me a rare service," said Eleazar, feeling in his breast while he spoke, and producing, from under his coarse garment, a jewel of considerable value, "a service neither thanks nor guerdon can requite; yet, I pray you, keep this trinket in remembrance of the Jew and the Jew's daughter, who come of a people that forgive not an injury, and forget not a benefit."

The colour mounted to Esca's forehead, and an expression of pain, almost of anger, came into his face, while he replied—

"I have done nothing to merit either thanks or reward. It is no such matter to put a fat eunuch on his back, or to defend an unprotected woman in a town like this. Take back your jewel, I pray you. Any other man would have done as much."

"It is not every man who could have interposed so effectually," replied Eleazar, with a glance of hearty approval at the thews and sinews of his friend, replacing the jewel meanwhile in his vestment, without the least sign of displeasure at its being declined. He would have bestowed it freely, no doubt, but if Esca did not want it, it would serve some other purpose: precious stones and gold would always fetch their value at Rome. "At least you will let me give you a safe-conduct home," he added; "the night is far advanced, and I should be loth that you should suffer wrong for your interposition in our behalf."

Esca burst out laughing now. In the pride of his strength, it seemed so impossible that he should require protection or assistance from anyone. He squared his large shoulders and drew himself to his full height.

"I should wish no better pastime," said he, "than a bout with a dozen of them! I, too, was brought up a warrior, in a land you have never heard of, many a long mile from Rome; a land fairer far than this, of green valleys and wooded hills, and noble rivers winding calmly towards the sea; a land where the oaks are lofty and the flowers are [pg 60]sweet, where the men are strong and the women fair. I have followed the chase afoot from sunrise to sunset through many a summer's day. I have fronted the invader, sword in hand, ever since my arm was long enough to draw blade from sheath, or I had not been here now. You too are a soldier, I see it in your eye—you can believe that my limbs grow stiff, my spirits droop for lack of martial exercise. In faith, it seems to me that even a vulgar broil in the street makes my blood dance in my veins once more!"

Mariamne was listening with parted lips and shining eyes. She drank in all he said of his distant home with its woodland scenery, its forest trees, its fragrant flowers, and, above all, its lovely women. She felt so kindly towards this bold young stranger, exiled from kin and country, she attributed her interest to pity and gratitude, nor could she help wondering to find these sentiments so strong.

Calchas looked up from his studies.

"Fare thee well!" said he. "Take an old man's warning, and strike not unless it be in self-defence. Mark well the turning from the main street to the Tiber, so shalt thou find thy way to our poor home again."

Esca promised faithfully to return, and fully intended to redeem his promise.

"Another cup of wine," said Eleazar, emptying the leathern bottle into a golden vessel; "the sun of Italy cannot ripen such a vintage as this."

But the rich produce of the Lebanon was all too cloying for the healthy palate and the thirst of youth. Esca prayed for a draught of fair water, and Mariamne brought him the pitcher and gave him to drink with her own hand. For the second time to-night their eyes met, and although they were instantly averted, the Briton felt that he was drinking from a cup more intoxicating than all the wine-presses of Syria could produce—a cup that made him unconscious of the past as of the future, and only too keenly sensible of the present by its joy. He forgot that he was a barbarian, he forgot that he was a slave.

He forgot everything but Mariamne and her dark imploring trustful eyes.

CHAPTER IX

THE ROMAN

It is time to give some account of Esca's anomalous position in the capital of the world—to explain how the young British noble (for that was indeed the rank he held in his own country) found himself a slave in the streets of Rome. In order to do so it is necessary to take a glimpse at the interior of a patrician's house about the hour of supper; perhaps also to intrude upon the reflections of its owner, as he paces up and down the colonnade in the cool air of sunset, absorbed in his own thoughts, and deep in the memories of the past.

His mansion is of stately proportion, and large size, but all its ornaments and accessories are chastened by a severe simplicity of taste. An observer might identify the man by the very nature of the objects that surround him. In his vestibule the columns are of the Ionic order, and their elaborate capitals have been wrought into the utmost degree of finish which that style will allow. In the smaller entrance-hall or lobby, which leads to the principal apartments, and which is guarded by an image of a dog, let into the pavement in mosaic, there are no florid sculptures nor carvings, nor any attempt at decoration beyond the actual beauty of the stonework and the scrupulous care with which it is kept clean. The doors themselves are of bronze, so well burnished as to need no mixture of gold or silver inlaid to enhance its brightness; whilst in the principal hall itself, the room in which friends are welcomed, clients received, and business transacted, the walls, instead of frescoes and such gaudy ornaments, are simply overlaid with entablatures of white and polished marble. The dome is very lofty, rising majestically towards the circular opening at the top, through which [pg 62]the sky is visible; and round the fountain or cistern immediately below this are ranged four colossal statues, representing the elements. These, with the busts of a long line of illustrious ancestors, are the only efforts of the sculptor's art throughout the apartment. A large banqueting-hall, somewhat more luxuriously furnished, opens from one side of the central room, and as much as can be seen of it displays considerable attention to convenience and personal comfort. Frescoes, representing scenes of military life, adorn the walls, and at one end stands a trophy, composed of deadly weapons and defensive armour, arranged so as to form a glittering and conspicuous ornament. Large flagons and chalices of burnished gold, some of them adorned with valuable jewels, are ranged upon a sideboard; but it is evident that no guests are expected to-night, for near the couch against the wall has been drawn a small table, laid for one person only, with a clean napkin, and a cup and platter of plain silver thereon. That person is none other than the master of the house, bodily pacing up and down his own colonnade in Rome, mentally gazing on a fair expanse of wood and vale and shining river, drinking in the cool breezes, the fragrant odours, and the wild luxuriant beauty of distant Britain.

Five-and-twenty years! and yet it seems but yesterday. The brow wrinkles, the hair turns grey, strength wastes, energy fails, the brain gets torpid, and the senses dull, but the heart never grows old. Business, ambition, pleasure, dangers, duties, difficulties, and successes have filled that quarter of a century, and passed away like a dream; but the touch of a hand, the memory of a face, have outlived them all. Caius Lucius Licinius, Roman patrician, general, prætor, consul, and procurator of the Empire, is the young commander of a legion once more, with the world before him, and the woman he loves by his side. This is what he sees now, as he has seen it so often in his dreams by night, and his waking visions by day.

An old oak-tree, a mossy sward soft and level as velvet, delicate fern bending and whispering in the summer breeze, fleecy clouds drifting across the blue sky, and a graceful form, in its white robes, coming shyly up the glade, with faltering step, and sidelong glance, and timid gesture, to keep her tryst with her Roman lover. She is in his arms now. The rich brown curls are scattered over his breastplate, and the blue eyes are looking up into his own, liquid with the love-light that thrills to a man's heart but from one pair of eyes in a lifetime. She is, indeed, no contemptible prize, in the glory [pg 63]of her beauty and the pride of her blooming womanhood. With the rounded form, the noble features, and the dazzling colour of her nation, she possesses the courage and constancy of a highborn race, and a witchery half imperious, half playful, peculiarly her own. There are women who find their way to the core of a man's heart, who pervade it all, and saturate it, so to speak, with their influence.

"Quo semel est imbuta recens, servabit odorem[4]

Testa diu"——

The vessel that has once held this rich and rare liquid is ever after impregnated with its fragrance, and even when it has been spilt every drop, and a fresh infusion poured in, the new wine smacks strangely and wildly of the old. She is one of them; he knows it too well.

They should have nothing in common, these two, the British chieftain's daughter and the Roman conqueror. But there is a truce between the nations; a truce in which the elements of discord are nevertheless smouldering, ready to blaze out afresh at the first opportunity, and they have seen each other accidentally, and been thrown together by circumstances, till curiosity has become interest, and interest grown into liking, and liking ripened into love. The British maiden might not be won lightly, and many a tear she wept in secret, and sore she strove against her own heart; but when it conquered her at last she gave it, as such women will, wholly and unreservedly. She would have lived for him, died for him, followed him to the end of the world. And Licinius worshipped her as a man worships the one woman who is the destiny of his life. Most men have at some time or other experienced this folly, infatuation, madness, call it what you will. They are not likely to forget it. Possibly—alas! probably—the bud they then watched opening has never expanded into bloom, at least for *them*. The worm may have destroyed it, or the cold wind cut it to the earth, or another's hand may have borne it away in triumph to gladden another's breast; but there is something in the May mornings that reminds them of the sweet flower still, and they wander round the fairest gardens of earth rather drearily to-day, because of the memory that has never faded, and the blank where *she* is not.

'Licinius holds the British maiden to his breast'

Licinius holds the British maiden to his breast, and they discourse of their own happiness and revel in the sunny hour, [pg 64]and plan schemes for the future—schemes in which each is to the other all in all, and dream not that when to-day is past for them there will be no to-morrow. The woman, indeed, heaves a gentle sigh at intervals, as though in the midst of her happiness some foreboding warned her of the brooding tempest; but the man is hopeful, buoyant, and impetuous, playful in his tenderness, and joyous in his own triumphant love. They parted that evening more reluctantly than usual. They lingered round the oak, they found excuse after excuse for another loving word, another fond caress. When at last they went their several ways, how often Licinius turned to look after the receding form that carried with it all his hope and all his happiness! Little did he think how, and when, and where, he would see Guenebra again.

Ten years went heavily by. The commander of a legion was the chief of an army now. Licinius had served Rome in Gaul, in Spain, in Syria. Men said he bore a charmed life; and, indeed, while his counsels showed the forethought, the caution, and the patience of a skilful officer, his personal conduct was remarkable for a reckless disregard of danger, which would have been esteemed foolhardy in the meanest soldier. It was observed, too, that a deep and abiding melancholy had taken possession of the once light-hearted patrician. He only seemed to brighten up into his former self under the pressure of imminent danger, in the confusion of a repulse, or the excitement of a charge. At other times he was silent, depressed, preoccupied; never morose, for his kindly heart was open to the griefs of others, and the legionaries knew that their daring general was the friend of all who were in sorrow or distress. But the men talked him over, too, by their watch-fires; they marvelled, those honest old campaigners, how one who was so ready in the field could be so sparing of the winecup; how the leader who could stoop to fill his helmet from the running stream under a storm of javelins, and drink composedly with a jest and a smile, should be so backward in the revel, should show such a disinclination to those material pleasures which they esteemed the keenest joys of life.

One old centurion, who had followed his fortunes from the Thames to the Euphrates, from the confines of Pannonia to the Pillars of Hercules, averred that he had never seen his chief discomfited but once, and that was on the day when he had been accorded a triumph for his services in the streets of Rome. The veteran used to swear he never could forget the dejected look upon those brows, encircled with their laurel [pg 65]garland, nor the weary listlessness of that figure, to which all eyes were directed in its gilded chariot; the object of admiration to the whole city, and, for that day, scarcely second even to Cæsar himself. It was a goodly triumph, no doubt; the spoils were rich, the car was lofty, the people shouted, and the victims fell. But what was glory without Guenebra? and the hero's eye could not rest in peace on one of all those gazing thousands, for lack of the loving face framed in its rich brown hair.

On the very night Licinius and Guenebra parted, a long-meditated rising had broken out among the islanders—conquered, but not subdued. Nothing but the cool courage of its young commander, and the immovable discipline of the legionaries, saved the Roman camp. Ere morning, Guenebra had been forced away by her tribe many miles from the scene of action; the Britons, too, retired into their strongholds, those natural fastnesses impregnable by regular troops. The whole country was once more in a state of open warfare. Prompt and decisive measures were taken; Publius Ostorius, the Roman general, in execution of a manœuvre by which he preserved his line of operation, despatched Licinius and his legion to a different part of the island, and with all his exertions and all his influence, the young officer could never obtain tidings of Guenebra again. It was after this event that the change came over Licinius which was so commented on by the soldiers under his command.

Ten years of brilliant and successful services had elapsed when he returned to Britain. Nero had but lately succeeded to the purple, nor had he then degenerated into the monster of iniquity which he afterwards became. Until sapped by his ungovernable passions, the Emperor's administrative abilities were of no mean order; and he selected Licinius for the important post assigned to him, as being a consummate soldier, and experienced in the country with which he had to deal. The latter accepted the appointment with alacrity; through all change of time and fortune, he had never forgotten his British love. Under the burning skies of Syria, by the frozen shores of the Danube, at home or abroad, in peace or war, Guenebra's face was ever present to him, fond and trustful as when they last parted under the old oak-tree. He longed but to see it once more. And so he did. Thus—

A partial insurrection had been quelled beyond the Trent. The Roman vanguard had surprised the Britons, and forced them to fly in great confusion, leaving their baggage, their valuables, in some cases even their arms, behind. When [pg 66]Licinius came up with the main body of his forces, he found, indeed, no prisoners taken, for everything animate had fled, but a goodly amount of spoil, over which Roman discipline had placed a strong guard. One of his tribunes approached him with a list of the captured articles; and when his general had perused it, the officer hesitated as though there was still some further report to make. At last he spoke out—

"There is a hut left standing within the lines of the enemy. I would not order it to be destroyed till I had provided for the burial of a dead body that lies beneath its shelter."

Licinius was counting the arms taken.

"A dead body!" said he carelessly; "is it an officer of rank?"

"'Tis a woman's corpse," answered the tribune; "a fair and stately woman, apparently the wife of some prince or chieftain at the least."

For Guenebra's sake, every woman, much more every British woman, was an object of respect and interest to Licinius.

"Lead on," said he. "I will give directions when I have seen it;" and the general followed his officer to the place already indicated.

It was but a rude hut made of a few planks and branches hastily thrown together. It seemed to have been erected at a moment's notice, probably to shelter an inmate in the last stage of dissolution. Through a wide rent in the roof the summer sun streamed in brilliantly, throwing a sheet of light on the dead face below. The prostrate form was swathed in its white robe, the bridal garment of the destroyer. A band of white encircled the head and chin, and the brown hair was parted modestly on the smooth forehead calm and womanly as of old. It was Guenebra's face that lay there so strangely still. Guenebra's face, how like and yet how changed! As he stooped over it, and looked on the closed eyes beneath their arching brows, the fair and noble features chiseled by the hand of death—the sweet lips wreathed even now with a chastened loving smile—he could not but mark that there were lines of thought upon the forehead, streaks of silver in the hair, the result it might be of regrets, and memories, and sorrows, and care for *him*.

Then the warm tears gushed up into the soldier's eyes, the pressure on his heart and brain seemed to be relieved. As when the spear is drawn out of a wound and the red stream spouts freely forth, the previous agony was succeeded by a dull hopeless resignation, that in comparison seemed [pg 67]almost akin to peace. He pressed his lips hard upon the cold dead forehead, and turned away—a man for whom from henceforth there was neither good to covet, nor evil to be feared.

And thus it was that here, on earth, Licinius looked once more upon his love.

Fresh victories crowned his arms in Britain—a fresh triumph awaited his return to Rome; but still as of old with Licinius, the glory seemed to count for nothing, the service seemed to be all-in-all. Only, now, the restless, eager look had left his face. He was always calm and unmoved, even in the uncertainty of conflict or the triumph of success. Still kindly in his actions, his outward demeanour was very stern and cold. He kept aloof from the intrigues, as from the pleasures, of the Court; but was ever ready to serve Rome with his sword, and on many occasions by his coolness and conduct redeemed the errors and incapacity of his colleagues or predecessors. Fortune smiled upon the man who was insensible to her frowns. Honours poured in on the soldier who seemed so careless of their attainment; and Caius Lucius Licinius was perhaps the object of more respect and less envy than any other person of his rank in Rome.

It fell out that shortly before the death of Nero, the general, in traversing the slave-market on the way from the Forum, felt his sleeve plucked by a notorious dealer in human wares, named Gargilianus, who begged him earnestly to come and examine a fresh importation of captives lately arrived from Britain. To mention their country was at once to excite the interest of Licinius, who readily acceded to the request, and spoke a few kind words in their native language to the unhappy barbarians as he passed through their ranks. His attention was, however, especially arrested by the appearance of one of the conquered, a fine young man of great strength and stature, who seemed to feel painfully the indignity of his position, placed as he was on a huge stone block, whereon his own towering height rendered him a conspicuous object in the throng. He had been severely wounded, too, in several places, as was apparent from the scars scarce yet healed over. Indeed, had it not been so, he would never probably have been here. There was something in his face, and the expression of his large blue eyes, that roused a painful thrill in the Roman general's breast. He felt a strange and undefinable attraction towards the captive, for which he could not account, and, pausing in his walk, scanned him with a wistful searching gaze, which was not lost on the practised perceptions of the dealer.

[pg 68]

"He should have been shown in private," whispered Gargilianus, with an important and mysterious air. "Indeed, my man was just taking him away, when I saw you coming, my honoured patron, and I called to him to stop. Ay! you may examine him all over—tall, young, and healthy. Sound, wind and limb, and stronger than any gladiator in the amphitheatre. They are men of iron, these barbarians, that's the truth, and he has only just come over. There! look for yourself, noble general; you will see the chalk-marks: on his feet."

"But he is badly wounded," observed Licinius, beginning to scan him, as the other instinctively felt, with the eye of a purchaser.

"That is nothing!" exclaimed Gargilianus. "Mere scratches, skin deep, and healed over now. You will not be able to run your nail against them in a week. Eyesores, I grant you, to-day, otherwise I would ask two thousand sesterces at least for him. These islanders are cheap at any price."

"I will give you a thousand," said Licinius quietly.

"Impossible!" burst out the dealer, with a quiver of his fingers, that expressed a most emphatic negative. "I should lose money by him, generous patron! What! A man must live. Cæsar would give more for him to die in the circus. Look at his muscles! He would stand up for a good five minutes against the tiger!"

This last consideration was probably not without its influence. After a little more haggling, the British captive became the property of Licinius at the cost of fifteen hundred sesterces; and Esca found the most indulgent and the kindest-hearted master in Rome.

We must return to that master, pacing thoughtfully up and down the colonnade, in the cool and pleasant evening air.

It is, perhaps, one of the most consoling and merciful dispensations of Providence that the human mind is so constituted as to dwell on past pleasures, rather than past pain. The sorrow that is done with, returns indeed at intervals vividly and bitterly enough; but every fresh recurrence is less cruel than the last, and we can look back to our sufferings at length with a calm and chastened humility which is the first step towards resignation and eventual peace. But the memory of a great happiness seems so interwoven with the [pg 69]imperishable part of our being, that it loses none of its reality by the lapse of time, none of its brightness from the effect of distance. Anger, sorrow, hatred, contentions, fleet away like a dream; but the smile that gladdened us long ago, has passed into the very sunlight of noonday; the whisper that softened our sternest moods, steals with the breeze of evening to our heart, gently and tenderly as of yore, and we know, we feel, that while crime, and misery, and remorse, are the temporary afflictions of humanity, pardon, and hope, and love are its inheritance for evermore.

Licinius, pacing his long shadowy colonnade, dwells not on the anxieties, and the separation, and the sorrows of years; on the loss of his dearest treasure and its possession by another; not even on the calm dead face bound with its linen band. No; he is back in Britain once more with his living love, in the green glade where the bending ferns are whispering under the old oak-tree.

A step in the hall rouses him from his meditations, and a kind grave smile steals over the general's face at the approach of his favourite slave.

The Roman patrician looks what he is—a war-worn veteran, bronzed and hardened by the influence of many campaigns in many climates. He is not yet past the prime of his bodily vigour, and there is a severe beauty about his noble features, and beard and hair already touched with grey, that possesses considerable attraction still. Valeria, no mean judge, asserts that he is, and always will be, a handsome man, but that he does not know it. She respects him much, likes him a good deal, and he is the only person on earth for whose good opinion she has the slightest value. In truth, though she would not confess it even to herself, she is a little afraid of her good-hearted, brave, and thoughtful kinsman.

A man who has reached mature age without forming family ties is always to a certain extent in a false position. No amount of public interest will stop up the little chinks and corners, so to speak, which are intended by Nature to contain the petty cares and pleasures and vexations of domestic life. Without the constant association—the daily friction—of wife and children, a cynical disposition becomes selfish and morose; a kind one, melancholy and forlorn. Licinius feels a blank in his existence, which nothing he has yet found serves to fill; and he often wonders in himself why the barbarian slave should be almost the only creature in Rome for whom he entertains a feeling of interest and regard.

As he takes his place on the couch by the supper-table, [pg 70]Esca gives him to drink; and the patrician cannot help thinking the while, how he would like to have such a son, tall and handsome, with so warlike an air; a son whom he could instruct in all the intricacies of his glorious profession, whose mind he could educate, whose genius he could foster, and whose happiness he could watch over and ensure. They converse freely enough during the general's temperate meal—an egg, a morsel of kid, a few grapes, and a flask of common Sabine wine. Esca tells his master the encounter of the previous evening, and the friendship he had made in consequence, after nightfall. Licinius laughs at his account of the skirmish, and the eunuch's discomfiture.

"Nevertheless," says he, "I trust he did not recognise you. It can have been none other than Spado, whom you treated so unceremoniously; and Spado is just now a prime favourite with Cæsar. I might find it difficult to protect you if he knew where to find you, for charms and philtres are deadlier weapons in such hands as his, than sword and spear in yours and mine. Did he take note of your person, think you, Esca, ere he went down?"

"I can hardly believe it," answered Esca. "The evening was dark, and the confusion great. Moreover, I fled with the poor girl they had surrounded, the very instant I could snatch her out of the throng."

"And you saw these Jews in their home, you say?" pursued Licinius gravely. "I have heard much of that people, and, indeed, served against them in Syria. Are they not morose, cruel, bloodthirsty? Slayers of men, devourers of children? Have they not fearful orgies in which they feast upon human flesh? And one day in the week that they devote to solitude and silence, and schemes of hatred against all mankind? Are you sure that your entertainers belonged to this detestable nation?"

"Christians and Jews," replied Esca, who had caught the sound of the former title in the course of his conversation with Calchas.

"Are they not the same?" returned Licinius, and to this question the barbarian was unable to furnish a reply.

CHAPTER X

A TRIBUNE OF THE LEGIONS

Under the porch of one of the most luxurious houses in Rome, two men jostled in the dubious light of early morning. Exclamations of impatience were succeeded by a mutual recognition, and a hearty laugh, as Damasippus and Oarses, freedmen and staunch clients of Julius Placidus, recognised each other's eagerness to pay court to their joint patron. They had risen from their beds while it was yet dark, and hurried hither in order to be the first to salute the tribune at his morning levée. Yet they found the great hall filling already with a bustling crowd of friends, retainers, clients, and dependants. Damasippus was a short, square, beetle-browed man, with a villainous leer; Oarses, a pale, sedate, and somewhat precise personage. But with this marked difference of exterior, an expression of unscrupulous and thorough-paced knavery was common to both. Said Damasippus to Oarses, with a shrug of affected disgust—

"It may be hours yet ere he will see us! Look at this wretched crowd of parasites and flatterers! They will follow the patron to his bath! They will besiege him in his very bed! Oh, my friend! Rome is no longer the place for an honest man."

To which Oarses replied, in subdued and humble tones—

"The flies gather round the honey, though it is only for what they can get. But the sincerest gratitude and affection draw you and me, my dear companion, to the side of the illustrious tribune."

"You speak truth," returned Damasippus. "It is sad to see how few clients are uninfluenced by mean and sordid thoughts. An honest man is becoming as rare at Rome as at Athens. It was not so in the days of the republic—in the golden age—in the good old times!"

"Oh for the good old times!" exclaimed Oarses, still in the same low and unmoved voice.

"Oh for the good old times!" echoed Damasippus; and [pg 72]the two knaves, with their arms on each other's shoulders, fell to pacing the extremity of the hall, and exchanging spiteful remarks on the concourse with which it was filled.

The tribune's house was the most perfect of its kind in the whole city. Standing apart and surrounded by a wall and garden of its own, it combined the luxurious splendour of a palace with the comfort and seclusion of a private residence. Everything of ornament that was most costly and gorgeous, had been procured by Placidus to decorate his mansion. Everything of art that was most conspicuous and effective hung on his walls, stood in picturesque groups about his apartments, or lay scattered in rich profusion on his floor. The hangings that veiled his own sleeping-room from the public eye, were of embroidered crimson silk, woven in the looms of Asia, and probably taken by the strong hand of the successful soldier as spoils of war. The very pavement of the hall was of the richest mosaic, traced in fanciful patterns and inlaid with gold. As the morning drew on, it was trodden by a multitude of feet. No one of his rank held so numerous a levée as Julius Placidus. In the concourse that thronged it now, might be seen men of all countries, classes, characters, professions, and denominations. Unlike Licinius, who, indeed, owed his influence solely to the firm consistency and unbending rectitude of his character, the tribune let no opportunity pass of binding an additional partisan to his cause by the ties of self-interest and expectation. They were crowding in now through the wide open doors; and while the spacious hall was nearly filled, the approach to it, and the street itself outside, were choked with applicants, who had one and all, directly or indirectly, something to get, or ask, or hope for, from the tribune. Here, an artist brought his picture carefully draped in the remains of an old garment; yet not so entirely concealed but that a varnished corner might be visible, and the painter, nothing loth, might be prevailed on by earnest solicitations to reveal, bit by bit, all the beauties of his production. There, a sculptor was diligently preserving the outlines of his model, wrapped in its wet cloth, from collision with the bystanders, and assuming credit for the mysterious beauties of a work, which, perhaps, if uncovered, would have grievously disappointed the eyes that scanned it so curiously. In one corner stood a jeweller, holding in his hand a gorgeous collar of pearls and rubies, prepared by the patrician's orders, and testifying at once to the ingenuity of the tradesman, [pg 73]and the munificence of his employer. In another, waited a common-looking slave, with a downcast eye and a bloated unwholesome face; who, nevertheless, assumed an important air that seemed to say he was sure of an early audience, as, indeed, was more than probable in consideration of his tidings, a message from venal beauty to the admirer who paid his welcome tribute in gold. Parasites and flatterers elbowed their way insolently in the midst, as though they had a right to be there, whilst honest men, brown with toil, and sighing wistfully for the fresh breezes of Tibur or Præneste, kept aloof, abashed and shrinking, though they had but come to ask for their due. Nearest the hangings that concealed the bedroom, stood a dirty slave, bespattered with the filth of the fish-market, and exhaling an odour of garlic that cleared for him an ample breathing-space even in a Roman crowd; but the knave knew the value of his intelligence, and how it would obtain him favour in the tribune's eyes. No less important a communication than this, that a mullet had been taken the night before of nearly six pounds weight, and that so lavish a patron as Placidus should have the first offer to purchase at a thousand sesterces[2] a pound. He waited with his eyes intently fastened on the curtains, and took no notice of the jabber and confusion that pervaded the hall.

Presently the crowd gave way a little, ebbing backward on either side, and forming a lane as it were for three men, who were regarded as they passed with glances of great awe and admiration. There was no mistaking the deep chest and broad shoulders of one of these, even apart from the loud frank voice in which Hirpinus the gladiator was wont to convey his observations, without much respect for persons. He was accompanied, on the present occasion, by two individuals, obviously of the same profession as himself—Hippias the fencing-master, and Euchenor the boxer. All three conversed and laughed boisterously. It was obvious that even at that early hour they had not broken their fast without a generous draught of wine.

"Talk not to me," said Hirpinus, rolling his strong shoulders, and observing with great complacency the attention he excited—"talk not to me: I have seen them all—Dacians, Gauls, Cimbrians, Ethiopians, every barbarian that ever put on a breastplate. By Hercules, they were fools to this lad. Why, the big yellow-haired German, whom Cæsar [pg 74]gave us for the lion last summer, would not have stood up to him for a quarter of an hour. He was taller, maybe, a little, but he hadn't the shape, man—he hadn't the shape! You'll hardly call *me* a kid that hasn't put his horns out, will ye? Well, he gave me so much to do with the *cestus*, that I wouldn't have taken it off for a flagon of cheap wine, I tell ye. What think ye of *that*, my little Greek? You don't call it so bad for a beginner, I hope?"

He turned to Euchenor as he spoke, a beautifully-made young man, of extraordinary strength and symmetry, with the regular chiseled features of his country, and as evil an expression as ever lowered on a fair face. The Greek pondered awhile before he answered. Then he made the apposite inquiry—

"Were you sober, Hirpinus, when you stood up to him? or had you sucked down a skinful of wine, before you took your bellyful of boxing?"

The other burst into a loud laugh.

"Drunk or sober," said he, "you know the stuff I am made of, just as well as I know your weight to an ounce, and your reach to an inch. Ay, and your mettle too, my lad! though it don't take a six-foot rod to get to the bottom of *that*. Harkye, this Briton of mine would *eat* such a man as you, body and bones and all, just as I would eat a thrush, and be ready for another directly, without so much as washing his mouth out."

A very sinister scowl passed across Euchenor's face, who did not quite relish this low valuation of his prowess, and, above all, his courage; but he was a professional boxer, and, as such, necessarily possessed thorough command of temper, so he only glanced a little scornfully over the other's frame, which was getting somewhat into flesh, and observed—

"There will be money to be made out of him then in the arena, if he falls into good hands, and is properly trained."

Hitherto, the fencing-master had joined but carelessly in the conversation, and, indeed, scarcely seemed aware of its purport; but the concluding sentence arrested his attention, and turning upon Hirpinus rather angrily, and with the air of one accustomed to command, he said abruptly—

"Why did you not bring him to me at once? If you have let him slip through those great fingers of yours, it will be the worst job you have been concerned in for many a day. Have a care, Hirpinus! Better men than you have been under the net ere now, and the great games are not so far off. It needs but a word from me to send you into the arena to-morrow, a [pg 75]fair prey for a clumsy trident and a fathom or two of twine. You know that as well as I do."

Hippias spoke truth. A retired gladiator, celebrated for his deadly swordsmanship and the number of his victories, he had been long ago invested by Nero with the wooden foil, which represented a free discharge and immunity from future services in the amphitheatre. Habituated, however, to the excitement of the fatal sport, and rejoicing in that spurious fame which so distinguished men of his class at Rome, he had set up a school for the express purpose of training swordsmen for the arena; and had won such favour, under two successive emperors, by the proficiency to which he brought his pupils, and his talent for arranging the deadly pageants in which they figured, that he had gradually become an incontrovertible authority on such matters, and the principal manager of the games in the amphitheatre. Of his reputation for gallantry, and the strange fascination such men possessed for the Roman ladies, we have already spoken; but if his smiles were courted amongst the fair spectators of their contests, his word was law with the gladiators themselves. He it was who paired the combatants, supplied them with weapons, adjusted their disputes, and, in most cases, held the balance on which their very lives depended. A threat from Hippias was more dreaded by these ruffians than the home-thrust of spear and sword.

Now, Hirpinus, although a fearless and skilful fighter, had his assailable point. On one occasion, when he had entered the circus as a *secutor*, that is to say, a combatant armed with sword and helmet, against the *retiarius*, who bore nothing but a trident and net, he had the misfortune to find himself involved in the meshes of the latter, and at the mercy of his antagonistic. The Roman crowd, though fickle in its approval, and uncertain in its antipathies, spared him in consideration of the gallant fight he had made; but Hirpinus never forgot his sensations at that moment. Bold and fierce as he was, it completely *cowed* him; and the boisterous, boastful prize-fighter would turn pale at the mention of a trident and a net. There was something ludicrous in the manner in which he now quailed before Hippias, eyeing him with the same sort of imploring glance that a dog casts at his master, and obviously persuaded of the speedy fulfilment of his threat.

"Patience, patron!" he growled apologetically. "I know where the lad is to be found. I can lay my hand on him at any time. I can bring him with me to the school. Why I [pg 76]talked myself well-nigh hoarse, and stayed out the drinking of two flagons of sour Sabine to boot, while I canvassed him to become one of *us* and join the Family forthwith. Why, you don't think, patron, I would be so thick-witted as to let him go without finding out where he lives? He is either a freedman, or a slave of"—

"Hush, fool!" interrupted Hippias angrily, observing that Damasippus and Oarses were hovering near, and listening intently for a piece of intelligence which he had resolved should be conveyed by himself, and none other, to the tribune's ear. "There is no occasion to publish it by the crier. Hadst thou but brains, man, in any sort of proportion to those great muscles of thine, I could tell thee why, with some hope of being understood. Enough! lose not sight of the lad; and, above all, keep thy tongue within thy teeth!"

The big gladiator nodded a sulky affirmative, puzzled, but obedient; and the two freedmen, with many courteous bows and gestures, accosted the champions with all the humility and deference to which such public characters were entitled.

"They say there will be two hundred pairs of swordsmen, matched at the same moment," observed Damasippus, in allusion to the coming games; "and not a plate of steel allowed in the circus, save sword and helmet. But of course, my Hippias, you know best if this is true."

"And three new lions from Libya, loose at once," added Oarses, "with a scene representing shepherds surprised over their watch-fires; real rocks, I have been told, and a stream of running water in the amphitheatre, with a thicket of live shrubs, from which the beasts are to emerge. Your taste, illustrious Hippias, the people say, is perfect. It has obviously been consulted here."

Hippias smiled mysteriously, and a little scornfully.

"There *is* a lion from Libya," said he; "I can tell you thus much. I, myself, saw him fed only yesterday at sunset."

"Is he large? is he strong? is he fierce?" questioned the two almost in a breath. "When did he come? is he quite full-grown? will they keep him without flesh? Of course the shepherds are not to be armed? Will they be condemned criminals, or only paid gladiators? Not that it matters much, if the lion is a pretty good one. We had a tiger, you know, last year, that killed five Ethiopian slaves, though they all set on him at once."

"But they were unarmed," interrupted Euchenor, whose cheek had turned a shade paler during the discussion. "Give [pg 77]me the proper weapons, and I fear no beast that walks the earth."

"Unarmed, of course!" repeated Damasippus, "and so was the tiger. A more beautiful creature was never seen. Do you not remember, Oarses, how he waved his long tail and stroked his face with his paws, like a kitten before it begins to play? And then, when he made his spring, the first black was rolled up like a ball? I was in the fifth row, my friends, yet I heard his bones crack, distinctly, even there."

"He was a great loss, that tiger," observed Oarses, more sadly than usual; "they should never have pitted him against a tusked elephant. The moment I saw the ivory, I knew how the fight must end, and I wagered against the smaller animal directly. I would have lost my sesterces, I think, willingly, for it to have won; but the beautiful beast never had a chance."

"It was the weight that did it, patrons—the weight," observed Hirpinus. "Man or beast, I will explain to you that weight must always"—

But here the gladiator's dissertation was broken off by the movement of the crimson hangings, and the appearance of Placidus emerging on his levée of expectants, bright and handsome, ready dressed for the day.

The tribune owned one advantage at least, which is of no small service to a man who embarks on a career demanding constant energy and watchfulness; he possessed that good digestion which is proverbially held to accompany an elastic conscience and a hard heart. Though supper the previous evening had been a luxurious and protracted meal—though the winecup had passed round very often, and the guests with singing brains had shown themselves in their own characters to their cool-headed and designing host—the latter, refreshed by a night's rest, now appeared with the glow of health on his cheek, and its lustre in his eye. As he looked about him on the throng of clients and dependants, his snow-white gown fastened and looped up with gold, his mantle adorned with a broad violet hem, his hair and beard carefully perfumed and arranged, a murmur of applause went round the circle which, perhaps, for once was really sincere, and even the rough gladiators could not withhold their approbation from a figure that was at once so richly attired, so manly, and so refined.

"Hail, my friends!" said the tribune, pausing in the entrance, and looking graciously around him on the crowd.

[pg 78]

"Hail, patron!" answered a multitude of voices, in every key, from the subdued and polished treble of Oarses to the deep hoarse voice of the gladiators.

Placidus moved from one to the other, with an easy though dignified cordiality of manner which he well knew how to assume when disposed to cultivate the favour of his inferiors. Clear-headed and discerning, in a wonderfully short space of time he had despatched the various matters which constituted the business of his morning levée. He had admired the model, declined the painting, ordered the statue, bought the jewels, answered the fair suppliant's message, and secured the mullet by sending to the market for it at once. The honest countrymen, too, he dismissed sufficiently well pleased, considering they had received nothing more substantial than smiles; and he now turned leisurely to Hippias, as if life had no duty so engrossing as the pursuit of pleasure, and asked him eagerly after the training of his gladiators, and the prospects of the amphitheatre.

Hippias knew his own value; he conversed with the patrician as an equal; but Hirpinus and Euchenor, appreciating the worth of a rich patron, gazed on Placidus with intense respect and admiration. The latter, especially, watched the tribune with his bright cunning eye, as if prepared to plant a blow on the first unguarded place.

"But your swordsmen are all too well known," urged the patrician on the fencing-master. "Here is old Hirpinus covers his whole body with two feet of steel as if it were a complete suit of armour, and never takes his point off his adversary's heart the while. The others are nearly as wary; if they encounter ordinary fencers they are sure to conquer; if we match them against each other and the people would see blood drawn, they must fight blindfolded,[1] and it becomes a matter of mere chance. No, what we want is a new man—one whom we can train without his being discovered, and bring out as an unknown competitor to try for the Emperor's prize. What say you, Hippias? 'Tis the only chance for a winning game now."

"I have heard of such a one," answered Hippias. "I think I can lay my hand on an untried blade, that a few weeks' training will polish up into the keenest weapon we have sharpened yet; at least, so Hirpinus informs me. What say'st thou, old Trojan? Tell the patron how thou camest to light on thy match at last."

Thus adjured, the veteran gladiator related at considerable [pg 79]length, interrupted by many exclamations of wonder from Damasippus and Oarses, his chance meeting with Esca in the Forum, and subsequent trial of strength and skill at the gymnasium. Somewhat verbose, as we have seen, when he could secure an audience, Hirpinus waxed eloquent on so congenial a theme as the beauty and stature of his new friend. "As strong as an ox, patron," said he, "and as lithe as a panther! Hand, and foot, and eye, all keeping time together like a dancing girl's. The spring of a wild-cat, and the light footfall of a deer. Then he would look so well in the arena, with his fair young face, set on his towering neck, like that of the son of Peleus. Indeed, if he should be vanquished, the women would save him every time. Why, one of the fairest and the noblest ladies in Rome stopped her litter in the crowded street while we walked together, and bade him come and speak to her from sheer goodwill. In faith, he was as tall, and twice as handsome, as the very Liburnians who carried her on their shoulders."

The tribune was laughing heartily at the athlete's eloquence; but Damasippus, who never took his eyes off his patron's face, thought the evil laugh was more malicious than usual at the mention of the Liburnians, and there was a false ring in the mirthful tones with which he asked for more information as to this young Apollo, and the dame on whom his appearance seemed to have made such an impression.

"I know most of the great ladies pretty well by sight," answered the honest swordsman. "Faith, a man does not easily forget the faces he sees turned on him in the arena, when he has his point at his adversary's throat, and they bid him drive it merrily home, and never spare. But of all the faces I see under the awning, there's not one looks down so calm and beautiful on a death-struggle as that of the noble Valeria."

"Like the moon on the torrent of Anio," observed Damasippus.

"Like the stars on the stormy Egean," echoed Oarses.

"Like nothing but herself," continued Hirpinus, who esteemed his own judgment incontrovertible on all matters relating to physical beauty, whether male or female. "The handsomest face and the finest form in Rome. It was not likely I could be mistaken, though I only caught a glimpse of her neck and arm for a moment, as she drew back the curtains of her litter, like"—and here Hirpinus paused for a simile, concluding with infinite relish,—"like a blade half drawn, and returned with a clash into the sheath."

Again Damasippus thought he perceived a quiver on his patron's face. Again there was something jarring in the tribune's voice, as he said to Hippias—

"We must not let this new Achilles escape us! See to it, Hippias. Who knows? He may make a worthy successor, even for thee, thou artist in slaughter, when he has worked his way up, step by step, and victory by victory, to the topmost branch of the tree."

Hippias laughed good-humouredly, turning at the same time his right thumb outward, and pointing with it to the roof. It was the gesture with which the Roman crowd in the amphitheatre refused quarter to the combatant who was down.

[pg 81]

CHAPTER XI

STOLEN WATERS

The broken column of one of the buildings destroyed in the great fire of Rome, and not yet restored, was glowing crimson in the setting sun. Beneath its base, the Tiber was gliding gently on towards the sea. There was a subdued hum even in the streets of the Imperial City that denoted how the burden and heat of the day were now past; and the languor of the hour seemed to pervade even those who were compelled to toil on in the struggle for bread, and who could only in imagination abandon themselves to repose. On a fragment of the ruin sat Esca, gazing intently on the water as it stole by. To all appearance his listless and dreamy mood was unconscious of surrounding objects, yet his attitude was that of one prepared to start into action at a moment's notice; and though his arms were folded and his head bent down, his ear was watching eagerly to catch the faintest sound.

It is a patience-wearing process, that same waiting for a woman; and under the most favourable circumstances is productive of much irritation, disappointment, and disgust. In the first place a man is invariably too soon, and this knowingly and as it were with *malice prepense*. Taking time thus by the forelock, delays his flight considerably, and indeed reduces his pace to the slowest possible crawl; so that when the appointed moment does arrive, it seems to the watcher that it has been past a considerable period, and that his vigil should be already over, when in reality it is only just begun. Then, as the minutes steal on, come the different misgivings and suspicions which only arise on such occasions, and which in his right senses the self-torturer would be incapable of harbouring. Circumstances which, when the appointment was made, seemed expressly adapted to further his designs, now change to insurmountable difficulties, or take their place as links in a chain of deception which he persuades himself has been forged with unheard-of duplicity, [pg 82]expressly for his discomfiture. He thinks badly of everyone, worst of all of her, whose unpardonable fault is that she is now some fifty seconds late. Then comes a revulsion of feeling, and his heart leaps to his mouth, for yonder, emerging on the long perspective, is a female figure obviously advancing this way. The expected object is tall, slim, pliant, and walks with the firm free step of a deer on the heather. The advancing shape is short, fat, awkward, and waddles in its gait; nevertheless, it is not till it has reached within arm's length that he will allow himself to be convinced of his disappointment. If its ears are pretty quick, the unoffending figure may well be shocked at the deep and startling execration which its presence calls forth. Then begins another phase of despondency, humiliation, and bitter self-contempt, through all which pleasant changes of feeling the old feverish longing remains as strong as ever. At last she comes round the corner in good earnest, with the well-known smile in her eyes, the well-known greeting on her lips, and he forgets in an instant, as if they had never been, his anxiety, his anger, his reproaches, all but the presence that brings light to his life and gladness to his heart once more.

Esca rose impatiently at intervals, walked a few paces to and fro, sat down again, and threw small fragments of the ruin into the water. Presently a figure, draped in black and closely veiled, moved down to the river's side near where the Briton sat, and began filling a pitcher from the stream. It could hardly have passed the column without seeing him, yet did it seem unconscious of his presence; and who could tell how the heart might be beating within the bosom, or the cheek blushing behind the veil? That veil was lifted, however, with an exclamation of surprise, when Esca stooped over her to take the pitcher from her hand, and Mariamne's cheek turned paler now than it had been even on the memorable night when he rescued her from the grasp of Spado and his fellow-bacchanals. He, too, murmured some vague words of astonishment at finding her here. If they were honest, for whom could he have been waiting so impatiently? and it is possible, besides, Mariamne might have been a little disappointed had she been allowed to fill her pitcher from the Tiber for herself.

The Jewess had been thinking about him a good deal more than she intended, a good deal more than she knew, for the last two days. It is strange how very insensibly such thoughts gain growth and strength without care or culture. There are plants we prune and water every day which never [pg 83]reach more than a sickly and stunted vitality after all, and there are others that we trample down, cut over, tear up by the very roots, which nevertheless attain such vigour and luxuriance that our walls are covered by their tendrils, and our dwellings pervaded by their fragrance.

Mariamne was no bigoted daughter of Judah, for whom the stranger was an outcast because a heathen. Her constant intercourse with Calchas had taught her nobler truths than she had derived from the traditions of her fathers. And with all her pride of race and national predilections, she had imbibed those principles of charity and toleration which formed the groundwork of a new religion, destined to shed its light upon all the nations of the earth.

It was not precisely as a brother, though, that Mariamne had yet brought herself to regard the handsome British slave. They were soon conversing happily together. The embarrassment of meeting had disappeared with the first affectation of surprise. It was not long before he told her how tired he had been of watching by the broken column at the riverside.

"How could you know I should come here?" asked the girl with a look of infinite simplicity and candour, though she must have remembered all the time, that she had not scrupled to hint at the daily practice in course of conversation with Calchas, on the night when Esca brought her safely home.

"I hoped it," he replied, with a smile. "I have been a hunter, you know, and have learned that the shyest and wildest of animals seek the waterside at sunset. I was here yesterday, and waited two long hours in vain."

She glanced quickly at him, but withdrew her eyes immediately, while the blood mounted to her pale face.

"Did you expect to see me?" she asked in a trembling voice; "and I never left the house the whole of yesterday! Oh, how I wish I had known it!"

Then she stopped in painful embarrassment, as having said too much. He appeared not to notice her confusion. He seemed to have some confession to make on his own part—something he hardly dared to tell her, yet which his honest nature could not consent should be withheld. At last he said with an effort—

"You know what I am! My time is not my own, my very limbs belong to another. It matters not that the master is kind, good, and considerate. Mariamne, I am a slave!"

[pg 84]

"I know it," she answered, very gently, with a loving pity beaming in her dark eyes. "My kinsman Calchas told me as much after you went away."

He drew a long breath as if relieved.

"And yet you wished to see me again?" he asked, while a gleam of happiness brightened his face.

"Why not?" she replied, with a kind smile. "Though that hand is a slave's, it struck my enemy down with the force of a hundred warriors; though that arm is a slave's, it bore me home with the care and tenderness of a woman. Ah! tell me not of slavery when the limbs are strong, and the heart is brave and pure. Though the body be chained with iron fetters, what matter so long as the spirit is free? Esca, you do not believe I think the worse of you because you are a heathen and a slave?"

Her voice was very soft and low while she spoke his name. No voice had ever sounded so sweetly in his ears before. A new, strange sense of happiness seemed to pervade his whole being, yet he had never felt his situation so galling and unendurable as now.

"I would not have you think the worse of me," he answered eagerly, "upon any account. Listen, Mariamne. I was taken captive in war and brought here with a hundred others to Rome. We were set up like cattle in the slave-market. Like cattle also we were purchased, one by one, by those who esteemed themselves practised judges of such human wares. I was bought by Caius Lucius Licinius at the price of a yoke of oxen, or a couple of chariot-horses. Bought and sold like a beast of the field, and driven home to my new master!"

He spoke with a scorn all the more bitter from having been repressed so long. Yet he kept back and smothered the indignation rising within him. This was the first ear that had ever been open to his wrongs, and the temptation was strong to pour them freely forth to so interested and partial a listener. To do him justice, he refrained from the indulgence. He had been taught from childhood that it was weak and womanish to complain; and the man had not forgotten the lessons of the boy.

Her gentle voice again interposed in soothing and consoling accents.

"But he is kind," she said, "kind and considerate—you told me so yourself. I could not bear to think him otherwise. Indeed, Esca, it would make me very unhappy to know that you"—

[pg 85]

Here she broke off suddenly, and snatched up the pitcher he had been filling for her with such haste as to spill half its contents over his dress and her own.

"There is someone watching us! Farewell!" she whispered in a breathless, frightened voice, and hurried away, turning her head once, however, to cast a glance over her shoulder, and then hastened home faster than before. Esca looked after her while she continued in sight, either unconscious of their vicinity, or at all events not noticing a pair of bold black eyes that were fixed upon him with an expression of arch and ludicrous surprise. He turned angrily, however, upon the intruder, when the black eyes had gazed their fill, and their owner burst out into a loud, merry, and mocking laugh.

[pg 86]

CHAPTER XII

MYRRHINA

Myrrhina's voice was at all times pitched in a high key; her accents were very distinct and shrill, admirably adapted for the expression of derision or the conveyance of sarcastic remarks.

"So I have run you into a corner at last," she said, "and a pretty hunt you have given me. 'Tis to draw water, of course, that you come down to the Tiber-side, just at sunset; and you met her quite by accident, I daresay, that slip of a girl in her wisp of black clothes, who flitted away just now like a ghost going back again to Proserpine. Ah! you gape like a calf when they put the garland on him for sacrifice, and the poor thing munches the very flower-buds that deck him for destruction. Well, you at least are reserved for a nobler altar, and a worthier fate than to give your last gasp to a sorceress in the suburbs. Jupiter! how you stare, and how handsome you look, you great, strong barbarian, when you are thoroughly surprised!"

She put her face so close up to his, to laugh at him, that the gesture almost amounted to a caress. Myrrhina had no slight inclination to make love to the stalwart Briton on her own account, pending the conclusion of certain negotiations she felt bound to carry out on her mistress's. These were the result of a conversation held that morning while the maid was as usual combing out her lady's long and beautiful hair.

Valeria's sleep had been broken and restless. She tossed and turned upon her pillow, and put back the hair from her fevered cheeks and throbbing temples in vain. It was weary work to lie gazing with eyes wide open at the flickering shadows cast by the night-lamp on the opposite wall. It was still less productive of sleep to shut them tight and abandon herself to the vision thus created, which stood out in life-like colours and refused to be dispelled. Do what she would to forget him, and conjure up some other object, there was the [pg 87]young barbarian, towering like a demigod over the mean effeminate throng; there were the waving linen garments, and the reeling symbols, and the tossing hands, and the scowling faces of the priests of Isis; there was the dark-clad girl with her graceful pliant form; and there, yes, always there, in his maddening beauty, was the tall brave figure, gathering itself in act to strike. She could not analyse her feelings; she believed herself bewitched. Valeria had not reached the prime of her womanhood, without having sounded, as she thought, every chord of feeling, tasted of every cup that promised gratification or excitement. She had been flattered by brave, courted by handsome, and admired by clever men. Some she fancied, some she liked, some she laughed at, and some she told herself she loved. But this was a new sensation altogether. This intense and passionate longing she had never felt before. But for its novelty it would have been absolutely painful. A timid girl might have been frightened at it; but Valeria was no timid girl. She was a woman, on the contrary, who, with all the eagerness and impetuosity of her sex, possessed the tenacity of purpose and the resolution of a man. Obviously, as she could not conquer the sentiment, it was her nature to indulge it.

"I have a message to Licinius," said she, turning at the same time from the mirror, and suffering her long brown hair to fall over her face like a veil; "a message that I do not care to write, lest it should be seen by other eyes. Tell me, Myrrhina, how can I best convey it to my kinsman?"

The waiting-maid was far too astute to suggest the obvious arrangement of a private interview, than which nothing could have been easier, or to offer her own services, as an emissary who had already proved herself trustworthy in many a well-conducted intrigue; for Myrrhina knew her business too well to hesitate in playing into the hands of her mistress. So she assumed a look of perplexity and deep reflection while, finger on forehead, as the result of profound thought, she made the following reply—

"It would be safest, madam, would it not, to trust the matter to some confidential slave?"

Valeria's heart was beating fast, and the fair cheek was pale again now, while she answered, with studied carelessness—

"Perhaps it would, if I could think of one. You know his household, Myrrhina. Can I safely confide in any of them?"

"Those barbarians are generally faithful," observed the maid, with the most unconscious air. "I know Licinius has [pg 88]a British slave in whom he places considerable trust. You have seen him yourself, madam."

"Have I?" answered Valeria, moving restlessly into a more comfortable attitude. "Should I know him again? What is he like?"

The blood had once more mounted to her forehead, beneath the long hair. Myrrhina, who was behind her, saw the crimson mantling even on her neck. She was a slave, and a waiting-maid, but she was also a woman, and she could not resist the temptation; so she answered maliciously—

"He is a big awkward-looking youth, of lofty stature, madam, and with light curly hair. Stupid doubtless, and as trusty, probably, as he is thick-witted."

It is not safe to jest with a tigress unless you are outside the bars of her cage. Valeria made a quick impatient movement that warned the speaker she had gone too far. The latter was not wanting in readiness of resource.

"I could bring him here, madam," she added demurely, "within six hours."

Her lady smiled pleasantly enough.

"This evening, Myrrhina," she said; "I shall scarcely be ready before. By the way, I am tired of those plain gold bracelets. Take them away, and don't let me see them again. This evening, you said. I suppose I had better leave it entirely to you."

Both maid and mistress knew what this meant well. It implied full powers and handsome remuneration on one side, successful manœuvring and judicious blindness on the other. Valeria disposed herself for a long day's dreaming: stretched indeed in bodily repose, but agitating her mind with all the harassing alternations of anticipation, and hope, and doubt, and fear—not without a considerable leavening of triumph, and a slight tinge of shame: while Myrrhina set herself energetically to work on the task she had undertaken; which, indeed, appeared to possess its difficulties, when she had ascertained at the first place she sought, namely, the house of Licinius, that Esca was abroad, and no one knew in what direction he was likely to be found.

A woman's wit, however, usually derives fresh stimulus from opposition. Myrrhina was not without a large circle of acquaintances; and amongst others owned a staunch friend, and occasional admirer, in the person of Hirpinus, the gladiator. That worthy took a sufficient interest in the athletic Briton to observe his movements, and was aware that Esca had spent some two or three hours by the Tiber-side on the [pg 89]previous evening—a fact which he imparted to Myrrhina, on cross-examination by the latter, readily enough, professing at the same time his own inability to account for it, inasmuch as there was neither wineshop nor quoit-ground in the vicinity. Not so his intriguing little questioner. "A man does not wait two or three hours in one spot," thought Myrrhina, "for anything but a woman. Also, the woman, if she comes at all, is never so far behind her time. The probability then is, that she disappointed him; and the conclusion, that he will be there again about sunset the following day."

Thus arguing, she resolved to attend at the trysting-place, and make a third in the interview, whether welcome or not; killing the intervening time, which might otherwise have hung heavily on her hands, by a series of experiments on the susceptibility of Hirpinus—an amusing pastime, but wanting in excitement from its harmlessness; for the gladiator had arrived at that period of life when outward charms, at least, are esteemed at their real value, and a woman must possess something more than a merry eye and a saucy lip if she would hope to rival the attraction of an easy couch and a flagon of old wine. Nevertheless, she laughed, and jested, and ogled, keeping her hand in, as it were, for practice against worthier occasions, till it was time to depart on her errand, when she made her escape from her sluggish admirer, with an excuse as false and as plausible as the smile on her lip.

Hirpinus looked after her as she flitted away, laughed, shook his head, and strode heavily off to the wineshop, with an arch expression of amusement on his brave, good-humoured, and somewhat stupid face. Myrrhina, drawing a veil about her head and shoulders so as effectually to conceal her features, proceeded to thread her way through the labyrinth of impoverished streets that led to the riverside, as if familiar with their intricacies. When she reached her destination at last, she easily hid herself in a convenient lurking-place, from which she took care not to emerge till she had learned all she wished to know about Esca and his companion.

"What do you want with me?" asked the Briton, a little disturbed by this saucy apparition, and not much pleased with the waiting-maid's familiar and malicious air.

"I am unwelcome, doubtless," answered the girl, with another peal of laughter; "nevertheless you must come with me whether you will or no. We Roman maidens take no denial, young man; we are not like your tall, pale, frozen women of the north."

[pg 90]

Subscribing readily to this opinion, Esca felt indignant at the same time to be so completely taken possession of. "I have no leisure," said he, "to attend upon your fancies. I must homeward; it is already nearly supper time."

"And you are a slave, I know," retorted Myrrhina with a gesture of supreme and provoking contempt. "*A slave!* You, with your strength, and stature, and courage, cannot call an hour of this fine cool evening your own."

"I know it," said he, bowing his head to conceal the flush of indignation that had risen to his brow. "I know it. A slave must clean his master's platter, and fill his cup to drink."

She could see that her thrust had pierced home; but with all her predilections for his handsome person, she cared not how she wounded the manly heart within.

"And being a slave," she resumed, "you may be loaded and goaded like a mule! You may be kicked and beaten like a dog! You cannot even resent it with hoofs and fangs as the dumb animal does when his treatment is harsher than he deserves! You are a *man*, you know, though a barbarian! You must cringe, and whine, and bite your lips, and be patient!"

Every syllable from that sharp tongue seemed to sting him like a wasp: his whole frame quivered with anger at her taunts; but he scorned to show it, and putting a strong constraint upon his feelings, he only asked quietly—

"What would you with me? It was not to tell me this that you watched and tracked me here."

Myrrhina thought she had now brought the metal to a sufficiently high temperature for fusion. She proceeded to mould it accordingly.

"I tracked you here," she said, "because I wanted you. I wanted you, because it is in my power to render you a great service. Listen, Esca; you must come with me. It is not every man in Rome would require so much persuasion to follow the steps of a pretty girl."

She looked very arch and tempting while she spoke, but her attractions were sadly wasted on the preoccupied Briton; and if she expected to win from him any overt act of admiration or encouragement, she was wofully disappointed.

"I cannot follow yours," said he; "my way lies in another direction. You have yourself reminded me that I am not my own master."

"That is the very reason," she exclaimed, clapping her hands exultingly. "I can show you the way to freedom. [pg 91]No one else can help you but Myrrhina; and if you attend to her directions you can obtain your liberty without delay."

"And why should *you* be disposed to confer on me such a benefit?" he asked, with instinctive caution, for the impulsive nature that jumps so hastily to conclusions, and walks open-eyed into a trap, is rarely born north of the Alps. "I am a barbarian, a stranger, almost an enemy. What have you and I in common?"

"Perhaps I have fallen in love with you myself," she laughed out; "perhaps you may be able to serve me in return. Come, you are as cold as the icy climate in which you were bred. You shall take your choice of the two reasons; only waste no more time, but gird yourself and follow me."

Though it had never been dormant, the desire for liberty had, within the last two days, acquired a painful intensity in Esca's breast. He had not indeed yet confessed to himself that he cherished an ardent attachment for Mariamne; but he was conscious that her society possessed for him an undefinable attraction, and that without her neither liberty nor anything else would be worth having. This new sensation made his position more galling than it had ever been before. He could not ignore the fact, that it was absurd for one whose existence was not his own, to devote that existence to another; and the degradation of slavery, which his lord's kindness had veiled from him as much as possible while in his household, now appeared in all its naked deformity. He felt that no effort would be too desperate, no sacrifice too costly, to make for liberty; and that he would readily risk life itself, and lose it, to be free, if only for a week.

"You have seen my mistress," resumed Myrrhina, as they hurried on through the now darkening streets; "the fairest lady and the most powerful in Rome; a near kinswoman, too, of your master. It needs but a word from her to make of you what she pleases. But she is wilful, you must know, and imperious, and cannot bear to be contradicted. Few women can."

Esca had yet to learn this peculiarity of the sex; but he heard Myrrhina mention her mistress with vague misgivings, and forebodings of evil far different from the unmixed feelings of interest such a communication would have called forth a while ago.

"Did she send for me expressly?" he asked, with some anxiety of tone. "And how did you know where to find me in such a town as this?"

"I know a great many things," replied the laughing [pg 92]damsel; "but I do not choose everyone to be as wise as myself. I will answer both your questions, though, if you will answer one of mine in return. Valeria did not mention you by name, and yet I think there is no other man in Rome would serve her turn but yourself; and I knew that I should find you by Tiber-side, because you cannot keep a goose from the water, nor a fool from his fate. Will you answer my question as frankly? Do you love the dark pale girl that fled away so hastily when I discovered you together?"

This was exactly what he had been asking himself the whole evening, with no very conclusive result; it was not likely, therefore, that Myrrhina should elicit a satisfactory reply. The Briton coloured a little, hesitated, and gave an evasive answer.

"Like tends to like," said he. "What is there in common between two strangers, from the two farthest extremities of the empire?"

Myrrhina clapped her hands in triumph.

"Like tends to like, say you?" she exclaimed exultingly. "You will tell another tale ere an hour be past. Hush! be silent now, and step softly; but follow close behind me. It is very dark in here, under the trees."

Thus cautioning him, she led Esca through a narrow door out of the by-street, into which they had diverged, and stepped briskly on, with a confidence born of local knowledge that he imitated with difficulty. They were now in a thickly planted shrubbery which effectually excluded the rays of a rising moon, and in which it was scarce possible to distinguish even Myrrhina's white dress. Presently they emerged upon a smooth and level lawn, shut in by a black group of cedars, through the lower branches of which peeped the crescent moon that had not long left the horizon, and turning the corner of a colonnade, under a ghostly-looking statue, traversed another door, which opened softly to Myrrhina's touch, and admitted them into a long carpeted passage, with a lamp at the farther end.

"Stay here while I fetch a light," whispered the damsel; and, gliding away for that purpose, returned presently to conduct Esca through a large dark hall into another passage; where she stopped abruptly, and lifting some silken hangings, that served for the door of an apartment, simply observed, "You will find food and wine there," and pushed him in.

Floods of soft and mellow light dazzled his eyes at first; but he soon realised the luxurious beauty of the retreat into which he had been forced. It was obvious that all the [pg 93]resources of wealth had been applied to its decoration with a lavish hand, guided by a woman's sensibility and a woman's taste. The walls were painted in frescoes of the richest colouring, and represented the most alluring scenes. Here the three jealous goddesses flashed upon bewildered Paris, in all the lustre of their immortal charms. A living envy sat on Juno's brow; a living scorn was stamped on Minerva's pale, proud face; and the living smile that won her the golden apple, shone in Aphrodité's winning eyes. There glowed imperial Circé in her magic splendour; and the very victims of her spell seemed yet to crave, with fiery glances and with thirsty lips, for one more draught from the tempting, luscious, and degrading cup. A shapely Endymion lay stretched in dreams of love. A frightened Leda shrank while she caressed. Here fair Adonis bled to death, ripped by the monster in the forest glade; there, where the broad-leaved lilies lay sleeping on the shady pool, bent fond Narcissus, to look and long his life away; an infant Bacchus rolled amongst the grapes, in bronze; a little Cupid mourned his broken bow, in marble. Around the cornices a circle of nymphs and satyrs, in bas-relief, danced hand-in-hand—wild woodland creatures, exulting in all the luxuriance of beauty, all the redundancy of strength; and yonder, just where the lamp cast its softest light on her attractions, stood the likeness of Valeria herself, depicted by the cunning painter in a loose flowing robe that enhanced, without concealing, the stately proportions of her figure, and in an attitude essentially her own—an attitude expressive of dormant passion, lulled by the languid insolence of power, and tinged with an imperious coquetry that she had found to be the most alluring of her charms.

It was bad enough to sit in that voluptuous room, under that mellow light, drinking the daintiest produce of Falernian vineyards, and gazing on such an image as Valeria's—an image of one who, beyond all women, was calculated to madden a heated brain, whose beauty could scarcely fail to captivate the outward senses, and take the heart by storm. It was bad enough to press the very couch of which the cushions still retained the print of her form—to see the shawl thrown across it, and trailing on the floor as though but now flung off—to touch the open bracelet hastily unclasped, yet warm from its contact with her arm. All this was bad enough, but worse was still to come.

Esca was in the act of setting down the goblet he had drained, and his eye was resting with an expression of [pg 94]admiration, not to be mistaken, on the picture opposite, when the rustling of the hangings caused him to turn his head. There was no more attraction now in bounding nymph or brilliant enchantress; haughty Juno, wise Minerva, and laughing Venus with her sparkling girdle, had passed into the shade. Valeria's likeness was no longer the masterpiece of the apartment, for there in the doorway appeared the figure of Valeria herself. Esca sprang to his feet, and thus they stood, that noble pair, confronting each other in the radiant light. The hostess and her guest—the lady and the slave—the assailant and the assailed.

[pg 95]

CHAPTER XIII

NOLENS—VOLENS

Valeria trembled in every limb; yet should she have remained the calmer of the two, inasmuch as hers could scarcely have been the agitation of surprise. Such a step, indeed, as that on which she now ventured, had not been taken without much hesitation and many changes of mind.

No woman, we believe, ever becomes utterly unsexed; and the process by which even the boldest lose their instinctive modesty, is gradual in the extreme. The power, too, of self-persuasion, which is so finely developed in the whole human race, loses none of its efficacy in the reasonings of the less logical and more impulsive half. People do not usually plunge headlong into vice. The shades are almost imperceptible by which the love of admiration deepens into vanity, and vanity into imprudence, and imprudence, especially if thwarted by advice and encouraged by opportunity, into crime. Nevertheless, the stone that has once been set in motion, is pretty sure to reach the bottom of the hill at last; and "I might" grows to "I will," and "I will," ere long, becomes "I must." Valeria's first thought had only been to look again upon an exterior that pleased her eye; then she argued that having sent for her kinsman's slave, there could be no harm in speaking to him—indeed, it would seem strange if she did not; and under any circumstances, of course there was no occasion that her colloquy should be overheard by all the maidens of her establishment, or even by Myrrhina, who, trusty as she might be, had a tongue of surpassing activity, and a love of gossip not to be controlled.

She ignored, naturally enough, that any unusual interest [pg 96]in the Briton should have caused her thus to summon him into her own private and peculiar retreat; thus to surround him with all that was dazzling to the eye, and alluring to the senses; thus to appear before him in the full glow of her personal beauty, set off by all the accessories of dress, jewels, lights, flowers, and perfumes, that she could command. If she sent for him, it was but natural that he should find her encircled by the usual advantages of her station. It was no fault of hers, that these were gorgeous, picturesque, and overpowering. He might as well blame the old Falernian for its seduction of the palate, and its confusion of the brain. Let him take care of himself! she would see him, speak to him, smile on him, perhaps, and be *guided by circumstances*. A wise resolution this last in all cases, and by no means difficult to keep when the circumstances are under our own control.

Valeria, womanlike, was the first to speak, though she scarcely knew what to say. With a very becoming air of hesitation she kept clasping and unclasping a bracelet, the fellow of the one on the couch. She was doubtless conscious that her round white arm looked rounder and whiter in the process.

"I have sent for you," she began, "because I am informed I can rely implicitly on your truth and secrecy. You are one, they tell me, who is incapable of betraying a trust. Is it not so?"

It is needless to say that Esca was already somewhat bewildered with the events of the evening, and in a mood not to be surprised at anything. Nevertheless, he could only bow his head in acknowledgment of this tribute to his honesty, and murmur a few indistinct syllables of assent. She seemed to gain confidence now the ice was broken, and went on more fluently.

"I have a secret to confide—a secret that none but yourself must know. Honour, reputation, the fame of a noble family, depend on its never being divulged. And yet I am going to impart this secret to you. Am I not rash, foolish, and impulsive, thus to place myself in the power of one whom I know so little? What must you think of me? What *do* you think of me?"

The latter question, propounded with a deepening colour and a glance that conveyed volumes, was somewhat difficult to answer. He might have said, "Think of you? Why, that you are the most alluring mermaiden who ever tempted a mariner to shipwreck on the rocks!" But what he did say was this—

"I have never feared man, nor deceived woman yet. I am not going to begin now."

She was a little disappointed at the coldness of his answer; yet her critical eye could not but approve the proud attitude he assumed, the stern look that came over his face, while he spoke. She edged a little nearer him and went on in a softened tone.

"A woman is always somewhat lonely and helpless, whatever may be her station, and oh! how liable we are to be deceived, and how we weep and wring our hands in vain when it is so! But I knew *you* from the first. I can read characters at a glance. Do you remember when I called you to my litter in the street while you were walking with Hirpinus, the gladiator?"

Again that warm crimson in the cheek—again that speaking flash from those dangerous eyes. Esca's head was beginning to turn, and his heart to beat with a strange sensation of excitement and surprise.

"I am not likely to forget it," said he, with a sort of proud humility. "It was such an honour as is seldom paid to one in my station."

She smiled on him more kindly than ever.

"I looked for you again," she murmured, "and saw you not. I wanted one in whom I could confide. I have no counsellor, no champion, no friend. I said what has become of him? who else will do my bidding, and keep my secret? Then Myrrhina told me that you would be here to-night."

She seemed to have something more to say that would not out. She looked at the Briton with expectant, almost imploring eyes; but Esca was young and frank and simple, so he waited for her to go on, and Valeria, discouraged and intimidated for the first time, proceeded in a colder and more becoming tone.

"The packet with which I intrust you must be delivered by yourself into the hands of Licinius. Not another creature must set eyes on it. No one must know that you have received it from me, nor, indeed, that you have been here to-night. If necessary you must guard it with your life! Can I depend upon you?"

He was beginning to feel that he could not depend upon himself much longer. The lights, the perfumes, the locality, the seductive beauty near him, so lovely and so kind, were making wild work with his senses and his reason. Nevertheless, the whole position seemed so strange, so impossible, [pg 98]that he could hardly believe he was awake. There was plenty of pride in his character, but no leavening of vanity; and, like many another gentle and inexperienced nature, he shrank from offending a woman's delicacy, with a repugnance that in some cases is exceedingly puzzling and provoking to the woman herself. So he put a strong constraint upon his feelings, and undertook the delivery of the missive with incredible simplicity and composure. The statue of Hermes at the door could not have looked colder and more impenetrable. She was a little at a loss. She must detain him at all hazards, for she felt that when once gone he would be gone for ever. She determined to lead him into conversation; and she chose the topic which, originating, perhaps, in the instinctive jealousy of a woman, was of all others the most subversive of her plans.

"I saw you once again," she said, "but it was in the hurry and confusion of that sudden broil. It was no fault of mine that the priests committed so gross an outrage on the poor thing you rescued. I would have helped you myself had you required assistance, but you carried her off as an eagle takes a kid. What became of the girl?"

The question was accompanied by a sharp inquisitive glance, and a forced smile of very perceptible annoyance wreathed her lip when she perceived Esca's embarrassed manner and reddening brow; but she had unwittingly called up the Briton's good genius, and for all women on earth, save one, he was a man of marble once more.

"I placed her in safety with her father," he replied; adding, with an assumption of deep humility, "Will you please to give me your commands and let me depart?"

Valeria was so totally unused to opposition in any of her whims or caprices that she could scarcely believe this obvious indifference was real. She persuaded herself that the Briton was so overpowered by her condescension, as to be only afraid of trespassing too far on such unexpected kindness, and she resolved that it should be no fault of hers if he were not quickly undeceived. She sank upon the couch in her most bewitching attitude, and, looking fondly up in his face, bade him fetch her tablets from the writing-stand. "For," said she, "I have not yet even prepared my communication to Licinius. Shall you be very weary of me, if I keep you my prisoner so long?"

Was it accident or design that entangled those rosy fingers with Esca's, as she took the tablets from his hand? Was it accident or design that shook the hair off her face, [pg 99]and loosed the rich brown clusters to fall across her glowing neck and bosom? It was surely strange that when she bent over the tablets her cheek turned pale, and her hand shook so that she could not form a letter on the yielding wax. She beckoned him nearer and bent her head towards him till the drooping curls trailed across her arm.

"I cannot write," said she, in trembling accents. "Something seems to oppress me—I am faint—I can scarcely breathe—Myrrhina shall give you the missive to-morrow. In the meantime, we are alone. Esca, you will not betray me. I can depend upon you. You are my slave, is it not so? This shall be your manacle!"

While she yet spoke, she took the bracelet from her arm and tried to clasp it round his wrist; but the glittering fetter was too narrow for the large-boned Briton, and she could not make it meet. Pressing it hard with both hands, she looked up in his face and laughed.

One responsive glance, the faintest shadow of yielding on those impassible features, and she would have told him all. But it came not. He shook the bracelet from his arm; and while he did so, she recovered herself, with the instantaneous self-command women seem to gather from an emergency.

"It was but to try your honesty!" she said, very haughtily, and rising to her feet. "A man who is not to be tempted, even by gold, can be safely trusted in such an affair as mine. You may go now," she added, with the slightest bend of her head. "To-morrow, if I require you, I shall take care that you hear from me through Myrrhina."

She looked after him as he disappeared under the silken hangings of the portal, her face quivered, her bosom heaved, and she clenched both hands till the round white arms grew hard as marble. Then she bit her lip once, savagely, and so seemed to regain her accustomed composure, and the usual dignity of her bearing. Nevertheless, when the despised bracelet caught her eye, lying neglected on the couch, she dashed it fiercely down, and stamped upon it, and crushed and ground the jewel beneath her heel against the floor.

CHAPTER XIV

CÆSAR

When a woman feels herself scorned, her first impulse seems to be revenge at any price. Some morbid sentiment, which the other sex can hardly fathom, usually prompts her in such cases to select for her instrument the man whom in her heart she loathes and despises, whose society is an insult, and whose attentions are a disgrace. Thus lowering herself in her own esteem, she knows that she inflicts a poisoned wound on the offender.

With all Valeria's self-command, her feelings had nearly got the better of her before Esca left the house. Had it been so, she would never have forgiven herself. But she managed to restrain them, and preserved an outward composure even while Myrrhina prepared her for repose. That damsel was much puzzled by the upshot of her manœuvres. From a method of her own, which long practice rendered familiar, she had made herself acquainted with all that occurred between her mistress and the handsome slave. Why their interview should have had no more definite result, she was at a loss to conceive. Altogether, Myrrhina was inclined to think that Esca had been so captivated by her own charms, as to be insensible to those of Valeria. This flattering supposition opened up a perspective of hazard, intrigue, and cross-purposes, that it was delicious to contemplate. The maid retired to her couch exulting. The mistress writhed in an agony of wounded pride and shame.

Morning, however, brought its unfailing accession of clear-sightedness and practical resolve. There are hours of the night in which we can abandon ourselves to love, hatred, despair, or sorrow with a helplessness that possesses in it some of the elements of repose; but with dawn reality resumes her sway, and the sufferer is indeed to be pitied, who can turn away from daylight without an impulse to be up and doing, who wishes only, in the lethargy of utter desolation, that it was evening once more.

[pg 101]

Valeria was not a woman to pass over the slight she had sustained. Few of them but will forgive an injury more readily than an insult. Long before she rose she had made up her mind where, and when, and how to strike; nothing remained but, to select the weapon, and put a keener edge upon the steel. Now Valeria had long been aware that, as far as was compatible with his disposition, Julius Placidus was devoted to her service. Indeed, he had told her so many a time, with an assumption of off-hand gallantry which, perhaps, she estimated at less than its proper value. Nevertheless, the compliments she received from the tribune were scarcely so well turned as might be expected from a man of his outward polish, refined manners, and general bad character. The woman's ear could detect the ring of truth, amidst all the jingle that accompanied it; and Valeria felt that the tribune loved her as much as it was possible for him to love anything but himself. To do her justice, she liked him none the better on that account. He was a man whom she must have hated under any circumstances, but perhaps she despised him a little less for this one redeeming quality of good taste. Here was a weapon, however, keen, and strong, and pliant, placed moreover, so to speak, within reach of her hand. She rose and dressed, languid, haughty, and composed as usual; but Myrrhina, who knew her, remarked a red spot burning on either cheek, and once a shudder, as of intense cold, passed over her, though it was a sunny morning in Rome.

Julius Placidus received a letter ere noon that seemed to afford him infinite satisfaction. The gilded chariot flashed brighter than ever in the sun, the white horses whirled it like lightning through the streets. Automedon's curls floated on the breeze, and the boy was even more insolent than usual without rebuke. Lolling on his velvet cushions the tribune's smile seemed to have lost something of its malice; and though the tiger-look was on him still, it was that of the sleek and satisfied tiger who has been fed. That look never left him all day, while he transacted business in the Forum, while he showed his grace and agility at ball in the Fives' Court, while he reposed after his exertions at the bath; but it was more apparent still when the hour of supper arrived, and he took his place in the banqueting-hall of Cæsar, with some of the bravest soldiers, the noblest senators, the greatest statesmen, wits, gluttons, and profligates in the empire.

A banquet with Vitellius was no light and simple repast. Leagues of sea and miles of forest had been swept to furnish [pg 102]the mere groundwork of the entertainment. Hardy fishermen had spent their nights on the heaving wave, that the giant turbot might flap its snowy flakes on the Emperor's table broader than its broad dish of gold. Many a swelling hill, clad in the dark oak coppice, had echoed to ringing shout of hunter, and deep-mouthed bay of hound, ere the wild boar yielded his grim life by the morass, and the dark grisly carcass was drawn off to provide a standing-dish that was only meant to gratify the eye. Even the peacock roasted in its feathers was too gross a dainty for epicures who studied the art of gastronomy under Cæsar; and that taste would have been considered rustic in the extreme, which could partake of more than the mere fumes and savour of so substantial a dish. A thousand nightingales had been trapped and killed, indeed, for this one supper, but brains and tongues were all they contributed to the banquet, while even the wing of a roasted hare would have been considered far too coarse and common food for the imperial board.

There were a dozen of guests reaching round the ivory table, and so disposed that the head of each was turned towards the giver of the feast. Cæsar was, indeed, in his glory. A garland of white roses crowned his pale and bloated face, enhancing the unhealthiness of its aspect. His features had originally been well-formed and delicate, expressive of wit, energy, and great versatility of character. Now the eyes were sunken, and the vessels beneath them so puffed and swollen as to discolour the skin; the jowl, too, had become large and heavy, imparting an air of sensual stupidity to the whole countenance, which brightened up, however, at the appearance of a favourite dish, or the smack of some rich luscious wine. He was busy at present with the eager, guzzling avidity of a pig; and he propped his unwieldy body, clad in its loose white gown, on one flabby arm, while with the other he fed himself on sharp-biting salads, salted herrings, pickled anchovies, and such stimulants as were served in the first course of a Roman entertainment, to provoke the hunger that the rest of the meal should satisfy. Now and then his eye wandered for an instant through the long shining vistas of the hall, amongst its marble pillars, its crimson hangings, its vases crowned with blushing fruit and flowers, its sideboards blazing with chalices, and flagons, and plates of burnished gold, as though he expected and winced from a blow; but the restless glance was sure to return to the table, and quench itself once more in the satisfaction of his favourite employment.

[pg 103]

Next to the Emperor was placed Paris, the graceful pantomimist, whose girlish face was already flushed with wine, and who turned his dark laughing eyes from one to another of the guests with the good-humoured insolence of incipient intoxication. The young actor's dress was extravagant in the extreme, and he wore a collar of pearls, the gift of an empress, that would have purchased a province. He was talking volubly to a fat, coarse-featured man, his neighbour, who answered him at intervals with a grunt of acquiescence, but in whose twinkling eye lurked a world of wit and sarcasm, and from whose thick sensual lips, engrossed as they were with the business of the moment, would drop ever and anon some pungent jest, that was sure to be repeated to-morrow at every supper-table in Rome. Montanus was a crafty statesman and a practised diplomatist, whose society was sought for at the Court, whose opinions carried weight in the Senate; but the old voluptuary had long discovered that there was no safety under the Empire for those who took a leading part in the council, but that certain distinction awaited proficiency at the banquet—so he devoted his powerful intellect to the study of gastronomy and the fabrication of witty sayings; nor did he ever permit the outward expression of his countenance to betray a consciousness of the good things that went into and came out of his mouth.

Beyond him again reclined Licinius; his manly face and noble bearing presenting a vivid contrast to those who surrounded him, and who treated him, one and all, including Cæsar himself, with marked deference and respect. The old soldier, however, appeared somewhat weary, and out of his element. He loathed these long entertainments, so opposed to his own simple habits; and regarded the company in his secret heart with a good-humoured, yet very decided, contempt. So he sat through the banquet as he would have kept watch on an outpost. It was tedious, it was disagreeable. There was nothing to be gained by it; but it was duty, and it must be done.

Far different, in the frank joyous expression he knew so well how to put on, was the mien of Julius Placidus, as he replied to a brief, indistinct question from the Emperor (murmured with his mouth full), by a sally that set everyone near him laughing, and even raised a smile on the pale face of Vitellius himself. It was the tribune's cue to make his society universally popular—to be all things to all men, especially to win the confidence of his imperial host. There is an art in social success, no less than in any other triumph [pg 104]of natural ability. The rein must never be completely loosed, the bow never stretched to its full compass. Latent power ready to be called forth, is the secret of all grace; and while the observed does well, it must be apparent to the observer that he could do better if he chose. Also, to be really popular, a man, though a good deal liked, should be a little feared. Julius Placidus excelled in the retort courteous, which he could deliver without the slightest hesitation or change of countenance; and a nickname or a sarcasm once inflicted by the ready-witted tribune clung afterwards to its object like a burr. Then he possessed besides the invaluable qualification of a discriminating taste in seasonings, the result of a healthy palate, refined, but not destroyed by the culture bestowed on it; and could drink every man of them, except Montanus, under the table, without his stomach or his brain being affected by the debauch.

Our acquaintance Spado was also of the party. Generally a buffoon of no mean calibre, and one whose special talent lay in such coarse and practical jests as served to amuse Vitellius when his intellects had become too torpid to appreciate the nicer delicacies of wit, the eunuch was to-night peculiarly dull and silent. He reclined, with his head resting on his hand, and seemed to conceal as much as he could of his face, one side of which was swollen and discoloured as from a blow. His fat unwieldy form looked more disgusting than usual in its sumptuous dress, fastened and looped up at every fold with clasps of emeralds and pearls; and though he ate slowly and with difficulty, he seemed determined to lose none of the gratifications of the meal.

There were a few more guests—one or two senators—who, with the caution, but not the genius of Montanus, were conspicuous for nothing but their fulsome adulation of the Emperor. A tall sullen-looking man, commander of the Prætorian Guard, who never laid aside the golden breastplate in which he was encased, and who seemed only anxious for the conclusion of the entertainment. Three or four unknown and undistinguished persons, called in Roman society by the expressive term "Shades," whose social position, and, indeed, whose very existence, depended on the patrons they followed. Amongst these were two freedmen of the Emperor, pale anxious-looking beings, with haggard eyes and careworn faces. It was their especial duty to guard against poison, by tasting of every dish served to their employer. It might be supposed that, as in previous reigns, one such functionary would have been enough; but the great variety of dainties in [pg 105]which the enormous appetite of Vitellius enabled him to indulge, rendered it impossible for any one stomach to keep pace with him throughout the whole of a meal, and these devoted champions took it by turns to guard their master with their lives. Keen appetites and jovial looks were not to be expected from men engaged on such a duty.

The first course, though long protracted, came to an end at last. Its greatest delicacy, consisting of dormice sprinkled with poppy-seed and honey, had completely disappeared. The tables were cleared by a band of Asiatic youths, richly habited, who entered to the sounds of wild Eastern music, and bore off the fragments that remained. As they emerged at one door, a troop of handsome fair-haired maidens—barbarian captives—simply clad in white muslin, and garlanded with flowers, entered at another, carrying the golden dishes and vessels that contained the second course. In the meantime, hanging curtains parted slowly from before a recess in the middle of the hall, and disclosed three Syrian dancing-girls, grouped like a picture, in different attitudes of voluptuous grace. Shaded lamps were so disposed as to throw a rosy light upon their limbs and faces; while soft thin vapours curled about them, rising from braziers burning perfumed incense at their feet. Simultaneously they clashed their cymbals, and bounded wildly out upon the floor. Then began a measure of alternate languor and activity, now swelling into frantic bacchanalian gestures, now sinking into tender lassitude or picturesque repose. The warm blood glowed in the dark faces of these daughters of the sun, the black eyes flashed under their long eyelashes, and their white teeth showed like pearls between the rich red lips; while the beautifully turned limbs, and the flexible, undulating forms, writhed themselves into attitudes suggestive of imperious conquest, coy reluctance, or yielding love.

The dance was soon over; wilder and faster flitted the glancing feet, and tossed the shapely hands, encircled with bracelets and anklets of tiny silver bells. When the measure was whirling at its speediest, the three stopped short, and at once, as if struck into stone, formed a group of rare fantastic beauty at the very feet of Cæsar's guests; who one and all broke into a murmur of unfeigned applause. As, touching their mouths and foreheads with their hands in Eastern obeisance, they retired, Placidus flung after them a collar of pearls, to be picked up by her who was apparently the leader of the three. One of the Emperor's freedmen seemed about to follow his example, for he buried his hand in his bosom, [pg 106]but either changed his mind or else found nothing there, since he drew it forth again empty; while Vitellius himself, plucking a bracelet from his arm, threw it after the retreating dancers, remarking that it was intended as a bribe to go away, for they only distracted attention from matters of real importance, now that the second course had come in; to which Montanus gave his cordial approval, fixing his eyes at the same time on the breast of a flamingo in which the skilful carver had just inserted the point of his long knife.

It would be endless to go into the details of such a banquet as that which was placed before the guests of Cæsar. Wild boar, pasties, goats, every kind of shellfish, thrushes, beccaficoes, vegetables of all descriptions, and poultry, were removed to make way for the pheasant, the guinea-hen, the turkey, the capon, venison, ducks, woodcocks, and turtledoves. Everything that could creep, or fly, or swim, and could boast a delicate flavour when cooked, was pressed into the service of the Emperor; and when appetite was appeased and could do no more, the strongest condiments and other remedies were used to stimulate fresh hunger and consume a fresh supply of superfluous dainties. But the great business of the evening was not yet half finished. Excess of eating was indeed the object; but it was to excess of drinking that the gluttons of that period looked as the especial relief of every entertainment, since the hope of each seemed to be, that when thoroughly flooded, and, so to speak, washed out with wine, he might begin eating again. The Roman was no drunkard like the barbarian, for the sake of that wild excitement of the brain which is purchased by intoxication. No, he ate to repletion that he might drink with gratification. He drank to excess that he might eat again.

Another train of slaves now cleared the table. These were Nubian eunuchs, clad in white turbans and scarlet tunics, embroidered with seed pearls and gold. They brought in the dessert—choice fruits heaped upon vases of the rarest porcelain, sweetmeats in baskets of silver filigree, Syrian dates borne by miniature golden camels of exquisite workmanship—masses of flowers in the centre, and perfumes burning at the corners of the table. Behind each couch containing its three guests stood a sable cup-bearer, deaf and dumb, whose only business it was to fill for his especial charge. These mutes were procured at vast expense from every corner of the empire; but Cæsar especially prided himself on their similarity in face and figure. To-day he would be served by [pg 107]Germans, to-morrow by Gauls, the next by Ethiopians, and so on; nor, though deprived of the organs of speech and hearing, were these ministers of Bacchus unobservant of what took place amongst the votaries on whom they waited; and it was said that the mutes in the palace heard more confidences, and told more secrets, than all the old women in Rome put together.

And now, taking his cue from the Emperor, each man loosened the belt of his tunic, shifted the garland of flowers off his brows, disposed himself in an easier attitude on his couch, and proffered his cup to be filled by the attendant. The great business of eating was for the present concluded, and deep drinking about to commence. When marvelling, however, at the quantity of wine consumed by the Romans in their entertainments, we must remember that it was the pure and unadulterated juice of the grape, that it was in general freely mixed with water, and that they thus imbibed but a very small portion of alcohol, which is in reality the destructive quality of all stimulants, to the welfare of the stomach and the brain.

CHAPTER XV

RED FALERNIAN

Cæsar's eye, though dim and sunken, flashed up for a moment with a spark of enthusiasm.

"The beccaficoes," said he, "were a thought over-seasoned, but the capon's liver stewed in milk was perfection. Varus, see that it is served again at the imperial table within the week."

The freedman took out his tablets and made a note of the royal commands with a somewhat unsteady hand, while Vitellius, draining his cup to the dregs, smacked his lips, and let his great chin sink on his breast once more.

The other guests conversed freely. Licinius and one of the senators were involved in an argument on military matters, with which the man of peace seemed almost as conversant as the man of war, and on which he laid down the law with far more confidence. Placidus was describing certain incidents of the campaign in Judæa, with an air of unassuming modesty and a deference to the opinions of others, which won him no little favour from those who sat near and listened, throwing in, every now and then, a chance expression or trifling anecdote, derogatory, by implication, to Vespasian's military skill, and eulogistic of Vitellius; for this reason doubly sweet in the ears of him at whose board the tribune sat. Montanus, whose cup was filled and emptied with startling rapidity, looked about him for a subject on which to vent some of the sarcasm with which he was charged, and found it in the woebegone appearance of Spado, who, despite the influence of food and wine, seemed unusually depressed and ill at ease. The eunuch on ordinary occasions was a prince of boon-companions, skilled in all the niceties of gastronomy, versed in the laws of drinking, overflowing with mirth and jollity, an adroit flatterer where flattery was acceptable, and a joyous buffoon who could give and take with equal readiness and good-humour, when banter was the order of the day. Now, less thirsty than usual, the feast seemed to have no enlivening effect on his disposition. He was silent, preoccupied, and, to all appearance, intent only on concealing his bruised cheek from the observation of those about him. He had never been struck in anger, never even stood face to face with a man before, and it had cowed him. The soft self-indulgent voluptuary could neither forget nor overcome his feelings of combined wrath, dismay, and shame. Montanus turned round and emptied a brimming goblet to his health.

"You are cheerless to-night, man!" quoth the senator; "you drink not, neither do you speak. What, has the red Falernian lost its flavour? or has some Canidia bewitched you with her evil eye? You used to be a prince of boon-companions, Spado, thirsty as a camel in the Libyan desert, insatiate as the sand on which he travels, and now your eye is dull, your face dejected, and your cup stands untasted, unnoticed, though bubbling to the brim. By the spear of Bacchus, 'tis not the fault of the liquor!" and Montanus emptied his own goblet with the air of a man who thoroughly appreciated the vintage he extolled.

Vitellius looked up for an instant, roused by the congenial theme.

"There is nothing the matter with the wine," said Cæsar. "Fill round."

The imperial hint was not to be disregarded, and Spado, with a forced smile, put his goblet to his lips and drained it to the last drop. In doing so the discoloration of his face was very apparent; and the guests, who had now arrived at that stage of conviviality where candour takes the place of politeness, proceeded to make their remarks without reserve.

"You have painted too thick," said one of the freedmen, alluding to an effeminacy of the times which the male sex were not ashamed to practise.

"You have taken off the paste and the skin with it," continued the other, whose own mistress was in the daily habit of spreading a kind of poultice over her whole countenance, and who might therefore be a good judge of the process and its results.

"You have been in the wars!" sneered one guest. "Or the amphitheatre!" echoed another. "'Tis a love-token from Chloe!" laughed a third. "Or a remembrance from Lydia!" added a fourth. "Nay," interposed Montanus, "our friend is too experienced a campaigner to come off second-best with a foe of that description. There must have been a warm [pg 110]encounter to leave such traces as those. She must have been a very Amazon, Spado, that could maul thee thus."

The eunuch looked from one to another of his tormentors with rather an evil smile. He well knew, however, that any appearance of annoyance would add tenfold to the ridicule which he must make up his mind to undergo, and that the best way for a man to turn a jest, even when to his own disadvantage, is to join in it himself; so he glanced at the Emperor, took a long draught of red Falernian, and assumed a face of quaint and good-humoured self-commiseration.

"Talk not to me of Amazons," said he, whereat there was a general laugh. "Tell me not of Chloes, and Lydias, and Lalages, and the rest. What's a Helen of Troy compared to a flask of this red Falernian? Why good wine gets better the longer you keep it, while woman loses her flavour year by year. 'Faith, if you only wait till she is old enough, she becomes very sour vinegar indeed. Even in the first flush of her beauty, I doubt whether any of you in your hearts think she is worth the trouble of catching. Still, you know, a man likes to look at a pretty face. Mine had not otherwise been so disfigured now. I had an adventure on that score but two nights ago. Would Cæsar like to hear it?"

Cæsar gave a nod and a grunt that signified acquiescence. Thus encouraged, Spado went on—

"It was the feast of Isis. I was coming from the worship of the goddess, and the celebration of those sacred rites, which may not be disclosed to the vulgar and the profane—mysteries too holy to be mentioned, save to pure and virgin ears." Here the countenance of Montanus assumed an expression that made even Cæsar smile, and caused the rest to laugh outright. "The procession was returning filled with inspiration from the goddess. The acolytes leaping and dancing in the van, the priests marching majestically under her symbols, and some of the noblest matrons in Rome bringing up the rear. The noblest and the fairest," repeated Spado, glancing round him complacently. "I name no names; but you all know that ours is not a vulgar worship, nor an illiberal creed."

Here Placidus stirred somewhat uneasily on his couch, and buried his face in his cup.

"The Roman people have ever paid the highest honours to our Egyptian goddess," proceeded the eunuch; "we lack the support of the plebeian no more than the worship of the patrician. Thus we flourish and drain draughts of plenty from the silver udders of our sacred cow. Well, they made [pg 111]way for us in the streets, both men and women—all but one slender girl dressed in black, who, coming quickly round a corner, found herself in the midst of us, and seemed too frightened to move. In another minute she would have been trampled to death by the crowd, when I seized hold of her in order to draw her into a place of safety while they passed."

"Or to see what sort of a face she hid under her black hood?" interrupted Montanus.

"Not so," replied the narrator, though obviously gratified by the impeachment. "Such follies I leave to senators, and statesmen, and soldiers. My object was simply to afford her my protection. I had better have plucked a nettle with my naked hand. The girl screamed and struggled as if she had never looked in a man's face before."

"She was frightened at your beard," said one of the freedmen, looking at Spado's smooth fat face. The latter winced, but affected not to hear. "Coax a frightened woman," said he, "and frighten an angry one. I flatter myself I know how to deal with them all. The girl would have been quiet enough had I been let alone; when just as she began to look kindly in my face, up comes an enormous barbarian, a hideous giant with waving yellow hair, and tries to snatch the maiden by main force from my grasp. I am a strong man, as you may perhaps have observed, my friends, and a fierce one when my blood is up. I showed fight. I struck him to the earth. He rose again with redoubled fury, and taking me at a disadvantage while I was protecting the girl, inflicted this injury on my face. I was stunned for an instant, and he seized that opportunity to make his escape. Well for him that he did so. Let him keep out of the way if he be wise. Should he cross my path again, he had better be in Euchenor's hands than mine; I will show him no mercy;" and Spado quaffed off his wine and squared his fat shoulders with the air of a gladiator.

"And what became of the girl?" asked Paris, who had hitherto listened to the recital with utter indifference.

"She was carried off by the barbarian," replied Spado. "Poor thing! I believe sorely against her will. Nevertheless, she was borne off by the Briton."

"A Briton!" exclaimed Licinius, whose intense contempt for Spado had hitherto kept him silent, and who had already heard the truth of the story from his slave.

"A Briton," repeated the eunuch. "It was impossible he could be otherwise from his size and ferocity. The Gaul, [pg 112]you see, is bigger than the Roman. The German than the Gaul. The Briton, by the same argument, must be bigger than the German; and this hideous giant must consequently have been one of those savage islanders. I take my logic from the Greeks."

"But not your boxing, it seems," observed Montanus, "We must have Euchenor to give you some lessons, if you run your head into these street brawls whenever you come across a woman with a veil."

"Nay," answered the eunuch, "he took me at a disadvantage; nevertheless he was a large and powerful athlete—there is no denying it."

"They are the finest men we have in the empire," said Licinius, thinking in his heart that the women were the fairest too.

"Their oysters are better than ours," observed Cæsar, with an air of profound and impartial judgment.

"I grant the oysters, but I deny the men," said Placidus, reflecting that his patriotism would be acceptable to his audience. "The Roman is the natural conqueror of the world. They cannot stand against our countrymen in the arena." The guests all joined in a cordial assent. Had it not been so, perhaps Licinius would have scarce thought it worth while to continue the argument. Now, though half ashamed of his warmth, he took up the matter with energy.

"There is a Briton in my house at this moment," said he, "who is a stronger and finer man than you will produce in Rome."

"You mean that long-legged lad with the mop of light hair?" said Placidus contemptuously. "I have seen him. I call him a boy, not a man."

Licinius felt somewhat irritated. He did not particularly like his company; and between two such opposite natures as his own and the tribune's there existed a certain hidden repugnance, which was sure sooner or later to break forth. He answered angrily—

"I will match him against any one you can produce to run, leap, wrestle, throw the quoit, and swim."

"Those are a boy's accomplishments," retorted the other coolly. "What I maintain is this, that, whether from want of courage or skill or both, these islanders are of no use with the steel. I would wish no better sport than to fight him myself in the arena, with the permission of Cæsar"—and the tribune bowed gracefully to his imperial host, who looked [pg 113]from one to the other of the disputants, without the slightest apparent interest in their discussion.

At this period of the Empire, when, although manners had become utterly dissolute, something was still left of the old audacity that had made the Roman a conqueror wherever he planted his foot, it was by no means unusual for men of patrician rank to appear in their own proper persons, a spectacle for the vulgar, in the amphitheatre. It was, perhaps, not unnatural that a desire for imitation should at last be aroused by the excessive fondness for these games of bloodshed, which pervaded all classes of the community. We have nothing in modern times that can at all convey to us the passion of the Roman citizen for the amusements of his circus. They were as necessary to his existence as daily bread. *Panem et Circenses* had passed into a familiar proverb. He would leave his home, neglect his business, forfeit his bath, to sit for hours on the benches of the amphitheatre, exposed to heat and crowding, and every sort of inconvenience, and would bring his food with him rather than run the risk of losing his place. And all this to see trained gladiators shedding each other's blood, wild beasts tearing foreign captives limb from limb, and imitation battles which differed in no respect from real, save that the wounded were not spared, and the slaughter consequently far greater in proportion to the number of combatants engaged. If a statesman wished to court popularity, if an emperor desired to blot out a whole page of enormities and crimes, he had but to give the people one of these free entertainments of blood—the more victims the better—and they were ready to approve of any measure, and to pardon any atrocity.

Ere long some fierce spirits panted to take part in the sports they so loved to contemplate; and the disgraceful exhibition ceased to be confined to hireling gladiators or condemned slaves. Knights and patricians entered the arena, to contend for the praises of the vulgar; and the noblest blood in Rome was shed for the gratification of plebeian spectators, who, sitting at ease munching cakes and sausages, could contemplate with placid interest the death-agonies of the Cornelii or the Gracchi.

Julius Placidus, like many other fashionable youths of the period, prided himself on his skill in the deadly exercises of the circus. He had appeared before the Roman public at different times, armed with all the various weapons of the gladiator; but the exercise in which he considered himself most perfect was that of the trident and the net. The [pg 114]contest between the *retiarius* and the *secutor* was always a favourite spectacle with the public. The former carried an ample casting-net upon his shoulders, a three-pronged spear in his hand; beyond this he was totally unarmed either for attack or defence. The latter with a short sword, vizored helmet, and oblong shield, would at first sight appear to have fought at great advantage over his opponent. Nevertheless the arts of the *retiarius* in entangling his adversary had arrived at such perfection that he was constantly the conqueror. Once down, and involved in the fatal meshes, there was no escape for the swordsman; and from some whimsical reason the populace seldom granted him quarter when vanquished. Great activity and speed of foot were the principal qualities required by the *retiarius*, for if he failed in his cast he was compelled to fly from his adversary while preparing his net for a fresh attempt, and if overtaken his fate was sealed. Placidus possessed extraordinary personal activity. His eye was very correct, and his throw generally deadly. It may be, too, that there was something pleasing to the natural cruelty of his disposition in the contemplation of an antagonist writhing and helpless on the sand. It was his delight to figure in the arena with the deadly net laid in careful festoons upon his shoulder, and the long barbed trident quivering in his grasp, Licinius fell into the snare, if snare it was, readily enough.

"I would wager a province on Esca," said he, "against anyone but a trained gladiator; and I think he could hold his own with the best of *them*, after a month's practice."

"Then you accept my challenge?" exclaimed Placidus, with a studied carelessness of manner that dissembled an eagerness he could scarcely control.

"Let us hear the terms over a fresh flask of Falernian," observed the Emperor, glad of such a stimulant with his wine.

"I ask for no weapons but the trident and the net," said Placidus, looking fixedly at Licinius. "Esca, if you so call him, may be armed as usual with sword and helmet."

"And shield," interrupted the other; too old a soldier, even in the excitement of the moment, to throw a chance away.

Placidus affected to demur.

"Well," said he, after a few moments' hesitation, "'tis but a young swordsman, and a barbarian; I give you the shield in."

A vision crossed the brain of Licinius, that already made [pg 115]him repent of his rashness. He saw the fine form writhing in those pitiless meshes, like a beast taken in the toils. He saw the frank blue eyes, looking upward, brave and kindly even in their despair. He saw the unsparing arm raised to strike, and the bright curling locks dabbled all in blood. But then he remembered the Briton's extraordinary strength and activity, his natural courage and warlike education—he was irritated, too, by the insolent malice that gleamed in the tribune's eyes; and he persuaded himself that nothing but renown and triumph could accrue to his favourite from such a contest.

"Be it so," said he; "*retiarius* and *secutor*. You will have no child's play, I can tell you; and now for the terms of the wager. I stake no man's life against a morsel of tinsel or a few polished pebbles, I warn you at once."

He glanced while he spoke, somewhat contemptuously, over the costly ornaments that decorated the tribune's dress. The latter laughed good-humouredly.

"A dozen slaves would scarce fetch the value of my sleeve-clasps. At least, a dozen of these islanders, whom you may capture by scores every time a legion moves its camp. Listen, I will wager two of my white horses against your picture of Daphne, or the bust of Euphrosyne that stands in your bath-room. Nay, I will give you more advantage still. I will stake the whole team, and the chariot into the bargain, against the British slave himself!"

Again had the other been watching him narrowly; he must have perceived a strange suppressed eagerness on the tribune's face, but he was preoccupied and annoyed; he had gone too far to retract, and a murmur from the listening guests denoted their opinion of the generosity displayed in this last proposal. When a man has placed himself in a false position, his efforts at extrication generally plunge him deeper than before. Quick as lightning, Licinius bethought him that the present bargain might probably save Esca's life, in the unlikely event of his being conquered, so he closed with it unhesitatingly, though he regretted doing so a moment afterwards.

The match was accordingly made upon the following terms: That Esca should enter the amphitheatre during the approaching games of Ceres, armed with sword, shield, and helmet, to oppose Placidus, whose only weapons were to be the trident and the net. That in the event of the latter being worsted, his four white horses and gilded chariot should become the property of Licinius; but that if he obtained [pg 116]the victory, and the populace permitted him to spare the vanquished, then his late antagonist should become his slave; and how enviable would be that position could only be known to the tribune himself and one other person from whom he had that day received kinder looks and smiles than she had ever before granted to an unwelcome suitor.

The business of drinking, which had been somewhat interrupted by these complicated discussions, was now resumed with greater energy than before; Placidus emptying his goblet with the triumphant air of one who has successfully accomplished a difficult task; Licinius like a man who seeks to drown anxiety and self-reproach in wine. The Emperor quaffed and quaffed again with his habitual greediness; and the remainder of the guests acted studiously in imitation of the Emperor.

[pg 117]

CHAPTER XVI

THE TRAINING-SCHOOL

But Licinius had an ordeal to go through on the following day, which was especially painful to the kind heart of the Roman general. When the terms of the combat were explained to the person chiefly interested, that young warrior eagerly accepted the challenge as affording an opportunity for indulgence in those feats of arms which early education had rendered so pleasing to his martial disposition. He could vanquish two such men as the tribune, he thought, at any exercise and with any weapons; but his face sank when he learned the penalty of failure, and a shudder passed through his whole frame at the bare possibility of becoming a slave to anyone but his present master. It nerved him, however, all the more in his resolution to conquer; and when Licinius, reproaching himself bitterly the while, promised him his liberty in the event of victory, Esca's heart beat fast with joy and hope and exultation once more.

A thousand vague possibilities danced through his brain; a thousand wild and visionary schemes, of which Mariamne formed the centre figure. Life that had seemed so dull but one short week ago, now shone again in the rosy light with which youth—and youth alone—can tinge the long perspective of the future. Alas for Licinius! he marked the glowing cheek and the kindling eye with a sensation of despondency weighing at his heart. Nevertheless the lot was cast, the offer was accepted. It was too late for looking back. Nothing remained but to strain every nerve to win.

In all bodily contests, in all mental labours, in everything which human nature attempts, systematic and continuous training is the essential element of success. The palm, as Horace says, can only flourish where the dust is plentiful; and he who would attain a triumph either as an athlete or a scholar, must cultivate his natural abilities with the utmost attention, and the most rigid self-denial, ere he enters for the prize. It is curious, too, how the mind, like the body, [pg 118]acquires vigour and elasticity by graduated exertion. The task that was an impossibility yesterday, is but a penance to-day, and will become a pleasure to-morrow. Let us follow Esca into the training-school, where his muscles are to be toughened, and his skill perfected for the deadly exercises of the arena.

It is a large square building, something like a modern riding-house, lighted and ventilated at the top, and is laid down three inches deep in sand, an arrangement which increases, indeed, the labour of all pedestrian exertion, but renders a fall comparatively harmless, and accustoms the pupil, moreover, to the yielding surface on which hereafter he will have to struggle for his life. Quoits, dumb-bells, ponderous weights, and massive clubs are scattered in the corners, or propped against the walls of the edifice, and a horizontal leaping-bar, placed at the height of a man's breast, denotes that activity is not neglected in the acquisition of strength. Beside these insignia of peaceful gymnastics, the *cestus* hangs conspicuous, and racks are placed at intervals supporting the deadly weapons and defensive armour with which the gladiator plies his formidable trade. There are also pointless spears, and blunted swords for practice, and a wooden figure, hacked and hewed out of all similitude to an enemy, on which the cuts and thrusts most in request have been dealt over and over again with increasing skill and severity.

At one end of the building paces the master to and fro; now glancing with wary eye at the movements of his pupils; now pausing to adjust some implement of instruction; now encouraging or chiding with a gesture; and anon catching up, as though in sheer absence of mind, one of the idle weapons, and whirling it round his head with a flourish that displays all the power and skill of the practised professional. Hippias, the retired gladiator, is a man of middle age, and of somewhat lofty stature, rendered more commanding by its lengthy proportions, and the peculiar setting on of the head. Constant exercise, pushed, indeed, to the verge of toil, and continued for many years, has toughened each shapely limb into the hardness and consistency of wire, and has rendered his large frame lean and sinewy, like a greyhound's. All his gestures have the graceful pliant ease which results from muscular strength, and his very walk—light, smooth, and noiseless—is like that of a panther traversing the floor of its cage. His swarthy complexion has been deeply tanned by exposure to heat and toil, but the blood courses healthfully [pg 119]beneath, and imparts a warm mellow tint to the skin. The fleshless face, in spite of a worn eager look, and a dash of grey in the hair and beard, is not without a wild defiant beauty of its own; and though its expression is somewhat dissolute and reckless, there is a bold keen flash in the eye, and the man is obviously enterprising, courageous, and steel to the backbone.

The Roman ladies, with that depravity of taste which marks a general deterioration of manners and morality, delighted at this period to choose their favourites from the ranks of the amphitheatre. There was a rage for warlike exercises, Amazonian dresses, imitations of the deadly sports, played out with considerable skill and ferocity, nay, for the very persons of the gladiators themselves. It was no wonder then, that the handsome fencing-master, with his reputation for strength and courage, should have been a marked man with the proud capricious matrons of the Imperial City. The favour of each, too, was doubtless his best recommendation to the good graces of the rest; and Hippias might have sunned himself in the smiles of the noblest ladies in Rome.

He made but little account, however, of his good fortune. The peaches fallen on the ground are doubtless the ripest, yet they never seem so tempting as those which sun themselves against the wall, a hand's-breadth above our reach. Nor can a man pay implicit obedience to more than one dominion (at a time); and unless the yoke be *very* heavy, it is scarce worth while to carry it at all. Hippias was neither dazzled nor flattered by the bright eyes that looked so kindly into his war-worn face. He loved a flask of wine nearly as well as a woman's beauty—two feet of pliant steel and a leathern buckler far better than either; nevertheless, amongst all the dainty dames of his acquaintance, he was least disposed to undervalue Valeria's notice, the more so, that she rarely condescended to bestow it on him; and he took more pains with her fencing lessons, than those of any other female pupil, and stayed longer in her house than in that of any lady in Rome. He approved of her strength, her resolution, her quickness, above all her cold manner and her pride, besides admiring her personal charms exceedingly, in his own practical way. There is a gleam of interest, almost of tenderness in his eyes, as he pauses every now and then in his walk, and reads a line or two from a scroll he carries in his hand, which Myrrhina brought him not an hour ago.

The scroll is from Valeria. She has heard of Esca's peril[pg 120]—nay, she has herself brought it on his head; and who knows the price it cost her haughty wilful heart? Yet in all her bitter anger, vexation, shame, she cannot bear to think of the noble Briton down on the sand, writhing and helpless at the mercy of his enemy. It is the weapon now she hates, and not the victim. It would give her intense pleasure, she feels, to see Placidus humbled, defeated, slain. Such is the sense of justice in a woman's breast; such are the advantages gained by submission at any sacrifice to do her bidding. We need not pity the tribune, however, in his dealings with either sex; he is well able to take care of himself.

Valeria accordingly sat her down and wrote a few friendly lines to the fencing-master, who had always stood high in her favour, and whose frank bold nature she felt she could trust. Womanlike, she thought it necessary to fabricate an excuse for her interest in the Briton, by affirming that she had staked heavily on his success in the coming contest. She adjured Hippias to spare no pains in counsel or instruction, and bade him come to see her without delay, and report the progress of his pupil. He raised his eyes from the scroll, and watched the said pupil holding his own gallantly at sword and buckler with Lutorius.

"One, two—Disengage the blade! A feint at the head, a cut at the legs, and come in over the shield with a lunge! Good! but scarce quick enough. Try that again—the elbow turned outwards, the wrist a little higher. So—once more. Now, look at me. Thus."

The combatants paused for breath, Hippias seized a wooden foil, and, beckoning to Hirpinus, engaged him in the required position, for Esca's especial benefit. Trained and wary, the old gladiator knew every feint and parry in the game. Yet had those blades been steel, Hirpinus would have been gasping his life out, at the master's feet, ere the close of their second encounter. Hippias never shifted his ground, never seemed to exert himself much, yet the quickest eye in Rome was puzzled to follow the movements of his point, the readiest hand to intercept it where it fell. Again he pitted Esca and Lutorius in the mimic strife, and stood with well-pleased countenance to watch the result. The Briton had, indeed, lost no time in beginning a course of instruction which he hoped was to ensure him victory and its reward—his much desired freedom. That morning Hirpinus had brought him to the school; and the veteran gladiator watched, with an interest that was almost touching, the preparations which were to fit his young friend for a career that at best must end [pg 121]ere long in a violent death. Hippias was delighted with the stature and strength of his new pupil. He had matched him at once with Lutorius, a wiry Gaul, who was supposed to be the most scientific swordsman of "the Family," and smiled to observe how completely, with an occasional hint from himself, the Briton was a match for his antagonist, who had expected an easy victory, and was even more disgusted than surprised. As the encounter was prolonged, and the combatants, warming to their work, advanced, retreated, struck, lunged and parried; now traversing warily at full distance—now dashing boldly in to close, the other gladiators gathered round, excited to unusual interest by the excellence of the play, and the dexterity of the barbarian.

"He is the best we've seen here for a lustre at least," exclaimed Rufus, a gigantic champion from Northern Italy, proud of his stature, proud of his swordsmanship, but above all, proud that he was a Roman citizen, though a gladiator; "those thrusts come home like lightning, and when he misses his parry, see, he jumps away like a wild-cat. Faith, Manlius, if they match him against thee at the games, thou wilt have a handful. I would stake my rights as a Roman citizen on him, toga and all, barbarian though he be. What, man! he would have thee down and disarmed in a couple of passes!"

Manlius seemed to think so too, though he was loth to confess it. He turned the subject by vowing that Lutorius must be masking his play, and not fighting his best, or he never could be thus worsted by a novice.

"Masking his play!" exclaimed Hirpinus indignantly, "let him unmask, then, as soon as he will! I tell thee this lad of mine hath not his match in the empire. I shall see him champion of the amphitheatre, and first swordsman in Rome, ere they give me the wooden foil with the silver guard,[2] and lay old Hirpinus on the shelf. I shall be satisfied to retire then, for I shall leave some good manhood to take my place."

"Well crowed!" replied Manlius, not quite pleased at the value placed on his own prowess in comparison. "To hear thee, a man would say there never was but one gladiator in Rome, and that this young mastiff must pull us all down by the throat, because he fences like thyself, wild and wide, and by main strength."

"It is no swordsmanship to run in like a bull and take [pg 122]more than you give," observed Euchenor, listening with his arms folded, and an expression of supreme contempt on his handsome features.

"Nevertheless his blows fall thick and fast, like a hailstorm, and Lutorius shifts his ground every time the young one makes the attack," argued honest Rufus, who had not a grain of either fear or jealousy in his disposition; and who considered his profession as a mere trade by which he could obtain a livelihood for wife and children in the meantime, and a remote chance of independence with a vineyard of his own beyond the Apennines, should he escape a violent death in the amphitheatre at last.

"He thrusts too often overhand," observed Manlius, "and his guard is always open for the wrist."

"He is a strong fencer, but he has no style," added Euchenor; and the boxer looked around him with the air of a man who closes a controversy by an unanswerable argument.

Hirpinus was boiling over with indignation; but his eloquence was by no means in proportion to his corporeal gifts, and he could not readily find words to express his dissent and his disdain. Banter, too, and a coarse, good-humoured sort of wrangling, was the usual form by which difference of opinion found expression in the training-school. Quarrelling, amongst men whose very trade it was to fight to the death, seemed simply absurd; and to come to blows except in public and for money, a mere childish waste of time. Indeed, with all their contempt for death, and their extraordinary courage when pitted against each other to amuse the populace, these gladiators, perhaps from the very nature of their profession, seem to have been unsuited for any sustained efforts of energy and endurance. When banded together under the eagles, they were often so undisciplined in camp, as by no means to be relied on before an enemy. Perhaps there was something of bravado in the flourish with which they entered the circus, and hailed Cæsar with their greetings from *those about to die*![10] Moreover, they had to fight in a corner, and with the impossibility of escape. Courage is of many different kinds. Men are brave from various motives—from ambition, from emulation, from the habit of confronting danger; some from a naturally chivalrous disposition, backed by strong physical nerves. The last alone are to be trusted in an emergency; and a really courageous man faces an unexpected and unaccustomed peril, if not with [pg 123]confidence, at least with an unflinching determination to do his best.

Hirpinus turned upon Euchenor, for whom he had no great liking at any time.

"You talk of your science," said he, "and your Greek skill, against which even our Roman thews and sinews are of no avail. Dare you stand up to this barbarian with the *cestus* on? Only to exchange half a dozen friendly buffets, you know, in sheer sport."

But Euchenor excused himself with great disdain. Like many another successful professor, he owed no inconsiderable share of his fame to his own assumption of superiority, and the judgment with which, when practicable, he matched himself against inferior performers. Champions who exist on their reputation, such as it is, are not to peril it lightly against the first tyro that comes, who has everything to gain and nothing to lose by an encounter with the celebrity; whereas the celebrity derives no additional laurels from a triumph, and a defeat tends to take the very bread out of his mouth. Euchenor said as much; but Hirpinus was not satisfied, till the subtle Greek, who had learned the terms of the match in which Esca was engaged, observed carelessly, that all the time the Briton had to spare should be devoted to practice in the part he was about to play before the Emperor. The suggestion took effect upon Hirpinus at once. He sprang across the school to where the master had resumed his walk. The old gladiator positively turned pale while he entreated Hippias to instruct his pupil in all the scientific devices by which those deadly meshes could be foiled.

"Nothing but art can save him," said he, in imploring accents, which seemed almost ludicrous from one of his Herculean exterior. "Courage and strength, ay, and the activity of a wild-cat, are all paralysed when that accursed twine is round your limbs. I know it! I have felt it! I was down under the net myself once. If a man is to die, he should die *like* a man, not like a thrush caught in a springe. He must learn, Hippias, he must practise day by day, and hour by hour; he must study every movement of the caster. Pit him against Manlius, he is the best netsman in the Family. If he learns to foil *him*, he will take the conceit out of Placidus readily enough. I tell you I shall not be easy till I see him with his foot on the gay tribune's breast!"

"Patience, man," replied Hippias, "thou fearest but one thing in the world, and that is a fathom of twine. Thinkest thou all others are scared at the same bugbear? Mind thine [pg 124]own training,—thou art yet too lusty by half to go into the circus,—and leave this young barbarian to me."

The master kept up his influence amongst these lawless pupils, partly by a reserved demeanour and a silent tongue, partly by never suffering his authority to be disputed for a moment. To have said as much as he now did was tantamount to a confession of interest in the Briton's success; and Hirpinus resumed his own labours with a lightened heart, whilst Esca, in all the delightful flush of youth and health, and muscular strength developing itself by scientific practice, plied his antagonist with redoubled vigour, and enjoyed his pastime to the utmost.

It was like taking an old friend by the hand to grasp a sword once more.

[pg 125]

CHAPTER XVII

A VEILED HEART

For three whole days Mariamne had not set eyes on the Briton, so she felt listless and dispirited. Not that she acknowledged, even to herself, the necessity of Esca's presence, nor that she was indeed aware how much it had influenced her thoughts and actions ever since she had known him—a period that seemed now of indefinite length. She found herself perpetually recalling the origin and growth of their acquaintance; she dwelt with a strange pleasure on the gross insult offered her by Spado, which scarce seemed an agreeable subject of contemplation; nor, be sure, did she forget its prompt and satisfactory redress. She remembered every step of her subsequent walk home, and every syllable of their conversation in that hasty and agitated progress; nay, every look and gesture of her companion's and of her own. It pleased her to think of the favourable impression made on her father and his brother by their guest; and the earthen pitcher, from which she gave the latter to drink, assumed a new and unaccountable value in her eyes. Also she strolled to Tiber-side, whenever she had a spare half-hour, and sat her down under the shadow of a broken column, with a strange persistency, and a vague expectation of something, she knew not what. For the first day this dreamy imaginative existence was delightful. Then came a feeling of want; a consciousness that there was a void, which it would be a great happiness to fill. Soon this grew to a thirst—a craving for a repetition of those hours which had glided by so sweetly and so fast. At rare intervals arose the startling thought, "suppose she should never see him again," and her heart stopped beating, and her cheek paled with the bare possibility; [pg 126]yet was there something not wholly painful in a consciousness of the sorrow such a privation would create.

Though young, Mariamne was no foolish and inexperienced girl. Her life had been calculated to elicit and bring to perfection some of woman's loftiest qualities. She had early learned the nobility of self-sacrifice, the necessity of self-reliance and self-denial. Like the generality of her nation she possessed considerable pride of race; suppressed, indeed, and kept down by the exigencies in which the Jews had so often found themselves, but none the weaker nor the less cherished on that account. Notwithstanding his many chastisements and reverses,—from his pilgrimage through the wilderness to his different captivities by the great Oriental powers, and final subjection under Rome,—the Jew never forgot that he sprang from a stem more especially planted by the hand of the Almighty; that he could trace his lineage back, unbroken and unstained, to those who held converse with Moses under the shadow of Mount Sinai; nay, to the Patriarch himself, who held his authority direct from Heaven, and who was thought worthy to entertain angels at his tent door on the plains of Mamre. Such a conviction imparted a secret pride to every one of his descendants. Man, woman, and child, were persuaded that to them belonged of right the dominion of the earth.

It may be supposed that one of Eleazar's disposition was not likely to bring up his family in any humble notions of their privileges and their importance. Mariamne had been early taught to consider her nationality as the first and dearest of her advantages; and, womanlike, she clung to it all the closer that her people had been forced to submit to the Roman yoke. Habits of patience, of reflection and endurance, had been engendered by the everyday life of the Jewish maiden, witnessing her father's continued impatience of the existing state of things, and his energetic, though secret, efforts to change the destinies of his countrymen; whilst all that such an education might have created of hard, cunning, and unfeminine in his daughter's mind, the society and counsels of Calchas were eminently qualified to counteract. Losing no opportunity of sowing the good seed; of teaching, both by precept and example, the lessons he had learned from those who had them direct from the Fountain-head; it was impossible to remain long uninfluenced by the constant kindliness and gentle bearing of one who understood Christianity to signify, not only faith, and purity, and devotion even to the death, but also that peace and goodwill [pg 127]amongst men, which its first teachers inculcated as its fundamental principle and essential element. Calchas, indeed, lacked not the fiery energy and the tameless instincts of his race. His nature, perhaps, was originally fierce and warlike as his brother's, but it had been subdued, softened, exalted by his religion; and, while his heart was pitiful and kindly, nothing remained of the warrior but his loyalty, his courage, and his zeal.

Cherishing a true attachment for that brother, it was doubtless a cause of daily sorrow to observe how totally Eleazar's principles and conduct were opposed to the meek and holy precepts of the new faith. It seemed to human reasoning impossible to convert the Jew from his grand and simple creed, to modify or to explain it, to add to it, or to take away from it, in the slightest degree to alter his belief in that direct thearchy, to which he was bound by the ties of gratitude, of tradition, of national isolation and characteristic pride of race. A religion which accepts the first great principles of truth, the omnipotence and eternity of the Deity, the immortality of souls, and the rewards and punishments of a life to come, stands already upon a solid basis from which it has little inclination to be removed; and in all ages, the Jew, as in a somewhat less degree the Mahometan, has been most unwilling to add to his own stern tenets the mild and loving doctrines of our revealed religion. Eleazar's was a character to which the outward and tangible ceremonials of his worship were essentially acceptable. To him the law, in its severest and most literal sense, was the only true guide for political measures as for private conduct; and where its burdens were multiplied or its severities enhanced by tradition, he upheld the latter gladly and inflexibly. To offer the sacrifices ordained by Divine command; to exact and rigidly fulfil the minutest points of observance which the priests enjoined; to keep the Sabbath inviolate by word and deed; also, when opportunity offered, to smite the heathen hip-and-thigh with the edge of the sword; these were the points of faith and practice on which Eleazar took his stand, and from which no consideration of affection, no temptation of ambition, no exigency of the times, would have induced him to waver one hair's-breadth. The fiercest soldier, the wildest barbarian, the most frivolous and dissolute patrician of the Imperial Court, would have been a more promising convert than such a man as this. Yet did not Calchas despair: well he knew that there is a season of seed-time and a season of harvest, that the soil once choked with weeds, or sown [pg 128]with tares, may thereafter produce a good crop; that waters have been known to flow freely from the bare rock, and that nothing is impossible under heaven. So he loved his brother and prayed for him, and took that brother's daughter to his heart as though she had been his own child.

It must have required no small patience, no small amount of self-control and humility, to engraft in Mariamne the good fruit, which her father held in such hatred and disdain. These, too, were difficulties with which the early Christians had to contend, and of which we now make small account. We read of their privations, their persecutions, their imprisonments, and their martyrdoms, with a thrill of mingled horror and indignation—we pity and admire, we even glorify them as the heroic leaders of that forlorn hope which was destined to head the armies of the only true conqueror, but we never consider the daily and harassing warfare in which they must have been engaged, the domestic dissensions, the insults of equals, the alienation of friends; above all, the cold looks and estranged affections of those whom they loved best on earth; whom they must give up here, and whom, with the new light that had broken in on them, they could scarce hope to see hereafter. So-called heroic deeds are not always deserving of that superiority which they claim over mortal weakness, when emblazoned on the glowing page of history. Many a man is capable, so to speak, of winding himself up for one great effort, even though it be to perish on the scaffold or the breach; but day after day, and year after year, to wage unceasing war against our nearest and dearest, our own comforts, our own prosperity, nay, our own weaknesses and inclinations, requires the aid of a sustaining power that is neither without nor within, nor anywhere below on earth, but must reach the suppliant directly and continuously from above.

Nevertheless the example of a true Christian, in the real acceptation of the word, is never without its effect on those who live under its constant influence. Even Eleazar loved and respected his brother more than anything on earth, save his ambition and his creed; while Mariamne, whose trusting and gentle disposition rendered her a willing recipient of those truths which Calchas lost no opportunity of imparting, gradually, and almost insensibly, imbibed the opinions and the belief of one whose everyday practice was so pure, so elevated, and so kindly; to whom, moreover, she was accustomed to look as her counsellor in difficulty, and her refuge in distress.

[pg 129]

It was Calchas, then, whose studies she interrupted as he sat with the scroll before him, that was seldom out of his hand, perusing those Syriac characters again and again, as a mariner consults his chart, never weary of storing information for his future course, and verifying the progress he has already made. It was to Calchas she had determined to apply for comfort because Esca came not, and for assistance to see him again—not that she admitted, even to herself, that this was her intention or her wish. Nevertheless, she hovered about the old man's seat, more caressingly than usual, and finding his attention still riveted on his employment, she laid one hand lightly on his shoulder, and with the other parted the thin grey hair that strayed across his forehead. He looked up with a pleasant smile.

"What is it, little one?" said he, with the endearing diminutive he had used in addressing her from her childhood. "You seem unusually busy with your household affairs to-day. Is this room to be decorated for a guest? My brother makes no acquaintances here in Rome; and we have given no stranger so much as a mouthful of food since we arrived, save that goodly barbarian you brought home with you the other evening. Is he coming again to-night?"

A bright blush swept over her face, yet when it faded, Calchas could not but remark that she was paler than her wont; and her manner, usually so gentle and composed, was now restless, anxious, and ill at ease.

"Nay," she replied, "what should I know of the barbarian's movements? It was but a chance meeting that led him to our quiet dwelling in the first instance; and save by the merest accident we are never likely to see him more."

She turned away while she spoke, trying to steady her voice and give it a tone of cold indifference, but failing utterly in the attempt.

"There is no such power as chance," said Calchas, looking her keenly in the face.

"I know it," replied Mariamne, smiling sadly; "and I know, too, that whatever befalls us is for the best. Yet some things are hard to bear, nevertheless. Not that I have aught to complain of," she added, shrinking instinctively from the very topic she wanted to bring on, "save my constant anxiety for my father in these tumultuous times."

"He is in God's hand," said Calchas, "who will bring him safe through all his perils, though they seem now to environ him as the breakers boil round a stranded galley, when the wild Adriatic is leaping and dashing for its prey. Take [pg 130]comfort, little one; I cannot bear to see your step so listless and your cheek so pale."

"How can they be otherwise?" returned the girl, not very candidly. "It is a weary lot to be a soldier's daughter. I could even find it in my heart to wish we had never left Judæa; never come to Rome."

He tried his best to soothe and comfort her—his best such as it was, for the good old man knew but little of a woman's heart—its wild hopes, its indefinite aims, its wayward feelings, and its inexplicable tendency to self-torture. He thought in his simplicity the real grievance was that which she avowed, and he strove to remove it in his own kind hopeful way.

"My child," said he, "the evils that are raging in Italy, the horrors that we hear of every day, cannot but make Eleazar's position more important and less hazardous, as they increase the difficulties of the imperial councils. It is, indeed, no child's play to bridle such a nation as ours with one hand, and to grasp at the imperial diadem with the other. It takes a bold heart to draw the sword against Judah, and a long arm to buffet Cæsar across the seas. Vespasian will have little leisure to persecute our race; and the Emperor, sore beset as he is, will surely lend a favourable ear to my brother's proposals for peace. Even now the legions are declaring, far and wide, against Vitellius; and civil war, the most dreadful of all scourges, is desolating the provinces and entering Italy herself. It was but yesterday that news reached Rome of the revolt of the whole fleet at Ravenna—and ere this Cremona has perhaps fallen into the power of Antonius, that soldier-orator, with the iron arm and the silver tongue. Well we know, for we have been told by One whose words shall never be forgotten, that a house divided against itself cannot stand; and is this a time, think you, my child, for the worn-out sensualist who wears the purple here, to make conditions with such a man as your father? It is all in God's hand, as I never cease to insist; yet I cannot but feel that a better day must at last be dawning upon Judæa, that her enemies will be confounded, her armies victorious, and her chiefs—but what have we to do with the sword?" he broke off abruptly, while his kindling eye and animated gestures bore witness to the ardent spirit that would flash out here and there even now. "Our weapon is the Cross, our warfare is not of this world, our triumph is in our humility, and when most we are brought low, then are we most exalted. Oh, that the time were come, as come it surely will, when Cæsar [pg 131]shall be content to take only that which is Cæsar's, and men shall be gathered under one banner, and in one brotherhood, from all corners of the world!"

It was no exaggerated account Calchas thus gave of the dilemma in which the empire was placed at this juncture. Vespasian, with great political talents, with coolness, patience, and audacity, was playing a game against which the besotted brains of Vitellius were powerless to compete. The former, adored by the army, who saw in him a successful general, an intrepid soldier, and a man of simple virtuous habits, contrasting nobly with the luxurious gluttony and sensuality of his rival, lost none of his influence by the moderation he displayed, and the modesty, real or affected, with which he declined the purple. Not afraid to wait till advantage ripened into opportunity, he could seize it when the time came with a bold and tenacious grasp, could turn it deftly to his own profit and guide those circumstances of which he seemed to be the mere puppet, with a master-hand. Though at a distance from the scene of warfare, and to all appearance little more than an unwilling observer of the disturbances carried on in his name, he directed as it were from behind a curtain the operations of his generals, and pulled the strings that set in motion his numerous partisans with a clear head, a delicate touch, and that tenacity of purpose which is the essential element of success. Vitellius, on the other hand, whose natural abilities had been weakened, nay destroyed, by an unceasing course of sensual gratification, wavered in council and hesitated in action; now determined to abdicate the diadem and retire into obscurity; anon persuaded to fight for dominion to the death; and ever paralysing the energies of his warmest partisans by the distrust he entertained for honest advisers, and the reliance he placed on the counsels of those traitors who surrounded him.

The empire was, perhaps, at this period in a more disheartening position than even under the ferocious sway of Nero. Monster as the latter was, he at least held the reins with a firm hand; and tyranny, however oppressive, is doubtless one degree better than anarchy and confusion. Now, the mighty fabric, of which Romulus laid the first stone and Augustus completed the pinnacle—the work of seven centuries, to which every generation had added its labours and its enterprise, till it embraced the confines of the known world—was beginning perceptibly to sink and crumble from its own enormous size and weight. The legions (and it must never be forgotten that the dominion of Rome was essentially [pg 132]that of the sword) were now recruited from natives of her distant colonies. The Syrian and the Ethiop guarded the eagles as well as the tall turbulent sons of Germany, and the ever-changing, ever-faithless Gaul. Armies thus gathered under one standard from such various climates could have but little in common save a certain professional ferocity, and an ardent liking for plunder, no less than pay. Mercenaries have in all ages been easily bought by the one and seduced by the other. Each legion gradually came to consider itself a separate and independent power, to be sold to the highest bidder. Perhaps the fairest vision of all was a march upon Rome, and a ten hours' sack of the city they were sworn to defend. A great and good man, backed by the glory of name, race, and illustrious actions, could alone have ruled such discordant elements, and united these conflicting interests for the common good; but fate ordained that the weak, worn-out, besotted Vitellius should be seated on the throne of the Cæsars, and that the cool, unflinching, and far-seeing Vespasian should be watching with sleepless eye and ready hand to snatch the diadem from his bewildered predecessor, and place it firmly on his own head.

While the destinies of the world were thus trembling in the balance, while her own nation was fighting for its very existence, and the storm gathering all around, obviously to burst in its greatest fury on the Imperial City, the care that weighed heaviest at Mariamne's heart was that she had that day noticed a barbarian slave walk into the training-school of a Roman gladiator.

"Is it true, then," asked the girl, "that civil war is indeed raging here, as we have seen it at home? That we shall have an enemy ere long at the very gates of the city?"

"Too true, my child," replied Calchas; "and the Roman people seem, as usual, to make light of the emergency, to eat, drink, buy, sell, and feast their eyes on bloodshed in the circus, as though their idolatrous temple, where Janus overlooks the usurers and money-changers of the city, were shut up once for all, never to be opened again."

She turned pale and shuddered at the mention of the circus.

"Are they making no preparations?" she asked timidly. "Did I not hear my father say they were collecting the gladiators, and—and—some of the nobles had enrolled their German and British slaves, and were arming them against an attack?"

"It may be so," answered Calchas; "but a slave can [pg 133]scarcely be expected to fight very stoutly for a cause which only serves to rivet his chains. As for the gladiators, those tigers in human form, it were surely better for them to perish in open warfare, than to tear one another to pieces in the arena, like the very beasts against which I have seen them pitted. Yet these, too, have souls to be saved."

"Surely have they," exclaimed Mariamne, with kindling eyes, "and none to help them; none to show them so much as a glimpse of the true light. These men go out to die as the citizen goes to his business or his bath; and who is answerable to man for their blood? who is answerable to God for their souls?"

His eye brightened while she spoke, and he raised his head like a soldier who hears the trumpet summoning him to the front.

"If I have a well in my court," said he, "and a man fall down and die of thirst at my gate, who is answerable? Surely I am guilty of my brother's blood, that I never so much as reached him the pitcher to drink. Shall these men go down daily to death, and shall I not stretch out a finger lest they perish everlastingly? Mariamne, it seems there is a task set to my hand, and I must accomplish it."

She was far from wishing to hinder him. Actuated as human nature too often is by mixed motives, she could yet respond, in her womanly generosity of heart, to that noble self-sacrifice which was so distinguishing a characteristic of the new religion; and could appreciate the devotion of Calchas, while she hoped through his intervention to obtain some alleviation of her anxiety on Esca's behalf. She had caught a glimpse of the slave's figure that very day as it entered the portals of the training-school; and this rapid glance had not served to quiet her misgivings on his account.

If Calchas should now think it right to interest himself about a class of men the most reckless and desperate of the whole Roman population, it was probable that he would at the same time learn something of Esca's movements; perhaps be able to dissuade him from joining the fierce band in which she now feared he was about to be enrolled. "It may be that he has some wild hope of thus obtaining his liberty," thought the girl; and her heart throbbed while she reflected that it was for her sake liberty had now become so dear to the barbarian. "It may be that he has extorted some vague promise from his lord, and, in his pride of strength and courage, he never dreams of danger or defeat; but oh! if he [pg 134]should come to harm for my sake, what will become of me? I would rather die a thousand times than that his white skin should be disfigured with a scratch!"

"They are practising for their deadly pastime in the next street," said she; "I can hear the blows as I go down to draw water. Blows dealt, as it were, in sport; what must they be in earnest?"

"There is no time to be lost," said Calchas. "The games of Ceres are to be soon celebrated, and the Roman crowd will think it but a poor show if some hundreds of gladiators are not slaughtered at the least. Child, I will visit these men to-morrow; they will revile me, but after a time they will listen. If I can even gain over one, be he the lowest and most degraded of the band, it will be a triumph greater than a thousand victories; a gain infinitely more precious than all the treasures of Rome."

"To-morrow may be too late," she returned, moving across the room at the same time so as to hide her face. "The school is full to-day. I—I think I saw that barbarian who was here lately go into it an hour or two ago."

"The Briton!" exclaimed Calchas, starting from his seat. "Why did you not tell me so before? Quick, girl, fetch me my gown and sandals. I will go there without delay."

She helped him, nothing loth. In a few minutes Calchas was ready to go forth, and as she watched him from the door, and saw him turn the corner of the street, Mariamne clasped her hands and muttered a thanksgiving for the success of her well-meant artifice; while the old man strode boldly to his destination, confident in the integrity of his purpose, and rejoicing in the breastplate of proof which covers a good heart bound on a pious mission. "It is no business of mine," was a maxim unknown to the early Christian. Fresh in his memory was the parable of the Good Samaritan; and it never occurred to him that, like the Pharisee, he might pass by on the other side. The world is some centuries older, yet is that tale of the friendless wounded wayfarer less suggestive now than it was then?

[pg 135]

CHAPTER XVIII

WINGED WORDS

The gladiators were pausing from their toil. Brawny chests heaved and panted, deep voices laughed and swore with returning breath; strong arms looked heavier and stronger as the athlete rested his wide hands upon his hips, and not unconsciously brought his huge muscles into full relief in the attitude. Esca and his late antagonist were wiping the sweat from their brows, and looking at one another with wistful eyes, as if by no means loth to renew the contest, so equally had the last bout been waged. Hirpinus laid down the weighty clubs he had been wielding, with a grunt of relief. No unpractised arm could have lifted those cumbrous instruments from the ground, yet they were but as reeds in the hands of the gladiator; nevertheless, he lamented piteously the tendency of his mighty frame to increasing bulk, which rendered such heavy and uninteresting work necessary to fit him for the arena.

"By the body of Hercules!" complained the giant, "I would I were but such a half-starved ape as thou, my Lutorius! See what the master calls training for a man of some solidity, and thank the gods that an hour's girls'-play with sword and buckler is enough to keep that slender waist of thine within the compass of a knight's finger-ring."

"Girls'-play, call you it?" answered Lutorius. "In faith 'tis a game that would put thy fat carcass on the sand, from sheer want of breath, in a quarter of the time. No more girls'-play for us, my lads, till after the feast of Ceres. The school will be thinner then, or I am mistaken. How many pairs are promised by the Consul for this coming bout? I heard the crier tell us in the street, but I have forgotten."

"One hundred at least, for sword and buckler alone. And twenty of them out of the Family!" answered Euchenor readily, and with a malicious smile. His profession as a boxer freed him from any fatal apprehensions; but he took none the less pleasure in recalling to his comrades the more [pg 136]deadly nature of their encounters. Rufus alone looked grave; perhaps he was thinking of his wife and children while he listened; perhaps that humble cottage in the Apennines seemed farther off than ever, and the more desirable on that account. The others smiled grimly, and a wolfish expression gleamed for an instant from their eyes—all but Esca, whose glowing young face displayed only courage, excitement, and hope.

"Bird of ill-omen!" said Hippias sternly. "What do you know of the clash of steel? Keep to your own boys'-play, and do not meddle with the game that draws blood at every stroke. I think I am master here!"

Euchenor would have answered sullenly, but a knock at the door arrested his attention. As it swung open, to the surprise of all, and of none more than Esca, Calchas stood before them.

"*Salve!*" said the old man kindly, as he looked around, his venerable head and calm dignified bearing contrasting nobly with the brute strength and coarser faces of the gladiators. "*Salve!*" he repeated, smiling at the astonishment his appearance seemed to call forth.

Hippias was not lacking in a certain rough courtesy of the camp. He advanced to the new-comer, bade him welcome as a stranger, and inquired the cause of his visit; "for," said he, "judging by your looks, O my father! it can scarcely be a mission connected either with me or my disciples here, whose trade, you may observe, is war."

"I too am a soldier," answered Calchas quietly, looking the astonished fencing-master full in the face. The gladiators had by this time gathered round; like schoolboys at play they were ripe for mischief, and, like schoolboys, it needed but the merest trifle to urge them into any extreme, either of good or evil.

"A soldier!" exclaimed Euchenor, "then you fear not steel!"—at the same moment he snatched a short two-edged sword from the wall, and delivered a thrust with it full at the old man's breast. Calchas moved not a muscle; his colour neither rose nor fell; his eyelash never quivered as he looked steadily at the Greek, who probably only intended a brutal jest, and cared but little how dangerous might be its result. The point had reached the folds of the visitor's gown, when Rufus dashed it aside with his hand, while Hippias dealt the offender a buffet, which sent him reeling to the opposite wall.

"What now?" exclaimed the professor, in a tone with [pg 137]which a man rates a disobedient hound. "What now? Am I not master here?"

The others looked on approvingly. The jest was well suited to their habits. They were amused at the discomfiture of the Greek, and pleased with the coolness shown by an old man of such unwarlike exterior. Esca, however, strode up to his friend's side, and glared about him in a manner that boded no good to the originator of any more such aggressions, either in sport or earnest.

"Thou hast hurt the youth," remarked Calchas, in as unmoved a tone as would have become the fiercest gladiator of the school. "Thou hast hurt him, and he was but in jest after all. In truth, Hippias, I have not seen so goodly a buffet dealt since I came to Rome. That arm of thine can strike to some purpose, and thy pupils are, like their master, brave, and strong, and skilful. I have heard of the legion called Invincible, surely I have found it here. My sons, are you not the Invincibles?"

He spoke so quietly they knew not whether he was jesting with them; but the flattering title tickled their ears pleasantly enough, and the gladiators crowded round him, with shouts of encouragement and mirth.

"Invincibles!" they laughed. "Invincibles! Well said, old man! yes, we are the Invincibles. Who can stand against the Family? Hast come to join us? We shall have plenty of space in the ranks ere another moon be old."

"Give him a sword, one of you!" exclaimed Rufus; "let us see what he can do with Lutorius. The Gaul has had a bellyful already; press him, old man, and he must go down!"

"Nay, let him have a bout with the wooden foils," laughed Hirpinus. "He is but young and tender. He would sicken at the sight of blood."

"Or a cast with the net and trident," continued Manlius.

"Or a round with the *cestus*," observed Euchenor; adding with a sneer, "I myself am ready to exchange a buffet or two with him, for sheer goodwill."

"Hold! my new comrades," interposed Esca, with rising colour. "In my country we are taught to venerate grey hairs. If ye are so keen for *cestus*, lance, and sword-play, here am I, untried and inexperienced, willing to stand against the best of you, from now till sundown."

The gladiators gathered round the last speaker somewhat angrily; the challenge was indeed a bold one in such company, and a contest begun in play amongst those [pg 138]turbulent spirits, might end, not improbably, in too fatal earnest; but Hippias cut the matter short by commanding silence, in loud imperious tones, and, turning to the new-comer, bade him state at once the business that had brought him there and have done with it.

"I came here," said the old man, looking round with a glance of mingled pity and admiration; "I came here to see, with my own eyes, the band of Invincibles. I have already told you that I too am a soldier, whose duty it is to go down, if need be, daily unto death."

There was something so quiet and earnest in the speaker's manner, such an absence of self-consciousness or apprehension, a sincerity and goodwill so frank and evident, that the rude fierce men whom he addressed could not but give him their attention. There was all the interest of novelty in beholding one whose appearance and habits were so at variance with their own, thus throwing himself fearlessly on their forbearance, and trusting, as it were, to that higher nature, which, dormant though it might be, each man felt to exist within himself. Even Hippias acknowledged the influence of his visitor's confidence, and answered graciously enough—

"If you are a soldier, I need not tell you that we are but on the drill-ground here. You will see my band to better advantage when they defile by Cæsar at the games of Ceres."

Calchas looked inquiringly round.

"And the chorus," said he, "that I have heard ring out in such a warlike tone, as your ranks marched past the imperial chair; are you perfect in it, my friends? Do you practise the chant as you do your sword-play and your wrestling?"

He had fixed their attention now. Half-interested, half-amused at his strange persistency, they looked laughingly at each other, and their deep voices burst out into the wild and thrilling cadence of their fatal dirge—

Ave, Cæsar! Morituri te salutant!

As the last notes died away, silence pervaded the school; to the rudest and most reckless, there was something suggestive in the sounds they knew too well would be the last music they should hear on earth. Calchas turned suddenly upon Hippias.

"And the wages Cæsar gives your men?" said he; "since he buys them body and bones, they must be very costly. How many thousand sesterces doth he pay for each?"

A brutal laugh echoed round him at the question.

"Sesterces!" answered Hippias. "Nay; Cæsar's generosity provides handsomely for the training and nourishment of his swordsmen."

"True enough!" added Rufus, at which there was another laugh. "He finds us in meat, and drink, and burial!"

"No more?" said Calchas. "Yet I have been told that in Rome everything fetches its price; but little did I think such men as these could be bought for less money than a Syrian dancing-girl, or a senator's white horses. So you are willing to toil day after day, harder than the peasant on the hillside, or the oarsman in the galley, to live simply, temperately, ay, virtuously, for months together, and then to face certain death, often in its ghastliest form, for the wages a Roman citizen gives his meanest slave—a morsel of meat and a draught of wine! If you conquer in the struggle, a branch of palm may be added to a handful of silver, and you deem your reward is more than enough. Truly, I am old and feeble, these hands are little worth to strike or parry, yet would I grudge to sell this worn-out body of mine at so mean a price."

"You told us you were a soldier," observed Rufus, on whom the argument of relative value seemed to make no slight impression.

"So I am," replied Calchas; "but not at such a low rate of pay as yours. My duties are not heavy. I am not forced to toil all day, nor to watch all night. My head aches with no weighty helmet; breastplate and greaves of steel do not gall my body nor cumber my limbs. I have neither trench to dig, nor mound to raise, nor eagles to guard. I need not stand, like you, against my comrade and my friend, with my point at his throat, and slay the man who has been to me even as a brother, lest he slay me. Yet, though my labours be so easy, and my service be so deficient and inadequate, all the gold and jewels you have seen glistening in a triumph, all the treasures of Cæsar and of Rome, would not equal the reward I hope to earn."

The gladiators looked from one to the other with glances of astonishment and curiosity. This was a subject that spoke to their personal interest, and roused their feelings accordingly.

"Are there vacancies in your ranks, comrade?" asked Hirpinus, using the military form of speech habitually affected by his profession. "Will you enrol a man of muscle like myself, who has been looking all his life for a service in which there is little to do and plenty to get? Take my word for it, you will not long want for recruits."

"There is room for all, and to spare," answered Calchas, raising his voice till it rung through every corner of the building. "My Captain will enlist you freely, and without reserve. Only you come to Him and range yourselves under His banner, and stand by Him for a few short watches, a week, a month, a decade or two of years at the most, and He will stand by you when Cæsar and his legions are scattered to the four winds of heaven; ay, and long after that, for ages and ages rolling on in a circle that has no end! Will you come, brave hearts? I have authority to receive you, man by man."

"Where is your Captain?" asked Hirpinus. "He must needs have a large following. Is he here in Rome? Can we see him ere we take the oaths and raise the standard? Comrades!" he added, looking round, "this old man speaks as though he were in earnest. Nay, he would scarcely dare to laugh in our very beards!"

"You might have seen Him," answered Calchas, "not forty years ago, as I myself did, on the sunny plains of Syria. You will not see Him now, till a pinch of dust has been sprinkled on your brow, and the death-penny put into your mouth. Then, when you have crossed the dark river, He will be waiting for you on the other side."

The gladiators looked at one another. "What means he?" said they. "Is he mad?" "Is he an augur?" "Doth he deal in magic?" Rufus reared his tall head above the throng. "Would you have us believe in what we cannot see?" was the apposite question of that practical swordsman. The old man drew his mantle round his shoulders with the air of one who prepares for argument. All he wanted was a fair hearing.

"Which is the nobler gift," he asked, "a strong body, or a gallant heart? Ye have fought many times, most of you, in the arena. Answer me truly—which is the conqueror, courage or strength?"

"Courage," they exclaimed, with one voice; all except Euchenor, who muttered something about skill and good fortune being preferable to either.

"And yet you cannot see it," resumed Calchas. "Will you therefore argue that it cannot exist? Is there one of you here that doth not feel a something wanting to complete his daily existence? Why do you long for the smiles of women, and the bubble of the winecup? Why can you [pg 141]not rest when the training of to-day is over, for thinking of the labours of to-morrow? Why are you always anxious, always anticipating, always dissatisfied? Because a man consists of two parts, the body and the spirit; because his life is made up of two phases, the present and the future. Your bodies belong to Cæsar, let him have them to do with them what he likes, to-day, to-morrow, at the games of Ceres, at the feast of Neptune, what matter? But the spirit, the man within you, is your own. He it is who doth not wince when the javelin pierces to the quick, or the wild beast rends to the marrow. He it is who quails not when the level sweep of sand seems to rock beneath him, and heave up against his face; when the white garments and eager faces of the crowd spin round him faster and faster as they fade upon his darkening eye. He is the better man of the two, and he will live for ever. Shall you not provide for *him*? What is your present? Much trouble, many hours of toil. A foot or two of steel in the hand, and a dash at a comrade's throat, then a back-fall below the equestrian benches, and so the future begins. Do you think there is nothing better there than old Charon's ferry-boat, and the pale misty banks of the uncertain river? I know the way to a golden land far brighter and fairer than the fabled islands of the West. There is a high wall round it, and the gate is low and narrow; but the key stands in the lock, and you need no death-penny to purchase entrance for the poorest of you. Go to the door in rags, with no other possession but the hope and trust that you may crawl in upon your knees, and it opens ere you have knocked."

Something in each man's heart told him, as he listened, that if he could but believe this, the conviction was worth more than all the treasures of the empire put together. Liable as were these gladiators to stand in the jaws of death at a day's notice, there was something inexpressibly elevating in the idea that the supreme moment which the most careless of them could not but sometimes picture to himself, was the mere passage to a nobler state of existence. The words of a man who is telling what he himself implicitly believes to be the truth, carry with them no small amount of persuasion; and when Calchas paused, the swordsmen looked doubtingly at him with eyes in which incredulity and admiration were strangely mingled; not without a certain wistful gleam of hope. Hippias, indeed, whose tastes inclined him to materialism, and his reflections to utter disbelief in every[pg 142]thing save the temper of a blade, seemed disposed to cut the matter short, as being a waste of valuable time; but the anxiety of his pupils, and especially of Esca, to hear more of the glowing promises held out, induced him to fold his arms and listen, with a smile of conscious superiority, not devoid of contempt.

"And the Captain who leads us?" asked the Gaul, after a whisper and a push from Hirpinus. "What of him? Your promises are fair enough, I grant you, but I would fain know with whom I serve."

Not one of them but noted the gleam on the old man's face, as he replied—

"The Captain went up to death with a patient, calm, and kindly face, for you, and you, and you, and me—for those who had never seen Him; for those who mistrusted Him; for those who failed Him, and turned back from Him at His need. Nay, for those who tortured and slew Him, and whom He forgave with the free full forgiveness of a God!—ay, of a God! Which of your gods has done as much for you? When did one of them leave their Mount Olympus, save for some human need, or some human mission of bloodshed and crime? Where is the king who would give up an earthly throne, and go voluntarily to a shameful death for the sake of his people? You are men, my friends—brave, resolute, hearty men; what would you have in him whom you serve? courage, patience, mercy, goodwill to all? What think ye of Him who left the rulership of the whole universe, and went so willingly to die, that He might buy you to be His own here and hereafter? Come and range yourselves under His standard. I will tell you of Him day by day. There is no jealousy amongst His soldiers. The service is easy; He has told us so Himself; and neither mine nor any mortal tongue can calculate the reward."

"Enough of this!" interrupted Hippias, noting the eager looks and excited gestures of the swordsmen; interpreting, as he did, the words of Calchas in their literal sense, and fearing lest he might, indeed, lose the services of the daring band, on whose blood it was his trade to live. "Enough of this, old man! We have heard you patiently, and now begone! My gladiators have enlisted under Cæsar, and they will not desert their standard for any inducement you can offer. I know not why I have listened to you so long; but trespass not further on my forbearance. This building is no Athenian school of rhetoric; and the only arguments acknowledged by Hippias, are those which may be parried [pg 143]with two foot of steel. Nevertheless, go in peace, old man, and fare you well."

So Calchas went out from amongst these fierce and turbulent spirits, unharmed and well satisfied. He had sown a handful of the good seed, and knew that somewhere it would take root. More than one of the gladiators was already pondering on his words; and the young Briton, with his ardent nature, his kind heart, and his predisposition in favour of Mariamne's kinsman, had resolved that he would hear more of these new doctrines, which seemed to dawn upon him like light from another world.

[pg 144]

CHAPTER XIX

THE ARENA

A hundred thousand tongues, whispering and murmuring with Italian volubility, send up a busy hum like that of an enormous beehive into the sunny air. The Flavian amphitheatre, Vespasian's gigantic concession to the odious tastes of his people, has not yet been constructed; and Rome must crowd and jostle in the great circus, if she would behold that slaughter of beasts, and those mortal combats of men, in which she now takes far more delight than in the innocent trials of speed and skill for which the enclosure was originally designed. That her luxurious citizens are dissatisfied even with this roomy edifice, is sufficiently obvious from the many complaints that accompany the struggling and pushing of those who are anxious to obtain a good place. To-day's bill-of-fare is indeed tempting to the morbid appetites of high and low. A rhinoceros and tiger are to be pitted against each other; and it is hoped that, notwithstanding many recent failures in such combats, these two beasts may be savage enough to afford the desired sport. Several pairs of gladiators, at least, are to fight to the death, besides those on whom the populace may show mercy, or from whom they may withhold it at will. In addition to all this, it has been whispered that one well-known patrician intends to exhibit his prowess on the deadly stage. Much curiosity is expressed, and many a wager has been already laid, on his name, his skill, the nature of his conflict, and the chances of his success. Though the circus be large enough to contain the population of a thriving city, no wonder that it is to-day full to the very brim. As usual in such assemblages, the hours of waiting are lightened by eating and drinking, by jests, practical and otherwise, by remarks, complimentary, sarcastic, or derisive, on the several notabilities who enter at short intervals, and take their places with no small stir and assumption of importance. The nobility and distinguished [pg 145]characters of this dissolute age are better known than respected by their plebeian fellow-citizens.

There is, however, one exception. Though Valeria's Liburnians lay themselves open to no small amount of insolence, by the emphatic manner in which they make way for their mistress, as she proceeds with her usual haughty bearing to her place near the patrician benches—an insolence of which some of the more pointed missiles do not spare the scornful beauty herself—it is no sooner observed that she is accompanied by her kinsman, Licinius, than a change comes over the demeanour even of those who feel themselves most aggrieved, by being elbowed out of their places, and pushed violently against their neighbours, while admiring glances and a respectful silence denote the esteem in which the Roman general is held by high and low.

It wants a few minutes yet of noon. The southern sun, though his intensity is modified by canvas awnings stretched over the spectators wherever it is possible to afford them shade, lights and warms up every nook and cranny of the amphitheatre; gleams in the raven hair of the Campanian matron, and the black eyes of the astonished urchin in her arms; flashes off the golden bosses that stud the white garments on the equestrian benches; bleaches the level sweep of sand so soon to bear the prints of mortal struggle, and flooding the lofty throne where Cæsar sits in state, deepens the broad crimson hem that skirts his imperial garment, and sheds a deathlike hue over the pale bloated face, which betrays even now no sign of interest, or animation, or delight. Vitellius attends these brutal exhibitions with the same immobility that characterises his demeanour in almost all the avocations of life. The same listlessness, the same weary vacancy of expression, pervades his countenance here, as in the senate or the council. His eye never glistens but at the appearance of a favourite dish; and the emperor of the world can only be said to *live* once in the twenty-four hours, when seated at the banquet.

Insensibility seems, however, in all ages to be an affectation of the higher classes; and here, while the plebeians wrangle, and laugh, and chatter, and gesticulate, the patricians are apparently bent on proving that amusement is for them a simple impossibility, and suffering or slaughter matters of the most profound indifference. And on common occasions who so impassible, so cold, so unmoved by all that takes place around her, as the haughty Valeria? but to-day there [pg 146]is an unusual gleam in the grey eyes, a quiver of the lip, a fixed red spot on either cheek; adding new charms to her beauty, not lost upon the observers who surround her.

Quoth Damasippus to Oarses (for the congenial rogues stand, as usual, shoulder to shoulder)—

"I would not that the patron saw her now. I never knew her look so fair as this. Locusta must have left her the secret of her love philtres."

"Oh, innocent!" replies the other. "Knowest thou not that the patron fights to-day? Seest thou her restless hands, and that fixed smile, like the mask of an old Greek player? She loves him; trust me, therefore, she has lost her power, were she subtle as Arachne. Dost not know the patron? To do him justice, he never prizes the stakes when he has won the game."

And the two fall to discussing the dinner they have brought with them, and think they are perfectly familiar with the intricacies of a woman's feelings. Meantime Valeria seems to cling to Licinius as though there were some spell in her kinsman's presence to calm that beating heart of which she is but now beginning to learn the wayward and indomitable nature. For the twentieth time she asks: "Is he prepared at all points? Does he know every feint of the deadly game? Are his health and strength as perfect as training can make them? And oh, my kinsman! is he confident in himself? Does he feel sure that he will win?"

To which questions, Licinius, though wondering at the interest she betrays in such a matter, answers as before—

"All that skill, and science, and Hippias can do, has been done. He has the advantage in strength, speed, and height. Above all, he has the courage of his nation. As they get fiercer they get cooler, and they are never so formidable as when you deem them vanquished. I could not sit here if I thought he would be worsted."

Then Valeria took comfort for a while, but soon she moved restlessly on her cushions.

"How I wish they would begin!" said she; yet every moment of delay seemed at the same time to be a respite of priceless value, even while it added to the torture of suspense.

Many hearts were beating in that crowd with love, hope, fear, and anxiety; but perhaps none so wildly as those of two women, separated but by a few paces, and whose eyes some indefinable attraction seemed to draw irresistibly towards each other. While Valeria, in common with many ladies of distinction, had encroached upon the space originally [pg 147]allotted to the vestal virgins, and established, by constant attendance in the amphitheatre, a prescriptive right to a cushioned seat for herself and her friends, women of lower rank were compelled to station themselves in an upper gallery allotted to them, or to mingle on sufferance with the crowd in the lower tier of places, where the presence of a male companion was indispensable for protection from annoyance, and even insult. Nevertheless, within speaking distance of the haughty Roman lady stood Mariamne, accompanied by Calchas, trembling with fear and excitement in every limb, yet turning her large dark eyes upon Valeria, with an expression of curiosity and interest that could only have been aroused by an instinctive consciousness of feelings common to both. The latter, too, seemed fascinated by the gaze of the Jewish maiden, now bending on her a haughty and inquiring glance, anon turning away with a gesture of affected disdain; but never unobservant, for many seconds together, of the dark pale beauty and her venerable companion.

When she was at last fairly wedged in amongst the crowd, Mariamne could hardly explain to herself how she came there. It had been with great difficulty that she persuaded Calchas to accompany her; and, indeed, nothing but his interest in Esca, and the hope that he might, even here, find some means of doing good, would have tempted the old man into such a scene. It was with many a burning blush and painful thrill that she confessed to herself, she must go mad with anxiety were she absent from the death-struggle to be waged by the man whom she now knew she loved so dearly; and it was with a wild defiant recklessness that she resolved if aught of evil should befall him to give herself up thenceforth to despair. She felt as if she was in a dream; the sea of faces, the jabber of tongues, the strange novelty of the spectacle, confused and wearied her; yet through it all Valeria's eye seemed to look down on her with an ominous boding of ill; and when, with an effort, she forced her senses back into self-consciousness, she felt so lonely, so frightened, and so unhappy, that she wished she had never come.

And now, with peal of trumpets and clash of cymbals, a burst of wild martial music rises above the hum and murmur of the seething crowd. Under a spacious archway, supported by marble pillars, wide folding-doors are flung open, and two by two, with stately step and slow, march in the gladiators, armed with the different weapons of their deadly trade. Four hundred men are they, in all the pride of perfect strength and symmetry, and high training, and practised skill. With [pg 148]head erect and haughty bearing, they defile once round the arena, as though to give the spectators an opportunity of closely scanning their appearance, and halt with military precision to range themselves in line under Cæsar's throne. For a moment there is a pause and hush of expectation over the multitude, while the devoted champions stand motionless as statues in the full glow of noon; then bursting suddenly into action, they brandish their gleaming weapons over their heads, and higher, fuller, fiercer, rises the terrible chant that seems to combine the shout of triumph with the wail of suffering, and to bid a long and hopeless farewell to upper earth, even in the very recklessness and defiance of its despair—

"Ave, Cæsar! Morituri te salutant!"

Then they wheel out once more, and range themselves on either side of the arena; all but a chosen band who occupy the central place of honour, and of whom every second man at least is doomed to die. These are the picked pupils of Hippias; the quickest eyes and the readiest hands in the Family; therefore it is that they have been selected to fight by pairs to the death, and that it is understood no clemency will be extended to them from the populace.

With quickened breath and eager looks, Valeria and Mariamne scan their ranks in search of a well-known figure: both feel it to be a questionable relief that he is not there; but the Roman lady tears the edge of her mantle to the seam, and the Jewish girl offers an incoherent prayer in her heart, for she knows not what.

Esca's part is not yet to be performed, and he is still in the background, preparing himself carefully for the struggle. The rest of the Family, however, muster in force. Tall Rufus stalks to his appointed station with a calm business-like air that bodes no good to his adversary, whoever he may be. He has fought too often not to feel confident in, his own invincible prowess; and when compelled to despatch a fallen foe, he will do it with sincere regret, but none the less dexterously and effectually for that. Hirpinus, too, assumes his usual air of jovial hilarity. There is a smile on his broad good-humoured face; and though, notwithstanding the severity of his preparation, his huge muscles are still a trifle too full and lusty, he will be a formidable antagonist for any fighter whose proportions are less than those of a Hercules. As the crowd pass the different combatants in review, none, with the exception perhaps of Rufus, have more backers than their old favourite. Lutorius, too, notwithstanding his Gallic origin, [pg 149]which places him but one remove, as it were, from a barbarian, finds no slight favour with those who pride themselves on their experience in such matters. His great activity and endurance, combined with thorough knowledge of his weapon, have made him the victor in many a public contest. As Damasippus observes to his friend, "Lutorius can always tire out an adversary and despatch him at leisure;" to which Oarses replies, "If he be pitted to-day against Manlius, I will wager thee a thousand sesterces blood is not drawn in the first three assaults."

The pairs had already been decided by lot; but amongst the score of combatants who were to fight to the death, these formidable champions were the most celebrated, and as such the especial favourites of the populace. Certain individuals in the crowd, who were sufficiently familiar with the gladiators to exchange a word of greeting, and to call them by their names, derived, in consequence, no small increase of importance amongst the bystanders. The swordsmen, although now ranged in order round the arena, are destined, for a time at least, to remain inactive. The sports are to commence with a combat between a lately imported rhinoceros, and a Libyan tiger, already familiarly known to the public, as having destroyed two or three Christian victims and a negro slave. It is only in the event of these animals being unwilling to fight, or becoming dangerous to the spectators, that Hippias will call in the assistance of his pupils for their destruction. In the meantime, they have an excellent view of the conflict, though perhaps it might be seen in greater comfort from the farther and safer side of the barrier.

Vitellius, with a feeble inclination of his head, signs to begin, and a portable wooden building which has been wheeled into the lists, creating no little curiosity, is now taken to pieces by a few strokes of the hammer. As the slaves carry away the dismembered boards, with the rapidity of men in terror of their lives, a huge, unwieldy beast stands disclosed, and the rhinoceros of which they have been talking for the last week bursts on the delighted eyes of the Roman public. These are perhaps a little disappointed at first, for the animal seems peaceably, not to say indolently, disposed. Taking no notice of the shouts which greet his appearance, he digs his horned muzzle into the sand in search of food, as though secure in the overlapping plates of armour that sway loosely on his enormous body, with every movement of his huge ungainly limbs. So intent are the spectators on this rare monster, that their attention is only directed to the [pg 150]farther end of the arena by the restlessness which the rhinoceros at length exhibits. He stamps angrily with his broad flat feet, his short pointed tail is furiously agitated, and the gladiators who are near him observe that his little eye is glowing like a coal. A long, low, dark object lies coiled up under the barrier as though seeking shelter, nor is it till the second glance that Valeria, whose interest, in common with that of the multitude, is fearfully excited, can make out the fawning, cruel head, the glaring eyes, and the striped sinewy form of the Libyan tiger.

In vain the people wait for him to commence the attack. Although he is sufficiently hungry, having been kept for more than a day without food, it is not his nature to carry on an open warfare. Damasippus and Oarses jeer him loudly as he skulks under the barrier; and Calchas cannot forbear whispering to Mariamne, that "a curse has been on the monster since he tore the brethren limb from limb, in that very place, for the glory of the true faith." The rhinoceros, however, seems disposed to take the initiative; with a short labouring trot he moves across the arena, leaving such deep footprints behind him, as sufficiently attest his enormous bulk and weight. There is a flash like real fire from the tiger's eyes, hitherto only sullen and watchful—his waving tail describes a semicircle in the sand—and he coils himself more closely together, with a deep low growl; even now he is not disposed to fight save at an advantage.

'with a short labouring trot he moves across the arena.'

A hundred thousand pairs of eyes, straining eagerly on the combatants, could scarce detect the exact moment at which that spring was made. All they can now discern is the broad mailed back of the rhinoceros swaying to and fro, as he kneels upon his enemy, and the grating of the tiger's claws against the huge beast's impenetrable armour can be heard in the farthest corner of the gallery that surrounds the amphitheatre. The leap was made as the rhinoceros turned his side for an instant towards his adversary; but with a quickness marvellous in a beast of such prodigious size, he moved his head round in time to receive it on the massive horn that armed his nose, driving the blunt instrument, from sheer muscular strength, right through the body of the tiger, and finishing his work by falling on him with his knees, and pressing his life out under that enormous weight. Then he rose unhurt, and blew the sand out of his nostrils, and left, as it seemed, unwillingly, the flattened, crushed, and mangled carcass, turning back to it once and again, with a horrible, yet ludicrous, pertinacity, ere he suffered the Ethiopians who [pg 151]attended him to lure him out of the amphitheatre with a bundle or two of green vegetable food.

The people shouted and applauded loudly. Blood had been drawn, and their appetite was sharpened for slaughter. It was with open undisguised satisfaction that they counted the pairs of gladiators, and looked forward to the next act of the entertainment.

Again the trumpets sound, and the swordsmen range themselves in opposite bodies, all armed alike with a deep concave buckler, and a short, stabbing, two-edged blade; but distinguished by the colour of their scarves. Wagers are rapidly made on the green and the red; so skilfully has the experienced Hippias selected and matched the combatants, that the oldest patrons of the sport confess themselves at a loss which to choose.

The bands advance against each other, three deep, in imitation of the real soldiers of the empire. At the first crash of collision, when steel begins to clink, as thrust and blow and parry are exchanged by these practised warriors, the approbation of the spectators rises to enthusiasm; but men's voices are hushed, and they hold their breath when the strife begins to waver to and fro, and the ranks open out and disengage themselves, and blood is to be seen in patches on those athletic frames, and a few are already down, lying motionless where they fell. The green is giving way, but their third rank has been economised, and its combatants are as yet fresh and untouched; these now advance to fill the gaps made among their comrades, and the fortunes of the day seem equalised once more.

And now the arena becomes a ghastly and forbidding sight; they die hard, these men, whose very trade is slaughter; but mortal agony cannot always suppress a groan, and it is pitiful to see some prostrate giant, supporting himself painfully on his hands, with drooping head and fast-closing eye fixed on the ground, while the life-stream is pouring from his chest into the thirsty sand. It is real sad earnest, this representation of war, and resembles the battle-field in all save that no prisoners are taken and quarter is but rarely given. Occasionally, indeed, some vanquished champion, of more than common beauty, or who has displayed more than common address and courage, so wins on the favour of the spectators, that they sign for his life to be spared. Hands are turned outwards, with the thumb pointing to the earth, and the victor sheathes his sword, and retires with his worsted antagonist from the contest; but more [pg 152]generally the fallen man's signal for mercy is neglected; ere the shout "A hit!" has died upon his ears, his despairing eye marks the thumbs of his judges pointing upwards, and he disposes himself to welcome the steel with a calm courage, worthy of a better cause.

The reserve, consisting of ten pairs of picked gladiators, has not yet been engaged. The green and the red have fought with nearly equal success; but when the trumpet has sounded a halt, and the dead have been dragged away by grappling-hooks, leaving long tracks of crimson in their wake, a careful enumeration of the survivors gives the victory by one to the latter colour. Hippias, coming forward in a suit of burnished armour, declares as much, and is greeted with a round of applause. In all her preoccupation, Valeria cannot refrain from a glance of approval at the handsome fencing-master; and Mariamne, who feels that Esca's life hangs on the man's skill and honesty, gazes at him with mingled awe and horror, as on some being of another world. But the populace have little inclination to waste the precious moments in cheering Hippias, or in calculating loss and gain. Fresh wagers are, indeed, made on the matches about to take place; but the prevailing feeling over that numerous assemblage is one of morbid excitement and anticipation. The ten pairs of men now marching so proudly into the centre of the lists, are pledged to fight to the death.

It would be a disgusting task to detail the scene of bloodshed; to dwell on the fierce courage wasted, and the brutal useless slaughter perpetrated in those Roman shambles; yet, sickening as was the sight, so inured were the people to such exhibitions, so completely imbued with a taste for the horrible, and so careless of human life, that scarcely an eye was turned away, scarcely a cheek grew paler, when a disabling gash was received, or a mortal blow driven home; and mothers with babies in their arms would bid the child turn its head to watch the death-pang on the pale stern face of some prostrate gladiator.

Licinius had looked upon carnage in many forms, yet a sad, grave disapproval sat on the general's noble features. Once, after a glance at his kinswoman's eager face, he turned from her with a gesture of anger and disgust; but Valeria was too intent upon the scene enacted within a few short paces to spare attention for anything besides, except, perhaps, the vague foreboding of evil that was gnawing at her heart, and to which such a moment of suspense as the present afforded a temporary relief.

[pg 153]

Rufus and Manlius had been pitted against each other by lot. The taller frame and greater strength of the former were supposed to be balanced by the latter's exquisite skill. Collars and bracelets were freely offered at even value amongst the senators and equestrians on each. While the other pairs were waging their strife with varying success in different parts of the amphitheatre, these had found themselves struggling near the barrier close under the seat occupied by Valeria. She could hear distinctly their hard-drawn breath; could read on each man's face the stern set expression of one who has no hope save in victory; for whom defeat is inevitable and instant death. No wonder she sat, so still and spell-bound, with her pale lips parted and her cold hands clenched.

The blood was pouring from more than one gash on the giant's naked body, yet Rufus seemed to have lost neither coolness nor strength. He continued to ply his adversary with blow on blow, pressing him, and following him up, till he drove him nearly against the barrier. It was obvious that Manlius, though still unwounded, was overmatched and overpowered. At length Valeria drew in her breath with a gasp, as if in pain. It seemed as if she, the spectator, winced from that fatal thrust, which was accepted so calmly by the gladiator whom it pierced. Rufus could scarcely believe he had succeeded in foiling his adversary's defence, and driving it deftly home, so unmoved was the familiar face looking over its shield into his own—so steady and skilful was the return which instantaneously succeeded his attack. But that face was growing paler and paler with every pulsation. Valeria, gazing with wild fixed eyes, saw it wreathed in a strange sad smile, and Manlius reeled and fell where he stood, breaking his sword as he went down, and burying it beneath his body in the sand. The other strode over him in act to strike. A natural impulse of habit or self-preservation bade the fallen man half raise his arm, with the gesture by which a gladiator was accustomed to implore the clemency of the populace, but he recollected himself, and let it drop proudly by his side. Then he looked kindly up in his victor's face.

"Through the heart, comrade," said he quietly, "for old friendship's sake;" and he never winced nor quailed when the giant drove the blow home with all the strength that he could muster.

They had fed at the same board, and drunk from the same winecup for years; and this was all he had it in his power to bestow upon his friend. The people applauded [pg 154]loudly, but Valeria, who had heard the dead man's last appeal, felt her eyes fill with tears; and Mariamne, who had raised her head to look, at this unlucky moment, buried it once more in her kinsman's cloak, sick and trembling, ready to faint with pity, and dismay, and fear.

[pg 155]

CHAPTER XX

THE TRIDENT AND THE NET

But a shout was ringing through the amphitheatre that roused the Jewish maiden effectually to the business of the day. It had begun in some far-off corner, with a mere whispered muttering, and had been taken up by spectator after spectator, till it swelled into a wild and deafening roar. "A Patrician! a Patrician!" vociferated the crowd, thirsting fiercely for fresh excitement, and palled with the vulgar carnage, yearning to see the red blood flow from some scion of an illustrious house. The tumult soon reached such a height as to compel the attention of Vitellius, who summoned Hippias to his chair, and whispered a few sentences in his ear. This somewhat calmed the excitement; and while the fencing-master's exertions cleared the arena of the dead and wounded, with whom it was encumbered, a general stir might have been observed throughout the assemblage, while each individual changed his position, and disposed himself more comfortably for sight-seeing, as is the custom of a crowd when anything of especial interest is about to take place. Ere long Damasippus and Oarses were observed to applaud loudly; and their example being followed by thousands of imitators, the clapping of hands, the stamping of feet, the cheers, and other vociferations rose with redoubled vigour, while Julius Placidus stepped gracefully into the centre of the arena, and made his obeisance to the crowd with his usual easy and somewhat insolent bearing.

The tribune's appearance was well calculated to excite the admiration of the spectators, no mean judges of the human form, accustomed as they were to scan and criticise it in its highest state of perfection. His graceful figure was naked and unarmed, save for a white linen tunic reaching to the knee, and although he wore rings of gold round his ankles, his feet were bare to ensure the necessary speed and activity demanded by his mode of attack. His long dark locks, [pg 156]carefully curled and perfumed for the occasion, and bound by a single golden fillet, floated carelessly over his neck, while his left shoulder was tastefully draped, as it were, by the folds of the dangling net, sprinkled and weighted with small leaden beads, and so disposed as to be whirled away at once without entanglement or delay upon its deadly errand. His right hand grasped the trident, a three-pronged lance, some seven feet in length, capable of inflicting a fatal wound; and the flourish with which he made it quiver round his head displayed a practised arm and a perfect knowledge of the offensive weapon.

To the shouts which greeted him—"Placidus! Placidus!" "Hail to the tribune!" "Well done the patrician order!" and other such demonstrations of welcome—he replied by bowing repeatedly, especially directing his courtesies to that portion of the amphitheatre in which Valeria was placed. With all his acuteness, little did the tribune guess how hateful he was at this moment to the very woman on whose behalf he was pledged to engage in mortal strife—little did he dream how earnest were her vows for his speedy humiliation and defeat. Valeria, sitting there with the red spots burning a deeper crimson in her cheeks, and her noble features set in a mask of stone, would have asked nothing better than to have leapt down from her seat, snatched up sword and buckler, of which she well knew the use, and done battle with him, then and there to the death.

The tribune now walked proudly round the arena, nodding familiarly to his friends, a proceeding which called forth raptures of applause from Damasippus, Oarses, and other of his clients and freedmen. He halted under the chair of Cæsar, and saluted the Emperor with marked deference; then, taking up a conspicuous position in the centre, and leaning on his trident, seemed to await the arrival of his antagonist. He was not kept long in suspense. With his eyes riveted on Valeria, he observed the fixed colour of her cheeks gradually suffusing face, neck, and bosom, to leave her as pale as marble when it faded, and turning round he beheld his enemy, marshalled into the lists by Hippias and Hirpinus—the latter, who had slain his man, thus finding himself at liberty to afford counsel and countenance to his young friend. The shouts which greeted the new-comer were neither so long nor so lasting as those that did honour to the tribune; nevertheless, if the interest excited by each were to be calculated by intensity rather than amount, the slave's suffrages would have far exceeded those of his adversary.

[pg 157]

Mariamne's whole heart was in her eyes as she welcomed the glance of recognition he directed exclusively to her; and Valeria, turning from one to the other, felt a bitter pang shoot to her very marrow, as she instinctively acknowledged the existence of a rival. Even at that moment of hideous suspense, a host of maddening feelings rushed through the Roman lady's brain. Many a sunburnt peasant woman, jostled and bewildered in the crowd, envied that sumptuous dame with her place apart, her stately beauty, her rich apparel, and her blazing jewels; but the peasant woman would have rued the exchange had she been forced to take, with these advantages, the passions that were laying waste Valeria's heart. Wounded pride, slighted love, doubt, fear, vacillation, and remorse, are none the more endurable for being clothed in costly raiment, and trapped out with gems and gold. While Mariamne, in her singleness of heart, had but one great and deadly fear—that he should fail—Valeria found room for a thousand anxieties and misgivings, of conflicting tendencies, and chafed under a distressing consciousness that she could not satisfy herself what it was she most dreaded or desired.

Unprejudiced and uninterested spectators, however, had but one opinion as to the chances of the Briton's success. If anything could have added to the enthusiasm called forth by the appearance of Placidus, it was the patrician's selection of so formidable an antagonist. Esca, making his obeisance to Cæsar, in the pride of his powerful form, and the bloom of his youth and beauty, armed, moreover, with helmet, shield, and sword, which he carried with the ease of one habituated to their use, appeared as invincible a champion as could have been chosen from the whole Roman Empire. Even Hirpinus, albeit a man experienced in the uncertainties of such contests, and cautious, if not in giving, at least in backing his opinion, whispered to Hippias that the patrician looked like a mere child by the side of their pupil, and offered to wager a flagon of the best Falernian "that he was carried out of the arena feet foremost within five minutes after the first attack, if he missed his throw!" To which the fencing-master, true to his habits of reticence and assumed superiority, vouchsafed no reply save a contemptuous smile.

The adversaries took up their ground with exceeding caution. No advantage of sun or wind was allowed to either, and having been placed by Hippias at a distance of ten yards apart in the middle of the arena, neither moved a limb for several seconds, as they stood intently watching each other, [pg 158]themselves the centre on which all eyes were fixed. It was remarked that while Esca's open brow bore only a look of calm resolute attention, there was an evil smile of malice stamped, as it were, upon the tribune's face—the one seemed an apt representation of Courage and Strength—the other of Hatred and Skill.

"He carries the front of a conqueror," whispered Licinius to his kinswoman, regarding his slave with looks of anxious approval. "Trust me, Valeria, we shall win the day. Esca will gain his freedom; the gilded chariot and the white horses shall bring him and me to your door to-morrow morning, and that gaudy tribune will have had a lesson, that I for one shall not be sorry to have been the means of bestowing on him."

A bright smile lighted up Valeria's face, but she looked from the speaker to a dark-haired girl in the crowd below, and the expression of her countenance changed till it grew as forbidding as the tribune's, while she replied with a careless laugh——

"I care not who wins now, Licinius, since they are both in the lists. To tell the truth, I did but fear the courage of this Titan of yours might fail him at the last moment, and the match would not be fought out after all. Hippias tells me the tribune is the best netsman he ever trained."

He looked at her with a vague surprise; but following the direction of his kinswoman's eyes, he could not but remark the obvious distress and agitation of the cloaked figure on which they were bent. Mariamne, when she saw the Briton fairly placed, front to front with his adversary, had neither strength nor courage for more. Leaning against Calchas, the poor girl hid her face in her hands and wept as if her heart would break.

Myrrhina, who no more than her mistress could have borne to be absent from such a spectacle, had forced her way into the crowd, accompanied by a few of Valeria's favourite slaves. Standing within three paces of the Jewess, that voluble damsel expatiated loudly on the appearance of the combatants, and her careless jests and sarcasms cut Mariamne to the quick. It was painful to hear her lover's personal qualities canvassed as though he were some handsome beast of prey, and his chance of life and death balanced with heartless nicety by the flippant tongue of a waiting-maid; but there was yet a deeper sting in store for her even than this. Myrrhina, having got an audience, was nothing loth to profit by their attention.

"I'm sure," said she, "whichever way the match goes I [pg 159]don't know what my mistress will do. As for the tribune, he would get out of his chariot any day on the bare stones to kiss the very ground she walks on; and yet, if he dare so much as to leave a scratch upon that handsome youth's skin, he need never come to our doors again. Why, time after time have I hunted that boy all over the city to bring him home with me. And it's no light matter for a slave and a barbarian to have won the favour of the proudest lady in Rome. See how he looks up at her now, before they begin!"

The light words wounded very sore; and Mariamne raised her head for one glance at the Briton, half in fond appeal, half to protest, as it were, against the slander she had heard. What she saw, however, left no room in her loving heart for any feeling save intense horror and suspense.

With his eye fixed on his adversary, Esca was advancing, inch by inch, like a tiger about to spring. Covering the lower part of his face and most of his body with his buckler, and holding his short two-edged sword with bended arm and threatening point, he crouched to at least a foot lower than his natural stature, and seemed to have every muscle and sinew braced, to dash in like lightning when the opportunity offered. A false movement, he well knew, would be fatal, and the difficulty was to come to close quarters, as, directly he was within a certain distance, the deadly cast was sure to be made. Placidus, on the other hand, stood perfectly motionless. His eye was unusually accurate, and he could trust his practised arm to whirl the net abroad at the exact moment when its sweep would be irresistible. So he remained in the same collected attitude, his trident shifted into the left hand, his right foot advanced, his right arm wrapped in the gathered folds of the net which hung across his body, and covered the whole of his left side and shoulder. Once he tried a scornful gibe and smile to draw his enemy from his guard, but in vain; and though Esca, in return, made a feint with the same object, the former's attitude remained immovable, and the latter's snake-like advance continued with increasing caution and vigilance.

An inch beyond the fatal distance, Esca halted once more. For several seconds the combatants thus stood at bay, and the hundred thousand spectators crowded into that spacious amphitheatre held their breath, and watched them like one man.

At length the Briton made a false attack, prepared to spring back immediately and foil the netsman's throw, but [pg 160]the wily tribune was not to be deceived, and the only result was that, without appearing to shift his ground, he moved an arm's length nearer his adversary. Then the Briton dashed in, and this time in fierce earnest. Foot, hand, and eye, all together, and so rapidly, that the tribune's throw flew harmless over his assailant's head, Placidus only avoiding his deadly thrust by the cat-like activity with which he leaped aside; then, turning round, he scoured across the arena for life, gathering his net for a fresh cast as he flew. "Coward!" hissed Valeria, between her set teeth; while Mariamne breathed once more—nay, her bosom panted, and her eye sparkled with something like triumph at the approaching climax.

She was premature, however, in her satisfaction, and Valeria's disdain was also undeserved. Though apparently flying for his life, Placidus was as cool and brave at that moment as when he entered the arena. Ear and eye were alike on the watch for the slightest false movement on the part of his pursuer; and ere he had half crossed the lists, his net was gathered up, and folded with deadly precision once more.

The tribune especially prided himself on his speed of foot. It was on this quality that he chiefly depended for safety in a contest which at first sight appeared so unequal. He argued from the great strength of his adversary, that the latter would not be so pre-eminent in activity as himself; but he omitted to calculate the effects of a youth spent in the daily labours of the chase amongst the woods and mountains of Britain. Those following feet had many a time run down the wild goat over its native rocks. Faster and faster fly the combatants, to the intense delight of the crowd, who specially affect this kind of combat for the pastime it thus affords. Speedy as is the tribune, his foe draws nearer and nearer, and now, close to where Mariamne stands with Calchas, he is within a stride of his antagonist. His arm is up to strike! when a woman's shriek rings through the amphitheatre, startling Vitellius on his throne, and the sword flies aimlessly from the Briton's grasp as he falls forward on his face, and the impetus rolls him over and over in the sand.

There is no chance for him now. He is scarcely down ere the net whirls round him, and he is fatally and helplessly entangled in its folds. Mariamne gazes stupefied on the prostrate form, with stony face and a fixed unmeaning stare. Valeria springs to her feet in a sudden impulse, forgetting for the moment where she is.

[pg 161]

Placidus, striding over his fallen enemy with his trident raised, and the old sneering smile deepening and hardening on his face, observed the cause of his downfall, and inwardly congratulated himself on the lucky chance which had alone prevented their positions being reversed. The blood was streaming from a wound in Esca's foot. It will be remembered that where Manlius fell, his sword was buried under him in the sand. On removing his dead body the weapon escaped observation, and the Briton, treading in hot haste on the very spot where it lay concealed, had not only been severely lacerated, but tripped up and brought to the ground by the snare.

All this flashed through the conqueror's mind, as he stood erect, prepared to deal a blow that should close all accounts, and looked up to Valeria for the fatal sign.

Maddened with rage and jealousy; sick, bewildered, and scarcely conscious of her actions, the Roman lady was about to give it, when Licinius seized her arms and held them down by force. Then, with a numerous party of friends and clients, he made a strong demonstration in favour of mercy. The speed of foot, too, displayed by the vanquished, and the obvious cause of his discomfiture, acted favourably on the majority of spectators. Such an array of hands turned outwards and pointing to the earth met the tribune's eye, that he could not but forbear his cruel purpose, so he gave his weapon to one of the attendants who had now entered the arena, took his cloak from the hands of another, and, with a graceful bow to the spectators, turned scornfully away from his fallen foe.

Esca, expecting nothing less than immediate death, had his eyes fixed on the drooping figure of Mariamne; but the poor girl had seen nothing since his fall. Her last moment of consciousness showed her a cloud of dust, a confused mass of twine, and an ominous figure with arm raised in act to strike; then barriers and arena, and eager faces and white garments, and the whole amphitheatre, pillars, sand, and sky, reeled ere they faded into darkness; sense and sight failed her at the same moment, and she fainted helplessly in her kinsman's arms.

[pg 162]

[pg 163]

Anteros

CHAPTER I

THE LISTENING SLAVE

Wounded, vanquished, transferred from his kind master, and farther from liberty than ever, Esca's was now indeed a pitiable lot. The tribune, entitled by the very terms of his wager to the life and person of his antagonist, was not the man to forego this advantage by any act of uncalled-for generosity. In the Briton he believed he now possessed a tool to use with effect, in furtherance of a work which the seductive image of Valeria rendered every day more engrossing; an auxiliary by whose aid he might eventually stand first in the good graces of the only woman who had ever obtained a mastery over his unyielding disposition and selfish heart. None the more on this account did he cherish the captive, nor alleviate his condition as a slave. From the effects of his injury, Esca could not be put to any harder kinds of labour, but in all menial offices, however degrading, he was compelled to take his share. Different, indeed, was his condition here from what it had been in the service of the high-minded Licinius, and bitterly did he feel the exchange.

Submitting to sarcasm, insult, continued ill-treatment, and annoyance, the noble barbarian would have failed under the trial, had it not been for a few well-remembered words, on the truth of which Calchas had so often insisted, and in which (for when were human thoughts without an earthly leavening?) Mariamne seemed to cherish an implicit belief. [pg 164]Those words breathed hope and consolation under the very worst misfortunes that life could offer; and Esca suffered on, very silent, and tolerably patient, although, perhaps, there was a fiercer fire smouldering in his breast than would have been approved by his venerable monitor—a fire that only waited occasion to blaze out all the more dangerously for being thus forcibly suppressed.

With a malicious pleasure, natural to his disposition, Placidus compelled the Briton to perform several domestic offices which brought him about his person. It flattered the tribune's vanity to have continually before his eyes the athletic frame he was so proud to have overcome; and it pleased him that his friends, guests, and clients should be thus led to converse upon his late encounter, which had created no small gossip in the fashionable world of Rome. It happened, then, that Esca, while preparing his master's bath, was startled to hear the name that was never long out of his own thoughts spoken in accents of caution and secrecy by the tribune himself, who was in the adjoining apartment, holding close consultation with Hippias the fencing-master and the two freedmen, Damasippus and Oarses. All were obviously interested in the subject under discussion, and, believing themselves safe from eaves-droppers, spoke energetically, though in tones somewhat lower than their wont.

He started, and the blood ebbed painfully from his heart. "Mariamne!" yes, the word was again repeated, and while Oarses said something in a whisper, he could clearly distinguish the tribune's low mocking laugh. It was plain they were unaware of his presence; and, indeed, it was at an earlier hour than usual that he had made ready the unguents, perfumes, strigil, and other appliances indispensable to the luxurious ablutions of a Roman patrician. The bathroom was inside the favourite apartment of Placidus, where he was now holding counsel, and could only be entered through the latter, from which it was separated by a heavy velvet curtain. Esca, surrounded by the materials of the toilet, had been sitting for a longer time than he knew, lost in thought, until aroused by the mention of Mariamne's name. Thus it was that the four others believed the bathroom empty, and their conversation unheard.

Anxious and excited, the Briton scarcely dared to draw his breath, but crept cautiously behind the folds of the heavy curtain, and listened attentively. The tribune was walking to and fro with the restless motions and stealthy gait of a tiger in its cage. Hippias, seated at his ease upon a couch, [pg 165]was examining the device of a breastplate, with his usual air of good-humoured superiority; and Damasippus, appealing with admiring looks to Oarses, who responded in kind, seemed to endorse, as it were, with a dependant's mute approval, the opinions and observations of his patron.

"Two-thirds of the legions have already come over," said Placidus, rapidly enumerating the forces on which Vespasian's party could count. "In Spain, in Gaul, in Britain, the soldiers have declared openly against Vitellius. The surrender of Cremona can no longer be concealed from the meanest populace. Alexandria, the granary of the empire, has fallen into the hands of Vespasian. Those dusky knaves, thy countrymen, Oarses, will see us starve, ere they send us supplies under the present dynasty; and think ye our greasy plebeians here will endure the girdle of famine, thus drawn tighter, day by day, round their luxurious paunches? The fleet at Misenum was secured long ago, but the news that Cæsar could not count upon a single galley in blue water only reached the capital to-day. Then the old Prætorians are ripe for mischief; you may trust them never to forget nor to forgive the disgrace of last year, when the chosen band was broke, dismissed, and, worst of all, deprived of rations and pay; I tell thee, Hippias, those angry veterans are ready to take the town without assistance, and put old and young to the sword. Fail! it is impossible we can fail; the new party outnumbers the old by ten to one!"

"You have told off a formidable list," replied Hippias quietly; "I cannot see that you are in need of any further help from me or mine."

Placidus shot a sharp questioning glance at the fencing-master, and resumed—

"Half the numbers that have given in their adhesion to Vespasian would serve to put my chariot-boy on the throne; Automedon's long curls might be bound by a diadem to-morrow, were he the favourite of the hour, so far as Rome is concerned. You know what the masses are, my Hippias, for it is your trade to pander to their tastes, and rouse their enthusiasm. It is true that the great general is, at this moment, virtually ruler of the empire, but a pebble might turn the tide in the capital. I would not trust Vespasian's own son, young and dissipated as he is, could he but make a snatch at the reins with any hope of holding them firmly when once within his grasp. Titus Flavius Domitian might be emperor to-morrow, if he would be satisfied to wear the purple but for a week, and then make room for someone [pg 166]else. Nay, the people are fickle enough to be capable of turning round at any moment, and retaining our present admirable ruler on the throne. Rome must be coerced, my Hippias; the barbers, and cobblers, and water-carriers must be kept down and intimidated; if need be, we must cut a few garlic-breathing throats. It may be necessary to remove Cæsar himself, lest the reactionary feeling should burst out again, and we should find ourselves left with nothing for our pains, but the choice of a cup of poison, a gasp in a halter, or three inches of steel. We *must* succeed this time, for not a man need hope for pardon if Cæsar is thoroughly frightened. Hippias, there must be no half-measures now!"

"Well said!" exclaimed the freedmen in a breath, with very pale faces, nevertheless, and an enthusiasm obviously somewhat against the grain.

Hippias looked quietly up from the breastplate resting on his lap.

"There will be shows," said he, "and blood flowing like water in the circus, whoever wears the purple. While Rome stands, the gladiator need never want for bread."

"Now you speak like a man of sense," replied the tribune, in the same tone; "for after all, the whole matter resolves itself into a mere question of money. The shows are tolerably lucrative, at least to their contriver, but it takes many a festival ere the sesterces count by tens of thousands; and Hippias loves luxury and wine, and women too—nay, deny it not, my comely hero; and if the Family and their trainer could be hired at a fair price, for an hour's work or so, why they need never enter the arena again, save as spectators; nay, poorer men than their chief might be have sat in the equestrian rows, ere now."

"You want to hire my chickens and myself for a forlorn hope," retorted Hippias impatiently. "Better say so at once, and be plain with me."

"It is even so," resumed Placidus, with an assumption of extreme candour. "For real work I have few I can depend upon but the old Prætorians; and though they stick at nothing, there are hardly enough of them for my purpose. With a chosen two hundred of thine, my dealer in heroes, I could command Rome for twenty-four hours; and when Placidus soars into the sky, he carries Hippias on his wings. Speak out; thy terms are high, but such a game as ours is not played for a handful of pebbles or a few brass farthings. What is the price, man by man?"

"You would require two hundred of them," observed [pg 167]the other reflectively. "Five thousand sesterces a man, and his freedom, which would come to nearly as much more."

"The killed not to count, of course," bargained the tribune.

"Of course not," repeated Hippias. "Listen, most illustrious; I will take all chances, and supply the best men I have, for eight thousand a-head. Two hundred swordsmen who would take Pluto by the beard without a scruple, if I only lifted my hand. Lads who can hold their own against thrice their number of any legion that was ever drilled. They are ready at two hours' notice."

He was speaking truth, for Hippias was honest enough in his own particular line. Amongst the thousands who owed their professional standing, and the very bread they ate, to the celebrated fencing-master, it was no hard task to select a company of dare-devils, such as he described, who would desire no better sport than to see their native city in flames, with the streets knee-deep in blood and wine, while they put men, women, and children indiscriminately to the sword. The tribune's eye brightened, as he thought of the fierce work he could accomplish with such tools as these ready to his hand.

"Keep them for me, from to-day," he answered, looking round the apartment, as though to assure himself that he was only heard by those in his confidence. "My plan cannot but succeed if we only observe common secrecy and caution. Ten picked men, and thyself, my Hippias, I bid to sup with me here, the rest of the band shall be distributed by twenties amongst the different streets opening on the palace, preserving their communication thus: one man at a time must continually pass from each post to the next, until every twenty has been changed. This secures us from treachery, and will keep our cut-throats on the alert. At a given signal, all are to converge on the middle garden-gate, which will be found open. Then they may lead the old Prætorians to the attack, and take the palace itself by assault, in defiance of any resistance, however desperate, that can be made. The German guard are stubborn dogs, and must be put to the sword directly the outer hall is gained. I would not have them burn down the palace if they can help it; but when they have done *my* work, they are welcome to all they can carry out of it on their backs, and you may tell them so."

Hippias noted in his own mind this additional incentive [pg 168] with considerable satisfaction. After a moment's pause, he looked fixedly in the tribune's face, and inquired—

"How would you wish your guests armed for the supper-party? Shall we bring our knives with us, kind host?"

Placidus flushed a dark red, and then grew pale. He averted his eyes from Hippias, while he answered—

"There are few weapons so true as the short two-edged sword. There will be work for our brave little party inside the palace, of which we must make no bungling. Is it such a grave matter, my Hippias, to slay a fat old man?" he added inquiringly.

The other's face assumed an expression of intense disgust.

"Nay," said he, "I will have no murder done in cold blood. As much fighting as you please, in the way of business, but we are no hired assassins, my men and I. To put one Cæsar off the throne, and another on, is a pretty night's amusement enough, and I have no objection to it; but to take an old man out of his bed, even though he be an emperor, and slay him as you slay a fat sheep, I'll none of it. Send for a butcher, tribune; this is no trade of ours!"

Placidus bit his lip, and seemed to think profoundly for a moment, then his brow cleared, and he resumed with a light laugh.

"Far be it from me to offend a gladiator's scruples. I know the morals of the Family, and respect their prejudices. Half the money shall be in your hands within an hour; the rest shall be paid when the job is done. I think we understand each other well enough. Is it a bargain, Hippias? Can I depend upon you?"

The fencing-master was not yet satisfied.

"About the guests," he asked sternly; "how are we to pay for our supper?"

Placidus clapped him on the shoulder, with a jovial laugh.

"I will be frank with thee," said he, "old comrade. Why should there be secrets between thee and me? We go from my supper-table to the palace. We enter with the storming-party. I know the private apartments of the Emperor. I can lead our little band direct to the royal presence. Here we will rally round Vitellius, and take his sacred person into our charge. Hippias, I will make it ten thousand sesterces a man, for each of the ten, and thou shalt name thine own price for thine own services. But the Emperor must not escape. Dost thou understand me now?"

[pg 169]

"I like it not," replied the other; "but the price is fair enough, and my men must live. I would it could be so arranged that some resistance might be made in the palace; you slay a man so much easier with his helmet on and his sword in his hand!"

"Pooh! prejudice!" laughed the tribune. "Professional fancies that spring from thy coarse material trade. Blood leaves no more stain than wine. You and I have spilt enough of both in our time. What matter, a throat cut or a cracked flagon of Falernian? Dash a pitcher of water over a marble floor like this, and you wash away the signs of both at once. Said I not well, Damasippus? Why, what ails thee, man? Thy face has turned as white as thy gown!"

Damasippus, indeed, whose eyes were fixed upon the floor to which his patron had just alluded, presented, at this juncture, an appearance of intense terror and amazement. The freedman's mouth was open, his cheeks were deadly pale, and his very hair seemed to bristle with dismay. Pointing a shaking finger to the slabs of marble at his feet, he could only stammer out in broken accents: "May the gods avert the omen!" over and over again.

The others, following the direction of his gaze, were no less astonished to see a narrow stream of crimson winding over the smooth white floor, as though the very stones protested against the tribune's reckless and inhuman sentiments. For an instant all stood motionless, then Placidus, leaping at the velvet curtain, tore it fiercely open, and discovered the cause of the phenomenon.

Listening attentively for some further mention of the name that had roused his whole being, not a syllable of the foregoing conversation had been lost upon Esca, who, kneeling on one knee, with his wounded foot bent under him, and his ear applied close to the heavy folds of the curtain, had never moved a hair's-breadth from his attitude of fixed and absorbing attention. In this constrained position, the wound in his foot, which was not yet healed over, had opened afresh, and though he was himself unconscious of all but the cruel and treacherous scheme he overheard, it bled so freely that a dark stream stole gradually beneath the curtains, and crept gently along the marble to the very feet of the horror-stricken Damasippus.

Esca sprang to his full height; in that moment his blood curdled, as it had done when he was down upon the sand, with his enemy's eye glaring on him through the cruel net. [pg 170]He knew the tribune, and he felt there was no hope. The latter laughed loud and long. It was his way of covering all disagreeable emotions, but it boded no good to the object of his mirth. When Esca heard that laugh he looked anxiously about him as though to seek a weapon. What was the use? He stood wounded and defenceless in the power of four reckless men, of whom two were armed.

"Hold him!" exclaimed Placidus to his freedmen, drawing at the same time a short two-edged sword from its sheath. "It is unfortunate for the barbarian that he has learned our language. The necessity is disagreeable, but there is only one way of ensuring silence. My bath, too, is prepared, so I can spare him for to-day, and my freedmen will see that his place is supplied by to-morrow. Hold him, cowards! I say; do you fear that he will bite you?"

Neither Damasippus nor Oarses, however, seemed much inclined to grapple with the stalwart Briton. Wounded and outnumbered as he was, without a chance of rescue or escape, there was yet a defiant carriage of the head, a fierce glare in the eye, that warned the freedmen to keep hands off him as long as they could. They looked at each other irresolutely, and shrank from the patron's glance. That moment's hesitation saved him. Hippias, who regarded every six feet of manhood with a brave heart inside it as his own peculiar property, had besides a kindly feeling for his old pupil. He put his muscular frame between the master and the slave.

"Give him a day or two, tribune," said he carelessly. "I can find a better use for him than to cut his throat here on this clean white floor, and an equally safe one in the end, you may be sure."

"Impossible, fool!" answered Placidus angrily. "He has heard enough to destroy every hair on the head of each of us. He must never leave this room alive!"

"Only twenty-four hours," pleaded the fencing-master, who well knew how much at that time in Rome a day might bring forth. "Put him in ward as close as you will, but let him live till to-morrow. Hippias asks it as a favour to himself, and you may not like to be refused by him, when it is *your* turn. What if I should say 'No' in the private apartments of the palace? Come, let us make a compromise."

The tribune reflected for a moment. Then striking his right hand into that of Hippias—

"Agreed," said he. "Twenty-four hours' grace on one [pg 171]side, and the sharpest blade in Rome at my disposal on the other. Ho! Damasippus, call some of my people in. Bid them put the new collar on the slave, and chain him to the middle pillar in the inner court."

The order was punctually obeyed, and Esca found himself a helpless prisoner, burdened with a secret that might save the empire, and with maddening apprehensions on behalf of Mariamne tearing at his heart.

[pg 172]

CHAPTER II

ATTACK AND DEFENCE

Such beauty as the Jewess's, although she seldom went abroad, and led as sequestered a life as was compatible with the domestic duties she had to perform, could not pass unnoticed in a place like Rome. Notwithstanding the utter contempt in which her nation was held by its proud conquerors, she had been observed going to market in the morning for the few necessaries of her household, or filling her pitcher from the Tiber at sunset; and amongst other evil eyes that had rested on her fair young face were those of Damasippus, freedman to Julius Placidus the tribune.

He had lost no time in reporting to his patron the jewel he had discovered, so to speak, in its humble setting; for, like the jackal, Damasippus never dared to hunt for himself, and followed after evil, not for its own sake, but for the lust of gold.

His patron, too, though he had only seen the girl once, and then closely veiled, was so inflamed by the description of her charms, on which the client dwelt at great length, that he resolved to possess himself of her, in the sheer insolence of a great man's whim, promising the freedman that after the lion was served he should have the jackal's reward. It was in consequence of this agreement that a plot was laid of which Esca overheard but half a dozen syllables, and yet enough to render him very uneasy when he reflected on the recklessness and cruelty of him with whom it originated, and the slavish obedience with which it was sure to be carried out. It would have broken the spirit of a brave man to be chained to a pillar, fasting and wounded, with only twenty-four hours to live; and a keen suspicion that the woman he loved was even then all unconsciously walking into the toils, added a pang to bodily suffering which might have turned the stoutest heart to water, but Esca never lost hope altogether. Something he could not analyse seemed to give him comfort and support, nor was he aware that the [pg 173]blind vague trust he was beginning to entertain in some power above and beyond himself, yet on which he felt he could implicitly rely, was the first glimmer of the true faith dawning on his soul.

Perhaps the slave in his chain, under sentence of death, bore a lighter heart than his luxurious master, washed, perfumed, and tricked out in all the glitter of dress and ornament, rolling in his gilded chariot to do homage to the woman who had really mastered his selfish heart. Automedon, whose eyes were of the sharpest, remarked that his lord was nervous and restless, that his cheek paled, and his lip shook more and more as they proceeded on their well-known way, and that when they neared the portals of Valeria's house the tribune's hand trembled so that he could scarcely fasten the brooch upon his shoulder. How white against the crimson mantle, dyed twice and thrice till it had deepened almost into purple, looked those uncertain fingers, quivering about the clasp of gold!

However reckless, unprincipled, and cunning a man may be, he is inevitably disarmed by the woman he really loves. This is even the case when his affection is returned; but when he has fallen into the hands of one who, disliking him personally, has resolved to make him her tool, his situation is pitiable indeed. These hopeless passions, too, have in all ages been of the fiercest and the most enduring. Ill-usage on the one side or the other has not produced the effect that might be expected, and the figurative shirt of Nessus, instead of being torn off in shreds and cast away, has been far oftener hugged closer and closer to the skin, burning and blistering into the very marrow. It generally happens, too, that the suitor, whose whole existence seems to hang upon his success, blunders into the course that leads him in a direction exactly contrary to his goal. He is pretty sure to say and do the wrong thing at the wrong time. He offers his attentions with a pertinacity that wearies and offends, or withdraws them with a precipitation so transparent as to compel remark. When he should be firm, he is plaintive; when he is expected to be cheerful, he turns sulky. To enhance his own value he becomes boastful to the extreme verge, and sometimes beyond it, of the truth; or in order to prove his devotion, he makes himself ridiculous, and thereby deals the final and suicidal blow, if such indeed be necessary, that is to shatter like glass the fabric of his hopes.

The tribune knew women thoroughly. He could plead no lack of experience, for ignorance of that intricate and [pg 174]puzzling labyrinth, a woman's heart. He had, indeed, broken more than one in the process of examination, and yet the boy Automedon, sitting by his side in the chariot, with the wind lifting his golden curls, would hardly have been guilty of so many false movements, such mistakes both of tactics and strategy, as disgraced his lord's conduct of the unequal warfare he waged with Valeria. Yet this engrossing affection, stained and selfish as it was, constituted perhaps the one redeeming quality of the tribune's character; afforded the only incentive by which his better and manlier feelings could be aroused.

Possibly Valeria expected him. Women have strange instincts on such matters, which seldom deceive. She was dressed with the utmost magnificence, as though conscious that simplicity could have no charms for Placidus, and sat in a splendour nearly regal, keeping Myrrhina and the rest of her maidens within call. Lovers are acute observers; as he walked up the cool spacious court to greet her, he saw that she was gentler, and more languid than her wont; she looked wearied and unhappy, as though she, too, acknowledged the sorrows and the weaknesses of her sex. Lover-like, he thought this unusual shade of softness became her well.

For days she had been fighting with her own heart, and she had suffered as such undisciplined natures must. The strife had left its traces on her pale proud face, and she felt a vague unacknowledged yearning for repose. The wild-bird had beat her wings and ruffled her plumage till she was tired, and a skilful fowler would have taken advantage of the reaction to lure her into his net. Perhaps she had been thinking what happiness it must be to have one in the world in whom she could confide, on whom she could rely; one loyal manly nature on which to rest her woman's heart, with all its caprices, and weaknesses, and capacity for love; perhaps she may have been even touched by the tribune's unshaken devotion to herself, by the constancy which could withstand the allurements of vice, and even the distractions of political intrigue; perhaps to-day she disliked him less than on any former occasion, though it could hardly have been for *his* sake that her eye was heavy, and her bosom heaved. If so, whatever favour he had unconsciously gained, was as unconsciously destroyed by his own hand. He approached her with an air of assumed confidence, that masked only too well the agitation of his real feelings.

"Fair Valeria," said he, "I have obeyed your commands, and I come like a faithful servant to claim my reward."

[pg 175]

Now a woman's commands are not always intended to be literally obeyed. Under any circumstances she seldom likes to be reminded of them; and as for *claiming* anything from Valeria, why the very word roused all the rebellion that was dormant in her nature. At that instant rose on her mind's eye the scene in the amphitheatre, the level sand, the tossing sea of faces, the hoarse roar of the crowd, the strong white limbs and the yellow locks lying helpless beneath a dark vindictive face, and a glitter of uplifted steel. How she hated the conqueror then! How she hated him now! She was clasping a bracelet carelessly on her arm, the fair round arm he admired so much, and that never looked so fair and round as in this gesture. It was part of his torture to make herself as attractive as she could. Her cold eyes chilled him at once.

"I had forgotten all about it," said she. "I am obliged to you for reminding me that I am in your debt."

Though somewhat hurt, he answered courteously, "There can be no debt from a mistress to her slave. You know, Valeria, that all of mine, even to my life, is at your disposal."

"Well?" she asked, with a provoking persistency of misapprehension.

He began to lose his head; he, ordinarily so calm, and cunning, and self-reliant.

"You bade me enter on a difficult and dangerous undertaking. It was perhaps a lady's caprice, the merest possible whim. But you expressed a wish, and I never rested till I had accomplished it."

"You mean about that wretched slave?" said she, and the colour rose faintly to her cheek. "But you never killed him after all."

How little he knew her! This, then, he thought, was the cause of her coldness, of her displeasure. Esca had in some way incurred her ill-will, and she was angry with the conqueror who had spared him so foolishly when in his power. What a heart must this be of hers that could only quench its resentment in blood! Yet he loved her none the less. How the fair round arm, and the stately head, and the turn of the white shoulder maddened him with a longing that was almost akin to rage. He caught her hand, and pressed it fervently to his lips.

"How can I please you?" he exclaimed, and his voice trembled with the only *real* emotion he perhaps had ever felt. "Oh! Valeria, you know that I love the very ground you tread on."

[pg 176]

She bade Myrrhina bring her some embroidery on which the girl was busied, and thus effectually checked any further outpouring of sentiments which are not conveniently expressed within earshot of a third person. The waiting-maid took her seat at her mistress's elbow, her black eyes dancing in malicious mirth.

"Is that all you have to tell me?" resumed Valeria, with a smile in which coquetry, indifference, and conscious power were admirably blended. "Words are but empty air. My favour is reserved for those who win it by deeds."

"He shall die! I pledge you my word he shall die!" exclaimed the tribune, still misunderstanding the beautiful enigma on which he had set his heart. "I have but spared him till I should know your pleasure, and now his fate is sealed. Ere this time to-morrow he will have crossed the Styx, and Valeria will repay me with one of her brightest smiles."

A shudder she could not suppress swept over the smooth white skin, but she suffered no trace of emotion to appear upon her countenance. She had a game to play now, and it must be played steadily and craftily to ensure success. She bade Myrrhina fetch wine and fruit to place before her guest, and while the waiting-maid crossed the hall on her errand, she suffered the tribune to take her hand once more—nay, even returned its caressing clasp, with an almost imperceptible pressure. He was intoxicated with his success, he felt he was winning at last; and the jewelled cup that Myrrhina brought him, as he thought all too soon, remained for a while suspended in his hand, while he uttered fervent protestations of love, which were received with an equanimity that ought to have convinced him they were hopelessly wasted on his idol.

"You profess much," said she, "but it costs men little to promise. We have but one faithful lover in the empire, and he is enslaved by a barbarian princess and another man's wife. Would *you* have turned back from all the pleasures of Rome, to fight one more campaign against those dreadful Jews, for the sake of Berenice's sunburnt face?"

"Titus had consulted the oracle of Venus," replied the tribune, with a meaning smile; "and doubtless the goddess had promised him a double victory. Valeria, you know there is nothing a man will not dare to win the woman he loves."

"Could you be as true?" she asked, throwing all the sweetness of her mellow voice, all the power of her winning eyes, into the question.

"Try me," answered he, and for one moment the man's nature was changed, and he felt capable of devotion, self-[pg 177]sacrifice, fidelity, all that constitutes the heroism of love. The next, nature reasserted her sway, and he was counting the cost.

"I have a fancy for your barbarian," said Valeria carelessly, after a pause. "Myrrhina loves him, and—and if you will give him to me I will take him into my household."

Placidus shot a piercing glance at the waiting-maid, and that well-tutored damsel cast down her eyes and tried to blush. There was something, too, in Valeria's manner that did not satisfy him, and yet he was willing to believe more than he hoped, and nearly all he wished.

"I seldom *ask* for anything," resumed Valeria, raising her head with a proud petulant gesture of which she knew the full effect. "It is far easier for me to grant a favour than to implore one. And yet, I know not why, but I do not feel it painful to beg anything to-day from you!"

A soft smile broke over the haughty face while she spoke, and she raised her eyes and looked full into his for an instant, ere she lowered them to toy with the bracelet once more. It was the deadliest thrust she had in all her cunning of fence, the antagonist could seldom parry or withstand it; would it foil him in their present encounter? He loved her as much as such a nature can love, but the question was one of life and death, and it was no time for child's play now, as Esca was in possession of a secret that might annihilate his lord in an hour. The tribune was not a man to sacrifice his very existence for a woman, even though that woman was Valeria. He hesitated, and she, marking his hesitation, turned pale, and shook with rage.

"You refuse me!" said she, in accents that trembled either with suppressed fury or lacerated feelings. "You refuse me. *You*, the only man living for whom I would have so lowered myself. The only man I ever stooped to entreat. Oh! it is too much, too much."

She bowed her head in her hands, and as the wealth of brown hair showered over her white shoulders, they heaved as if she wept. Myrrhina looked reproachfully at the tribune, and muttered, "Oh! if he knew, if he only *knew*!"

In his dealings with the other sex Placidus had always been of opinion that it is better to untie a knot than to cut it.

"Fair Valeria," said he, "ask me anything but this. I am pledged to slay this man within twenty-four hours; will not that content you?"

The exigency of the situation, the danger of him for whom she had conceived so wild and foolish a passion, sharpened her powers of deception, and made her reckless of [pg 178]her own feelings, her own degradation. Shaking the hair back from her temples, beautiful in her disorder and her tears, she looked with wet eyes in the tribune's face, while she replied—

"Do you think I care for the barbarian? What difference can it make to Valeria if such as this Briton were slain by hecatombs? It is for Myrrhina's sake I grieve; and more, far more than this, to think that you can refuse me anything in the whole world!"

Duplicity was no new effort for the tribune. He had often, ere now, betaken himself to this mode of defence when driven to his last ward. He raised her hands respectfully to his lips.

"Be it as you will," said he; "I make him over to you to do with him what you please. Esca is your property, beautiful Valeria, from this hour."

A dark thought had flitted through his brain, that it would be no such difficult matter to destroy an inconvenient witness, and retain the favour of an exacting mistress at the same time. It was but a grain or two of poison in the slave's last meal, and he might depart in peace, a doomed man, to Valeria's mansion. He would take the chance of his silence for the few hours that intervened, and after all, the ravings of one whose brow was already stamped with death would arouse little suspicion. Afterwards it would be easy to pacify Valeria, and shift the blame on some over-zealous freedman, or officious client. He did not calculate on the haste with which women jump to conclusions. Valeria clapped her hands with unusual glee. "Quick! Myrrhina," said she, "my tablets to the tribune. He shall write the order here, and my people can go for the slave and bring him back, before Placidus departs."

"Nay," interposed the latter in some confusion, "it is indispensable that I go home at once. I have already lingered here too long. Farewell, Valeria. Ere the sun goes down you shall see that Placidus is proud and happy to obey your lightest whim."

With these words, he made a low obeisance, and, ere his hostess could stop him, had traversed the outer hall, and mounted in his chariot. Valeria seemed half stupefied by this sudden departure, but ere the rolls of his wheels had died away, a light gleamed in her eyes, and summoning the little negro, who had lain unnoticed and coiled up within call during the interview, she bade him run out and see which direction the chariot took, then she stared wildly in Myrrhina's face, and burst into a strange, half-choking laugh.

CHAPTER III

"FURENS QUID FŒMINA"

"The chariot has turned into the Flaminian Way," said the urchin, running breathlessly back to his mistress. "Oh! so fast! so fast!" and he clapped his little black hands with the indescribable delight all children take in rapidity of movement.

"The Flaminian Way!" repeated Valeria. "He must go round by the Great Gate and the Triumphal Arches to get home. Myrrhina, if we make haste, we shall yet be in time."

In less than ten minutes the two women had crossed the wide pleasure-grounds which skirted Valeria's mansion, and had let themselves out by a pass-key into the street. So complete, however, was their transformation that the most intimate friend would have failed to recognise in these shrouded, hurrying figures, the fashionable Roman lady and her attendant. A wig of curling yellow hair covered Valeria's nut-brown tresses, and the lower part of her face was concealed by a mask, whilst Myrrhina, closely-veiled and wrapped in a dark-coloured mantle, stained and threadbare with many a winter's storm, looked like some honest child of poverty, bound on one of the humble errands of daily plebeian life. As they tripped rapidly along a narrow and little frequented street,—one of the many inconvenient thoroughfares which Nero's great fire had spared, and which still intersected the magnificence of the Imperial City,—they had to pass a miserable-looking house, with a low shabby doorway, which was yet secured by strong fastenings of bolts and bars, as though its tenant had sufficient motives for affecting privacy and retirement. The women looked meaningly at each other while they approached it, for the dwelling of Petosiris the Egyptian was too well known to all who led a life of pleasure or intrigue in Rome. He it was who provided potions, love philtres, charms of every description, and whom the superstitious of all classes, no trifling majority, young and old, rich and poor, male and female, consulted in matters of interest and affection; the supplanting of a rival, the acquisition of a heart, and the removal of those who stood in the way either of a fortune or a conquest. It is needless to observe that the Egyptian's wealth increased rapidly; and that humbler visitors had to turn from his door disappointed, day after day, waiting the leisure of the celebrated magician.

But if Valeria hurried breathlessly through the dirty and ill-conditioned street, she stopped transfixed when she reached its farthest extremity, and beheld the tribune's chariot, standing empty in the shade, as though waiting for its master. The white horses beguiled their period of inaction in the heat, by stamping, snorting, and tossing their heads, while Automedon, now nodding drowsily, now staring vacantly about him, scarcely noticed the figures of the two women, so well were they disguised.

"What can he be doing there?" whispered Valeria anxiously; and Myrrhina replied in the same cautious tones, "If Placidus be trafficking for philtres with the Egyptian, take my word for it, madam, there will be less of love than murder in the draught!"

Then they hurried on faster than before, as if life and death hung upon the rapidity of their footsteps.

Far back, up a narrow staircase, in a dark and secluded chamber, sat Petosiris, surrounded by the implements of his art. Enormous as his wealth was supposed to be, he suffered no symptoms of it to appear, either in his dwelling or his apparel. The walls of his chamber were bare and weather-stained, totally devoid of ornament, save for a mystic figure traced here and there on their surface, while the floor was scorched, and the ceiling blackened, with the burning liquids that had fallen on the one, and the heavy aromatic vapours that clung about the other. The magician's own robe, though once of costly materials, and surrounded with a broad border, on which cabalistic signs and numerals were worked in golden thread, now sadly frayed, was worn to the last degree of tenuity, and his linen head-dress, wound in a multiplicity of folds, till it rose into a peak some two feet high, was yellow with dirt and neglect. Under this grotesque covering peered forth a pair of shrewd black eyes, set in a grave emaciated face. They denoted cunning, audacity, and that restless vigilance which argued some deficiency or warping of the brain, a tendency, however remote, to insanity, from which, with all their mental powers, these impostors are seldom free. There was nothing else remarkable about the man. He had [pg 181]the deep yellow tint with the supple figure and peculiar nostril of the Egyptian, and when he rose in compliment to his visitor, his low stature afforded a quaint contrast to his trailing robes and real dignity of bearing.

The tribune—for he it was whose entrance disturbed the calculations on which the magician was engaged—accosted the latter with an air of abrupt and almost contemptuous familiarity. It was evident that Placidus was a good customer, one who bought largely while he paid freely; and Petosiris, throwing aside all assumption of mystery or preoccupation, laughed pleasantly as he returned the greeting. Yet was there something jarring in his laugh, something startling in his abrupt transition to the profoundest gravity; and though his small glittering eyes betrayed a schoolboy's love of mischief, gleams shot from them at intervals which expressed a diabolical malice, and love of evil for evil's sake.

"Despatch, my man of science!" said the tribune, scarcely noticing the obeisance and expressions of regard lavished on him by his host. "As usual I have little time to spare, and less inclination to enter into particulars. Give me what I want—you have it here in abundance—and let me begone out of this atmosphere, which is enough to stifle the lungs of an honest man!"

"My lord! my illustrious patron! my worthiest friend!" replied the other, with evident enjoyment of his customer's impatience, "you have but to command, you know it well, and I obey. Have I not served you faithfully in all my dealings? Was not the horoscope right to a minute? Did not the charm protect from evil? and the love philtre ensure success? Have I ever failed, my noble employer? Speak, mighty tribune; thy slave listens to obey."

"Words! words!" replied the other impatiently. "You know what I require. Produce it, there is the price!"

At the same time he threw a bag of gold on the floor, the weight of which inferred that secrecy must constitute no small portion of the bargain it was to purchase. Though he affected utter unconsciousness, the Egyptian's eyes flashed at the welcome chink of the metal against the boards; none the more, however, would he abstain from tantalising the donor by assuming a misapprehension of his meaning.

"The hour," said he, "is not propitious for casting a horoscope. Evil planets are in the ascendant, and the influence of the good genius is counteracted by antagonistic spells. Thus much I can tell you, noble tribune, they are of barbarian [pg 182]origin. Come again an hour later to-morrow, and I will do your bidding."

"Fool!" exclaimed Placidus impatiently, at the same time raising his foot as though to spurn the magician like a dog. "Does a man give half a helmetful of gold for a few syllables of jargon scrawled on a bit of scorched parchment? You keep but one sort of wares that fetch a price like this. Let me have the strongest of them."

Neither the gesture, nor the insult it implied, was lost on the Egyptian. Yet he preserved a calm and imperturbable demeanour, while he continued his irritating inquiries.

"A philtre, noble patron? A love philtre? They are indeed worth any amount of gold. Maid or matron, vestal virgin or Athenian courtesan, three drops of that clear tasteless fluid, and she is your own!"

The tribune's evil smile was deepening round his mouth—it was not safe to jest with him any further; he stooped over the magician and whispered two words in his ear; the latter looked up with an expression in which curiosity, horror, and a perverted kind of admiration, were strangely blended. Then his eyes twinkled once more with the schoolboy's mirth and malice, while he ransacked a massive ebony cabinet, and drew forth a tiny phial from its secret drawer. Wrapping this in a thin scroll, on which was written the word *Cave* (beware!) to denote the fatal nature of its contents, he hurried it into the tribune's hands, hid away the bag of gold, and in a voice trembling with emotion, bade his visitor begone, an injunction which Placidus obeyed with his usual easy carelessness of demeanour, stepping daintily into his chariot, as though his errand had been of the most benevolent and harmless kind.

In the meantime, Valeria, accompanied by her attendant, had reached the tribune's house, which she entered with a bold front indeed, but with shaking limbs. Despite her undaunted nature, all the fears and weaknesses of her sex were aroused by the task she had set herself to fulfil, and her woman's instinct told her that, whatever might be her motives, the crossing of this notorious threshold was an act she would bitterly repent at some future time. Myrrhina entertained no such misgivings; she looked on the whole proceeding as an opportunity to display her own talents for intrigue, and make herself, if possible, more necessary than ever to the mistress with whose secrets she was so dangerously familiar.

In the outer hall were lounging a few slaves and freedmen, who welcomed the entrance of the two women with consider[pg 183]ably less respect than one of them at least was accustomed to consider her due. Damasippus, indeed, with a coarse jest, strove to snatch away the mask that concealed the lower part of Valeria's face, but she released herself from his hold so energetically as to send him reeling back half a dozen paces, not a little discomfited by the unexpected strength of that shapely white arm. Then drawing herself to her full height, and throwing her disguise upon the floor, she confronted the astonished freedman in her own person, and bade him stand out of her way.

"I am Valeria!" said she, "and here by your master's invitation, slave! for what are you better than a mere slave after all? If I were to hint at your insolence, he would have you tied to that doorpost, in despite of your citizenship, and scourged to death, like a disobedient hound. Pick up those things," she added loftily, "and show me, some of you, to the private apartment of your lord. Myrrhina, you may remain outside, but within call."

Completely cowed by her demeanour, and no whit relishing the tone in which she threatened him, Damasippus did as he was commanded; while a couple of slaves, who had remained till now in the background, ushered the visitor into another apartment, where they left her with many obsequious assurances that their lord was expected home every moment.

Every moment! Then there was no time to lose. How her heart beat, and what a strange instinct it was that made her feel she was in the vicinity of the man she loved! As yet she had formed no plan, she had made no determination, she only knew he was in danger, he was to die, and come what might, at any risk, at any sacrifice, her place was by his side. Imminent as was the peril, critical as was the moment, through all the tumult of her feelings, she was conscious of a vague wild happiness to be near him; and as she walked up and down the polished floor, counting its tesselated squares mechanically, in her strong mental excitement, she pressed both hands hard against her bosom, as though to keep the heart within from beating so fiercely, and to collect all its energies by sheer strength and force of will.

Thus pacing to and fro, running over in her mind every possible and impossible scheme for the discovery and release of the slave, whose very prison she had yet to search out, her quick ear caught the dull and distant clank of a chain. The sound reached her from an opposite direction to that of the principal entrance; and as all Roman houses were constructed on nearly the same plan, Valeria had no fear of losing her [pg 184]way among the roomy halls and long corridors of her admirer's mansion. She held her breath as she hurried on, fortunately without meeting a human being, for the household slaves of both sexes had disposed themselves in shady nooks and corners to sleep away the sultriest hours of the day; nor did she stop till she reached a heavy crimson curtain, screening an inner court, paved and walled by slabs of white stone that refracted the sun's rays with painful intensity. Here she stood still and listened, while her very lips grew white with emotion, then she drew the curtain, and looked into the court.

He had dragged himself as far as his chain would permit, to get the benefit of some two feet of shade close under the stifling wall. A water-jar, long since emptied, stood on the floor beside him, accompanied by a crust of black mouldy bread. A heavy iron collar, which defied alike strength and ingenuity, was round his throat, while the massive links that connected it with an iron staple let into the pavement would have held an elephant. It was obvious the prisoner could neither stand nor even sit upright without constraint; and the white skin of his neck and shoulders was already galled and blistered in his efforts to obtain relief by occasional change of posture. Without the key of the heavy padlock that fastened chain and collar, Vulcan himself could scarcely have released the Briton; and Valeria's heart sank within her as she gazed helplessly round, and thought of what little avail were her own delicate fingers for such a task. There seemed no nearer prospect of help even now that she had reached him; and she clenched her hand with anger while she reflected how he must have suffered from heat, and thirst, and physical pain, besides the sense of his degradation and the certainty of his doom.

Nevertheless, extended there upon the hard glowing stones, Esca was sleeping as sound and peacefully as an infant. His head was pillowed on one massive arm, half hidden in the clustering yellow locks that showered across it, and his large shoulders rose and fell regularly with the measured breathing of a deep and dreamless slumber. She stole nearer softly, as afraid to wake him, and for a moment came upon Valeria's face something of the deep and holy tenderness with which a mother looks upon a child. Yet light as was that dainty footstep it disturbed, without actually rousing, the watchful instincts of the sleeper. He stirred and turned his face upwards with a movement of impatience, while she, hanging over him and drinking in the beauty that [pg 185]had made such wild work with her tranquillity, as if her life had neither hope nor fear beyond the ecstasy of the moment, gazed on his fair features and his closed eyes, till she forgot time and place and hazard, the emergency of the occasion, and the errand on which she had herself come. Deeper and deeper sank into her being the dangerous influence of the hour and the situation. The summer sky above, the hot dreamy solitude around, and there, down at her feet—nay, so near, that, while she bent over him, his warm breath stirred the very hair upon her brow—the only face of man that had ever thrilled her heart, sleeping so calmly close to her own, and now made doubly dear by all it had suffered, all it was fated to undergo. Lower and lower, nearer and nearer, bent her dainty head to meet the slave's; and as he stirred once more in his sleep, and a quiet smile stole over his unconscious countenance, her lips clung to his in one long, loving, and impassioned kiss.

[pg 186]

CHAPTER IV

THE LOVING CUP

As he opened his dreamy eyes she started to her feet, for voices now broke in on the silence that had hitherto reigned throughout the household, and the tread of slaves bustling to and fro announced the return of their lord, a master who brooked no neglect, as well they knew, from those who were in his service. She had scarcely risen from her posture of soothing and devoted affection; scarcely had time to shake the long hair off her face, when Julius Placidus entered the court and stood before her with that inscrutable expression of countenance which most she hated, and which left her in complete ignorance as to whether or not he had been in time to witness the caresses she had lavished on the captive. And now Valeria vindicated the woman's nature of which, with all her faults, she partook so largely. At this critical moment her courage and presence of mind rose with the occasion; and though, womanlike, she had recourse to dissimulation, that refuge of the weak, there was something on her brow that argued, if need were, she would not shrink from the last desperate resources of the strong. Turning to the tribune with the quiet dignity and the playful smile that she knew became her so well, she pointed to the recumbent figure of the Briton, and said gently—

"You gave him to me, and I am here to fetch him. Why is it that of late I value your lightest gift so much? Placidus, what must you think of me, to have come unbidden to your house?"

Then she cast down her eyes and drooped her stately head, as though ready to sink in an agony of love and shame. Deceiver, intriguer, as he had been ever since the down was on his chin, he was no match for her. He shot, indeed, one sharp inquisitive glance at Esca, but the slave's bewildered gaze reassured him. The latter, worn out with trouble and privation, was only half awake, and almost [pg 187]imagined himself in a dream. Then the tribune's looks softened as they rested on his mistress; and, although there was a gleam of malicious triumph on his brow, the hard unmeaning expression left his face, which brightened with more of kindness and cordiality than was its wont.

"It is no longer house of mine," said he, "but of yours, beautiful Valeria! Here you are ever welcome, and here you will remain, will you not, with him who loves you better than all the world besides?"

Even while he spoke she had run over in her mind the exigencies and difficulties of her position. In that instant of time she could think of Esca's danger—of the necessity that she should herself be present to save him from the fate with which, for some special reason that she was also determined to find out, he was obviously threatened—of the tribune's infamous character, and her own fair fame; for Cornelia might not have left such a house as that with her reputation unscathed, and Valeria could far less afford to tamper with so fragile and shadowy a possession than the severe mother of the Gracchi. Yet her brow was unclouded, and there was nothing but frank good-humour in her tone while she replied—

"Nay, Placidus. You know that even we of the patrician order cannot do always as we would. Surely I have risked enough already; because—because I fancied you left me in anger, and I could not bear the thought even for an hour. I will but ask you for a cup of wine and begone. Myrrhina accompanied me here, and we can return, unknown and unsuspected, as we came."

He wished nothing better. A cup of wine, a sumptuous feast spread on the moment, garlands of flowers, heavy perfumes loading the sultry air; soft music stealing on the senses gently as the faint breeze that whispered through the drowsy shade. All the voluptuous accessories so adapted to a pleading tongue and so dangerous to a willing ear. He had never known them fail; it should not be the fault of master or household if they proved useless now.

He took Valeria respectfully by the hand, and led her to the large banqueting-hall with as much deference as though she had been Cæsar's wife. None knew better than the tribune how scrupulously all the honours of war must be paid to a fortress about to capitulate. As he bent before her, the phial he had purchased from Petosiris peeped forth in the bosom of his tunic, and her quick eye did not fail to detect it. In an instant she turned back as though [pg 188]stumbling on the skirt of her robe, and in the action made a rapid sign to Esca by raising her hand to her mouth, accompanied by a warning shake of the head and a glance from her eloquent eyes, that she trusted he would understand as forbidding him to taste either food or drink till her return. Once more, whilst she made this covert signal, the set and passionless look came over the tribune's face. Cunning, cautious as she might think herself, his snake-like eye had seen enough. At that moment Placidus had resolved Esca should die within the hour. Then those two walked gracefully into the adjoining hall, and seated themselves at the banquet with a scrupulous courtesy and strict observance of the outward forms of good breeding; while the slaves who waited believed that the whole proceeding was but one of their lord's usual affairs of gallantry, and that the noble pair before them loved each other well.

The tribune, like the rest of his sex, was no large eater when making love; and an appetite that could accompany Vitellius through the most elaborate banquets of the gluttonous Cæsar was satisfied with a handful of dates and a bunch or two of grapes in the presence of Valeria. She, too, in her anxiety and agitation, felt as if every morsel would choke her; but she pledged her host willingly in a goblet of red Falernian, with a vague idea that every moment she could keep his attention employed was of priceless value, clingingly almost hopelessly to the chance of obtaining by some means the possession of the fatal phial before it was too late.

He was in high spirits,—voluble, witty, eloquent, sarcastic, but devoted to her. In the moment, as he hoped, of his triumph he could afford to show, or rather to affect, more of delicacy and generosity than she had believed him to possess, and she loathed and hated him all the more. Once, when, after enunciating a sentiment of the warmest regard and attachment, she caught the expression of his eyes as they looked into her own, she glanced wildly round the room, and clenched her hand with rage to observe that the walls were bare of weapons. He was no stately, high-spirited Agamemnon, this supple intriguer, yet had there been sword, axe, or dagger within reach of that white arm, she would have asked nothing better than to enact the part of Clytemnestra. How she wished to be a man for the moment—ay, and a strong one! She felt she could have strangled him there, hateful and smiling on the couch! Oh! for Esca's thews and sinews! Esca—so fair, and brave, [pg 189]and honest! Her brain swam when she thought of him chained, like a beast, within ten paces of her. An effort must be made to save him at any risk and at any sacrifice.

Placidus talked gaily on, broaching in turn those topics of luxury, dissipation, and even vice, which constituted the everyday life of the patrician order at Rome, and she forced herself to reply with an affected levity and indifference that nearly drove her mad. Cæsar's banquets; Galeria's yellow head-gear, and the bad taste in which her jewels were set, so inexcusable in an emperor's wife; the war in Judæa; the last chariot race; and the rival merits of the Red and Green factions, were canvassed and dismissed with a light word and a happy jest. Such subjects inevitably led to a discussion on the arena and its combatants, the magnificence of the late exhibition, and the tribune's own prowess in the deadly game. Placidus turned suddenly, as if recollecting himself, called for a slave, whispered an order in his ear, and bade him begone. The man hastened from the room, leaving lover and mistress once more alone.

The presence of mind and self-command on which she prided herself now completely deserted Valeria. In an agony of alarm for Esca, she jumped at once to the conclusion that his doom was gone forth. The tribune, turning to her with some choice phrase, half-jest, half-compliment, was startled to observe her face colourless to the very lips, while her large eyes shone with a fierce, unnatural light. Uttering a low stifled cry, like that of some wild animal in its death-pang, she fell at his feet, clasping him round the knees, and gasped out—

"Spare him! spare him! Placidus—beloved Placidus! spare him—for *my* sake!"

Her host, whose whole mind at that moment was occupied with thoughts very foreign to bloodshed, and whose whispered mandate had reference to nothing more deadly than orders for a strain of unexpected music, gazed in astonishment at the proud woman thus humbled before him to the dust. He had, indeed, intended to despatch Esca quietly by poison before nightfall, and so get rid at once of an inconvenient witness and a possible rival; but for the present he had dismissed the slave completely from his mind. If, an hour ago, he had allowed himself to harbour such a wild fancy, as that a mere barbarian should have captivated the woman on whom he had set his affections, her voluntary acceptance of his hospitality and her cordial demeanour since, had dispelled so foolish and unjust a suspicion, which he [pg 190]wondered he could have entertained even for a moment. Now, however, a chill seemed to curdle the blood about his heart. Very quietly he raised her from the floor; but, though he was not conscious of it, his grasp left a mark upon her wrist. Very distinct and steady were the tones in which he soothed her, asking courteously—

"Whom do you wish me to spare? What is it, Valeria? Surely you are not still dwelling on that barbarian slave? What is he, to come between you and me? It is too late—too late!"

"Never! never!" she gasped out, seizing his hand in both her own, and folding it to her breast. "It is no time now for concealment; no time for choice phrases, and mock reserve, and false shame! I love him, Placidus! I love him!—do you hear? Grant me but his life, and ask me for everything I have in return!"

She looked beautiful as she knelt before him once more, so dishevelled and disordered, with upturned face and streaming hair. It seemed to the tribune as though a knife had been driven home to his heart; but he collected all his energies for a revenge commensurate to the hurt, as he threw himself indolently on the couch, a worse man by a whole age of malice than he had risen from it a few seconds before.

"Why did you not tell me sooner?" said he, in accents of the calmest courtesy and self-command. "Fair Valeria! not more bargains are driven every day in the Forum than in the courts of Love! You offer liberal terms. It seems to me we have nothing left to do but to settle the remainder of the agreement."

What a price was she paying for her interference! Not a woman in Rome could have felt more deeply the degradation she was accepting, the insult to which she was submitting; and through it all she was miserably conscious of a false move in the game she had the temerity to play against this formidable adversary. Still she had resolved that she would shrink from no humiliation to save Esca, and she blushed blood-red with anger and shame as she rose from her knees, hid her face in her hands, while she summoned her woman's wit and her woman's powers of endurance to help her in the emergency.

He, too, had bethought him of an appropriate revenge. The tribune never forgave; for such an offence as the present it was his nature to seek reprisals, exceeding, in their subtle cruelty, the injury they were to atone. There is no venom so deadly as a bad man's love turned to gall. It would be [pg 191]fine sport, thought Placidus, to make her slay this yellow-haired darling of hers with her own hand. The triumph would be complete, when he had outwitted her at every point, and could sneer politely over the dead body of the man, and the passionate reproaches of the woman. The first step to so tempting a consummation was, of course, to put her off her guard, and for this it would be necessary to assume some natural displeasure and pique; too open a brow would surely arouse suspicions, so he spoke angrily, in the harsh excited tones of a generous man who has been wronged.

"I have been deceived," said he, striking his hand against the board; "deceived, duped, scorned, and by you, Valeria, from whom I did not deserve it. Shame on the woman who could thus wring an honest heart for the mere triumph of her vanity! And yet," he added, with an admirable appearance of wounded feeling in his lowered voice and relenting accents, "I can forgive, because I would not others should suffer as I do now. Yes, Valeria's wishes are still laws to me; I *will* spare him for your sake, and you shall bear the news to him yourself. But he must be half dead ere this, of thirst and exhaustion; take him a cup of wine with your own fair hands, and tell him he will be a free man before sunset!"

While he spoke, he turned from her to a sideboard, on which stood a tall jar of Falernian, flanked by a pair of silver goblets. She had sunk from the couch beside him, and was resting her head upon the table; but she looked up quickly for a moment, and saw his back reflected in the burnished surface of a gold vase that stood before her. By the motion of his shoulders she was aware that he had taken something from his bosom while he filled the wine. The whole danger of the situation flashed upon her at once; she felt intuitively that one of the cups was poisoned; she could risk her life to find out which. Her tears were dried, her nerves were strung, as if by magic; like a different being she rose to her feet now, pale and beautiful, but perfectly calm and composed.

"You do love me, Placidus," said she, raising one of the goblets from the salver on which they stood. "Such truth as yours might win any woman. I pledge you, to show that we are friends again at least, if nothing more!"

She was in the act of putting it to her lips, when he interposed, somewhat hurriedly, and with a voice not so steady as usual—

[pg 192]

"One moment!" he exclaimed, taking it from her hand, and setting it down again in its place, "we have not made our terms yet; the treaty must be signed and sealed; a libation must be poured to the gods. It is a strong rough wine, that Falernian: I have some Coan here you would like better. You see I have not forgotten your tastes."

He laughed nervously, and his lip twitched; she knew now that it was the right-hand goblet which held the poison. Both were equally full, and they stood close together on the salver.

"And this man could not slay me after all," was the thought that for a moment softened her heart, and bade her acknowledge some shadow of compunction for her admirer. Bad as he was, she could not help reflecting that to her influence he owed the only real feeling his life had ever known, and it made her waver, but not for long. Soon the image of Esca, chained and prostrate, passed before her, and the remembrance of her odious bargain goaded her into the bitterest hatred once more.

She placed her hand in the tribune's with the abandonment of a woman who really loves, she turned her eyes on his with the swimming glance of which she had not miscalculated the power.

"Forgive me," she murmured. "I have never valued you, never known you till now. I was heartless, unfeeling, mad; but I have learned a lesson to-day that neither of us will ever forget. No, we will never quarrel again!"

He clasped her in his arms, he took her to his heart, his brain reeled, his senses failed him, that bewitching beauty seemed to pervade his being, to surround him with its fragrance like some intoxicating vapour; and whilst his frame thrilled, and his lips murmured out broken words of fondness, the white hand thrown so confidingly across his shoulder had shifted the position of the goblets, and the heart that beat so wildly against his own had doomed him remorselessly to die.

She extricated herself from his embrace, she put her hair back from her brow; love is blind, indeed, or it must have struck him that instead of blushing with conscious fondness, her cheek was as white and cold as marble, though she kept her eyes cast down as if they dared not meet his own.

"Pledge me," said she, in a tone of the utmost softness, and forcing a playful smile that remained, carved as it were, in fixed lines round her mouth; "drink to me in token of [pg 193]forgiveness; it will be the sweetest draught I have ever tasted when your lips have kissed the cup."

He reached his hand out gaily to the salver. Her heart stood still in the agony of her suspense, lest he should mark the change she had made so warily; but the goblets were exactly alike, and he seized the nearest without hesitation, and half-emptied it ere he set it down. Laughing, he was in the act of handing to her what remained, when his eye grew dull, his jaw dropped, and, stammering some broken syllables, he sank back senseless upon the couch.

She would have almost given Esca's life now to undo the deed. But it was no time for repentance or indecision; keeping her eyes off the white vacant face, which yet seemed ever before her, she felt resolutely in the bosom of the tribune's tunic for the precious key, and having found it, walked steadily to the door and listened. It was well she did so, for a slave's step was heard rapidly approaching, and she had but time to return, on tiptoe, and take her place upon the couch ere the domestic entered; disposing of the tribune's powerless head upon her lap as though he had sunk to sleep in her embrace. The slave discreetly retired, but short as was its duration, the torture of those few seconds was hardly inadequate to the guilt that had preceded them. Then she hurried through the well-known passages, and reached the court in which Esca was confined. Not a word of explanation, not a syllable of fondness escaped her lips as she calmly liberated the man for whom she had risked so much. Mechanically, and like a sleep-walker, she unlocked the collar round his neck, signing to him at the same time, for she seemed incapable of speech, to rise and follow her. He obeyed, scarce knowing what he did, astonished at the apparition of his deliverer, and almost scared by her ghastly looks and strange imperious gestures. Thus they threaded, without interruption, the passages of the house, and emerged from the private entrance into the now silent and deserted street. Then came the reaction; Valeria could bear up no longer, and trembling all over while she clung to Esca, but for whose arm she must have fallen, she burst into a passion of sobs upon his breast.

[pg 194]

CHAPTER V

SURGIT AMARI

She had known but few moments of happiness, that proud unbending woman, in the course of her artificial life. Now, though remorse was gnawing at her heart, there was such a wild delight in the Briton's presence, such ecstasy in the consciousness of having saved him, though at the price of a hateful crime, that the pleasure kept down and stifled the pain. It was a new sensation to cling to that stalwart form and acknowledge him for her lord whom others deemed a mere barbarian and a slave. It was intense joy to think that she had penetrated his noble character; that she had given him her love unasked, when such a gift could alone have saved him from destruction; and that she had grudged no price at which to ransom him for herself. It was the first time in Valeria's whole existence that she had vindicated her woman's birthright of merging her own existence in another's, and for the moment this engrossing consciousness completely altered the whole character and training of the patrician lady. Myrrhina, walking discreetly some ten paces behind, could hardly believe in the identity of that drooping form, faltering in step, and timid in gesture, with her imperious and wilful mistress. This vigilant damsel, who was never flurried nor surprised, had effected her escape from the domestics of the tribune's household, at the moment her practised ear caught the light footstep of Valeria making its way to the door; and although she scarcely expected to see the latter pacing home with the captive at her side, as oblivious of her waiting-maid's existence, as of everything else in the world, she was quite satisfied to observe that this preoccupation was the result of interest in her companion. So long as an intrigue was on foot, it mattered little to Myrrhina who might be its originators or its victims.

[pg 195]

They had not proceeded far before Esca stopped, waking up like a man from a dream.

"I owe you my life," he said, in his calm voice and foreign accent, that made such music to her ear. "How shall I ever repay you, noble lady? I have nothing to give but the strength of my right arm, and of what service can such as I be to such as you?"

She blushed deeply, and cast down her eyes.

"We are not safe yet," she answered. "We will talk of this when we get home."

He looked before him down the stately street, with its majestic porticoes, its towering palaces, and its rows of lofty pillars, stretching on in grand perspective till they met the dusky crimson of the evening sky; and perhaps he was thinking of a free upland, and blue hills, and laughing sunshine glittering on the mere and trembling in the green wood far away at home, for he only answered by repeating her last word with a sigh, and adding: "There is none for me; a wanderer, an outcast, and a degraded man."

She seemed to check the outburst that was rising to her lips, and she kept her eyes off his face, while she whispered—

"I have determined to save you. Do you not know that there is nothing you can ask me which I will not grant?"

He raised her hand to his lips, but the gesture partook more of the dependant's homage than the lover's rapture. She felt instinctively that it was a tribute of gratitude and loyalty, not an impassioned caress. For the second time, something seemed to warn her she had better have left that day's work undone. Then she began to talk rapidly of the dangers they might undergo from pursuit, of the necessity for immediate flight to her house, and close concealment when there; wandering wildly on from one subject to another, and apparently but half-conscious of anything she said. At last he asked her eagerly, even sternly—

"And the tribune? What of him? How could you release me from his power? I tell you, I had the life of Placidus in my hand, as completely as if I had been standing over him in the amphitheatre with my foot on his neck. Would any price have purchased me from him, with all I knew?"

The crimson rose to her brow as she answered hurriedly, "No price! Believe me, no price that man could offer, or woman either! Esca, do not think worse of me than I deserve!"

"Then why am I here?" he continued, with a softened [pg 196]look; "I would like well to discover the secret by which Valeria can charm such a man as Placidus to her will."

She was very pale now.

"The tribune will claim you no more," said she; "I have settled that account for ever."

He did not understand her, yet he dropped the hand he held and walked on a little farther from her side. She felt her punishment had already commenced, and when she spoke again it was in hard cold accents quite unlike her own.

"He crossed my path, Esca, and he met the fate of all who are rash enough to oppose Valeria. What motives of pity, or love, or honour, would avail with Placidus? When did he ever swerve a hair's-breadth from his goal for any consideration but self? I knew him, ah! too well. There was but one invincible argument for the tribune, and I used it. I slew him—slew him there, upon his couch; but it was to save you!"

Perhaps he felt he was ungrateful. Perhaps he tried to think that he, at least, had no right to judge her harshly; that such devotion for his sake should have made him look with indulgent eye, even on so foul a crime as murder; but he could not control the repugnance and horror that now rose in him for this beautiful, reckless, and unscrupulous woman: but while he strove to conceal his feelings, and to mask them with an air of deference and gratitude, she knew by the instinct of love all that was passing in his breast, and suffered, as those only can suffer, who have thrown honour, virtue, conscience, everything to the winds, to purchase but the conviction that their shameful sacrifice has been in vain. She determined to put a period to the tortures she was enduring. Ere this, they had reached the street, from which opened the private entrance into her own grounds. Myrrhina, though within sight, still kept discreetly in the rear. This was the situation, this was the moment that Valeria had pictured to herself in many a rapturous day-dream, that seemed too impossibly happy ever to come to pass. To have ransomed him from some great danger at some equivalent price; to have led him off with her in triumph; those two pacing by themselves through the deserted streets at the witching sunset hour; to have brought him home her own, her very own, to this identical gate exactly in this manner; to have none between them, none to watch them, except faithful Myrrhina, and to see before her a long future of uninterrupted sunshine, this it had been ecstasy to dream of—and now it had come, and brought with it a dull sickening [pg 197]sensation that was worse than pain. She had a brave rebellious nature, in keeping with the haughty head and stately form hereditary in her line. No scion of that noble old house would shrink or quiver under mental, any more than under bodily, torture. Among the ancestral busts that graced her cornices, was that of one who endured with a calm set face to watch his own hand shrivelled up and crackling in the glowing coals. His descendants, male and female, partook of that unflinching character; and not Mutius Scævola himself, erect and stern before the Tuscan king, had more of the desperate tenacity which sets fate itself at defiance, than lurked under the soft white skin, and the ready smile, and the voluptuous beauty of proud Valeria.

She looked prouder and fairer than ever now, as she stopped at her own gate and confronted the Briton.

'You are safe she said'

"You are safe," she said, and what it cost her to say it none knew but herself. "You are free besides, and at liberty to go where you will."

The rapture with which he kissed her hand while she spoke, the gleam of delight that lit up his whole face, the intense gratitude with which he bowed himself to the ground before her, smote like repeated strokes of a dagger to her heart. She continued in accents of well-acted indifference, though a less preoccupied observer might have marked the quivering eyelid and dilated nostril—

"You may have friends whom you long to see—friends who have been anxious about your safety. Though it seems," she added, ironically, "they have taken but little pains to set you out of danger."

Esca was always frank and honest; this was, perhaps, the charm that, combined with his yellow locks and broad shoulders, so endeared him to the Roman lady. She was unaccustomed to these qualities in the men she usually met.

"I have no friends," he answered, rather sadly; "none in the whole of this great city, except perhaps yourself, noble lady, who care whether I am alive or dead. Yet I have one mission, for the power of performing which this very night I thank you far more than for saving my life. To-morrow, it would be too late."

The tone was less that of a question than an assertion, in which she forced out the words—

"It concerns that dark-eyed girl! Esca, do not fear to tell me the truth."

A faint red stole over the young man's brow. They were [pg 198]standing together within the garden-wall on the smooth lawn that sloped towards the house. The black cedars cut clear and distinct against the pure serene opal of the fading sky. A star or two were dimly visible, and not a breath stirred the silent foliage of the holm-oaks, folded as it were in sleep, or the drooping flowers, drowsy with the very weight of fragrance they exhaled. It was the time and place for a confession of love. What a mockery it seemed to Valeria to stand there and watch his rising colour, and listen to the faltering voice in which he betrayed his secret!

"I must save her, noble lady," said he; "I must save her this very night, whatever else be left undone. Be he dead or alive, she shall not enter the tribune's house, whilst I can strike a blow or grasp an enemy by the throat. Lady, you have earned my eternal gratitude, my eternal service; give me but this one night, and I return to-morrow to be the humblest and most willing of your slaves for ever after."

"And see her no more?" asked Valeria, with a choking throat and a strong tendency to burst into tears.

"And see her no more," repeated Esca, sadly and resignedly.

There was no mistaking the tone of manly, unselfish, and utterly hopeless love. Valeria passed her hand across her face, and tried more than once to speak. At last she muttered in a hoarse hard voice—

"You love her then very dearly?"

He raised his head proudly, and a smile came on his lips, a light into his blue eyes. She remembered how he had looked so in the arena, when he gave his salute before the imperial chair. She remembered, too, a pair of dark eyes and a pale face that followed his every movement.

"So dearly," was his answer, "that can I but rescue her I will gladly bargain to give her up and never even look on her again. How can I think of myself when the question is of her happiness and her safety?"

Valeria with all her faults was a woman. She had indeed dreamed of an affection such as this, an affection purified from the dross and alloy that combine to form so much of what men call love. She might not be capable of feeling it, but, womanlike, she could admire and appreciate the nobility of its aspirations, and the ideal standard to which it stretched. Womanlike, too, she was not to be outdone in generosity, and Esca's proposal of returning to her household, and submitting to her will directly he had accomplished his errand, disarmed her completely. She was not accustomed [pg 199]to analyse her feelings, or to check the reckless impulse which always bade her act on the spur of the moment. She did not stop to consider to-morrow's repentance, nor the grudging regrets which would goad her when the excitement of her self-denial had died out, and the blank that had hitherto rendered existence so dreary would be even less tolerable than before. If a shadowy misgiving that she would repent her concession hereafter passed for a moment across her mind, she hastened to repress it, ere it should warp her better intentions; and she could urge him to leave her now, with all the more importunity, that she dared not trust her heart to waver for an instant in the sacrifice.

"You are alone," said she, calming herself with a great effort, and speaking very quick. "Alone in this great city, but you are loyal and brave. Such men are rare here and are worth a legion. Still, you must have gold in your bosom and steel at your belt, if you would succeed. You shall take both from me, and you will tell the dark-eyed girl that it was Valeria who saved her and you."

His blue eyes turned upon her with looks of the deepest, the most fervent gratitude, and again the wild love surged up in her heart, and threatened to swamp every consideration but its own irresistible longing. His answer, however, sent it ebbing coldly back again.

"We shall be ever grateful; oh! that either of us could prove it! We shall not forget Valeria."

Myrrhina thought her mistress had never looked so queenly, as when she called her up at this juncture, and bade her fetch a purse of gold from her own cabinet, and one of the swords that hung in the vestibule, and deliver them to Esca. Then, very erect and pale, Valeria walked towards the house, apparently insensible to his thanks and protestations, but turned round ere she had reached the threshold, and gave him her hand to kiss. Myrrhina returning from her errand, saw the face that was bent over him as he stooped in act of homage, and even that hollow-hearted girl was touched by its wild, tender, and mournful expression, but ere he could look up, it was cold and passionless as marble once more. Then she disappeared slowly through the porch, and Myrrhina with all her daring had not the courage to follow her into the privacy of her own chamber.

CHAPTER VI

DEAD LEAVES

The stars shone brilliantly down on the roofs of the great city—roofs that covered in how various a multitude of hopes, fears, wishes, crimes, joys, study, debaucheries, toil, and repose. What enormities were veiled by a tile some half an inch thick! What contrasts separated by a partition of a deal plank, and a crevice stopped with mortar! Here, a poor worn son of toil, working with bleared eyes and hollow cheeks to complete the pittance that a whole day's labour was insufficient to attain; there, a sleek pampered slave, snoring greasily on his pallet, drenched with pilfered wine, and gorged with the fat leavings of his master's meal. On this side the street, a whole family penned helplessly together in a stifling garret; on that, a spacious palace, with marble floors, and airy halls, and lofty corridors, devoted to the occasional convenience and the shameful pleasures of one man—a patrician in rank, a senator in office; yet, notwithstanding, a profligate, a coward, a traitor, and a debauchee. Could those roofs have been taken off; could those chambers have been bared to the million eyes of night that seemed to be watching her so intently, what a mass of corruption would Imperial Rome have laid bare! There were plague-spots under her purple, festering and spreading and eating into the very marrow of the mistress of the world. Up six storeys, under the slanting roof, in a miserable garret, a scene was being enacted, bad as it was, far below the nightly average of vice and treachery in Rome.

Dismissed from their patron's house when he had no further need of their attendance, and, so to speak, off duty for the day, Damasippus and Oarses had betaken themselves to their home in order to prepare for the exploits of the night. That home was of the cheapest and most wretched among the many cheap and wretched lodgings to be found in the overgrown yet crowded city. Four bare walls bulging and [pg 201]blistered with the heat, supported the naked rafters on which rested the tiles, yet glowing from an afternoon sun. A wooden bedstead, rickety and creaking, with a coarse pallet, through the rents of which the straw peeped and rustled, occupied one corner, and a broken jar of common earthenware, but of a sightly design copied from the Greek, half-full of tepid water, stood in another. These constituted the only furniture of the apartment, except a few irregular shelves filled with unguents, cosmetics, and the inevitable pumice-stone, by which the fashionable Roman studied to eradicate every superfluous hair from his unmanly cheek and limbs. A broken Chiron, in common plaster, yet showing marks of undoubted genius where the shoulders and hoofs of the Centaur had escaped mutilation, kept guard over these treasures, and filled a place that in the pious days of the old Republic, however humble the dwelling, would have been occupied by the Lares and Penates of the hearth. A mouldy crust of bread, slipped from the lid of an open trunk full of clothing, lay on the floor, and a wine-jar emptied to the dregs stood by its side. The two inhabitants, however, of this squalid apartment betrayed in their persons none of the misery in keeping with their dwelling-place. They were tolerably well fed, because their meals were usually furnished at their patron's expense; they contrived to be well dressed, because a decent and even wealthy appearance was creditable to their patron's generosity, and indispensable to many of the duties he called upon them to perform—dirty work indeed, but only to be done, nevertheless, with clean clothes and an assured countenance; so that the exterior both of Damasippus and Oarses would have offered no discredit to the ante-room of Cæsar himself. But they were men of pleasure as the word is understood in great cities—men who lived solely for the sensual indulgences of the body; and it was their nature to spend their gains, chiefly ill-gotten, in those debasing luxuries which an insatiable demand enabled Rome to supply to her public at the lowest possible cost, to sun themselves, as it were, in the glare of that gaudy vice which walks abroad in the streets, and then creep back into their loathsome hole, like reptiles as they were.

Damasippus, whose plump well-rounded form and clear colour afforded a remarkable contrast to the lithe shape and sallow tint of Oarses, was the first to speak. He had been watching the Egyptian intently, while the latter went through the painful and elaborate ceremonies of a protracted toilet, rasping his chin with pumice-stone, smoothing and greasing [pg 202]his dark locks with a preparation of lard and perfumed oil, and finally drawing a needle charged with lampblack carefully and painfully through his closed eyelids, in order to lengthen the line of the eye, and give it that soft languishing expression so prized by Orientals of either sex. Damasippus, waxing impatient, then, at the evident satisfaction with which his friend pursued the task of adornment, broke out irritably—

"And of course it is to be the old story again! As usual, mine the trouble, and, by Hercules! no small share of the danger, now that the town is swarming with soldiers, all discontented and ill-paid. While yours, the credit, and very likely the reward, and nothing to do but to whine out a few coaxing syllables, and make yourself as like an old woman as you can. No difficult task either," he added, with a half-sarcastic, half-good-humoured laugh.

The other lingered before a few inches of cracked mirror, which seemed to rivet his attention, and put the finishing touches to either eyelid with infinite care, ere he replied—

"Every tool to its own work; and every man to his special trade. The wooden-headed mallet to drive home the sharp wedge. The brute force of Damasippus to support the fine skill of Oarses."

"And the sword of a Roman," retorted the other, who, like many untried men, was somewhat boastful of his mettle, "to hew a path for the needlework of an Egyptian. Well, at least the needle is in appropriate hands. By all the fountains of Caria thou hast the true feminine leer in thine eye, the very swing of thy draperies seems to say, 'Follow me, but not too near.' The clasp of Salmacis herself could not have effected a more perfect transformation. Oarses, thou lookest an ugly old woman to the life!"

In truth the Egyptian's disguise was now nearly complete. The dark locks, smoothed and flattened, were laid in modest bands about his head; the matronly stole, or gown, gathered at the breast by a broad girdle, and fastened with a handsome clasp high on the shoulder, descended in long sweeping lines to his feet, where it was ornamented by a broad and elaborate flounce of embroidery. Over the whole was disposed in graceful folds a large square shawl of the finest texture, dark-coloured but woven through with glistening golden threads, and further set off by a wide golden fringe. It formed a veil and cloak in one, and might easily be arranged to conceal the figure as well as the face of the wearer. Oarses was not a little proud of the dainty feminine grace with which he wore the head-gear, and as he tripped to and fro across the narrow [pg 203]floor of his garret, it would have taken a sharper eye than that of keen Damasippus himself to detect the disguise of his wily confederate.

"A woman, my friend," he replied, somewhat testily, "but not such an ugly one, after all; as thou wilt find to thy cost when we betake ourselves to the streets. I look to thee, my Damasippus," he added maliciously, "to protect thy fair companion from annoyance and insult."

Damasippus was a coward, and he knew it, so he answered stoutly—

"Let them come, let them come! a dozen at a time if they will. What! a good blade and a light helmet is enough for me, though you put me at half-sword with a whole maniple of gladiators! The patron knows what manhood is, none better. Why should he have selected Damasippus for this enterprise, but that he judges my arm is iron, and my heart is oak?"

"And thy forehead brass," added the Egyptian, scarcely concealing a contemptuous smile.

"And my forehead brass," repeated the other, obviously gratified by the compliment. "Nay, friend, the shrinking heart, and the failing arm, and the womanly bearing, are no disgrace, perhaps, to a man born by the tepid Nile; but we who drink from the Tiber here (and very foul it is)—we of the blood of Romulus, the she-wolf's litter, and the war-god's line—are never so happy as when our feet are reeling in the press of battle, our hearts leaping to the clash of shields, and our ears deafened by the shout of victory. Hark! what is that?"

The boaster's face turned very pale, and he hastily unbuckled the sword he had been girding on while he spoke; for a wild, ominous cry came sweeping over the roofs of the adjoining houses, rising and falling, as it seemed, with the sway of deadly strife, and boding, in its fierce fluctuations, to some a cruel triumph, to others a merciless defeat.

Oarses heard it too. His dark face scarce looked like a woman's now, with its gleam of malicious glee and exulting cunning.

"The old Prætorians are up," said he quietly. "I have been expecting this for a week. Brave soldier, there will be a fill of fighting for thee this night in the streets; and goodly spoils, too, for the ready hand, and love and wine, and all the rest of it, without the outlay of a farthing."

"But it will not be safe to be seen in arms now," gasped Damasippus, sitting down on the tester-bed, with a white [pg 204]flabby face, and a general appearance of being totally unstrung. "Besides," he added, with a ludicrous attempt at reasserting his dignity, "a brave Roman should not engage in civil war."

Oarses reflected for a moment, undisturbed by a second shout, that made his frightened companion tremble in every limb; then he smoothed his brows, and spoke in soothing and persuasive tones.

"Dost thou not see, my friend, how all is in favour of our undertaking? Had the city been quiet, we might have aroused attention, and a dozen chance passengers half as brave as thyself might have foiled us at the very moment of success. Now, the streets will be clear of small parties, and it is easy for us to avoid a large body before it approaches. One act of violence amongst the hundreds sure to be committed to-night, will never again be heard of. The three or four resolute slaves under thine orders, will be taken to belong to one or other of the fighting factions, and thus even the patron's spotless character will escape without a blemish. Besides, in such a turmoil as we are like to have by sundown, a woman might scream her heart out, and nobody would think of noticing her. On with that sword again, my hero, and let us go softly down into the street."

"But if the old Prætorians succeed," urged the other, evincing a great disinclination for the adventure, "what will become of Cæsar? and with Cæsar's fall down goes the patron too, and then who is to bear us harmless from the effects of our expedition to-night?"

"Oh! thick-witted Ajax!" answered the Egyptian, laughing; "bold and strong in action as the lion; but in council innocent as the lamb. Knowest thou the tribune so little as to think he will be on the losing side? If there is tumult in Rome, and revolt, and the city boils and seethes like a huge flesh-pot casting up its choicest morsels to the surface, dost thou suppose that Placidus is not stirring the fire underneath? I tell thee that, come what may of Cæsar to-night, to-morrow will behold the tribune more popular and more powerful than ever; and I for one will beware of disobeying his behests."

The last argument was not without its effect. Damasippus, though much against the grain, was persuaded that of two perils he had better choose the lesser; and it speaks well for the ascendency gained by Placidus over his followers, that the cleverer and more daring knave should have obeyed him unhesitatingly from self-interest, the ruffian and the coward [pg 205]from fear. Damasippus, then, girding on his sword once more, and assuming as warlike a port as was compatible with his sinking heart, marched down into the street to accompany his disguised companion on their nefarious undertaking, with many personal fears and misgivings for the result.

How different, save in its disquietude, was the noble nature at the same moment seeking repose and finding none, within half a bow-shot of the garret in which these two knaves were plotting. Despite his blameless life, despite his distinguished career, Caius L. Licinius sat and brooded, lonely and sorrowful, in his stately home. In that noble palace, long ranges of galleries and chambers were filled with objects of art and taste, beautiful, and costly, and refined. If a yard of the wall had looked bare, it would have been adorned forthwith by some trophy of barbaric arms taken in warfare. If a corner had seemed empty, it would have been at once filled with an exquisite group of marble, wrought into still life by some Greek artist's chisel. Not a recess in that pile of building, but spoke of comfort, complete in every respect, and the only empty chamber in the whole was its owner's heart. Nay, more than empty, for it was haunted by the ghost of a beloved memory, and the happiness that was never to come again.

Cold and dreary is the air of that mysterious tenement where we buried our treasures long ago. Cold and dreary, like the atmosphere of the tomb, but a perfume hangs about it still, because love, being divine, is therefore eternal; and though the turf be laid damp and heavy over the beloved head, our tears fall like the blessed rain from heaven, and water the very barrenness of the grave, till at length, through weary patience and humble resignation, the flowers of hope begin to spring, and faith tells us they shall bloom hereafter, in another and a better world.

Licinius was very lonely, and at a time of life when, perhaps, loneliness is most oppressive to the mind. Youth has so much to anticipate, is so full of hope, is so sanguine, so daring, that its own dreams are sufficient for its sustenance; but in middle age, men have already found out that the mirage is but sand and sunshine after all; they look forward, indeed, still, yet only from habit, and because the excitement that was once such intoxicating rapture, is now but a necessary stimulant. If they have no ties of family, no affections to take them out of themselves, they become pompous triflers, or despondent recluses, according as their temperaments lead them to inordinate self-importance or excessive humility. [pg 206]Not so when the quiver is full, and the hearth is merry with the patter of little feet, and the ring of childish laughter. There is a charm to dispel all the evil, and call up all the good, even of the worst man's nature, in the soft white brow, pure from the stamp of sin and care, in the bold bright eyes that look up so trustingly to his own. There is a sense of protection and responsibility, that few natures are so depraved as to repudiate, in the household relationship which acknowledges and obeys the father as its head; and there is no man so callous or so reckless, but he would wish to appear nobler and better than he is in the eyes of his child. Licinius had none of these incentives to virtue; but the lofty nature and the loving heart that could worship a memory, and feel that it was a reality still, had kept him pure from vice. He had never of late attached himself much to anything, till Esca became an inmate of his household; but since he had been in habits of daily intercourse with the Briton, a feeling of content and well-being, he would have found it difficult to analyse, had gradually crept over him. Perhaps he would have remained unconscious of his slave's influence, had it not been for the blank occasioned by his departure. He missed him sadly now, and wondered why, at every moment of the day, he found himself thinking of the pleasant familiar face and frank cordial smile.

So much alone, he had acquired grave habits of reflection, even of that self-examination which is so beneficial an exercise when impartially performed, but which men so rarely practise without a self-deception that obviates all its good effects. This evening he was in a more thoughtful mood than common; this evening, more than ever, it seemed to him that his was an aimless, fruitless life; that he had let the material pleasures of existence slip through his fingers, and taken nothing in exchange. Of what availed his toils, his enterprise, his love of country, his self-denial, his endurance of hardship and privation? What was he the better now, that he had marched, and watched, and bled, and preserved whole colonies for the empire; and sat glorious, crowned with laurels in the triumphal car? He looked round on his stately walls, and the trophies that adorned them, thinking the while that even such a home as this might be purchased too dear at the expense of a lifetime. Gold and marble, corridors and columns, ivory couches and Tyrian carpets, were these equivalents for youth's toil and manhood's care, and at last a desolate old age? What was this ambition that led men so irresistibly up the steepest paths, by the brink of such fatal precipices? [pg 207]Had he ever experienced its temptations? He scarcely knew; he could not realise them now. Had Guenebra lived, indeed, and had she been his own, he might have prized honour and renown, and a name that was on all men's lips, for her dear sake. To see the kind eyes brighten; to call up a smile into the beloved face, that would surely have been reward enough, and that would never be. Then he fell to thinking of the bright days when they were all in all to each other, when the very sky seemed fairer, while he watched for her white dress under the oak-tree. Was he not perfectly happy then? Would he not at least have been perfectly happy could he have called her, as he hoped to do, his own? Honesty answered, No. At the very best there was a vague longing, a something wanting, a sense of insufficiency, of insecurity, and even discontent. If it was so then, how had it been since? Passing over the sharp sudden stroke, so numbing his senses at the time that a long interval had to elapse ere he awoke to its full agony—passing over the subsequent days of yearning, and nights of vain regret, the desolation that laid waste a heart which would bear fruit no more, he reviewed the long years in which he had striven to make duty and the love of country fill the void, and was forced to confess that here, too, all was barren. There was a something ever wanting, even to complete the dull torpor of that resignation which philosophy inculcated, and common sense enjoined. What was it? Licinius could not answer his own question, though he felt that it must have some solution, at which man's destiny intended him to arrive.

All the Roman knew, all he could realise, was that the spring was gone long ago, with her buds of promise, and her laughing morning skies; that the glory of summer had passed away, with its lustrous beauty and its burnished plains, and its deep dark foliage quivering in the heat; that the blast of autumn had strewn the cold earth now with faded flowers and withered leaves, and all the wreck of all the hopes that blossomed so tenderly, and bloomed so bright and fair. The heaven was cold and grey, and between him and heaven the bare branches waved and nodded, mocking, pointing with spectral fingers to the dull cheerless sky. Could he but have believed, could he but have vaguely imaged to himself that there would come another spring; that belief, that vague imagining, had been to Licinius the one inestimable treasure for which he would have bartered all else in the world.

In vain he sought, and looked about him for something [pg 208]on which to lean; for something out of, and superior to himself, inspiring him with that sense of being protected, for which humanity feels so keen, yet so indefinite, a desire. What is the bravest and wisest of mankind, but a child in the dark, groping for the parental hand that shall guide its uncertain steps? Where was he to find the ideal that he could honestly worship, on the superiority of which he could heartily depend? The mythology of Rome, degraded as it had become, was not yet stripped of all the graceful attributes it owed to its Hellenic origin. That which was Greek, might indeed be evil, yet it could scarce fail to be fair; but what rational man could ground his faith on the theocracy of Olympus, or contemplate with any feeling save disgust that material Pantheism, in which the lowest even of human vices was exalted into a divinity? As well become a worshipper of Isis at once, and prostitute, to the utter degradation of the body, all the noblest and fairest imagery of the mind. No, the deities that Homer sang were fit subjects for the march of those Greek hexameters, sonorous and majestic as the roll of the Ægean sea; fit types of sensuous perfection, to be wrought by the Greek chisel, from out the veined blocks of smooth, white Parian stone; but for man, intellectual man, to bow down before the crafty Hermes, or the thick-witted god of forges, or the ambrosial front of father Jove himself, the least ideal of all, was a simple absurdity, that could scarce impose upon a woman or a child.

Licinius had served in the East, and he bethought him now of a nation against whom he had stood in arms, brave fierce soldiers, men instinct with public virtue and patriotism; whose rites, different from those of all other races, were observed with scrupulous fidelity and self-denial. This people, he had heard, worshipped a God of whom there was no material type, whose being was omnipresent and spiritual, on whom they implicitly depended when all else failed, and trusting in whom they never feared to die. But they admitted none to partake with them in their advantages, and their faith seemed to inculcate hatred of the stranger no less than dissensions and strife amongst themselves.

"Is there nothing, alas! but duty, stern cold duty, to fill this void?" thought Licinius. "Be it so, then; my sword shall be once more at the service of my country, and I will die in my harness like a Roman and a soldier at the last!"

CHAPTER VII

"HABET!"

Hippias, the fencing-master, had completed his preparations for the night. With a certain military instinct, as necessary to his profession as to that of the legitimate soldier, he could rely upon his own dispositions, when they were once made, with perfect confidence, and a total absence of anxiety for the result. Like all men habituated to constant strife, he was never so completely in his element as when surrounded by perils, only to be warded off by cool, vigilant courage; and though he may have had moments in which he longed for the softer joys of affection and repose, it needed but the clang of a buckler, or the gleam of a sword, to rouse him into his fiercer self once more.

It had been his habit to attend Valeria, for the purpose of instructing her in swordsmanship, by an hour's practice on certain appointed days. Everything connected with the amphitheatre possessed at this period such a morbid fascination for all classes of the Roman people, that even ladies of rank esteemed it a desirable accomplishment to understand the use of the sword; and it is said that on more than one occasion women of noble birth had been known to take part in the deadly games themselves. These, however, were rare instances of such complete defiance of all modesty and even natural feeling; but to thrust, and shout, and stamp, in the conflict of mimic warfare, was simply esteemed the regular exercise and the healthy excitement of every patrician dame who aspired to a fashionable reputation. Such sudorifics, accompanied by excessive use of the bath and a free indulgence in slaking the thirst, arising from so severe a course of treatment, must have been highly detrimental to female beauty; but even this consideration was postponed to the absorbing claims of fashion, and then, as now, a woman was content and pleased to disfigure herself by any process, however painful and inconvenient, providing other women did the same.

[pg 210]

It is possible, too, that the manly symmetry of form, the tough thews and sinews of their instructors, were not without effect on pupils, whose hearts softened in proportion as their muscles became hard, and whose whole habits and education tended to interest them in the person and profession of the gladiator. Be this as it may, the fencing-masters of Rome had but little time left on their hands, and, of these, Hippias was doubtless the most sought after by the fair. It was his custom to neglect nothing, however trifling, connected with his calling. No details were too small to be attended to by one whose daily profession taught him that life and victory might depend on the mere quiver of an eyelid, the accidental slip of a buckle; and, besides, he took a strange pride in his deadly trade, and especially in the methodical regularity with which he carried it out. Though bound to-night for the desperate enterprise which should make or mar him; though confident that, in either event, he would to-morrow be far beyond the necessities of a gladiator, it was part of his character to play out his part thoroughly to-day. Valeria would expect him, as usual, before the bathing-hour on the following morning. It was but decent he should leave a message at her house that he might be detained. The very wording of his excuse brought to his mind the possibilities of the next few hours—the many chances of failure in the enterprise, failure which, to him at least, the leader of desperate men, was synonymous with certain death.

To-day, for the first time, as he turned his steps towards her mansion, a soft, half-sorrowful, yet not unpleasing sensation stole into his heart as the image of its mistress rose before him in all the pride of her stately beauty. He had often admired the regularity of her haughty features—had scanned, in his own critical way, with unqualified approval the lines of her noble figure, and the symmetry of her firm, well-turned limbs; had even longed to touch that wealth of silken hair when it shook loose in her exertions, and yet—a strange sensation for such a man—had flinched and felt oppressed when, placing her once in a position of defence, a tress of it had fallen across his hand. Now, it seemed to him that he would give much to live those few moments over again; that he would like to see her once more, if, indeed, as was probable, it would be for the last time; that there was no other woman to be compared with her in Rome; and that, with all her glowing beauty and all her physical attractions, her pride was her greatest charm.

He was a desperate man, about to play a desperate [pg 211]game for life. Such thoughts in such a heart and at such a time quicken with fearful rapidity into evil. Admiration, untempered by the holier leavening of that affection which can only exist in the breast that has kept itself pure, soon grows to cruelty and selfishness. The love of beauty, poisoned by the love of strife, seethes into a fierce passionate longing, less that of the lover for his mistress than of the tiger for its prey. Valeria was a proud woman, the proudest and the fairest in Rome. He drew his breath hard as he thought what a wild triumph it would be to bend that stately neck, and humble that pride to his very feet. Methodical and soldierlike, he had seen to everything with his own eyes. The plot was laid, the conspirators were armed and instructed, there was yet an hour or two to spare before the appointed gathering at the tribune's house, and that time he resolved should be devoted to Valeria; at least, he would feast his eyes once more on that glorious beauty, of which he now seemed to acknowledge the full power. He would see her, would bid her farewell. She had always welcomed him cordially and kindly; perhaps she would be sorry to lose him altogether. He smiled a very evil smile, though his heart beat faster than it had done since he was a boy, as he halted under the statue of Hermes in her porch.

And Valeria was sitting in her chamber, with her head buried in her hands, and her long brown hair sweeping like a mantle to her feet. All the feelings that could most goad and madden a woman were tearing at her heart. She dared not—for the sake of tottering reason she dared not—think of the tribune's white face and dropping jaw, and limbs strewed helpless on the couch. She suffered the vision, indeed, to weigh upon her like some oppressive nightmare; but she abstained, with an effort of which she was yet fully conscious, from analysing its meaning or recalling its details, above all, from considering its origin and its effect. No! the image of Esca still filled her brain and her heart. Esca in the amphitheatre; Esca chained and sleeping on the hard hot pavement; Esca walking by her side through the shady streets; and Esca turning away with his noble figure and his manly step, exulting in the liberty that set him free from *her*!

Then came a rush of those softer feelings, that were required to render her torture unbearable: the sting of what might have been; the picture of herself (she could see herself in her mind's eye—beautiful and fascinating, in all the advantages of dress and jewels) leaning on that strong [pg 212]arm, and the kind brave face looking down into hers with the protective air that became it so well. To give him all; to tell him all she had risked, all she had done for his sake, and to hear his loving accents in reply! She almost fancied in her dream that this had actually come to pass, so vividly did her heart imagine to itself its dearest longings. Then she saw another figure in the place that ought to be her own—another face into which he was looking as he had never looked in hers. It was the dark-eyed girl's! The dark-eyed girl, who had been her rival throughout! Would she have done as much for him with her pale face and her frightened, shrinking ways? And now, ere this, he had reached her home, was whispering in her ear, with his arm round her waist. Perhaps he was boasting of the conquest he had made over the haughty Roman lady, and telling her that he had scorned Valeria for her dear sake. Then all that was evil in her nature gained the ascendant, and with the bitter recklessness that has ruined so many an undisciplined heart, she said to herself—"There is no reality but evil. Life is an illusion, and hope a lie. It matters little what becomes of me now!"

When Myrrhina entered she found her lady busied in rearranging the folds of her robe and her disordered tresses. It was no part of Valeria's character to show by her outward bearing what was passing in her mind, and least of all would she have permitted her attendant to guess at the humiliation she had undergone. The waiting-maid, indeed, was a little puzzled; but she had gained so much knowledge, both by observation and experience, of the strange effects produced by over-excitement on her sex, that she never suffered herself to be surprised at a feminine vagary of any description. Now, though she wondered why Esca was gone, and why her mistress was so reserved and haughty, she refrained discreetly from question or remark, contenting herself with a silent offer of her services, and arranging the brown hair into a plaited coronet on Valeria's brows, without betraying by her manner that she was conscious anything unusual had taken place.

After a few moments' silence, her mistress's voice was sufficiently steadied for her to speak.

"I did not send for you," said she. "What do you want here?"

Myrrhina's hands were busied with the long silken tresses, and she held a comb between her teeth. Nevertheless, she answered volubly.

[pg 213]

"I would not have disturbed you, madam, this warm, sultry evening—and I rebuked the porter soundly for letting him in; only as he said, to be sure, he never was denied before, and I thought, perhaps, you would not be displeased to see him, if it was only for a few minutes, and he seemed so anxious and hurried—and, indeed, he never has much time to spare, so I bade him wait in the inner hall while I came to let you know."

Hoping even against hope! She knew it was impossible, yet her heart leapt as she thought—"Oh! if it were only Esca who had turned back!"

"I will see him," said she quietly, prolonging the illusion by purposely avoiding to ask who this untimely visitor might be.

In another minute Hippias stood before her—Hippias, the fencing-master, a man in whose dangerous career she had always taken a vague interest; whose personal prowess she admired, and whose reputation, such as it was, possessed for her a wild fascination of its own. He was reckless, too, from the very nature of his profession; and she, in her present mood, more reckless, more desperate than any gladiator of them all. It would have done her good to stand, with naked steel, against some fierce wild beast or deadly foe. There was nothing, she felt, that she could not dare to-day. Nerve and brain wound up to the highest pitch of excitement—heart and feelings crushed, and wounded, and sore. When the reaction came, it would necessarily be fatal; when the tide ebbed, it would leave a wearied, helpless sufferer on the shore.

Such was the frame of mind in which Valeria received the gladiator; outwardly impassive—for her colour did not even deepen, nor her breath come quicker at his unexpected appearance—inwardly vexed by a conflict of tumultuous feelings, and longing for any change—any anodyne that could deaden or alleviate her pain. How could she but respond to his manly, respectful farewell? How could she but listen to the few burning words in which he spoke of long-suppressed and hopeless adoration, or pretend not to be interested in the desperate enterprise which he hinted might prevent his ever looking on her fair face again. He soothed her self-love; he roused her curiosity; he set her pride on its broken pedestal again, and propped it with a strong, yet gentle hand; and so the two thunder-clouds drew nearer still and nearer, ere they met, to be destroyed and riven by the lightning their own contact had engendered.

[pg 214]

CHAPTER VIII

TOO LATE!

Esca, treading on air, hastened from Valeria's house with the common selfishness of love, ignoring all the pain and disappointment he had left behind him. The young blood coursed merrily through his veins, and, in spite of his anxiety, he exulted in the sense of being at liberty once more. He was alive, doubtless, to the generosity and devotion of the woman who had set him free, nor was he so blind as to be unaware of the affection that had driven her to such desperate measures for his sake; and in the first glow of a gratitude, that had in it no vestige of tenderer feelings, he had resolved, when his mission was accomplished and Mariamne placed in safety, he would return and throw himself at the Roman lady's feet once more. But the farther he left her stately porch behind, the weaker became this generous resolution, and ere long he had little difficulty in persuading himself that his first duty was to the Jewess, and that in his future actions he must be guided by circumstances, or, in other words, follow the bent of his own inclinations. Meanwhile, in spite of his wounded foot, he sped on towards the Tiber as fast as, in years gone by, he had followed the lean wolf, or the foam-flecked boar, over the green hills of Britain. The sun had not been down an hour when he entered the well-known street that was now enchanted ground; yet, while he looked up into the darkening sky, his heart turned sick within him at the thought that he might be too late, after all.

The garden-door was open, as she must have left it. She was not, therefore, in the house. He might find her at the riverside, and have the happiness of a few minutes alone with her, ere he brought her back and placed her, for the second time, in safety within her father's walls. The more prudent course, he confessed to himself at the time, would have been to alarm Eleazar, and put him on the defensive at once; but he had been so long without seeing Mariamne, the peril in which she was placed had so endeared her to him, [pg 215]and his own near approach to death had stamped her image so vividly on his heart, that he could not resist the temptation of seeking her at the water-side, and telling her, unwatched by other ears or eyes, all he had felt and endured since they last parted, and how, for both their sakes, they must never part again.

Full of such thoughts, he ran down to the water's edge, and sought the broken column where she was accustomed to descend and fill her pitcher from the stream. In vain his eager eye watched for the dark-clad figure and the dear pale face. Once in the deepening twilight his heart leapt as he thought he saw her crouching low beneath the bank, and sank again to find he had been deceived by a fallen slab of stone. Then he turned for one more searching look ere he departed, and his glance rested on a pitcher, broken into a dozen fragments, at his feet. He did not know that it was Mariamne's. How should he, when a thousand pitchers carried by a thousand women to the Tiber every evening were precisely alike? Yet his blood ran cold through his veins and his fears hurried him back, almost insensibly, to Eleazar's door, which he burst open without going through the ceremony of knocking.

Her father and his brother were in the house. The former leapt to his feet and snatched a javelin from the wall ere he recognised his visitor. The latter, less prone to do battle at a moment's notice, laid his hand on Eleazar's arm, and calmly said—

"It is the friend who is always welcome, and whom we have expected day by day in vain."

Everything looked so much as usual that for a moment Esca felt almost reassured. It was possible Mariamne might be even now busied with household affairs, safe in the inner chamber. A lover's bashfulness brought the blood to his cheeks, as he reflected if it were so it would be difficult to account for his unceremonious entrance; but the recollection of her danger soon stifled all such trivial considerations, and he confronted her father impetuously, and asked him, almost in a threatening tone—

"Where is Mariamne?"

Eleazar looked first simply astonished, then somewhat offended. He answered, however, with more command of temper than was his wont.

"My daughter has but now left the house with her pitcher. She will be home again almost immediately; but what is this to thee?"

[pg 216]

"What is it to me?" repeated Esca in a voice of thunder, catching hold of his questioner's arm at the same time with an iron grasp for which the fierce old Jew liked him none the worse—"What is it to thee, to him, to all of us? I tell thee, old man, whilst we are drivelling here, they are bearing her off into captivity ten thousand times worse than death! I heard the plot—I heard it with my own ears, lying chained like a dog on the hard stones. The wicked tribune was to make her his own this very night, and though he has met his reward, the villains that do his bidding have got her in their power ere this. The pure—the loved—the beautiful—Mariamne—Mariamne!"

He hid his face in his hands, and his strong frame shook with agony from head to heel.

It was the turn of Calchas now to start to his feet, and look about him as if in search of a weapon. His first impulse was resistance to oppression, even by the strong hand. With Eleazar, on the contrary, the instincts of the soldier predominated, and the very magnitude of the emergency seemed to endow him with preternatural coolness and composure. He knit his thick brows indeed, and there was a smothered glare in his eye that boded no good to an enemy when the time for an outbreak should arrive, but his voice was low and distinct, as in a few sharp eager questions he gathered the outline of the plot that was to rob him of his daughter. Then he thought for a few seconds ere he spoke.

"The men that were to take her? What were they like? I would fain know them if I came across them."

His white teeth gleamed like a wild beast's with a smile ominous of his intentions on their behalf.

"Damasippus and Oarses," replied the Briton. "The former stout, sleek, heavy, and beetle-browed. The latter pale, dark, and thin. An Egyptian with an Egyptian's false face, and more than an Egyptian's cruelty and cunning."

"Where live they?" asked the Jew, buckling at the same time a formidable two-edged sword to his side.

"In the Flaminian Way," replied the other. "High up in some garret where we should never find them. But they will not take her there. She is by this time at the other end of the city in the tribune's house." And again he groaned in anguish of spirit at the thought.

"And that house?" asked Eleazar, still busied with his warlike preparations. "How is it defended? I know its outside well, and an easy entrance from the wall to the [pg 217]inner court; but what resistance shall we encounter within? what force can the tribune's people raise at a moment's outcry?"

"Alas!" answered Esca. "To-night of all nights, the house of Placidus is garrisoned like a fortress. A chosen band of gladiators are to sup with the tribune, and afterwards to take possession of the palace and drag Cæsar from the throne. When they find the banquet prepared for them, I know them too well to think they will separate without partaking of it, even though their host be lying dead on the festal couch. She will become the prey of men like Hippias, Lutorius, and Euchenor. But if we cannot rescue her, at least we may die in the attempt."

Even in his anxiety for his daughter, such news as this could not but startle the emissary of the Jewish nation. In an instant's time he had run over its importance, as it regarded his own mission and the probable influence on the destinies of his country. Should the conspiracy succeed,

Vitellius might already be numbered with the dead, and instead of that easy self-indulgent glutton, over whom he had already obtained considerable influence, he would have to do with the bold, sagacious, far-seeing general, the remorseless enemy of his nation, whom neither he nor any of his countrymen had ever succeeded in deceiving by stratagem or worsting by force of arms. When the purple descended on Vespasian the doom of Jerusalem was sealed. Nevertheless, Eleazar concentrated his mind on the present emergency. In a few words he laid out his plan for the rescue of his daughter.

"The freedmen's garret must be our first point of attack," said he. "The tribune would scarce have ordered them to bring their prize to his house to-night, where there would be so many to dispute it with him, and where dissension would be fatal to his great enterprise. Calchas and I will proceed immediately to the dwelling of this Damasippus and his fellow-villain. Your directions will enable us to find it. You, Esca, speed off at once to the tribune's house. You will soon learn whether she has been brought there. If so, come to us without delay in the Flaminian Way. I am not entirely without friends even here, and I will call on two or three of my people to help as I go along. Young man, you are bold and true. We will have her out of the tribune's house if we pull the walls down with our naked hands; and let me but come within reach of the villains who take shelter there"—here his face darkened and his frame quivered in a [pg 218]paroxysm of suppressed fury—"may my father's tomb be dishonoured, and the name of my mother defiled, if I dip not my hands to the very elbows in their hearts' blood!"

To be told he was brave and true by her father added fuel to Esca's enthusiasm. It was indeed much for Eleazar to confess on behalf of a stranger and a heathen, but the fierce old warrior's heart warmed to a kindred nature that seemed incapable of selfish fear, and he approved hugely, moreover, of the implicit attention with which the Briton listened to his directions, and his readiness for instantaneous action, however desperate. Calchas, too, clasped the young man warmly by the hand.

"We are but three," said he, "three against a host. Yet I have no fear. I trust in One who never failed His servants yet. One to whom emperors and legions are as a handful of dust before the wind, or a few dried thorns on the beacon-fire. And so do you, my son, so do you, though you know it not. But the time shall come when His very benefits shall compel you to confess your Master, and when in sheer gratitude you shall enrol yourself amongst those who serve Him faithfully even unto death."

Many a time during that eventful and anxious night had Esca occasion to remember the old man's solemn words. Its horrors, its catastrophes, its alternations of hope and fear, might have driven one mad, who had nothing to depend upon but his own unaided strength and resolution. Few great actions have been performed, few tasks exacting the noble heroism of endurance fulfilled successfully, without extraneous aid, without the help of some leading principle out of, and superior to, the man. Honour, patriotism, love, loyalty, all have supported their votaries through superhuman exertions and difficulties that seemed insurmountable, teaching them to despise dangers and hardships with a courage sterner than mortals are expected to possess; but none of these can impart that confidence which is born of faith in the believer's breast;—that confidence which enables him to take good and evil with an equal mind, to look back on the past without a sigh, forward on the future without a fear; and though the present may be all a turmoil of peril, uncertainty, and confusion, to stand calmly in the midst, doing the best he can with a stout heart and an unruffled brow, while he leaves the result fearlessly and trustfully in the hand of God.

Eleazar and Calchas were already equipped for the pursuit. The one armed to the teeth, and looking indeed a formidable enemy; the other mild and hopeful as usual, [pg 219]venerable with his white hair and beard, and carrying but a simple staff for his weapon. In grave silence, but with a grasp of the hand more emphatic than any spoken words, the three parted on their search; Esca threading his way at once through the narrow and devious streets that led towards the tribune's house—that house which he had left so gladly but a few short hours ago when, rescued by Valeria, he bade her farewell, exulting in the liberty that enabled him to seek Mariamne's side once more. He soon reached the hated dwelling. All there seemed quiet as the grave. From other quarters of the city indeed there came, now and again, the roar of distant voices which rose and fell at intervals as the tide of tumult ebbed and flowed, but, preoccupied as he was, Esca took little heed of these ominous sounds, for they bore him no intelligence of Mariamne. All was silent in the porch, all was silent in the vestibule and outer hall, but as he ventured across its marble pavement, he heard the bustle of preparation, and the din of flagons within.

It was at the risk of liberty and life, that he crept noiselessly forward, and peeped into the banqueting-hall, which was already partially lighted up for the feast. Shrinking behind a column, he observed the slaves, many of whom he knew well by sight, laying covers, burnishing vases, and otherwise making ready for a sumptuous entertainment. He listened for a few moments, hoping to gather from their conversation some news of the Jewess and her captors. All at once he started and trembled violently. Bold as he was, in common with his northern countrymen a vein of superstition ran through his nature, and though he feared nothing tangible or corporeal, he held in considerable dread all that touched upon the confines of the spiritual and the unknown. There within ten paces of him, ghastly pale, with dark circles round his eyes, and clad in white, stood the figure of the tribune, pointing, as it seemed to him, with shadowy hand at the different couches, and giving directions in a low sepulchral voice for the order of the banquet.

"Not yet!" he heard the apparition exclaim in tones of languid, fretful impatience. "Not come yet! the idle loiterers! Well, she must preside there at the supper-table and take her place at once as mistress here. Ho! slaves! bring more flowers! Fill the tall golden cup with Falernian and set it next to mine!"

Well did Esca know to whom these directions must refer. Though his blood had been chilled for an instant by this reappearance, as he believed it, of his enemy from the grave, [pg 220]he soon collected his scattered energies and summoned his courage back, with the hateful conviction that, alive or dead, the tribune was resolved to possess himself of Mariamne. And this he vowed to prevent, ay, though he should slay his dark-eyed love with his own hand.

It was obvious now that Damasippus and Oarses would bring the captive straight to their patron's house, that Eleazar and Calchas had gone upon a fool's errand to the freedmen's garret in the Flaminian Way. What would he have given to be cheered by the wise counsels of the one, and backed by the strong arm of the other! Would there be time for him to slip from here unobserved, and to summon them to his aid? Three desperate men might cut their way through all the slaves that Placidus could muster, and if they had any chance of success at all it must be before the arrival of the gladiators. But then she was obviously expected every minute. She might arrive—horrible thought!—while he was gone for help, and once in the tribune's power it would be too late. In his despair the words of Calchas recurred forcibly to his mind. "We are but three," said the old man, "three against a host, yet I have no fear." And Esca resolved that though he was but one, he too would have no fear, but would trust implicitly in the award of eternal justice, which would surely interfere to prevent this unholy sacrifice.

Feeling that his sword was loose in its sheath and ready to his hand, holding his breath, and nerving himself for the desperate effort he might be called upon at any moment to make, the Briton stole softly back through the vestibule, and concealed himself behind a marble group in the darkest corner of the porch. Here, with the dogged courage of his race, he made up his mind that he would await the arrival of Mariamne, and rescue her at all hazards, against any odds, or die with her in the attempt.

CHAPTER IX

THE LURE

Like other great cities, the poorer quarters of Rome were densely crowded. The patricians, and indeed all the wealthier class, affected rural tastes even in the midst of the capital, and much space was devoted to the gardens and pleasure-grounds which surrounded their dwellings. The humbler inhabitants were consequently driven to herd together in great numbers, with little regard to health or convenience, and the streets leading to and adjoining the Tiber were perhaps the most thickly populated of all. That in which Eleazar's house stood, was seldom empty of passengers at any hour of the twenty-four, and least of all about sunset when the women thronged out of their dwellings to draw water for the household consumption of the following day. Oarses was well aware of this, and therefore it was that the cunning Egyptian had protested against an abduction of the Jewish maiden by open force from her father's door.

"Leave it to me," said this finished villain, in discussing their infamous project with his patron. "I know a lure to wile such birds as these off the bough into my open hand. Stratagem first, force afterwards. There is no need to waken the tongues of all the women in the quarter. It was the cackling of a goose, my patron, that foiled the attack on the Capitol."

'she was accosted by a dark sallow old woman'

Mariamne, anxious and sad, was carrying her pitcher listlessly down to the Tiber and letting her thoughts wander far from her occupation, into a few sweet memories, and a thousand dreary apprehensions, when she was accosted by a dark sallow old woman, whose speech and manners, as well as her dress, betrayed an Eastern origin. The stranger [pg 222]asked some trifling questions about her way, and prayed for a draught of cold water when the pitcher should be filled. Mariamne, whose heart unconsciously warmed to the homely Syriac, entered freely into conversation with one of her own sex, and whose language denoted, moreover, that she was familiar with her nation. Willingly she drew her a measure from the stream, which the other quaffed with the moderation of one whose thirst is habitually quenched with wine rather than water.

"It is somewhat muddy, I fear," said the girl kindly, reverting in her own mind to the sparkling fountains of her native land, and yet acknowledging how she loved this turbid stream better than them all. "If you will come back with me to my father's house I can offer you a draught of wine and a morsel of bread to cheer you on your way."

The other, though with no great avidity, took a second pull at the pitcher.

"Nay," said she, "my daughter, I will not tax your hospitality so far. Nor have I need. There is lore enough left under these faded locks of mine, to turn the foulest cesspool in Rome as clear as crystal. Ay, to change this tasteless draught to wine of Lebanon, and the pitcher that contains it to a vase of gold."

Mariamne shrank from her with a gesture of dismay. Believing implicitly in their power, her religion forbade her to hold any intercourse with those who professed the black art. The other marked her repugnance.

"My child," she continued, in soothing tones, "be not afraid of the old woman's secret gifts. Mine is but a harmless knowledge, gained by study of the ancient Chaldæan scrolls, such as your own wise king possessed of old. It is but white magic, such as your high-priest himself would not scruple to employ. Fear not, I say—I, who have pored over those mystic characters till mine eyes grew dim, can read your sweet pale face as plain as the brazen tablets in the Forum, and I can see in it sorrow, and care, and anxiety for him you love."

Mariamne started. It was true enough, but how could the wise woman have found it out? The girl looked wistfully at her companion, and the latter, satisfied she was on the right track, proceeded to answer that questioning glance.

"Yes," she said, "you think he is in danger or in grief. You wonder why you do not see him oftener. Sometimes you fear he may be false. What would you not give, my poor child, to look on the golden locks, and the white brow, [pg 223]now, at this very moment? And I can show them to you if you will. The old woman is not ungrateful even for a draught of the Tiber's muddy stream."

The blood mounted to Mariamne's brow, but the light kindled at the same time in her eyes, and the soft gleam swept over her face that comes into every human countenance when the heart vibrates with an allusion to its treasure as though the silver cord thrilled to the touch of an angel's wing. It was no clumsy guess of the wise woman, to infer that this dark-eyed damsel cherished some fair-haired lover.

"What mean you?" asked the girl eagerly. "How can you show him to me? What do you know of him? Is he safe? Is he happy?"

The wise woman smiled. Here was a bird flying blindfold into the net. Take her by her affections, and there would be little difficulty in the capture.

"He is in danger," she replied. "But you could save him if you only knew how. He might be happy too, if he would. But with another!"

To do Mariamne justice she heard only the first sentence.

"In danger!" she repeated, "and I could save him! Oh, tell me where he is, and what I can do for his sake!"

The wise woman pulled a small mirror from her bosom.

"I cannot tell you," she answered, "but I can show him to you in this. Only not here, where the shadow of a passer-by might destroy the charm. Let us turn aside to that vacant space by the broken column, and you shall look without interruption on the face you love."

It was but a short way off, though the ruins which surrounded it made the place lonely and secluded; had it been twice the distance, however, Mariamne would have accompanied her new acquaintance without hesitation in her eagerness for tidings of Esca's fate. As she neared the broken column, so endeared to her by associations, she could not repress a faint sigh, which was not lost on her companion.

"It was here you met him before," whispered the wise woman. "It is here you shall see his face again."

This was scarcely a random shaft, for it required little penetration to discover that Mariamne had some tender associations connected with a spot thus adapted for the meeting of a pair of lovers; nevertheless the apparent familiarity with her previous actions was sufficient to convince the Jewess of her companion's supernatural knowledge, and though it roused alarm, it excited curiosity in a still greater degree.

"Take the mirror in your hand," whispered the wise woman, when they had reached the column, casting, at the same time, a searching glance around. "Shut your eyes whilst I speak the charm that calls him, three times over, and then look steadily on its surface till I have counted a hundred."

Mariamne obeyed these directions implicitly. Standing in the vacant space with the mirror in her hand, she shut her eyes and listened intently to the solemn tones of the wise woman chanting in a low monotonous voice some unintelligible stanzas, while from the deep shadow behind the broken column, there stole out the portly figure of Damasippus, and, at the same moment, half a dozen strong well-armed slaves rose from the different hiding-places in which they lay concealed amongst the ruins. Ere the incantation had been twice repeated, Damasippus threw a shawl over the girl's head, muffling her so completely, while he caught her in his strong arms, that an outcry was impossible. The others snatched her up ere she could make a movement, and bore her swiftly off to a chariot with four white horses waiting in the next street, whilst the wise woman, following at a rapid pace, and disencumbering herself of her female attire as she sped along, disclosed the cunning features and the thin wiry form of Oarses the Egyptian. Coming up with Damasippus, who was panting behind the slaves and their burden, he laughed a low noiseless laugh.

"My plan was the best," said he, "after all. What fools these women are, O my friend! Is there any other creature that can be taken with a bait so simple? Three inches of mirror and the ghost of an absent face!"

But Damasippus had not breath to reply. Hurrying onward, he was chiefly anxious to dispose of his prize in the chariot without interruption; and when he reached it he mounted by her side, and bidding Oarses and the slaves follow as near as was practicable, he drove off at great speed in the direction of the tribune's house.

But this was an eventful night in Rome, and although for that reason well adapted to a deed of violence, its tumult and confusion exacted great caution from those who wished to proceed without interruption along the streets. The shouts that had disturbed the two freedmen in their garret whilst preparing the enterprise they had since so successfully carried out, gave no false warning of the coming storm. That storm had burst, and was now raging in its fury throughout a wide portion of the city. Like all such outbreaks it gathered [pg 225]force and violence in many quarters at once, and from many sources unconnected with its original cause.

Rome was the theatre that night of a furious civil war, consequent on the intrigues of various parties which had now grown to a head. The old Prætorian guard had been broken up by Vitellius, and dismissed without any of the honours and gratuities to which they considered themselves entitled, in order to make way for another body of troops on whose fidelity the Emperor believed he could rely, and who were now called, in contradistinction to their predecessors, the New Prætorians. Two such conflicting interests carried in them the elements of the direst hatred and strife. The original body-guard hoping to be restored by Vespasian, should he attain the purple, had everything to gain by a change of dynasty, and were easily won over by the partisans of that successful general to any enterprise, however desperate, which would place him on the throne. Trusting to this powerful aid, these partisans, of whom Julius Placidus, the tribune, though he had wormed himself into the confidence of Vitellius, was one of the most active and unscrupulous, were ready enough to raise the standard of revolt and had no fear for the result. The train was laid, and to-night it had been decided that the match should be applied. In regular order of battle, in three ranks with spears advanced and eagles in the centre, the Old Prætorians marched at sundown to attack the camp of their successors. It was a bloody and obstinate contest. The new body-guard, proud of their promotion, and loyal to the hand that had bought them, defended themselves to the death. Again and again was the camp almost carried. Again and again were the assailants obstinately repulsed. It was only when slain, man by man, falling in their ranks as they stood, with all their wounds *in front*, that a victory was obtained—a victory which so crippled the conquerors as to render them but inefficient auxiliaries in the other conflicts of that eventful night. But this was only one of the many pitched battles, so to speak, of which Rome was the unhappy theatre. The Capitol after an obstinate defence had been taken by the partisans of the present Emperor and burned to the ground.

This stronghold having been previously seized and occupied by Sabinus, who declared himself Governor of Rome in the name of Vespasian, and who even received in state several of the principal nobility and a deputation from the harassed and vacillating senate, had been alternately the object of attack and defence to either party. Its possession [pg 226]seemed to confer a spurious sovereignty over the whole city, and it was held as obstinately as it was vigorously and desperately attacked.

An hour or two before sunset, an undisciplined body of soldiers, armed only with their swords, and formidable chiefly from the wild fury with which they seemed inspired, marched through the Forum and ascended the Capitoline Hill. The assailants having no engines of war either for protection or offence, suffered severely from the missiles showered upon them by the besieged, till the thought struck them of throwing flaming torches into the place from the roofs of the houses which surrounded it, and which, erected in time of peace, had been suffered to overtop the Roman citadel. In vain, after the flames had consumed the gate, did they endeavour to force an entrance; for Sabinus, with the unscrupulous resource of a Roman soldier, had blocked the way by a hundred prostrate statues of gods and men, pulled down from the sacred pedestals on which they had stood for ages; but the contiguous houses catching fire, and all the woodwork of the Capitol being old and dry, the flames soon spread, and in a few hours the stronghold of Roman pride and Roman history was levelled with the ground. Callous to the memories around him, forgetful of the Tarquins, and the Scipios, and the many hallowed names that shed their lustre on this monument of his country's greatness, Sabinus lost his presence of mind in proportion as the necessity for preserving it became more urgent. He was no longer able to control his troops, and the latter, panic-stricken with the entrance of their enemies, disbanded, and betook themselves to flight. The majority, including one woman of noble birth, were put ruthlessly to the sword, but a few, resembling their assailants, as they did, in arms, appearance, and language, were fortunate enough to catch the password by which they recognised each other, and so escaped.

In another quarter of the mighty city, a large body of troops who had hoisted the standard of Vespasian, and had already suffered one repulse which rather excited their animosity than quelled their ardour, were advancing in good order, and, according to sound warlike tactics, in three divisions. The gardens of Sallust, laid out by that elegant and intellectual sensualist, with a view to pursuits far removed from strife and bloodshed, were the scene of an obstinate combat, in which, however, one of these columns succeeded in establishing itself within the walls; and now the struggle that had heretofore been carried on in its outskirts, penetrated [pg 227]to the heart of the Roman capital. The citizens beheld war brought into their very homes and hearths—the familiar street slippery with blood—the wounded soldier reeling on the doorsill, where the children were wont to play—the dead man's limbs strewed helpless by the fountain, where the girls assembled with shrill laughing voices on the calm summer evenings,—and worse than all, instead of the kindly grasp of friends and fellow-countrymen, the brother's hand clutching at the brother's throat.

Such horrors, however, did but more demoralise a population already steeped to the very lips in cruelty, vice, and foul iniquity. Trained to bloodshed by the ghastly entertainments of the amphitheatre, the Roman citizen gloated on no spectacle with so keen a pleasure as on the throes of a fellow-creature in the agony of violent death. The populace seemed now to consider the contest waged at their doors as a goodly show got up for their especial amusement. Loud shouts encouraged the combatants as either party swayed and wavered in the mortal press, and *Euge!—Bene!* were cried as loudly for their encouragement, as if they had been paid gladiators, earning their awful livelihood on the sand. Nay, worse, when some wounded soldier dragged himself into a house for safety, instead of succour, he was received with yells of reprobation, and thrust out into the street that he might be despatched by his conquerors according to the merciless regulations of the amphitheatre.

Nor was man the only demon on the scene. Unsexed women with bare bosoms, wild eyes, streaming hair, and white feet stained with blood, flew to and fro amongst the soldiers, stimulating them to fresh atrocities with wine and caresses and odious ribald mirth. It was a festival of Death and Sin. She had wreathed her fair arms around the spectral king, and crowned his fleshless brows with her gaudy garlands, and wrapped him in her mantle of flame, and pressed the blood-red goblet to his lips, maddening him with her shrieks of wild, mocking laughter, the while their mutual feet trampled out the lives and souls of their victims on the stones of Rome.

Through a town in such a state of turmoil and confusion, Damasippus took upon himself to conduct in safety the prize he had succeeded in capturing, not, it must be confessed, without many hearty regrets that he had ever embarked in the undertaking. Devoutly did he now wish that he could shift the whole business on to the shoulders of Oarses; but of late he had been concerned to observe in the patron's manner a certain sense of his own inutility as compared with [pg 228]the astute Egyptian; and if the latter were now permitted to conclude, as he had undoubtedly inaugurated, the adventure, Placidus might be satisfied that there was little use in entertaining two rogues to do the work of one. He knew his patron well enough to be aware of the effect such a conviction would have on his own prospects. The tribune would no more scruple to bid him go starve or hang, than he would to pull out a superfluous hair from his beard. Therefore, at all risks, thought Damasippus, he must be the man to bring Mariamne into his lord's house. It was a difficult and a dangerous task. There was only room for himself and one stout slave besides the charioteer and the prisoner. The latter had struggled violently, and required to be held down by main force, nor in muffling her screams was it easy to observe the happy medium between silence and suffocation. Also, it was indispensable, in the present lawless state of affairs, to avoid observation; and the spectacle of a handsomely gilded chariot with a female figure in it, held down and closely veiled, the whole drawn by four beautiful white horses, was not calculated to traverse the streets of a crowded city without remark. Oarses, indeed, had suggested a litter, but this had been overruled by his comrade on the score of speed, and now the state of the streets made speed impossible. To be sure this enabled the escort to keep up with him, and Damasippus, who was no fighter at heart, derived some comfort from their presence. The darkness, however, which should have favoured him, was dispelled by the numerous conflagrations in various parts of the city; and when the chariot was stopped and forced to turn into a by-street to avoid a crowd rushing towards the blazing Capitol, Damasippus felt his heart sink within him in an access of terror, such as even he had never felt before.

CHAPTER X

FROM SCYLLA TO CHARYBDIS

Up one street, down another, avoiding the main thoroughfares, now rendered impassable by the tumult, his anxious freedmen threaded their way with difficulty in the direction of the tribune's house. Mariamne seemed either to have fainted, or to have resigned herself to her fate, for she had ceased to struggle, and cowered down on the floor of the chariot, silent and motionless. Damasippus trusted his difficulties were nearly over, and resolved never again to be concerned in such an enterprise. Already he imagined himself safe in his patron's porch, claiming the reward of his dexterity, when he was once more arrested by a stoppage which promised a hazardous and protracted delay.

Winding its slow length along, in all the pomp and dignity affected by the maiden order, a procession of Vestals crossed in front of the white horses, and not a man in Rome but would have trembled with superstitious awe at the bare notion of breaking in on the solemn march of these sacred virgins, dedicated to the service of a goddess, whose peculiar attributes were mystery, antiquity, and remorseless vengeance for offence. Dressed in their long white garments, simple and severe, with no relief save a narrow purple border round the veil, they swept on in slow majestic column, like a vision from the other world, led by a stately priestess, pale and calm, of lofty stature and majestic bearing. They believed that to them was confided the welfare of the State, the safety of the city; nay, that with the mysterious symbols in their temple, they guarded the very existence of the nation; therefore on all public occasions of strife or disorder, the Vestal Virgins were accustomed to show themselves confidently in the streets, and use their influence for the restoration of peace. Nor had they need to fear either injury or insult. To touch the person of a Vestal, even to obstruct the litter in which she was carried, was punishable with death, and public opinion in such a case was even more exacting than the law. [pg 230]Immunities and privileges of many kinds were granted to the order by different enactments. When the Vestal went abroad, she was preceded and followed by the lictors of the State; and if she met a criminal under sentence of death, honestly by accident, during her progress, he was pardoned and set free for her sake, on the spot.

It may be that Mariamne had some vague recollection of this custom, for no sooner were the horses stopped to let the procession pass, than she uttered a loud shriek, which brought it to a halt at once, and caused her own guards to gather round the chariot and prepare for resistance, Oarses wisely keeping aloof, and Damasippus, while he strove to wear a bold front, quaking in every limb. At a signal from the superior priestess, the long white line stood still, while her lictors seized the horses, and surrounded the chariot. Already a crowd of curious bystanders was gathering, and the glare of the burning Capitol shed its light even here, on their dark, eager faces, contrasting strangely with the veiled figures that occupied the middle of the street, cold and motionless as marble.

Two lictors seized on Damasippus, each by a shoulder, and brought him unceremoniously to within a few paces of the priestess. Here he dropped upon his knees, and began wringing his hands in ludicrous dismay, whilst the populace, gathering round, laughed and jeered at him, only refraining from violence on account of the Vestal's presence.

"She is a slave, our slave, bought with our own money in the market, sacred virgin. I can swear it. I can prove it. Here is the man who paid for her. O accursed Oarses, hast thou left me in the lurch at last?"

The wily Egyptian now came up, composed and sedate, with the air of a man confident in the justice of his cause. Mariamne, meanwhile, could but strive to release herself in vain. So effectually had she been bound and muffled, that she could scarcely move, and was unable to articulate. She struggled on, nevertheless, in the wild hope of succour, writhing her whole body to set her lips free from the bandages that stifled them. With the quiet dignity which was an especial attribute of her office, the priestess pointed to the chariot containing the prisoner, and from beneath her veil, in clear, low tones, while the bystanders listened with respectful awe, came the question—

"What crime has she committed?"

"No crime, sacred virgin, no crime whatsoever," replied the wily Oarses, well knowing that the privilege of pardon, [pg 231]which the Vestals loved to exercise, was less likely to be exerted for a refractory bondswoman than a condemned criminal. "She is but a runaway slave, a mere dancing-girl. How shall I tell it in your august presence? I bought her scarce a week ago, as my friend here knows, and can swear. Canst thou not, Damasippus, worthy citizen? I gave but two thousand sesterces, nevertheless it was a large sum for me, who am a poor man; and I borrowed the half of it from my friend here. I bought her in the open market, and I took her home with me to my wife and children, that she might beat flax and card wool, and so gain an honest livelihood—an honest livelihood, sacred virgin; and that is why she ran away from me; so I informed the ædile, and I sought her diligently, and to-day I found her with her cheeks painted, and her bosom gilt, in her old haunts, drunk with wine. Then I bound her, and placed her in a litter, and the litter breaking down, for I am poor, sacred virgin, and of humble birth, though a Roman citizen—the litter, I say, breaking down, and my patron's chariot passing by, I placed her within it, that I might take her home, for she is insensible still. All this I swear, and here is my friend who will swear it too. Damasippus, wilt thou not?"

The latter worthy had indeed been accompanying every syllable of his confederate's statement with those eager Italian gestures which signify so much of argument and expostulation. These were not without effect on the bystanders, predisposed as such generally are to believe the worst, and prone to be influenced by the last speaker, especially when supported by testimony, however unworthy of reliance. They crowded in as near as their awe of the priestess would allow, and angry looks were shot at the poor, dark figure lying helpless in the chariot.

Under the Vestal's long white veil, there might have been a gleam of pity or a flash of scorn on the unseen face, according as she felt a kindly sympathy or womanly indignation for the sins of an erring sister. But whatever was her private opinion, with a priestess of her order, such an appeal as that of Oarses could have but one result. The pale slender hand made a gesture of contempt and impatience. The tall ghostly figure moved on with a prouder, sterner step, and the procession swept by, carrying away with it the last fragile hope of succour that had comforted Mariamne's heart. Like a poor hunted hind caught in a net, when the sharp muzzle of the deerhound touches her flank, the Jewess made one convulsive effort that loosened [pg 232]the shawl about her mouth. In her agony, the beloved name flew instinctively to her lips, and hopelessly, unconsciously, she called out, "Esca! Esca!" in loud piercing tones of terror and despair.

The Vestals had indeed passed by, and the chariot was again set in motion, but the Briton's name seemed to act as a talisman on the crowd, for no sooner had she pronounced it, than the bystanders were seen to give way on each side to the pressure of a huge pair of shoulders, surmounted by the fearless, honest face of Hirpinus the gladiator. That professional, in common with a few chosen comrades, had found the last few hours hang exceedingly heavy on his hands. Bound by oath to keep sober, and, what was perhaps even a more galling restriction, to abstain from fighting, this little party had seen themselves deprived at once of their two principal resources, the favourite occupations which gave a zest to their existence. But the saying that there is "Honour among thieves" dates farther back than the institution of an amphitheatre; and as soon as the gladiator had made his bargain, he considered himself, body and soul, the property of his purchaser. So, when Hippias gave his final orders, insisting on the appearance of his myrmidons at a given place and a given time, fresh, sober, and without a scratch, he had no fear but that they would be punctually and honestly obeyed.

Accordingly, Hirpinus, Rufus, Lutorius, and a few of the surest blades in the Family, had been whiling away their leisure with a stroll through the principal streets of Rome, and had met with not a few incidents peculiarly pleasing to men of their profession. They had been good enough to express their approval of the soldierlike manner in which the gardens of Sallust were attacked and carried; they had also marked, with a certain grim satisfaction, the assault on the Capitol, though they complained that when it was fired the thick volumes of smoke that swept downwards from its walls obstructed their view of the fighting, which was to them the chief attraction of the entertainment, and which they criticised with many instructive and professional remarks; it was difficult, doubtless, to abstain from taking part in any of these skirmishes, more particularly as each man was armed with the short, two-edged Roman sword; but, as they reminded one another, it was only a temporary abstinence, and for a very short period, since, from all they could gather, before midnight they might be up to their necks in wine, and over their ankles in blood. [pg 233]Now, supper-time was approaching, and the athletes were getting fierce, hungry, and weary of inaction. They had stood still to watch the procession of Vestals pass by, and even these wild, unscrupulous men had refrained from word or gesture that could be construed into disrespect for the maiden order; but they had shown little interest in the cause of stoppage, and scarce condescended to notice a discussion that arose from so mean a subject as a runaway slave. Suddenly, however, to the amazement of his comrades and the discomfiture of the bystanders, Hirpinus burst hastily through the crowd, unceremoniously thrusting aside those who stood in his way, and lifting one inquisitive little barber clean off his legs, to hurl him like a plaything into a knot of chattering citizens, much to their indignation and the poor man's own physical detriment. Hands were clenched, indeed, and brows bent, as the strong square form forged through the press, like some bluff galley through the surf, but *Cave! cave!* was whispered by the more cautious, and in such dread was a gladiator held by his peaceful fellow-citizens, that the boldest preferred submission under insult to a quarrel with a man whose very trade was strife. The chariot was already in motion, when a strong hand forced the two centre horses back upon their haunches, and the bold, frank voice of Hirpinus was heard above the trampling hoofs and general confusion.

"Easy, my little fellow, for a moment," said he to the indignant Automedon. "I heard a comrade's name spoken just now, from within that gilded shell of thine. Halt! I tell thee, lad, and keep that whip quiet, lest I brain thee with my open hand!"

Automedon, little relishing the business from the beginning, pulled his horses together, and looked very much disposed to cry. Damasippus, however, confident in the support of his companion, and the presence of half a dozen armed slaves, stepped boldly forward, and bade the gladiator "make way there" in a high, authoritative voice. Hirpinus recognised the freedman at once, and laughed loud and long.

"What now?" said he, "my old convive and boon-companion. By Pollux! I knew thee not in thy warlike array of steel. In faith, a garland of roses becomes that red nose of thine better than the bosses of a helmet, and the stem of a goblet would fit thy hand more deftly than the haft of that gaudy sword. What stolen goods are these, old parasite? I'll wager now that the jackal is but taking home a lump of carrion to the lion's den."

[pg 234]

"Stay me not, good friend," replied the other, with importance. "It is even as you say, and I am about the business of your employer and mine, Julius Placidus the tribune."

Hirpinus, in high good-humour, would have bade him pass on, but Mariamne, whose mouth was now released, gathered her exhausted energies for a last appeal.

"You are his comrade! you said so even now. Save me, save me, for Esca's sake!"

Again at that name the gladiator's eye glistened. He loved the young Briton like a son—he who had so little to love in the world. He had brought him out, as he boasted twenty times a day. He had made a man—more, a swords-man—of him. Now he had lost sight of him, and, as far as his nature permitted, had been anxious and unhappy ever since. If a dog had belonged to Esca, he would have dashed in to rescue it from danger at any risk.

"Stand back, fool!" he shouted to Damasippus, as the latter interposed his person between the gladiator and the chariot. "Have a care, I tell thee! I want the woman out into the street. What! you will, will you?—One—two.—Take it then, idiot! Here! comrades, close in, and keep off this accursed crowd!"

Damasippus, confident in the numbers of his escort, and believing, too, that his adversary was alone, had, indeed, drawn his sword, and called up the slaves to his assistance, when the gladiator moved towards the chariot containing his charge. To dash the blade from his unaccustomed grasp, to deal him a straight, swift, crushing blow, that sent him down senseless on the pavement, and then, drawing his own weapon, to turn upon the shrinking escort a point that seemed to threaten all at once, was for Hirpinus a mere matter of professional business, so simple as to be almost a relaxation. His comrades, laughing boisterously, made a ring round the combatants. The slaves hesitated, gave ground, turned and fled; Hirpinus dragged the helpless form of Mariamne from the chariot, and Oarses, who had remained in the background till now, leaped nimbly in, to assume the vacant place, and, whispering Automedon, went off at a gallop.

The poor girl, terrified by the danger she had escaped, and scarcely reassured by the mode of her rescue, or the appearance of her deliverers, clung, half-fainting, to the person of her supporter, and the old swordsman, with a delicacy almost ludicrous in one of his rough exterior, [pg 235]soothed her with such terms of encouragement as he could summon at the moment: now like a nurse hushing a child off to sleep, anon like a charioteer quieting a frightened or fretful horse.

In the meantime, the crowd, gathering confidence from the sheathed swords and obvious good-humour of the gladiators, pressed round with many rude gestures and insulting remarks, regardless of the fallen man, who, on recovering his senses, wisely remained for a while where he was, and chiefly bent on examining the features of the cloaked and hooded prize, that had created this pretty little skirmish for their diversion. Such unmannerly curiosity soon aroused the indignation of Hirpinus.

"Keep them off, comrades!" said he angrily; "these miserable citizens. Keep them off, I say! Have they never seen a veiled woman before, that they gape and stare, and pass their rancid jests, as they do on you and me when we are down on our backs for their amusement in the arena? Let her have air, my lads, and she will soon come to. Pollux! She looks like the lily thy wife was watering at home, when we stopped there this morning, Rufus, for a draught of the five-year-old wine, and a gambol with those bright-haired kids of thine."

The tall champion to whom this remark was addressed, and who had that very morning, in company with his friend, bidden a farewell, that might be eternal, to wife and children, as indeed it was nothing unusual for him to do, softened doubtless by the remembrance, now exerted himself strenuously to give the fainting woman room. Without the use of any but nature's weapons, and from sheer weight, strength, and resolution, the gladiators soon cleared an ample space in the middle of the street for their comrade and his charge; nor did they seem at all indisposed to a task which afforded opportunities of evincing their own physical superiority, and the supreme contempt in which they held the mass of their fellow-citizens. Perhaps it was pleasant to feel how completely they could domineer over the crowd by the use of those very qualities which made their dying struggles a spectacle for the vulgar; perhaps they enjoyed the repayment in advance of some of the ribaldry and insult that would too surely accompany their end. At anyrate they shouldered the mob back with unnecessary violence, drove their spiked sandals into the feet of such as came under their tread, and scrupled not to strike with open hand or clenched fist any adventurous citizen who was fool enough to put [pg 236]himself forward for appeal or resistance. These, too, seemed terror-stricken by this handful of resolute men. Accustomed to look on them from a safe distance in the amphitheatre, like the wild beasts with whom they often saw them fight, they were nearly as unwilling to beard the one as the other; and to come into collision with a gladiator in the street, was like meeting a tiger on the wrong side of his bars. So Hirpinus had plenty of room to undo the girl's bands, and remove the stifling folds that muffled her head and throat.

"Where am I?" she murmured, as she began to breathe more freely, looking round bewildered and confused. "You are Esca's friend. Surely I heard you say so. You will take care of me, then, for Esca's sake."

Instinctively she addressed herself to Hirpinus, instinctively she seemed to appeal to him for protection and encouragement. The veil had been taken from her head, and the beauty of the sweet pale face was not lost on the surrounding gladiators. Old Hirpinus looked at her with a comical expression, in which admiration and pity were blended with astonishment and a proud sense of personal appropriation in the defenceless girl who seemed utterly dependent on him. He had never seen anything so beautiful in his life. He had never known the happiness of a home; never had wife nor child: but at that moment his heart warmed to her as a father's to a daughter.

"Where are you," he repeated, "pretty flower? You are within a hundred paces of the Flaminian Way. How came you here? Ay, that is more than I can tell you. Yonder knave lying there.—What? he is gone, is he? Ay! I could not hit hard enough at a man with whom I have emptied so many skins of Sabine.—Well, Damasippus brought thee here, he best knows why, in his master's gaudy chariot. I heard thee speak, my pretty one, and who loves Esca, loves me, and I love him, or her, or whoever it may be. So I knocked him over, that fat freedman, and took thee from the chariot, and pulled off these wraps that were stifling thee, and indeed I think it was about time."

He had raised her while he spoke, and supported her on his strong arm, walking slowly on, while the gladiators, closing round them, moved steadily along the street, followed, though at a safe distance, by much verbal insult and abuse. At intervals, two or three of the rear-guard would turn and confront the mob, who immediately gave back and were silent. Thus the party proceeded on its way, more, it would [pg 237]seem, with the view of leaving the crowd than of reaching any definite place of shelter.

"Where are we going? and who are those who guard us?" whispered Mariamne, clinging close to her protector. "You will take care of me, will you not?" she added, in a confiding tone.

"They are my comrades," he answered soothingly; "and old Hirpinus will guard you, pretty one, like the apple of his eye. We will take you straight home, or wherever you wish to go, and not one of these will molest you while I am by—never fear!"

Just then, Euchenor, who was one of the band, and had overheard this reassuring sentence, clapped the old swordsman on the shoulder.

"You seem to forget our compact," said he, with his evil, mocking laugh.

The face of Hirpinus fell, and his brow lowered, for he remembered then that Mariamne was not much better off here than in the captivity from which he had rescued her.

[pg 238]

CHAPTER XI

THE RULES OF THE FAMILY

The Jewess had indeed but escaped one danger to fall into another. Bold and lawless as were these professional swordsmen, they acknowledged certain rules of their own, which they were never known to infringe. When a band of gladiators had been mustered, and told off for a particular service, it was their custom to bind themselves by oath, as forming one body, unanimous and indivisible, until that service was completed. They swore to stand by each other to the death, to obey their chief implicitly, and to take orders from him alone—to make common cause with their fellows, in defiance of all personal feelings of interest or danger, even to the cheerful sacrifice of life itself; and to consider all booty of arms, gold, jewels, captives, or otherwise, however obtained, as the property of the band; subject to its disposal, according to the established code of their profession. Therefore it was that Hirpinus felt his heart sink at Euchenor's malicious observation. Therefore it was that though he strove to put on an appearance of good-humour and confidence, a perceptible tremor shook his voice while he replied—

"I found her first. I dragged her from the chariot. I put that foolish citizen on his back to make sport for you all. I am the oldest swordsman in the band. I think you might leave her to me!"

Euchenor's eye was on the frightened girl, and, meeting its glance, she shrank yet closer to her protector, while the Greek observed, with a sneer—

"You had better make a new set of rules for us then, since you seem inclined to break through the old. Comrades, I appeal to you; doth not the booty belong to us all, share and share alike?"

The others were crowding in now, having reached a narrower street, and left the populace behind.

"Of course, of course!" was re-echoed on all sides; "who doubts it? who disputes it?"

[pg 239]

"What would you have, man?" exclaimed Hirpinus, waxing wroth. "You cannot cut a captive into twenty pieces and give every man a portion! I tell you, she is mine. Let her alone!"

"You cannot cut a wineskin into twenty pieces, nor need you," replied the Greek; "but you pass it round amongst your comrades, till every man's thirst be slaked. 'Faith, after that, you may keep the empty skin for your own share, if you like!"

He spoke in a cold derisive tone, and although Mariamne could not understand half he said, garnished as his speech was with the cant terms of his calling, she gathered enough of its import to be terrified at the prospect before her. Old Hirpinus lost patience at last.

"Will you take her from me?" he burst out, knitting his bushy brows, and putting his face close to the Greek's. "Stand up then like a man and try!"

Euchenor turned very pale. It was no part of his scheme to provoke his robust old comrade to a personal encounter; and, indeed, the pugilist was a coward at heart, owing his reputation chiefly to the skill with which he had always matched himself against those whom he was sure to conquer. Now he fell back a step or two from his glaring adversary, and appealed once more to their companions. These gathered round, speaking all at once, Hirpinus turning from one to the other, and ever shielding his charge with his body, as an animal shields its young. He was determined to save the girl, because he understood dimly that she belonged in some way to Esca, and the loyal old swordsman would not have hesitated one moment in flinging his life down, then and there, to purchase her safety.

"Hold, comrades!" shouted he, in a stentorian voice that made itself heard above the din. "Will ye bay me altogether like a pack of Molossian wolf-hounds? Hounds, forsooth! nay, the Molossians are true-bred, and there is one cur amongst us here at least, to my knowledge. Rather, like a knot of jabbering old women in a market-place! Talk of rules! Of course we abide by our rules, ay, and stick to our oath. Rufus, old friend, we have stood with our swords at each other's throats for hours together, many a time during the last ten years, and never had an angry word or an unkindly thought. Thou wilt not fail me now? Thou wilt not see old Hirpinus wronged?"

The champion thus appealed to by such tender associations, thrust his tall person forward in the throng. Slow of speech, [pg 240]calm, calculating, and reflective, Rufus was held an oracle of good sense amongst his fellow-swordsmen.

"You are both wrong," said he sententiously. "The girl belongs to neither of you. If this had happened yesterday, Hirpinus would have had a right to carry her where he chose. But we have taken the oath since then, old comrade, and she is the joint property of the band by all our laws."

"I said so!" exclaimed Euchenor triumphantly. "The prize belongs to us all. Every man his turn. The apple seems fair and ripe enough. Mine shall be the hand to pare its rind."

As he spoke, he pulled aside the veil which Mariamne had modestly drawn once more about her head, and the girl, flushing scarlet at the insult, stamped passionately with her foot, and then, as if acknowledging her helplessness, burst into tears, and hid her face in her hands. Hirpinus caught the aggressor by the shoulder, and sent him reeling back amongst the rest. His beard bristled with anger, and the foam stood on his lip like some old boar at bay.

"Hands off!" roared the veteran. "Rules or no rules, another such jest as that and I drive a foot of steel through the jester's brisket! What! Rufus, I came not into the Family yesterday. I was eating raw flesh and lentil porridge when most of these were sucking their mothers' milk. I tell thee, man, the old law was this: When gladiators disputed on any subject whatever—pay, plunder, or precedence—they were to take short swords, throw away their shields, and fight it out by pairs, till they were agreed. Stand round, comrades! Put the little Greek up at half-sword distance; clear a space of seven feet square, not an inch more, and I'll show you how we used to settle these matters when Nero wore the purple!"

"Nay, nay!" interposed Mariamne, wringing her hands in an agony of terror and dismay. "Shed not blood on my account. I am a poor, helpless girl. I have done no one any harm. Let me go, for pity's sake! Let me go!"

But to this solution of the difficulty objections were offered on all sides. Rufus indeed, and one or two of the older swordsmen, moved by the youth and tears of the captive, would willingly have permitted her to escape; but Euchenor, Lutorius, and the rest, objected violently to the loss of so beautiful a prize. Rufus, too, when appealed to, though he would fain have supported his old comrade, was obliged to confess that justice, according to gladiator's law, was on Euchenor's side. Even the proposal to fight for her possession [pg 241]by pairs, popular as it was likely to be in such a company, was rendered inadmissible by the terms of the late oath. The band, indeed, when purchased as they had been by Hippias for a special duty to be performed that night, had become pledged, according to custom, not only to the usual brotherhood and community of interests, but also to refrain from baring steel upon any pretence or provocation either amongst themselves or against a common foe, until ordered to do so by their employer. Hirpinus, though he chafed and swore vehemently, and kept Mariamne close under his wing through it all, was obliged to acknowledge the force of his comrade's arguments; and the puzzled athlete racked his unaccustomed brains till his head ached to find some means of escape for the girl he had resolved to save. In the meantime, delay was dangerous. These men were not used to hesitate or refrain, and already the hour was approaching at which they were to muster for their night's work, whatever it might be, in the tribune's house. The old swordsman felt he must dissemble, were it but to gain time; so he smoothed his brows, and, much against the grain, assumed an appearance of good-humour and satisfaction.

"Be it as you will," said he; "old Hirpinus is the last man to turn round upon his comrades, or to break the laws of the Family, for the sake of a cream-coloured face and a wisp of black hair. I will abide by the decision of Hippias. We shall find him at the tribune's house, and it is time we were there now. Forward, my lads! Nay, hands off! I tell thee once more, Euchenor, till we have brought her to the master's she belongs to me."

Euchenor grumbled, but was compelled to submit; for the other's influence amongst the gladiators was far greater than his own. And the little party, with Mariamne in the centre, still clinging fast to Hirpinus, moved on in the direction of the tribune's house.

Esca, crouching in his place of concealment, silent and wary, as he had ofttimes crouched long ago, when watching for the dun deer on the hillside, was aware of the tramp of disciplined men approaching the porch in which he lay in ambush. Every faculty was keenly, painfully on the stretch. Once, at the sound of wheels, he had started from his lair, ready to make one desperate attempt for the rescue of his love; but greatly to his consternation, the gilded chariot returned empty, save of Automedon, looking much scared and bewildered. The wily Oarses, indeed, having made his escape from the gladiators, had betaken himself to his lodging, [pg 242]and there determined to remain, either till his patron's wrath should be exhausted, or till the events which he foresaw the night would bring forth should have diverted it into another channel. So Automedon went home in fear and trembling by himself. As the Briton revolved matters in his mind, he knew not whether to be most alarmed or reassured by this unforeseen contingency. Though the chariot had returned without Mariamne, the freedmen and armed slaves were still absent. Could they have missed their prey, and were they still searching for her? or had they carried her elsewhere?—to the freedmen's garret, perhaps, there to remain concealed till the night was further advanced. Yet the words of Placidus, or of his ghost, which he had overheard, seemed to infer that the Jewess was expected every minute. Every minute indeed! and those racking minutes seemed to stretch themselves to hours. With the natural impatience of inaction, which accompanies uncertainty, he had almost made up his mind to return in search of Eleazar, when the steady footfall of the approaching party arrested his attention.

There was a bright moon shining above, and the open space into which the gladiators advanced was clear as day. With a keen feeling of confidence he recognised the square frame of Hirpinus, and then, as he caught sight of the dark-robed figure at the swordsman's side, for one exulting moment, doubt, fear, anxiety, all were merged in the delight of seeing Mariamne once more. With the bound of a wild deer, he was in the midst of them, clasping her in his arms, and the girl sobbing on his breast felt safe and happy, because she was with him. Hirpinus gave a shout that startled the slaves laying the tables in the inner hall.

"Safe, my lad!" he exclaimed, "and in a whole skin. Sound and hearty, and fit to join us in to-night's work. Better late than never. Swear him, comrades! swear him on the spot! Send in for a morsel of bread and a pinch of salt. Here, Rufus, cross thy blade with mine! Thou art in the nick of time, lad, to take thy share with the rest, of peril, and pleasure, and profit to boot!"

This speech he eked out with many winks and signs to his young friend, for Hirpinus, guessing how matters stood between the pair, could think of no better plan by which Esca should at least claim a share in the prey they had so recently acquired. His artifice was, however, lost upon the Briton, who seemed wholly occupied with Mariamne, and to whom the girl was whispering her fears and distresses, and [pg 243]entreaties that he would save her from the band. The young man drew her to his side.

"Give way," said he haughtily, as Euchenor and Lutorius closed in upon him. "She has made her choice, she goes with me. I take her home to her father's house."

The others set up a shout of derision.

"Hear him!" they cried. "It is the prætor who speaks! It is the voice of Cæsar himself! Yes, yes, go in peace, if thou wilt. We have had enough and to spare of your yellow-haired barbarians, but the girl remains with us."

She was not trembling now. She was past all fear in such a crisis as this. Erect and defiant she stood beside her champion—pale indeed as the dead, but with eyes in which flashed the courage of despair. His lips were white with the effort of self-command as he strove to keep cool and to use fair words.

"I am one of yourselves," said he. "You will not turn against me all at once. Let me but take the maiden home, and I will come back and join you, true as the blade to the haft."

"Ay, let them go!" put in Hirpinus. "He speaks fairly, and these barbarians never fail their word!"

"No, no," interposed Euchenor. "He has nothing to do with us. Why, he was beaten in the open circus by a mere patrician. Besides, he is not engaged for to-night. He has no interest in the job. Who is he, this barbarian, that we should give up to him the fairest prize we are like to take in the whole business?"

"Will you fight for her?" thundered Esca, hitching his swordbelt to the front.

Euchenor shrank back amongst his comrades. "Our oath forbids me," said he; and the others, though they could not refrain from jeering at the unwilling Greek, confirmed his decision.

Esca's mind was made up.

"Pass your hands under my girdle," he whispered to Mariamne. "Hold fast, and we shall break through!"

His sword was out like lightning, and he dashed amongst the gladiators, but he had to do with men thoroughly skilled in arms and trained to every kind of personal contest. A dozen blades were gleaming in the moonlight as ready as his own. A dozen points were threatening him, backed by fearless hearts, and strong supple practised hands. He was at bay; a desperate man penned in by a circle of steel. He glanced fiercely round, defiant yet bewildered, then down at [pg 244]the pale face at his breast, and his heart sank within him. He was at his wits' end. She looked up—loving, resolute, and courageous.

"Dear one," she said softly, "let me rather die by your hand. See, I do not fear. Strike! You only have the right, for I am yours!"

Even then a faint blush came into her cheek, while the pale hands busied themselves with her dress to bare her bosom for the blow. He turned his point upon her, and she smiled up in his face. Old Hirpinus dashed the tears from his shaggy eyelashes.

"Hold! hold!" said he, in a broken voice; "not till I am down and out of the game for one! Enough of this!" he added in an altered tone, and with a ludicrous assumption of his usual careless manner. "Here comes the master—no more wrangling, lads! we will refer the matter to him!"

While he spoke, Hippias entered the open space in front of the tribune's house, and the gladiators gathered eagerly around him, Euchenor alone remaining somewhat in the background.

[pg 245]

CHAPTER XII

A MASTER OF FENCE

Hippias knew well how to maintain discipline amongst his followers. While he interested himself keenly in their training and personal welfare, he permitted no approach to familiarity, and above all never suffered a syllable of discussion on a command, or a moment's hesitation in its fulfilment. He came now to put himself at their head for the carrying out of a hazardous and important enterprise. The consciousness of coming danger, especially when it is of a kind with which habit has rendered him familiar, and which practice has taught him to baffle by his own skill and courage, has a good moral effect on a brave man's character. It cheers his spirits, it exalts his imagination, it sharpens his intellects, and, above all, it softens his heart. Hippias felt that to-night he would need all the qualities he most prized to carry him safely through his task—that while failure must be inevitable destruction, success would open out to him a career of which the ultimate goal might be a procuratorship or even a kingdom. How quickly past, present, and possible future, flitted through his brain! It was not so long since his first victory in the amphitheatre! He remembered, as if it were but yesterday, the canvas awnings, the blue sky, and the confused mass of faces, framing that dazzling sweep of sand, all of which his sight took in at once, though his eyes were fixed on those of the watchful Gaul, whom he disarmed in a couple of passes, and slew without the slightest remorse. He could feel again, even now, the hot breath of the Libyan tiger, as he fell beneath it, choked with sand and covered by his buckler, stabbing desperately at that sinewy chest in which the life seemed to lie so deep. The tiger's claws had left their marks upon his brawny shoulder, but he had risen from the contest victorious, and Red and Green through the whole crowded building, from the senators' cushions to the slaves' six inches of standing-room, cheered him to a man. After this triumph, who such a favourite with the Roman people as handsome Hippias? Again, he was the centre of [pg 246]all observation, as, confessedly the head of his profession, he set in order Nero's cruel shows, and catered with profuse splendour for the tastes of Imperial Rome. Yes, he had reached the pinnacle of a gladiator's fame, and from that elevation a prospect opened itself that he had scarcely even dreamed of till now. A handful of determined men, a torch or two for every score of blades, a palace in flames, a night of blood (he only hoped and longed that there might be resistance enough to distinguish strife from murder), another dynasty, a grateful patron, and a brave man's services worthily acknowledged and repaid. Then the future would indeed smile in gorgeous hues. Which of Rome's dominions in the East would most fully satisfy the thirst for royal luxury that he now experienced for the first time? In which of his manlier qualities was he so inferior to the Jew, that Hippias the gladiator should make a lowlier monarch than Herod the Great? and men had not done talking of that warlike king, even now!—his wisdom, his cruelty, his courage, his splendour, and his crimes. A Roman province was but another name for an independent government. Hippias saw himself enthroned in the blaze of majesty under a glowing Eastern sky. Life offering all it had to give of pomp and pageantry and rich material enjoyment. Slaves, horses, jewels, banquets, dark-eyed women, silken eunuchs, and gaudy guards with burnished helmets and flashing shields of gold. Nothing wanting, not even one with whom to share the glittering vision. Valeria would be his. Valeria was born to be a queen. It would, indeed, be a triumph to offer the half of a throne to the woman who had hitherto condescended by listening to his suit. There was a leavening of generosity in Hippias that caused him to reflect with intense pleasure on the far deeper homage he would pay her after so romantic a consummation of his hopes. He felt as if he could almost love her then, with the love he had experienced in his boyhood—that boyhood which seemed now to have been another's rather than his own. He had put it away long since, and it had not come back to him for years till to-day; but gratified vanity, the pleasure which most hearts experience in grasping an object that has been dangling out of reach, beyond all, the power exerted by a woman, over one who has been accustomed to consider himself either above or below such pleasing influences, had softened him strangely, and he hardly felt like the same man who made his bargain with the tribune for a certain quantity of flesh and blood and mettle, so short a time ago.

[pg 247]

It is not to be thought, however, that in his dreams of the future, the fencing-master neglected the means by which that future was to be attained. He had mustered and prepared his band with more than common care; had seen with his own eyes that their arms were bright and sharp and fit for work; had placed them at their appointed posts and visited them repeatedly, enjoining, above all things, extreme vigilance and sobriety. Not one of those men saw beneath his unruffled brow and quiet stern demeanour anything unusual in the conduct of their leader; not one could have guessed that schemes of ambition far beyond any he had ever cherished before, were working in his brain—that a strange, soft, kindly feeling was nestling at his heart. He stood in the moonlight amongst his followers, calm, abrupt, severe as usual; and when Hirpinus looked into his stern set face, the hopes of the old gladiator fell as did his countenance, but Mariamne perceived at once with a woman's eye something that taught her an appeal to his pity on this occasion would not be made in vain.

With habitual caution, his first proceeding was to count the band ere he took note of the two figures in their centre. Then he cast a scrutinising glance at their arms to satisfy himself all were ready for immediate action. After that he turned with a displeased air to Hirpinus, and asked—

"What doth the woman amongst us? You heard my orders this morning? Who brought her here?"

Half a dozen voices were raised at once to answer the master's question; only he to whom it was especially addressed kept silence, knowing the nature with which he had to do. Hippias raised but his sheathed sword and the clamour ceased. Not a maniple in all Rome's well-drilled legions seemed in better discipline than this handful of desperate men. Then he turned to Esca, still speaking in short incisive tones.

"Briton!" said he, "you are not one of us to-night. Go your ways in peace!"

"Well said!" shouted the gladiators. "He is no comrade of ours! He hath no share in our spoil!"

But Hippias only wished to save the Briton from the perils of the coming night, and this from some vague feeling he could hardly explain to himself, that Valeria was interested in the stalwart barbarian. It was not in the fencing-master's nature to entertain sentiments of jealousy upon uncertain grounds. And he was just fond enough of Valeria to value anyone she liked for her sake. Moreover Esca knew their [pg 248]plans. He would alarm the palace, and there would be a fight. He wished nothing better.

Esca was about to make his appeal, but Mariamne interposed.

"Where he goeth I will go," said she, almost in the words of her own sacred writings. "I have to-night lost father, and home, and people. This is the second time he hath saved me from captivity worse than death. Part us not now, I beseech thee, part us not!"

Hippias looked kindly on the sweet face with its large imploring eager eyes.

"You love him," said he, "foolish girl. Begone then, and take him with you."

But again a fierce murmur rose amongst the gladiators. Not even the master's authority was sufficient to carry out such a breach of all laws and customs as this. Euchenor, ever prone to wrangle, stepped forward from the background, where he had remained so as to appear an impartial and uninterested observer.

"The oath!" exclaimed the Greek. "The oath—we swore it when the sun was up—shall we break it ere the moon goes down? She is ours, Hippias, by all the laws of the Family, and we will not give her up."

"Silence!" thundered the master, with a look that made Euchenor shrink back once more. "Who asked for your vote? Hirpinus, Rufus, once again, how came this woman here?"

"She was bound hand and foot in a chariot," answered the former, ignoring, however, with less than his usual frankness, to whom that chariot belonged. "She was carried away by force. I protected her from ill-usage," he added stoutly, "as I would protect her again."

The girl gave him a grateful look, which sank into the old swordsman's heart. Esca, too, muttered warm broken words of thanks, while the band assented to the truth of this statement.

"Even so!" they exclaimed. "Hirpinus speaks well. That is why she belongs to us, and we claim every man his share."

Hippias was too experienced a commander not to know that there are times when it is necessary to yield with a good grace, and to use artifice if force will not avail. It is thus the skilful rider rules his steed, and the judicious wife her husband—the governing power in either case inducing the governed to believe that it obeys entirely of its own free will. He [pg 249]smiled, therefore, pleasantly on his followers, and addressed them in careless good-humoured tones.

"She belongs to us all without doubt," said he, "and, by the sandals of Aphrodité, she is so fair that I shall put in my claim with the rest! Nevertheless there is no time to be wasted now, for the sake of the brightest eyes that ever flashed beneath a veil. Put her aside for a few hours or so. You, Hirpinus, as you captured her, shall take care that she does not escape. For the Briton, we may as well keep him safe too—we may find a use for those long arms of his when to-night's business is accomplished. In the meantime, fall in, my heroes, and make ready for your work. Supper first (and it's laid even now) with the noblest patrician and the deepest drinker in Rome, Julius Placidus the tribune!"

Euge! exclaimed the gladiators in a breath, forgetful at the moment of their recent dissatisfaction, and eager to hear more of the night's enterprise, about which they entertained the wildest and most various anticipations; nothing loth, besides, to share the orgies of a man whose table was celebrated for its luxuries amongst all classes in Rome. Hippias looked round on their well-pleased faces, and continued—

"Then what say you, my children, to a walk through the palace gardens? We will take our swords, by Hercules, for the German guards are stubborn dogs, and best convinced by the argument each of us carries at his belt. It may be dark, too, ere we get there, for the moon is early to-night, and we have no need to stir till we have tasted the tribune's wine, so we must not forget a few torches to light us on our way. There are a score at least lying ready in the corner of that porch. So we will join our comrades in a fair midnight frolic under Cæsar's roof. Cæsar's, forsooth! my children, there will be a smouldering palace and another Cæsar by to-morrow!"

Euge! exclaimed the gladiators once more. "Hail, Cæsar! Long live Cæsar!" they repeated with shouts of fierce mocking laughter.

"It is well," remarked Rufus sagaciously, when silence was restored. "The pay is good and the work no heavier than an ordinary prætor's show. But I remember a fiercer lion than common, that Nero turned loose upon us once in the arena, and we called him Cæsar amongst ourselves, because he was dangerous to meddle with. If the old man's purple is to be rent, we should have something over the regular pay. They have not lasted long of late; but still, Hippias, 'tis somewhat [pg 250]out of the usual business. We don't change an emperor every night, even now."

"True enough," answered the master good-humouredly. "And you have never been within the walls of a palace in your life. Something beyond your pay, said you? Why, man, the pay is but a pretext, a mere matter of form. Once in Cæsar's chambers, a large-fisted fellow like Rufus here, may carry away a king's ransom in either hand. Then think of the old wine! Fifty-year-old Cæcuban, in six-quart cups of solid gold, and welcome to take the goblet away with you, besides, if you care to be encumbered with it. Shawls from Persia, lying about for mere coverings to the couches. Mother-of-pearl and ivory gleaming in every corner. Jewels scattered in heaps upon the floor. Only get the work done first, and every man here shall help himself unquestioned, and walk home with whatever pleases him best."

It was not often Hippias treated his followers to so long a speech, or one, in their estimation, so much to the purpose. They marked their approval with vehement and repeated shouts. They ceased to think of Esca, and forgot all about Mariamne and their late dissatisfaction; nay, they seemed now but to be impatient of every subject unconnected with their enterprise, and to grudge every minute that delayed them from their promised spoil. At a signal from Hippias and his intimation that supper was ready, and their host awaiting them, they rushed tumultuously through the porch, leaving behind them Mariamne and Esca, guarded only by old Hirpinus and Euchenor, the latter appearing alone to be unmoved by the glowing prospects of plunder held out, and obstinately standing on his rights, determined not to lose sight of the captured girl, the more so that she was now overlooked by the rest of his comrades.

This man, though deficient in the dashing physical daring which is so popular a quality amongst those of his profession, possessed, nevertheless, a dogged tenacity of purpose, totally unqualified by any moral scruples or feelings of shame, which rendered him formidable as an antagonist, and generally successful in any villany he attempted. As in the combats he waged with or without the heavy lacerating *cestus*, his object was to tire out his adversary by protracted and scientific defence, taking as little punishment as possible, and never hazarding a blow save when it could not be returned, so in everything he undertook, it was his study to reach the goal by unrelaxing vigilance, and unremitting recourse to the means which experience and common sense pointed out for [pg 251]its attainment. Slinking behind the broad back of Hirpinus, he concealed himself in the darkest corner of the porch, and watched the result of Mariamne's appeal to the fencing-master.

Hippias pushed the gladiators on before him, with boisterous good-humour and considerable violence; as they crowded through the narrow entrance, he remained behind for a moment, and whispered to Esca—

"You will take the girl home, comrade. Can I trust you?"

"Trust me!" was all the Briton answered, but the tone in which he spoke, and the glance he exchanged with Mariamne, might have satisfied a more exacting inquirer than the captain of gladiators.

"Fare thee well, lad," said Hirpinus, "and thee, too, my pretty flower. I would go with you myself, but it is a long way from here to Tiber-side, and I must not be missing to-night, come what may."

"Begone, both of you!" added Hippias hurriedly. "Had it not been for the plunder, I should scarce have found my lambs so reasonable to-night; were you to fall in with them again, the Vestals themselves could not save you. Begone, and farewell."

They obeyed and hastened off, while the fencing-master, with a well-pleased smile, clapped Hirpinus on the shoulder, and accompanied him into the house.

"Old comrade," said he, "we will drink a measure of the tribune's Cæcuban to-night, come what may. To-morrow we shall either be on our backs gaping for the death-fee, or pressing our lips to nothing meaner than a chalice of burnished gold. Who knows? Who cares?"

"Not I for one," replied Hirpinus; "but I am strangely thirsty in the meantime, and the tribune's wine, they tell me, is the best in Rome."

[pg 252]

CHAPTER XIII

THE ESQUILINE

With attentive ears, and faculties keenly on the stretch, Euchenor, lurking in the corner of the porch, listened to the foregoing conversation. When he gathered that Tiber-side was the direction the fugitives meant to take, his quick Greek intellect formed its plan of operation at once.

There was a post of his comrades, consisting of some of the gladiators purchased by Placidus, and placed there a few hours since by the orders of Hippias, in the direct road for that locality. He would follow the pair, noiseless and unsuspected, for he had no mind to provoke an encounter with the Briton till within reach of assistance, then give the alarm, seize the wayfarers, and appeal to the club-law they all held sacred, for his rights. Esca would be sure to defend the girl with his life, but he would be overpowered by numbers, and it would be strange if he could not be quieted for ever in the struggle. There would still be time enough, thought Euchenor, after his victory to join his comrades at the tribune's table, leaving the girl to the tender mercies of the band. He could make some excuse for his absence to satisfy his companions, heated as they would by that time be with wine. Indeed, for his own part, he had no great fancy for the night's adventure, promising as it did more hard knocks than he cared to exchange in a fight with the German guard, fierce blue-eyed giants, who would give and take no quarter. He did not wish, indeed, to lose his share of the plunder, for no one was more alive to the advantages of a full purse, but he trusted to his own dexterity for securing [pg 253]this, without running unnecessary risk. Meanwhile, it was his method to attend to one thing at a time; he waited impatiently, therefore, till Hippias entered the house, and left him at liberty to emerge from his hiding-place.

No sooner was the master's back turned than the Greek sped into the street, glancing eagerly down its long vista, lying white in the moonlight, for the two dark figures he sought. Agile and noiseless as a panther, he skulked swiftly along under the shadow of the houses, till he reached the corner which a passenger would turn who was bound for Tiber-side. Here he made sure that he must sight his prey; but no, amongst the few wayfarers who dotted this less solitary district he looked in vain for Esca's towering shoulders or the shrinking figure of the Jewess. In vain, like a hound, he quested to and fro, now casting forward upon a vague speculation, now trying back with untiring perseverance and determination. Like a hound, too, whose game has foiled him, he was obliged to slink home at length, ashamed and baffled, to the porch of the tribune's house, inventing as he went a plausible excuse to host and comrades for his tardy appearance at the banquet. He had passed, nevertheless, within twenty paces of those he hunted, but he knew it not.

With the first rapture of intense joy for their escape, it was in the nature of Mariamne that her predominant feeling should be one of gratitude to Heaven for thus preserving both herself and him whose life was dearer to her than her own. In common with her nation, she believed in the constant and immediate interposition of the Almighty in favour of His servants; and the new faith, which was rapidly gaining ground in her heart, had tempered the awe in which His worshipper regards the Deity, with the implicit trust, and love, and confidence, entertained for its father by a child. Such feelings can but find an outlet in thanksgiving and prayer. Before Mariamne had gone ten paces from the tribune's house, she stopped short, looked up in Esca's face, and said: "Let us kneel together, and thank God for our deliverance."

"Not here at least!" exclaimed the Briton, whose nerves, good as they were, had been somewhat unstrung by the vicissitudes of the night, and the apprehensions that had racked him for his beloved companion. "They may return at any moment. You are not safe even now. If you are so exhausted you cannot go on (for she was leaning heavily on his arm, and her head drooped), I will carry you in my [pg 254]arms from here to your father's house. My love, I would carry you through the world."

She smiled sweetly on him, though her face was very pale. "Let us turn in at this ruined gateway," said she; "a few moments' rest will restore me; and, Esca, I must give thanks to the God of Israel, who has saved both thee and me."

They were near a crumbling archway, with a broken iron gate that had fallen in. It was on the opposite side of the street to the tribune's house; and as they passed beneath its mouldering span, they saw that it formed an entrance into one of those wildernesses, which, after the great fire of Nero, existed here and there, not only in the suburbs, but at the very heart of Rome. They were, in truth, in that desolate waste which had once been the famous Esquiline Gardens, originally a burial-ground, and granted by Augustus to his favourite, the illustrious Mæcenas, to plant and decorate according to his prolific fancy and unimpeachable taste. That learned nobleman had taken advantage of his emperor's liberality to build here a stately palace, which had not, however, escaped the great fire, and to lay out extensive pleasure-grounds, which had been devastated by the same calamity. Little, indeed, now remained, save the trees that had originally shadowed the Roman's grave in the days of the old Republic. The "unwelcome cypresses" so touchingly described in his most reflective ode, by him whose genius Mæcenas fostered, and whose gratitude paid his princely patron back by rendering him immortal.

Many a time had Horace lounged in these pleasant shades, musing with quaint and varied fancies, half pathetic, half grotesque, on the business and the pleasures, the sunshine and the shadows, the aim and the end, of that to him inexplicable problem, a man's short life. Here, too, perhaps, he speculated on the mythology, to the beauty of which his poetic imagination was so keenly alive, while his strong common sense and somewhat material character must have been so utterly incredulous of its truth. Nay, on this very spot did he not ridicule certain superstitions of his countrymen, with a coarseness that is only redeemed by its wit? and preserve, in pungent sarcasm, for coming ages, the memory of an indecent statue on the Esquiline, as he has preserved in sweet and glowing lines the glades of cool Præneste, or the terraced vineyards basking in the glare and glitter of noonday on Tibur's sunny slopes? Here, [pg 255]perhaps, many a time may have been seen the stout sleek form, so round and well-cared for, with its clean white gown, and dainty shining head, crowned with a garland of festive roses, and not wanting, be sure, a festive goblet in its hand. Here may the poet have sat out many a joyous hour in the shade, with mirth, and song, and frequent sips of old Falernian, and a vague dreary fancy the while ever present, though unacknowledged—like a death's-head at the banquet—that feast, and jest, and song could not last for ever, but that the time must come at length, when the empty jar would not be filled again, when the faded roses could be bound together no longer in a chaplet for the unconscious brows, and the string of the lyre, once snapped, must be silent henceforward for evermore. The very waterfall that had soothed its master to his noonday slumber in the drowsy shade, was now dried up, and in the cavity above, a heap of dusty rubbish alone remained, where erst the cool translucent surface shone, fair and smooth as glass. Weeds were growing rank and tall, where once the myrtle quivered and the roses bloomed. Where Chloe gambolled and where Lydia sang, the raven croaked and fluttered, and the night-owl screamed. Instead of velvet turf and trim exotic shrubs, and shapely statues framed in bowers of green, the nettle spread its festering carpet, and the dock put out its pointed leaf; and here and there a tombstone showed its slab of marble, smooth and grim, like a bone that has been laid bare. All was ruin or decay—a few short years had done the work of ages; and whether they waked or whether they slept, poet and patron had gone hence, never to return.

'Her eyes grew dim, her senses seemed failing'

Under the branches of a spectral holm-oak, blackened, withered, and destroyed by fire, Mariamne paused, and clung with both hands to her companion's arm. Bravely had the girl borne up for hours against terrible mental anxiety, as well as actual bodily pain, but with relief and comparative safety came the reaction. Her eyes grew dim, her senses seemed failing, and her limbs trembled so that she was unable to proceed. He hung over her in positive fear. The pale face looked so deathlike that his bold heart quailed, as the possibility presented itself of life without her. Propped in his strong grasp she soon recovered, and he told her as much, in a few frank simple words.

"And yet it must come at last," said she gently. "What is the short span of a man's life, Esca, for such love as ours? Even had we everything we can wish, all the world can [pg 256]give, there would be a sting in each moment of happiness at the thought that it must end so soon."

"Happiness!" repeated Esca. "What is it? Why is there so little of it on earth? *My* happiness is to be with you; and see, I win it but for an hour at a time, at a cost to yourself I cannot bear to think of."

She looked lovingly in his face.

"Do you suppose *I* would count the cost?" said she. "Ever since the night you took me from those fearful revellers, and brought me so gently and so courteously to my father's house, I—I have never forgotten what I owe you."

He raised her hand to his lips, with the action of an inferior doing homage. Alone with the woman he loved, the very depth and generosity of his young affection made him look on her as something sacred and apart She hesitated, for she had yet more to say, which maiden shame repressed, lest it should disclose her feelings too openly; but she loved him well: she could not keep silence on so vital a subject, and after a pause, she took courage and asked—

"Esca, could you bear to think we were never to meet again?"

"I would rather die at once!" he exclaimed fervently.

She shook her head, and smiled rather sadly.

"But *after* death," she insisted; "after death do you believe you will see me no more?"

He looked blank and confused. The same question had been present almost unconsciously in his mind, but had never taken so definite a shape before.

"You would make me a coward, Mariamne," said he; "when I think of you, I almost fear to die."

They were standing under the holm-oak, where the moonlight streamed down clear and cold through the bare branches. It shone on a slab of marble, half defaced, half overgrown with moss. Nevertheless, on that surface was distinctly carved the horse's head with which the Roman loved to decorate the stone that marked his last resting-place.

"Do you know what that means?" said she, pointing to this quaint and yet suggestive symbol. "Even the proud Roman feels that death and departure are the same,—that he is going on a journey he knows not where, but one from which he never shall return. It is a journey we must all take, none can tell how soon; for you and me the horse may be harnessed this very night. But I know where I am [pg 257]going, Esca. If you had slain me an hour ago with your sword, I should have been there even now."

"And I?" he exclaimed. "Should I have been with you? for I would have died amongst the gladiators as I have seen a wolf die in my own country, overmatched by hounds. Mariamne, you would not have left me for ever? What would have become of me?"

Again she shook her head with the same pitiful plaintive smile.

"You do not know the way," said she. "You have no guide to take you by the hand; you would be lost in the darkness; and I—I should see you no more. Oh! Esca, I can teach you, I can show it you. Let us travel it together, and, come what may, we need never part again!"

Then the girl knelt down under that dead tree, with the moonbeams shining on her pale face, and her lips moved in whispered thanksgiving for the late escape, and prayer for him who now stood by her side, and who watched her with wistful looks, as a child watches a piece of mechanism of which he sees plainly the effect, while he strives in vain to comprehend the cause. It seemed to Esca that the woman he loved must have found the talisman that all his youth he had felt a vague consciousness he wanted—something beyond manly courage, or burning patriotism, or the dogged obstinacy that fortifies itself by defying the worst. Moreover, the course of his past life, above all, the trials he had lately undergone, could not but have prepared the ground for the reception of that good seed which brings forth such good fruit,—could not but have shown him the necessity for a strength superior to the bravest endurance of mere humanity, for a hope that was fixed beyond the grave. A few minutes she remained on her knees, praying fervently for herself,—for him. He felt that it was so, and while his eyes were riveted on the dear face, so pure and peaceful, turned upward to the sky, he knew that his own being was elevated by her holy influence, that the earthly affection of a lover for his mistress, was in his breast refined by the adoration of a worshipper for a saint.

Then she rose, and taking him by the arm, walked leisurely on her way, discoursing, as she went, on certain truths which she had learnt from Calchas, and which she believed with the faith of those who have been taught by one, himself an eye-witness of the wonders he relates. There were no dogmas in those early days of the Christian Church to distract the minds of its votaries from the simple tenets of their creed. The grain of mustard-seed had not yet shot up [pg 258]into that goodly tree which has since borne so many branches, and the pruning-knife, hereafter to lop away so many redundant heresies, was not as yet unsheathed. The Christian of the first century held to a very simple exposition of his faith as handed down to him from his Divine Master.

Trust and love were the fundamental rules of his order. Trust that in the extremity of mortal agony could penetrate beyond the gates of death, and brighten the martyr's face with a ray of splendour "like the face of an angel." Love that embraced all things, downward from the Creator to the lowest of the created, that opened its heart freely and ungrudgingly to each, the sinner, the prodigal, and the traveller who fell among thieves. Other faiths, indeed, and other motives have fortified men to march proudly to the stake, to bear without wincing tortures that forced the sickening spectator to turn shuddering away. A heathen or a Jew could front the lion's sullen scowl, or the grin and glare of the cruel tiger, in the amphitheatre, with the dignified composure that brave men borrow from despair; could behold unmoved the straight-cut furrow in the sand that marked the arena of his sufferings, soon to run crimson with his blood. Even athwart the dun smoke, amidst the leaping yellow flames, pale faces have been seen to move, majestic and serene as spectres, with no sustaining power beyond that of a lofty courage, the offspring of education and of pride. But it was the Christian alone who could submit to the vilest degradations and the fiercest sufferings with a humble and even cheerful thankfulness; who could drink from the bitter cup and accept the draught without a murmur, save of regret for his own unworthiness; nay, who could forgive and bless the very tyranny that extorted, the very hand that ministered to, the tortures he endured.

In its early days, fresh from the fountain-head, the Christian's was, indeed, essentially and emphatically, a religion of love. To feed the hungry, to clothe the naked, to stretch a hand to the fallen, to think no evil, to judge not, nor to condemn, in short, to love "the brother whom he *had* seen," were the direct commands of that Great Example who had so recently been here on earth. His first disciples strove, hard as fallible humanity can, to imitate Him, and in so striving, failed not to attain a certain peaceful composure and contentment of mind, that no other code of morality, no other system of philosophy, had ever yet produced. Perhaps this was the quality that, in his dealings with his victim, the Roman executioner found most mysterious and inexplicable. [pg 259]Fortitude, resolution, defiance, these he could understand: but the childlike simplicity that accepted good and evil with equal confidence; that was thankful and cheerful under both, and that entertained neither care for to-day nor anxiety for to-morrow, was a moral elevation, at which, with all their pretensions, his own countrymen had never yet been able to arrive. Neither Stoic nor Epicurean, Sophist nor Philosopher, could look upon life, and death also, with the calm assurance of these unlearned men, leaning on a hand the Roman could not see, convinced of an immortality the Roman was unable to conceive.

With this happy conviction beaming in her face, Mariamne inculcated on Esca the tenets of her noble faith; explaining, not logically, indeed, but with woman's persuasive reasonings of the heart, how fair was the prospect thus open to him, how glorious the reward, which, though mortal eye could not behold it, mortal hand could not take away. Promises of future happiness are none the less glowing that they fall on a man's ear from the lips he loves. Conviction goes the straighter to his heart when it pervades another's that beats in unison with his own. Under that moonlit sky, reddened in the horizon with the glare of a distant quarter of the city already set on fire by the insurgents; in that dreary waste of the Esquiline, with its blasted trees, its shrieking night-birds, and its scattered grave-stones, the Briton imbibed the first principles of Christianity from the daughter of Judah, whom he loved; and the girl's face beamed with a holy tenderness more than mortal, while she showed the way of everlasting happiness, and life, and light, to him whose soul was dearer to her than her own.

And meanwhile around them on all sides, murder, rapine, and violence were stalking abroad unchecked. Riotous parties of Vespasian's supporters met, here and there, detached companies of Cæsar's broken legions; and when such collisions took place, the combatants fought madly, as it would seem from mere wanton love of bloodshed, to the death; whichever conquered, neither spared the dissolute citizens, who indeed, when safe out of reach, from roofs or windows encouraged the strife heartily with word and gesture. Sparks fell in showers through the streets of Rome, and blood and wine ran in streams along the pavement; nor were the deserted gardens of the Esquiline undisturbed by the tumult and devastation that pervaded the rest of the unhappy city.

CHAPTER XIV

THE CHURCH

When they sought to leave their place of refuge, Esca and Mariamne found themselves hemmed in and drawn back by the continued tumult that was raging through the surrounding quarters. On all sides were heard the shouts of victory, the shrieks of despair, and the mad riot of drunken mirth. Occasionally, flying parties of pursuers or pursued swept through the very outskirts of the gardens themselves, compelling the Briton and his charge to plunge deeper into its gloomy solitudes for concealment.

At length they reached a place of comparative safety, under a knot of dark cypresses that had escaped the general conflagration, and here they paused to take breath and listen, Mariamne becoming every moment more composed and tranquil, while Esca, with a beating heart, calculated the many chances that must still be risked ere they could reach her home beyond the Tiber, and he could place the daughter in safety under her father's roof once more. It was very dark where they were, for the cypresses grew thick and black between them and the sky. The place had probably in former times been a favourite resort in the noonday heat. There were the remains of a grotto or summer-house not yet wholly destroyed, and the fragments of a wide stone basin, from which a fountain had once shot its sparkling drops into the summer air. Several alleys, too, cut in the young plantations, had apparently converged at this spot; and although these were much overgrown and neglected, one still formed, so to speak, a broad white street of turf, hemmed in by walls of quivering foliage, dark and massive, but sprinkled here and there with points of silver in the moonlight.

Mariamne crept closer to her companion's side.

"I feel so safe and so happy with you," said she caressingly. "We seem to have changed places. You are the one who is now anxious and—no, not frightened—but ill at ease. Esca! what is it?" she asked with a start, as, [pg 261]looking fondly up in his face, she caught its expression of actual terror and dismay.

His blue eyes were fixed like stone. With parted lips and rigid features, his whole being seemed concentrated into the one effort of seeing, and backed by the dark shadows of the cypress, his face, usually so frank and fearless, was paler even than her own. Following with her eyes the direction of his glance, she, too, was something more than startled at what she saw. Two black figures, clad in long and trailing garments, moved slowly into sight, and crossed the sheet of moonlight which flooded the wide avenue, with solemn step and slow. These again were followed by two in white, looking none the less ghostly that their outlines were so indistinctly defined, the head and feet being alone visible, and the rest of the figure wrapped, as it were, in mist. Then came two more in black, and thus in alternate pairs the unearthly procession glided by; only, ere the half of it had passed, a something, not unlike the human form, draped in a white robe, seemed to float horizontally, at a cubit's height, above the line. A low and wailing chant, too, rose and fell fitfully on the listeners' ears. It was the "Kyrie Eleison," the humble plaintive dirge in which the Christian mourned, not without hope, for his dead.

Fear was no familiar sentiment in Esca's breast. It could not remain there long. He drew himself up, and the colour rushed back redly to his brow.

"They are spirits!" said he; "spirits of the wood, on whose domains we have trespassed. Good or evil, we will resist them to the last. They will sacrifice us to their vengeance if we show the least signs of fear."

She was proud of his courage even then—the courage that could defy, though it had not been able to shake off, the superstitions of his northern birthplace. It was sweet, too, to think that from her lips he must learn what was truth, both of this world and of the next.

"They are no spirits!" she answered. "They are Christians burying their dead. Esca, we shall be safe with them, and they will show us how to leave this place unobserved."

"Christians?" he replied doubtfully; "and we, too, are Christians, are we not? I would they were armed, though," he added reflectively. "With twenty good swordsmen, I would engage to take you unmolested from one end of Rome to the other; but these, I fear, are only priests. Priests! and the legions are loose even now all over the city!"

[pg 262]

He was but a young disciple, thought his loving teacher, and many a defeat must be experienced, many a rebuff sustained, ere dependence on his own courage is rooted out of a brave man's heart, to be replaced by that nobler fortitude which relies solely on the will of Heaven. Yet a brave man is no bad material out of which to form a good one.

They left their hiding-place, and hastened down the alley after the departing Christians. In a secluded place, where the remaining trees grew thickest and most luxuriant—where the noontide ray had least power to penetrate, the procession had halted. The grave was already being dug. As spadeful after spadeful of loose earth fell with a dull grating sound on the sward, or trickled back into the cavity, the dirge wailed on, now lowered and repressed like the stifled sob of one who weeps in secret, now rising into notes of chastened triumph, that were almost akin to joy. And here, where Mæcenas, and his poets and his parasites, had met, with garland and goblet, to while away the summer's day in frivolous disputations, arguing on the endless topics of here and hereafter, life and death, body and soul; groping blindly and in vain throughout the labyrinth for a clue—sneering at Pythagoras, refuting Plato, and maligning Socrates—the body of the dead Christian was laid humbly and trustfully in the earth, and already the departed spirit had learned the efficacy of those truths it had imbibed through scorn and suffering in its lifetime—truths that the heathen sages would have given goblets and garlands, and riches and empire, and all the world besides, but to know and believe in that supreme moment, when all around the dying fades and fails as though it had never been, and there is but one reality from which is no escape.

The Jewess and her champion waited a few paces off while the spade threw its last handfuls to the surface. Then the Christians gathered solemnly and silently round the open grave, and the corpse was lowered gently into its resting-place, and the faces that watched it sink, and stop, and waver, and sink again out of sight, even like the life of the departed, beamed with a holy triumph, for they knew that with this wayfarer, at least, the journey was over and the home attained. Two mourners, somewhat conspicuous from the rest, stood at either end of the grave. The one was a woman, still in the meridian of her beauty; the other a strong warlike man, scarcely of middle age. The woman's face was turned to heaven, rapt, as it seemed in an ecstasy of prayer. She was not thinking of the poor remains, the [pg 263]empty shell, consigned beneath her feet to its kindred dust; but with the eye of faith she watched the spirit in its upward flight, and for her the heavens were opened, and her child was even now disappearing through the golden gate. But on the man's contracted features might be read the pain of him who is too weak to bear, and yet too strong to weep. His eye followed with sad wistful glances clod after clod, as they fell in to cover up the loved and lost. When the earth was flattened down above her head, and not till then, he seemed to look inquiringly at the vacant space amongst the bystanders, and to know that she was gone. He clenched his strong hands tight, and raised his eyes at last. "It is hard to bear," he muttered; "it is very hard to say, 'Thy will be done.' " Then he thought of the empty place at home, and hid his face and wept.

A young girl, on the verge of womanhood, had been called away—called suddenly away—the pride and the flower and the darling of her father's house. He was a good man and a brave, and a believer, yet every time his child's face rose up before him, with its bright hair and its loving eyes, something smote him, sharp and cold, like the thrust of a knife.

When the grave was finally closed, the Christians gathered round it in prayer. Mariamne, taking Esca by the hand, came silently among them, and joined in their devotions. It was a strange and solemn sight to the barbarian. A circle of cloaked figures kneeling round an empty space, to worship an unseen power. On either hand a wilderness of ruin and devastation in the heart of a great city; above, an angry glare on the midnight sky, and the shouts of maddened combatants rising and falling on the breeze. By his side, the woman he loved so dearly, and whom he had thought he should never look on again. He knelt with the others, to offer his tribute from a grateful heart. Their prayers were short and fervent, nor did they omit the form their Master had given them expressly for their use. When they rose to their feet, one figure stood forth amongst the rest, and signed for silence with uplifted hand. This man was obviously a Roman by birth, and spoke his language with the ease, but at the same time with the accent and phrases of the lowest plebeian class. He seemed a handicraftsman by trade, and his palm, when he raised it impressively to bespeak attention, was hardened and scarred with toil. Low of stature, mean in appearance, coarsely clothed, with bare head and feet, there was little in his exterior to command interest or respect; [pg 264]but his frame, square and strongly built, seemed capable of sustaining a vast amount of toil or hardship, while his face, notwithstanding its plain features, denoted repressed enthusiasm, earnest purpose, and honest singleness of heart. He was indeed one of the pioneers of a religion, destined hereafter to cover the surface of the earth. Such were the men who went forth in their master's name, without scrip or sandals, or change of raiment, to overrun and conquer the world—who took no thought what they should say when brought before the kings, and governors, and great ones of the earth, trusting only in the sanctity of their mission, and the inspiration under which they spoke. Having little learning, they could refute the wisest philosophers. Having neither rank nor lineage, they could beard the Proconsul on his judgment-seat or the Cæsar on his throne. Homely and ignorant, they feared not to wander far and wide through strange countries, and hostile nations, spreading the good tidings with a simple ungrudging faith that forced men to believe. Weak by nature it may be, and timid by education, they descended into the arena to meet their martyrdom from the hungry lion, with a quiet fortitude such as neither soldier nor gladiator had courage to display. It was a moral their Master never ceased to inculcate, that His was a message sent not to the noble, and the prosperous, and the distinguished, for these, if they wished to find Him, might make their own opportunities to seek Him out; but to the poor and lowly, the humble and forlorn, especially to those who were in distress and sorrow, who, having none to help them here, might rely all the more implicitly on His protection, who is emphatically the friend of the friendless.

Therefore, the men who did His work seem to have been chosen principally from the humbler classes of society, from such as could speak to the multitude in homely phrases and with familiar imagery; whose authority the most careless and unthinking might perceive originated in no aid of extraneous circumstances, but came directly from above.

As the speaker warmed to his subject, Esca could not but observe the change that came over the bearing and appearance of his outward man. At first the eye was dull, the speech hesitating, the manner diffident. Gradually a light seemed to steal over his whole countenance, his form towered erect as though it had actually increased in stature, his words flowed freely in a torrent of glowing and appropriate language, his action became dignified, and the whole man [pg 265]clothed himself, as it were, in the majesty of the subject on which he spoke.

That subject was indeed simple enough, sad, it may be, from an earthly point of view, and yet how comforting to the mourners gathered round him beside the new-made grave! At first he contented himself with a short and earnest tribute, clothed in the plainest form of speech, to the worth and endearing qualities of that young girl whom they had just laid in the earth. "She was precious to us all," said he, "yet words like these seem but a mockery to some present here, for whom she was the hope and the joy, and the very light of an earthly home. Grieve, I say, and weep, and wring your hands, for such is man's weak nature, and He who took our nature upon Him sympathises with our sorrows, and, like the good physician, pities while He heals. To-day your wounds are fresh, your hearts are full, your eyes are blind with tears, you cannot see the truth. To-morrow you will wonder why you mourn so bitterly; to-morrow you will say, 'It is well; we are labouring in the sun, she is resting in the shade; we are hungry and thirsty in a barren land, she is eating the bread and drinking the waters of life, in the garden of Paradise; we are weary and footsore, wayfarers still upon the road, but she has reached her home.'

"Yea, now at this very hour, standing here where the earth has just closed over the young face, tender and delicate even in death, would you have her back to you if you could? Those who have considered but the troubles that surround us now, and to whom there is no hereafter, who call themselves philosophers, and whose wisdom is as the wisdom of a blind man walking on the brink of a precipice, have themselves said 'whom the gods love die young'; and will you grudge that your beloved one should have been called out of the vineyard, to take her wages and go to her rest, before the burden and heat of the day? Think what her end might have been. Think that you might have offered her up to bear witness to the truth, tied to a stake in the foul arena, face to face with the crouching wild beast gathered for his spring. Ay! and worse even than this might have befallen the child, whom you remember, as it were but yesterday, nestling to her mother's bosom, or clinging round her father's knees! 'The Christians to the panther, and the maidens to the pandar!'[u] You have heard the brutal shouts and shuddered with fear and anger while you heard. And [pg 266]you would have offered her, as Abraham offered Isaac, beating your breasts, and holding your breath for very agony the while. But is it not better thus? She has earned the day's wages, labouring but for an hour at sunrise; she has escaped the cross, and yet has won the crown!

"But you who hear me, envy not this young maiden, though she be now arrived where all so long to go. Rather be proud and happy, that your Master cannot spare you, that He has yet work for you to do. To every man's hand is set his appointed task, and every man shall find strength given him to fulfil it when the time arrives. Some of you will bear witness before Cæsar, and for such the scourges are already knotted and the cross is reared; but to these I need scarcely speak of loyalty, for to them the very suffering brings with it its own fortitude, and they are indeed blessed who are esteemed worthy of the glory of martyrdom! Some must go forth to preach the gospel in wild and distant lands; and well I know that neither toil, nor hardship, nor peril, will cause them to waver an hair's-breadth from their path, yet have they difficulties to meet, and foes to contend with, that they know not of. Let them beware of pride and self-sufficiency, lest, in raising the altar, they make the sacrifice of more account than the spirit in which it is offered; lest in building the church they take note of every stone in the edifice, and lose sight of the purpose for which it was reared. But ye cannot all be martyrs, nor preachers, nor prophets, nor chief-priests, yet every one of you, even the weakest and the lowest here present—woman, child, slave, or barbarian—is none the less a soldier and a servant of the cross! Every one has his duty to do, his watch to keep, his enemy to conquer. It is not much that is required of you—little indeed in comparison with all you have received—but that little must be given without reserve, and with the whole heart. Has any one of you left a duty unfulfilled? when he departs from hence let him go home and accomplish it. Has any one an enemy? let him be reconciled. Has he done his brother a wrong? let him make amends. Has he sustained an injury? let him forgive it. Even as you have laid in the grave the perishable body of the departed, so lay down here every earthly weakness, every unholy wish, and every evil thought. Nay, as these chief mourners have to-night parted and weaned themselves from that which they loved best on earth, so must you tear out and cast away from you the truest and dearest affections that stand between you and your service, ay, even though you rend [pg 267]them from the very inner chambers of your heart. And then, with constant effort and never-ceasing prayer, striving, step by step, and winning, inch by inch, now slipping back it may be where the path is treacherous, and the hill is steep, to rise from your knees, humbled and therefore stronger, gaining more than you have lost, you shall arrive at last, where there is no strife, and no failing, where she for whom you weep to-night is even now in glory, where He whom you follow has already prepared a place for you, and where you who have loved and trusted, shall be happy for evermore!"

Ceasing, he spread his hands abroad, and implored a blessing on those who heard him, after which the Christians breaking up their circle, gathered round the bereaved parents with a few quiet words and gestures of sympathy, such as those offer who have themselves experienced the sorrows they are fain to assuage.

"I am in safety here," whispered Mariamne to the Briton, as she pointed out a dark figure, with white flowing locks, whom he now recognised as Calchas. In another moment she was in the old man's arms, who raised his eyes to heaven, and thanked God with heartfelt gratitude for her deliverance.

"Your father and I," said he, "have sought you with fearful anxiety, and even now he is raising some of his countrymen to storm the tribune's house, and take you from it with the strong hand. Mariamne, you hardly know how much your father loves his child. And I too was disturbed for your safety, but I trusted—trusted in that Heaven which never fails the innocent. Nevertheless, I sought for aid among my brethren, and they have raised, even the poorest of them, such a sum as would have tempted the prætor to interfere, even against a man like Placidus. I did but remain with them to say a prayer while they buried their dead. But now you are safe, and you will come back with me to your father's house, and one of these whom I can trust shall go to tell him at the place where his friends were to assemble; and Esca, thy preserver for the second time, who is to me as a son, shall accompany us home—though we shall not need a guard, for thy father's friends, tried warriors every man, and armed, will meet us ere we leave the wilderness for the streets."

It was a strong temptation to the Briton, but the words he had so lately heard had sunk deep into his heart. He, too, would fain cast in his lot amongst these earnest men. He, too, he thought, had a task to perform—a cherished [pg 268]happiness to forego. With a timely warning, it might be in his power to save the Emperor's life, and his very eagerness to accompany Mariamne but impressed him the more with the conviction that it was his duty to leave her, now she was in comparative safety, and hasten on his errand of mercy. Calchas, too, insisted strongly on this view, and though Mariamne was silent, and even pleaded with her eyes against the risk, he turned stoutly from their influence, and ere she was clasped in her father's arms, the new Christian was already half-way between the Esquiline and the palace of Cæsar.

[pg 269]

CHAPTER XV

REDIVIVUS

Many had been the debauch at which, himself its chief originator and promoter, the tribune had assisted; nor had he escaped the penalties that Nature exacts even from the healthiest constitutions, when her laws are habitually outraged in the high-tide of revelry and mirth; but never, after his longest sittings with the Emperor, had he experienced anything to compare with the utter prostration of mind and body in which he came to himself, waking from the deathlike sleep that followed his pledge to Valeria. With returning consciousness came a sense of painful giddiness, which, as the velvet cushions of the couch rose and heaved beneath his sight, confused him utterly as to where he was, or how he got there; then, sitting up with an effort that seemed to roll a ball of lead across his brain, he was aware that every vein throbbed at fever-heat, that his hands were numbed and swollen, that his mouth was parched, his lips cracked, and that he had a racking headache—the latter symptom was sufficiently familiar to be reassuring; he sprang to his feet, regardless of the pang so sudden a movement shot through his frame, then seizing a goblet from the table, filled it to the brim with Falernian, and in defiance of the nausea with which its very fragrance overpowered him, emptied it to the dregs. The effect, as he expected, was instantaneous; it enabled him to stand erect, and, passing his hand across his brow, by a strong effort of the will, he forced himself to connect and comprehend the events that had led to this horrible and bewildering trance. By degrees, one after another, like links in a chain, he traced the doings of the day, beginning a long way back, somewhere about noon, till the immediate past, so to speak, came more and more tangibly within his grasp. It was with a thrill of triumphant pleasure that he remembered Valeria's visit, and his own arm winding round her handsome form on that very couch. Where was she [pg 270]now? He looked about him vacantly, almost expecting to find her in the room; as he did so, his eye lighted on the two goblets, one of them half-emptied, still standing on their salver.

To say that Placidus had a conscience would be simply a perversion of terms; for that monitor, never very troublesome, had since his manhood been so stifled and silenced as to have become a mere negative quality, yet in his present unhinged state, a shudder of horror did come over him, as he recalled the visit to Petosiris, and the poison with which he had resolved to ensure the silence of his slave. But ere that shudder passed away, the dark secret Esca knew, the plot from which it was now too late to draw back, the desperate adventure that every hour brought nearer, and that must be attempted to-night—all these considerations came flooding in on his memory at once, and for a moment he felt paralysed by the height of the precipice on the brink of which he stood. With the emergency, however, as was always the case in the tribune's character, came the energy required to encounter it. "At least," he muttered, steadying himself by the table with one hand, "the cup is nearly empty; the drug cannot but have done its work. First, I must make sure of the carrion, and then it will be time enough to find Valeria." Had he suffered less in body, he would have laughed his own low malicious laugh, to think how deftly he had outwitted the woman he professed to love. The laugh, however, died away in a grin that betrayed more pain than mirth; and the tribune, with chattering teeth and shaking frame, and wavering uncertain steps, betook himself to the outer court to make sure with his own eyes that the stalwart frame of him whom he feared was stiff and cold in death.

His first feeling would have been one of acute apprehension, had not anger so completely mastered that sensation, when he perceived the slave's chain and collar lying coiled on the pavement. Obviously, Esca had escaped; and was gone, moreover, with his late master's life completely in his power; but Placidus possessed a keen intellect and one familiar with sudden combinations; it flashed upon him at once, that he had been outwitted by Valeria, and the two had fled together.

The sting was very sharp, but it roused and sobered him. Pacing swiftly back through the corridors, and stopping for a few minutes to immerse his head and face in cold water, he returned to the banqueting-hall, and eagerly scrutinised with [pg 271] look and smell, and, notwithstanding all that had happened, even with a sparing taste, the cup from which he had last drunk. The opiate, however, had been so skilfully prepared that nothing suspicious could be detected in the flavour of the wine; nevertheless, reflecting on all the circumstances with a clearer head, as the strength of his constitution gradually asserted itself, he arrived at the true conclusion, and was satisfied that Valeria had changed the cups while his attention was distracted by her charms; that he had purchased a poison he never doubted for a moment, nor suspected that Petosiris could have dared, from sheer love of trickery, to substitute an opiate for the deadlier draught; but he exulted to think that his powerful organisation must have resisted its effects, and that he who had so often narrowly escaped death in the field must indeed bear a charmed life. If a suspicion haunted him that the venom might still be lurking in his system, to do its work more completely after a short respite, the vague horror of such a thought did but goad him to make use of the intervening time all the more ardently for business and pleasure, not forgetting the sacred duty of revenge. *Dum vivimus vivamus!* was the tribune's motto, and if he had been granted but one hour to live, he would have divided that hour systematically, between the delights of love, wine, and mischief.

Rapidly, though coolly, he reviewed his position, as though he had been commanding a cohort hemmed in by the Jewish army. To-night would make or mar him. The gladiators would be here within an hour. Esca must, ere this, have reached the palace and given the alarm. Why had a centurion of Cæsar not yet arrived with a sufficient guard to arrest him in his own house? They might be expected at any moment. Should he fly while there was yet time? What! and lose the brilliant future so nearly within his reach? No—he would weather this as he had weathered other storms, by skilful and judicious steering. A man who has no scruples need never be deficient in resource. To leave his house now, would be a tacit admission of guilt. To be found alone, undefended, unsuspicious, a strong presumption of innocence. He would at least have sufficient interest to be taken into the presence of Cæsar. There, what so easy as to accuse the slave of treachery, to persuade the Emperor the barbarian had but hatched a plot against his master's life; to make the good-humoured old glutton laugh with an account of the drugged goblet, and finish the night by a debauch with his imperial host?

Then, he must be guided by the preparations for defence which he observed in the palace. If they were weak, he must find some means of communicating with Hippias, and the attack would be facilitated by his own presence inside. If, on the contrary, there was an obvious intention of firm resistance, the conspirators must be warned to postpone their enterprise. If worst came to the worst, he could always save his own head by informing against his confederates, and so handing over Hippias and the gladiators to death.

Some slight compunction visited him at the thought of such an alternative, but he soon stifled it with the arguments of his characteristic philosophy. Should he be found, indeed, presiding at a supper-party composed of these desperate men, they might defend the gate whilst he fled directly to Cæsar, and sacrificed them at once. Under any circumstances, he argued, he had bought them, and had a right to make use of them.

In the meantime, Mariamne would be here directly. She ought to have been here long ago. Whatever the future threatened, an hour, half an hour, a quarter, should be devoted to her society, and after that, come what might, at least he would not have been foiled in every event of the day. It was when he had arrived at this conclusion, that Esca from his hiding-place saw the figure of the tribune, pale, wan, and ghostly, giving directions for the preparation of the supper-table.

The evening stole on, the sun-dial no longer showed the hour, and the slave whose duty it was to keep count of time by the water-clock[12] then in vogue, announced that the first watch of the night was already advanced. He was followed by Automedon, who came into the presence of his master, with hanging head and sheepish looks, sadly mistrusting how far his own favour would bear him harmless in the delivery of the tidings he had to impart. It was always a perilous duty to inform Placidus of the failure of any of his schemes. He listened, indeed, with a calm demeanour and an unmoved countenance, but sooner or later he surely contrived to visit on the unfortunate messenger the annoyance he himself experienced from the message.

The tribune's face brightened as the boy came into the [pg 273]hall; with characteristic duplicity, however, he veiled even from his charioteer the impatience in which he had waited his return.

"Have you brought the horses in cool?" said he, with an affectation of extreme indifference.

Automedon looked greatly relieved.

"Quite cool," he answered, "most illustrious! and Oarses came part of the way home, but he got down near the Sacred Gate, and I had no one with me in the chariot the whole length of the Flaminian Way; and the slaves will be back presently; and Damasippus—Oh! my lord, do not be angry!—Damasippus—I fear I have left him dead in the street."

Here the lad's courage failed him completely; he had indeed been thoroughly frightened by the events of the night; and making a piteous face, he twined his fingers in his long curls and wept aloud.

"What, fool!" thundered the tribune, his brow turning black with rage. "You have not brought her after all! Silly child," he added, controlling himself with a strong effort. "Where is the—the passenger—I charged Damasippus to bring here with him to-night?"

"I will tell you the truth," exclaimed the boy, flinging himself down on his knees, and snatching at the hem of his master's garment. "By the Temple of Vesta, I will tell you the truth. I drove from here across Tiber, and I waited in the shadow by Tiber-side; and Jugurtha wouldn't stand still, and presently Damasippus brought a—a passenger in his arms, and put it into the chariot, and bade me go on fast; and we went on at a gallop till we tried to cross the Appian Way, and then we had to turn aside, for the houses were burning and the people fighting in the street, and Scipio was frightened and pulled, and Jugurtha wouldn't face the crowd, and I drove on to cross a little farther down, but we were stopped again by the Vestals, and I couldn't drive through *them*! So we halted to let them pass, and then a fierce terrible giant caught the horses and stopped them once more, and a thousand soldiers, nay, a legion at least, surrounded the chariot, and they killed Damasippus, and they tore the passenger out, and killed it too, and Scipio kicked, and I was frightened, and drove home as fast as I could—and indeed it wasn't my fault!"

Automedon's fears had magnified both the number of the assailants and the dangers undergone. He had not recognised the gladiators, and was altogether in too confused a state, as the tribune perceived at a glance, to afford his master any [pg 274]more coherent information than the foregoing. Placidus bit his lip in baffled anger, for he could not see his way; nevertheless the boy-charioteer was a favourite, and he would not visit the failure of the enterprise on him.

"I am glad the horses are safe," said he good-humouredly. "Go, get some supper and a cup of wine. I will send for you again presently."

Automedon, agreeably surprised, glanced up at his master's face ere he departed, and observed that, although deadly pale, it had assumed the fixed resolute expression his dependants knew so well.

Placidus had indeed occasion to summon all the presence of mind on which he prided himself, for even while he spoke, his quick ear caught the tramp of feet, and the familiar clink of steel. The blood gathered round his heart as he contemplated the possibility that a maniple of Cæsar's guards might even now be occupying the court. It was with a sigh of intense relief that, instead of the centurion's eagle crest, he recognised the tall form of Rufus, accompanied by his comrades, advancing respectfully, and even with awkward diffidence, through the outer hall. The tribune could assume—none better—any character it suited him to play at a moment's notice; nevertheless there was a ring of real cordiality in his greeting, for the visitors were more welcome than they guessed.

"Hail! Rufus, Lutorius, Eumolpus!" he shouted boisterously. "Gallant swordsmen and deep drinkers all! What! old Hirpinus, do I not see thy broad shoulders yonder in the rear? and Hippias too, the king of the arena! Welcome, every man of you! Even now the feast is spread, and the Chian cooling yonder amongst the flowers. Once again, a hearty welcome to you all!"

The gladiators, still somewhat abashed by the unaccustomed splendour which met their eyes on every side, responded with less than their usual confidence to their entertainer. Rufus nudged Lutorius to reply in polite language, and the Gaul, in a fit of unusual modesty, passed the signal on to Eumolpus of Ravenna—a beetle-browed, bow-legged warrior, with huge muscles and a heavy, sullen face. This champion looked helplessly about him and seemed inclined to turn tail and fly, when, to his great relief, Hippias advanced from the rear of his comrades, and created a diversion in his favour, of which he availed himself by slinking incontinently into the background. Placidus clapped his hands, an Asiatic fashion affected by the more luxurious [pg 275]Romans; and two or three slaves appeared in obedience to the summons. The gladiators looked on in awe at the sumptuous dresses and personal beauty of these domestics.

"Hand round wine here amongst my friends. I will but say three words to your captain, and we will go to supper forthwith."

So speaking, the tribune led Hippias apart, having resolved that in the present critical state of affairs it would be better to take him entirely into his confidence, and trust to the scrupulous notions of fidelity to their bargains, which such men entertained, for the result.

"There is no time to lose," observed he anxiously, when he had led Hippias apart from his followers. "Something has occurred which was out of all our calculations. Can they overhear us, think ye?"

The fencing-master glanced carelessly at his band. "Whilst they are at *that* game," said he, "they would not hear the assembly sounding from all four quarters of the camp. Never fear, illustrious! it will keep them busy till supper time."

The band had broken up into pairs, and were hard at work with their favourite pastime, old as the Alban hills, and handed down to the Roman Empire from the dynasty of the Pharaohs. It consisted in gambling for small coins at the following trial of skill:—the players sat or stood, face to face; each held the left hand erect, on which he marked the progress of his game. With the right he shot out any one or more of his four fingers and thumb, or all together, with immense rapidity, guessing aloud at the same time the sum-total of the fingers thus brandished by himself and his adversary, who was employed in the same manner. Whoever guessed right won a point, which was immediately marked on the left, held immovable at shoulder-height for the purpose, and when five of these had been won the game began again. Nothing could be more simple, nothing apparently less interesting, and yet it seemed to engross the attention of the gladiators to the exclusion of all other subjects, even the prospect of supper and the flavour of the Falernian.[14]

"They are children now," said Placidus contemptuously. "They will be men presently, and tigers to-night. Hippias, the slave has escaped. We must attack the palace forthwith."

[pg 276]

"I know it," replied the other quietly. "But the Germans are relieving guard at this hour. My own people are hardly ready, and it is not dark enough yet."

"You know it," repeated Placidus, even more irritated than astonished by his companion's coolness, "you *know* it, and yet you have not hastened your preparations? Do you know, too, that this yellow-haired barbarian has got your head, and mine, and all the empty skulls of our intelligent friends who are amusing themselves yonder, under his belt? Do you know that Cæsar, true to his swinish propensities, will turn like a hunted boar, when he suspects the least shadow of danger? Do you know that not one of us may live to eat the very supper waiting for us in the next room? What are you made of, man, that you can thus look me so coolly in the face with the sword at both our throats?"

"I can keep my own throat with my hand," replied the other, totally unmoved by his host's agitation. "And I am certainly not accustomed to fear danger before it comes. But that the barbarian has escaped I saw with my own eyes, for I left him ten minutes since within a hundred paces of your own gate."

The tribune's eyebrows went up in unfeigned surprise.

"Then he has not reached the palace!" he exclaimed, speaking rather to himself than his informant.

"Not reached the palace certainly," replied the latter calmly, "since I tell you I saw him here. And in very good company too," he added with a smile.

The tribune's astonishment had for once deprived him of his self-command.

"With Valeria?" he asked unguardedly; and directly he had spoken, a vague suspicion made him wish that he had held his tongue.

The fencing-master started and knit his brows. His head was more erect and his voice sterner when he answered—

"I have seen the lady Valeria too, within the last hour. She had no slaves with her beyond her usual attendants."

Anger, curiosity, uncertainty, jealousy, a hundred conflicting emotions were rankling at the tribune's heart. What had this handsome gladiator to do at Valeria's house? and was it possible that she did not care for the slave after all? Then what could have been her object throughout? He marked too the alteration in manner betrayed by Hippias at the mention of this fair and flighty dame; nor did it seem [pg 277]improbable under all the circumstances that he entertained a kindly feeling, if nothing more, for his pupil. Judging men and women by his own evil nature, and knowing well the favour with which their female admirers regarded these votaries of the sword, the tribune did not hesitate to put its true construction on such kindly feelings, and their probable result. From that moment he hated Hippias—hated him all the more that in the tumult and confusion of the coming night he might find an opportunity of gratifying his hatred by the destruction of the gladiator. Many a bold leader has been struck down from behind by the very followers he was encouraging; and who would ask how a conspirator met his death, in the attack on a palace and the murder of an emperor? Even while the thought crossed his mind he took the other by the hand, and laughed frankly in his face.

"Thou art at home in the private apartments of every lady in Rome, I believe, my warlike Apollo," said he. "But, indeed, it is no question now of such trifling; the business of to-night must be determined on—ay, and disposed of—without delay. If my slave had reached the palace our whole plan must have been altered. I wish, as you did come across him, you had treated him to that deadly thrust of yours under the short-ribs, and brought him in here dead or alive."

"He will not trouble us," observed the other coolly. "Take my word for it, tribune, he is disposed of for the present."

"What mean you?" asked Placidus, a devilish joy lighting up his sallow face. "Did you bribe him to secrecy then and there with the metal you are accustomed to lavish so freely? Gold will buy silence for a time, but steel ensures it for ever."

"Nay, tribune," answered Hippias, with a frank laugh. "We have been fencing too long in the dark. I will tell you the whole truth. This young giant of yours is safe enough for the present. I saw him depart with a pale-faced girl, in a black hood, whom he promised to take care of as far as Tiber-side. Depend upon it, he will think of nothing else to-night. For all his broad shoulders the down is yet upon his chin. And a man's beard must be grey before he leaves such a fair young lass as that to knock his head against a wall, even though it be the wall of a palace. No, no, tribune, he is safe enough, I tell you, for the next twelve hours, at least!"

[pg 278]

"A pale-faced girl?" repeated Placidus, still harping on Valeria. "What and who was she? Did you know her? did you speak to her?"

"My people had some wild tale," replied the fencing-master, "about a chariot with white horses, that had been upset in the street, and a girl all gagged and muffled, whom they pulled out of it, and for whom, of course, they quarrelled amongst themselves. In faith, had it not been for to-night's business and the oath, you might have seen some sweet practice in your own porch, for I have two or three here that can make as close and even work with a sword as a tailor does with his needle. They said something about her being a Jewess. Very likely she may be, for they swam across Tiber since we have lost Nero. And the lad might as well be a Jew as a Briton for that matter. Are you satisfied now, tribune? By the belly of Bacchus, I must wash my mouth out with Falernian! All this talking makes a man as thirsty as a camel."

Satisfied! and after what he had just learnt! Chariot! White horses! Jewess! There could be no doubt of it. These gladiators must have blundered on her, thought the tribune, and slain my freedman, and rescued her from my people, and handed her over to the man whom most I hate and fear on earth. Satisfied! Perhaps I shall be better satisfied when I have captured her, and humbled Valeria, and put you out of the way, my gallant cut-throat, and seen the slave scourged to death at my own doorpost! Then, and not till then, shall I be able to drink my wine without a heartburn, and lay my head on the pillow with some chance of sleep. In the meantime, to-night's work must be done. To-night's work, that puts Vespasian virtually on the throne (for this boy[12] of his shall only keep the cushion warm till his father takes his seat), that makes Placidus the first man in the empire. Nay, that might even open a path to the purple itself. The general is well advanced in years; already somewhat broken and worn with his campaigns. Titus, indeed, is the darling of the legions, but all the heart black-browed Berenice has left him, is wrapped up in war. He loves it, I verily believe—the daring fool!—for the mere braying of trumpets, and the clash of steel. Not a centurion exposes himself half so freely, nor so often. Well, a Zealot's javelin, or a stone from the ramparts of some nameless town in Judæa, may dispose of him at any time. Then there is but Domitian—a clever youth indeed, and an unscrupulous. So [pg 279]much the worse for him! A mushroom is not the only dish that may be fatal to an emperor, and if the knot be so secure as to baffle all dexterity, why, it must be cut with steel. Ay, the Macedonian knew well how the great game should be played. Satisfied! Like him, I shall never be satisfied while there is anything more to win! These being the tribune's thoughts, it is needless to say that he assumed a manner of the utmost frankness and carelessness.

"Thirsty!" he repeated, in a loud voice, clapping Hippias on the shoulder. "Thirsty—I could empty an aqueduct! Welcome again, and heartily, my heroes all! See, the supper waits. Let us go in and drink out the old Falernian!"

CHAPTER XVI

"MORITURI"

Knowing well with whom he was to deal, Placidus had ordered a repast to be prepared for his guests on a scale of magnificence unusual even in his luxurious dwelling. It was advisable, not only to impose on these rude natures with unaccustomed pomp and parade, but also to excite their cupidity by the display of gold and jewels while their fiercer passions were inflamed with wine. The more reckless and desperate they could be rendered, the more fit would they be for his purpose. There were the tools, sharp and ready for use, but he thought they would admit of a yet finer edge, and prepared to put it on accordingly. Therefore, he had ordered the supper to be laid in an inner apartment, reserved for occasions of especial state, and in which it was whispered that Vitellius himself had more than once partaken of his subject's hospitality; nay, had even expressed gratification with his entertainment; and which, while blazing with as much of ornament and decoration as could be crowded into a supper-room, was of such moderate dimensions as to bring all the costly objects it contained within notice of the guests. The tesselated pavement was of the richest and gaudiest squares, laid together as smooth and bright as glass. The walls were of polished citron-wood, heavily gilded round the skirting and edges, while the panels were covered in the florid and gradually deteriorating taste of the period, with paintings, brilliant in colour, and beautiful in execution. These represented mythological subjects not of the purest nature, but fauns, nymphs, and satyrs were to be found in the majority, while Bacchus himself was more than once repeated in all the glory of his swaying paunch; his garland of vine-leaves, his ivy-covered wand, and surrounding clusters of rich, ripe, purple grapes. To fill the niches between these panels, the goat—an animal always associated in the Roman mind with wine, perhaps because he drinks no water—was imitated in precious metals, and in every attitude. Here they butted, [pg 281]there they browsed, in another corner a pair of them frisked and gambolled in living kid-like glee, while yonder, horned and bearded, a venerable sage in silver gazed upon the guests with a wise Arcadian simplicity that was almost ludicrous. The tables, which were removed with every change of dishes, were of cedar, supported on grotesque claws of bronze, heavily gilt; the couches, framed of ivory and gold, were draped in various coloured shawls of the softest Asiatic texture, and strewed with cushions of so rich a crimson as to border nearly on imperial purple. No dish was of a meaner metal than gold, and the drinking-cups, in which Falernian blushed, or Chian sparkled, were studded with rubies, emeralds, pearls, and other precious stones. The sharp nail of a gladiator might at any moment have picked out, unobserved, that which would have purchased his freedom and his life, but the men were honest, as they understood the term, and the gems were as safe here, and indeed a good deal safer, than they would have been in the temple of Vesta, or of the Capitoline Jove himself. In a recess at one end of the apartment, reared like an altar upon three wide low carpeted steps, from each of which censers exhaled aromatic odours, stood the sideboard of polished walnut, carved in exquisite imitation of birds, insects, reptiles, flowers, and fruit. This was covered by a snowy cloth, and on it glittered, richly chased and burnished, the tribune's store of golden cups and vases, which men quoted at every supper-table in Rome.

Lutorius, reclining opposite this blaze of magnificence, shaded his eyes with his hand.

"What is it, my bold Gaul?" asked his host, raising himself on his elbow to pledge him, and signing to a slave to fill the swordsman's cup. "Hast thou got thy guard up already to save thy face?"

"They dazzle me, most illustrious!" answered the ready Gaul. "I had rather blink at the sunrise flashing on the blue waters from Ostia. I did not think there had been so much gold in Rome."

"He has not seen the palace yet," said Placidus, laughing, as he emptied his cup and turned to the other guests. "Some of us will indeed be dazzled to-night, if I mistake not. What think ye, my friends, must be the plates and drinking-vessels where the very shields and helmets of the guards are solid gold? Meantime, let us wash our eyes with Falernian, lest we mistake our way and intrude on the privacy of Cæsar in the dark."

So appropriate a sentiment met with universal approval. [pg 282]The gladiators laughed loudly, and proffered their cups to be filled. There was no question now of secrecy or disguise; there was even no further affectation of ignoring the purpose for which they had met, or the probable result of the night's enterprise. Eumolpus, indeed, and one or two more of the thicker-witted, satisfied to know that the present moment brought a magnificent reception and an abundance of good cheer, were willing to remain in uncertainty about the future, resolving simply to obey the orders of their captain, and to ask no questions; but even these could not help learning by degrees that they had before them no work of ordinary bloodshed, but that they were involved in a conspiracy which was to determine the empire of the world. It did not destroy their appetite, though it may have increased their thirst.

In proportion as the wine flowed faster the guests lost their diffidence and found their tongues. Their host exerted himself to win golden opinions from all, and entered with ready tact into the characteristics and peculiarities of each.

"Eumolpus!" said he, as a slave entered bearing an enormous turbot on a yet larger dish, "fear not to encounter him. He is a worthy foe, and a countryman of thine own. He left Ravenna but yesterday. In truth, that fair-built town sends us the widest turbots and the broadest shoulders in the empire. Taste him, man, with a cup of Chian, and say if the trainer's rations have spoiled thy palate for native food."

Half-brutalised as he was by nature and education, the gladiator had still a kindly feeling for his birthplace. Even now a memory of his boyhood would sometimes steal across him like a dream. The stretch of sand, the breezy Adriatic, the waves dashing against the harbour-walls, and a vision of curly-headed, black-eyed children, of whom he was one, tumbling and playing on the shore. He felt more human when he thought of such things. While the tribune spoke he rose in his own esteem; for his host treated him like a man rather than a beast; and those few careless words gained a champion for Placidus who was ready to follow him to the death.

So was it with the rest. To Rufus he enlarged on the happiness of a country life, and the liberty—none the less dear for being imaginary—enjoyed by a Roman citizen, who, within easy distance of the capital, could sit beneath his own porch to watch the sunset crimsoning the Apennines, and tread into home-made wine the grapes of his own vineyard. He talked of pruning the elms and training the vines, of shearing sheep and goading oxen, as though he had been a [pg 283]rustic all his life, seasoning such glowing descriptions, to suit his listener's palate, with the charms even of winter in the snow amongst the hills—the boar driven through the leafless copse, the wild-fowl lured from the half-frozen lake, the snug and homely roof, the crackling fire, and the children playing on the hearth.

"'Tis but another night-watch," said he cordially, "and it will be my turn to sup with thee in thy mountain-home. Half a dozen such strokes as I have seen thee deal in mere sport, my hero! and thou wilt never need to meddle with steel again, save in the form of a ploughshare or a hunting-spear. By the fillet of Ceres! my friends, there is a golden harvest to-night, only waiting for the sickle!"

And Rufus, for whom a few acres of Italian soil, and liberty to cultivate them in peace, with his wife and children, comprised all of happiness that life could give, contemplated the prospect thus offered with an imagination heated by wine, and a determination, truly formidable in a man of his quiet, dogged resolution, if hard fighting was to count for anything, not to fail in at least deserving his reward.

"Hirpinus!" exclaimed the host, turning to the veteran, who was a sworn lover of good cheer, and had already consumed supper enough for two ordinary men, washed down by proportionate draughts of wine, "thy favourite morsel is even now leaving the spit. Pledge me in Falernian ere it comes. Nay, spoil it not with honey, which I hold to be a mistake unworthy of a gladiator. We will pour a libation to Diana down our throats, in her capacity of huntress only, my friend; I care not for the goddess in any other. Ho! slaves! bring here some wild boars!"

As he spoke the domestics reappeared, in pairs, carrying between them as many wild boars, roasted whole, as there were guests. One of these huge dishes was set aside for each man, and the carvers proceeded to their duty, unmoved by the ejaculations of amazement that broke from the gladiators at such prodigal magnificence.

Their attention was, however, somewhat distracted at this stage of the feast by the entrance of Euchenor, who slunk to the place reserved for him with a shade of sullen disappointment lowering on his brow. The host, however, had resolved that nothing should occur to mar the success of his entertainment, so refrained from asking any questions as to his absence, and motioned him courteously to a couch, with as frank a greeting as though he had been aware of its cause. He suspected treachery notwithstanding, none the less that [pg 284]Euchenor hastened to explain his tardy arrival. "He had heard a tumult in the neighbourhood," he said, "whilst the guests were entering the house, and had visited the nearest post of his comrades to ascertain that they had not been attacked. It was some distance to the palace-gardens, and he could not avoid missing the earlier stages of the banquet."

"You must make up for lost time," observed Placidus, signing to the slaves to heap the new-comer's plate and fill his cup to the brim. "The later, the warmer welcome; the earlier, the better cheer;" and whilst he spoke the friendly words he was resolving that the Greek should be placed in front that whole night, under his immediate supervision. At the slightest symptom of treachery or wavering he would slay him with his own hand.

And now the gigantic hunger of these champions seemed to be appeased at last. Dish had succeeded dish in endless variety, and they had applied themselves to each as it came with an undiminished energy that astonished the domestics accustomed to the palled appetites of jaded men of pleasure like their lord. Even the latter—though he tried hard, for he especially prided himself on his capacity of eating and drinking—found it impossible to keep pace with his guests. Their great bodily powers, indeed, increased by severe and habitual training, enabled them to consume vast quantities of food, without experiencing those sensations of lassitude and repletion which overcome weaker frames. It seemed as though most of what they ate went at once to supply the waste created by years of toil, and as soon as swallowed, fed the muscles instead of burdening the stomach. It was equally so with wine. Such men can drink draught after draught, and partake freely in the questionable pleasures of intoxication, whilst they pay none of its penalties. A breath of fresh air, a few minutes' exercise, and their brains are cool, their eyes clear, their whole system strengthened for the time, and stimulated, rather than stupefied, by their excess.

The gladiators lay back on their couches in extreme bodily content. The cups were still quickly filled and emptied, but more in compliance with the customs of conviviality than the demands of thirst. They were all talking at once, and every man saw both present and future through the rosy medium of the wine he had imbibed.

There were two, however, of the party who had not suffered their real inmost attention to stray for an instant from the actual business of the night, who calculated the [pg 285]time exactly as it passed—who watched the men through the succeeding phases of satisfaction, good-humour, conviviality, and recklessness, stopping just short of inebriety, and seized the very moment at which the iron was hot enough to strike. The same thought was in the brain of each, when their eyes met; the same words were springing to their lips, but Hippias spoke first.

"No more wine to-night, tribune, if work is to be done! The circus is full; the arena swept; the show paid for. When the prætor takes his seat we are ready to begin."

Placidus glanced significantly in his face, and rose, holding a brimming goblet in his hand. The suddenness of the movement arrested immediate attention. The men were all silent, and looking towards their host.

"Good friends!" said he. "Trusty swordsmen! Welcome guests! Listen to me. To-night we burn the palace—we overthrow the empire—we hurl Cæsar from his throne. All this you know, but there is something more you do not know. One has escaped who is acquainted with the plot. In an hour it may be too late. We are fast friends; we are in the same galley—the land is not a bowshot off. But the wind is rising—the water rushing in beneath her keel. Will you bend your backs forthwith and row the galley safe home with me?"

The project was a favourite one, the metaphor suited to their tastes. As the tribune paused, acclamations greeted him on all sides, and "We will! We will!" "Through storm and sunshine!" "Against wind and weather!" sprang from many an eager lip. It was obvious the men were ready for anything. "One libation to Pluto!" added the host, emptying his cup, and the guests leaping to their feet followed his example with a mad cheer. Then they formed in pairs, as they were accustomed in the amphitheatre, and Euchenor with a malicious laugh exclaimed—*Morituri te salutant.*

It was enough! The ominous words were caught up and repeated in wild defiance and derision, boding small scruples of mercy or remorse. Twice they marched round the supper-room to the burden of that ghastly chant, and when shaking off the fumes of wine they snatched eagerly at their arms, Placidus put himself at their head with a triumphant conviction that, come what might, they would not fail him in his last desperate throw for the great game.

CHAPTER XVII

THE GERMAN GUARD

All was in confusion at the palace of the Cæsars. The civil war that had now been raging for several hours in the capital, the tumults that pervaded every quarter of the city, had roused the alarm, and to a certain extent the vigilance of such troops as still owned allegiance to Vitellius. But late events had much slackened the discipline for which Roman soldiers were so famous, and that could be but a spurious loyalty which depended on amount of pay and opportunities for plunder, which was accustomed moreover to see the diadem transferred from one successful general to another at a few months' interval. Perhaps his German guards were the only soldiers of Vitellius on whom he could place any reliance; but even these had been reduced to a mere handful by slaughter and desertion, while the few who remained, though unimpeachable in their fidelity, were wanting in every quality that constitutes military efficiency, except the physical strength and desperate courage they brought with them from the north.

They were, however, the Emperor's last hope. They occupied palace-gardens to-night, feeding their bivouac-fires with branches from its stately cedars, or uprooting its exotic shrubs to hurl them crackling in the blaze. The Roman citizens looking on their gigantic forms moving to and fro in the glare, shuddered and whispered, and pointed them out to each other as being half men, half demons, while a passing soldier would raise his eagle crest more proudly, relating how those were the foes over whom the legions had triumphed, and would turn forthwith into a wineshop to celebrate his prowess at the expense of some admiring citizen in the crowd.

[pg 287]

One of these German mercenaries may be taken as a sample of the rest. He was standing sentry over a narrow wicket that afforded entrance to the palace-gardens, and was the first obstacle encountered by Esca, after the latter had hastened from the Esquiline to give intelligence of the design against Cæsar's life. Leaning on his spear, with his tall frame and large muscles thrown into strong relief by the light of the bivouac-fire behind him, he brought to the Briton's mind many a stirring memory of his own warlike boyhood, when by the side of just such champions, armed in such a manner, he had struggled, though in vain, against the discipline and the strategy of the invader. Scarcely older than himself, the sentry possessed the comely features and the bright colouring of youth, with a depth of chest and squareness of shoulder that denoted all the power of mature manhood. He seemed indeed a formidable antagonist for any single foe, and able to keep at bay half a score of the finest men who stood in the front rank of the legions. He was clad in a long white garment of linen, reaching below the knee, and fastened at the neck by a single clasp of gold; his shield and helmet too, although this was no state occasion, but one on which he would probably be massacred before morning, were of the same metal, his spear-head and sword of the finest-tempered steel. The latter, especially, was a formidable weapon.

Considerably longer than the Roman's, which was only used for the thrust at close quarters, it could deal sweeping blows that would cleave a headpiece or lop a limb, and managed lightly as a riding-wand by the German's powerful arm, would hew fearful gaps in the ranks of an enemy, if their line wavered, or their order was in any degree destroyed.

Notwithstanding the warlike nature of his arms and bearing, the sentry's face was fair and smooth as a woman's; the flaxen down was scarcely springing on his chin, and the golden locks escaped beneath his helmet, and clustered in curls upon his neck. His light blue eye, too, had a mild and rather vacant expression as it roved carelessly around; but the Romans had long ago learned that those light blue eyes could kindle into sparks of fire when steel was crossed, could glare with invincible hatred and defiance even when fixed in death.

Esca's heart warmed to the barbarian guardsman with a feeling of sympathy and kindred. The latter sentiment may have suggested the plan by which he obtained entrance to the palace, for the difficulty of so doing had presented itself [pg 288]to him in brighter colours every moment as he approached. Pausing, therefore, at a few paces from the sentry, who levelled his spear and challenged when he heard footsteps, the Briton unbuckled his sword and cast it down between them, to indicate that he claimed protection and had no intention of offence. The other muttered some unintelligible words in his own language. It was obvious that he knew no Latin and that their conversation must be carried on by signs. This, however, rather smoothed than enhanced the difficulty; and it was a relief to Esca that the first impulse of the German had not been to alarm his comrades and resort to violence. The latter seemed to entertain no apprehension from any single individual, whether friend or foe, and looked, moreover, with favourable eyes on Esca's appearance, which bore a certain family likeness to that of his own countrymen. He suffered him therefore to approach his post, questioning him by signs, to which the Briton replied in the same manner, perfectly ignorant of their meaning, but with a fervent hope that the result of these mysterious gestures might be his admission within the wall.

Under such circumstances the two were not likely to arrive at a clear understanding. After a while the German looked completely puzzled, and passed the word in his own language to a comrade within hearing, apparently for assistance. Esca heard the sound repeated in more than one voice, till it died away under the trees; there was obviously a strong chain of sentries round Cæsar's palace. In the meantime the German would not permit Esca to approach within spear's-length of his post, though he kept him back good-humouredly with the butt-end of that weapon, nor would he suffer him to pick his sword up and gird it round his waist again—making nevertheless, all the while, signs of cordiality and friendship; but though Esca responded to these with equal warmth, he was no nearer the inside than at first.

Presently the heavy tramp of armed men smote his ear, and a centurion, accompanied by half a dozen soldiers, approached the wicket. These bore a strong resemblance, both in form and features, to the sentry who had summoned them; but their officer spoke Latin, and Esca, who had gained a little time to mature his plan, answered the German centurion's questions without hesitation.

"I belong to your own division," said he, "though I come from farther north than your troop, and speak a different dialect. We were disbanded but yesterday, by a [pg 289]written order from

Cæsar. It has turned out to be a forgery. We have been scattered through half the wineshops in Rome, and a herald came round and found me drinking, and bade me return to my duty without delay. He said we were to muster somewhere hereabouts, that we should find a post at the palace, and could join it till our own officers came back. I am but a barbarian, I know little of Rome, but this is the palace, is it not? and you are a centurion of the German guard?"

He drew himself up as he spoke with military respect, and the officer had no hesitation in believing his tale, the more so that certain of Cæsar's troops had lately been disbanded at a time when their services seemed to be most in requisition. Taking charge of Esca's weapon, he spoke a few words in his own language to the sentry, and then addressed the Briton.

"You may come to the main-guard," said he. "I should not mind a few more of the same maniple. We are likely to want all we can get to-night."

As he conducted him through the gardens, he asked several questions concerning the strength of the opposing party, the state of the town, and the general feeling of the citizens towards Vitellius, all which Esca parried to the best of his abilities, hazarding a guess where he could, and accounting for his ignorance where he could not, on the plea that he had spent his whole time since his dismissal in the wineshops—an excuse which the centurion's knowledge of the tastes and habits of his division caused him to accept without suspicion of its truth.

Arrived at the watch-fire, Esca's military experience, slight as it had been, was enough to apprise him of the imminent dangers that threatened the palace in the event of an attack. The huge Germans lounged and lay about in the glare of the burning logs, as though feast, and song, and revelry were the objects for which they were mustered. Wine was flowing freely in large flagons, commensurate to the noble thirst of these Scandinavian warriors; and even the sentries leaving their posts at intervals, as caprice or indolence prompted, strode up to the watch-fire, laughed a loud laugh, drained a full beaker, and walked quietly back again, none the worse, to their beat. All hailed a new comrade with the utmost glee, as a further incentive to drink; and although Esca was pleased to find that none but their centurion was familiar with Latin, and that he was consequently free from much inconvenient cross-[pg 290]examination, it was obvious that there was no intention of letting him depart without pledging them in deep draughts of the rough and potent Sabine wine.

With youth, health, and a fixed resolve to keep his wits about him, the Briton managed to perform this part of a soldier's duty to the satisfaction of his entertainers. The moments seemed very long, but whilst the Germans were singing, drinking, and making their remarks upon him in their own language, he had time to think of his plans. To have declared at once that he knew of a plot against Cæsar, and to call upon the centurion to obtain his admittance to the person of the Emperor, would, he was well aware, only defeat his own object, by throwing suspicion on himself as a probable assassin and confederate of the conspirators. To put the officer on the alert, would cause him, perhaps, to double his sentries, and to stop the allowance of wine in course of consumption; but Esca saw plainly that no resistance from within the palace could be made to the large force his late master would bring to bear upon it. The only chance for the Emperor was to escape. If he could himself reach his presence, and warn him personally, he thought he could prevail upon him to fly. This was the difficulty. A monarch in his palace is not visible to everyone who may wish to see him, even when his own safety is concerned; but Esca had already gained the interior of the gardens, and that success encouraged him to proceed.

The Germans, though believing themselves more vigilant than usual (to such a low state the boasted discipline of Cæsar's body-guard had fallen), were confused and careless under the influence of wine, and their attention to the new-comer was soon distracted by a fresh chorus and a fresh flagon. Esca, under pretence that he required repose, managed to withdraw himself from the glare of the firelight, and borrowing a cloak from a ruddy comrade with a stentorian voice, lay down in the shadow of an arbutus, and affected profound repose. By degrees, coiling himself along the sward like a snake, he slipped out of sight, leaving his cloak so arranged as to resemble a sleeping form, and sped off in the direction of the palace, to which he was guided by numerous distant lights.

Some alarm had evidently preceded him even here. Crowds of slaves, both male and female, chiefly Greeks and Asiatics, were pouring from its egresses and hurrying through the gardens in obvious dismay. The Briton could not but remark that none were empty-handed, and the value of [pg 291]their burdens denoted that those who now fled had no intention ever to return. They took little notice of him when they passed, save that a few of the more timid, glancing at his stalwart figure, turned aside and ran the swifter; while others, perceiving that he was unarmed, for he had left his sword with the Germans, shot at him some contemptuous gesture or ribald jest, which they thought the barbarian would not understand in time to resent.

Thus he reached the spacious front of the palace, and here, indeed, the trumpets were sounding, and the German guard forming, evidently for resistance to an attack. There was no mistaking the expression of the men's faces, nor the clang of their heavy weapons. Though they filled the main court, however, a stream of fugitives still poured from the side-doors, and through one of these, the Briton determined he would find no difficulty in effecting an entrance. Glancing at the fine men getting under arms with such business-like rapidity, he thought how even that handful might make such a defence as would give Cæsar time to escape, either at the back of the palace, or, if that were invested, disguised as one of the slaves who were still hurrying off in motley crowds; and notwithstanding his new-born feelings, he could not help, from old association, wishing that he might strike a blow by the side of these stalwart guardsmen, even for such a cause as theirs.

Observing a door opening on a terrace which had been left completely undefended, Esca entered the palace unopposed, and roamed through hall after hall without meeting a living creature. Much of value had already been cleared away, but enough remained to have excited the cupidity of the richest subject in Rome. Shawls, arms, jewels, vases, statues, caskets, and drinking-cups were scattered about in a waste of magnificent confusion, while in many instances rapacious ignorance had carried off that which was comparatively the dross, and left the more precious articles behind. Esca had never even dreamed of such gorgeous luxury as he now beheld. For a few minutes his mind was no less stupefied than his eye was dazzled, and he almost forgot his object in sheer wonder and admiration; but there was no time to be lost, and he looked about in vain for some clue to guide him through this glittering wilderness to the presence of the Emperor.

The rooms seemed endless, opening one into another, and each more splendid than the last. At length he heard the sound of voices, and darting eagerly forward, found [pg 292]himself in the midst of half a dozen persons clad in robes of state, with garlands on their heads, reclining round the fragments of a feast, a flagon or two of wine, and a golden cornucopia of fruit and flowers. As he entered, these started to their feet, exclaiming, "They are upon us!" and huddled together in a corner, like a flock of sheep when terrified by a dog. Observing, however, that the Briton was alone and unarmed, they seemed to take courage, and a fat figure thrusting itself forward, exclaimed in one breath, "He is not to be disturbed! Cæsar is busy. Are the Germans firm?"

His voice shook and his whole frame quivered with fear, nevertheless Esca recognised the speaker. It was his old antagonist Spado, a favourite eunuch of the household, in dire terror for his life, yet showing the one redeeming quality of fidelity to the hand that fed him. His comrades kept behind him, taking their cue from his conduct as the bellwether of the flock, yet trusting fervently his wisdom would counsel immediate flight.

"I know you," said Esca hurriedly. "I struck you that night in anger. It is all over now. I have come to save your lives, all of you, and to rescue Cæsar."

"How?" said Spado, ignoring his previous injuries in the alarm of the hour. "You can save us? You can rescue Cæsar? Then it *is* true. The tumult is grown to a rebellion! The Germans are driven in, and the game is lost!"

The others caught up their mantles, girded themselves, and prepared for instant flight.

"The guard can hold the palace for half an hour yet," replied Esca coolly. "But the Emperor must escape. Julius Placidus will be here forthwith, at the head of two hundred gladiators, and the tribune means to murder his master as surely as you stand trembling there."

Ere he had done speaking, he was left alone in the room with Spado. The tribune's character was correctly appreciated, even by the eunuchs of the palace, and they stayed to hear no more; but Spado only looked blankly in the Briton's face, wringing his fat hands, and answered to the other's urgent appeals, "His orders were explicit. Cæsar is busy. He must not be disturbed. He said so himself. Cæsar is busy!"

[pg 293]

CHAPTER XVIII

THE BUSINESS OF CÆSAR

Thrusting Spado aside without ceremony, and disregarding the eunuch's expostulations in obedience to the orders he had received, Esca burst through a narrow door, tore down a velvet curtain, and found himself in the private apartment of the Emperor. Cæsar's business was at that moment scarcely of an urgency to weigh against the consideration of Cæsar's life. Vitellius was reclining on a couch, his dress disordered and ungirt, a garland of roses at his feet, his heavy face, of which the swollen features had lost all their early comeliness, expressing nothing but sullen torpid calm; his eye fixed on vacancy, his weak nerveless hands crossed in front of his unwieldy person, and his whole attitude that of one who had little to occupy his attention, save his own personal indulgence and comfort. Yet for all this, the mind was busy within that bloated form. There are moments in existence, when the past comes back to us day by day, and incident by incident, shining out in colours vivid and lifelike as the present. On the eve of an important crisis, during the crisis itself if we are not permitted to take an active part in it but compelled to remain passive, the mere sport of its contingencies, for the few minutes that succeed a complete demolition of the fabric we have been building all our lives, we become possessed of this faculty, and seem, in a strange dream-like sense, to live our time over again.

For the last few days, even Vitellius had awoke to the conviction that his diadem was in danger, for the last few hours he had seen cause to tremble for his life; nevertheless, none of the usual habits of the palace had been altered; and even when Primus, the successful general of his dangerous rival, Vespasian, occupied the suburbs, his reverses did but elicit from the Emperor a call for more wine and a heartless jest. To-day he must have seen clearly that all was lost, yet the supper to which he sat down with half a dozen favourite eunuchs, was no less elaborate than usual, the wine flowed as [pg 294]freely, the Emperor ate as enormously, and when he could eat no more, retired to pass his customary half-hour in perfect silence and repose, nor suffered the important process of digestion to be disturbed by the fact that his very gates must ere midnight be in possession of the enemy.

Nevertheless, as if in warning of what was to come, the pageant of his life seemed to move past his half-closed eyes; and who shall say how vain and empty such a pageant may have appeared even to the besotted glutton, who, though he had the address to catch the diadem of the Cæsars, when it was thrown to him by chance, knew but too well that he had no power to retain it on his head when wrested by the grasp of force. Though feeble and worn out, he was not old, far short of threescore years, yet what a life of change and turmoil and vicissitudes his had been! Proconsul of Africa, favourite of four emperors, it must have been a certain versatility of talent that enabled him to rule such an important province with tolerable credit, and yet retain the good graces of successive tyrants, resembling each other in nothing save incessant caprice. An informer with Tiberius; a pander to the crimes, and a proselyte to the divinity of mad Caligula; a screen for Messalina's vices, and an easy adviser to her easy and timid lord; lastly, everything in turn with Nero—chariot-driver, singer, parasite, buffoon, and in all these various parts, preserving the one unfailing characteristic of a consummate and systematic debauchee. It seemed but yesterday that he had thrown the dice with Claudius, staking land and villas as freely as jewels and gold, losing heavily to his imperial master; and, though he had to borrow the money at high usury, quick-witted enough to perceive the noble reversion he had thus a chance of purchasing. It seemed but yesterday that he flew round the dusky circus, grazing the goal with practised skill, and, by a happy dexterity, suffering Caligula to win the race so narrowly, as to enchance the pleasure of imperial triumph. It seemed but yesterday that he sang with Nero, and flattered the monster by comparing him with the sirens, whose voices charmed mariners to their destruction.

And now was it all over? Must he indeed give up the imperial purple and the throne of blazing gold?—the luxurious banquets and the luscious wines? He shuddered and sickened while he thought of a crust of brown bread and a pitcher of water. Nay, worse than this, was he sure his life was safe? He had seen death often—what Roman had not? But at his best, in the field, clad in corselet and head[pg 295]piece, and covered with a buckler, he had thought him an ugly and unwelcome visitor. Even at Bedriacum, when he told his generals as he rode over the slain, putrefying on the ground, that "a dead enemy smelt sweet, and the sweeter for being a citizen," he remembered now that his gorge had risen while he spoke. He remembered, too, the German body-guard that had accompanied him, and the faithful courage with which his German levies fought. There were a few of them in the palace yet. It gave him confidence to recollect this. For a moment the soldier-spirit kindled up within, and he felt as though he could put himself at the head of those blue-eyed giants, lead them into the very centre of the enemy, and die there like a man. He rose to his feet, and snatched at one of the weapons hanging for ornament against the wall, but the weak limbs failed, the pampered body asserted itself, and he sank back helpless on the couch.

It was at this moment that Esca burst so unceremoniously into the Emperor's presence.

Vitellius did not rise again, less alarmed, perhaps, than astonished. The Briton threw himself upon his knees, and touched the broad crimson binding of the imperial gown.

"There is not a moment to lose!" said he. "They are forcing the gates. The guard has been driven back. It is too late for resistance; but Cæsar may yet escape if he will trust himself to me."

Vitellius looked about him, bewildered. At that moment a shout was heard from the palace-gardens, accompanied by a rush of many feet, and the ominous clash of steel. Esca knew that the assailants were gladiators. If they came in with their blood up, they would give no quarter.

"Cæsar must disguise himself," he insisted earnestly. "The slaves have been leaving the palace in hundreds. If the Emperor would put on a coarse garment and come with me, I can show him the way to safety; and Placidus, hastening to this apartment, will find it empty."

With all his sensual vices, there was yet something left of the old Roman spirit in Vitellius, which sparkled out in an emergency. After the first sudden surprise of Esca's entrance, he became cooler every moment. At the mention of the tribune's name he seemed to reflect.

"Who are you?" said he, after a pause; "and how came you here?"

Short as had been his reign he had acquired the tone of royalty; and could even assume a certain dignity, notwith[pg 296]standing the urgency of his present distress. In a few words Esca explained to him his danger, and his enemies.

"Placidus," repeated the Emperor thoughtfully, and as if more concerned than surprised; "then there is no chance of the design failing; no hope of mercy when it has succeeded. Good friend! I will take your advice. I will trust you, and go with you, where you will. If I am an Emperor to-morrow, you will be the greatest man in Rome."

Hitherto he had been leaning indolently back on the couch. Now he seemed to rouse himself for action, and stripped the crimson-bordered gown from his shoulders, the signet-ring from his hand.

"They will make a gallant defence," said he, "but if I know Julius Placidus, he will outnumber them ten to one. Nevertheless they may hold him at bay with their long swords till we get clear of the palace. The gardens are dark and spacious; we can hide there for a time, and take an opportunity of reaching my wife's house on Mount Aventine; Galeria will not betray me, and they will never think of looking for me there."

Speaking thus coolly and deliberately, but more to himself than his companion, Cæsar, divested of all marks of splendour in his dress and ornaments, stripped to a plain linen garment, turning up his sleeves and girding himself the while, like a slave busied in some household work requiring activity and despatch, suffered the Briton to lead him into the next apartment, where, deserted by his comrades, and sorely perplexed between a vague sense of duty and a strong inclination to run away, Spado was pacing to and fro in a ludicrous state of perturbation and dismay. Already the noise of fighting was plainly distinguished in the outer court. The gladiators, commanded by Hippias and guided by the treacherous tribune, had overpowered the main body of the Germans who occupied the imperial gardens, and were now engaged with the remnant of these faithful barbarians at the very doors of the palace.

The latter, though outnumbered, fought with the desperate courage of their race. The Roman soldier in his cool methodical discipline, was sometimes puzzled to account for that frantic energy, which acknowledged no superiority either of position or numbers, which seemed to gather a fresher and more stubborn courage from defeat; and even the gladiators, men whose very livelihood was slaughter, and whose weapons were never out of their hands, found themselves no match for these large savage warriors in the struggle [pg 297]of a hand-to-hand combat, recoiled more than once in baffled rage and astonishment from the long swords, and the blue eyes, and the tall forms that seemed to tower and dilate in the fierce revelry of battle.

The military skill of Placidus, exercised before many a Jewish rampart, and on many a Syrian plain, had worsted the main body of the Germans by taking them in flank. Favoured by the darkness of the shrubberies, he had contrived to throw a hundred practised swordsmen unexpectedly on their most defenceless point. Surprised and outnumbered, they retreated nevertheless in good order, though sadly diminished, upon their comrades at the gate. Here the remaining handful made a desperate stand, and here Placidus, wiping his bloody sword upon his tunic, whispered to Hippias—

"We must put Hirpinus and the supper-party in front! If we can but carry the gate, there are a score of entrances into the palace. Remember! we give no quarter, and we recognise no one."

Whilst the chosen band who had left the tribune's table were held in check by the guard, there was a moment's respite, during which Cæsar might possibly escape. Esca, rapidly calculating the difficulties in his own mind, had resolved to hurry him through the most secluded part of the gardens into the streets, and so running the chance of recognition which in the darkness of night, and under the coarse garb of a household slave, was but a remote contingency, to convey him by a circuitous route to Galeria's house, of which he knew the situation, and where he might be concealed for a time without danger of detection. The great obstacle was to get him out of the palace without being seen. The private door by which he had himself entered, he knew must be defended, or the assailants would have taken advantage of it ere this, and he dared not risk recognition, to say nothing of the chances of war, by endeavouring to escape through the midst of the conflict at the main gate. He appealed to Spado for assistance.

"There is a terrace at the back here," stammered the eunuch; "if Cæsar can reach it, a pathway leads directly down to the summer-house in the thickest part of the gardens; thence he can go between the fish-ponds straight to the wicket that opens on the Appian Way."

"Idiot!" exclaimed the Emperor angrily, "how am I to reach the terrace? There is no door, and the window must be a man's height at least from the ground."

[pg 298]

"It is your only chance of life, illustrious!" observed Esca impatiently. "Guide us to the window, friend," he added, turning to Spado, who looked from one to the other in helpless astonishment, "and tear that shawl from the couch; we may want it for a rope to let the Emperor down."

A fresh shout from the combatants at the gate, while it completely paralysed the eunuch, seemed to determine Vitellius. He moved resolutely forward, followed by his two companions, Spado whispering to the Briton, "You are a brave young man. We will all escape together, I—I will stand by you to the last!"

They needed but to cross a passage and traverse another room. Cæsar peered over the window-sill into the darkness below, and drew back.

"It is a long way down," said he. "What if I were to break a limb?"

Esca produced the shawl he had brought with him from the adjoining apartment, and offered to place it under his arms and round his body.

"Shall I go first?" said Spado. "It is not five cubits from the ground."

But the Emperor thought of his brother Lucius and the cohorts at Terracina. Could he but gain the camp there he would be safe, nay more, he could make head against his rival; he would return to Rome with a victorious army; he would retrieve the diadem and the purple, and the suppers at the palace once more.

"Stay where you are!" he commanded Spado, who was looking with an eager eye at the window. "I will risk it. One draught of Falernian, and I will risk it and be gone."

He turned back towards the banqueting-room, and while he did so another shout warned him that the gate was carried, and the palace in possession of the conspirators.

Esca followed the Emperor, vainly imploring him to fly. Spado, taking one more look from the window ere he risked his bones, heard the ring of armour and the tramp of feet coming round the corner of the palace, on the very terrace he desired to reach. White and trembling, he tore the garland from his head and gnawed its roses with his teeth in the inpotence of his despair. He knew the last chance was gone now, and they must die.

The Emperor returned to the room where he had supped; seized a flagon of Falernian, filled himself a large goblet which he half-emptied at a draught, and set it down on the [pg 299]board with a deep sigh of satisfaction. The courtyard had been taken at last, and the palace surrounded. Resistance was hopeless, and escape impossible. The Germans were still fighting, indeed, within the rooms, disputing inch by inch the glittering corridors, and the carved doorways, and the shining polished floors, now more slippery than ever with blood. Pictures and statues seemed to look down in calm amazement at thrust and blow and death-grapple, and all the reeling confusion of mortal strife. But the noise came nearer and nearer; the Germans, falling man by man, were rapidly giving ground. Esca knew the game was lost at last, and he turned to his companions in peril with a grave and clouded brow.

"There is nothing for it left," said he, "but to die like men. Yet if there be any corner in which Cæsar can hide," he added, with something of contempt in his tone, "I will gain him five minutes more of life, if this glittering toy holds together so long."

Then he snatched from the wall an Asiatic javelin, all lacquered and ornamented with gold, cast one look at the others, as if to bid them farewell, and hurried from the room. Spado, a mass of shaking flesh, and tumbled garments and festive ornaments strangely out of keeping with his attitude, cowered down against the wall, hiding his face in his hands; but Vitellius, with something akin even to gratification on his countenance, returned to the half-emptied cup, and raising it to his lips, deliberately finished his Falernian.

CHAPTER XIX

AT BAY

It was not in Esca's nature to be within hearing of shrewd blows and yet abstain from taking part in the fray. His recent sentiments had indeed undergone a change that would produce timely fruit; and neither the words of the preacher in the Esquiline, nor the example of Calchas, nor the sweet influence of Mariamne, had been without their effect. But it was engrained in his very character to love the stir and tumult of a fight. From a boy his blood leaped and tingled at the clash of steel. His was the courage which is scarcely exercised in the tide of personal conflict, and must be proved rather in endurance than in action—so naturally does it force itself to the front when men are dealing blow for blow. His youth, too, had been spent in warfare, and in that most ennobling of all warfare which defends home from the aggression of an invader. He had long ago learned to love danger for its own sake, and now he experienced besides a morbid desire to have his hand on the tribune's throat, so he felt the point and tried the shaft of his javelin with a thrill of savage joy, while, guided by the sounds of combat he hurried along the corridor to join the remnant of the faithful German guard. Not a score of them were left, and of these scarce one but bled from some grievous wound. Their white garments were stained with crimson, their gaudy golden armour was hacked and dinted, their strength was nearly spent, and every hope of safety gone; but their courage was still unquenched, and as man after man went down, the survivors closed in and fought on, striking desperately with their faces to the foe. The tribune and his chosen band, supported by a numerous body of inferior gladiators, were pressing them sore. Placidus, an expert swordsman, and in no way wanting physical courage, was conspicuous in the front. Hippias alone seemed to vie with the tribune in reckless daring, though Hirpinus, Eumolpus, Lutorius, and the others, were all earning their wages with scrupulous [pg 301]fidelity, and bearing themselves according to custom, as if fighting were the one business of their lives.

When Esca reached the scene of conflict the tribune had just closed with a gigantic adversary. For a minute they reeled in the death-grapple, then parted as suddenly as they met, the German falling backward with a groan, the tribune's blade as he brandished it aloft dripping with blood to the very hilt.

"*Euge!*" shouted Hippias, who was at his side, parrying at the same moment, with consummate address, a sweeping sword-cut dealt at him from the dead man's comrade. "That was prettily done, tribune, and like an artist!"

Esca, catching sight of his enemy's hated face, dashed in with the bound of a tiger, and taking him unawares, delivered at him so fierce and rapid a thrust as would have settled accounts between them, had Placidus possessed no other means of defence than his own skilful swordsmanship; but the fencing-master, whose eye seemed to take in all the combatants at once, cut through the curved shaft of the Briton's weapon with one turn of his short sword, and its head fell harmless on the floor. His hand was up for a deadly thrust when Esca found himself felled to the ground by some powerful fist, while a ponderous form holding him down with its whole weight, made it impossible for him to rise.

"Keep quiet, lad," whispered a friendly voice in his ear; "I was forced to strike hard to get thee down in time. Faith! the master gives short warning with his thrusts. Here thou'rt safe, and here I'll take care thou shalt remain till the tide has rolled over us, and I can pass thee out unseen. Keep quiet! I tell thee, lest I have to strike thee senseless for thine own good."

In vain the Briton struggled to regain his feet; Hirpinus kept him down by main force. No sooner had the gladiator caught sight of his friend, than he resolved to save him from the fate which too surely threatened all who were found in the palace, and with characteristic promptitude, used the only means at his disposal for the fulfilment of his object. A moment's reflection satisfied Esca of his old comrade's good faith. Life is sweet, and with the hope of its preservation came back the thought of Mariamne. He lay still for a few minutes, and by that time the tide of fight had rolled on, and they were left alone. Hirpinus rose first with a jovial laugh.

"Why, you went down, man," said he, "like an ox at an [pg 302]altar. I would have held my hand a little—in faith I would—had there been time. Well, I must help thee up, I suppose, seeing that I put thee down. Take my advice, lad, get outside as quick as thou canst. Keep the first turning to the right of the great gate, stick to the darkest part of the gardens, and run for thy life!"

So speaking, the gladiator helped Esca to his feet, and pointed down the corridor where the way was now clear. The Briton would have made one more effort to save the Emperor, but Hirpinus interposed his burly form, and finding his friend so refractory, half-led, half-pushed him to the door of the palace. Here he bade him farewell, looking wistfully out into the night, as though he would fain accompany him.

"I have little taste for the job here, and that's the truth," said he, in the tone of a man who has been unfairly deprived of some expected pleasure. "The Germans made a pretty good stand for a time, but I thought there were more of them, and that the fight would have lasted twice as long. Good luck go with thee, lad; I shall perhaps never see thee again. Well, well, it can't be helped. I have been bought and paid for, and must go back to my work."

So, while Esca, hopeless of doing any more good, went his way into the gardens, Hirpinus re-entered the palace to follow his comrades, and assist in the search for the Emperor. He was somewhat surprised to hear loud shouts of laughter echoing from the end of the corridor. Hastening on to learn the cause of such strangely-timed mirth, he came upon Rufus lying across the prostrate body of a German, and trying hard to stanch the blood that welled from a fatal gash inflicted by his dead enemy, ere he went down. Hirpinus raised his friend's head, and knew it was all over.

"I have got it," said Rufus, in a faint voice; "my foot slipped and the clumsy barbarian lunged in over my guard. Farewell, old comrade! Bid the wife keep heart. There is a home for her at Picenum, and—the boys—keep them out of the Family. When you close with these Germans—disengage—at half distance, and turn your wrist down with the—old—thrust, so as to"—

Weaker and weaker came the gladiator's last syllables, his head sank, his jaw dropped, and Hirpinus, turning for a farewell look at the comrade with whom he had trained, and toiled, and drank, and fought, for half a score of years, dashed his hand angrily to his shaggy eyelashes, for he saw him through a mist of tears.

Another shout of laughter, louder still and nearer, roused [pg 303]him to action. Turning into the room whence it proceeded, he came upon a scene of combat, nearly as ludicrous as the last was pitiful. Surrounded by a circle of gladiators, roaring out their applause and holding their sides with mirth, two most unwilling adversaries were pitted against each other. They seemed, indeed, very loth to come to close quarters, and stood face to face with excessive watchfulness and caution.

In searching for the Emperor, Placidus and his myrmidons had scoured several apartments without success. Finding the palace thus unoccupied, and now in their own hands, the men had commenced loading themselves with valuables, and prepared to decamp with their plunder, each to his home, as having fulfilled their engagement, and earned their reward. But the tribune well knew that if Vitellius survived the night, his own head would be no longer safe on his shoulders, and that it was indispensable to find the Emperor at all hazards; so gathering a handful of gladiators round him, persuading some and threatening others, he instituted a strict search in one apartment after another, leaving no hole nor corner untried, persuaded that Cæsar must be still inside the palace, and consequently within his grasp. He entertained, nevertheless, a lurking mistrust of treachery roused by the late appearance of Euchenor at supper, which was rather strengthened than destroyed by the Greek's unwillingness to engage in personal combat with the Germans. Whilst he was able to do so, the tribune had kept a wary eye upon the pugilist, and had indeed prevented him more than once from slipping out of the conflict altogether. Now that the Germans were finally disposed of, and the palace in his power, he kept the Greek close at hand with less difficulty, jeering him, half in jest and half in earnest, on the great care he had taken of his own person in the fray. Thus, with Euchenor at his side, followed by Hippias, and some half-dozen gladiators, the tribune entered the room in which the Emperor had supped, and from which a door, concealed by a heavy curtain, led into a dark recess originally intended for a bath. At the foot of this curtain, half-lying, half-sitting, grovelled an obese unwieldy figure, clad in white, which moaned and shook and rocked itself to and fro, in a paroxysm of abject fear. The tribune leapt forward with a gleam of diabolical triumph in his eyes. The next instant his face fell, as the figure, looking up, presented the scared features of the bewildered Spado. But even in his wrath and disappointment Placidus could indulge himself with a brutal jest.

[pg 304]

"Euchenor," said he, "thou hast hardly been well blooded to-night. Drive thy sword through this carrion, and draw it out of our way."

The Greek was only averse to cruelty when it involved personal danger. He rushed in willingly enough, his blade up, and his eyes glaring like a tiger's; but the action roused whatever was left of manhood in the victim, and Spado sprang to his feet with the desperate courage of one who has no escape left. Close at his hand lay a Parthian bow, one of the many curiosities in arms that were scattered about the room, together with a sandal-wood quiver of puny painted arrows.

"Their points are poisoned," he shouted; "and a touch is death!"

"'Their points are poisoned', he shouted"

Then he drew the bow to its full compass, and glared about him like some hunted beast brought to bay. Euchenor, checked in his spring, stood rigid as if turned to stone. His beautiful form indeed, motionless in that lifelike attitude, would have been a fit study for one of his own country's sculptors; but the surrounding gladiators, influenced only by the ludicrous points of the situation, laughed till their sides shook, at the two cowards thus confronting each other.

"To him, Euchenor!" said they, with the voice and action by which a man encourages his dog at its prey. "To him, lad! Here's old Hirpinus come to back thee. He always voted thee a cur. Show him some of thy mettle now!"

Goaded by their taunts, Euchenor made a rapid feint, and crouched for another dash. Terrified and confused, the eunuch let the bowstring escape from his nerveless fingers, and the light gaudy arrow, grazing the Greek's arm and scarcely drawing blood, fell, as it seemed, harmless to the floor between his feet. Again there was a loud shout of derision, for Euchenor, dropping his weapon, applied this trifling scratch to his mouth; ere the laugh subsided, however, the Greek's face contracted and turned pale. With a wild yell he sprang bolt upright, raising his arms above his head, and fell forward on his breast, dead.

The gladiators leaping in, passed half a dozen swords through the eunuch's body, almost ere their comrade touched the floor. Then Lutorius and Eumolpus tearing down the curtain disappeared in the dark recess behind. There was an exclamation of surprise, a cry for mercy, a scuffling of feet, the fall of some heavy piece of furniture, and the two [pg 305]emerged again, dragging between them, pale and gasping, a bloated and infirm old man.

"Cæsar is fled!" said he, looking wildly round. "You seek Cæsar?" then perceiving the dark smile on the tribune's face, and abandoning all hope of disguise, he folded his arms with a certain dignity that his coarse garments and disordered state could not wholly neutralise, and added—

"I am Cæsar! Strike! since there is no mercy and no escape!"

The tribune paused an instant and pondered. Already the dawn was stealing through the palace, and the dead upturned face of Spado looked grey and ghastly in the pale cold light. Master of the situation, he did but deliberate whether he should slay Cæsar with his own hand, thus bidding high for the gratitude of his successor, or whether, by delivering him over to an infuriated soldiery, who would surely massacre him on the spot, he should make his death appear an act of popular justice, in the furtherance of which he was himself a mere dutiful instrument. A few moments' reflection on the character of Vespasian, decided him to pursue the latter course. He turned to the gladiators, and bade them secure their prisoner.

Loud shouts and the tramp of many thousand armed feet announced that the disaffected legions were converging on the palace, and had already filled its courtyard with masses of disciplined men, ranged under their eagles in all the imposing precision and the glittering pomp of war. The increasing daylight showed their serried files, extending far beyond the gate, over the spacious gardens of the palace, and the cold morning breeze unfurled a banner here and there, on which were already emblazoned the initials of the new emperor, "Titus Flavius Vespasian Cæsar." As Vitellius with his hands bound, led between two gladiators, passed out of the gate which at midnight had been his own, one of these gaudy devices glittered in the rising sun before his eyes.

Then his whole frame seemed to collapse, and his head sank upon his breast, for he knew that the bitterness of death had indeed come at last.

But it was no part of the tribune's scheme that his victim's lineaments should escape observation. He put his own sword beneath the Emperor's chin, and forced him to hold his head up while the soldiers hooted and reviled, and ridiculed their former lord.

"Let them see thy face," said the tribune brutally. "Even now thou art still the most notorious man in Rome."

Obese in person, lame in gait, pale, bloated, dishevelled, and a captive, there was yet a certain dignity about the fallen emperor, while he drew himself up, and thus answered his enemy—

"Thou hast eaten of my bread and drunk from my cup. I have loaded thee with riches and honours. Yesterday I was thine emperor and thy host. To-day I am thy captive and thy victim. But here, in the jaws of death, I tell thee that not to have my life and mine empire back again, would I change places with Julius Placidus the tribune!"

They were the last words he ever spoke, for while they paraded him along the Sacred Way, the legions gathered in and struck him down, and hewed him in pieces, casting the fragments of his body into the stream of Father Tiber, stealing calm and noiseless by the walls of Rome. And though the faithful Galeria collected them for decent interment, few cared to mourn the memory of Vitellius the glutton; for the good and temperate Vespasian reigned in his stead.

CHAPTER XX

THE FAIR HAVEN

In a land-locked bay sheltered by wooded hills, under a calm cloudless sky, and motionless as some sleeping seabird, a galley lay at anchor on the glistening surface of the Mediterranean. Far out at sea, against a clear horizon the breeze just stirred the waters to a purer deeper blue, but here, behind the sharp black point, that shot boldly from the shore, long sheets of light, unshadowed by a single ripple traversed the bay, basking warm and still in the glaring sunshine. The very gulls that usually flit so restless to and fro, had folded their wings for an interval of repose, and the hush of the hot southern noon lay drowsily on the burnished surface of the deep.

The galley had obviously encountered her share of wind and weather. Spars were broken and tackle strained. Her large square sail, rent and patched, was under process of repair; heaped up, neglected for the present, and half unfurled upon the deck, while the double-banked seats of her rowers were unoccupied, and the long oars shipped idly in her sides. Like the seabird she resembled, and whose destiny she shared, it seemed as though she also had folded her wings, and gone peacefully to sleep.

Two figures were on the deck of the galley, drinking in the beauty that surrounded them, with the avidity of youth, and health, and love. They thought not of the dangers they had so narrowly escaped—of the perils by sea and perils by land that were in store for them yet, of the sorrows they must undergo, the difficulties they must encounter, the frail thread on which their present happiness depended. It was enough for them that they were gazing on the loveliness of one of the fairest isles in the Ægean, and that they were together.

Surely there is a Fair Haven in the voyage of each of us, to which we reach perhaps once in a lifetime, where we pause and furl the sail and ship the oar, not that we are weary [pg 308]indeed, nor unseaworthy, but that we cannot resist, even the strongest and bravest of us, the longing of poor humanity for rest. Such seasons as these come to remind us of our noble destiny, and our inherent unworthiness—of our capacity for happiness, and our failure in attaining it—of the sordid casket, and the priceless jewel we are sure that it contains. At such seasons shall we not rejoice and revel in the happiness they bring? Shall we not bathe in the glorious sunshine, and snatch at the glowing fruit, and empty the golden cup, ay to the very dregs? What though there be a cloud behind the hill, a bitter morsel at the fruit's core, a drop of wormwood in the sparkling draught?—a consciousness of insecurity, a foresight of sorrow, a craving for the infinite and the eternal, which goads and guides us at once on the upward way? Would we be without it if we could? We cannot be more than human; we would not willingly be less. Is not failure the teacher of humility? Is not humility the first step to wisdom? Where is least of self-dependence, there is surely most of faith; and are not pain and sorrow the title-deeds of our inheritance hereafter?

It is a false moral, it is a morbid and unreal sentiment, beautifully as it is expressed, which teaches us that "a sorrow's crown of sorrows, is remembering happier things." All true happiness is of spiritual origin. When we have been brushed, though never so lightly by the angel's wing, we cannot afterwards entirely divest ourselves of the fragrance breathed by that celestial presence. Even in those blissful moments, something warned us they would pass away; now that they have faded here, something assures us that they will come again, hereafter. Hope is the birthright of immortality. Without winter there would be no spring. In decay is the very germ of life, and while suffering is transitory, mercy is infinite, and joy eternal.

The sailors were taking their noonday rest below, to escape the heat. Eleazar, the Jew, sat at the stern of the vessel, deep in meditation, pondering on his country's resources and his nation's wrongs—the dissensions that paralysed the Lion of Judah, and the formidable qualities of the princely hunter who was bringing him warily and gradually to bay. It would be hard enough to resist Titus with both hands free, how hopeless a task when one neutralised the efforts of the other! Eleazar's outward eye, indeed, took in the groves of olives, and the dazzling porches, the jagged rocks and the glancing water; but his spirit was gazing the while upon a very different scene. He saw his tumultuous countrymen [pg 309]armed with sword and spear, brave, impetuous, full of the headlong courage which made their race irresistible for attack, but lacking the cool methodical discipline, the stern habitual self-reliance so indispensable for a wearing and protracted defence; and he saw also the long even lines under the eagles, the impregnable array of the legions; their fortified camp, their mechanical discipline, their exact manœuvres, and the calm confident strength that was converging day by day for the downfall and destruction of his people. Then he moved restlessly, like a man impatient of actual fetters about his limbs, for he would fain be amongst them again, with his armour on and his spear in his hand. Calchas, too, was on board the anchored galley. He looked on the fair scene around as those look who see good in everything. And then his eye wandered from the glowing land, and the cloudless heaven, and the sparkling sea, to the stately form of Esca, and Mariamne with her gentle loving face, ere it sought his task again, the perusal of his treasured Syriac scroll; for the old man, who took his share of all the labours and hardships incidental to a sea-voyage, spent in sacred study many of the hours devoted by others to rest; his lips moved in prayer, and he called down a blessing on the head of the proselyte he had gained over, and the kinsman he loved.

After the success of the tribune's plot, and the escape of Esca from the imperial palace, Rome was no longer a place in which the Briton might remain in safety. Julius Placidus, although, from the prominent part taken by Domitian in public affairs, he had not attained such power as he anticipated, was yet sufficiently formidable to be a fatal enemy, and it was obvious that the only chance of life was immediately to leave the neighbourhood of so implacable an adversary. The murder, too, of Vitellius, and the accession of Vespasian, rendered Eleazar's further stay at Rome unnecessary, and even impolitic, while the services rendered to Mariamne by her champion and lover, had given him a claim to the protection of the Jewish household, and the intimacy of its members. On condition of his conforming to certain fasts and observances, Eleazar therefore willingly gave Esca the shelter of his roof, concealed him whilst he himself made preparations for a hasty departure, and suffered him to accompany the other two members that constituted his family, on their voyage home to Jerusalem. After many storms and casualties, half of that voyage was completed, and the attachment between Esca and Mariamne [pg 310]which sprang up so unexpectedly at the corner of a street in Rome, had now grown to the engrossing and abiding affection which lasts for life, perhaps for eternity. Floating in that fair haven, with the glow of love enhancing the beauty of an earthly paradise, they quaffed at the cup of happiness without remorse or misgiving, thankful for the present and trusting for the future. As shipwreck had threatened them but yesterday, as to-morrow they might again be destined to weather stormy skies, and ride through raging seas, so, although they had suffered great dangers and hardships in life, greater were yet probably in store. Nevertheless, to-day all was calm and sunshine, contentment, security, and repose. They took it as it came, and standing together on the galley's deck, the beauty of those two young creatures seemed god-like, in the halo of their great joy.

"We shall never be parted here," whispered Esca, while they stooped over the bulwark, and his hand stealing to his companion's, pressed it in a gentle timid clasp.

With her large loving eyes full of tears, she leaned towards him, nearer, nearer, till her cheek touched his shoulder, and, pointing upward, she answered in the low earnest tones that acknowledge neither doubt nor fear: "Esca, we shall never be parted hereafter."

Moira

CHAPTER I

A HOUSE DIVIDED AGAINST ITSELF

The Feast of the Passover was at hand; the feast that was wont to call the children of Israel out of all parts of Syria to worship in the Holy City; the feast that had celebrated their deliverance from the relentless grasp of Pharaoh: that was ordained to mark the fulfilment of prophecy in the downfall of the chosen people, and their national extinction under the imperial might of Rome. Nevertheless, even this, the last Passover held in that Temple of which Solomon was the founder, and in the destruction of which, notwithstanding its sacred character, not one stone was permitted to remain upon another, had collected vast multitudes of the descendants of Abraham from all parts of Judæa, Samaria, Galilee, Perea, and other regions, to increase the sufferings of famine, and enhance the horrors of a siege. True to the character of their religion, rigidly observant of outward ceremonies, and admitting no exemptions from the requirements of the law, they swarmed in thousands and tens of thousands to their devoted city, round which even now Titus was drawing closer and closer the iron band of blockade, over which the Roman eagles were hovering, ere they swooped down irresistible on their prey.

There was the hush of coming destruction in the very stillness of the Syrian noon, as it glowed on the white carved pinnacles of the temple, and flashed from its golden roof. There was a menace in the tall black cypresses, pointing as it were with warning gesture towards the sky. There was [pg 312]a loathsome reality of carnage about the frequent vulture, poised on his wide wings over every open space, or flapping heavily away with loaded gorge and dripping beak, from his hideous meal. Jerusalem lay like some royal lady in her death-pang; the fair face changed and livid in its ghastly beauty, the queenly brow warped beneath its diadem, and the wasted limbs quivering with agony under their robe of scarlet and gold.

Inside the walls, splendour and misery, unholy mirth and abject despair, the pomp of war and the pressure of starvation, were mingled in frightful contrast. Beneath the shadow of princely edifices dead bodies lay unburied and uncared-for in the streets. Wherever was a foot or two of shelter from the sun, there some poor wretch seemed to have dragged himself to die. Marble pillars, lofty porches, white terraces, and luxuriant gardens denoted the wealth of the city, and the pride of its inhabitants; yet squalid figures crawling about, bent low towards the ground, sought eagerly here and there for every substance that could be converted into nourishment, and the absence of all offal and refuse on the pavement denoted the sad scarcity even of such loathsome food.

The city of Jerusalem, built upon two opposite hills, of which the plan of the streets running from top to bottom in each, and separated only by a narrow valley, exactly corresponded, was admirably adapted to purposes of defence. The higher hill, on which was situated the upper town and the holy Temple, might, from the very nature of its position, be considered impregnable; and even the lower offered on its outside so steep and precipitous an ascent as to be almost inaccessible by regular troops. In addition to its natural strength, the city was further defended by walls of enormous height and solidity, protected by large square towers, each capable of containing a formidable garrison, and supplied with reservoirs of water and all other necessaries of war. Herod the Great, who, notwithstanding his vices, his crimes, and his occasional fits of passion amounting to madness, possessed the qualities both of a statesman and a soldier, had not neglected the means at his disposal for the security of his capital. He had himself superintended the raising of one of these walls at great care and expense, and had added to it three lofty towers, which he named after his friend, his brother, and his ill-fated wife.[16] These were constructed [pg 313]of huge blocks of marble, fitted to each other with such nicety, and afterwards wrought out by the workman's hand with such skill, that the whole edifice appeared to be cut from one gigantic mass of stone. In the days, too, of that magnificent monarch, these towers were nothing less than palaces within, containing guest-chambers, banqueting-rooms, porticoes, nay, even fountains, gardens, and cisterns, with great store of precious stones, gold and silver vessels, and all the barbaric wealth of Judæa's fierce and powerful king. Defended by Herod, even a Roman army might have turned away discomfited from before Jerusalem.

Agrippa, too, the first of that name, who was afterwards stricken with a loathsome disease, and "eaten of worms," like a mere mortal, while he affected the attributes of a god, commenced a system of fortification to surround the city, which would have laughed to scorn the efforts of an enemy; but the Jewish monarch was too dependent on his imperial master at Rome to brave his suspicion by proceeding with it; and although a wall of magnificent design was begun, and even raised to a considerable height, it was never finished in the stupendous proportions originally intended. The Jews, indeed, after the death of its founder, strengthened it considerably, and completed it for purposes of defence, but not to the extent by which Agrippa proposed to render the town impregnable.

And even had Jerusalem been entered and invested by an enemy, the Temple, which was also the citadel of the place, had yet to be taken. This magnificent building, the very stronghold of the wealth and devotion of Judæa, the very symbol of that nationality which was still so prized by the posterity of Jacob, was situated on the summit of the higher hill, from which it looked down and commanded both the upper and lower cities. On three sides it was artificially fortified with extreme caution, while on the fourth, it was so precipitous as to defy even the chances of a surprise. To possess the Temple was to hold the whole town as it were in hand; nor was its position less a matter of importance to the assailed than its splendour rendered it an object of cupidity to the assailants. Every ornament of architecture was lavished upon its cloisters, its pillars, its porticoes, and its walls. Its outward gates even, according to their respective positions, were brass, silver, and gold; its beams were of cedar, and other choice woods inlaid with the precious metal, which was also thickly spread over doorposts, candlesticks, cornices—everything that would admit of such costly [pg 314]decoration. The fifteen steps that led from the Court of the Women to the great Corinthian gate, with its double doors of forty cubits high, were worth as many talents of gold as they numbered.[12]

To those who entered far enough to behold what was termed the Inner Temple, a sight was presented which dazzled eyes accustomed to the splendour of the greatest monarchs on earth. Its whole front was covered with plates of beaten gold; vines bearing clusters of grapes the size of a man's finger, all of solid gold, were twined about and around its gates, of which the spikes were pointed sharp, that birds might not pollute them by perching there. Within were golden doors of fifty-five cubits in height; and before this entrance hung the celebrated veil of the Temple. It consisted of a curtain embroidered with blue, fine linen, scarlet and purple, signifying by mystical interpretation, a figure of the universe, wherein the flax typified earth; the blue, air; the scarlet, fire; and the purple, water. Within this sumptuous shrine were contained the candlestick, the table of shew-bread, and the altar of incense: the seven lamps of the first denoting the seven planets of heaven; the twelve loaves on the second representing the circle of the zodiac and the year; while the thirteen sweet-smelling spices on the third, reminded men of the Great Giver of all good things in the whole world. In the inmost part, again, of this Inner Temple was that sacred space, into which mortal eye might not look, nor mortal step enter. Secluded, awful, invisible, divested of all material object, it typified forcibly to the Jew the nature of that spiritual worship which was taught him through Abraham and the Patriarchs, direct from heaven.

All men, however, of all creeds and nations, might gaze upon the outward front of the Temple, and judge by the magnificence of the covering the costly splendour of the shrine it contained. While a dome of pure white marble rose above it like a mountain of snow, the front itself of the Temple was overlaid with massive plates of gold, so that when it flashed in the sunrise men could no more look upon it than on the god of day himself. Far off in his camp, watching the beleaguered city, how often may the Roman soldier have pondered in covetous admiration, speculating on the strength of its defenders and the value of his prey!

The Temple of Jerusalem then was celebrated through all the known earth for its size, its splendour, and its untold wealth. The town, strong in its natural position and its [pg 315]artificial defences, garrisoned, moreover, by a fierce and warlike people, whose impetuous valour could be gauged by no calculations of military experience, was justly esteemed so impregnable a fortress, as might mock the attack of a Roman army even under such a leader as the son of Vespasian. Had it been assailed by none other than the enemy outside the walls, the Holy Place need never have been desecrated and despoiled by the legions, the baffled eagles would have been driven westward, balked of their glorious prey. But here was a "house divided against itself." The dissension within the walls was far more terrible than the foe without. Blood flowed faster in the streets than on the ramparts. Many causes originating in his past history, had combined to shake the loyalty and undermine the nationality of the Jew. Perhaps, for the wisest purposes, it seems ordained that true religion should be especially prone to schism. Humanity, however high its aspirations, cannot be wholly refined from its earthly dross; and those who are the most in earnest are sometimes the most captious and unforgiving. While worship for his Maker appears to be a natural instinct of man, it needed a teacher direct from heaven to inculcate forbearance and brotherly love. The Jews were sufficiently ill-disposed to those of their own faith, who differed with them on unimportant points of doctrine, or minute observance of outward ceremonies; but where the heresy extended to fundamental tenets of their creed, they seemed to have hated each other honestly, rancorously, and mercilessly, as only brethren can.

Now for many generations they have been divided into three principal sects, differing widely in belief, principle, and practice. These were distinguished by the names of Pharisees, Sadducees, and Essenes. The first, as is well known, were rigid observers of the traditional law, handed down to them from their fathers, attaching fully as much importance to its letter as to its spirit. With a vague belief in what is understood by the term predestination, they yet allowed to mankind the choice between good and evil, confounding, perhaps, the foreknowledge of the Creator with the freewill of the creature, and believed in the immortality of souls, and the doctrine of eternal punishment. Their failings seem to have been inordinate religious pride, and undue exaltation of outward forms to the neglect of that which they symbolised; a grasping ambition of priestly power, and an utter want of charity for those who differed in opinion with themselves.

The Sadducees, though professing belief in the Deity, [pg 316]argued an entire absence of influence from above on the conduct of the human race. Limiting the dispensation of reward and punishment to this world, they esteemed it a matter of choice with mankind to earn the one or incur the other; and as they utterly ignored the life to come, were content to enjoy temporal blessings, and to deprecate physical evil alone. Though wanting a certain genial philosophy on which the heathen prided himself, the Sadducee, both in principles and practice, seems closely to have resembled the Epicurean of ancient Greece and Rome.

But there was also a third sect which numbered many votaries throughout Judæa, in whose tenets we discover several points of similarity with our own, and whose ranks, it is not unfair to suppose, furnished numbers of the early converts to Christianity. These were the Essenes, a persuasion that rejected pleasure as a positive evil, and with whom a community of goods was the prevailing and fundamental rule of the order. These men, while they affected celibacy, chose out the children of others to provide for and educate. While they neither bought nor sold, they never wanted the necessaries of life, for each gave and received ungrudgingly, according to his own and his neighbour's need. While they despised riches, they practised a strict economy, appointing stewards to care for and dispense that common patrimony which was raised by the joint subscription of all. Scattered over the whole country, in every city they were sure of finding a home, and none took on a journey either money, food, or raiment, because he was provided by his brethren with all he required wherever he stopped to rest. Their piety, too, was exemplary. Before sunrise not a word was spoken referring to earthly concerns, but public prayer was offered, imploring the blessing of light day by day before it came. Then they dispersed to their different handicrafts, by which they earned wages for the general purse. Meeting together once more, they bathed in cold water and sat down in white garments to their temperate meal, in which a sufficiency and no more was provided for each person, and again separated to labour till the evening, when they assembled for supper in the same manner before going to rest.

The vows taken by all who were admitted into their society, and that only after a two years' probation, sufficiently indicated the purity and benevolence of their code. These swore to observe piety towards God, and justice towards men; to do no one an injury, either voluntarily or by command of [pg 317]others; to avoid the evil, and to aid the good; to obey legal authority as coming from above; to love truth, and openly reprove a lie; to keep the hands clean from theft, and the heart from unfair gain; neither to conceal anything from their own sect, nor to discover their secrets to others, but to guard them with life; also to impart these doctrines to a proselyte literally and exactly as each had received them himself. If one of the order committed any grievous sin, he was cast out of their society for a time; a sentence which implied starvation, as he had previously sworn never to eat save in the presence of his brethren. When in the last stage of exhaustion he was received again, as having suffered a punishment commensurate with his crime, and which, by the maceration of the body, should purify and save the soul.

With such tenets and such training, the Essenes were conspicuous for their confidence in danger, their endurance of privation, and their contempt for death. The flesh they despised as the mere corruptible covering of the spirit, that imperishable essence, of which the aspiration was ever upwards, and which, when released from prison, in obedience to the dictates of its very nature, flew direct to heaven. Undoubtedly such doctrines as these, scattered here and there throughout the land, partially redeemed the Jewish character from the fierce unnatural stage of fanaticism, to which it had arrived at the period of the Christian era—afforded, it may be, a leavening which preserved the whole people from utter reprobation; and helped, perhaps, to smooth the way for those pioneers, who carried the good tidings first heard beneath the star of Bethlehem, westward through the world.

But at the period when Jerusalem lay beleaguered by Titus and his legions, three political parties raged within her walls, to whose furious fanaticism her three religious sects could offer no comparison. The first and most moderate of these, though men who scrupled not to enforce their opinions with violence, had considerable influence with the great bulk of the populace, and were, indeed, more than either of the others, free from selfish motives, and sincere in their desire for the common good. They affected a great concern for the safety and credit of their religion, making no small outcry at the fact that certain stones and timber, provided formerly by Agrippa for the decoration of the Temple, had been desecrated by being applied to the repair of the defences and the construction of engines of war. They observed, also, how the rivalry of faction, in which, nevertheless, they took a prominent part, devastated the city more than any efforts of [pg 318]the enemy; and they did not scruple to paralyse the energies of the besieged, by averring that the military rule of the Romans, wise and temperate, though despotic, was preferable to the alternations of tyranny and anarchy under which they lived.

This numerous party was especially displeasing to Eleazar, whose restless force of character and fanatical courage were impatient of any attempt at capitulation, who was determined on resistance to the death, and the utter destruction of the Holy City rather than its surrender. He was now living in the element of storm and strife, which seemed most congenial to his nature. No longer a foreign intriguer, disguised in poor attire, and hiding his head in a back street of Rome, the Jew seemed to put on fresh valour every day with his breastplate, and walked abroad in the streets or directed operations from the ramparts; a mark for friend and foe, in his splendid armour, with the port of a warrior, a patriarch and a king. He was avowedly at the head of a numerous section of the seditious, who had adopted the title of Zealots; and who, affecting the warmest enthusiasm in the cause of patriotism and religion, were utterly unscrupulous as to the means by which they furthered their own objects and aggrandisement. Their practice was indeed much opposed to the principles they professed, and to that zeal for religion from which they took their name. They had not scrupled to cast lots for the priesthood, and to confer the highest and holiest office of the nation on an illiterate rustic, whose only claim to the sacerdotal dignity consisted in his relationship with one of the pontifical tribes. Oppression, insult, and rapine inflicted on their countrymen, had rendered the very name of Zealot hateful to the mass of the people; but they numbered in their ranks many desperate and determined men, skilled in the use of arms, and ready to perpetrate any act of violence on friend or foe. In the hands of a bold unscrupulous leader, they were sharp and efficient weapons. As such Eleazar considered them, keeping them under his own control and fit for immediate use.

The third of these factions, which was also perhaps the most numerous, excited the apprehensions of the more peaceably disposed no less than the hatred of the last-mentioned party who had put Eleazar at their head. It was led by a man distinguished alike for consummate duplicity and reckless daring—John of Gischala, so called from a small town in Judæa, the inhabitants of which he had influenced to hold out against the Romans, and whence he had himself escaped [pg 319]by a stratagem, redounding as much to the clemency of Titus as to his own dishonour.

Gischala being inhabited by a rural and unwarlike population, unprovided besides with defences against regular troops, would have fallen an easy prey to the prince with his handful of horsemen, had it not been for that disposition to clemency which Titus, in common with other great warriors, seems to have indulged when occasion offered. Knowing that if the place were carried by storm it would be impossible to restrain his soldiers from putting the inhabitants to the sword, he rode in person within earshot of the wall, and exhorted the defenders to open their gates and trust to his forbearance, a proposal to which John, who with his adherents completely overmastered and dominated the population, took upon himself to reply. He reminded the Roman commander that it was the Sabbath, a day on which not only was it unlawful for the Jews to undertake any matters of war, policy, or business, but even to treat of such, and therefore they could not so much as entertain the present proposals of peace; but that if the Romans would give them four-and-twenty hours' respite, during which period they could surround the city with their camp, so that none could escape from it, the keys of the gate should be given up to him on the following day, when he might enter in triumph and take possession of the place. Titus withdrew accordingly, probably for want of forage, to a village at some distance, and John with his followers, accompanied by a multitude of women and children, whom he afterwards abandoned, made his escape in the night and fled to Jerusalem.

After such a breach of faith, he could expect nothing from the clemency of the Roman general; so that John of Gischala, like many others of the besieged, might be said to fight with a rope round his neck.

Within the city there had now been a fierce struggle for power between the Zealots under Eleazar, and the reckless party called by different opprobrious terms, of which "Robbers" was the mildest, who followed the fortunes of John. The peaceful section, unable to make head against these two, looked anxiously for the entrance of the eagles, many indeed of the wealthier deserting when practicable to the camp of the enemy. Meanwhile the Romans pushed the siege vigorously. Their army now consisted of Vespasian's choicest legions, commanded by his son in person. Their engines of war were numerous and powerful. Skilful, scientific, exact in discipline, and unimpeachable in courage, they [pg 320]were gradually but surely converging, in all their strength, for one conclusive effort on the devoted city. Already the second wall had been taken, retaken in a desperate struggle by the besieged, and once more stormed and carried by the legions. Famine, too, with her cruel hand, was withering the strongest arms and chilling the bravest hearts in the city. It was time to forget self-interest, faction, fanaticism, everything but the nationality of Judæa, and the enemy at the gate.

[pg 321]

CHAPTER II

THE LION OF JUDAH

Eleazar had resolved to obtain supreme command. In a crisis like the present, no divided authority could be expected to offer a successful resistance. John of Gischala must be ruined by any means and at any sacrifice. His unscrupulous rival, regardless of honour, truth, every consideration but the rescue of his country, laid his plans accordingly. With a plausible pretence of being reconciled, and thus amalgamating two formidable armies for the common good, he proposed to hold a conference with John in the Outer Court of the Temple, where, in presence of the elders and chief men of the city, they should arrange their past differences and enter into a compact of alliance for the future. The Great Council of the nation, ostensibly the rulers of public affairs, and influenced alternately by the two antagonists, were to be present. Eleazar thought it would go hard, but that, with his own persuasive powers and public services, he should gain some signal advantage over his adversary ere they separated.

He appeared, accordingly, at the place of conference, splendidly armed indeed in his own person, but accompanied by a small retinue of adherents all attired in long peaceful robes, as though inviting the confidence of his enemy. Observant eyes, it is true, and attentive ears, caught the occasional clank and glitter of steel under these innocent linen mantles, and the friends, if few in number, were of tried valour and fidelity, while a mob of warlike men outside, who had gathered ostensibly to look idly on, belonged obviously to the party of the Zealots. Nevertheless, Eleazar had so contrived matters that, while he guarded against surprise, he should appear before the Council as a suppliant imploring justice rather than a leader dictating terms. He took up his position, accordingly, at the lower end of the court, and after a deep obeisance to the assembled elders, stood, as it were, in the background, assuming an air of [pg 322]humility somewhat at variance with his noble and warlike exterior.

His rival, on the contrary, whose followers completely blocked up the entrance from the Temple, through which he had thought it becoming to arrive, strode into the midst with a proud and insolent bearing, scarcely deigning to acknowledge the salutations he received, and glancing from time to time back amongst his adherents, with scornful smiles, that seemed to express a fierce contempt for the whole proceeding. He was a man who, though scarcely past his youth, wore in his face the traces of his vicious and disorderly career. His features were flushed and swollen with intemperance; and the deep lines about his mouth, only half concealed by the long moustache and beard, denoted the existence of violent passions, indulged habitually to excess. His large stature and powerful frame set off the magnificence of his dress and armour, nor was his eye without a flash of daring and defiance that boded evil to an enemy; but his bearing, bold as it was, smacked rather of the outlaw than the soldier, and his rude, abrupt gestures contrasted disadvantageously with the cool self-possession of his rival. The latter, asking permission, as it were, of the Senate by another respectful obeisance, walked frankly into the middle of the court to meet his foe. John changed colour visibly, and his hand stole to the dagger at his belt. He seemed to expect the treachery of which he felt himself capable; but Eleazar, halting a full pace off, looked him steadily in the face, and held out his right hand in token of amity and reconciliation. A murmur of approval ran through the Senate, which increased John's uncertainty how to act; but after a moment's hesitation, unwillingly and with a bad grace, he gave his own in return.

Eleazar's action, though apparently so frank and spontaneous, was the result of calculation. He had now made the impression he desired on the Senate, and secured the favourable hearing which he believed was alone necessary for his triumph.

"We have been enemies," said he, releasing the other's hand and turning to the assembly, while his full voice rang through the whole court, and every syllable reached the listeners outside. "We have been fair and open enemies, in the belief that each was opposed to the interests of his country; but the privations we have now undergone in the same cause, the perils we have confronted side by side on the same ramparts, must have convinced us that however we may differ in our political tenets, nay, in our religious practices, [pg 323]we are equally sincere in a determination to shed our last drop of blood in the defence of the Holy City from the pollution of the heathen. This is no time for any consideration but one—Jerusalem is invested, the Temple is threatened, and the enemy at the gate. I give up all claim to authority, save as a leader of armed men. I yield precedence in rank, in council, in everything but danger. I devote my sword and my life to the salvation of Judæa! Who is on my side?"

Loud acclamations followed this generous avowal; and it was obvious that Eleazar's influence was more than ever in the ascendant. It was no time for John to stem the torrent of popular feeling, and he wisely floated with the stream. Putting a strong control upon his wrath, he expressed to the Senate in a few hesitating words, his consent to act in unison with his rival, under their orders as Supreme Council of the nation; a concession which elicited groans and murmurs from his own partisans, many of whom forced their way with insolent threats and angry gestures into the court. Eleazar did not suffer the opportunity to escape without a fresh effort for the downfall of his adversary.

"There are men," said he, pointing to the disaffected, and raising his voice in full clear tones, "who had better have swelled the ranks of the enemy than stood side by side with Judah on the ramparts of Agrippa's wall. They may be brave in battle, but it is with a fierce undisciplined courage more dangerous to friend than foe. Their very leader, bold and skilful soldier as he is, cannot restrain such mutineers even in the august presence of the Council. Their excesses are laid to his charge; and a worthy and patriotic commander becomes the scapegoat of a few ruffians whose crimes he is powerless to prevent. John of Gischala, we have this day exchanged the right hand of fellowship. We are friends, nay, we are brothers-in-arms once more. I call upon thee, as a brother, to dismiss these robbers, these paid cut-throats, whom our very enemies stigmatise as 'Sicarii,' and to cast in thy lot with thine own people, and with thy father's house!"

John shot an eager glance from his rival to his followers. The latter were bending angry brows upon the speaker, and seemed sufficiently discontented with their own leader that he should listen tamely to such a proposal. Swords, too, were drawn by those in the rear, and brandished fiercely over the heads of the seething mass. For an instant the thought crossed his mind, that he had force enough to put the opposing assemblage, Senate and all, to the sword; but his quick practised glance taught him at the same time, that [pg 324]Eleazar's party gathered quietly towards their chief, with a confidence unusual in men really without arms, and a methodical precision that denoted previous arrangement; also that certain signals passed from them to the crowd, and that the court was filling rapidly from the multitude without. He determined then to dissemble for a time, and turned to the Senate with a far more deferential air than he had yet assumed.

"I appeal to the elders of Judah," said he, repressing at the same time by a gesture the turbulence of his followers—"I am content to abide by the decision of the National Council. Is to-day a fitting season for the reduction of our armament? Shall I choose the present occasion to disband a body of disciplined soldiers, and turn a host of outraged and revengeful men loose into the city with swords in their hands? Have we not already enough idle mouths to feed, or can we spare a single javelin from the walls? My *brother*"—he laid great stress upon the word, and gripped the haft of his dagger under his mantle while he spoke it—"My brother gives strange counsel, but I am willing to believe it sincere. I too, though the words drop not like honey from my beard as from his, have a right to be heard. Did I not leave Gischala and my father's vineyard for a prey to the enemy? Did I not fool the whole Roman army, and mock Titus to his face, that I might join in the defence of Jerusalem? and shall I be schooled like an infant, or impeached for a traitor to-day? Judge me by the result. I was on the walls this morning; I saw not my brother there. The enemy were preparing for an assault. The engine they call Victory had been moved yet nearer by a hundred cubits. While we prate here the eagles are advancing. To the walls! To the walls, I say! Every man who calls himself a Jew; be he Priest or Levite, Pharisee or Sadducee, Zealot or Essene. Let us see whether John and his Sicarii are not as forward in the ranks of the enemy as this *brother* of mine, Eleazar, and the bravest he can bring!"

Thus speaking, and regardless of the presence in which he stood, John drew his sword and placed himself at the head of his adherents, who with loud shouts demanded to be led instantly to the ramparts. The enthusiasm spread like wildfire, and even communicated itself to the Council. Eleazar's own friends caught the contagion, and the whole mass poured out of the Temple, and, forming into bands in the streets, hurried tumultuously to the walls.

What John had stated to the Council was indeed true. [pg 325]The Romans, who had previously demolished the outer wall and a considerable portion of the suburbs, had now for the second time obtained possession of the second wall, and of the high flanking tower called Antonia, which John, to do him justice, had defended with great gallantry after he had retaken it once from the assailants. It was from this point of vantage that an attack was now organised by the flower of the Roman army, having for its object the overthrow of her last defences and complete reduction of the city. When Eleazar and his rival appeared with their respective bands they proved a welcome reinforcement to the defenders, who, despite of their stubborn resistance, were hardly pressed by the enemy.

Every able-bodied Jew was a soldier on occasion. Troops thus composed are invariably more formidable in attack than defence. They have usually undaunted courage and a blind headlong valour that sometimes defies the calculations of military science or experience; but they are also susceptible of panic under reverses, and lack the cohesion and solidity which is only found in those who make warfare the profession of a lifetime. The Jew armed with spear and sword, uttering wild cries as he leaped to the assault, was nearly irresistible; but once repulsed, his final discomfiture was imminent. The Roman, on the contrary, never suffered himself to be drawn out of his ranks by unforeseen successes, and preserved the same methodical order in the advance as the retreat. He was not, therefore, to be lured into an ambush however well disguised; and even when outnumbered by a superior force, could retire without defeat.

The constitution of the legion, too, was especially adapted to enhance the self-reliance of well-drilled troops. Every Roman legion was a small army in itself, containing its proportion of infantry, cavalry, engines of war, and means for conveyance of baggage. A legion finding itself never so unexpectedly detached from the main body, was at no loss for those necessaries without which an army melts away like snow in the sunshine, and was capable of independent action, in any country and under any circumstances. Each man too had perfect confidence in himself and his comrades; and while it was esteemed so high a disgrace to be taken prisoner that many soldiers have been known rather to die by their own hands than submit to such dishonour, it is not surprising that the imperial armies were often found to extricate themselves with credit from positions which would have ensured the destruction of any other troops in the world.

[pg 326]

The internal arrangement, too, of every cohort, a title perhaps answering to the modern word regiment, as does the legion to that of division, was calculated to promote individual intelligence and energy in the ranks. Every soldier not only fought, but fed, slept, marched, and toiled, under the immediate eye of his *decurion* or captain of ten, who again was directly responsible for those under his orders to his centurion, or captain of a hundred. A certain number of these centuries or companies, varying according to circumstances, constituted a maniple, two of which made up the cohort. Every legion consisted of ten cohorts, under the charge of but six tribunes, who seem to have entered on their onerous office in rotation. These were again subservient to the general, who, under the different titles of prætor, consul, etc., commanded the whole legion. The private soldiers were armed with shield, breastplate, helmet, spear, sword, and dagger; but in addition to his weapons every man carried a set of intrenching tools, and on occasion two or more strong stakes, for the rapid erection of palisades. All were, indeed, robust labourers and skilful mechanics, as well as invincible combatants.

The Jews, therefore, though a fierce and warlike nation, had but little chance against the conquerors of the world. It was but their characteristic self-devotion that enabled them to hold Titus and his legions so long in check. Their desperate sallies were occasionally crowned with success, and the generous Roman seems to have respected the valour and the misfortunes of his foe; but it must have been obvious to so skilful a leader, that his reduction of Jerusalem and eventual possession of all Judæa was a question only of time.

At an earlier period of the siege the Romans had made a wide and shallow cutting capable of sheltering infantry, for the purpose of advancing their engines closer to the wall, but from the nature of the soil this work had been afterwards discontinued. It now formed a moderately-secure covered-way, enabling the besieged to reach within a short distance of the Tower of Antonia, the retaking of which was of the last importance—none the less that from its summit Titus himself was directing the operations of his army. There was a breach in this tower on its inner side, which the Romans strove in vain to repair, harassed as they were by showers of darts and javelins from the enemy on the wall. More than once, in attempting to make it good at night, their materials had been burnt and themselves driven back upon their works with great loss, by the valour of the besieged. The Tower of Antonia was indeed the key to the possession of the second [pg 327]wall. Could it but be retaken, as it had already been, the Jews might find themselves once more with two strong lines of defence between the upper city and the foe.

When Eleazar and John, at the head of their respective parties, now mingled indiscriminately together, reached the summit of the inner wall, they witnessed a fierce and desperate struggle in the open space below.

Esca, no longer in the position of a mere household slave, but the friend and client of the most influential man in Jerusalem, who had admitted him, men said, as a proselyte to his faith, and was about to bestow on him his daughter in marriage, had already so distinguished himself by various feats of arms in the defence of the city, as to be esteemed one of the boldest leaders in the Jewish army. Panting to achieve a high reputation, which he sometimes dared to hope might gain him all he wished for on earth—the hand of Mariamne—and sharing to a great extent with the besieged their veneration for the Temple and abhorrence of a foreign yoke, the Briton lost no opportunity of adding a leaf to the laurels he had gained, and thrust himself prominently forward in every enterprise demanding an unusual amount of strength and courage. His lofty stature and waving golden hair, so conspicuous amongst the swarthy warriors who surrounded him, were soon well known in the ranks of the Romans, who bestowed on him the title of the Yellow Hostage, as inferring from his appearance that he must have lately been a stranger in Jerusalem; and many a stout legionary closed in more firmly on his comrade, and raised his shield more warily to the level of his eyes, when he saw those bright locks waving above the press of battle, and the long sword flashing with deadly strokes around that fair young head. He was now leading a party of chosen warriors, along the covered-way that has been mentioned, to attack the

Tower of Antonia. For this purpose, the trench had been deepened during the night by the Jews themselves, who had for some days meditated a bold stroke of this nature; and the chosen band had good reason to believe that their movements were unseen and unsuspected by the enemy.

As they deployed into the open space, but a few furlongs from the base of the tower, the Jews caught sight of Titus on the summit, his golden armour flashing in the sun, and, with a wild yell of triumph, they made one of their fierce, rushing, disorderly charges to the attack. They had reached within twenty paces of the breach, when swooping round the angle of the tower, like a falcon on his prey, came Placidus, at the [pg 328]head of a thousand horsemen, dashing forward with lifted shields and levelled spears amongst the disorganised mass of the Jews, broken by the very impetus of their own advance.

The tribune had but lately joined the Roman army, having been employed in the subjugation of a remote province of Judæa—a task for which his character made him a peculiarly fit instrument. Enriched by a few months of extortion and rapine, he had taken care to rejoin his commander in time to share with him the crowning triumphs of the siege. Julius Placidus was a consummate soldier. His vigilance had detected the meditated attack, and his science was prepared to meet it in the most effectual manner. Titus, from the summit of his tower, could not but admire the boldness and rapidity with which the tribune dashed from his concealment, and launched his cavalry on the astonished foe.

But he had to do with one, who, though his inferior in skill and experience, was his equal in that cool hardihood which can accept and baffle a surprise. Esca had divided his force into two bodies, so that the second might advance in a dense mass to the support of the first, whether its disorderly attack should be attended by failure or success. This body, though clear of the trench, yet remaining firm in its ranks, now became a rallying point for its comrades, and although a vast number of the Jews were ridden down and speared by the attacking horsemen, there were enough left to form a bristling phalanx, presenting two converging fronts of level steel impervious to the enemy. Placidus observed the manœuvre and ground his teeth in despite; but though his brow lowered for one instant, the evil smile lit up his face the next, for he espied Esca, detached from his band and engaged in rallying its stragglers; nor did he fail to recognise at a glance the man he most hated on earth. Urging his horse to speed, and even at that moment of gratified fury glancing towards the tower to see whether Titus was looking on, he levelled his spear and bore down upon the Briton in a desperate and irresistible charge. Esca stepped nimbly aside, and receiving the weapon on his buckler, dealt a sweeping sword-cut at the tribune's head, which stooping to avoid, the latter pulled at his horse's reins so vigorously as to check the animal's career and bring it suddenly on its haunches. The Briton, watching his opportunity, seized the bit in his powerful grasp, and with the aid of his massive weight and strength, rolled man and horse to the ground in a crashing fall. The tribune was undermost, and for the moment at the mercy of his adversary. Looking [pg 329]upward with a livid face and deep bitter hatred glaring in his eye, he did but hiss out "Oh, mine enemy!" from between his clenched teeth, and prepared to receive his deathblow; but the hand that was raised to strike, fell quietly to Esca's side, and he turned back through the press of horsemen, buffeting them from him as a swimmer buffets the waves, till he reached his own men. Placidus, rising from the ground, shook his clenched fist at the retreating figure; but he never knew that he owed his preservation to the first-fruits of that religion which had now taken root in the breast of his former slave. When he groaned out in his despair "Oh, mine enemy!" the Briton remembered that this man had, indeed, shown himself the bitterest and most implacable of his foes. It was no mere impulse, but the influence of a deep abiding principle that bade him now forgive and spare for the sake of One whose lessons he was beginning to learn, and in whose service he had resolved to enter. Amongst all the triumphs and the exploits of that day, there was none more noble than Esca's, when he lowered his sword and turned away, unwilling, indeed, but resolute, from his fallen foe.

The fight raged fiercely still. Eleazar with his Zealots—John of Gischala with his Robbers—rushed from the walls to the assistance of their countrymen. The Roman force was in its turn outnumbered and surrounded, though Placidus, again on horseback, did all in the power of man to make head against the mass of his assailants. Titus at length ordered the Tenth Legion, called by his own name and constituting the very flower of the Roman army, to the rescue of their countrymen. Commanded by Licinius, in whose cool and steady valour they had perfect confidence, these soon turned the tide of combat, and forced the Jews back to their defences; not, however, until their general had recognised in the Yellow Hostage the person of his favourite slave, and thought, with a pang, that the fate of war would forbid his ever seeing him face to face again, except as a captive or a corpse.

CHAPTER III

THE WISDOM OF THE SERPENT

Ever since the night which changed the imperial master of Rome, Esca had dwelt with Eleazar as if he were a member of the same family and the same creed. Though Mariamne, according to the custom of her nation, confined herself chiefly to the women's apartments, it was impossible that two who loved each other so well as the Jewess and the Briton should reside under the same roof without an occasional interview. These usually took place when the latter returned to unarm after his military duties; and though but a short greeting was interchanged, a hurried inquiry, a few words of thanksgiving for his safety, and assurances of her continued affection, these moments were prized and looked forward to by both, as being the only occasions on which they could enjoy each other's society uninterrupted and alone.

After the repulse of the tribune's attack beneath the Tower of Antonia, Esca returned in triumph to Eleazar's house. He was escorted to the very door by the chief men of the city, and a band of those chosen warriors who had witnessed and shared in his exploits. Mariamne, from the gallery which surrounded it, saw him enter her father's court at the head of her father's friends, heard that father address him before them all in a few soldierlike words of thanks and commendation—

nay, even observed him lead the successful combatant away with him as though for some communication of unusual confidence. The girl's heart leaped within her; and vague hopes, of which she could not have explained the grounds, took possession of her mind. She loved him very dearly: they slept under the same roof, they ate at the same board; notwithstanding the perils of warfare to which she was now habituated, they met every day: but this was not enough; something was wanting still; so she watched him depart with her father, and grudged not the loss of her own short interview with [pg 331]its congratulations that she so longed to pour into his ear, because the indefinite hopes that dawned on her, seemed to promise more happiness than she could bear.

Eleazar took the helmet from his brow, and signed to Esca to do the same. Then he filled a measure of wine, and draining the half of it eagerly, handed the rest to his companion. For a few minutes he paced up and down the room, still wearing his breastplate, and with his sword girded to his side, deep in thought, ere turning abruptly to his companion he placed his hand on his shoulder, and said—

"You have eaten my bread—you have drunk from my cup. Esca, you are to me as a son; will you do my bidding?"

"Even as a son," replied the Briton; to whom such an address seemed at once to open the way for the fulfilment of his dearest wishes.

Eleazar ignored the emphasis on the word. It may be that his mind was too entirely engrossed with public interests to admit a thought upon private affairs; it may be that he considered Esca, like the sword upon his thigh, as a strong and serviceable weapon, to be laid aside when no longer wanted for conflict; or it may be that his purpose was honest, and that, after the salvation of his country, he would have been actuated by the kindlier motives of a father and a friend; but in the meantime he had a purpose in view, and no considerations of affection or partiality would have led him to swerve from it by a hair's-breadth.

"Look around you," said he, "and behold the type of Judæa, and especially of Jerusalem, in this very building. See how fair and stately are the walls of my house, how rich its ornaments, how costly its hangings and decorations. Here are ivory, and sandal-wood, and cedar; webs of divers colours; robes of purple, stores of fine linen, vessels of silver, and drinking-cups of gold; frankincense and wine are here in plenty, but of barley we have scarce a few handfuls; and if the same visitors that my father Abraham entertained on the plains of Mamre were at my door to-day, where should I find a kid that I might slay it, and set it before them to eat? I have everything here in the house, save that alone without which everything else is of no avail—the daily bread that gives man strength for his daily task. And so is it with my country: we have men, we have weapons, we have wealth; but we lack that which alone renders those advantages efficient for defence—the constant [pg 332]unshrinking reliance on itself and its faith, from which a nation derives its daily resources as from its daily bread. There are men here in the city now who would hand Jerusalem over to the heathen without striking another blow in her defence."

"Shame on them!" answered the other warmly. "Barbarian, stranger as I am, I pledge myself to die there, ere a Roman soldier's foot shall pollute the threshold of the Temple."

"You are a warrior," answered Eleazar; "you have proved it to-day. As a warrior I consult with you on the possibility of our defence. You saw the result of the conflict under the Tower of Antonia, and the bravery of the Tenth Legion; we cannot resist another such attack till our defences are repaired. We must gain time; at all hazards, and at any sacrifice, we must gain time."

"In two days the breach might be strengthened," replied the other; "but Titus is an experienced soldier; he was watching us to-day from the summit of his tower. He will hardly delay the assault beyond to-morrow."

"He must!" answered Eleazar vehemently. "I have my preparations for defence, and in less than two days the city shall be again impregnable. Listen, Esca; you little know the opposition I have met with, or the hatred I have incurred in overcoming it. I have sought means to preserve the city from all quarters, and have thus given a handle to my enemies that they will not fail to use for my destruction. Have I not taken the holy oil from the sacrifice, to pour boiling on the heads of the besiegers? and will not John of Gischala and the Robbers fling this sacrilege in my teeth when it becomes known? Even at this moment I have seized the small quantity of chaff there is yet remaining in the city, to fill the sacks with which we may neutralise the iron strokes of that heavy battering-ram, which the soldiers themselves call Victory. There is scarce a grain of wheat left, and many a hungry stomach must sleep to-night without even the miserable meal it had promised itself, for want of this poor measure of chaff. Men will curse Eleazar in their prayers. It is cruel work,—cruel work. But, no! I will never abandon my post, and the seed of Jacob shall eat one another for very hunger in the streets, ere I deliver the Holy City into the keeping of the heathen."

Something almost like a tear shone in the eye of this iron-hearted fanatic while he spoke, but his resolution was not to be shaken; and he only spoke the truth when he [pg 333]avowed that famine, stalking abroad in its most horrible form, would be a less hateful sight to him than the crest of a Roman soldier within the walls of Jerusalem. His brain had been hard at work on his return from the conflict of the day; and he had woven a plan by which he hoped to gain such a short respite from attack as would enable him to bid defiance to Titus once more. This could only be done, however, with the aid of others, and by means of a perfidy that even he could scarcely reconcile to himself—that he could not but fear must be repugnant to his agent.

The well-known clemency of the Roman commander, and his earnest wish to spare, if it were possible, the beautiful and sacred city from destruction, had caused him to listen patiently at all times to any overtures made by the Jews for the temporary suspension of hostilities. Titus seemed not only averse to bloodshed, but also extended his goodwill in an extraordinary degree to an enemy whose religion he respected, and whose miseries obtained his sincere compassion. On many occasions he had delayed his orders for a final and probably irresistible assault, in the hope that the city might be surrendered; and that he could hand over to his father this beautiful prize, undefaced by the violence inflicted on a town taken by storm. The great Roman commander was not only the most skilful leader of his day, but a wise and far-sighted politician, as well as a humane and generous man. Eleazar knew the character with which he had to deal; but he stifled all scruples of honour in the one consideration, that his first and only duty was to the cause of Judah; yet in his breast were lying dormant the instincts of a brave man, and it was not without misgivings of opposition from his listener, that he disclosed to Esca the scheme by which he hoped to overreach Titus and gain a few hours' respite for the town.

"Two days," said he, resuming his restless walk up and down the apartment—"two days is all I ask—all I require. Two days I *must* have. Listen, young man. I have proved you, I can trust you; and yet the safety of Judah hangs on your fidelity. Swear, by the God of Israel, that you will never reveal the secret I disclose to you this day. It is but known to my brother, my daughter, and myself. You are the adopted son of my house. Swear!"

"I swear!" replied Esca solemnly; and his hopes grew brighter as he found himself thus admitted, as it were, to a place in the family of the woman he loved.

Eleazar looked from the casement and through the door, [pg 334]to assure himself against listeners; then he filled the Briton's cup once more, and proceeded with his confidences.

"Around that dried-up fountain," said he, pointing to the terraces on which his stately house was built, "there lie seven slabs of marble, with which its basin is paved. If you put the point of your sword under the left-hand corner of the centre one, you may move it sufficiently to admit your hand. Lift it, and you find a staircase leading to a passage; follow that passage, in which a full-grown man can stand upright, and along which you may grope your way without fear, and you come to an egress choked up with a few faggots and briers. Burst through these, and, lo! you emerge beyond the Tower of Antonia, and within fifty paces of the Roman camp. Will you risk yourself amongst the enemy for Judah's sake?"

"I have been nearer the Romans than fifty paces," answered Esca proudly. "It is no great service you ask; and if they seize upon me as an escaped slave, and condemn me to the cross, what then? It is but a soldier's duty I am undertaking after all. When shall I depart?"

Eleazar reflected for a moment. The other's unscrupulous, unquestioning fidelity touched even his fierce heart to the quick. It would be, doubtless, death to the messenger, who, notwithstanding his character of herald, would be too surely treated as a mere runaway; but the message must be delivered, and who was there but Esca for him to send? He bent his brows, and proceeded in a harder tone—

"I have confided to you the secret way, that is known to but three besides in Jerusalem. I need keep nothing from you now. You shall bear my written proposals to Titus for a truce till the sun has again set twice, on certain terms; but those terms it will be safer for the messenger not to know. Will you run the risk, and when?"

"This instant, if they are ready," answered the other boldly; but even while he spoke, Calchas entered the apartment; and Eleazar, conscious of the certain doom to which he was devoting his daughter's preserver and his own guest, shrank from his brother's eye, and would have retired to prepare his missive without further question.

Fierce and unscrupulous as he was, he could yet feel bitterly for the brave, honest nature that walked so unsuspiciously into the trap he laid. It was one thing to overreach a hostile general, and another to sacrifice a faithful and devoted friend. He had no hesitation in affecting treason to Titus, and promising the Romans that, if they would but grant him [pg 335]that day and the next, to obtain the supremacy of his own faction and chief power within the walls, he would deliver over the city, with the simple condition that the Temple should not be demolished, and the lives of the inhabitants should be spared. He acknowledged no dishonour in the determination, which he concealed in his own breast, to employ that interval strenuously in defensive works, and when it had elapsed to break faith unhesitatingly with his foe. In the cause of Judah—so thought this fanatic, half-soldier, half-priest—it was but a fair stratagem of war, and would, as a means of preserving the true faith, meet with the direct approval of Heaven. But it seemed hard—very hard—that, to secure these advantages, he must devote to certain destruction one who had sat at his board and lived under his roof for months; and a pang, of which he did not care to trace the origin, smote the father's heart when he thought of Mariamne's face, and her question to-morrow, "Where is Esca? and why is he not come back?"

He took his brother aside, and told him, shortly, that Esca was going as a messenger of peace to the Roman camp. Calchas looked him full in the face, and shook his head.

"Brother," said he, "thy ways are tortuous, though thy bearing is warlike and bold. Thou trustest too much to the sword of steel and the arm of flesh—the might of man's strength, which a mere pebble on the pavement can bring headlong to the ground; and the scheming of man's brain, which cannot foresee, even for one instant, the trifle that shall baffle and confound it in the next. It is better to trust boldly in the right. This youth is of our own household: he is more to us than friend and kindred. Wouldst thou send him up with his hands bound to the sacrifice? Brother, thou shalt not do this great sin!"

"What would you?" said Eleazar impatiently. "Every man to his duty. The priest to the offering; the craftsman to his labour; the soldier to the wall. He alone knows the secret passage. Whom have I but Esca to send?"

"I am a man of peace," replied Calchas, and over his face stole that ray of triumphant confidence which at seasons of danger seemed to brighten it like a glory; "who so fitting to carry a message of peace as myself? You have said, everyone to his appointed task. I cannot—nay, I *would* not—put a breastplate on my worthless body, and a helmet on my old grey head, and brandish spear, or javelin, or deadly weapon in my feeble hands; but do you think it is because I fear? Remember, brother, the blood of the sons of Manahem runs in [pg 336]my veins as in yours, and I, too, have a right to risk every drop of it in the service of my country! Oh! I have sinned! I have sinned!" added the old man, with a burst of contrition, after this momentary outburst. "What am I to speak such words? I, the humblest and least worthy of my master's servants!"

"You shall not go!" exclaimed Eleazar, covering his face with his hands as the horrid results of such a mission rose before his eyes. Should the Romans keep the herald for a hostage, as most probably they would, until the time of surrender had elapsed, what must be his certain fate? Had they not already crucified more than one such emissary in face of the walls? and could they be expected to show mercy in a case like this? His love for his brother had been the one humanising influence of Eleazar's life. It tore his heart now with a grief that was something akin to rage, when he reflected that even that brother, if requisite, must be sacrificed to the cause of Jerusalem.

Esca looked from one to the other, apparently unmoved. To him the whole affair seemed simply a matter of duty, in the fulfilment of which he would himself certainly run considerable risk, that did not extend to Calchas. He was perfectly willing to go; but could not, at the same time, refrain from thinking that the latter was the fitter person to undertake such a mission at such a time. He could not guess at the perfidy which Eleazar meditated, and which brought with it its own punishment in his present sufferings for his brother. "I am ready," said he quietly, resting his hand on his helmet, as though prepared to depart forthwith.

"You shall not go," repeated Calchas, looking fixedly at his brother the while. "I tell thee, Eleazar," he added, with kindling eye and heightened tone, "that I will not stand by and see this murder done. As an escaped slave, Esca will be condemned to death unheard. It may be that they will even subject him to the scourge, and worse. As the bearer of terms for a truce, our enemies will treat me as an honoured guest. If thou art determined to persevere, I will frustrate thine intention by force. I need but whisper to the Sanhedrim that Eleazar is trafficking with those outside the walls, and where would be the house of Ben-Manahem? and how long would the Zealots own allegiance to their chief? Nay, brother, such discord and such measures can never be between thee and me. When have we differed in our lives, since we clung together to our mother's knees? Prepare thy missive. I will take it to the Roman camp forthwith, and return in [pg 337]safety as I went. What have I to fear? Am I not protected by Him whom I serve?"

When Eleazar withdrew his hands from his face it was deadly pale, and large drops stood upon his forehead. The struggle had been cruel indeed, but it was over. "Jerusalem before all," was the principle from which he had never been known to swerve, and now he must sacrifice to it that life so much dearer than his own.

"Be it as you will," said he, commanding himself with a strong effort; "you can only leave the city by our secret passage. The scroll shall be ready at midnight. It must be in the hand of Titus by dawn!"

[pg 338]

CHAPTER IV

THE MASTERS OF THE WORLD

An hour before sunrise Calchas was stopped by one of the sentinels on the verge of the Roman camp. He had made his escape from the city, as he hoped, without arousing the suspicions of the besieged. The outskirts of Jerusalem were, indeed, watched almost as narrowly by its defenders as its assailants, for so many of the peaceful inhabitants had already taken refuge with the latter, and so many more were waiting their opportunity to fly from the horrors within the walls, and trust to the mercy of the conquerors without, that a strict guard had been placed by the national party on the different gates of the city, and all communication with the enemy forbidden and made punishable with death. It was no light risk, therefore, that Calchas took upon himself in carrying his brother's proposals to the Roman general.

Following the high-crested centurion, who, summoned by the first sentinel that had challenged, offered to conduct him at once to the presence of Titus; the emissary, man of peace though he was, could not but admire the regularity of the encampment in which he found himself, and the discipline observed by those who occupied it. The line of tents was arranged with mathematical order and precision, forming a complete city of canvas, of which the principal street, so to speak, stretching in front of the tents occupied by the tribunes and other chief officers, was not less than a hundred feet wide. From this great thoroughfare all the others struck off at right angles, completing a simple figure, in which communication was unimpeded and confusion impossible, whilst an open space of some two hundred feet was preserved between the camp and the ramparts that encircled the whole. In this interval troops might parade, spoil and baggage be stored, or beasts of burden tethered, whilst its width afforded comparative security to those within from darts, firebrands, or other missiles of offence.

If Calchas had ever dreamed of the possibility that his [pg 339]countrymen would be able to make head against the Romans, he abandoned the idea now. As he followed his conductor through the long white streets in which the legions lay at rest, he could not but observe the efficient state of that army which no foe had ever yet been able to resist—he could not fail to be struck by the brightness of the arms, piled in exact symmetry before each tent; by the ready obedience and cheerful respect paid by the men to their officers, and by the abundant supplies of food and water, contrasting painfully with the hunger and thirst of the besieged. Line after line he traversed in silent wonder, and seemed no nearer the pavilion of the general than at first; and he could not conceal from himself that the enemy were no less formidable to the Jews in their numerical superiority than in discipline, organisation, and all the advantages of war.

His conductor halted at length in front of a large canvas dome, opposite to which a strong guard of the Tenth Legion were resting on their arms. At a sign from the centurion, two of these advanced like machines, and stood motionless one on each side of Calchas. Then the centurion disappeared, to return presently with a tribune, who, after a short investigation of the emissary, bade him follow, and, lifting a curtain, Calchas found himself at once in the presence of the Roman conqueror and his generals. As the latter gave way on each side, the hero advanced a step and confronted the ambassador from the besieged. Titus, according to custom, was fully armed, and with his helmet on his head. The only luxury the hardy soldier allowed himself was in the adornment of his weapons, which were richly inlaid with gold. Many a time had he nearly paid the penalty of this warlike fancy with his life; for, in the thick of battle, who so conspicuous as the bold prince in his golden armour? Who such a prize, alive or dead, as the son of Vespasian, and heir to the sovereignty of the world? He stood now, erect and dignified, a fitting representative of the mighty engine he wielded with such skill. His firm and well-knit frame wore its steel covering lightly and easily as a linen tunic. His noble features and manly bearing bore witness to the generous disposition and the fearless heart within; and his gestures denoted that self-reliance and self-respect which spring from integrity and conscious power combined. He looked every inch a soldier and a prince.

But there was a peculiarity in the countenance of Titus which added a nameless charm to his frank and handsome [pg 340]features. With all its manly daring, there was yet in the depths of those keen eyes a gleam of womanly compassion and tenderness, that emboldened a suppliant and reassured a prisoner. There was a softness in the unfrequent smile that could but belong to a kindly guileless nature. It was the face of a man capable, not only of lofty deeds and daring exploits, but of gentle memories, loving thoughts, home affections, generosity, commiseration, and self-sacrifice.

Close behind the general, affording a striking contrast in every respect to his chief, stood the least-trusted, but by no means the least efficient, of his officers. Almost the first eye that Calchas met when he entered the tent was that of Julius Placidus, whose services to Vespasian, though never thoroughly understood, had been rewarded by a high command in the Roman army. The most right-thinking of Cæsars could not neglect the man whose energies had helped him to the throne; and Titus, though he saw through the character he thoroughly despised, was compelled to do justice to the ready courage and soldierlike qualities of the tribune. So Julius Placidus found himself placed in a position from which he could play his favourite game to advantage, and was still courting ambition as zealously as when he intrigued at Rome against Vitellius, and bargained with Hippias over a cup of wine for the murder of his emperor.

That retired swordsman, too, was present in the tent; no longer the mere trainer of professional gladiators, but commanding a band that had made itself a name for daring at which the besieged grew pale, and which the Tenth Legion itself could hardly hope to emulate. After the assassination of the last Cæsar, this host of gladiators had formed themselves into a body of mercenaries, with Hippias at their head, and offered their services to the new emperor. Under the ominous title of "The Lost Legion," these desperate men had distinguished themselves by entering on all such enterprises as promised an amount of danger to which it was hardly thought prudent to expose regular troops, and had gained unheard-of credit during the siege, which from its nature afforded them many opportunities for the display of wild and reckless courage. Their leader was conspicuous, even in the general's tent, by the lavish splendour of his arms and appointments; but, though his bearing was proud and martial as ever, his face had grown haggard and careworn, his beard was thickly sprinkled with grey. Hippias had played for the heaviest stakes of life boldly, and had [pg 341]won. He seemed to be little better off, and little better satisfied, than the losers in the great game.

Near him stood Licinius,—staid, placid, determined; the commander of the Tenth Legion; the favoured councillor of Titus; the pride of the whole army; having all the experiences, all the advantages, all the triumphs of life at his feet. Alas! knowing too well what they were worth. It was a crown of parsley men gave the young athlete who conquered in the Isthmian Games; and round the unwrinkled brows that parsley was precious as gold. Later in life the converse holds too true, and long before the hair turns grey, all earthly triumphs are but empty pageantry; all crowns but withered parsley at the best.

Titus, standing forward from amongst his officers, glanced with a look of pity at the worn hungry face of the messenger. Privation, nay, famine, was beginning to do its work even on the wealthiest of the besieged, and Calchas could not hide under his calm, dignified bearing, the lassitude and depression of physical want.

"The proposal is a fair one," said the prince, turning to his assembled captains. "Two days' respite, and a free surrender of the city, with the simple condition that the holy places shall be respected, and the lives of the inhabitants spared. These Jews may do me the justice to remember that my wish throughout the war has ever been to avoid unnecessary bloodshed, and had they treated me with more confidence, I would long ago have shown them how truly I respected their Temple and their faith. It is not too late now. Nevertheless, illustrious friends, I called you not together so soon after cock-crow[1] for a council of war, without intending to avail myself of your advice. I hold in my hand a proposal from Eleazar, an influential patrician, as it appears, in the city, to deliver up the keys of the Great Gate, within forty-eight hours, provided I will pledge him my word to preserve his Temple from demolition, and his countrymen from slaughter; provided also, that the Roman army abstain during that time from all offensive measures, whatever preparations for resistance they may observe upon the walls. He further states that the city contains a large party of desperate men, who are opposed to all terms of capitulation, and that he must labour during these two days to coerce some and cajole others to his own opinion. It is a fair proposal enough, I repeat. The Tenth [pg 342]Legion is the first in seniority as in fame—I call upon its commander for his opinion."

Licinius, thus appealed to, earnestly advised that any terms which might put an end to the loss of life on both sides, should be entertained from motives of policy as well as humanity.

"I speak not," said the general, "for myself or my legion. Our discipline is unshaken, our supplies are regular, our men have been inured by long campaigning to a Syrian climate and a Syrian sun. We have lost comparatively few from hardships or disease. But no commander knows better than Titus, how an army in the field melts by the mere influence of time, and the difference that a few weeks can make in its efficiency and numerical strength is the difference between victory and defeat. Other divisions have not been so fortunate as my own. I will put it to the leader of the Lost Legion, how many men he could march to-day to the assault?"

Hippias stroked his beard gravely, and shook his head.

"Had I been asked the question five days ago," said he frankly, "I could have answered a thousand. Had I been asked it yesterday, seven hundred. Great prince, at noon, to-day, I must be content to muster five hundred swordsmen. Nevertheless," he added, with something of his old abrupt manner, "not one of them but claims his privilege of leading the other cohorts to the breach!"

It was too true that the influence of climate, acting upon men disposed to intemperance in pleasure, added to the severity of their peculiar service, had reduced the original number of the gladiators by one half. The remnant, however, were still actuated, like their commander, by the fierce reckless spirit of the amphitheatre. Titus, looking from one to the other, pondered for a few moments in earnest thought, and Placidus, seizing the opportunity, broke in with his smooth courteous tones.

"It is not for me," said he, "to differ with such illustrious leaders as those who have just spoken. The empire has long acknowledged Licinius as one of her bravest commanders; and Hippias the gladiator lives but in his natural element of war. Still, my first duty is to Cæsar and to Rome. Great prince, when a short while ago you bade a noble Jewish captive address his countrymen on the wall, what was the result? They knew him to be a patrician of their oldest blood, and, I believe, a priest also of their own superstitions. They had proved him a skilful general, and [pg 343]I myself speak of him without rancour, though he foiled me before Jotapata. Till taken prisoner by Vespasian Cæsar, he had been their staunchest patriot and their boldest leader. When he addressed them, notwithstanding the length of his appeal, they had no reason but to believe him sincere. And what, I say, was the result? A few hours gained for resistance; a fiercer defiance flung at Rome; a more savage cruelty displayed towards her troops. I would not trust them, prince. This very proposal may be but a stratagem to gain time. The attack of yesterday, covered by my cavalry, must have shaken them shrewdly. Probably their stores are exhausted. The very phalanx that opposed us so stubbornly looked gaunt and grim as wolves. Observe this very emissary from the most powerful man in Jerusalem. Is there not famine in his hollow cheeks and sunken eyes? Give him to eat. See how his visage brightens at the very name of food! Give him to eat, now, in presence of the council of war, and judge by his avidity of the privations he has endured behind the walls."

"Hold!" exclaimed Titus indignantly; "hold, tribune, and learn, if you have one generous feeling left, to respect misfortune, most of all when you behold it in the person of your enemy. This venerable man shall indeed be supplied with wine and food; but he shall not be insulted in my camp by feeling that his sufferings are gauged as the test of his truth. Licinius, my old and trusty counsellor, my very instructor in the art of war, I confide him to your care. Take him with you to your tent; see that he wants for nothing. I need not remind you to treat an enemy with all the kindness and courtesy compatible with the caution of a soldier. But you must not lose sight of him for a moment, and you will send him back with my answer under a strong guard to the chief gate of Jerusalem. I will have no underhand dealings with this unhappy people; though much, I fear, my duty to my father and the empire will not permit me to grant them the interval of repose that they desire. This is for my consideration. I have taken your opinions, for which I thank you. I reserve to myself the option of being guided by them. Friends and comrades, you are dismissed. Let this man be forthcoming in an hour, to take my answer back to those who sent him. *Vale!*"

Vale! repeated each officer, as he bowed and passed out of the tent.

Hippias and Placidus lingered somewhat behind the rest, and halting when out of hearing of the sentinel who guarded [pg 344]the eagles planted before the commander's quarters, or Prætorium, as it was called, looked in each other's faces, and laughed.

"You put it pointedly," said the former, "and took an ugly thrust in return. Nevertheless, the assault will be delayed after all, and my poor harmless lambs will scarce muster in enough force to be permitted to lead the attack."

"Fear not," replied the tribune; "it will take place to-morrow. It would suit neither your game nor mine, my Hippias, to make a peaceable entry by the Great Gate, march in order of battle to the Temple, and satisfy ourselves with a stare at its flashing golden roof. I can hardly stave off my creditors. You can scarce pay your men. Had it not been for the prospect of sacking the Holy Place, neither of us would have been to-day under a heavy breastplate in this scorching sun. And we *shall* sack it, I tell you, never fear."

"You think so?" said the other doubtfully; "and yet the prince spoke very sternly, as if he not only differed with you, but disapproved of your counsel. I am glad I was not in your place; I should have been tempted to answer even the son of Vespasian."

The tribune laughed gaily once more. "Trifles," said he; "I have the hide of a rhinoceros when it is but a question of looks and words, however stern and biting they may be. Besides, do you not yet know this cub of the old lion? The royal beast is always the same; dangerous when his hair is rubbed the wrong way. Titus was only angry because his better judgment opposed his inclinations, and agreed with me—me to whom he pays the compliment of his dislike. I tell you we shall give the assault before two days are out, with my cohort swarming on the flanks, and thy Lost Legion, my Hippias, maddening to the front. So now for a draught of wine and a robe of linen, even though it be under one of these suffocating tents. I think when once the siege is over and the place taken, I shall never buckle on a breastplate again."

[pg 345]

CHAPTER V

GLAD TIDINGS

The eye of Calchas did indeed brighten, and his colour went and came when food was placed before him in the Roman general's tent. It was with a strong effort that he controlled and stifled the cravings of hunger, never so painful as when the body has been brought down by slow degrees to exist on the smallest possible quantity of nourishment. It was long since a full meal had been spread even on Eleazar's table; and the sufferings from famine of the poorer classes in Jerusalem had reached a pitch unheard-of in the history of nations. Licinius could not but admire the self-control with which his guest partook of his hospitality. The old man was resolved not to betray, in his own person, the straits of the besieged. It was a staunch and soldierlike sentiment to which the Roman was keenly alive, and Licinius turned his back upon his charge, affecting to give long directions to some of his centurions from the tent-door, in order to afford Calchas the opportunity of satisfying his hunger unobserved.

After a while, the general seated himself inside, courteously desiring his guest to do the same. A decurion, with his spearmen, stood at the entrance, under the standard where the eagles of the Tenth Legion hovered over his shining crest. The sun was blazing fiercely down on the white lines of canvas that stretched in long perspective on every side, and flashing back at stated intervals from shield, and helm, and breastplate, piled in exact array at each tent-door. It was too early in the year for the crackling locust; and every trace of life, as of vegetation, had disappeared from the parched surface of the soil, burnished and slippery with [pg 346]the intense heat. It was an hour of lassitude and repose even in the beleaguering camp, and scarce a sound broke the drowsy stillness of noon, save the stamp and snort of a tethered steed, or the scream of an ill-tempered mule. Scorched without, and stifled within, even the well-disciplined legionary loathed his canvas shelter; longing, yearning vainly in his day-dreams for the breeze of cool Præneste, and the shades of darkling Tibur, and the north wind blowing through the holm-oaks off the crest of the snowy Apennines.

In the general's pavilion the awning had been raised a cubit from the ground, to admit what little air there was, so faint as scarce to stir the fringe upon his tunic. Against the pole that propped the soldier's home, rested a mule's pack-saddle, and a spare breastplate. On the wooden frame which served him for a bed, lay the general's tablets, and a sketch of the Tower of Antonia. A simple earthenware dish contained the food offered to his guest, and, like the coarse clay vessel into which a wineskin had been poured, was nearly empty. Licinius sat with his helmet off, but otherwise completely armed. Calchas, robed in his long dark mantle, fixed his mild eye steadily on his host.

The man of war and the man of peace seemed to have some engrossing thought, some all-important interest in common. For a while they conversed on light and trivial topics, the discipline of the camp, the fertility of Syria, the distance from Rome, and the different regions in which her armies fought and conquered. Then Licinius broke through his reserve, and spoke out freely to his guest.

"You have a hero," said the Roman, "in your ranks, of whom I would fain learn something, loving him as I do like a son. Our men call him the Yellow Hostage; and there is not a warrior among all the brave champions of Jerusalem whom they regard with such admiration and dread. I myself saw him but yesterday save your whole army from destruction beneath the walls."

"It is Esca!" exclaimed Calchas. "Esca, once a chief in Britain, and afterwards your slave in Rome."

"The same," answered Licinius; "and, though a slave, the noblest and the bravest of men. A chief, you say, in Britain. What know you of him? He never told me who he was, or whence he came."

"I know him," replied Calchas, "as one who lives with us like a kinsman, who takes his share of hardship, and far more than his share of danger, as though he were a very chief in Israel—who is to me, indeed, and those dearest to [pg 347]me, far more precious than a son. We escaped together from Rome—my brother, my brother's child, and this young Briton. Many a night on the smooth Ægean has he told me of his infancy, his youth, his manhood, the defence his people made against your soldiers, the cruel stratagems by which they were foiled and overcome, how nobly he himself had braved the legions; and yet how the first lessons he learned in childhood were to feel kindly for the invader, how the first accents his mother taught him were in the Roman tongue."

"It is strange," observed Licinius, musing deeply, and answering, as it seemed, his own thought. "Strange lesson for one of that nation to learn. Strange, too, that fate seems to have posted him continually in arms against the conqueror."

"They were his mother's lessons," resumed Calchas; "and that mother he has not forgotten even to-day. He loves to speak of her as though she could see him still. And who shall say she cannot? He loves to tell of her stately form, her fond eyes, and her gentle brow, with its lines of thought and care. He says she had some deep sorrow in her youth, which her child suspected, but of which she never spoke. It taught her to be kind and patient with all; it made her none the less loving for her boy. Ay, 'tis the same tale in every nation and under every sky. The garment has not yet been woven in which the black hank of sin and sorrow does not cross and recross throughout the whole web. She had her burden to bear, and so has Esca, and so hast thou, great Roman commander, one of the conquerors of the earth; and so have I, but I know where to lay mine down, and rest in peace."

"They are a noble race, these women of Britain," said Licinius, following out the thread of his own thoughts with a heavy heart, on which one of them had impressed her image so deeply, that while it beat, a memory would reign there, as it had reigned already for years, undisturbed by a living rival. "And so the boy loves to talk of his childhood, and his lost mother—lost," he added bitterly, "surely lost, because so loved!"

"Even so," replied Calchas; "and deep as was the child's grief, it carried a sharper sting from the manner of her death. Too young to bear arms, he had seen his father hurry away at the head of his tribe to meet the Roman legions. His father, a fierce, imperious warrior, of whom he knew but little, and whom he would have dreaded rather than loved, had [pg 348]the boy dreaded anything on earth. His mother lay on a bed of sickness; and even the child felt a nameless fear on her account, that forbade him to leave her side. With pain and difficulty they moved her on her litter to a fastness in their deep, tangled forests, where the Britons made a last stand. Then certain long-bearded priests took him by force from his mother's side, and hid him away in a cavern, because he was a chief's son. He can recall now the pale face and the loving eyes, turned on him in a last look, as he was borne off struggling and fighting like a young wolf-cub. From his cavern he heard plainly the shouts of battle and the very clash of steel; but he heeded them not, for a vague and sickening dread had come over him that he should see his mother no more. It was even so. They hurried the child from his refuge by night. They never halted till the sun had risen and set again. Then they spoke to him with kind, soothing words; but when he turned from them, and called for his mother, they told him she was dead. They had not even paid her the last tribute of respect. While they closed her eyes, the legions had already forced their rude defences; her few attendants fled for their lives, and the high-born Guenebra was left in the lonely hut wherein she died, to the mercy of the conquerors."

When Calchas ceased speaking, he saw that his listener had turned ghastly pale, and that the sweat was standing on his brow. His strong frame, too, shook till his armour rattled. He rose and crossed to the tent-door as if for air, then turned to his guest, and spoke in a low but steady voice—

"I knew it," said he—"I knew it must be so; this Esca is the son of one whom I met in my youth, and why should I be ashamed to confess it? whose influence has pervaded my whole life. I am old and grey now. Look at me; what have such as I to do with the foolish hopes and fears that quicken the young fresh heart, and flush the unwrinkled cheek? But now, to-day, I tell thee, warworn and saddened as I am, it seems to me that the cup of life has been but offered, and dashed cruelly away ere it had so much as cooled my thirsty lips. Why should I have known happiness, only to be mocked by its want? What! thou hast a human heart? Thou art a brave man, too, though thy robes denote a vocation of peace, else thou hadst not been here to-day in the heart of an enemy's camp. Need I tell thee, that when I entered that rude hut in the Briton's stronghold, and saw all I loved on earth stretched cold and inanimate on her litter [pg 349]at my feet, had I not been a soldier of Rome my own good sword had been my consolation, and I had fallen by her there, to be laid in the same grave; and now I shall never see her more!" He passed his hand across his face, and added, in a broken whisper, "Never more! never more!"

"You cannot think so. You cannot believe in such utter desolation," exclaimed Calchas, roused like some old war-horse by the trumpet sound, as he saw the task assigned him, and recognised yet another traveller on the great road, whom he could guide home.

"Do you think that you or she, or any one of us, were made to suffer, and to cause others suffering—to strive and fail, and long and sorrow, for a little while, only to drop into the grave at last, like an over-ripe fig from its branch, and be forgotten? Do you think that life is to end for you, or for me, when the one falls in his armour, at the head of the Tenth Legion, pierced by a Jewish javelin, or the other is crucified before the walls for a spy, by Titus, or stoned in the gate for a traitor, by his own countrymen? And this is the fate which may await us both before to-morrow's sun is set. Believe it not, noble Roman! That frame of yours is no more Licinius than is the battered breastplate yonder on the ground, which you have cast aside because it is no longer proof against sword and spear; the man himself leaves his worn-out robe behind, and goes rejoicing on his journey—the journey that is to lead him to his home elsewhere."

"And where?" asked the Roman, interested by the earnestness of his guest, and the evident conviction with which he spoke. "Is it the home to which, as our own poets have said, good Æneas, and Tullus, and Ancus have gone before? the home of which some philosophers have dreamed, and at which others laugh—a phantom-land, a fleeting pageant, impalpable plains beyond a shadowy river? These are but dreams, the idle visions of men of thought. What have we, who are the men of action, to do with aught but reality?"

"And what is reality?" replied Calchas. "Is it without or within? Look from your own tent-door, noble Roman, and behold the glorious array that meets your eye—the even camp, the crested legionaries, the eagles, the trophies, and the piles of arms. Beyond, the towers and pinnacles of Jerusalem, and the white dome of the Temple with its dazzling roof of gold. Far away, the purple hills of Moab looking over the plains of the Dead Sea. It is a world of beautiful reality. There cometh a flash from a thunder-cloud or an arrow off [pg 350]the wall, and your life is spared, but your eyesight is gone: which is the reality now, the light or the darkness? the wide expanse of glittering sunshine, or the smarting pain and the black night within? So is it with life and death. Titus in his golden armour, Vespasian on the throne of the Cæsars, that stalwart soldier leaning yonder on his spear, or the wasted captive dying for hunger in the town—are they beings of the same kind? and why are their shares so unequal in the common lot? Because it matters so little what may be the different illusions that deceive us now, when all may attain equally to the same reality at last."

Licinius pondered for a few minutes ere he replied. Like many another thinking heathen, he had often speculated on the great question which forces itself at times on every reflective being, "Why are these things so?" He, too, had been struck ere now with the obvious discrepancy between man's aspirations and his efforts—the unaccountable caprices of fortune, the apparent injustice of fate. He had begun life in the bold confidence of an energetic character, believing all things possible to the resolute strength and courage of manhood. When he failed, he blamed himself with something of contempt; when he succeeded, he gathered fresh confidence in his own powers and in the truth of his theories. But in the pride of youth and happiness, sorrow took him by the hand, and taught him the bitter lesson that it is good to learn early rather than late; because, until the plough has passed over it, there can be no real fertility, no healthy produce on the untilled soil. The deeper they are scored, the heavier is the harvest from these furrows of the heart. Licinius, in the prime of life, and on the pinnacle of success, became a thoughtful, because a lonely and disappointed, man. He saw the complications around him; he acknowledged his inability to comprehend them. While others thought him so strong and self-reliant, he knew his own weakness and his own need; the broken spirit was humble and docile as a child's.

"There must be a *reason* for everything," he exclaimed at last; "there must be a clue in the labyrinth, if a man's hand could only find it. What is truth? say our philosophers. Oh, that I did but know!"

Then, in the warlike tent, in the heart of the conquering army, the Jew imparted to the Roman that precious wisdom to which all other learning is but an entrance and a path. Under the very shadow of the eagles that were gathered to devastate his city, the man to whom all vicissitudes were alike, [pg 351]to whom all was good, because he knew "what was truth," showed to his brother, whose sword was even then sharpened for the destruction of his people, that talisman which gave him the mastery over all created things: which made him superior to hunger and thirst, pain and sorrow, insult, dishonour, and death. It is something, even in this world, to wear a suit of impenetrable armour, such as is provided for the weakest and the lowest who enter the service that requires so little and that grants so much. Licinius listened eagerly, greedily, as a blind man would listen to one who taught him how to recover his sight. Gladdening was the certainty of a future to one who had hitherto lived so mournfully in the past. Fresh and beautiful was the rising edifice of hope to one whose eye was dull with looking on the grey ruins of regret.

There was comfort for him, there was encouragement, there was example. When Calchas told, in simple, earnest words, all that he himself had heard and seen of glorious self-sacrifice, of infinite compassion, and of priceless ransom, the soldier's knee was bent, and his eyes were wet with tears.

By the orders of his commander, Licinius conducted his guest back to the Great Gate of Jerusalem with all the customary honours paid to an ambassador from a hostile power. He bore the answer of Titus, granting to the besieged the respite they desired. Placidus had been so far right that the prince's better judgment condemned the ill-timed reprieve; but in this, as in many other instances, Titus suffered his clemency to prevail over his experience in Jewish duplicity and his anxiety to terminate the war.

CHAPTER VI

WINE ON THE LEES

The commander of the Lost Legion, when he parted with Placidus after the council of war, retired moodily to his tent. He, too, was disappointed and dissatisfied, wearied with the length of the siege, harassed and uneasy about the ravages made by sickness among his men, and anxious moreover as to his share of the spoil. Hippias, it is needless to say, was lavish in his expenses, and luxurious in his personal habits: like the mercenaries he commanded, he looked to the sacking of Jerusalem as a means of paying his creditors, and supplying him with money for future excesses. Not a man of the Lost Legion but had already calculated the worth of that golden roof, to which they looked so longingly, and his own probable portion when it was melted into coin. Rumour, too, had not failed to multiply by tens the amount of wealth stored in the Temple, and the jewels it contained. The besiegers were persuaded that every soldier who should be fortunate enough to enter it sword in hand, would be enriched for life; and the gladiators were the last men to grudge danger or bloodshed for such an object.

But there is a foe who smites an army far more surely than the enemy that meets it face to face in the field. Like the angel who breathed on the host of the Assyrians in the night, so that when the Jews rose in the morning, their adversaries were "all dead men," this foe takes his prey by scores as they sleep in their tents, or pace to and fro watching under their armour in the sun. His name is Pestilence; and wherever man meets man for mutual destruction, he hovers over the opposing multitudes, and secures the lion's share of both. Partly from their previous habits, partly from their looser discipline, he had been busier amongst the gladiators than in any other quarter of the camp. Dwindling day by day in numbers and efficiency, Hippias began to fear that they would be unable to take the prominent part he [pg 353]had promised them in the assault, and the chance of such a disappointment was irritating enough; but when to this grievance was added the proposal he had just heard, for the peaceful surrender of the city—a proposal which Titus seemed to regard with favourable eyes, and which would entail the distribution in equal portions of whatever treasure was considered the spoil of the army, so that the gladiator and legionary should but share alike—the contingency was nothing less than maddening. He had given Titus a true report of his legion in council; for Hippias was not a man to take shelter in falsehood, under any pressure of necessity, but he repented, nevertheless, of his frankness; and, cursing the hour when he embarked for Syria, began to think of Rome with regret, and to believe that he was happier and more prosperous in the amphitheatre after all. Passing amongst the tents of his men, he was distressed to meet old Hirpinus, who reported to him that another score had been stricken by the sickness since watch-setting the previous night. Every day was of the utmost importance now, and here were two more to be wasted in negotiations, even if the assault should be ordered to take place after all. The reflection did not serve to soothe him, and Hippias entered his own tent with a fevered frame, and a frown of ill-omen on his brow.

For a soldier it was indeed a luxurious home; adorned with trophies of arms, costly shawls, gold and silver drinking-vessels, and other valuables scattered about. There was even a porcelain vase filled with fresh flowers standing between two wineskins; and a burnished mirror, with a delicate comb resting against its stand, denoted either an extraordinary care for his personal appearance in the owner, or a woman's presence behind the crimson curtain which served to screen another compartment of the tent. Kicking the mirror out of his way, and flinging himself on a couch covered with a dressed leopard-skin, Hippias set his heavy headpiece on the ground, and called angrily for a cup of wine. At the second summons, the curtain was drawn aside, and a woman appeared from behind its folds.

Pale, haughty, and self-possessed, tameless, and defiant, even in her degradation, Valeria, though fallen, seemed to rise superior to herself, and stood before the man whom she had never loved, and yet to whom, in a moment of madness, she had sacrificed her whole existence, with the calm, quiet demeanour of a mistress in the presence of her slave. Her [pg 354]beauty had not faded—far from it—though changed somewhat in its character, growing harder and colder than of old. If less womanly, it was of a deeper and loftier kind. The eyes, indeed, had lost the loving, laughing look which had once been their greatest charm, but they were keen and dazzling still; while the other features, like the shapely figure, had gained a severe and majestic dignity in exchange for the flowing outlines and the round comeliness of youth. She was dressed sumptuously, and with an affectation of Eastern habits that suited her beauty well. Alas! that beauty was her only weapon left; and although she had turned it against herself, a true woman to the end, she had kept it bright and pointed still.

When Valeria left her home to follow the fortunes of a gladiator, she had not even the excuse of blindness for her folly. She knew that she was abandoning friends, fortune, position—all the advantages of life for that which she did not care to have. She believed herself to be utterly desperate, depraved, and unsexed. It was her punishment that she could not rid herself of her woman's nature, nor stifle the voice that no woman ever *can* stifle in her heart. For a time, perhaps, the change of scene, the voyage, the excitement of the step she had taken, the determination to abide by her choice and defy everything, served to deaden her mind to her own misery. It was her whim to assume on occasions the arms and accoutrements of a gladiator; and it was even said in the Lost Legion, that she had fought in their ranks more than once in some of their desperate enterprises against the town. It was certain that she never appeared abroad in the female dress she wore within her tent: Titus, indeed, would have scarcely failed to notice such a flagrant breach of camp-discipline; and many a fierce swordsman whispered to his comrade, with a thrill of interest, that in a force like theirs she might mingle unnoticed in their ranks, and be with them at any time. It was but a whisper, though, after all, for they knew their commander too well to canvass his conduct openly, or to pry into matters he chose to keep secret.

These outbreaks, however, so contrary to all the impulses and instincts of a woman's nature, soon palled on the high-born Roman lady; and as the siege, with its various fortunes, was protracted from day to day, the yoke under which she had voluntarily placed her proud white neck, became too galling to endure. She hated the long glistening line of tents; she hated the scorching Syrian sky, the flash of armour, [pg 355]the tramp of men, the constant trumpet-calls, the eternal guard-mounting, the wearisome and monotonous routine of a camp. She hated the hot tent, with its stifling atmosphere and its narrow space; above all, she was learning daily to hate the man with whom she shared its shelter and its inconveniences.

She handed him the wine he asked for without a word, and standing there in her cold scornful beauty, never noticed him by look or gesture. She seemed miles away in thought, and utterly unconscious of his presence.

He remembered when it was so different. He remembered how, even when first he knew her, his arrival used to call a smile of pleasure to her lips, a glance of welcome to her eye. It might be only on the surface, but still it was there; and he felt for his own part, that as far as he had ever cared for any woman, he had cared for her. It was galling, truly, this indifference, this contempt. He was hurt, and his fierce undisciplined nature urged him to strike again.

He emptied the cup, and flung it from him with an angry jerk. The golden vessel rolled out from under the hangings of the tent; she made no offer to pick it up and fetch it back. He glared fiercely into her eyes, and they met his own with the steady scornful gaze he almost feared; for that cold look chilled him to the very heart. The man was hardened, depraved, steeped to the lips in cruelty and crime; but there was a defenceless place in him still that she could stab when she liked, for he would have loved her if she had let him.

"I am very weary of the siege," said he, stretching his limbs on the couch with affected indifference, "weary of the daily drudgery, the endless consultations, the scorching climate, above all, this suffocating atmosphere, where a man can hardly breathe. Would that I had never seen this accursed tent, or aught that it contains!"

"You cannot be more weary of it than I am," she replied, in the same contemptuous quiet tone that maddened him.

"Why did you come?" he retorted, with a bitter laugh. "Nobody wanted such a delicate dainty lady in a soldier's tent—and certainly nobody ever asked you to share it with him!"

She gave a little gasp, as though something touched her to the quick, but recovered herself on the instant, and answered calmly and scornfully, "It is kindly said, and [pg 356]generously, considering all things. Just what I might have expected from a gladiator!"

"There was a time you liked the Family well enough!" he exclaimed angrily; and then, softened by his own recollections of that time, added in a milder tone, "Valeria, why will you thus quarrel with me? It used not to be so when I brought the foils and dumbbells to your portico, and spared no pains to make you the deadliest fencer, as you were the fairest, in Rome. Those were happy days enough, and so might these be, if you had but a grain of common sense. Can you not see, when you and I fall out, who must necessarily be the loser? What have you to depend on now but me?"

He should have stopped at his tender recollections. Argument, especially if it has any show of reason in it, is to an angry woman but as the *bandillero's* goad to the Iberian bull. Its flutter serves to irritate rather than to scare, and the deeper its pointed steel sinks in, the more actively indeed does the recipient swerve aside, but returns the more rapidly and the more obstinately to the charge. Of all considerations, that which most maddened Valeria, and rendered her utterly reckless, was that she should be dependent on a gladiator. The cold eyes flashed fire; but she would not give him the advantage over her of acknowledging that he could put her in a passion, so she restrained herself, though her heart was ready to burst. Had she cared for him she might have stabbed him to death in such a mood.

"I thank you for reminding me," she answered bitterly. "It is not strange that one of the Mutian line should occasionally forget her duty to Hippias, the retired prize-fighter. A patrician, perhaps, would have brought it more delicately to her remembrance; but I have no right to blame the fencing-master for his plebeian birth and bringing up."

"Now, by the body of Hercules, this is too much!" he exclaimed, springing erect on the couch, and grinding his teeth with rage. "What! you tax me with my birth! You scout me for my want of mincing manners and white hands, and syllables that drop like slobbered wine from the close-shaven lip! You, the dainty lady, the celebrated beauty, the admired, forsooth, of all admirers, whose porch was choked with gilded chariots, whose litter was thronged with every curly-headed, white-shouldered, crimson-cloaked, young Narcissus in Rome, and yet who sought her chosen lovers in the amphitheatre—who scanned with judicious eye the points [pg 357]and the vigour and the promise of naked athletes, and could find at last none to serve her turn, but war-worn old Hippias, the roughest and the rudest, and the worst-favoured, but the strongest, nevertheless, amongst them all!"

The storm was gathering apace, but she still tried hard to keep it down. An experienced mariner might have known by the short-coming breath, the white cheek, and the dilated nostril, that it was high time to shorten sail, and run for shelter before the squall.

"It was indeed a strange taste," she retorted. "None can marvel at it more than myself."

"Not so strange as you think," he burst out, somewhat inconsistently. "Do not fancy you were the only lady in Rome who was proud to be admired by Hippias the gladiator. I tell you I had my choice amongst a hundred maids and matrons, nobler born, fairer, ay, and of better repute than yourself! any one of whom would have been glad to be here to-day in your place. I was a fool for my pains; but I thought you were the fittest to bear the toil of campaigning, and the least able to do without me, so I took you, more out of pity than of love!"

"Coward!" she hissed between her clenched teeth. "Traitor and fool, too! Must you know the truth at last? Must you know what I have spared you this long time? what alone has kept me from sinking under the weight of these weary days with their hourly degradation? what has been disease and remedy, wound and balm, bitterest punishment, and yet dearest consolation? Take it then, since have it you will! Can you think that such as I could ever love such as you? Can you believe you could be more to Valeria than the handle of the blade, the shaft of the javelin, the cord of the bow, by which she could inflict a grievous wound in another's bosom? Listen! When you wooed me, I was a scorned, an insulted, a desperate woman. I loved one who was nobler, handsomer, better. Ay, you pride yourself on your fierce courage and your brutal strength. I tell you who was twice as strong, and a thousand times as brave as the best of you. I loved him, do you hear? as men like you never can be loved—with an utter and entire devotion, that asked but to sacrifice itself without hope of a return, and he scorned me, not as you would have done, with a rough brutal frankness that had taken away half the pain, but so kindly, so delicately, so generously, that even while I clung to him, and he turned away from me, I felt he was dearer than ever to my heart. Ay, you may sit there and look at me with your eyes glaring [pg 358]and your beard bristling like some savage beast of prey; but you brought it on yourself, and if you killed me I would not spare you now. I had never *looked* at you but for your hired skill, which you imparted to the man I loved. I took you because he scorned me, as I would have taken one of my Liburnians, had I thought it would have wounded him deeper, or made him hate me more. You are a fencer, I believe—one who prides himself on his skill in feints and parries, in giving and taking, in judging accurately of the adversary's strength and weakness at a glance. Have I foiled you to some purpose? You thought you were the darling of the high-born lady, the favourite of her fancy, the minion to whom she could refuse nothing, not even her fair fame, and she was using you all the time as a mere rod with which to smite a slave! A *slave*, do you hear? Yes, the man I preferred, not only to you, but to a host of your betters, the man I loved so dearly, and love so madly still, is but your pupil Esca, a barbarian, and a slave!"

Her anger had supported her till now, but with Esca's name came a flood of tears, and, thoroughly unstrung, she sat down on the ground and wept passionately, covering her face with her hands. He could have almost found it in his heart to strike her, but for her defenceless attitude, so exasperated was he, so maddened by the torrent of her words. He could think of nothing, however, more bitter than to taunt her with her helplessness, whilst under his charge.

"Your minion," said he, "is within the walls at this moment. From that tent door, you might almost see him on the rampart, if he be not skulking from his duty like a slave as he is. Think, proud lady, you who are so ready, asked or unasked, for slave or gladiator, you need but walk five hundred paces to be in his arms. Surely, if they knew your mission, Roman guards and Jewish sentries would lower their spears to you as you passed! Enough of this! Remember who and what you are. Above all, remember *where* you are, and how you came here. I have forborne too long, my patience is exhausted at last. You are in a soldier's tent, and you must learn a soldier's duty—unquestioning obedience. Go! pick up that goblet I let fall just now. Fill it, and bring it me here, without a word!"

Somewhat to his surprise, she rose at once to do his bidding, leaving the tent with a perfectly composed step and air. He might have remarked, though, that when she returned with his wine, the red drops fell profusely over her white trembling fingers, though she looked in his face as [pg 359]proudly and steadily as ever. The hand might, indeed, shake, but the heart was fixed and resolute. In the veins of none of her ancestors did the Mutian blood, so strong for good and evil, ebb and flow with a fuller, more resistless tide, than in hers. Valeria had made up her mind in the space of time it took to lift a goblet from the ground.

[pg 360]

CHAPTER VII

THE ATTAINDER

John of Gischala would never have obtained the ascendency he enjoyed in Jerusalem, had he not been as well versed in the sinuous arts of intrigue, as in the simpler stratagems of war. After confronting his rival in the Council, and sustaining in public opinion the worst of the encounter, he was more than ever impressed with the necessity of ruining Eleazar at any price; therefore, keeping a wary eye upon all the movements of the Zealots, he held himself ready at every moment to take advantage of the first false step on the part of his adversary.

Eleazar, with the promptitude natural to his character, had commenced a repair of the defences, almost before his emissary was admitted to the Roman camp, thinking it needless to await the decision of Titus, either for or against his proposal. Labouring heart and soul at the works, with all the available force he could muster, he left John and his party in charge of the Great Gate, and it happened that his rival was present there in person, when Calchas was brought back to the city by the Roman guard of honour Titus had ordered for his safe-conduct—a compliment his brother never expected, and far less desired. Eleazar made sure his messenger would be permitted to return the way he came, and that his own communications with the enemy would remain a secret from the besieged.

John saw his opportunity, and availed himself of it on the instant. No sooner had Calchas placed his foot once more within the town, than his head was covered, so that he might not be recognised; and he was carried off by a guard of John's adherents, and placed in secure ward, their chief adroitly arresting him by a false name, for the information of the populace, lest the rumour should reach Eleazar's ears. He knew his rival's readiness of resource, and determined to take him by surprise. Then he rent his garment, and ran bareheaded through the streets towards the Temple, calling [pg 361]with a great voice, "Treason! Treason!" and sending round the fragments of his gown amongst the senators, to convoke them in haste upon a matter of life and death, in their usual place of deliberation. So rapidly did he take his measures that the Outer Court was already filled and the Council assembled, ere Eleazar, busied with his labours at the wall far off, opposite the Tower of Antonia, knew that they had been summoned. Covered with sweat and dust, he obeyed at once the behest of the Levite who came breathlessly to require his presence, as an elder of Israel; but it was not without foreboding of evil that he observed the glances of suspicion and mistrust shot at him by his colleagues when he joined them. John of Gischala, with an affectation of extreme fairness, had declined to enter upon the business of the State, until this, the latest of her councillors, had arrived; but he had taken good care, by means of his creatures, to scatter rumours amongst the Senate, and even amongst the Zealots themselves, deeply affecting the loyalty of their chief.

No sooner had Eleazar, still covered with the signs of his toil, taken his accustomed station, than John stood forth in the hall and spoke out in a loud, clear voice.

"Before the late troublous times," said he, "and when every man in Judæa ate of his own figs from his own fig-tree, and trod out his own grapes in his own vineyard; when we digged our wells unmolested, and our women drew water unveiled, and drank it peacefully at sundown; when our children played about our knees at the door, and ate butter and honey, and cakes baked in oil; when the cruse was never empty, and the milk mantled in the milking-vessels, and the kid seethed in the pot—yea, in the pleasant time, in the days of old, it chanced that I was taking a prey in the mountain by the hunter's craft, in the green mountain, even the mountain of Lebanon. Then at noon I was wearied and athirst, and I laid me down under a goodly cedar and slept, and dreamed a dream. Behold, I will discover to the elders my dream and the interpretation thereof.

"Now the cedar under which I lay was a goodly cedar, but in my dream it seemed that it reached far into the heavens, and spread its roots abroad to the springs of many waters, and sheltered the birds of the air in its branches, and comforted the beasts of the field with its shade. Then there came a beast out of the mountain—a huge beast with a serpent between its eyes and horns upon its jaws—and leaned against the cedar, but the tree neither bent nor broke. So there came a great wind against the cedar—a mighty [pg 362]wind that rushed and roared through its branches, till it rocked to and fro, bending and swaying to the blast—but the storm passed away, and the goodly tree stood firm and upright as before. Again the face of heaven was darkened, and the thunder roared above, and the lightning leaped from the cloud, and smote upon the cedar, and rent off one of its limbs with a great and terrible crash; but when the sky cleared once more, the tree was a fair tree yet. So I said in my dream, 'Blessed is the cedar among the trees of the forest, for destruction shall not prevail against it.'

"Then I looked, and behold, the cedar was already rotting, and its arms were withered up, and its head was no longer black, for a little worm, and another, and yet another were creeping from within the bark, where they had been eating at its heart. Then one drew near bearing fagots on his shoulders, and he built the fagots round the tree, and set a light to them, and burned them with fire, and the worms fell out by myriads from the tree, and perished in the smoke.

"Then said he unto me, 'John of Gischala, arise! The cedar is the Holy City, and the beast is the might of the Roman Empire, and the storm and the tempest are the famine and the pestilence, and none of these shall prevail against it, save by the aid of the enemies from within. Purge them therefore with fire, and smite them with the sword, and crush them, even as the worm is crushed beneath thy heel into the earth!'

"And the interpretation of the dream hath remained with me to this day, for is it not thus even now when the Roman is at the gate, as it hath ever been with the Holy City in the times of old? When the Assyrian came up against her, was not his host greater in number than the sands of the seashore? But he retired in discomfiture from before her, because she was true to herself. Would Nebuzaradan have put his chains on our people's neck, and Gedaliah scorned to accept honour from the conqueror, and to pay him tribute? When Pompey pitched his camp at Jericho and surrounded the Holy City with his legions, did not Aristobulus play the traitor and offer to open the gate? and when the soldiers mutinied, and prevented so black a treason, did not Hyrcanus, who was afterwards high-priest, assist the besiegers from within, and enable them to gain possession of the town? In later days, Herod, indeed, who was surnamed the Great, fortified Jerusalem like a soldier and a patriot; but even Herod, our warrior king, soiled his hands with Roman gold, and bowed his head to the Roman [pg 363]yoke. Will you tell me of Agrippa's wall, reared by the namesake and successor of the mighty monarch? Why was it never finished? Can you answer me that? I trow ye know too well; there was fear of displeasing Cæsar, there was the old shameful truckling to Rome. This is the leaven that leaveneth all our leaders; this is the palsy that withereth all our efforts. Is not the chief who defended Jotapata now a guest in the tent of Titus? Is not Agrippa the younger a staunch adherent of Vespasian? Is he not a mere procurator of the Empire, for the province, forsooth, of Judæa? And shall we learn nothing from our history? Nothing from the events of our own times, from the scenes we ourselves witness day by day? Must the cedar fall because we fail to destroy the worms that are eating at its core? Shall Jerusalem be desecrated because we fear to denounce the hand that would deliver her to the foe? We have a plague-spot in the nation. We have an enemy in the town. We have a traitor in the Council, Eleazar Ben-Manahem! I bid thee stand forth!"

There is an instinct of danger which seems to warn the statesman like the mariner of coming storms, giving him time to trim his sail, while they are yet below the horizon. When the assembled Senate turned their startled looks on Eleazar, they beheld a countenance unmoved by the suddenness and gravity of the accusation, a bearing that denoted, if not conscious innocence, at least a fixed resolution to wear its semblance without a shadow of weakness or fear. Pointing to his dusty garments, and the stains of toil upon his hands and person, he looked round frankly among the elders, rather, as it seemed, appealing to the Senate than answering his accuser, in his reply.

"These should be sufficient proofs," said he, "if any were wanting, that Eleazar Ben-Manahem hath not been an instant absent from his post. I have but to strip the gown from my breast, and I can show yet deeper marks to attest my loyalty and patriotism. I have not grudged my own blood, nor the blood of my kindred, and of my father's house, to defend the walls of Jerusalem. John of Gischala hath dealt with you in parables, but I speak to you in the plain language of truth. This right hand of mine is hardened with grasping sword and spear against the enemies of Judah; and I would cut it off with its own fellow, ere I stretched it forth in amity to the Roman or the heathen. Talk not to me of thy worms and thy cedars! John of Gischala, man of blood and rapine—speak out thine accusation plainly, that I may answer it!"

John was stepping angrily forward, when he was arrested by the voice of a venerable long-bearded senator.

"It is not meet," said the sage, "that accuser and accused should bandy words in the presence of the Council. John of Gischala, we summon thee to lay the matter at once before the Senate, warning thee that an accusation without proofs will but recoil upon the head of him who brings it forward."

John smiled in grim triumph.

"Elders of Israel," said he, "I accuse Eleazar Ben-Manahem of offering terms to the enemy."

Eleazar started, but recovered himself instantaneously. It was war to the knife, as well he knew, between him and John. He must not seem to hesitate now when his ascendency amongst the people was at such a crisis. He took the plunge at once.

"And I reply," he exclaimed indignantly, "that rather than make terms with the Roman, I would plunge the sword into my own body."

A murmur of applause ran through the assembly at this spirited declaration. The accused had great weight amongst the nobility and the national party in Jerusalem, of which the Council chiefly consisted. Could Eleazar but persevere in his denial of communication with Titus, he must triumph signally over his adversary; and, to do him justice, there was now but little personal ambition mingled with his desire for supremacy. He was a fanatic, but he was a patriot as well. He believed all things were lawful in the cause of Jerusalem, and trusting to the secret way by which Calchas had left the city for the Roman camp, and by which he felt assured he must have returned, as, thanks to John's precautions, nothing had been heard of his arrival at the Great Gate and subsequent arrest, he resolved to persevere in his denial, and trust to his personal influence to carry things with a high hand.

"There hath been a communication made from his own house, and by one of his own family, to the Roman commander," urged John, but with a certain air of deference and hesitation, for he perceived the favourable impression made on the Council by his adversary, and he was crafty enough to know the advantage of reserving his convincing proofs for the last, and taking the tide of opinion at the turn.

"I deny it," said Eleazar firmly. "The children of Ben-Manahem have no dealings with the heathen!"

"It is one of the seed of Ben-Manahem whom I accuse," replied John, still addressing himself to the elders. "I can prove he hath been seen going to and fro, between the camp and the city."

"His blood be on his own head!" answered Eleazar solemnly.

He had a vague hope that after all they might but have intercepted some poor half-starved wretch whom the pangs of hunger had driven to the enemy. John looked back amongst his adherents crowding in the gate that led towards the Temple.

"I speak not without proofs," said he; "bring forward the prisoner!"

There was a slight scuffle amongst the throng, and a murmur which subsided almost immediately as two young men appeared in the court, leading between them a figure, having its hands tied, and a mantle thrown over its head.

"Eleazar Ben-Manahem!" said John, in a loud, clear voice that seemed to ring amongst the porticoes and pinnacles of the overhanging Temple, "stand forth, and speak the truth! Is not this man thy brother?"

At the same moment, the mantle was drawn from the prisoner's head, revealing the mild and placid features of Calchas, who looked round upon the Council, neither intimidated nor surprised. The Senate gazed in each other's faces with concern and astonishment: John seemed, indeed, in a fair way of substantiating his accusation against the man they most trusted in all Jerusalem. The accuser continued, with an affectation of calm unprejudiced judgment, in a cool and dispassionate voice—

"This man was brought to the Great Gate to-day, under a guard of honour, direct from the Roman camp. I happened to be present, and the captain of the gate handed him over at once to me. I appeal to the Council whether I exceeded my duty in arresting him on the spot, permitting him no communication with anyone in the town until I had brought him before them in this court. I soon learned that he was the brother of Eleazar, one of our most distinguished leaders, to whom more than to any other the defence of the city has been entrusted, who knows better than anyone our weakness and the extremity of our need. By my orders he was searched, and on his person was found a scroll, purporting to be from no less a person than the commander of the Tenth Legion, an officer second only in authority to Titus himself, and addressed to one Esca, a Gentile, living in the very house, and I am informed a member of the very family, of Eleazar Ben-Manahem, this elder in Judah, this chief of the Zealots, this member of the Senate, this adviser in Council, this man whose right hand is hardened with sword and spear, but who would cut it off with his left, rather than that it should traffic with the enemy! I demand from the Council an order for the arrest of Esca, that he too may be brought before it, and confronted with him whose bread he eats. From the mouth of three offenders, our wise men may peradventure elicit the truth. If I have erred in my zeal let the Senate reprove me. If Eleazar can purge himself from my accusation, let him defile my father's grave, and call me liar and villain to my very beard!"

The Senate, powerfully affected by John's appeal, and yet unable to believe in the treachery of one who had earned their entire confidence, seemed at a loss how to act. The conduct of the accused, too, afforded no clue whereby to judge of his probable guilt or innocence. His cheek was very pale, and once he stepped forward a pace, as if to place himself at his brother's side. Then he halted and repeated his former words, "His blood be on his own head," in a loud and broken voice, turning away the while, and glaring round upon the senators like some fierce animal taken in the toils. Calchas, too, kept his eyes fixed on the ground; and more than one observer remarked that the brothers studiously abstained from looking each other in the face. There was a dead silence for several seconds. Then the senator who had before spoken, raised his hand to command attention, and thus addressed the Council—

"This is a grave matter, involving as it does not only the life and death of a son of Judah, but the honour of one of our noblest houses, and the safety, nay, the very existence of the Holy City. A grave matter, and one which may not be dealt with, save by the highest tribunal in the nation. It must be tried before our Sanhedrim, which will assemble for the purpose without delay. Those of us here present who are members of that august body, will divest their minds of all they have heard in this place to-day, and proceed to a clear and unbiassed judgment of the matters that shall be then brought before them. Nothing has been yet proved against Eleazar Ben-Manahem, though his brother, and the Gentile who has to answer the same accusation, must be kept in secure ward. I move that the Council, therefore, be now dissolved, holding itself ready, nevertheless, seeing the imminent peril of the times, to reassemble at an hour's notice, for the welfare of Judah, and the salvation of the Holy City."

[pg 367]

Even while he ceased speaking, and ere the grave senators broke up, preparing to depart, a wail was heard outside the court that chilled the very heart of each, as it rose and fell like a voice from the other world, repeating ever and again, in wild unearthly tones, in solemn warning—

"Woe to Jerusalem! Woe to the Holy City! Sin, and sorrow, and desolation! Woe to the Holy City! Woe to Jerusalem!"

[pg 368]

CHAPTER VIII

THE SANHEDRIM

The highest tribunal acknowledged by the Jewish law, taking cognisance of matters especially affecting the religious and political welfare of the nation, essentially impartial in its decisions, and admitting of no appeal from its sentence, was that assembly of Seventy, or rather of Seventy-three members, which was called the Sanhedrim. This court of justice was supposed to express and embody the opinions of the whole nation, consisting as it did of a number which subdivided would have given six representatives for each tribe, besides a president to rule the proceedings of the whole. The latter, who was termed the *Nasi* or Prince of the Sanhedrim, was necessarily of illustrious birth, venerable years, and profound experience in all matters connected with the law—not only the actual law as laid down by inspiration for the guidance of the Chosen People, but also the traditional law, with its infinite variety of customs, precedents, and ceremonious observances, which had been added to, and as it were overlaid on the other, much to the detriment of that simpler code, which came direct from heaven. The members themselves of this supreme council were of noble blood. In no nation, perhaps, was the pride of birth more cherished than amongst the Jews; and in such an assemblage as the Sanhedrim, untainted lineage was the first indispensable qualification. The majority, indeed, consisted of priests and Levites; but other families of secular distinction who could count their ancestors step by step, from generation to generation, through the Great Captivity, and all the vicissitudes of their history, back to the magnificence of Solomon and the glories of David's warlike reign, had their representatives in this solemn conclave.

Not only was nobility a requirement, but also maturity of years, a handsome person, and a dignified bearing; nor were mental attainments held in less regard than the adventitious advantages of appearance and station. Every elder of the [pg 369]Sanhedrim was obliged to study physic, to become an adept in the science of divination in all its branches, comprising astrology, the casting of nativities and horoscopes, the prediction of future events, and those mysteries of White Magic, as it was called, which bordered so narrowly on the forbidden limits of the Black Art. He was also required to be an excellent linguist; and was indeed supposed to be proficient in the seventy languages, believed to comprise all the tongues of the habitable earth. No eunuch nor deformed person could aspire to hold a place in this august body, no usurer, no Sabbath-breaker, none who were in the practice of any unlawful business or overt sin. Those who sat in the highest place of the Jewish nation, who ruled her councils and held the right of life and death over her children, must be prudent, learned, blameless men, decked with the patent of true nobility both in body and mind.

The Sanhedrim, in its original constitution, was the only Court which had the right of judging capital cases; and this right, involving so grave a responsibility, it was careful to preserve during all the calamities of the nation, until it fell under the Roman yoke. The Empire, however, reserved to itself the power of condemning its criminals to death; but no sooner had the Jews broken out once more in open resistance to their conquerors, than the Sanhedrim resumed all its former privileges and sat again in judgment upon its countrymen.

In a large circular chamber, half within and half without the Temple, this awful Court held its deliberations, the members, ranged in order by seniority, occupying the outer semicircle, as it was not lawful to sit down in the sacred precincts. That chamber was now the theatre of a solemn and imposing scene. The hall itself, which, though wide and lofty, appeared of yet larger proportions from its circular form, was hung round with cloth of a dark crimson colour, that added much to the prevailing sentiments of gloom which its appearance called forth. Over its entrance was suspended a curtain of the same hue; and the accused who underwent examination in this dreaded locality, found themselves encircled by an unbroken wall the colour of blood. A black carpet was spread on the floor, bordered with a wide yellow margin, on which were written in black Hebrew characters certain texts of the law, inculcating punishment rather than pardon, inflexible justice rather than a leaning towards mercy and forbearance. The heart of the guilty died within him as he looked uneasily around; and even the innocent might [pg 370]well quail at these preparations for a trial over which an exacting severity was so obviously to hold sway.

The Sanhedrim were accustomed to assemble in an outer chamber, and march in grave procession to the court of trial. The crimson curtain, drawn by an unseen hand, rolled slowly from the door, and the members, dressed in black, came in by pairs and took their places in order. As they entered, their names were called over by an official concealed behind the hangings; and each man notified his arrival as he passed on to his seat, by the solemn answer: "Here! In the presence of the Lord!" Last of all, the president made his appearance, and assumed a higher chair, set apart a little from the rest. Then the youngest member offered up a short prayer, to which the whole assembly responded with a deep and fervent Amen! The Court was now considered to be opened, and qualified for the trial of all causes that should be brought before it during its sitting.

On the present occasion the junior member was a Levite, nearly threescore years of age, of a stately presence, which he had preserved notwithstanding the hardships of the siege, and who retained much of his youthful comeliness with the flowing beard and grave countenance of maturer years. Phineas Ben-Ezra possessed the exterior qualities by which men are prone to be influenced, with a ready tongue, a scheming brain, and an unscrupulous heart. He was attached to John's faction, and a bitter enemy of the Zealots, by whom he had himself been formerly accused of treasonable correspondence with Vespasian; an accusation that he refuted to his own exultation and the utter confusion of his enemies, but which those who had the best means of judging believed to be true nevertheless. He took his seat now with an expression of cold triumph on his handsome features, and exchanged looks with one or two of the colleagues who seemed deepest in his confidence, that the latter knew too well boded considerable danger to the accused whom they were about to try.

The Prince of the Sanhedrim, Matthias the son of Boethus, who had already filled the office of high-priest, was a stern and conscientious man of the old Jewish party, whose opinions indeed were in accordance with those of Eleazar, and who entertained, besides, a personal friendship for that determined enthusiast, but whose inflexible obstinacy was to be moved by no earthly consideration from the narrow path of duty which he believed his sacred character compelled him to observe. His great age and austere bearing commanded [pg 371]considerable influence among his countrymen, enhanced by the high office he had previously filled; nor was he the less esteemed that his severe and even morose disposition, while it gained him few friends, yielded no confidences and afforded no opportunity for the display of those human weaknesses by which a man wins their affections, while he loses the command over his fellow-creatures. His face was very pale and grave now, as he moved haughtily to the seat reserved for him; and his dark flowing robes, decorated, in right of his former priesthood, with certain mystic symbols, seemed well-fitted to the character of a stern and inflexible judge. The other members of the assembly, though varying in form and feature, were distinguished one and all by a family likeness, originating probably in similarity of habits and opinions, no less than in a common nationality and the sharing of a common danger, growing daily to its worst. The dark flashing eye, the deep sallow tint, the curving nostril and the waving beard, were no more distinguishing marks of any one individual in the assembly, than were his long black gown and his expression of severe and inscrutable gravity; but even these universal characteristics were not so remarkable as a certain ominous shadow that cast its gloom upon the face of each. It was the shadow of that foe against whom sword and spear and shield and javelin, bodily strength, dauntless courage, and skill in the art of war, were all powerless to make head—the foe who was irresistible because he lay at the very heart of the fortress. The weary, anxious, longing look of hunger was on the faces even of these, the noblest and the most powerful behind the wall. They had stores of gold and silver, rich silks, sparkling jewels, costly wines within their houses; but there was a want of bread, and gaunt uneasy famine had set his seal, if not as deeply at least as surely, upon these faces in the Sanhedrim as on that of the meanest soldier, who girded his sword-belt tighter to stay his pangs, as he stood pale and wasted in his armour on the ramparts, over against the foe.

There was a hush for several seconds after the Prince of the Sanhedrim had taken his seat, and the general prayer had been offered up. It was broken at length by Matthias, who rose with slow impressive gestures, drew his robe around him so as to display the sacred symbols and cabalistic figures with which its hem was garnished, and spoke in stern and measured tones—

"Princes of the House of Judah," said he, "elders and nobles, and priests and Levites of the nation, we are met [pg 372]once more to-day, in accordance with our ancient prerogative, for the sifting of a grave and serious matter. In this, the highest Council of our country, we adhere to the same forms that have been handed down to us by our fathers from the earliest times, even from their sojourn in the wilderness, that have been preserved through the Great Captivity of our nation, that may have been prohibited by our conquerors, but that we have resumed with that independence which we have recently asserted, and which the Ruler to whom alone we owe allegiance will assuredly enable us to attain. We will not part with one iota of our privileges, and least of all with our jurisdiction in matters involving life and death; a jurisdiction as inseparable from our very existence as the Tabernacle itself, which we have accompanied through so many vicissitudes, and with which we are so closely allied. That inferior assemblage from which our chosen body is selected has already considered the heavy accusation which has collected us here. They have decided that the matter is of too grave a character to be dealt with by their own experience—that it involves the condemnation to death of one if not two members of the illustrious family of Ben-Manahem—that it may deprive us of a leader who claims to be among the staunchest of our patriots, who has proved himself the bravest of our defenders. But what then, princes of the House of Judah, elders and nobles, and priests and Levites of the nation? Shall I spare the pruning-hook, because it is the heaviest branch in my vineyard that is rotting from its stem? Shall I not rather lop it off with mine own hand, and cast it from me into the consuming fire? If my brother be guilty shall I screen him, brother though he be? Shall I not rather hand him over to the Avenger, and deliver my own soul? We are all assembled in our places, ready to hear attentively, and to try impartially, whatsoever accusations may be brought before us. Phineas Ben-Ezra, youngest member of the Sanhedrim, I call on thee to count over thy colleagues, and proclaim aloud the sum thereof."

In compliance with established usage, Phineas, thus adjured, rose from his seat, and walking gravely through the hall, told off its inmates one by one, in a loud and solemn voice, then finding the tale to be correct, stopped before the high chair of the Nasi, and proclaimed thrice—

"Prince of the Sanhedrim, the mystic number is complete!"

The president addressed him again in the prescribed formula—

[pg 373]

"Phineas Ben-Ezra, are we prepared to try each cause according to the traditions of our nation, and the strict letter of the law? Do we abide by the decisions of wisdom without favour, and justice without mercy?"

Then the whole Sanhedrim repeated as with one voice, "Wisdom without favour, and justice without mercy!"

The president now seated himself, and looked once more to Phineas, who, as the youngest member present, was entitled to give his opinion first. The latter, answering his glance, rose at once and addressed his fellows in a tone of diffidence which would have seemed misplaced in one of his venerable appearance, had he not been surrounded by men of far greater age than himself.

"I am but as a disciple," said he, "at the feet of a master, in presence of Matthias the son of Boethus, and my honoured colleagues. Submitting to their experience, I do but venture to ask a question, without presuming to offer my own opinion on its merits. Supposing that the Sanhedrim should be required to try one of its own number, is it lawful that he should remain and sit, as it were, in judgment upon himself?"

Eleazar, who was present in his place as a member of the august body, felt that this attack was specially directed against his own safety. He knew the virulence of the speaker, and his rancorous enmity to the Zealots, and recognised the danger to himself of exclusion from the coming deliberations. He was in the act of rising in indignant protest against such an assumption, when he was forestalled by Matthias, who replied in tones of stern displeasure—

"He must indeed be a mere disciple, and it will be long ere he is worthy of the name of master in the Sanhedrim, who has yet to learn, that our deliberations are uninfluenced by aught we have heard or seen outside the chamber—that we recognise in our august office no evidence but the proofs that are actually brought before us here. Phineas Ben-Ezra, the Court is assembled; admit accusers and accused. Must I tell thee that we are still ignorant of the cause we are here to try?"

The decision of the Nasi, which was in accordance with traditional observance and established custom, afforded Eleazar a moment's respite, in which to resolve on the course he should adopt; but though his mind was working busily, he sat perfectly unmoved, and to all outward appearance calm and confident; whilst the hangings were again drawn back, and the tread of feet announced the approach of accuser [pg 374]and accused. The latter were now two in number: for by John's orders a strong guard had already proceeded to Eleazar's house, and laid violent hands on Esca, who, confident in his own innocence and in the influence of his host, accompanied them without apprehension of danger into the presence of the awful assembly. The Briton's surprise was, however, great, when he found himself confronted with Calchas, of whose arrest, so skilfully had John managed it, he was as unconscious as the rest of the besieged. The two prisoners were not permitted to communicate with each other; and it was only from a warning glance shot at him by his fellow-sufferer, that Esca gathered they were both in a situation of extreme peril.

It was not without considerable anxiety that Eleazar remarked, when the curtains were drawn back, how a large body of armed men filled the adjoining cloister of the Temple: like the guard who watched the prisoners, these were partisans of John; and so well aware were the Sanhedrim of that fierce soldier's lawless disposition, that they looked uneasily from one to the other, with the painful reflection that he was quite capable of massacring the whole conclave then and there, and taking the supreme government of the city into his own hands.

It was the influence, however, of no deliberative assembly that was feared by a man like John of Gischala. Fierce and reckless to the extreme, he dreaded only the violence of a character bold and unscrupulous as his own. Could he but pull Eleazar from the pinnacle on which he had hitherto stood, he apprehended no other rival. The chief of the Zealots was the only man who could equal him in craft as well as in courage, whose stratagems were as deep, whose strokes were even bolder, than his own. The opportunity he had desired so long was come, he believed, at last. In that circular chamber, thought John, before that council of stern and cruel dotards, he was about to throw the winning cast of his game. It behoved him to play it warily, though courageously. If he could enlist the majority of the Sanhedrim on his own side, his rival's downfall was certain. When he had assumed supreme power in Jerusalem—and he made no doubt that would be his next step—it would be time enough to consider whether he too might not ensure his own safety, and make terms with Titus by delivering up the town to the enemy.

Standing apart from the prisoners, and affecting an air of extreme deference to his audience, John addressed the Nasi, [pg 375]in the tones rather of an inferior who excused himself for an excess of zeal in the performance of his duty, than of an equal denouncing a traitor and demanding justice for an offence.

"I leave my case," said he, "in the hands of the Sanhedrim, appealing to them whether I have exceeded my authority, or accused any man falsely of a crime which I am unable to prove. I only ask for the indulgence due to a mere soldier, who is charged with the defence of the city, and is jealous of everything that can endanger her safety. From each member here present without a single exception, from Matthias the son of Boethus to Phineas Ben-Ezra of the family of Nehemiah, I implore a favourable hearing. There stands the man whom I secured at noon this day, coming direct from Titus, with a written scroll upon his person, of which the superscription was to a certain Gentile dwelling in the house of Eleazar, who is also present before you, and purporting to be in the writing of that warrior of the heathen who commands the Tenth Legion. Was it not my duty to bring such a matter at once before the Council? and was it not expedient that the Council should refer so grave a question to the Sanhedrim?"

Matthias bent his brows sternly upon the speaker, and thus addressed him—

"Thou art concealing thy thoughts from those to whose favour thou makest appeal. John of Gischala, thou art no unpractised soldier to draw a bow at a venture, and heed not where the shaft may strike. Speak out thine accusation, honestly, boldly, without fear of man, before the assembly, or for ever hold thy peace!"

Thus adjured, John of Gischala cast an anxious glance at the surrounding faces turned towards him, with varying expressions of expectation, anger, encouragement, and mistrust. Then he looked boldly at the president, and made his accusation before the Sanhedrim as he had already made it before the Council—

"I charge Eleazar Ben-Manahem," said he, "with treason, and I charge these two men as his instruments. Let them clear themselves if they can!"

CHAPTER IX

THE PAVED HALL

All eyes were now turned on Eleazar, who sat unmoved in his place, affecting a composure which he was far from feeling. His mind, indeed, was tortured to agony, by the conflict that went on within. Should he stand boldly forward and confess that he had sent his own brother into the Roman camp, with proposals for surrender? Well he knew that such a confession would be tantamount to placing his neck at once under John of Gischala's foot. Who amongst his most devoted partisans would have courage to profess a belief in his patriotic motives, or allow that he was satisfied with the explanation offered for such a flagrant act of treason? The condemnation of the Sanhedrim would be the signal for his downfall and his death. When he was gone who would be left to save Jerusalem? This was the consideration that affected him, far more than any personal apprehensions of danger or disgrace. On the other hand, should he altogether renounce his brother, and disavow the authority he had given him? It has already been said, that as far as he loved any living being, he loved Calchas; perhaps had it not been so, he might have shrunk from the disgrace of abandoning one who had acted under his own immediate orders, and risked so much in obeying them; but in the depths of his fierce heart, something whispered that self-sacrifice was essentially akin to duty, and that *because* he loved him, therefore he must offer up his brother, as a man offers up a victim at the altar.

Nevertheless, he ran his eye hastily over his seventy-two colleagues, as they sat in grave deliberation, and summed up rapidly the score of friends and foes. It was nearly balanced, [pg 377]yet he knew there were many who would take their opinions from the Nasi; and from that stern old man he could expect nothing but the severity of impartial justice. He dared not look at Calchas, he dared not cover his face with his hand to gain a brief respite from the cold grave eyes that were fixed upon him. It was a bitter moment, but he reflected that, in the cause of Jerusalem, shame and suffering and sorrow, and even sin, became sacred, and he resolved to sacrifice all, even his own flesh and blood, to his ascendency in the town.

He was spared the pain, however, of striking the fatal blow with his own hand. Matthias, scrupulous in all matters of justice, had decided that until the accusation against him was supported by some direct evidence, no member of the Sanhedrim could be placed in the position of a culprit. He therefore determined to interrogate the prisoners himself, and ascertain whether anything would be elicited of so grave a nature as to cause Eleazar's suspension from his present office, and the consequent reassembling of the whole Sanhedrim; a delay that in the present critical state of matters it was desirable to avoid, the more so that the day was already far advanced, and the morrow was the Sabbath. He therefore ordered the two prisoners to be placed in the centre of the hall; and, looking sternly towards the accused, began his interrogations in the severe accents of one who is an avenger rather than a judge.

The mild eye and placid demeanour of Calchas afforded a strong contrast to the frowning brows and flashing glances of the Nasi.

"Your name, old man," said the latter abruptly. "Your name, lineage, and generation?"

"Calchas the son of Simeon," was the reply, "the son of Manahem, of the house of Manahem, and of the tribe of Judah."

"Art thou not the brother of Eleazar Ben-Manahem, who is sitting yonder in his place as a member of the Sanhedrim, before whom thou hast to plead?"

Ere he replied, Calchas stole a look at Eleazar, who forced himself to return it. There was something in the elder brother's face that caused the younger to turn his eyes away, and bend them on the ground. The fierce old president, impatient of that momentary delay, broke out angrily—

"Nay, look up, man! no subterfuges will avail thee here. Remember the fate of those who dare to lie in the presence of the Sanhedrim!"

[pg 378]

Calchas fixed his eye on the president's in mild rebuke.

"I am in a higher presence than thine, Matthias son of Boethus," said he; "neither need the children of Manahem be adjured to speak truth before God and man!"

"Hast thou heard the accusation brought against thee by John of Gischala?" proceeded the Nasi. "Canst thou answer it with an open brow and a clean heart?"

"I heard the charge," replied Calchas, "and I am ready to answer it for myself, and for him who is in bonds by my side. Have I permission to clear myself before the Sanhedrim?"

"Thou wilt have enough to do to slip thine own neck out of the yoke," answered Matthias sternly. "Colleagues," he added, looking round, "ye have heard the accuser—will ye now listen to the accused?"

Then Phineas, speaking for the rest, answered: "We will hear him, Nasi, without favour, we will judge him without mercy."

Thus encouraged, Calchas shook the white hair from his brow, and entered boldly on his defence.

"It is true," said he, "that I have been outside the walls. It is true that I have been in the Roman camp, nay, that I have been in the very presence of Titus himself. Shall I tell the assembly of the strength of Rome, of the discipline of her armies, of the late reinforcement of her legions? Shall I tell them that I saw the very auxiliaries eating wheaten bread and the flesh of kids and sheep, whilst my countrymen are starving behind the walls? Shall I tell them that we are outnumbered by our foes, and are ourselves weakened by dissensions, and wasting our strength and courage day by day? Shall I tell them that I read on the face of Titus confidence in himself and reliance on his army, and, even with a conviction that he should prevail, a wish to show pity and clemency to the vanquished? All this they already know, all this must make it needless for me to enter into any defence beyond a simple statement of my motives. Nay, I have gathered intelligence from the Roman camp," he added, now fixing his eyes on his brother, to whom he had no other means of imparting the answer, which the prince had confided to him through Licinius by word of mouth,—"intelligence, the importance of which should well bear me harmless, even had I committed a greater offence than escaping from a beleaguered town to hold converse with the enemy. Titus," he spoke now in a loud clear voice, of which every syllable rang through the [pg 379]building—"Titus bade me be assured that his determination was unalterable, to grant no further delay, but, surrender or no surrender, to enter Jerusalem the day after the Sabbath, and if he encountered resistance, to lay waste the Holy City with fire and sword!"

Eleazar started to his feet, but recollected himself, and resumed his seat instantaneously. The action might well be interpreted as the mere outbreak of a soldier's energy, called, as it were, by the sound of the trumpet to the wall. This, then, was what he had gained, a respite, a reprieve of one day, and that one day he had purchased at the dear price of his brother's life. Yet even now the fierce warrior reflected with a grim delight, how judiciously he had used the time accorded him, and how, when the proud Roman did make his threatened assault, he would meet with a reception worthy of the warlike fame so long enjoyed by the Jewish nation.

The rest of the Sanhedrim seemed scared and stupefied. Every man looked in his neighbour's face, and read there only dismay and blank despair. The crisis had been long threatening, and now it was at hand. Resistance was hopeless, escape impossible, and captivity insupportable. The prevailing feeling in the assembly was, nevertheless, one of indignation against the bearer of such unwelcome tidings. The Nasi was the first to recover himself, yet even he seemed disturbed.

"By whose authority," said he—and every eye was turned on Eleazar while he spoke—"by whose authority didst thou dare to enter the camp of the enemy, and traffic with the Gentile who encompasseth the Holy City with bow and spear?"

The chief of the Zealots knew well that he was the observed of all his colleagues, many of whom would triumph at his downfall, whilst even his own partisans would detach themselves from it, each to the best of his abilities, when his faction ceased to be in the ascendant. He knew, too, that on his brother's answer hung not only his life—which indeed he had risked too often to rate at a high value—but the stability of the whole fabric he had been building for months—the authority by which he hoped to save Jerusalem and Judæa, for which he grudged not to peril his immortal soul; and knowing all this, he forced his features into a sedate and solemn composure. He kept his eye away from the accused indeed, but fixed sternly on the president, and sat in his place the only man in the whole of that panic-stricken assembly who appeared master of the situation, and confident [pg 380]in himself. Calchas paused before he answered, waiting till the stir was hushed, and the attention which had been diverted to his brother settled once more on his own case. Then he addressed the Nasi in bold sonorous accents, his form dilating, his face brightening as he spoke—

"By the authority of Him who came to bring peace on earth—by the authority that is as far greater than that of Sanhedrim, or priest, or conqueror, as the heavens are higher than the sordid speck of dust on which, but for that authority, we should only swarm and grovel and live one little hour, like the insects dancing in the sunbeams, to die at the close of day—I am a man of peace! Could I bear to see my country wasted by the armed hand, and torn by the trampling hoof? I love my neighbour as myself. Could I bear to know that his grasp was day by day on his brother's throat? I have learned from my Master that all are brethren, besieger and besieged, Roman and barbarian, Jew and Gentile, bond and free. Are they at variance, and shall I not set them at one? Are their swords at each other's breasts, and shall I not step between and bid them be at peace? By whose authority, dost thou ask me, Matthias son of Boethus? By His authority who came to you, and ye knew Him not. Who preached to you, and ye heeded Him not. Who would have saved you in His own good time from the great desolation, and ye reviled Him, and judged Him, and put Him to death on yonder hill!"

Even the Prince of the Sanhedrim was staggered at the old man's boldness. Like other influential men of his nation, he could not ignore the existence of a well-known sect, which had already exchanged its title of Nazarenes for that of Christians, the name in which it was hereafter to spread itself over the whole earth; but the very mention of these self-devoted men was an abomination in his ears, and the last house in which he could have expected to find a votary of the cross, was that of Eleazar Ben-Manahem, chief of such a party as the Zealots, and grounding his influence on his exclusive nationality and strict adhesion to the very bigotry of the Jewish law. He looked on Calchas for a space, as if scarcely believing his eyes. Then there came over his features, always stern and harsh, an expression of pitiless severity, and he addressed his colleagues, rather than the accused.

"This is even a graver matter than I had thought for," said he, in a low yet distinct voice, that made itself heard in the farthest corner of the Court. "Princes of the house of [pg 381]Judah, elders and nobles, and priests and Levites of the nation, I am but the instrument of your will, the weapon wielded by your collective might. Is it not the duty of mine office that I smite and spare not?"

"Smite and spare not!" repeated Phineas; and the whole assembly echoed the merciless verdict.

There was not one dissentient, not even Eleazar, sitting gloomy and resolved in his place. Then Matthias turned once more to Calchas, and said, still in the same suppressed tones—

"Thou speakest in parables, and men may not address the Sanhedrim save in the brief language of fact. Art thou then one of those accursed Nazarenes who have called themselves Christians of late?"

"I am indeed a Christian," answered Calchas, "and I glory in the name. Would that thou, Matthias son of Boethus, and these the elders of Judah, were partakers with me in all that name affords."

Then he looked kindly and joyfully in Eleazar's face, for he knew that he had saved his brother. The corselet of the latter rattled beneath his long black robe with the shiver that ran through his whole frame. The tension was taken off his nerves at last, and the relief was great, but it was purchased at too dear a price. Now that it was doomed, he felt the value of his brother's life. He was totally unmanned, and shifted uneasily in his seat, not knowing what to do or say. They seemed to have changed places at last—Calchas to have assumed the bold unyielding nature, and Eleazar the loving tender heart. He recovered himself, however, before long. The ruling passion triumphed once more, as he anticipated the discomfiture of his rival, and the speedy renewal of his own ascendency amongst his countrymen.

The Prince of the Sanhedrim reflected for a few moments ere he turned his severe frown on Esca, and said—

"What doth this Gentile here in the Court of the Sanhedrim? Let him speak what he knoweth in this matter, ere he answer his own crime. Thy testimony at least may be valid," he added scornfully, "for thou surely art not a Christian?"

The Briton raised his head proudly to reply. If there was less of holy meekness in his demeanour than in that of Calchas, there was the same bold air of triumph, the same obvious defiance of consequences, usually displayed by those who sealed their testimony with their blood.

"I *am* a Christian," said he. "I confess it, and I too, like [pg 382]my teacher there, glory in the name! I will not deny the banner under which I serve. I will fight under that banner, even to the death."

The Nasi's very beard bristled with indignation; he caught up the skirt of his mantle, and tore it asunder to the hem. Then, raising the pieces thus rent above his head, he cried out in a loud voice, "It is enough! They have spoken blasphemy before the Sanhedrim. There is nothing more but to pronounce immediate sentence of death. Phineas Ben-Ezra, bid thy colleagues adjourn to the Stone-paved Hall!"

Then the assembly rose in silence, and, marching gravely two by two, passed out into an adjoining chamber, which was paved, and roofed, and faced with stone. Here alone was it lawful to pass sentence of death on those whom the Sanhedrim had condemned; and here, while their judges stood round them in a circle, the prisoners with their guard fronting the Nasi took their position in the midst. The latter stooping to the ground went through the form of collecting a handful of dust and throwing it into the air.

"Thus," said he, "your lives are scattered to the winds, and your blood recoils on your own heads. You, Calchas the son of Simeon, the son of Manahem, of the house of Manahem, and you, Gentile, called Esca on the scroll which has been delivered into my hand, shall be kept in secure ward till to-morrow be past, seeing that it is the Sabbath, and at morning's dawn on the first day of the week ye shall be stoned with stones in the Outer Court adjoining the Temple until ye die; and thus shall be done, and more also, to those who are found guilty of blasphemy in the presence of the Sanhedrim!"

Then turning to Eleazar, who still retained his forced composure throughout the hideous scene, he added—

"For thee, Eleazar Ben-Manahem, thy name is still untarnished in the nation, and thy place still knows thee amongst thy brethren. The testimony of a Nazarene is invalid; and no accusation hath yet been brought against thee supported by any witness save these two condemned and accursed men. That thou hast no portion, my brother, with blasphemers scarcely needs thine own unsupported word in the ears of the Sanhedrim!"

Eleazar, with the same fixed white face, looked wildly round him on the assembled elders, turning up the sleeves of his gown the while, and moving his hands over each other as though he were washing them.

"Their blood be on their own head," said he. "I renounce them from my family and my household—I abjure them, I wash my hands of them—their blood be on their own head!"

And while he spoke, the warning voice was heard again outside the Temple, causing even the bold heart of the Nasi to thrill with a wild and unaccustomed fear—the voice of the wailing prophet crying, "Woe to Jerusalem! Woe to the Holy City! Sin and sorrow and desolation! Woe to the Holy City! Woe to Jerusalem!"

CHAPTER X

A ZEALOT OF THE ZEALOTS

The man who has resolved that he will shake himself free from those human affections and human weaknesses which, like the corporeal necessities of hunger and thirst, seem to have been given us for our enjoyment rather than our discomfort, will find he undertakes a task too hard for mortal courage and for mortal strength. Without those pleasant accessories, like water and sunshine, the simple and universal luxuries of mankind, existence may indeed drag on, but it can scarcely be called life. The Great Dispenser of all knows best. His children are not meant to stand alone, independent of each other and of Him. While they help their fellows, and trust in His strength, they are strong indeed; but no sooner do they lean on the staff themselves have fashioned, than they stumble and fall. It wounds the hand that grasps it, and breaks too surely when it is most needed at the last.

Eleazar believed, when he quitted the Paved Hall in which the Sanhedrim pronounced their sentence, that the bitterest drop was drained in the cup he had forced himself to quaff. He had not anticipated the remorseful misery that awaited him in his own home—the empty seats, where *they* were not—the tacit reproach of every familiar object—worst of all, the meeting with Mariamne, the daughter of his affections, the only child of his house. All that dreary Sabbath morning the Zealot sat in his desolate home, fearing—yes, he who seemed to fear nothing; to whom the battle-cry of shouting thousands on the wall was but as heart-stirring and inspiring music—fearing the glance of a girl's dark eye, the tone of her gentle voice—and that girl his own daughter. There was no daily sacrifice in the Temple now; that last cherished prerogative of the Jewish religion had been suspended. His creed forbade him to busy himself in any further measures of defence which would involve labour on the Sacred Day. He might not work with lever and [pg 385]crowbar at the breach. All that could be done in so short a space of time had been done by his directions yesterday. He must sit idle in his stately dwelling, brooding darkly over his brother's fate, or traverse his marble floor in restless strides, with clenched hands, and gnashing teeth, and a wild despair raging at his heart. Yet he never yielded nor wavered in his fanatical resolve. Had it all to be done once more, he would do the same again.

One memory there was that he could not shake off—a vague and dreary memory that sometimes seemed to soothe, and sometimes to madden him. The image of Mariamne would come up before his eyes, not as now in her fair and perfect womanhood, but as a helpless loving little child, running to him with outstretched arms, and round cheeks wet with tears, asking him for the precious favourite that had gone with the rest of the flock to one of those great sacrifices with which the Jews kept their sacred festivals—the kid that was his child's playfellow—that he would have ransomed, had he but known it in time, with whole hecatombs of sheep and oxen, ere it should have been destroyed. The child had no mother even then; and he remembered, with a strange clearness, how he had taken the weeping little girl on his knee and soothed her with unaccustomed tenderness, while she put her arms round his neck, and laid her soft cheek against his own, accepting consolation, and sobbing herself to sleep upon his breast.

After this there seemed to grow up a tacit confidence—a strong though unspoken affection—between father and daughter. They seldom exchanged many words in a day, sometimes scarcely more than a look. No two human beings could be much less alike, or have less in common. There was but this one slender link between them, and yet how strong it had been! After a while it angered him to find this memory softening, while it oppressed him, whether he would or no. He resolved he would see Mariamne at once and face the worst. She knew he had avoided her, and held him in too great awe to risk giving offence by forcing herself upon him. Ignorant of Esca's arrest, the instinctive apprehension of a woman for the man she loves had yet caused her to suspect some threatened danger from his prolonged absence. She watched her opportunity, therefore, to enter her father's presence and gain tidings, if possible, of his brother and the Briton.

The hours sped on, and the fierce Syrian noon was already glaring down upon the white porches and dazzling [pg 386]streets of the Holy City. The hush of the Sabbath was over all; but it seemed more like the brooding, unnatural hush that precedes earthquake or tempest, than the quiet of a day devoted to peaceful enjoyment and repose. Her father was accustomed to drink a cup of wine at this hour, and Mariamne brought it him, trembling the while to learn the certainty of that which she could not yet bear to leave in doubt. She entered the room in which he sat with faltering steps, and stood before him with a certain graceful timidity that seemed to deprecate his resentment. His punishment had begun already. She reminded him of her mother, standing there pale and beautiful in her distress.

"Father," she said softly, as he took the cup from her hand and set it down untasted, without speaking, "where is our kinsman, Calchas? and—and Esca, the Briton? Father! tell me the worst at once. I am your own daughter, and I can bear it."

The worst, had she allowed herself to embody her vague fears, would have applied to the younger of the absent ones. It would have assumed that he was gravely wounded, even dangerously. Not killed—surely not killed! He turned his eyes upon her sternly, nay, angrily; but even then he could not tell her till he had lifted the cup and drained it every drop. His lip was steady now, and his face was harder, gloomier, than before, while he spoke—

"Daughter of Ben-Manahem!" said he, "henceforth thou hast no portion with him who was thy kinsman but yesterday, neither with him the Gentile within my gate, who has eaten of my bread and drunk from my cup, and stood with me shoulder to shoulder against the Roman on the wall."

She clasped her hands in agony, and her very lips turned white; but she said true—she was his own daughter, and she neither tottered nor gave way. In measured tones she repeated her former words.

"Tell me the worst, father. I can bear it."

He found it easier now that he had begun, and he could lash himself into a spurious anger as he went on, detailing the events of the previous day; the charges brought forward by John of Gischala, the trial before the Sanhedrim, his own narrow escape, and the confession of the two culprits, owning, nay, glorying in their mortal crime. He fenced himself in with the sophistry of an enthusiast and a fanatic. He deluded himself into the belief that he had been injured and aggrieved by the apostasy of the condemned. He poured forth all the eloquence that might have vindicated him before [pg 387]Matthias and his colleagues, had John's accusation been ever brought to proof. The girl stood petrified and overpowered with his violence: at last he denounced herself, for having listened so eagerly to the gentle doctrines of her own father's brother, for having consorted on terms of friendship with the stranger whom he had been the first to encourage and welcome beneath his roof. Once she made her appeal on Esca's behalf, but he silenced her ere she had half completed it.

"Father," she urged, "though a Gentile, he conformed to the usages of our people; though a stranger, I have heard yourself declare that not a warrior in our ranks struck harder for the Holy City than your guest, the brave and loyal Esca!"

He interrupted her with a curse.

"Daughter of Ben-Manahem! in the day in which thou shalt dare again to speak that forbidden name, may thine eye wax dim, and thy limbs fail, and thy heart grow cold within thy breast—that thou be cut off even then, in thy sin—that thou fall like a rotten branch from the tree of thy generation—that thou go down into the dust and vanish like water spilt on the sand—that thy name perish everlastingly from among the maidens of Judah and the daughters of thy father's house!"

Though his fury terrified it did not master her. Some women would have fled in dismay from his presence; some would have flung themselves on their knees and sought to move him to compassion with prayers and tears. Mariamne looked him fixedly in the face with a quiet sorrow in her own that touched him to the quick, and maddened him the more.

"Father," she said softly, "I have nothing left to fear in this world. Slay me, but do not curse me."

The vision of her childhood, the memory of her mother, the resigned sadness of her bearing, and the consciousness of his own injustice, conspired to infuriate him.

"Slay thee!" he repeated between his set teeth. "By the bones of Manahem—by the head of the high-priest—by the veil of the Temple itself, if ever I hear thee utter that accursed name again, I will slay thee with mine own hand!"

It was no empty threat to a daughter of her nation. Such instances of fanaticism were neither unknown to the sterner sects of the Jews, nor regarded with entirely unfavourable eyes by that self-devoted and enthusiastic people. The tale of Jephthah's daughter was cherished rather as an example of [pg 388]holy and high-minded obedience, than a warning from rash and inconsiderate vows. The father was more honoured as a hero than the daughter was pitied for a victim. And in later times, one Simon of Scythopolis, who had taken up arms against his own countrymen, and repented of his treachery, regained a high place in their estimation by putting himself to death, having previously slain every member of his family with his own hand.[a] It would have only added one more incident, causing but little comment, to the horrors of the siege, had the life of Mariamne been taken by her own father on his very threshold. She looked at him more in surprise than fear, with a hurt reproachful glance that pierced him to the heart. "Father!" she exclaimed, "you cannot mean it. Unsay those cruel words. Am I not your daughter? Father! father! you used to love me, when I was a little girl!"

Then his savage mood gave way, and he took her to him and spoke to her in gentle soothing accents, as of old.

"Thou art a daughter of Manahem," said he, "a maiden of Judah. It is not fit for thee to consort with the enemies of thy nation and of thy father's house. These men have avowed the pernicious doctrines of the Nazarenes, who call themselves Christians. Therefore they are become an abomination in our sight, and are to be cut off from amongst our people. Mariamne, if I can bear unmoved to see my brother perish, surely it is no hard task for thee to give up this stranger guest. It is not that my heart is iron to the core, though thou seest me ofttimes so stern, even with thee; but the men of to-day, who have taken upon themselves the defence of Jerusalem from the heathen, must be weaned from human affections and human weaknesses, even as the child is weaned from its mother's milk. I tell thee, girl, I would not count the lives of all my kindred against one hour of the safety of Judah; and Mariamne, though I love thee dearly, ay, better far than thou canst know—for whom have I now but thee, my daughter?—yet, if I believed that thou, too, couldst turn traitor to thy country and thy faith—I speak it [pg 389]not in anger—flesh and blood of mine own though thou be, I would bury my sword in thy heart!"

Had Eleazar's looks corresponded with his words, such a threat, in her present frame of mind, might have caused Mariamne to avow herself a Christian, and brave the worst at once; but there was a weight of care on her father's haggard brow, a mournful tenderness in his eyes, that stirred the very depths of her being in compassion—that merged all other feelings in one of intense pity for the misery of that fierce, resolute, and desolate old man. For the moment she scarcely realised Esca's danger in her sympathy for the obvious sufferings of one usually so self-reliant and unmoved. She came closer to his side, and placed her hand in his without speaking. He looked fondly down at her.

"Abide with me for a space," said he; "Mariamne, thou and I are left alone in the world."

Then he covered his face with his hands, and remained without speaking, wrapped, as it seemed, in gloomy reflections that she dare not disturb. So the two sat on through the weary hours of that long hot Sabbath day. Whenever she made the slightest movement, he looked up and signed for her to remain where she was. Though it was torture, she dared not disobey; and while the time slipped on and the shadows lengthened, and the breeze began to stir, she knew that every minute, as it passed, brought her lover nearer and nearer to a cruel death. Thus much she had learned too surely; but with the certainty were aroused all the energies of her indomitable race, and she resolved that he should be saved. Many a scheme passed through her working brain, as she sat in her father's presence, fearing now, above all things, to awake his suspicion of her intentions by word or motion, and so make it impossible for her to escape. Of all her plans there was but one that seemed feasible; and even that one presented difficulties almost insurmountable for a woman.

She knew that he was safe at least till the morrow. No execution could take place on the Sabbath; and although the holy day would conclude at sundown, it was not the custom of her nation to put their criminals to death till after the dawn, so that she had the whole night before her in which to act. But, on the other hand, her father would not leave his home during the Sabbath, and she would be compelled to remain under his observation till the evening. At night, then, she had resolved to make her escape, and taking advantage of the private passage, only known to her father's [pg 390]family, by which Calchas had reached the Roman camp, to seek Titus himself, and offer to conduct his soldiers by that path into the city, stipulating as the price of her treachery an immediate assault, and the rescue of her kinsman, Calchas, with his fellow-sufferer. Girl as she was, it never occurred to her that Titus might refuse to believe in her good faith towards himself, and was likely to look upon the whole scheme as a design to lead his army into an ambush. The only difficulty that presented itself was her own escape from the city. She never doubted but that, once in the Roman camp, her tears and entreaties would carry everything before them, and, whatever became of herself, her lover would be saved.

It was not, however, without a strong conflict of feelings that she came to this desperate resolve. The blood that flowed in her veins was loyal enough to tingle with shame ever and anon, as she meditated such treachery against her nation. Must she, a daughter of Judah, admit the enemy into the Holy City? Could the child of Eleazar Ben-Manahem, the boldest warrior of her hosts, the staunchest defender of her walls, be the traitor to defile Jerusalem with a foreign yoke? She looked at her father sitting there, in gloomy meditation, and her heart failed her as she thought of his agony of shame, if he lived to learn the truth, of the probability that he would never survive to know it, but perish virtually by her hand, in an unprepared and desperate resistance. Then she thought of Esca, tied to the stake, the howling rabble, the cruel mocking faces, the bare arms and the uplifted stones. There was no further doubt after that—no more wavering—nothing but the dogged immovable determination that proved whose daughter she was.

When the sun had set, Eleazar seemed to shake off the fit of despondency that had oppressed him during the day. The Sabbath was now past, and it was lawful for him to occupy mind and body in any necessary work. He bade Mariamne light a lamp, and fetch him certain pieces of armour that had done him good service, and now stood in need of repair. It was a task in the skilful fulfilment of which every Jewish warrior prided himself. Men of the highest rank would unwillingly commit the renewal of these trusty defences to any fingers but their own; and Eleazar entered upon it with more of cheerfulness than he had shown for some time. As he secured one rivet after another, with the patience and precision required, every stroke of the hammer seemed to smite upon his daughter's brain. There she was compelled [pg 391]to remain a close prisoner, and the time was gliding away so fast! At length, when the night was already far advanced, even Eleazar's strong frame began to feel the effects of hunger, agitation, labour, and want of rest. He nodded two or three times over his employment, worked on with redoubled vigour, nodded again, let his head sink gradually on his breast, while the hammer slipped from his relaxing fingers, and he fell asleep.

CHAPTER XI
THE DOOMED CITY

Mariamne watched her father for a few impatient minutes, that seemed to lengthen themselves into hours, till she had made sure by his deep respiration that her movements would not wake him. Then she extinguished the lamp and stole softly from the room, scarcely breathing till she found herself safe out of the house. The door through which she emerged was a private egress, opening on the wide terrace that overhung the gardens. Its stone balustrades and broad flight of steps were now white and glistening in the moonlight, which shone brighter and fairer in those mellow skies than doth many a noonday in the misty north. While she paused to draw breath, and concentrate every faculty on the task she had undertaken, she could not but admire the scene spread out at her very feet. There lay the gardens in which she had followed many a childish sport, and dreamed out many a maiden's dream, sitting in the shade of those black cypresses, and turning her young face to catch the breeze that stirred their whispering branches, direct from the hills of Moab, blending in the far distance with the summer sky. And lately, too, amid all the horrors and dangers of the siege, had she not trod these level lawns with Esca, and wondered how she could be so happy while all about her was strife, and desolation, and woe? The thought goaded her into action, and she passed rapidly on; nevertheless, in that one glance around, the fair and gorgeous picture stamped itself for ever on her brain.

Beneath her—here black as ebony, there glistening like sheets of burnished steel—lay the clear-cut terraces and level lawns of her father's stately home, dotted by tall tapering cypresses pointing to the heavens, and guarded by the red stems of many a noble cedar, flinging their twisted branches aloft in the midnight sky. Beyond, the spires and domes and pinnacles of the Holy City glittered and shone in the mellow light, or loomed in the alternate shade, fantastic, gloomy, and [pg 393]indistinct. Massive blocks of building, relieved by rows of marble pillars supporting their heavy porticoes, denoted the dwellings of her princes and nobles; while encircling the whole could be traced the dark level line of her last defensive wall, broken by turrets placed at stated intervals, and already heightened at the fatal breach opposite the Tower of Antonia, from the summit of which glowed one angry spot of fire, a beacon kindled for some hostile purpose by the enemy. High above all, like a gigantic champion guarding his charge, in burnished armour and robes of snowy white, rose the Temple, with its marble dome and roof of beaten gold. It was the champion's last watch—it was the last sleep of the fair and holy city. Never again would she lie in the moonlight, beautiful, and gracious, and undefaced. Doomed, like the Temple in which she trusted, to be utterly demolished and destroyed, the plough was already yoked that should score its furrows deep into her comeliness; the mighty stones, so hewn and carved and fashioned into her pride of strength, were even now vibrating to that shock which was about to hurl them down into such utter ruin, that not one should be left to rear itself upon the fragments of another!

The moonbeams shone calm and pleasant on the doomed city, as they shone on the stunted groves of the Mount of Olives, on the distant crest of the hills of Moab, and, far away below these, on the desolate plains that skirt the waters of the Dead Sea. They shone down calm and pleasant, as though all were in peace and safety, and plenty and repose; yet even now the arm of the avenger was up to strike, the eagle's wing was pruned, his beak whetted; and Mariamne, standing on the terrace by her father's door, could count the Roman watch-fires already established in the heart of the Lower City, twinkling at regular distances along the summit of Mount Calvary.

The view of the enemy's camp, the thought of Esca's danger, spurred her to exertion. She hurried along the terrace, and down into the garden, following the path which she knew was to lead her to the marble basin with its hidden entrance to the secret passage. Her only thought now was one of apprehension that her unassisted strength might be unable to lift the slab. Full but of this care, she advanced swiftly and confidently towards the disused fountain, to stop within ten paces of it, and almost scream aloud in the high state of tension to which her nerves had been strung—so startled was she and scared at what she saw. Sitting with its back to her, a long lean figure stooped and cowered over [pg 394]the empty basin, waving its arms, and rocking its body to and fro with strange unearthly gestures, and broken, muttered sentences, varied by gasps and moans. Her nation are not superstitious, and Mariamne had too many causes for fear in this world to spare much dread for the denizens of another; nevertheless she stood for a space almost paralysed with the suddenness of the alarm, and the unexpected nature of the apparition, quaking in every limb, and unable either to advance or fly.

There are times when the boldest of human minds become peculiarly susceptible to supernatural terrors—when the hardest and least impressionable persons are little stronger than their nervous and susceptible brethren. A little anxiety, a little privation, the omission of a meal or two, nay, even the converse of such abstinence in too great indulgence of the appetites, bring down the boasted reason of mankind to a sad state of weakness and credulity. The young, too, are more subject to such fantastic terrors than the old. Children suffer much from fears of the supernatural, conceiving in their vivid imaginations forms and phantoms and situations, which they can never have previously experienced, and of which it is therefore difficult to account for the origin. But all classes, and all ages, if they speak truth, must acknowledge, that at one time or another, they have felt the blood curdle, the skin creep, the breath come quick, and the heart rise with that desperate courage which springs from intense fear, at the fancied presence or the dreaded proximity of some ghostly object which eludes them after all, leaving a vague uncertainty behind it, that neither satisfies their curiosity nor ensures them against a second visitation of a similar nature.

Mariamne was in a fit state to become the victim of any such supernatural delusion. Her frame was weakened by the want of food; for like the rest of the besieged, she had borne her share of the privations that created such sufferings in the city for many long weeks before it was finally reduced. She had gone through much fatigue of late—the continuous unbroken fatigue that wears the spirits even faster than the bodily powers; and above all she had been harassed for the last few hours by the torture of inaction in a state of protracted suspense. It was no wonder that she should suffer a few moments of intense and inexplicable fear.

The figure, still with its back to her, and rocking to and fro, was gathering handfuls of dust from the disused basin of the fountain, and scattering them with its long lean arms upon its head and shoulders, chanting at the same time, in [pg 395]wild, mournful tones, the words "Wash and be clean," over and over again. It obviously imagined itself alone, and pursued its monotonous task with that dreary earnestness and endless repetition so peculiar to the actions of the insane.

After a while, Mariamne, perceiving that she was not observed, summoned courage to consider what was best to be done. The secret of the hidden passage was one to be preserved inviolate under any circumstances; and to-night everything she most prized depended on its not being discovered by the besieged. While the figure remained in its present position, she could do nothing towards the furtherance of her scheme. And yet the moments were very precious, and Esca's life depended on her speed.

There was no doubt, the unfortunate who had thus wandered into her father's gardens was a maniac; and those who suffered under this severe affliction were held in especial horror among her people. Unlike the Eastern nations of to-day, who believe them to be not only under its special protection, but even directly inspired by Providence, the Jews held that these sufferers were subject to the great principle of evil; that malignant spirits actually entered into the body of the insane, afflicting, mocking, and torturing their victim, goading it in its paroxysms to the exertion of that supernatural strength with which they endowed its body, and leaving the latter prostrate, exhausted, and helpless when they had satiated their malice upon its agonies. To be possessed of a devil was indeed the climax of all mental and corporeal misery. The casting out of devils by a mere word or sign, was perhaps the most convincing proof of miraculous power that could be offered to a people with whom the visitation was as general as it was mysterious and incomprehensible.

Mariamne hovered about the fountain, notwithstanding her great fear, as a bird hovers about the bush under which a snake lies coiled, but which shelters nevertheless her nest and her callow young. Standing there, in long dark robes, beneath a flood of moonlight, her face and hands white as ivory by the contrast, her eyes dilating, her head bent forward, her whole attitude that of painful attention and suspense, she might have been an enchantress composing the spell that should turn the writhing figure before her into stone, cold and senseless as the marble over which it bent. She might have been a fiend, in the form of an angel, directing its convulsions, and gloating over its agonies; or she might have been a pure and trusting saint, exorcising the [pg 396]evil spirit, and bidding it come out of a vexed fellow-creature in that name which fiends and men and angels must alike obey.

Presently the night-breeze coming softly over the Roman camp, brought with it the mellow notes of a trumpet, proclaiming that the watch was changed, and the centurions, each in his quarter, pacing their vigilant rounds. Ere it reached Mariamne's ears, the maniac had caught the sound, and sprang to his feet, with his head thrown back and his muscles braced for a spring like some beast of chase alarmed by the first challenge of the hound. Gazing wildly about him, he saw the girl's figure standing clear and distinct in the open moonlight, and raising a howl of fearful mirth, he leaped his own height from the ground, and made towards her with the headlong rush of a madman. Then fear completely overmastered her, and she turned and fled for her life. It was no longer a curdling horror that weighed down the limbs like lead, and relaxed the nerves like a palsy, but the strong and natural instinct of personal safety, that doubled quickness of perception for escape and speed of foot in flight.

Between herself and her father's house lay a broad and easy range of steps, leading upward to the terrace. Instinctively she dared not trust the ascent, but turned downwards over the level lawn into the gardens, with the maniac in close pursuit. It was a fearful race. She heard his quick-drawn breath, as he panted at her very heels. She could almost fancy that she felt it hot upon her neck. Once the dancing shadow of her pursuer, in the moonlight, actually reached her own! Then she bounded forward again in her agony, and eluded the grasp that had but just missed its prey. Thus she reached a low wall, dividing her father's from a neighbour's ground; feeling only that she must go straight on, she bounded over it, she scarce knew how, and made for an open doorway she saw ahead, trusting that it might lead into the street. She heard his yell of triumph as he rose with a vigorous leap into the air, the dull stroke of his feet as he landed on the turf so close behind her, and the horror of that moment was almost beyond endurance. Besides, she felt her strength failing, and knew too well that she could not sustain this rate of speed for many paces farther; but escape was nearer than she hoped, and reaching the door a few yards before the madman, she gained slightly on him as she shot through it, and sped on, with weakening limbs and choking breath, down the street.

[pg 397]

She heard his yell once again, as he caught sight of her, but two human figures in front restored her courage, and she rushed on to implore their protection from her enemy; yet fear had not so completely mastered her self-possession, as to drive her into an obvious physical danger, even to escape encounter with a lunatic. Nearing them, and indeed almost within arm's-length, she perceived that one was blasted with the awful curse of leprosy. The moon shone bright and clear upon the white glistening surface of his scarred and mortifying flesh. On his brow, on his neck, in the patches of his wasting beard and hair, on his naked arms and chest, nay, in the very garment girt around his loins, the plague-spots deepened, and widened, and festered, and ate them all away. It would be death to come in contact, even with his garments—nay, worse than death, for it would entail a separation from the touch of human hand, and the help of human skill.

Yet grovelling there on the bare stones of the street, the leper was struggling for a bone with a strong active youth, who had nearly overpowered him, and whom famine had driven to subject himself to the certainty of a horrible and loathsome fate, rather than endure any longer its maddening pangs. There was scarcely a meal of offal on the prize, and yet he tore it from the leper whom he had overpowered, and gnawed it with a greedy brutish muttering, as a dog mumbles a bone.

Gathering her dress around her to avoid a chance of the fatal contact, Mariamne scoured past the ghastly pair, even in her own imminent terror and distress feeling her heart bleed for this flagrant example of the sufferings endured by her countrymen. The maniac, however, permitted his attention to be diverted for a few moments, by the two struggling figures, from his pursuit; and Mariamne, turning quickly aside into a narrow doorway, cowered down in its darkest corner, and listened with feelings of relief and thankfulness to the steps of her pursuer, as, passing this unsuspected refuge, he sped in his fruitless chase along the street.

[pg 398]

CHAPTER XII

DESOLATION

Panting like a hunted hind, yet true to the generous blood that flowed in her veins, Mariamne recovered her courage even before her strength. No sooner was the immediate danger passed, than she cast aside all thoughts of personal safety, and only considered how she might still rescue the man she loved. Familiar with the street in which she had taken refuge, as with every other nook and corner of her native city—for the Jews permitted their women far more liberty than did their Eastern neighbours—she bethought her of taking a devious round in case she should be followed, and then returning by the way she had come, to her father's gardens. It was above all things important that Eleazar should not be made aware of his daughter's absence; and she calculated, not without reason, that the fatigues he had lately gone through, would ensure a few hours at least of sound unbroken sleep. The domestics, too, of his household, worn out with watching and hunger, were not likely to be aroused before morning; she had, therefore, sufficient time before her to put her plan into execution.

She reflected that it was impossible to approach her father's garden unnoticed at this hour, save by the way she had taken in her flight. To go through his house from the street was not to be thought of, as the entrance was probably secured, and she could not gain admittance without giving an explanation of her absence, and exciting the observation she most wished to avoid. Then she fell to thinking on the paths she had followed in her headlong flight, tracing them backward in her mind with that clear feminine perception, which so nearly approaches instinct, and is so superior to the more logical sagacity of man. She knew she could thread them step by step, to the marble basin of the fountain; and once again at that spot she felt as if her task would be half accomplished, instead of scarce begun. Doubtless the exertion of mind served to calm her recent terrors, and to [pg 399]distract attention from the dangers of her present situation—alone in a strange house, with the streets full of such horrors as those she had lately witnessed, and thronged by armed parties of lawless and desperate men.

She had gathered her robes about her, and drawn her veil over her head preparatory to emerging from her hiding-place, when she was driven back by the sound of footsteps, and the clank of weapons, coming up the street. To be seen was to accept the certainty of insult, and to run the risk of ill-usage, and perhaps death. She shrank farther back, therefore, into the lower part of the house; and becoming more accustomed to the gloom, looked anxiously about, to ascertain what further chance she had within for concealment or escape.

It was a low irregular building, of which the ground-floor seemed to have been used but as a space for passage to and from the upper apartments, and, perhaps, before the famine consumed them, as a shelter for beasts of burden, and for cattle. Not a particle of their refuse, however, had been left on the dry earthen floor; and though a wooden manger was yet standing, not a vestige remained of halter or tethering ropes, which had been long since eaten in the scarcity of food.[20] A boarded staircase, fenced by carved wooden balustrades, led from this court to the upper chambers, which were carefully closed; but a glimmer of light proceeding from the chinks of an ill-fitting door at its head, denoted that the house was not deserted. It was probably inhabited by some of the middle class of citizens; a rank of life that had suffered more than the higher, or even the lower during the siege—lacking the means of the one, and shrinking from the desperate resources of the other.

Mariamne, listening intently to every sound, was aware of a light step passing to and fro, within the room, and perceived besides a savoury smell as of roasted flesh, which pervaded the whole house. She knew by the quiet footfall and the rustle of drapery, that it was a woman whose motions she overheard, and for an instant the desire crossed her mind to beg for a mouthful of strengthening food, ere she departed on her way—a request she had reason to believe [pg 400]would be refused with anger. She blushed as she thought how a morsel of bread was now grudged, even at her own father's gate; and she remembered the time when scores of poor neighbours thronged it every morning for their daily meal; when sheep and oxen were slain and roasted at a moment's notice, on the arrival of some chance guest with his train of followers.

"It is a judgment!" thought the girl, regarding the afflictions of her people in the light of her new faith. "It may be, we must be purified by suffering, and so escape the final doom. Woe is me for my kindred and for my father's house! What am I, that I should not take my share in the sorrows of the rest?"

Then in a pure and holy spirit of self-sacrifice, she turned wearily away, resolving rather to seek the enemy weak and fasting, than shift from her own shoulders one particle of the burden borne by her wretched fellow-citizens; and ere long the time came when she was thankful she had not partaken, even in thought, of the food that was then being prepared.

Seeking the street once more, she found, to her dismay, that the armed party had halted immediately before the door. She was forced again to shrink back into the gloom of the lower court, and wait in fear and trembling for the result. These, too, had been arrested before the house by the smell of food. Wandering up and down the devoted city, such hungry and desperate men scrupled not to take with the strong hand anything of which they had need. By gold and silver, and soft raiment, they set now but little store—of wine they could procure enough to inflame and madden them, but food was the one passionate desire of their senses. Besides his own party, John of Gischala had now attached to his faction numbers of the Sicarii—a band of paid assassins who had sprung up in the late troubles to make a trade of murder—and had also seduced into his ranks such of the Zealots as were weary of Eleazar's rigid though fervent patriotism, finding the anarchy within the walls produced by the siege more to their taste than the disciplined efforts of their chief to resist the enemy. The party that now prevented Mariamne's egress consisted of a few fierce pitiless spirits from these three factions, united in a common bond of recklessness and crime. It was no troop for a maiden to meet by night in the house of a lone woman, or on the stones of a deserted street, and the girl, trembling at the conversation she was forced to overhear, needed all her [pg 401]courage to seize the first opportunity for escape. The clang of their arms made her heart leap, as they halted together at the door; but it was less suggestive of evil and violence than their words.

"I have it!" exclaimed one, striking his mailed hand against the post, with a blow that vibrated through the building. "Not a bloodhound of Molossis hath a truer nose than mine, or hunts his game more steadily to its lair. I could bury my muzzle, I warrant ye, in the very entrails of my prey, had I but the chance. There is food here, comrades, I tell ye, cooking on purpose for us. 'Tis strange if we go fasting to the wall to-night!"

"Well said, old dog!" laughed another voice. "Small scruple hast thou, Sosas, what the prey may be, so long as it hath but the blood in it. Come on; up to the highest seat with thee! No doubt we are expected, though the doors be closed and we meet with a cold welcome!"

"Welcome!" repeated Sosas; "who talks of welcome? I bid ye all welcome, comrades. Take what you please, and call for more. Every man what he likes best, be it sheep or lamb, or delicate young kid, or tender sweet-mouthed heifer. My guests ye are, and I bid you again walk up and welcome!"

"'Twere strange to find a morsel of food here, too," interposed one of the band. "Say, Gyron, is not this the house thou and I have already stripped these three times? By the beard of old Matthias, there was but half a barley-cake left when we made our last visit!"

"True," replied Gyron, with a brutal laugh, "and the woman held on to it like a wild-cat. I was forced to lend her a wipe over the wrist with my dagger, ere she let go, and then the she-wolf sucked her own blood from the wound, and shrieked out that we would not even leave her *that*. We might let her alone this time, I think, and go elsewhere!"

"Go to!" interrupted Sosas. "Thou speakest like one for whom the banquet is spread at every street corner. Art turning tender, and delicate even as a weaned child, with that grizzled beard on thy chin? Go to! I say. The supper is getting cold. Follow me!"

With these words the last speaker entered the house, and proceeded to ascend the staircase, followed by his comrades, who pushed and shouldered each other through the door with ribald jest and laughter, that made their listeners' blood run cold. Mariamne, in her retreat, was thus compelled to retire step by step before them to the top of the stairs, [pg 402] dreading every moment that their eyes, gradually accustomed to the gloom, which was rendered more obscure by the moonlight without, should perceive her figure, and their relentless grasp seize upon her too surely for a prey. It was well for her that the stairs were very dark, and that her black dress offered no contrast in colour to the wall against which she shrank. The door of the upper chamber opened outwards, and she hid herself close behind it, hoping to escape when her pursuers had entered one by one. To her dismay, however, she found that, with more of military caution than might have been expected, they had left a scout below to guard against surprise. Mariamne heard the unwilling sentinel growling and muttering his discontent, as he paced to and fro on the floor beneath.

Through the hinges of the open door, the upper apartment was plainly visible, even by the dim light of a solitary lamp that stood on the board, and threw its rays over the ghastly banquet there set forth. Sick, faint, and trembling with the great horror she beheld, Mariamne could not yet turn her eyes away. A gaunt grim woman was crouching at the table, holding something with both hands to her mouth, and glaring sidelong at her visitors, like a wild beast disturbed over its prey. Her grisly tresses were knotted and tangled on her brow; dirt, misery, and hunger were in every detail of her dress and person. The long lean arms and hands, with their knotted joints and fleshless fingers, like those of a skeleton, the sunken face, the sallow tight-drawn skin, through which the cheek-bones seemed about to start, the prominent jaw, and shrivelled neck, denoted too clearly the tortures she must have undergone in a protracted state of famine, bordering day by day upon starvation.

And what was that ghastly morsel hanging from those parched thin lips?

Mariamne could have shrieked aloud with mingled wrath and pity and dismay. Often had she seen a baby's tiny fingers pressed and mumbled in a mother's mouth, with doting downcast looks and gentle soothing murmurs and muttered phrases, fond and foolish, meaningless to others, yet every precious syllable a golden link of love between the woman and her child. But now, the red light of madness glared in the mother's eye; she was crouching fierce and startled, like the wild wolf in its lair, and her teeth were gnashing in her accursed hunger over the white and dainty limbs of her last-born child. Its little hand was in her [pg 403]mouth when the ruffians entered, whose violence and excesses had brought this abomination of desolation upon her house. She looked up with scarce a trace of humanity left in her blighted face.

"You have food here, mother!" shouted Sosas, rushing in at the head of his comrades. "Savoury food, roasted flesh, dainty morsels. What! hast got no welcome for thy friends? We have come to sup with thee unbidden, mother, for we know of old[2] the house of Hyssop is never ill-provided. Ay, Gyron there, watching down below, misled us sadly. His talk was but of scanty barley-cakes and grudging welcome, while lo! here is a supper fit to set before the high-priest, and the mother gives a good example, though she wastes no breath on words of welcome. Come on, comrades, I tell you; never wait to wash hands, but out with your knives, and fall to!"

While he spoke, the ruffian stretched his brawny arm across the table, and darted his long knife into the smoking dish. Mariamne behind the door, saw him start, and shiver, and turn pale. The others looked on, horror-struck, with staring eyes fixed upon the board. One, the fiercest and strongest of the gang, wiped his brow, and sat down, sick and gasping, on the floor. Then the woman laughed out, and her laughter was terrible to hear.

"I did it!" she cried, in loud, triumphant tones. "He was my own child, my fair, fat boy. If I had a hundred sons I would slay them all. All, I tell you, and set them before you, that you might eat and rejoice, and depart full and merry from the lonely woman's house. I slew him at sundown, my masters, when the Sabbath was past, and I roasted him with my own hands, for we were alone in the house, I and my boy. What! will ye not partake? Are you so delicate, ye men of war, that ye cannot eat the food which keeps life in a poor, weak woman like me? It is good food, it is wholesome food, I tell ye, and I bid you hearty welcome. Eat your fill, my masters; spare not, I beseech you. But we will keep a portion for the child. The child!" she repeated, like one who speaks in a dream: "he must be hungry ere now; it is past his bedtime, my masters, and I have not given him his supper yet!"

Then she looked on the dish once more, with a vacant, bewildered stare, rocking herself the while, and muttering [pg 404]in strange, unintelligible whispers, glancing from time to time stealthily at her guests, and then upon the horrid fragment she held, which, as though fain to hide it, she turned over and over in her gown. At length she broke out in another wild shriek of laughter, and laid her head down upon the table, hiding her face in her hands.

Pale and horror-struck, with quiet steps, and heads averted from the board, the gang departed one by one. Gyron, who was already wearied of his watch, met them on the stairs, to receive a whispered word or two from Sosas, with a muttered exclamation of dismay, and a frightful curse. The rest, who had seen what their comrade only heard, were speechless still, and Mariamne, listening to their clanking, measured tread as it traversed the lower court and passed out into the street, heard it die away in the distance, unbroken by a single exclamation even of disgust or surprise. The boldest of them dared not have stood another moment face to face with the hideous thing from which he fled.

Mariamne, too, waited not an instant after she had made sure that they were gone. Not even her womanly pity for suffering could overcome her feelings of horror at what she had so lately beheld. She seemed stifled while she remained under the roof where such a scene had been enacted; and while she panted to quit it, was more than ever determined to seek the Roman camp, and call in the assistance of the enemy. It was obvious even to her, girl as she was, that there was now no hope for Jerusalem within the walls. While her father's faction, and that of John, were neutralising each other's efforts for the common good—while to the pressure of famine, and the necessary evils of a siege, were added the horrors of rapine and violence, and daily bloodshed, and all the worst features of civil war—it seemed that submission to the fiercest enemy would be a welcome refuge, that the rule of the sternest conqueror would be mild and merciful by comparison.

She remembered, too, much that Calchas had explained in the sacred writings they had studied together, with the assistance of that Syrian scroll which proclaimed the good tidings of the new religion, elucidating and corroborating the old. She had not forgotten the mystical menaces of the prophets, the fiery denunciations of some, the distinct statements of others—above all, the loving, merciful warning of the Master himself. Surely the doom had gone forth at length. Here, if anywhere, was the carcass. Yonder, where she was going, was the gathering of the eagles. Was not [pg 405]she in her mission of to-night an instrument in the hands of Providence? A means for the fulfilment of prophecy? If she had felt patriotic scruples before, they vanished now. If she had shrunk from betraying her country, dishonouring her father, and disgracing her blood, all such considerations were as nothing now, compared to the hope of becoming a divine messenger, that, like the dove with its olive-branch, should bring back eventual peace and safety in its return. She had seen to-night madness and leprosy stalking abroad in the streets. Within a Jewish home she had seen a more awful sight even than these. It was in her power, at least, to put an end to such horrors, and she doubted whether the task might not have been specially appointed her from heaven; but she never asked herself the question if she would have been equally satisfied of her celestial mission, had Esca not been lying under the wall of the Temple, bound and condemned to die with the light of to-morrow's sun.

CHAPTER XIII

THE LEGION OF THE LOST

Nerving herself with every consideration that could steel a woman's heart, Mariamne sought her father's gardens by the way she had already come. They were deserted now, and the house, at which she could not forbear taking a look that would probably be her last, was still quiet and undisturbed. She would fain have seen her father once more, even in his sleep—would fain have kissed his unconscious brow, and so taken a fancied pardon for the treason she had resolved to commit—but it was too great a risk to run, and with a prayer for divine protection and assistance, she bent down to lift the slab of marble that concealed the secret way. Having been moved so lately in the egress of Calchas, it yielded easily to her strength, and she descended, not without considerable misgivings, a damp, winding stair, that seemed to lead into the bowels of the earth.

As the stone fell back to its former place, she was enveloped in utter darkness; and while she groped her way along the slimy arch that roofed-in the long, mysterious tunnel, she could not forbear shuddering with dread of what she might encounter, ere she beheld the light of day once more. It was horrible to think of the reptiles that might be crawling about her feet; of the unknown shapes with which, at any moment, she might come in contact; of the chances that might block her in on both sides, and so consign her, warm and living, to the grave: worst of all, of the possibility that some demoniac, like him from whom she had so recently escaped, might have taken up his abode here, in the strange infatuation of the possessed, and that she must assuredly become his prey, without the possibility of escape.

Such apprehensions made the way tedious indeed; and it was with no slight feeling of relief, and no mere formal thanksgiving, that Mariamne caught a glimpse of light stealing through the black, oppressive darkness, that seemed to take her breath away, and was aware that she had reached the other extremity of the passage at last. A few armfuls of brushwood, skilfully disposed, concealed its egress. These had been replaced by Calchas, in his late visit to the Roman camp, and Mariamne, peering through, could see without being seen, while she considered what step she should take next.

She was somewhat uneasy, nevertheless, to observe that a Roman sentinel was posted within twenty paces; she could hear the clank of his armour every time he stirred; she could even trace the burnished plumage of the eagle on the crest of his helmet. It was impossible to emerge from her hiding-place without passing him; and short as his beat might be, he seemed indisposed to avail himself of it by walking to and fro. In the bright moonlight there was no chance of slipping by unseen, and she looked in vain for a coming cloud on the midnight sky. He would not even turn his head away from the city, on which his gaze was fastened; and she watched him with a sort of dreary fascination, pondering what was best to be done.

Even in her extremity she could not but remark the grace of his attitude, and the beautiful outline of his limbs, as he leaned wearily on his spear. His arms and accoutrements, too, betrayed more splendour than seemed suitable to a mere private soldier, while his mantle was of rich scarlet, looped up and fastened at the shoulder with a clasp of gold. Such details she took in mechanically and unconsciously, even as she perceived that, at intervals, he raised his hand to his eyes, like one who wipes away unbidden tears. Soon she summoned her presence of mind, and watched him eagerly, for he stretched his arms towards Jerusalem with a pitiful, yearning gesture, and, bowing wearily, leant his crested head upon both arms, resting them against the spear.

'she walked boldly up to him'

It was her opportunity, and she seized it; but at the first movement she made the sentinel's attention was aroused, and she knew she was discovered, for he challenged immediately. Even then, Mariamne could not but observe that his voice was unsteady, and the spear he levelled trembled like an aspen in his grasp. She thought it wisest to make no attempt at deception, but walking boldly up to him, implored his safe-conduct, and besought him to take her to the tent of the [pg 408]commander at once. The sentinel seemed uncertain how to act, and showed, indeed, but little of that military promptitude and decision for which the Roman army was so distinguished. After a pause, he answered—and the soft tones, musical even in their trouble, that rang in Mariamne's ears, were unquestionably those of a woman—a woman, too, whose instincts of jealousy had recognised her even before she spoke.

"You are the girl I saw in the amphitheatre," she said, laying a white hand, which trembled violently, on the arm of the Jewess. "You were watching him that day, when he was down in the sand beneath the net. I know you, I say! I marked you turned pale when the tribune's arm was up to strike. You loved him then. You love him now! Do not deny it, girl! lest I drive this spear through your body, or send you to the guard to be treated like a spy taken captive in the act. You look pale, too, and wretched," she added, suddenly relenting. "Why are you here? Why have you left him behind the walls alone? I would not have deserted you in your need, Esca, my lost Esca!"

Mariamne shivered when she heard the beloved name pronounced in such fond accents by another's lips. Womanlike, she had not been without suspicions from the first, that her lover had gained the affections of some noble Roman lady—suspicions which were confirmed by his own admission to herself, accompanied by many a sweet assurance of fidelity and devotion; but yet it galled her even now, at this moment of supreme peril, to feel the old wound thus probed by the very hand that dealt it; and, moreover, through all her anxiety and astonishment, rose a bitter and painful conviction of the surprising beauty possessed by this shameless woman, clad thus inexplicably in the garb of a Roman soldier. Nevertheless, the Jewish maiden was true as steel. Like that mother of her nation who so readily gave up all claim to her own flesh and blood, to preserve it from dismemberment under the award of the wisest and greatest of kings, she would have saved her cherished Briton at any sacrifice, even that of her own constant and unfathomable love. She knelt down before the sentinel, and clasped the scarlet mantle in both hands.

"I will not ask you what or who you are," she said; "I am in your power, and at your mercy. I rejoice that it is so. But you will help me, will you not? You will use all your beauty and all your influence to save him whom—whom we both love?"

[pg 409]

She hesitated while she spoke the last sentence. It was as if she gave him up voluntarily, when she thus acknowledged another's share. But his very life was at stake; and what was her sore heart, her paltry jealousy, to stand in the way at such a moment as this? The other looked scornfully down on the kneeling girl.

"You, too, seem to have suffered," said the sentinel. "It is true then, all I have heard of the desolation and misery within the walls? But boast not of your sorrows; think not you alone are to be pitied. There are weary heads and aching hearts here in the leaguer, as yonder in the town. Tell me the truth, girl! What of Esca? You know him. You come from him even now. Where is he, and how fares it with him?"

"Bound in the Outer Court of the Temple!" gasped Mariamne, "and condemned to die with the first light of to-morrow's sun!"

His fate seemed more terrible and more certain, now that she had forced herself to put it into words. The Roman soldier's face turned deadly pale. The golden-crested helmet, laid aside for air, released a shower of rich brown curls, that fell over the ivory neck, and the smooth shoulders, and the white bosom panting beneath its breastplate. There could be no attempt at concealment now. Mariamne was obliged to confess that, even in her male attire, the woman whom she so feared, yet whom she must trust implicitly, was as beautiful as she seemed to be reckless and unsexed.

They were a lawless and a desperate band, that body of gladiators which Hippias had brought with him to the siege of Jerusalem. None of them but were deeply stained with blood; most of them were branded with crime; all were hopeless of good, fearless and defiant of evil. In many a venturous assault, in many a hand-to-hand encounter, fought out with enemies as fierce and almost as skilful as themselves, they had earned their ominous title; and the very legionaries, though they sneered at their discipline, and denied their efficiency in long-protracted warfare, could not but admit that to head a column of attack, to run a battering-ram under the very ramparts of a citadel, to dash in with a mad cheer over the shattered ruins of a breach, or to carry out any other hot and desperate service, there were no soldiers in the army like the Legion of the Lost. They had dwindled away, indeed, sadly from slaughter and disease; yet there were still some five or six hundred left, and this remnant consisted of the strongest and staunchest in the band. They still con[pg 410]stituted a separate legion, nor would it have been judicious to incorporate them with any other force, which, indeed, might have been as unwilling to receive them as they could be to enrol themselves in its ranks; and they performed the same duties, and made it their pride to guard the same posts they had formerly watched when thrice their present strength. Under these circumstances a fresh draft would have been highly acceptable to the Legion of the Lost; and in their daily increasing want of men, even a single recruit was not to be despised. Occasionally one of the Syrian auxiliaries, or a member of any of the irregular forces attached to the Roman army, who had greatly distinguished himself by his daring, was admitted into their band, and these additions became less rare as the original number decreased day by day.

An appeal to the good-nature of old Hirpinus, backed by a heavy bribe to one of his centurions, ensured Valeria's enrolment into this wild, disorderly, and dangerous force; nor in their present lax state of discipline, with the prospect of an immediate assault, had she much to dread from the curiosity of her new comrades. Even in a Roman camp, money would purchase wine, and wine would purchase everything else. Valeria had donned in earnest the arms she had often before borne for sport. "Hippias taught me to use them," she thought, with bitter, morbid exultation; "he shall see to-morrow how I have profited by his lessons!" Then she resolved to feed her fancy by gazing at the walls of Jerusalem; and she had little difficulty in persuading a comrade to whom she brought a jar of strong Syrian wine, that he had better suffer her to relieve him for the last hour or two of his watch.

The Amazons of old, with a courage we might look for in vain amongst the other sex, were accustomed to amputate their right breast that it might not hinder the bowstring when they drew the arrow to its head. Did they never feel, after the shapely bosom was thus mutilated and defaced, a throb of anguish, or a weight of dull dead pain where the flesh was now scarred, and hardened, and cicatrised—nay, something worse than pain beneath the wound, when they beheld a mother nursing a sucking-child? Valeria, too, had resolved, so to speak, that she would cut the very heart from out of her breast—that she would never feel as a woman feels again. She knew she was miserable, degraded, desperate—she believed she could bear it nobly now, because she was turned to stone. Yet, as she leaned on her spear in the [pg 411]moonlight, and gazed on the city which contained the prize she had so coveted and lost, she was compelled to acknowledge that the fibres of that heart she had thought to tear out and cast away, retained their feelings still. For all that was come and gone, she loved him, oh! so dearly, yet; and the eyes of the lost, maddened, desperate woman filled with tears of as deep and unselfish affection as could have been shed by Mariamne herself in her pure and stainless youth.

Valeria, as Hippias had learned by painful experience, was resolute for good and evil. It was this decision of character, joined to the impulsive disposition which springs from an undisciplined life, that had given him his prey. But it was this that thwarted all the efforts he made to obtain the ascendency over her which generally follows such a link as theirs; and it was this, too, that ere long caused her to tear the link asunder without a moment's apprehension or remorse. With all his energy and habits of command, the gladiator found he could not control the proud Roman lady, who in a moment of caprice had bowed her head to the very dust for the sake of following him. He could neither intimidate her into obedience, nor crush her into despair, though he tried many a haughty threat, and many an unmanly taunt at her shame. But all in vain; and as he would not yield an inch in their disputes, there was but little peace in the tent of the brave leader who ruled so sternly over the Legion of the Lost. The pair, indeed, went through the usual phases that accompany such bonds as those they chose to wear; but the changes were more rapid than common, as might well be expected, when their folly had not even the excuse of true affection on both sides. Valeria indeed tired first; for as far as the gladiator was capable of loving anything but his profession, he loved her, and this perhaps only embittered the guilty cup that was already sufficiently unpalatable to both. Weariness, as usual, followed fast on the heels of satiety, to be succeeded by irritation, discontent, and dislike; then came rude words, angry gestures, and overt aggression from the man, met by the woman with trifling provocations, mute defiance, and sullen scorn. To love another, too, so hopelessly and so dearly, made Valeria's lot even more difficult to bear, rendering her fretful, intolerant, and inaccessible to all efforts at reconciliation. Thus the breach widened hour by hour; and on the day when Hippias returned to his tent from the council of war before which Calchas had been brought, Valeria quitted it, vowing never to return. She had but one object left for which to live. [pg 412]Maddened by shame, infuriated by the insults of the gladiator, her great love yet surged up in her heart with an irresistible tide; and she resolved that she would see Esca once more, ay, though the whole Jewish army stood with levelled spears between them. After that, she cared not if she died on the spot at his feet!

To get within the works was indeed no easy matter; and so close a watch was kept by the Romans on all movements between the lines of the hostile forces, now in such dangerous proximity, that it was impossible to escape from the camp of Titus and join the enemy behind the wall, though the Jews, notwithstanding the vigilance of their countrymen, were trooping to the besiegers' camp by scores, to implore the protection of the conqueror, and throw themselves on his well-known clemency and moderation.

Valeria, then, had taken the desperate resolution of entering the city with the assault on the morrow. For this purpose she had adopted the dress and array of the Lost Legion. She would at least, she thought in her despair, be as forward as any of those reckless combatants. She would, at least, see Esca once more. If he met her under shield, not knowing her, and hurled her to the ground, the arm that smote her would be that of her glorious and beloved Briton. There was a wild, sweet sadness in the thought that she might perhaps die at last by his hand. Full of such morbid fancies—her imagination over-excited, her courage kindled, her nerves strung to their highest pitch—it brought with it a fearful reaction to learn that even her last consolation might be denied her—that the chance of meeting her lover once more was no longer in her own hands. What! had she undergone all these tortures, submitted to all this degradation, for nothing? And was Esca to die after all, and never learn that she had loved him to the last? She could not have believed it, but for the calm, hopeless misery that she read in Mariamne's eyes.

For a while Valeria covered her face and remained silent; then she looked down scornfully on the Jewess, who was still on her knees, holding the hem of the Roman lady's garment, and spoke in a cold, contemptuous tone—

"Bound and condemned to death, and you are here? You must indeed love him very dearly to leave him at such a time!"

Mariamne's despair was insensible to the taunt.

"I am here," said she, "to save him. It is the only chance. Oh, lady, help me! help me if only for his dear sake!"

"What would you have me do?" retorted the other impatiently. "Can I pull down your fortified wall with my naked hands? Can you and I storm the rampart at point of spear, and bear him away from the midst of the enemy to share him afterwards between us, as the legionaries share a prey?"—and she laughed a strange, choking laugh while she spoke.

"Nay," pleaded the kneeling Jewess, "look not down on me so angrily. I pray—I implore you only to aid me! Ay! though you slay me afterwards with your hand if I displease you by word or deed. Listen, noble lady; I can lead the Roman army within the walls; I can bring the soldiers of Titus into Jerusalem, maniple by maniple, and cohort by cohort, where they shall surprise my countrymen and obtain easy possession of the town; and all I ask in return—the price of my shame, the reward of my black treachery—is, that they will rescue the two prisoners bound in the Outer Court of the Temple, and spare their lives for her sake who has sold honour, and country, and kindred here to-night!"

Valeria reflected for a few seconds. The plan promised well; her woman's intuition read the secret of the other woman's heart. A thousand schemes rose rapidly in her brain; schemes of love, of triumph, of revenge. Was it feasible? She ran over the position of the wall, the direction from which Mariamne had come, her own knowledge gained from the charts she had studied in the tent of Hippias—charts that, obtained partly by treachery and partly by observation, mapped out every street and terrace in Jerusalem—and she thought it was. Of her suppliant's good faith she entertained no doubt.

"There is then a secret passage?" she said, preserving still a stern and haughty manner to mask the anxiety she really felt. "How long is it, and how many men will it take in abreast?"

"It cannot be far," answered the Jewess, "since it extends but from that heap of brushwood to the terrace of my father's house. It might hold three men abreast. I entreat you take me to Titus, that I may prevail on him to order the attack ere it be too late. I myself will conduct his soldiers into the city."

Valeria's generosity was not proof against her selfishness. Like many other women, her instincts of possession were strong; and no sooner had she grasped the possibility of saving Esca, than the old fierce longing to have him for her very own returned with redoubled force.

"That I may rescue the Briton for the Jewess!" she retorted, with a sneer. "Do you know to whom you speak? Listen, girl: I, too, have loved this Esca: loved him with a love to which yours is but as the glimmer on my helmet compared to the red glare of that watch-fire below the hill—loved him as the tigress loves her cubs—nay, sometimes as the tigress loves her prey! Do you think I will save him for another?"

Mariamne's face was paler than ever now, but her voice was clear, though very low and sad, while she replied—

"You love him too! I know it, lady, and therefore I ask you to save him. Not for me; oh! not for me! When he is once set free, I will never see him more: this is your price, is it not? Willingly, heartily I pay it; only save him—only save him! You will, lady; will you not? And so you will take me direct to Titus? See! the middle watch of the night is already nearly past."

But Valeria's plotting brain began now to shape its plans; she saw the obstacles in her way were she to conduct the girl at once into the presence of Titus. Her own disguise would be discovered, and the Roman commander was not likely to permit such a flagrant breach of discipline and propriety to pass unnoticed. If not punished, she would probably be at least publicly shamed, and placed under restraint. Moreover, the prince might hesitate to credit Mariamne's story, and suspect the whole scheme was but a plot to lead the attacking party into an ambush. Besides, she would never yield to the Jewess the credit and the privilege of saving her lover. No: she had a better plan than this. She knew that Titus had resolved the city should fall on the morrow. She knew the assault would take place at dawn; she would persuade Mariamne to return into the town; she would mark the secret entrance well. When the gladiators advanced to the attack, she would lead a chosen band by this path into the very heart of the city; she would save Esca at the supreme moment; and surely his better feelings would acknowledge her sovereignty then, when she came to him as a deliverer and a conqueror, like some fabulous heroine of his own barbarian nation. She would revenge on Hippias all the past weary months of discord; she would laugh Placidus to scorn with his subtle plans and his venturous courage, and the skill he boasted in the art of war. Nay, even Licinius himself would be brought to acknowledge her in her triumph, and be forced to confess that, stained, degraded as she was, his kinswoman had at last [pg 415]proved herself a true scion of their noble line, worthy of the name of Roman! There was a sting, though, in a certain memory that Mariamne's words brought back; their very tone recalled his, when he too had offered to sacrifice his love that he might save its object—and she thought how different were their hearts to hers. But the pain only goaded her into action, and she raised the still kneeling girl with a kindly gesture, and a reassuring smile.

"You can trust me to save him," said she; "but it would be unwise to declare your plan to Titus. He would not believe it, but would simply make you a prisoner, and prevent me from fulfilling my object till too late. Show me the secret path, girl; and by all a woman holds most sacred, by all I have most prized, yet lost, I swear to you that the eagles shall shake their wings in the Temple by to-morrow's sunrise; that I will cut Esca's bonds with the very sword that hangs here in my belt! Return the way you came; be careful to avoid observation; and if you see Valeria again alive, depend upon her friendship and protection for his sake whom you and I shall have saved from death before another day be past!"

So strangely constituted are women, that something almost like a caress passed between these two, as the one gave and the other received the solemn pledge; although Mariamne yielded but unwillingly to Valeria's arguments, and sought the secret way on her return with slow reluctant steps. But she had no alternative; and the Roman lady's certainty of success imparted some of her own confidence to the weary and desponding Jewess. "At least," thought Mariamne, "if I cannot save him, I can die with him, and then nothing can separate us any more!" Sad as it was, she yet felt comforted by the hopeless reflection, while it urged her to hasten to her lover at once.

There was no time to be lost. As she looked back to the Roman sentinel, once more motionless on his post, and waved her hand with a gesture that seemed to implore assistance, while it expressed confidence, ere she stooped to remove the brushwood for her return, a peal of Roman trumpets broke on the silence, sounding out the call which was termed "cock-crow," an hour before the dawn.

[pg 416]

CHAPTER XIV

FAITH

There is nothing in the history of ancient or modern times that can at all help us to realise the feelings with which the Jews regarded their Temple. To them the sacred building was not only the very type and embodiment of their religion, but it represented also the magnificence of their wealth, the pride of their strength, the glory, the antiquity, and the patriotism of the whole people—noble in architecture, imposing in dimensions, and glittering with ornament, it was at once a church, a citadel, and a palace. If a Jew would express the attributes of strength, symmetry, or splendour, he compared the object of his admiration with the Temple. His prophecies continually alluded to the national building as being identical with the nation itself; and to speak of injury or contamination to the Temple was tantamount to a threat of defeat by foreign arms, and invasion by a foreign host—as its demolition was always considered synonymous with the total destruction of Judæa; for no Jew could contemplate the possibility of a national existence apart from this stronghold of his faith. His tendency thus to identify himself with his place of worship was also much fostered by the general practice of his people, who annually flocked to Jerusalem in great multitudes to keep the feast of the Passover; so that there were few of the posterity of Abraham throughout the whole of Syria who had not at some time in their lives been themselves eye-witnesses of the glories in which they took such pride. At the period when the Roman army invested the Holy City, an unusually large number of these worshippers had congregated within its walls, enhancing to a great degree the scarcity of provisions, and all other miseries inseparable from a state of siege.

The Jews defended their Temple to the last. While the terrible circle was contracting day by day, while suburb after suburb was taken, and tower after tower destroyed, [pg 417]they were driven, and, as it were, condensed gradually and surely, towards the upper city and the Holy Place itself.

They seemed to cling round the latter and to trust in it for protection, as though its very stones were animated by the sublime worship they had been reared to celebrate.

It was a little before the dawn, and the Outer Court of the Temple, called the Court of the Gentiles, was enveloped in the gloom of this, the darkest hour in the whole twenty-four. Nothing could be distinguished of its surrounding cloisters, save here and there the stem of a pillar or the segment of an arch, only visible because brought into relief by the black recesses behind. A star or two were faintly twinkling in the open sky overhead; but the morning was preceded by a light vapoury haze, and the breeze that wafted it came moist and chill from the distant sea, wailing and moaning round the unseen pillars and pinnacles of the mighty building above. Except the sacred precincts themselves, this was perhaps the only place of security left to the defenders of Jerusalem; and here, within a spear's-length of each other, they had bound the two Christians, doomed by the Sanhedrim to die. Provided with a morsel of bread, scarce as it was, and a jar of water, supplied by that spurious mercy which keeps the condemned alive in order to put him to death, they had seen the Sabbath, with its glowing hours of fierce pitiless heat, pass slowly and wearily away; they had dragged through the long watches of the succeeding night, and now they were on the brink of that day, which was to be their last on earth.

Esca stirred uneasily where he sat; and the movement seemed to rouse his companion from a fit of deep abstraction, which, judging by the cheerful tones of his voice, could have been of no depressing nature.

"It hath been a tedious watch," said Calchas, "and I am glad it is over. See, Esca, the sky grows darker and darker, even like our fate on earth. In a little while day will come, and with it our great and crowning triumph. How glorious will be the light shining on thee and me, in another world, an hour after dawn!"

The Briton looked admiringly at his comrade, almost envying him the heartfelt happiness and content betrayed by his very accents. He had not himself yet arrived at that pinnacle of faith, on which his friend stood so confidently; and, indeed, Providence seems to have ordained, that in most cases such piety should be gradually and insensibly attained, [pg 418]that the ascent should be won slowly step by step, and that even as a man breasting a mountain scales height after height, and sees his horizon widening mile by mile as he strains towards its crest, so the Christian must toil ever upwards, thankful to gain a ridge at a time, though he finds that it but leads him to a higher standard and a farther aim; and that, though his view is extending all around, and increasing knowledge takes in much of which he never dreamed before, the prospect expands but as the eye ascends, while every summit gained is an encouragement to attempt another, nobler, and higher, and nearer yet to heaven.

"It will be daylight in an hour," said Esca, in a far less cheerful voice, "and the cowards will be here to pound us to death against this pavement with their cruel stones. I would fain have my bonds cut, and a weapon within reach at the last moment, Calchas, and so die at bay amongst them, sword in hand!"

"Be thankful that a man's death is not at his own choice," replied Calchas gently. "How would poor human nature be perplexed, to take the happy method and the proper moment! Be thankful, above all things, for the boon of death itself. It was infinite mercy that bade the inevitable deliverer wait on sin. What curse could equal an immortality of evil? Would you live for ever in such a world as ours if you could? nay, you in your youth, and strength, and beauty, would you wish to remain till your form was bent, and your beard grey, and your eyes dim? Think, too, of the many deaths you might have died,—stricken with leprosy, crouching like a dog in some hidden corner of the city, or wasted by famine, gnawing a morsel of offal from which the sustenance had long since been extracted by some wretch already perished. Or burnt and suffocated amongst the flaming ramparts, like the maniple of Romans whom you yourself saw consumed over against the Tower of Antonia but a few short days ago!"

"That, at least, was a soldier's death," replied Esca, to whose resolute nature the idea of yielding up his life without a struggle seemed so hard. "Or I might have fallen by sword-stroke, or spear-thrust, on the wall, like a man. But to be stoned to death, as the shepherds stone a jackal in his hole! It is a horrible and an ignoble fate!"

"Would you put away from you the great glory that is offered you?" asked Calchas gravely. "Would you die but as a heathen, or one of our own miserable Robbers and Zealots, of whom the worst do not hesitate to give their blood [pg 419]for Jerusalem? Are you not better, and braver, and nobler than any of these? Listen, young man, to him who speaks to you now words for which he must answer at the great tribunal ere another hour be past. Proud should you be of His favour whom you will be permitted to glorify to-day. Ashamed, indeed, as feeling your own unworthiness, yet exulting that you, a young and inexperienced disciple, should have been ranked amongst the leaders and the champions of the true faith. Look upon me, Esca, bound and waiting here like yourself for death. For two-score years have I striven to follow my Master, with feeble steps, indeed, and many a sad misgiving and many a humbling fall. For two-score years have I prayed night and morning; first, that I might have strength to persevere in the way that I had been taught, so that I might continue amongst His servants, even though I were the very lowest of the low. Secondly, that if ever the time should come when I was esteemed worthy to suffer for His sake, I might not be too much exalted with that glory which I have so thirsted to attain. I tell thee, boy, that in an hour's time from now, thou and I shall be received by those good and great men of whom I have so often spoken to thee, coming forward in shining garments, with outstretched arms, to welcome our approach, and lead us into the eternal light of which I dare not speak even now, in the place which eye hath not seen, nor ear heard, nor the heart of man conceived. And all this guerdon is for thee, coming into the vineyard at the eleventh hour, yet sharing with those who have borne the labour and heat of the day. Oh, Esca, I have loved thee like a son, yet from my heart, I cannot wish thee anywhere but bound here by my side this night."

The other could not but kindle with his companion's enthusiasm. "Oh, when they come," said he, "they shall find me ready. And I too, Calchas, believe me, would not flinch from thee now if I could. Nay, if it be His will that I must be stoned to death here in the Outer Court of the Temple, I have learned from thee, old friend, gratefully and humbly to accept my lot. Yet I am but human, Calchas. Thou sayest truly, I lack the long and holy training of thy two-score years. I have a tie that binds me fast to earth. It is no sin to love Mariamne, and I would fain see her once again."

A tear rose to the old man's eye. Chastened, purified, as was his spirit, and ready to take its flight for home, he could yet feel for human love. Nay, the very ties of kindred were [pg 420]strong within him, here in his place of suffering, as they had been at his brother's hearth. It was no small subject of congratulation to him, that his confession of faith before the Sanhedrim, while it vindicated his master's honour, should at the same time have preserved Eleazar's character in the eyes of the nation, while his exultation at the prospect of sharing with his disciple the glory of martyrdom, was damped by the reflection that Mariamne must grieve bitterly, as the human heart will, ere her nobler and holier self could become reconciled to her loss. For a moment he spoke not, though his lips moved in silent prayer for both, and Esca pursued the subject that occupied most of his thoughts even at such an hour as this.

"I would fain see her," he repeated dreamily. "I loved her so well; my beautiful Mariamne. And yet it is a selfish and unworthy wish. She would suffer so much to look on me lying bound and helpless here. She will know, too, when it is over, that my last thought was of her, and it may be she will weep because she was not here to catch my last look before I died. Tell me, Calchas, I shall surely meet her in that other world? It can be no sin to love her as I have loved!"

"No sin," repeated Calchas gravely; "none. The God who bears such love for them has called nine-tenths of His creatures to His knowledge through their affections. When these are suffered to become the primary object of the heart, it may be that He will see fit to crush them in the dust, and will smite, with the bitterest of all afflictions, yet only that He may heal. How many men have followed the path to heaven that was first pointed out by a woman's hand? That a woman hath perhaps gone on to tread, beckoning him after her as she vanished, with a holy hopeful smile. No, Esca, it is not sin to love as thou hast done; and because thou hast not scrupled to give up even this, the great and precious treasure of thy heart, for thy master's honour, thou shalt not lose thy reward."

"And I shall see her again," he insisted, clinging yet somewhat to earthly feelings and earthly regrets, for was he not but a young and untrained disciple? "It seems to me, that it would be unjust to part her from me for ever. It seems to me that heaven itself would not be heaven away from her!"

"I fear thou art not fit to die," replied Calchas, in a low and sorrowful voice. "Pray, my son, pray fervently, unceasingly, that the human heart may be taken away from thee, [pg 421]and the new heart given which will fit thee for the place whither thou goest to-day. It is not for thee and for me to say, 'Give me here, Father, a morsel of bread, or give me there a cup of wine.' We need but implore in our prayers, of Infinite Wisdom and Infinite Mercy, to grant that which it knows is best for our welfare; and He who has taught us how to pray, has bidden us, even before we ask for food, acknowledge a humble unquestioning resignation to the will of our Father which is in heaven. Leave all to Him, my son, satisfied that He will grant thee what is best for thy welfare. Distress not thyself with weak misgivings, nor subtle reasonings, nor vain inquiries. Trust, only trust and pray, here in the court of death, as yonder on the rampart, or at home by the beloved hearth, so shalt thou obtain the victory; for, indeed, the battle draweth nigh. The watches of the night are past, and it is already time to buckle on our armour for the fight."

While he spoke the old man pointed to the east, where the first faint tinge of dawn was stealing up into the sky. Looking into his companion's face, only now becoming visible in the dull twilight, he was struck with the change that a few hours of suffering and imprisonment had wrought upon those fair young features. Esca seemed ten years older in that one day and night; nor could Calchas repress a throb of exultation, as he thought how his own time-worn frame and feeble nature had been supported by the strong faith within. The feeling, however, was but momentary, for the Christian identified himself at once with the suffering and the sorrowful; nor would he have hesitated in the hearty self-sacrificing spirit that his faith had taught him, that no other faith either provides or enjoins, to take on his own shoulders the burden that seemed so hard for his less-advanced brother to bear. It was no self-confidence that gave the willing martyr such invincible courage; but it was the thorough abnegation of self, the entire dependence on Him, who alone never fails man at his need, the fervent faith, which could see so clearly through the mists of time and humanity, as to accept the infinite and the eternal for the visible, and the tangible, and the real.

They seemed to have changed places now; that doomed pair waiting in their bonds for death. The near approach of morning seemed to call forth the exulting spirit of the warrior in the older man, to endow the younger with the humble resignation of the saint.

"Pray for me that I may be thought worthy," whispered [pg 422]the latter, pointing upwards to the grey light widening every moment above their heads.

"Be of good cheer," replied the other, his whole face kindling with a triumphant smile. "Behold, the day is breaking, and thou and I have done with night, henceforth, for evermore!"

[pg 423]

CHAPTER XV

FANATICISM

While faith has its martyrs, fanaticism also can boast its soldiers and its champions. Calchas in his bonds was not more in earnest than Eleazar in his breastplate; but the zeal that brought peace to the one, goaded the other into a restless energy of defiance, which amounted in itself to torture.

The chief of the Zealots was preparing for the great struggle that his knowledge of warfare, no less than the words of his brother before the Sanhedrim (words which yet rang in his ears with a vague monotony of repetition), led him to expect with morning. Soon after midnight, he had woke from the slumber in which Mariamne left him wrapped, and without making inquiry for his daughter, or indeed taking any thought of her, he had armed himself at once and prepared to visit the renewed defences with the first glimpse of day. To do so he was obliged to pass through the Court of the Gentiles, where his brother and his friend lay bound; for in the strength of the Temple itself consisted the last hopes of the besieged, and its security was of the more importance now that the whole of the lower town was in possession of the enemy. Eleazar had decided that if necessary he would abandon the rest of the city to the Romans, and throwing himself with a chosen band into this citadel and fortress of his faith, would hold it to the last, and rather pollute the sacred places with his blood, than surrender them into the hand of the Gentiles. Sometimes, in his more exalted moments, he persuaded himself that even at the extremity of their need, Heaven would interpose for the rescue of the chosen people. As a member of the Sanhedrim and one of the chief nobility of the nation, he had not failed to acquire the rudiments of that magic lore, which was called the science of divination. Formerly, while in compliance with custom he mastered the elements of the art, his strong intellect laughed to scorn the power it pretended to confer, and the mysteries [pg 424]it professed to expound. Now, harassed by continual anxiety, sapped by grief and privation, warped by the unvaried predominance of one idea, the sane mind sought refuge in the shadowy possibilities of the supernatural, from the miseries and horrors of its daily reality.

He recalled the prodigies, of which, though he had not himself been an eye-witness, he had heard from credible and trustworthy sources. They could not have been sent, he thought, only to alarm and astonish an ignorant multitude. Signs and wonders must have been addressed to him, and men like him, leaders and rulers of the people. He never doubted now that a sword of fire had been seen flaming over the city in the midnight sky; that a heifer, driven there for sacrifice, had brought forth a lamb in the midst of the Temple; or that the great sacred gate of brass in the same building had opened of its own accord in the middle watch of the night; nay, that chariots and horsemen of fire had been seen careering in the heavens, and fierce battles raging from the horizon to the zenith, with alternate tide of conquest and defeat, with all the slaughter and confusion and vicissitudes of mortal war.[a]

These considerations endowed him with the exalted confidence which borders on insanity. As the dreamer finds himself possessed of supernatural strength and daring, attempting and achieving feats which yet he knows the while are impossibilities, so Eleazar, walking armed through the waning night towards the Temple, almost believed that with his own right hand he could save his country—almost hoped that with daylight he should find an angel or a fiend at his side empowered to assist him, and resolved that he would accept the aid of either, with equal gratitude and delight.

Nevertheless, as he entered the cloisters that surrounded the Court of the Gentiles, his proud crest sank, his step grew slower and less assured. Nature prevailed for an instant, and he would fain have gone over to that gloomy corner, and bidden his brother a last kind farewell. The possibility even crossed his brain of drawing his sword and setting the prisoners free by a couple of strokes, bidding them escape in the darkness, and shift for themselves; but the fanaticism which had been so long gaining on his better judgment, checked the healthy impulse as it arose. "It may be," thought [pg 425]the Zealot, "that this last great sacrifice is required from me—from me, Eleazar Ben-Manahem, chosen to save my people from destruction this day. Shall I grudge the victim, bound as he is now with cords to the altar? No, not though my father's blood will redden it when he dies. Shall I spare the brave young Gentile, who hath been to me as a kinsman, though but a stranger within my gate, if his life too be required for an oblation? No! not though my child's heart will break when she learns that he is gone forth into the night, never to return. Jephthah grudged not his daughter to redeem his vow; shall I murmur to yield the lives of all my kindred, freely as mine own, for the salvation of Jerusalem?" And thus thinking, he steeled himself against every softer feeling, and resolved he would not even bid the prisoners farewell. He could not trust himself. It might unman him. It might destroy his fortitude; nay, it might even offend the vengeance he hoped to propitiate. Besides, if he were known to have held communication with two professed Christians, where would be the popularity and influence on which he calculated to bear him in triumph through the great decisive struggle of the day? It was better to stifle such foolish yearnings. It was wiser to harden his heart and pass by on the other side.

Nevertheless he paused for a moment and stretched his arms with a yearning gesture towards that corner in which his brother lay bound, and, while he did so, a light step glided by in the gloom; a light figure passed so near that it almost touched him, and a woman's lips were pressed to the hem of his garment with a long clinging kiss, that bade him a last farewell.

Mariamne, returning to the city by the secret way from her interview with Valeria in the Roman camp, had been careful not to enter her father's house, lest her absence might have been discovered, and her liberty of action for the future impaired. She would have liked to see that father once more; but all other considerations were swallowed up in the thought of Esca's danger, and the yearning to die with him if her efforts had been too late to save. She sped accordingly through the dark streets to the Temple, despising, or rather ignoring, those dangers which had so terrified her in her progress during the earlier part of the night. While she stole under the shadow of the cloisters towards her lover, her ear recognised the sound of a familiar step, and her eye, accustomed to the gloom, and sharpened by a child's affection, made out the figure of her father, armed and on his way to the wall. She could not but remember that the morning light which [pg 426]was to bring certain death to Esca, might not, improbably shine upon Eleazar's corpse as well. He would defend the place she knew to the last drop of his blood; and the Roman would never enter the Temple but over the Zealot's body. She could never hope to see him again, the father whom, notwithstanding his fierceness and his faults, she could not choose but love. And all she could do was to shed a tear upon his garment, and wish him this silent and unacknowledged farewell. Thus it was that Eleazar bore with him into the battle the last caress he was ever destined to receive from his child.

[pg 427]

CHAPTER XVI

DAWN

The day soon broke in earnest, cold and pale on the towers and pinnacles of the Temple. The lofty dome that had been looming in the sky, grand and grey and indistinct, like the mass of clouds that rolls away before the pure clear eye of morning, glowed with a flush of pink; and changed again to its own glittering white of polished marble, as its crest caught the full beams of the rising sun. Ere long the golden roof was sparkling here and there in points of fire, to blaze out at last in one dazzling sheet of flame; but still the Court of the Gentiles below was wrapped in gloom, and the two bound figures in its darkest corner, turned their pale faces upward to greet the advent of another day—their last on earth.

But their attention was soon recalled to the court itself; for through the dark recesses of the vaulted cloisters, was winding an ominous procession of those who had been their judges, and who now approached to seal the fiat of their doom. Clad in long dark robes, and headed by their "Nasi," they paced slowly out, marching two by two with solemn step and stern unpitying mien: it was obvious that the Sanhedrim adhered strictly to that article of their code, which enjoined them to perform justice without mercy. Gravely advancing with the same slow step, gradual and inevitable as time, they ranged themselves in a semicircle round the prisoners—then halted every man at the same moment; while all exclaimed as with one voice, to notify their completion and their unanimity—

"Here in the presence of the Lord!"

Again a deathlike silence, intolerable, and apparently interminable to the condemned. Even Calchas felt his heart burn with a keen sense of injustice and a strange instinct of resistance; while Esca, rising to his full height, and in spite of his bonds, folding his brawny arms across his chest, frowned back at the pitiless assembly a defiance that [pg 428]seemed to challenge them to do their worst. Matthias the son of Boethus then stepped forward from amongst his fellows; and addressed, according to custom, the youngest member of the Sanhedrim.

"Phineas Ben-Ezra. Hath the doom gone forth?"

"It hath gone forth through the nation," answered Phineas, in deep sonorous tones. "To north and south, to east and west; to all the people of Judæa hath the inevitable decree been made manifest. The accuser hath spoken and prevailed. The accused have been judged and condemned. It is well. Let the sentence be executed without delay!"

"Phineas Ben-Ezra," interposed Matthias, "can the condemned put forth no plea for pardon or reprieve?"

It was according to ancient custom that the Nasi should even at the last moment urge this merciful appeal—an appeal that never obtained a moment's respite for the most innocent of sufferers. Ere Calchas or Esca could have said a word on their own behalf, Phineas took upon himself the established reply—

"The voice of the Sanhedrim hath spoken! There is no plea; there is no pardon; there is no reprieve."

Then Matthias raised both hands above his head, and spoke in low grave accents—

"For the accused, justice; for the offender, death. The Sanhedrim hath heard; the Sanhedrim hath judged; the Sanhedrim hath condemned. It is written, 'If a man be found guilty of blasphemy, let him be stoned with stones until he die!' Again I say unto you, Calchas Ben-Manahem, and you, Esca the Gentile, your blood be upon your own heads."

Lowering his hands, the signal was at once answered by the inward rush of some score or two of vigorous young men, who had been in readiness outside the court. These were stripped to the waist, and had their loins girt. Some bore huge stones in their bare arms; others, loosening the pavement with crow and pick-axe, stooped down and tore it up with a fierce and cruel energy, as though they had already been kept waiting too long. They were followers of John of Gischala, and their chief, though he took no part in the proceeding, stood at their head. His first glance was one of savage triumph, which faded into no less savage disappointment, as he saw Eleazar's place vacant in the assembly of judges—that warrior's duties against the enemy excusing his attendance on the occasion. John had counted on this critical moment for the utter discomfiture of his rival; but [pg 429]the latter, whose fortitude, strung as it had been to the highest pitch, could scarcely have carried him through such a trial as was prepared for him, had escaped it by leading a chosen band of followers to the post of danger, where the inner wall was weakest, and the breach so lately made had been hastily and insufficiently repaired.

John saw in this well-timed absence another triumph for his invincible enemy. He turned away with a curse upon his lips, and ordered the young men to proceed at once in the execution of their ghastly duty. It seemed to him that he must not lose a moment in following his rival to the wall, yet he could not resist the brutal pleasure of witnessing that rival's brother lying defaced and mangled in the horrible death to which he had been condemned. Already the stones were poised, the fierce brows knit, the bare arms raised, when even the savage executioners held their hands, and the grim Sanhedrim glanced from one to another, half in uncertainty, half in pity, at what they beheld. The figure of a woman darting from the gloomy cloister, rushed across the court to fall in Esca's arms with a strange wild cry, not quite a shout of triumph, not quite a shriek of despair; and the Briton looking down upon Mariamne, folded her head to his breast, with a murmur of manly tenderness that even such a moment could not repress, while he shielded her with his body from the threatened missiles, in mingled gentleness and defiance, as a wild animal turned to bay protects its young.

She passed her hands across his brow with a fond impulsive caress. With a woman's instinct, too, of care and compassion, she gently stroked his wrist where it had been chafed and galled by his bonds; then she smiled up in his face, a loving happy smile, and whispered, "My own, my dear one; they shall never part us. If I cannot save thee, I can die with thee; oh! so happy. Happier than I have ever been before in my life."

It was a strange feeling for him to shrink from the beloved presence, to avoid the desired caress, to entreat his Mariamne to leave him; but though his first impulse had been to clasp her in his arms, his blood ran cold to think of the danger she was braving, the fate to which those tender limbs, that fair young delicate body, would too surely be exposed.

"No, no," he said, "not so. You are too young, too beautiful to die. Mariamne, if you ever loved me—nay, as you love me, I charge you to leave me now."

[pg 430]

She looked at Calchas, whom she had not yet seemed to recognise, and there was a smile—yes! a smile on her face, while she stood forth between the prisoners, and fronted that whole assembly with dauntless forehead and brave flashing eyes; her fair slight figure the one centre of all observation, the one prominent object in the court.

"Listen," she said, in clear sweet tones, that rang like music to the very farthest cloisters. "Listen all, and bear witness! Princes of the House of Judah, elders and nobles, and priests and Levites of the nation! ye cannot shrink from your duty, ye cannot put off your sacred character. I appeal to your own constitution and your own awful vow. Ye have sworn to obey the dictates of wisdom without favour; ye have sworn to fulfil the behests of justice without mercy. I charge ye to condemn me, Mariamne, the daughter of Eleazar Ben-Manahem, to be stoned with stones until I die; for that I too am one of those Nazarenes whom men call Christians. Yea, I triumph in their belief, as I glory in their name. Ye need no evidence, for I condemn myself out of my own mouth. Priests of my father's faith, here in its very Temple I deny your holiness, I abjure your worship, I renounce your creed! This building that overshadows me shall testify to my denunciations. It may be that this very day it shall fall in upon you and cover you with its ruins. If these have spoken blasphemy, so have I; if these are offenders worthy of death, so am I. I bear witness against you! I defy you! I bid you do your worst on those who are proud and happy to die for conscience' sake!"

Her cheek glowed, her eye flashed, her very figure dilated as she shook her white hand aloft, and thus braved the assembled Sanhedrim with her defiance. It was strange how like Eleazar she was at that moment, while the rich old blood of Manahem mounted in her veins; and the courage of her fathers, that of yore had smitten the armed Philistine in the wilderness, and turned the fierce children of Moab in the very tide of conquest, now blazed forth at the moment of danger in the fairest and gentlest descendant of their line. Even her very tones thrilled to the heart of Calchas, not so much for her own sake, as for that of the brother whom he so loved, and whose voice he seemed to hear in hers. Esca gazed on her with a fond astonishment; and John of Gischala quailed where he stood, as he thought of his noble enemy, and the hereditary courage he had done more wisely not to have driven to despair.

But the tension of her nerves was too much for her [pg 431]woman's strength. Bravely she hurled her challenge in their very teeth; and then, shaking in every limb, she leaned against the Briton's towering form, and hid her face once more on his breast.

Even the Nasi was moved. Stern, rigid, and exacting, yet apart from his office he too had human affections and human weaknesses. He had mourned for more than one brave son, he had loved more than one dark-eyed daughter. He would have spared her if he could, and he bit his lip hard under the long white beard, in a vain effort to steady the quiver he could not control. He looked appealingly amongst his colleagues, and met many an eye that obviously sympathised with his tendency to mercy; but John of Gischala interposed, and cried out loudly for justice to be done without delay.

"Ye have heard her!" he exclaimed, with an assumption of holy and zealous indignation; "out of her own mouth she is condemned. What need ye more proof or further deliberation? The doom has gone forth. I appeal to the Sanhedrim that justice be done, in the name of our faith, our nation, our Temple, and our Holy City, which such righteous acts as these may preserve even now from the desolation that is threatening at the very gate!"

With such an assembly, such an appeal admitted of no refusal. The Seventy looked from one to another and shook their heads, sorrowfully indeed, but with knitted brows and grave stern faces that denoted no intention to spare. Already Phineas Ben-Ezra had given the accustomed signal; already the young men appointed as executioners had closed round the doomed three, with huge blunt missiles poised, and prepared to launch them forth, when another interruption arrived to delay for a while the cruel sacrifice that a Jewish Sanhedrim dignified with the title of justice.

A voice that had been often heard before, though never so wild and piercing as at this moment, rang through the Court of the Gentiles, and seemed to wail among the very pinnacles of the Temple towering in the morning air above. It was a voice that struck to the hearts of all who heard it—such a voice as terrifies men in their dreams; chilling the blood, and making the flesh creep with a vague yet unendurable horror, so that when the pale sleeper wakes, he is drenched with the cold sweat of mortal fear. A voice that seemed at once to threaten and to warn, to pity and to condemn; a voice of which the moan and the burden were ever unbroken and the same— "Woe to Jerusalem! Woe to the Holy City! Sin, [pg 432]and sorrow, and desolation! Woe to the Holy City! Woe to Jerusalem!"

Naked, save for a fold of camel's hair around his loins, his coarse black locks matted and tangled, and mingled with the uncombed beard that reached below his waist—his dark eyes gleaming with lurid fire, and his long lean arms tossing aloft with the wild gestures of insanity— a tall figure stalked into the middle of the court, and taking up its position before the Nasi of the Sanhedrim, began scattering around it on the floor the burning embers from a brazier it bore on its head; accompanying its actions with the same mournful and prophetic cry. The young men paused with their arms up in act to hurl; the Nasi stood motionless and astonished; the Sanhedrim seemed paralysed with fear; and the Prophet of Warning, if prophet indeed he were, proceeded with his chant of vengeance and denunciation against his countrymen.

"Woe to Jerusalem!" said he once more. "Woe to the Holy City! A voice from the East, a voice from the West, a voice from the four winds; a voice against Jerusalem and the holy house; a voice against the bridegrooms and the brides; and a voice against the whole people!"

Then he turned aside and walked round the prisoners in a circle, still casting burning ashes on the floor. Matthias, like his colleagues, was puzzled how to act. If this were a demoniac, he entertained for him a natural horror and aversion, enhanced by the belief he held, in common with his countrymen, that one possessed had the strength of a score of men in his single arm; but what if this should be a true prophet, inspired directly from heaven? The difficulty would then become far greater. To endeavour to suppress him might provoke divine vengeance on the spot;

whereas, to suffer his denunciations to go abroad amongst the people as having prevailed with the Great Council of the nation, would be to abandon the inhabitants at once to despair, and to yield up all hope of offering a successful defence to the coming attack. From this dilemma the Nasi was released by the last person on whom he could have counted for assistance at such a time. Pointing to the prisoners with his wasted arm, the prophet demanded their instant release, threatening divine vengeance on the Sanhedrim if they refused; and then addressing the three with the same wild gestures and incoherent language, he bade them come forth from their bonds, and join him in his work of prophecy through the length and breadth of the city.

"I have power to bind," he exclaimed, "and power to [pg 433]loose! I command you to rend your bonds asunder! I command you to come forth, and join me, the Prophet of Warning, in the cry that I am commissioned to cry aloud, without ceasing—'Woe to Jerusalem! Woe to the Holy City! Woe to Jerusalem!' "

Then Calchas, stretching out his bound hands, rebuked him, calmly, mildly, solemnly, with the patience of a good and holy man—with the instinctive superiority of one who is standing on the verge of his open grave.

"Wilt thou hinder God's work?" he said. "Wilt thou dare to suppress the testimony we are here to give in His presence to-day? See! even this young girl, weak indeed in body yet strong in faith, stands bold and unflinching at her post! And thou, O man! what art thou, that thou shouldst think to come between her and her glorious reward? Be still! be still! Be no more vexed by the unquiet spirit, but go in peace, or rather stay here in the Court of the Gentiles, and bear witness to the truth, for which we are so thankful and so proud to die!"

The prophet's eye wandered dreamily from the speaker's face to those of the surrounding listeners. His features worked as though he strove against some force within that he was powerless to resist; then his whole frame collapsed, as it were, into a helpless apathy, and placing his brazier on the ground, he sat down beside it, rocking his body to and fro, while he moaned out, as it seemed unconsciously, in a low and wailing voice, the burden of his accustomed chant.

To many in the assembly that scene was often present in their after lives. When they opened their eyes to the light of morning they saw its glow once more on the bewildered faces of the Sanhedrim; on the displeasure, mingled with wonder and admiration, that ruffled the austere brow of Matthias; on the downward scowl that betrayed how shame and fear were torturing John of Gischala; on the clear-cut figures of the young men he had marshalled, girded and ready for their cruel office; on Esca's towering frame, haughty and undaunted still; on Mariamne's drooping form, and pale patient face; above all, on the smile that illumined the countenance of Calchas, standing there in his bonds, so venerable, and meek, and happy, now turning to encourage his companions in affliction, now raising his eyes thankfully to heaven, his whole form irradiated the while by a flood of light, that seemed richer and more lustrous than the glow of the morning sun.

But while the prophet, thus tranquillised and silenced by [pg 434]the rebuke he had provoked, sat muttering and brooding amongst his dying embers on the floor; while the Sanhedrim, with their Nasi, stood aghast; while John of Gischala gnawed his lip in impatient vindictive hatred; and the young men gathered closer round their victims, as the wolves gather in upon their prey,—Mariamne raised her head from Esca's breast, and, pushing the hair back from her ears and temples, stood for an instant erect and motionless, with every faculty absorbed in the one sense of listening. Then she turned her flashing eyes, lit up with great hope and triumph, yet not untinged by wistful mournful tenderness, upon the Briton's face, and sobbed in broken accents, between tears and laughter—

"Saved! Saved! beloved. And by my hand, though lost to me!"

Sharpened by intense affection, her ear alone had caught the distant note of the Roman trumpets sounding for the assault.

CHAPTER XVII

THE FIRST STONE

But the young men would hold their hands no longer. Impatient of delay, and encouraged by a sign from their leader, they rushed in upon the prisoners. Esca shielded Mariamne with his body. Calchas, pale and motionless, calmly awaited his fate. Gioras, the son of Simeon, a prominent warrior amongst the Sicarii, hurling on him a block of granite with merciless energy, struck the old man bleeding to the earth; but while the missile left his hands—while he yet stood erect and with extended arms, a Roman arrow quivered in the aggressor's heart. He fell upon his face stone dead at the very feet of his victim. That random shaft was but the first herald of the storm. In another moment a huge mass of rock, projected from a powerful catapult against the building, falling short of its mark, struck the prophet as he sat moaning on the ground, and crushed him a lifeless, shapeless mass beneath its weight. Then rose a cry of despair from the outer wall—a confused noise of strife and shouting, the peal of the trumpets, the cheer of the conquerors, the wild roar of defiance and despair from the besieged. Ere long fugitives were pouring through the court, seeking the shelter of the Temple itself. There was no time to complete the execution—no time to think of the prisoners. John of Gischala, summoning his adherents, and bidding the young men hasten for their armour, betook himself to his stronghold within the Sacred Place. The Sanhedrim fled in consternation, although Matthias and the braver of his colleagues died afterwards in the streets, as became them, under shield. In a few minutes the Court of the Gentiles was again clear, save for the prisoners, one of whom was bound, and one mangled and bleeding on the pavement, tended by Mariamne, who bent over her kinsman in speechless sorrow and consternation. The fragment of rock, too, which had been propelled against the Temple, lay in the centre, over the crushed and flattened body of the prophet, whose hand and arm alone protruded from beneath the mass. The place did not thus remain in solitude for long. Fighting their retreat step by step, and, although driven backward, contesting every yard with their faces to the enemy, the flower of the Jewish army soon passed through, in the best order they could maintain, as they retired upon the Temple. Among the last of these was Eleazar; hopeless now, for he knew all was lost, but brave and unconquered still. He cast one look of affection at his brother's prostrate form, one of astonishment and reproof on his kneeling child; but ere he could approach or even speak to her, he was swept on with the resistless tide of the defeated, ebbing before the advance of the Roman host.

And now Esca's eye kindled, and his blood mounted, to a well-known battle-cry. He had heard it in the deadly circus; he had heard it on the crumbling breach; he had heard it wherever blows rained hard and blood flowed free, and men fought doggedly and hopelessly, without a chance or a wish for escape. His heart leaped to the cheer of the gladiators, rising fierce, reckless, and defiant above all the combined din of war, and he knew that his old comrades and late antagonists had carried the defences with their wonted bravery, as they led the Roman army to the assault.

The Legion of the Lost had indeed borne themselves nobly on this occasion. Their leader had not spared them; for Hippias well knew that to-day, with the handful left him by slaughter and disease, he must play his last stake for riches and distinction; nor had his followers failed to answer gallantly to his call. Though opposed by Eleazar himself and the best he could muster, they had carried the breach at the first onset—they had driven the Jews before them with a wild headlong charge that no courage could resist, and they had entered the outskirts of the Temple almost at the same moment with its discomfited defenders. It was their trumpets sounding the advance that reached Mariamne's ear as she stood in the Court of the Gentiles, awaiting the vengeance she had defied. And amongst this courageous band two combatants had especially signalised themselves by feats of reckless and unusual daring. The one was old [pg 437]Hirpinus, who felt thoroughly in his element in such a scene, and whose natural valour was enhanced by the consciousness of the superiority he had now attained as a soldier over his former profession of a gladiator. The other was a comrade whom none could identify; who was conspicuous no less from his flowing locks, his beautiful form, and his golden armour, than from the audacity with which he courted danger, and the immunity he seemed to enjoy, in common with those who display a real contempt for death.

As he followed the golden headpiece and the long brown hair, that made way so irresistibly through the press, more than one stout swordsman exulted in the belief that some tutelary deity of his country had descended in human shape to aid the Roman arms; and Titus himself inquired, and waited in vain for an answer, "Who was that dashing warrior, with white arms and shining corselet, leading the gladiators so gallantly to the attack?"

But old Hirpinus knew, and smiled within his helmet as he fought. "The captain is well rid of her," thought he, congratulating himself the while on his own freedom from such inconveniences. "For all her comely face and winning laugh, I had rather have a tigress loose in my tent than this fair, fickle, fighting fury, who takes to shield and spear as other women do to the shuttle and the distaff!"

Valeria, in truth, deserved little credit for her bravery. While apprehension of danger never for a moment overmastered her, the excitement of its presence seemed to offer a temporary relief to her wounded and remorseful heart. In the fierce rush of battle she had no leisure to dwell on thoughts that had lately tortured her to madness; and the very physical exertion such a scene demanded, brought with it, although she was unconscious of its severity, a sure anodyne for mental suffering. Like all persons, too, who are unaccustomed to bodily perils, the impunity with which she affronted each imparted an overweening confidence in her good fortune, and an undue contempt for the next, till it seemed to herself that she bore a charmed life; and that, though man after man might fall at her side as she fought on, *she* was destined to fulfil her task unscathed, and reach the presence of Esca in time to save him from destruction, even though she should die the next minute at his feet.

The two first assailants who entered the Court of the Gentiles were Valeria, in her golden armour, and Hirpinus, brandishing the short deadly weapon he knew how to use [pg 438]so well. They were close together; but the former paused to look around, and the gladiator, rushing to the front, made for his old comrade, whom he recognised on the instant. His haste, however, nearly proved fatal. The heavily-nailed sandals that he wore afforded but a treacherous foothold on the smooth stone pavement, his feet slipped from under him, and he came with a heavy back-fall to the ground. *Habet!*[a] exclaimed Hippias, from the sheer force of custom, following close upon his tracks; but he strained eagerly forward to defend his prostrate comrade while he spoke, and found himself instantly engaged with a score of Jewish warriors, who came swarming back like bees to settle on the fallen gladiator. Hirpinus, however, covered his body skilfully under his shield, and defended himself bravely with his sword—dealing more than one fatal thrust at such of his assailants as were rash enough to believe him vanquished because down. As more of the gladiators came pouring in, they were opposed by troops of the Jews, who, with Eleazar at their head, made a desperate sally from the Temple to which they had retired, and a fierce hand-to-hand struggle, that lasted several minutes, took place round Hirpinus in the centre of the court. When he at length regained his feet, his powerful aid soon made itself felt in the fray, and the Jews, though fighting stubbornly still, were obliged once more to retreat before the increasing columns of the besiegers.

Valeria, in the meantime, rushing through the court to where she spied a well-known form struggling in its bonds, came across the path of Eleazar, at whom she delivered a savage thrust as she met him, lest he should impede her course. The fierce Jew, who had enough on his hands at such a moment, and was pressing eagerly forward into the thickest of the struggle, was content to parry the stroke with his javelin, and launch that weapon in return at his assailant, while he passed on. The cruel missile did its errand only too well. The broad thirsty point clove through a crevice in her golden corselet, and sank deep in her white tender side, to drink the life-blood of the woman-warrior as she sped onward in fulfilment of her fatal task. Breaking the javelin's shaft in her hands, and flinging the fragments from her with a scornful smile, Valeria found strength to cross the court, nor did her swift step falter, nor did her proud bearing betray wounds or weakness, till she reached Esca's side. A loving smile of recognition, two strokes of [pg 439]her sharp blade, and he was free! but as the severed bonds fell from his arms, and he stretched them forth in the delight of restored liberty, his deliverer, throwing away sword and shield, seized his hand in both her own, and, pressing it convulsively to her bosom, sank down helpless on the pavement at his feet.

Sank down helpless on the pavement at his feet.

CHAPTER XVIII

THE COST OF CONQUEST

Mariamne turned from the still insensible form of Calchas to the beautiful face, that even now, though pale from exhaustion and warped with agony, it pained her to see so fair. Gently and tenderly she lifted the golden helmet from Valeria's brows; gently and tenderly she smoothed the rich brown hair, and wiped away the dews of coming death. Compassion, gratitude, and an ardent desire to soothe and tend the sufferer left no room for bitterness or unworthy feeling in Mariamne's breast. Valeria had redeemed her promise with her life—had ransomed the man whom they both loved so dearly, at that fatal price, for *her*! and the Jewess could only think of all she owed the Roman lady in return; could only strive to tend and comfort her, and minister to her wants, and support her in the awful moment she did not fail to see was fast approaching. The dying woman's face was turned on her with a sweet sad smile; but when Mariamne's touch softly approached the head of her father's javelin, still protruding from the wound, Valeria stayed her hand.

"Not yet," she whispered with a noble effort that steadied voice and lips, and kept down mortal agony; "not yet; for I know too well I am stricken to the death. While the steel is there it serves to stanch the life-blood. When I draw it out, then scatter a handful of dust over my forehead, and lay the death-penny on my tongue. I would fain last a few moments longer, Esca, were it but to look on thy dear face! Raise me, both of you. I have somewhat to say, and my time is short."

The Briton propped her in his strong arms, and she leaned her head against his shoulder with a gesture of contentment and relief. The winning eyes had lost none of their witchery yet, though soon to be closed in death. Perhaps they never shone with so soft and sweet a lustre as now, while they looked upon the object of a wild, foolish, and [pg 441]impossible love. While one white hand was laid upon the javelin's head, and held it in its place, the other wandered over Esca's features in a fond caress, to be wetted with his tears. Her voice was failing, her strength was ebbing fast, but the brave spirit of the Mutian line held out, tameless and unshaken still.

"I have conquered," gasped the Roman lady, in broken accents and with quick-coming breath. "I have conquered, though at the cost of life. What then? Victory can never be bought too dear. Esca, I swore to rescue thee. I swore thou shouldst be mine. Now have I kept my oath. I have bought thee with my blood, and I give thee—*give* thee, my own, to this brave girl, who risked her life to save thee too, and who loves thee well; but not so well, not half so well, as I have done. Esca, my noble one, come closer, closer yet." She drew his face down nearer and nearer to her own while she guided his hand to the javelin's head, still fast in her side. "I can bear this agony no longer," she gasped, "but it is not hard to die in thine arms, and by thy dear hand!"

Thus speaking, she closed his grasp within her own, round the steel, and drew it gently from the wound. The blood welled up in dark-red jets to pour forth, as it cleared its channel, in one continuous stream that soon drained life away. With a quiver of her dainty limbs, with a smile deepening in her fair face, with her fond eyes fixed on the man she loved, and her lips pressed against his hand, the spirit of that beautiful, imperious, and wilful woman passed away into eternity.

Blinded by their tears, neither Esca nor Mariamne were, for the moment, conscious of aught but the sad fate of her who had twice saved the one from death, and to whom the other had so lately appealed as the only source of aid in her great need. Dearly as he loved the living woman by his side, the Briton could not refrain from a burst of bitter sorrow while he looked on the noble form of Valeria lying dead at his feet; and Mariamne forgot her own griefs, her own injuries, in holy pity for her who had sacrificed virtue, happiness, wealth, life itself in his behalf, whom she, too, loved more dearly than it behoves human weakness to love anything this side the grave.

But the living now claimed that attention which it availed no longer to bestow upon the dead. Calchas, though sadly bruised and mangled, began to show signs of restored life. The stone that stretched him on the pavement had, indeed, dealt a fatal injury; but though it stunned him for a time, [pg 442]had failed to inflict instantaneous death. The colour was now returning to his cheek, his breath came in long deep sighs, and he raised his hand to his head with a gesture of renewed consciousness, denoted by a sense of pain. Esca, careless and almost unaware of the conflict raging around, bent sorrowfully over his old friend, and devoted all his faculties to the task of aiding Mariamne in her efforts to alleviate his sufferings.

In the meantime, the tide of battle surged to and fro, with increasing volume and unmitigated fury. The Legion of the Lost, flushed with success, and secure of support from the whole Roman army in their rear, pressed the Jews, with the exulting and unremitting energy of the hunter closing in on his prey. These, like the wild beasts driven to the toils, turned to bay with the dreadful courage of despair. Led by Eleazar, who was ever present where most needed, they made repeated sallies from the body of the Temple, endeavouring to regain the ground they had lost, at least as far as the entrance to the Court of the Gentiles. This became, therefore, an arena in which many a mortal combat was fought out hand to hand, and was several times taken and retaken with alternate success.

Hippias, according to his wont, was conspicuous in the fray. It was his ambition to lead his gladiators into the Holy Place itself, before Titus should come up, and with such an object he seemed to outdo to-day the daring feats of valour for which he had previously been celebrated.

Hirpinus, who had no sooner regained his feet than he went to work again as though, like the fabled Titan, he derived renewed energy from the kisses of mother Earth, expostulated more than once with his leader on the dangers he affronted, and the numerical odds he did not hesitate to engage, but received to each warning the same reply. Pointing with dripping sword at the golden roof of the Temple flashing conspicuously over their heads, "Yonder," said the fencing-master, "is the ransom of a kingdom. I will win it with my own hand for the legion, and share it amongst you equally, man by man." Such a prospect inspired the gladiators with even more than their usual daring; and though many a stout swordsman went down with his face to the enemy, and many a bold eye looked its last on the coveted spoil, ere it grew dark for ever, the survivors did but close in the fiercer, to fight on, step by step, and stroke by stroke, till the court was strewed with corpses, and its pavement slippery with blood.

[pg 443]

During a pause in the reeling strife, and while marshalling his men, who had again driven the Jews into the Temple, for a fresh and decisive attack, Hippias found himself in that corner of the court where Esca and Mariamne were still bending over the prostrate form of Calchas. Without a symptom of astonishment or jealousy, but with his careless half-contemptuous laugh, the fencing-master recognised his former pupil, and the girl whom he had once before seen in the porch of the tribune's mansion at Rome. Taking off his heavy helmet, he wiped his brows, and leaned for a space on his shield.

"Go to the rear," said he, "and take the lass with thee, man, since she seems to hang like a clog round thy neck, wherever there is fighting to be done. Give yourselves up to the Tenth Legion, and tell Licinius, who commands it, you are my prisoners. 'Tis your only chance of safety, my pretty damsel, and none of your sex ever yet had cause to rue her trust in Hippias. You may tell him also, Esca, that if he make not the more haste, I shall have taken the Temple, and all belonging to it, without his help. Off with thee, lad! this is no place for a woman. Get her out of it as quick as thou canst."

But the Briton pointed downward to Calchas, who had again become unconscious, and whose head was resting on Mariamne's knees. His gesture drew the attention of Hippias to the ground, cumbered as it was with slain. He had begun with a brutal laugh to bid his pupil "leave the carrion for the vultures," but the sentence died out on his lips, which turned deadly white, while his eyes stared vacantly, and the shield on which he had been leaning fell with a clang to the stones.

There at his very feet over the golden breastplate was the dead face of Valeria; and the heart of the brave, reckless, and unprincipled soldier smote him with a cruel pang, for something told him that his own wilful pride and selfishness had begun that work, which was completed, to his eternal self-reproach, down there.

He never thought he loved her so dearly. He recalled, as if it were but yesterday, the first time he ever saw her, beautiful and sumptuous and haughty, looking down from her cushioned chair by the equestrian row, with the well-known scornful glance that possessed for him so keen a charm. He remembered how it kindled into approval as it met his own, and how his heart thrilled under his buckler, though he stood face to face with a mortal foe. He remembered how fondly he clung to that mutual glance of [pg 444]recognition, the only link between them, renewed more frankly and more kindly at every succeeding show, till, raising his eyes to meet it once too often in the critical moment of encounter, he went down badly wounded under the blow he had thus failed to guard. Nevertheless, how richly was he rewarded when fighting stubbornly on his knee, and from that disadvantageous attitude vanquishing his antagonist at last, he distinguished amidst the cheers of thousands her marked and musical *Euge!* syllabled so clearly though so softly, for his special ear, by the lips of the proud lady, whom from that moment he dared to love! Afterwards, when admitted periodically to her house, how delightful were the alternations of hope and fear with which he saw himself treated; now as an honoured guest, now as a mere inferior, at another time with mingled kindness and restraint, that, impassible as he thought himself, woke such wild wishes in his heart! How sweet it was to be sure of seeing her at certain stated hours, the recollection of one meeting bridging over the intervening period so pleasantly, till it was time to look forward to another! She was to him like the beautiful rose blooming in his garden, of which a man is content at first only to admire the form ere he learns to long for its fragrance, and at last desires to pluck it ruthlessly from the stem that he may wear it on his breast. How soon it withers there and dies, and then how bitterly, how sadly, he wishes he had left it blushing where it grew! There are plenty more flowers in the garden, but none of them are quite equal to the rose.

It was strange how little Hippias dwelt on the immediate past—how it was the Valeria of Rome, not the Valeria of Judæa, for whom his heart was aching now. He scarcely reverted even to the delirious happiness of the first few days when she accompanied him to the East; he did not dwell on his own mad joy, nor the foolish triumph that lasted so short a time. He forgot, as though they had never been, her caprice, her wilfulness, her growing weariness of his society, and the scorn she scarcely took the trouble to conceal. It was all past and gone now, that constraint and repugnance in the tent, that impatience of each other's presence, those angry recriminations, those heartless biting taunts and the final rupture that could never be pardoned nor atoned for now. She was again Valeria of the olden time, of the haughty bearing, and the winning eyes, and the fresh glad voice that sprang from a heart which had never known a struggle nor a fall—the Valeria whose every [pg 445]mood and gesture were gifted with a dangerous witchery, a subtle essence that seems to pervade the very presence of such women—a priceless charm, indeed, and yet a fatal, luring the possessor to the destruction of others and her own.

Oh, that she could but speak to him once more! Only once, though it were in words of keen reproach or bitter scorn! It seemed like a dream that he should never hear her voice again; and yet his senses vouched that it was waking cold reality, for was she not lying there before him, surrounded by the slain of his devoted legion? The foremost, the fairest, and the earliest lost, amongst them all!

He took no further note of Calchas nor of Esca. He turned not to mark the renewed charge of his comrades, nor the increased turmoil of the fight, but he stooped down over the body of the dead woman, and laid his lips reverently to her pale cold brow. Then he lifted one of her long brown tresses, dabbled as they were in blood, to sever it gently and carefully with his sword, and unbuckling his corselet, hid it beneath the steel upon his heart. After this, he turned and took leave of Esca. The Briton scarcely knew him, his voice and mien were so altered. But watching his figure as he disappeared, waving his sword, amidst the press of battle, he knew instinctively that he had bidden Hippias the gladiator a long and last farewell.

CHAPTER XIX

THE GATHERING OF THE EAGLES

Shouting their well-known war-cry, and placing himself at the head of that handful of heroes who constituted the remnant of the Lost Legion, Hippias rallied them for one last desperate effort against the defenders of the Temple. These had formed a hasty barricade on the exigency of the moment from certain beams and timbers they had pulled down in the Sacred Place. It afforded a slight protection against the javelins, arrows, and other missiles of the Romans, while it checked and repulsed the impetuous rush of the latter, who now wavered, hesitated, and began to look about them, making inquiry for the battering-rams and other engines of war that were to have supported their onset from the rear. In vain Hippias led them, once and again, to carry this unforeseen obstacle. It was high and firm, it bristled with spears and was lined with archers; above all, it was defended by the indomitable valour of Eleazar, and the gladiators were each time repulsed with loss. Their leader, too, had been severely wounded. He had never lifted his shield from the ground where it lay by Valeria's side; and, in climbing the barricade, he had received a thrust in the body from an unknown hand. While he stanched the blood with the folds of his tunic, and felt within his breastplate for the tress of Valeria's hair, he looked anxiously back for his promised reinforcements, now sorely needed, convinced that his shattered band would be unable to obtain possession of the Temple without the assistance of the legions. Faint from loss of blood, strength and courage failing him at the same moment, an overpowering sense of hopeless sorrow succeeding the triumphant excitement of the last hour, his thoughts were yet for his swordsmen; and collecting them with voice and gesture, he bade them form with their shields the figure that was called "the tortoise," as a screen against the shower of missiles that overpowered them from the barricade. Cool, confident, and well-drilled, the gladiators soon settled into this impervious order of defence; and the word of command had hardly died on his lips ere the leader himself was the only soldier left out of that movable fortress of steel.[a]

Turning from the enemy to inspect its security, his side was left a moment exposed to their darts. The next, a Jewish arrow quivered in his heart. True to his instincts, he waved his sword over his head, as he went down, with a triumphant cheer; for his failing ear recognised the blast of the Roman trumpets—his darkening eye caught the glitter of their spears and the gleam of their brazen helmets, as the legions advanced in steady and imposing order to complete the work he and his handful of heroes had begun.

Even in the act of falling, Esca, looking up from his charge, saw the fencing-master wheel half-round that his dead face might be turned towards the foe; perhaps, too, the Briton's eye was the only one to observe a thin dark stream of blood steal slowly along the pavement, till it mingled with the red pool in which Valeria lay.

Effectual assistance had come at last. From the Tower of Antonia to the outworks of the Temple a broad and easy causeway had been thrown up in the last hour by the Roman soldiers. Where every man was engineer as well as combatant, there was no lack of labour for such a task. A large portion of the adjoining wall, as of the tower itself, had been hastily thrown down to furnish materials; and while the gladiators were storming the Court of the Gentiles, their comrades had constructed a wide, easy, and gradual ascent, by which, in regular succession, whole columns could be poured in to the support of the first assailants. These were led by Julius Placidus with his wonted skill and coolness. In his recent collision with Esca he had sustained such severe injuries as incapacitated him from mounting a horse; but with the Asiatic auxiliaries were several elephants of war, and on one of these huge beasts he now rode exalted, directing from his movable tower the operations of his own troops, and galling the enemy when occasion offered with the shafts of a few archers who accompanied him on the patient and sagacious animal.

The elephant, in obedience to its driver, a dark supple [pg 448]Syrian, perched behind its ears, ascended the slope with ludicrous and solemn caution. Though alarmed by the smell of blood, it nevertheless came steadily on, a formidable and imposing object, striking terror into the hearts of the Jews, who were not accustomed to confront such enemies in warfare. The tribune's arms were more dazzling, his dress even more costly than usual. It seemed that with his Eastern charger he affected also something of Eastern luxury and splendour; but he encouraged his men, as he was in the habit of doing, with jeer and scoff, and such coarse jests as soldiers best understand and appreciate in the moment of danger.

No sooner had he entered the court, through its battered and half-demolished gateway, than his quick eye caught sight of the still glowing embers scattered by the Prophet of Warning on the pavement. These suggested a means for the destruction of the barricade, and he mocked the repulsed gladiators, with many a bitter taunt, for not having yet applied them to that purpose. Calling on Hirpinus, who now commanded the remnant of the Lost Legion, to collect his followers, he bade them advance under the *testudo* to pile these embers against the foundations of the wooden barrier.

"The defenders cannot find a drop of water," said he, laughing; "they have no means of stifling a fire kindled from without. In five minutes all that dry wood will be in a blaze, and in less than ten there will be a smoking gap in the gateway large enough for me to ride through, elephant and all!"

Assisted by fresh reinforcements, the gladiators promptly obeyed his orders. Heaps of live embers were collected and applied to the wooden obstacle so hastily erected. Dried to tinder in the scorching sun, and loosely put together for a temporary purpose, it could not fail to be sufficiently inflammable; and the hearts of the besieged sank within them as the flame began to leap and the woodwork to crackle, while their last defences seemed about to consume gradually away.

The tribune had time to lean over from his elephant and question Hirpinus of his commander. With a grave sad brow and a heavy heart, the stout old swordsman answered by pointing to the ground where Hippias lay, his face calm and fixed, his right hand closed firmly round his sword.

"*Habet!*" exclaimed the tribune with a brutal laugh; adding to himself, as Hirpinus turned away sorrowful and [pg 449]disgusted, "My last rival down; my last obstacle removed. One more throw for the Sixes, and the great game is fairly won!"

Placidus was indeed now within a stride of all he most coveted, all he most wished to grasp on earth. A dozen feet below him, pale and rigid on the ground, lay the rival he had feared might win the first place in the triumph of to-day; the rival whom he knew to possess the favour of Titus; the rival who had supplanted him in the good graces of the woman he loved. He had neither forgotten nor forgiven Valeria; but he bore none the less ill-will against him with whom she had voluntarily fled. When he joined the Roman army before Jerusalem, and found her beautiful, miserable, degraded, in the tent of the gladiator, he had but dissembled and deferred his revenge till the occasion should arrive when he might still more deeply humiliate the one and inflict a fatal blow on the other. Now the man was under his elephant's feet; and the woman left alone yonder, friendless and deserted in the camp, could not, he thought, fail eventually to become his prey. He little knew that those who had made each other's misery in life were at last united in the cold embrace of death. He had arrived, too, in the nick of time, to seize and place on his own brows the wreath that had been twined for him by the Lost Legion and their leader. A little earlier and Hippias, supplied by himself with fresh troops, would have won the credit of first entering the Temple; a little later, and his triumph must have been shared by Licinius, already with the Tenth Legion close upon his rear. But now, at the glorious opportunity, there was nothing between him and victory save a score of Jewish spearmen and a few feet of blazing wood.

Leaning over to the unwilling driver, he urged him to goad the elephant through the flames, that its weight might at once bear down what remained of the barricade and make a way for his followers into the Temple. Ambition prompted him not to lose a moment. The Syrian unwound the shawl from his waist, and spread it over the animal's eyes, while he persuaded it, thus blindfolded, to advance. Though much alarmed, the elephant pushed on, and there was small hope that the shattered smouldering barrier would resist the pressure of its enormous weight. The last chance of the besieged seemed to fail them, when Eleazar leaped out through the smoke, and, running swiftly to meet it, dashed under the beast's uplifted trunk, and stabbed it fiercely with [pg 450]quick repeated thrusts in the belly. At each fresh stroke the elephant uttered a loud and hideous groan, a shriek of pain and fear, mingled with a trumpet-note of fury, and then sinking on its knees, fell slowly and heavily to the ground, crushing the devoted Zealot beneath its huge carcass, and scattering the band of archers, as a man scatters a handful of grain, over the court.

Eleazar never spoke again. The Lion of Judah died as he had lived—fierce, stubborn, unconquered, and devoted to the cause of Jerusalem. Mariamne recognised him as he sallied forth, but no mutual glance had passed between the father and the child. Pale, erect, motionless, she watched him disappear under the elephant, but the scream of horror that rang from her white lips when she realised his fate was lost in the wild cry of pain, and anger, and dismay, that filled the air, while the huge quivering mass tottered and went down. Placidus was hurled to the pavement like a stone from a sling. Lying there, helpless, though conscious, he recognised at once the living Esca and the dead Valeria; but baffled wrath and cherished hatred left no room in his heart for sorrow or remorse. His eye glared angrily on the Briton, and he ground his teeth with rage to feel that he could not even lift his powerless hand from the ground; but the Jewish warriors were closing in with fierce arms up to strike, and it was but a momentary glimpse that Esca obtained of the tribune's dark, despairing, handsome face. It was years, though, ere he forgot the vision. The costly robes, the goodly armour, the shapely writhing form, and the wild hopeless eyes that gleamed with hatred and defiance both of the world he left and that to which he went.

And now the court was filling fast with a dun lurid smoke that wreathed its vapours round the pinnacles of the Temple, and caused the still increasing troops of combatants to loom like phantom shapes struggling and fighting in a dream. Ere long, bright tongues of flame were leaping through the cloud, licking the walls and pillars of the building, gliding and glancing over the golden surface of its roof, and shooting upwards here and there into shifting pyramids of fire. Soon was heard the hollow rushing roar with which the consuming element declares its victory, and showers of sparks, sweeping like storms across the Court of the Gentiles, proclaimed that the Temple was burning in every quarter.

One of the gladiators, in the wild wantonness of strife, had caught a blazing fragment of the barricade, as its remains were carried by a rush of his comrades, after the fall of [pg 451]Eleazar, and flung it into an open window of the Temple over his head. Lighting on the carved woodwork, with which the casement was decorated, it soon kindled into a strong and steady flame, that was fed by the quantity of timber, all thoroughly dry and highly ornamented, which the building contained; thus it had communicated from gallery to gallery, and from storey to storey, till the whole was wrapped in one glowing sheet of fire. From every quarter of the city, from Agrippa's wall to the Mount of Olives, from the camp of the Assyrians to the Valley of Hinnom, awestruck faces of friend and foe, white with fear, or anger, or astonishment, marked that rolling column, expanding, swaying, shifting, and ever rising higher into the summer sky, ever flinging out its red forked banner of destruction broader, and brighter, and fiercer, with each changing breeze.

Then the Jews knew that their great tribulation was fulfilled—that the curse which had been to them hitherto but a dead letter and a sealed book, was poured forth literally in streams of fire upon their heads—that their sanctuary was desolate, their prosperity gone for ever, their very existence as a nation destroyed, and "the place that had known them should know them no more"! The very Romans themselves, the cohorts advancing in serried columns to support their comrades, the legions massed in solid squares for the completion of its capture, in all the open places of the town, gazed on the burning Temple with concern and awe. Titus, even, in the flush of conquest, and the exulting joy of gratified ambition, turned his head away with a pitying sigh, for he would have spared the enemy had they but trusted him, would fain have saved that monument of their nationality and their religion, as well for their glory as his own.

And now with the flames leaping, and the smoke curling around, the huge timbers crashing down on every side to throw up showers of sparkling embers as they fell—the very marble glowing and riven with heat—the precious metal pouring from the roof in streams of molten fire—Esca and Mariamne, half suffocated in the Court of the Gentiles, could not yet bring themselves to seek their own safety, and leave the helpless form of Calchas to certain destruction. Loud shouts, cries of agony and despair, warned them that even the burning Temple, at furnace heat, was still the theatre of a murderous and useless conflict. The defenders had set the example of merciless bloodshed, and the Romans, exasperated to cruelty, now took no prisoners and gave no quarter. John of Gischala and his followers, driven to bay by the legions, [pg 452]still kept up a resistance the more furious that it was the offspring of despair. Hunted from wall to wall, from roof to roof, from storey to storey, they yet fought on while life and strength remained. Even those whose weapons failed them, or who were hemmed in by overwhelming numbers, leaped down like madmen, and perished horribly in the flames.

But although steel was clashing, and blood flowing, and men fighting by myriads around it, the Court of the Gentiles lay silent and deserted under its canopy of smoke, with its pavement covered by the dead. The only living creatures left were the three who had stood there in the morning, bound and doomed to die. Of these, one had his foot already on the border-land between time and eternity.

"I will never desert him," said Esca to his pale companion; "but thou, Mariamne, hast now a chance of escape. It may be the Romans will respect thee if thou canst reach some high commander, or yield thee to some cohort of the reserve, whose blood is not a-fire with slaughter. What said Hippias of the Tenth Legion and Licinius? If thou couldst but lay hold on his garment, thou wert safe for my sake!"

"And leave thee here to die!" answered Mariamne. "Oh, Esca! what would life be then? Besides, have we not trusted through this terrible night, and shall we not trust still? I know who is on my side. I have not forgotten all he taught me who lies bruised and senseless here. See, Esca! He opens his eyes. He knows us! It may be we shall save him now!"

Calchas did indeed seem to have recovered consciousness; and the life so soon to fade glowed once more on his wasted cheek, like an expiring lamp that glimmers into momentary brightness ere its flame is extinguished for ever.

[pg 453]

CHAPTER XX

THE VICTORY

The Tenth Legion, commanded by Licinius and guarding the person of their beloved prince, were advancing steadily upon the Temple. Deeming themselves the flower of the Roman army, accustomed to fight under the eye of Titus himself, there was no unseemly haste in the movements of these highly disciplined troops. None even of that fiery dash, which is sometimes so irresistible, sometimes so dangerous a quality in the soldier. The Tenth Legion would no more have neglected the even regularity of their line, the mechanical precision of their step, in a charge than in a retreat. They were, as they boasted, "equal to either fortune."[a] Not flushed by success, because they considered victory the mere wages to which they were entitled—not discouraged by repulse, because they were satisfied that the Tenth Legion could do all that was possible for soldiers; and the very fact of their retiring, was to them in itself a sufficient proof that sound strategy required such a movement.

Thus, when the Legion of the Lost dashed forward with wild cheers and an impetuous rush to the attack, the Tenth supported them with even ranks and regular pace and a scornful smile on their keen, bronzed, quiet faces. They would have taken the Temple, they thought, if they had the order, with half the noise and in half the time, so they closed remorselessly in, as man after man fell under the Jewish missiles, and preserved through their whole advance the same stern, haughty, and immovable demeanour, which was the favourite affectation of their courage. Titus had addressed them, when he put himself at their head, to recommend neither steadiness, valour, nor implicit compliance with orders, for in all such requirements he could depend on them, as if they were really what he loved to call them, "his own children"! but he exhorted them to spare the lives of the vanquished, and to respect as far as possible the property as [pg 454]well as the persons of the citizens. Above all, he had hoped to save the Temple; and this hope he expressed again and again to Licinius, who rode beside him, even until gazing sorrowfully on the mass of lowering smoke and yellow flame, his own eyes told him that his clemency was too late.

Even then, leaving to his general the duty of completing its capture and investing its defences, he put spurs to his horse and rode at speed round the building, calling on his soldiers to assist him in quenching the flames, shouting, signing, gesticulating; but all in vain.[a] Though the Tenth Legion were steady as a rock, the rest of the army had not resisted the infection of success; and stimulated by the example of the gladiators, were more disposed to encourage than to impede the conflagration—nor, even had they wished, would their most strenuous efforts have been now able to extinguish it.

Though fighting still went on amongst the cloisters and in the galleries of the Temple; though John of Gischala was still alive, and the Robbers held out, here and there, in fast diminishing clusters; though the Zealots had sworn to follow their leader's example, dying to a man in defence of the Holy Place; and though the Sicarii were not yet completely exterminated—Jerusalem might nevertheless be considered at length in possession of the Roman army. Licinius, leading the Tenth Legion through the Court of the Gentiles, more effectually to occupy the Temple, and prevent if possible its total destruction, was accosted at its entrance by Hirpinus, who saluted him with a sword dripping from hilt to point in blood. The old gladiator's armour was hacked and dinted, his dress scorched, his face blackened with smoke; but though weary, wounded, and exhausted, his voice had lost none of its rough jovial frankness, his brow none of the kindly good-humoured courage it had worn through all the hardships of the siege.

"Hail, prætor!" said he, "I shall live to see thee sitting [pg 455]yet once again, high on the golden car, in the streets of Rome. The Temple is thine at last, and all it contains, if we can only save it from these accursed flames. The fighting is over now; and I came back to look for a prisoner who can tell me where water may be found. The yellow roof yonder is flaring away like a torch in an oil-cask, and they must be fond of gold who can catch it by handfuls, guttering down like this in streams of fire. Our people, too, have cut their prisoners' throats as fast as they took them, and I cannot find a living Jew to show me well or cistern. Illustrious! I have won spoil enough to-day to buy a province—I would give it all for as much clear water as would go into my helmet. The bravest old man in Syria is dying in yonder corner for want of a mouthful!"

Returning through the court, in obedience to the prince's orders, to collect men and procure water, if possible, for the extinction of the conflagration, Hirpinus had recognised his young friend Esca with no little surprise and delight. Seeing Calchas, too—for whom, ever since his bold address to the gladiators in the training-school, he had entertained a sincere admiration—lying half suffocated, and at his last gasp, on the stones, the old swordsman's heart smote him with a keen sense of pity, and something between anger and shame at his own helplessness to assist the sufferer. He said nothing but truth, indeed, when he declared that he would give all his share of spoil for a helmetful of water; but he might have offered the price of a kingdom rather than a province, with as little chance of purchasing what he desired. Blood there was, flowing in streams, but of water not a drop! It was more in despair than hope that he told his sad tale to Licinius, on whom it seemed natural for every soldier in the army to depend when in trouble, either for himself or for others. Giving his orders, clear, concise, and imperative to his tribunes, the Roman general accompanied Hirpinus to the corner of the court where Calchas lay. Fallen beams and masses of charred timber were smouldering around, dead bodies, writhed in the wild contortions of mortal agony, in heaps on every side—he was sick and faint, crushed, mangled, dying from a painful wound, yet the Christian's face looked calm and happy; and he lay upon the hard stones, waiting for the coming change, like one who seeks refreshing slumber on a bed of down.

As the kind eyes turned gently to Licinius, in glance of friendly recognition, they were lit with the smile that is never worn but by the departing traveller whose barque has already [pg 456]cast off its moorings from the shore—the smile in which he seems to bid a hopeful, joyful farewell to those he leaves for a little while, with which he seems to welcome the chill breeze and the dark waters because of the haven where he would be. Mariamne and Esca, bending over with tender care, and watching each passing shade on that placid countenance, knew well that the end was very near.

His strength was almost gone; but Calchas pointed to his kinswoman and the Briton, while looking at Licinius he said, "They will be your care now. I have bestowed on you countless treasures freely yonder in the camp of the Assyrians. This you shall promise me in return."

Licinius laid his shield on the ground and took the dying man's hand in both his own.

"They are my children," said he, "from this day forth. Oh! my guide, I will never forget thy teaching nor thy behest."

Calchas looked inquiringly in the face of Hirpinus. The gladiator's rugged features bore a wistful expression of sorrow, mingled with admiration, sympathy, and a dawning light of hope.

"Bring him into the fold with you," he murmured to the other three, and then his voice came loud and strong in full triumphant tones. "It may be that this man of blood, also, shall be one of the jewels in my crown. Glory to Him who has accepted my humble tribute, who rewards a few brief hours of imperfect service; a blow from a careless hand with an eternity of happiness, an immortal crown of gold! I shall see you, friends, again. We shall meet ere we have scarcely parted. You will not forget me in that short interval. And you will rejoice with me in humble thankful joy that I have been permitted to instruct you of heaven, and to show you myself the way."

Exhausted with the effort, he sank back ere he had scarce finished speaking, and his listeners, looking on the calm dead face, from which the radiant smile had not yet faded, needed to keep watch no longer, for they knew that the martyr's spirit was even now holding converse with the angels in heaven.

PRINTED BY MORRISON AND GIBB LIMITED, EDINBURGH

Footnotes

1.

The dinner or *prandium* of Rome was the first meal in the day.

2.

A technical term for a school of gladiators trained by the same master.

3.

"*Sicarii*," or homicides—bands of assassins, regularly organised in Judæa, who made a trade of murder.

4.

"You may break, you may ruin, the vase if you will;

But the scent of the roses will hang round it still."

5.

According to Pliny, the distinguishing sign of newly-arrived slaves.

6.

About twelve pounds sterling.

7.

The *sestercius* was at this period about 1¾d., or rather more. The *sestercium*, or thousand sesterces, about £7, 16s.

8.

This inhuman practice was actually in vogue.

9.

The form by which a gladiator, who had repeatedly distinguished himself, received his dismissal and immunity from the arena for life.

10.

The well-known "Morituri te salutant!"

11.

About forty pounds sterling.

12.

"Christiani ad leones! virgines ad lenones!"—a sentence that found no small favour with the Roman crowd.

13.

The *clepsydra*, or water-clock—a Greek invention for the division of time—consisting of a hollow globe made of glass, or some transparent substance, from which the water trickled out through a narrow orifice, in quantities so regulated, that the sinking level of the element marked with sufficient exactitude the time that had elapsed since the vessel was filled.

14.

This game is played to-day with equal zest, under its Italian name of "Morro." Perhaps its nature was best rendered by the Latin phrase *micare digitos*, "to flash the fingers."

15.

Domitian.

16.

Hippicus, Phasaelus, and lovely Mariamne, for whom, in the dead of night, the great king used to call out in his agony of remorse when she was no more.

17.

Josephus, *Wars of the Jews*, book v. sec. 5.

18.

The first call of the Roman trumpets in camp, about two hours before dawn, was distinguished by that name.

19.

Now when he had said this he looked round about him, upon his family, with eyes of commiseration and of rage (that family consisted of a wife and children, and his aged parents), so in the first place he caught his father by his grey hairs, and ran his sword through him, and after him he did the same to his mother, who willingly received it; and after them he did the like to his wife and children, every one almost offering themselves to his sword, as desirous to prevent being slain by their enemies; so when he had gone over all his family he stood upon their bodies, to be seen by all, and stretching out his right hand, that his action might be observed by all, he sheathed his entire sword into his own bowels. This young man was to be pitied, on account of the strength of his body, and the courage of his soul.—Josephus, *Wars of the Jews*, book ii. sec. 18.

20.

Moreover, their hunger was so intolerable, that it obliged them to chew everything, while they gathered such things as the most sordid animals would not touch, and endured to eat them; nor did they at length abstain from girdles and shoes; and the very leather which belonged to their shields they pulled off and gnawed: the very wisps of old hay became food to some; and some gathered up fibres, and sold a very small weight of them for four Attic (drachmæ).—Josephus, *Wars of the Jews*, book vi. sec. 3.

21.

This frightful supper is said to have been eaten in the dwelling of one Mary of Bethezub, which signifies the House of Hyssop.—Josephus, *Wars of the Jews*, book vi. sec. 3.

22.

    For a description of these portentous appearances, both previous to and during the siege of Jerusalem, see Josephus, *Wars of the Jews*, book vi. sec. 5, as related by the historian with perfect good faith, and no slight reproaches to the incredulity of his obdurate countrymen—that generation of whom the greatest authority has said, "Except ye see signs and wonders, ye will not believe."

23.

    The exclamation with which the spectators notified a conclusive thrust or blow in the circus.

24.

    In bringing forward their heavy battering-rams, or otherwise advancing to the attack of a fortified place, the Roman soldiers were instructed to raise their shields obliquely above their heads, and, linking them together, thus form an impervious roof of steel, under which they could manœuvre with sufficient freedom. This formation was called the *testudo*, or tortoise, from its supposed resemblance to the defensive covering with which nature provides that animal.

25.

    "Utrinque parati."

26.

    Then did Cæsar, both by calling to the soldiers that were fighting, with a loud voice, and by giving a signal to them with his right hand, order them to quench the fire; but they did not hear what he said, though he spake so loud, having their ears already dinned by a greater noise another way; nor did they attend to the signal he made with his hand neither, as still some of them were distracted with passion, and others with fighting, neither any threatenings nor any persuasions could restrain their violence, but each one's own passion was his commander at this time; and as they were crowding into the Temple together many of them were trampled on by one another, while a great number fell among the ruins of the cloisters, which were still hot and smoking, and were destroyed in the same miserable way with those whom they had conquered.—Josephus, *Wars of the Jews*, book vi. sec. 4.

27.

    The ground occupied by the Roman lines during the siege.

Transcriber's Note

The illustrations have been placed between paragraphs in the electronic text.

Variations in hyphenation have not been changed.

Other changes, which have been made to the text:

page 9, exclamation mark added after "Jugurtha"

page 98, quote mark removed after "plans."

page 114, quote mark removed before "after"

page 137, "wel" changed to "well"

page 164, "Brition" changed to "Briton"

page 259, "inbibed" changed to "imbibed"

page 335, "Where s" changed to "Where is"

page 433, "Jeruslaem" changed to "Jerusalem"

Printed in Great Britain
by Amazon